More acclaim for

FIFTY-THREE
TUESDAYS

"*Fifty-Three Tuesdays* would be worthy resource material in the psychology of self-esteem, or in international studies on cultural differences, or just a good read in a bookstore's self-help section. The experience is slow, fast, benevolent, frustrating—in other words, *human*. I had to search inside myself to discover and accept that the kind of trauma in these pages actually exists."

—Yvette Lee, human resources professional

"Here are two people with big hearts and sincere spirits, who yearn to nurture one another and settle down. But at the same time, attention from others leads to conflict and self-sabotage, before their true feelings can be revealed. It's a solid and intriguing storyline that will appeal to readers over a broad spectrum."

—Azsa Heitkamp, documents manager

"*Fifty-Three Tuesdays* revolves around themes of love and loss, particularly the fatal dangers of lack of self-love when unaddressed. It also touches upon what happens when patience and perseverance are applied in the most dire situations, and the fact that surviving the worst tragedies can result in some of the biggest triumphs in life."

—Kathleen L., communications consultant

i

FIFTY-THREE
TUESDAYS

FIFTY-THREE TUESDAYS

G. K. NAKATA

LEGACY ISLE
PUBLISHING

ISBN 978-1-948011-81-5 (print edition)
ISBN 978-1-948011-82-2 (e-book)

Library of Congress Control Number: 2022908143

Cover photography
iStock/benjavisa (couple)
iStock/Taras Dubov (calendar)

Design and production
Jen Tadaki Catanzariti

Legacy Isle Publishing
1000 Bishop St., Ste. 806
Honolulu, HI 96813
Toll-free 1-866-900-BOOK
www.legacyislepublishing.net
info@legacyislepublishing.net

Printed in the United States

CONTENTS

PART THREE

PART FOUR

PART ONE

1

UNDER THE APPLE TREE

On a cold, drafty February morning, a little boy wearing only his underwear ran from room to room in the shack he called home. Looking for his mother, he was panicking. Heart beating faster. Alone. Face crumpled with fear, his sniffs turned to sobs as he called out, "Mommy! Where are you?"

He wiped tears from his eyes, walked into the kitchen and spied the back door ajar. *I found her*, he thought. The toddler ran barefoot out the door to the backyard, where he saw his mother's slipper under an apple tree. Searching for the other one, he looked up and saw her—hanging from a tree branch, a garden hose wrapped around her neck.

"Noooo! Noooo! Mommy!" Cries of pure animal anguish pierced the early morning.

The retired fire captain who lived next door had just stepped out to get the morning paper. He would remember the scene for life. As he came running around the corner, he saw over the fence a little boy screaming at the top of his lungs. Little Glenn was jumping up and down, trying to reach his mother, wanting to bring her down, wanting his mommy back.

The fireman hopped the fence in one vault and in one swift movement cut the woman down. He laid her down softly onto the grass below and unwrapped the hose. Glenn whimpered. "Mommy? Wake up, Mommy!" Sonny, the fire captain, a large Polynesian man, scooped the little boy up and held him tight.

Sonny feared for Glenn and pondered the worst. As a youth coach on the poorer side of town, he'd seen what could happen in broken homes. *This kid's screwed. For sure jail, or an early grave.* Sonny hugged Glenn tighter and silently prayed for God to watch over the boy.

In the distance, a siren blared. The giant man whispered in the little boy's ear, "Glenn, she's still with you no matter what. Her love for you is forever. You will be okay. Love conquers all. Remember that, okay?"

Glenn nodded, burying those words somewhere deep in his psyche. But now he just wanted his mama and reached out to her. Sonny set Glenn down tenderly by his mother's side.

She was still warm, with a peaceful look on her face. Glenn hugged her around her neck, then took her hand and wiped his face with it—the way she always did to wipe his tears away. He put his arm around her and cradled himself by her side. "Wake up, Mommy. Don't go. Come back. Don't go. You said you wouldn't leave. I'm sorry. What did I do?" He cried hot, heavy tears. A gentle breeze felt like a hand wiping tears from his face. He pretended it was her. And cried some more.

2

CHILD FORSAKEN

As they did so often, Mommy and Daddy had fought the night before. Glenn had watched in terror as Daddy slapped his mother against the wall, then chased her with a knife. He heard Daddy screaming, asking who the father was. She had her back to the front door, calling for Glenn, but Daddy grabbed his hair and wouldn't let him go to her. Glenn screamed, "Mommy, Mommy! Don't go!"

She caught the look in his innocent puppy dog eyes and sank to the floor, reaching out to her son. With a triumphant sneer, Daddy let go, and Glenn ran to Mommy. Burrowing his face in her neck, Glenn whimpered, "Don't go, Mommy, don't go . . . "

She cupped his face, then wiped away his tears, kissing his forehead as if to seal a deal. "Don't worry. I won't leave this house ever again."

Glenn's head jerked back hard as Daddy pulled him off of Mommy. With a swift kick, the boy was sent stumbling to his room. No dinner. He was sent straight to bed and not allowed to come out. Like so many nights before, he lay in the dark, asking God to make things okay. He listened. He wondered, would there be more yelling? Or would Mommy and Daddy play their game, jumping up and down on the bed and laughing?

He heard Daddy yell, then Mommy scream, and their door slammed. He lay shaking under the covers, holding a toy gun for protection. He breathed quietly till he heard the bedsprings sound. No laughter, but he thought surely things were okay again.

Sometime during the night, Glenn woke to Mommy caressing his face, wiping his cheek with the palm of her hand as if drying tears. This act of love always soothed him. Placing her hand on his heart, she whispered, "I will always be with you. Even when I'm not here, I will be here in your heart. And remember what I told you, when I'm not here, you can always talk to God."

Rubbing his eyes, he murmured, "Okay, Mommy."

She reached down to hug him and instead pulled him up onto her. He sat in her lap facing her, his face buried in her neck. She nuzzled the side of his face with her nose. Then pressing her cheek to his, she said firmly, "You're a big boy now, Glenn. You be a good boy okay, for Mommy?"

He didn't catch the sadness in her voice. "Okay, Mommy. Don't worry. I'm a big boy now."

He yawned as she lay him down gently. Fast asleep, he didn't feel her tear that fell on his cheek.

And now she was gone. The only person he had ever loved, the only person that ever loved him, was gone.

3

BEATEN TEMPTED

Fourth grade

Dear Mama,
I miss you. Why you go? You promised you
not leave. I said stay but you went. Why you
leave me with daddy? He cry on me. Then he
hit me. He said I killed you. I sorry mama.

Forty-five years later
"What the hell?!" Glenn Forrester woke with a start. Summer sunlight forced its way between the narrow slits of his sleep-filled eyes. He reached for his phone. *What time is it?* "Shit, I'm late! What happened to the alarm?" As he jumped out of bed, the fog cleared slowly. He sat back down and reality set in. So did the hangover. The room was spinning. He collapsed backward. *Too many drinks last night. What did I drink? Can't remember.*

He wondered how it had all come to all this. Three days before, he'd been a member of the mayor's cabinet and his trusted advisor on community affairs. Then he was shown the door. He ran through his impressive list of credits: decorated military veteran, law school standout, respected and feared lawyer, banking wizard, CFO with the Midas touch, mayor's confidant. A real people's champion. He sighed. *The great Glenn Forrester. I've been on an upward trajectory all my life. Now what? The great Glenn Forrester—unemployed nobody.*

Deputy mayor Clifford Schumaker had outflanked him. He could've fought it, and in his mind, he should have put up a fight, at least called a press conference. But he had too much respect for the mayor. Instead, the mayor had allowed Schumaker free reign to handle Glenn's exit, making sure he wouldn't work anywhere after that. All the contractors and city vendors got the word—*Don't hire Forrester if you want city work*—followed by a memo falsely claiming that Glenn had left because of a bad audit.

Real bona fide assholes, he thought, as he slowly lifted himself out of bed. He was no longer thinking of three days ago. *Damn, I need to pee or puke. Or both.*

Watching last night's beer drain from his body, he wondered what was next.

He could still hear his supporters asking him to stay. The civil servant folks said fight. The Council said persevere. So many people counted on him. To him, these were all good people. He had worked all his life to be an essential player at City Hall. He wanted to help those in real need. And in one prideful misstep, he had let it all go.

He took two steps to the sink and splashed water on his face, letting himself drip dry, the droplets falling off his face like tears. Leaning on the bathroom sink, he stared into the mirror and ran his fingers through his hair as he often did when lost in thought.

He was about to turn fifty-four years old and thanked God he had all his hair, only now starting to gray at the sides. With his hair kept short, he easily passed for law enforcement or military, especially since he'd trimmed fifty pounds off his 225-pound-plus bulk in the last three years. His boyish features, hard piercing dark eyes and chiseled jawline were reminiscent of naval aviators in the movies. So youthful was his face, most thought he was in his thirties at first meeting.

Neither short nor tall, he still looked like the sleek bulldog he'd been in college, this after a renewed interest in bodybuilding and mixed martial arts the past year. He sucked in and flexed his abdomen. A faint trace of a six-pack showed through what some women considered just the right amount of hair on his chest and gut.

Surveying his image, he turned one way and the other and wondered how long he would last, given the drinking binge he'd been on. He slapped his gut. Big mistake. He erupted in dry heaves, and the room started spinning again.

Head sore. Need more sleep. Taking two steps, he jumped back into the king-sized bed, targeting the comfort spot right in the center. The bed felt big without her, and he was getting used to sleeping in the middle of it all.

He rolled away from the sun, right into his drool pool. *What the shit! Man, I can't catch a break.*

He crawled out of bed, wiping his face on his blanket and trudged over to the fridge for a longneck. The smell of stale pizza hung in the air, and the rug reeked like spilled beer and whiskey. The whole place smelled like a scuzzy bar—the morning after. He hobbled out to the living room and pushed open the lanai door of his condo.

He lived on the twentieth floor of a high-rise, built mere miles from where he'd grown up, and across the dotted line separating the haves and have-nots. They'd purchased it right after getting married and spent the first ten years eating cold cuts and ramen to make the mortgage payments. That is, until he moved up in the world and spaghetti became the weekly luxury.

After they'd decided against having children, the second bedroom became a walk-in closet for her and a workout room for him. The living room had a large sofa against one wall facing a large flatscreen fixed on the opposite wall. The open kitchen was opposite the patio, which looked out on a view of the city and the ocean in the distance.

The place was comfortable, and the décor reflected the days when money was scarce. Pictures of her family and their early days together adorned the shelf above the large flatscreen, along with the family Bible. The glass coffee table in between the couch and TV was where they had their meals. It had been a while since they'd eaten together. Now the table was littered with beer bottles and three days' worth of pizza boxes and Chinese takeout containers.

The master bedroom still looked like she slept there. Nothing had been moved or touched.

He sat back on his end of the couch thinking, *It's been three days since I left City Hall. I can't just sit here feeling sorry for myself.* Looking over at her end of the couch, he sensed that she'd tell him to get up and get out. *I miss her. Talk everything out. Score some nods, maybe a hug, just to know things are okay.*

He shook his head, willing himself back to reality. *She's not here. I could go see her. Nah. It isn't the same anymore.*

He nuked a burrito. Turned on the TV and tried watching his usual morning shows, expertly shuffling between his thirteen favorite channels. Nothing appealed to him, and he turned it off.

His watch read noon. He'd already wasted three hours. It was a disorienting feeling to be busy all your life and suddenly not have anything to do. *Man, I'm so lost. No more 300 emails a day. No more being on the phone or in meetings all day. No more sparring with issues and people with personal agendas. No more.*

He'd only been up a few hours before he reached for the hard stuff. Johnny Walker and José Cuervo were his only friends now. Remorse and guilt waged war on whatever good feelings he had left about working at the city. It was a running debate that was going on its fourth day.

He questioned quitting the cabinet and why it had to be him or Clifford. *Always my way or no way. What a shit. I left the staff, my peeps. I left all the people that need help. What a selfish wuss. Left things unfinished. Left those I loved behind.*

He'd done so much but now imagined Clifford and his cronies undoing everything he'd accomplished. He was lost with nothing to do and no one to do it with. He had no friends outside of work. His staff doubled as family. *I could see it in their eyes when I left—I was deserting them. I left them with no rudder, no compass. Of course they understood—had watched me take the beatings over time. And yet, it was like leaving children behind. I'm so sorry.*

The words "fall from grace" kept coming back to him. On his third scotch, he sat back on his couch and babbled to no one in particular. "Feel like shit. Like this small." He pinched his thumb and index finger together.

The empty glass fell out of his hands. His thoughts drifted in and out. *God, I know you put me there to do good. I know you didn't want me to leave, but I did, and I'm so sorry. I failed you too. And now I'm a nobody who nobody cares to know.*

Half asleep, he slurred, "Why couldn't you take my side and get rid of Clifford? Why me, God?" He tried to sit back up and continued his monologue. "I'm so sorry, God. You gave me something important to do. To help people. What I wanted to do all my life. I just needed to take Clifford's shit like everyone else. But I couldn't let it slide. Oh Father, I failed You. I feel so . . . so . . ."

He struggled to define how he was feeling. *What's the word? Beaten.*

He sank into the couch and passed out.

It was evening when he woke. *Gotta get out of here. Grab some fresh air.* Instead of the treadmill, he decided to walk around the neighborhood. In twenty years, he had only crossed the street on foot once.

It was a nice enough neighborhood, with a mix of condos, mini-marts and other stores, and on the outskirts, a bunch of seedy looking bars. He knew what these were. Hostess bars. Made famous in faraway places like Thailand, Vietnam, the Philippines, Korea, and Japan. The so-called service industry born of the Vietnam war had made its way across the Pacific to US soil.

He stood at the corner, hands folded, contemplating his next move. Whenever it came up in conversations, he'd say that he never understood what guys saw in these "buy me drinky" places, shelling out twenty dollars for ten minutes of conversation, and if they got lucky, copping a feel of the girl's ass.

Conventional wisdom was that the more drinks you bought, the more touching occurred. And depending on how much the schmuck emptied his wallet—the back room.

He paused. Cocked his head to one side. As if listening to some wise sage offering advice.

Aw man, who am I kidding. I've wanted to go back and get my itch scratched ever since Tomo took me five years ago.

Kashiwazaki Tomohiro, Tomo for short, was the number two guy in the Japanese construction conglomerate that built a hundred thousand temporary housing units for people displaced by Japan's massive earthquake and tsunami several years prior. With life moving on, these units started to look like ghost towns.

Glenn worked a deal to have these shipped to the state to create a new homeless housing project. He and Tomo hit the town to celebrate, forming a bond over Japanese whiskey and midnight raids on several hostess bars. Tomo stood six foot two and could pass for Daniel Dae Kim. The kind of guy women swooned over. His chiseled looks and body were intimidating. Saying his name was even more intimidating. Glenn simply called him Tomo.

He wanted to go back to the bars after Tomo left. God, the job, the wife, all kept him in check. He couldn't risk getting caught in one of these places while working for the mayor, so he buried his itch deep down inside. And Katie, for better or for worse—*well,* he thought, *she isn't here anymore, is she?* For a split second, he saw her face, remembering all the good times. But then he pushed back, suppressing it all, somewhere in his memory vault.

So what's holding me back now?

He looked up. *God, are you there? I just want to chill somewhere. Maybe it's not that bad. I really could use someplace to unwind. Tomo told me about the no-touch zone. I'll hang there. Do some people watching.*

Deep inside, he just wanted to feel good again. Adrenaline, dopamine and oxytocin, the brain's happy chemicals, were swirling into an intoxicating cocktail in his head and other parts. The church warned about this. They called it temptation, and he was about to fall hard.

4

SINFUL SUMMER SEX

Fifth grade

Mama,
Daddy said we broke. We eat grass and
leaves from the yard with gray hamburger. I
don't know why broke. Daddy spend plenty
money on beer and cigarettes. I miss you
Mommy.

Every day since you gone, I watch Billy across
the street come home from school and his
mama always waiting with a big hug. I see
them play in the yard. I wish you was here
with me Mommy.

With nothing to lose—no reputation, no status, no one waiting at home, and not much help from God—Glenn rolled the dice on a sin splurge. He spent his first full week out of City Hall visiting almost every hostess bar he could find. There was no more suppressing that pent-up desire he'd had since his first experience. He indulged himself with bargirls a couple times a night for a week and returned home each night reeking of alcohol and cheap perfume.

Many nights, many bars, many bargirls. He wasn't sure how things worked. It didn't go down each time the way Tomo had explained. The rules differed from bar to bar. He was looking for a place to chill, someplace where he could feel sorry for himself and lick his wounds. That's what he told himself to soothe the Judeo-Christian guilt he harbored.

Most of the time, someone pulled him into a backroom after a few drinks, some groping, and the room spinning. One night his mind wandered as he watched a girl putting her clothes back on. *Man, this is getting old. I must look desperate to them.*

Two sin-filled weeks later, he woke with the usual massive headache. It was mid-afternoon on a warm summer day. The bedsheets reeked of an alcoholic's sweat, stale makeup, and cheap vinegary smelling perfume.

He flipped on the TV and blindly clicked through the news channels. He thought there had to be more than this. It was becoming routine. Dark bars with purplish neon giving off just enough light to do things better done in the dark. He always started at the no-fly bar zone, where they're not supposed to approach you, and always lied to himself that he was only going to chill that night.

Even the girls started to look the same. Fly zone or no-fly zone, he always ended up in a booth with someone, usually Asian, exotic, pretty, and aggressive and submissive at the same time. He tried small talk, but their English consisted of "honey I make you happy tonight" or "baby you have good time tonight." Most girls talked with their hands, and by that time, there was no going back.

Still clutching the remote control, he settled on some mind-numbing game show. After a few minutes, he turned off the TV and wondered, trying to remember through the prior night's fog. *What was last night? Oh yeah, a grand opening. Geez, these places seem to have grand openings and new management every year or two.*

It had been a raucous affair. *Shit,* he thought, checking to see if his charge cards were still in his wallet. Extremely parched, he dragged himself into the shower, then washed his bedsheets and downed a Diet Coke and a burrito. He ran a couple of miles on the treadmill and took another shower.

His head still hurt. He had the dry heaves. He vaguely recalled holding shot glasses with his beer last night. Shots of what, he wondered? Then he fell asleep on the couch.

Daniel Dae Kim appeared out of nowhere. It was Tomo.

"Hey Tomo, so what does private room mean?"

"Private room is code for all out-sex. You pay some egregious amount for a bottle of cheap champagne, which they serve you privately in a back room. In some places, they don't even serve you champagne. They call it a private room fee so you two can have a private conversation."

"A conversation? That's it?"

"No, bean-brain. That's what they call it. It's whatever you can negotiate. Oh geez, you truly didn't know this stuff?"

"Just some, was not really into it. Married and all."

"Well, good. I know lots of guys, get hooked into it. Buy them condos

and shit. One put a car, whole freaking car, on his MasterCard for one of these girls. He's still paying it off."

"Sounds criminal, man."

"It's a business. We're wads of cash walking in the door, and it's a question of what you want and what they're willing to give up to you. It's economics, supply and demand. We have a supply of money and a demand for a good time. They have a demand for money, and a supply of whatever it takes to get that money."

"Sounds cold."

"They're great actors. They'll want to make you a regular. They'll probe you for what you do to see if you're a cash cow. They'll want to know your job, where you live, and what kind of car you drive. They'll ask for your name, your phone number and your email so they can sweet talk you the rest of the week to get you to come back. It's all about assuring themselves of a return customer."

"Not sure if I'll ever go again, but tonight . . . it was interesting."

"Always take care of the mama-san, one drink just to say hello and pay respects. No fuss, no muss.

Ignore the compliments. Cute, Handsome. Muscular. Nice. Smart. They'll get to your inside psyche faster than interrogators at Guantanamo."

Glenn nodded.

Tomo hauled off and punched Glenn in the arm. "And one more thing—never, ever, fall in love in those places."

Glenn got up with a start, rubbing his arm. *That punch felt real.* He walked over to his lanai. The sun had long set. Staring out at nothing, he came to a decision. *I've had enough of this shit.*

He took five steps back to the shelf above the TV and reached for his Bible, the one she gave to him on their first Valentine's Day. It had been over a month since he last read scripture. He'd always been faithful to her and had never even felt up a stripper at all those parties the firm used to host. But something had snapped this past month, and he knew it had to stop.

He considered himself a man of faith. As a young child, he turned to prayer when Mommy and Daddy fought. Through all the shouting and screaming and the dull sounds of flesh and bone pounding flesh and bone, he kept praying to God to make it stop. Through blurred tears and sobbing, he looked at God's picture on the wall and kept asking for the awful thuds and screaming to stop. Eventually, the chaos quieted as he fell asleep.

He'd wake up in the dark, with Mommy next to him, stroking his hair. She had a way of soothing him by wiping his face with the palm of her hand. "Don't worry Glenn. Mommy's not hurt. Daddy just drink too much. Mommy's here now. Daddy's gone." In the morning, Glenn was happy. Mommy looked okay. Mommy hid all the bruises on her body with an oversized dress. Daddy knew just where to hit.

Mommy always ended their nights with prayer. She always said, "If Mommy no stay and you scared, talk to God, okay?" She had given him her crucifix when he turned four, and he'd held this crucifix tightly at her funeral.

Am I really a man of God? He plodded over to the couch. He knew he was sinning. He had started a prayer group at City Hall, and he'd been personal counselor to many friends he'd brought to Christ. *What kind of witness am I? If they saw me now, would they lose faith in me and quit God?*

From somewhere deep within, he heard a small still voice: *You're more worried about your own reputation than about peoples' relationship with me.*

Glenn dismissed the voice quickly. It had been a month since he'd had a serious conversation with God. Sitting on the couch, he sighed and looked upward and ahead, at nothing in particular, but in his mind saw a very familiar vision.

"Hi, Father. Long time. Sorry. I hope You're not too pissed at me. Can I still come to heaven? Say hi to Mommy for me. I'm screwing up here and could use Your help. You know, just snap Your fingers and my horniness is gone."

He'd had this conversation with God for many years. The human weakness never went away. It didn't seem any different this time as he sent his words upward. "I'm so tired of it all, Father. Just empty, you know? These bars. I go inside, a quick intro, some conversation I don't understand. A few beers in, and my inhibition and guilt are both gone. Her hand in my crotch, then fifteen minutes later I'm zipping up and it's on to the next bar. I'm done. I wanna find someplace I can chill and not be bothered. Geez, isn't there one place in the neighborhood that just lets you chill?"

Glenn poured his heart out to God on other things as well. The job that just ended. The betrayal. The knife wounds in his back. How he let pride take over. All familiar topics. The answer was always the same. *What did you learn?*

Social media was filled with screenshots, saying God leads you through the dark so that you can learn and be blessed. Glenn was wondering where the blessings were now. "Well, Father, bless me and bless you. Talk to you later."

Glenn's walk with God was always just that personal. Something that did not sit well with some church leaders. He was a supportive member of his last church until the elders told him to stop talking about his relationship with God. If there were a facepalm emoji back then, Glenn would have replied with it in the email. Instead, he never went back. After three months of emails and voicemails unanswered by Glenn, they stopped calling. Last he heard, the church had counted him as one of the fallen.

So be it. His last thought before passing out again.

5

FIRST ENCOUNTER

Sixth grade

Happy Mother day Mama!
Billy's mama still hugs him every day. I really
wish you could give me a Billy mom hug.

He woke early and spent the day cleaning the condo. Wrestling with the vacuum cleaner, he yelled over the whirring of the appliance, arguing to no one in particular. "I'm done with this shit! This bar life. Tomo can have it. Every night, I get drunk then have sex. Every morning feel like shit. This is getting old. Time for a new leaf. And I'm running out of money!!"

He sprayed the place with Febreze and flopped back on the couch with a Diet Coke. Looking upward, he half prayed, half argued. "God, if You're out there. Take my life and make straight my crooked ways. I want to be happy, Father. Like she and I used to be. Enough of this sex stuff." A little calmer, he bowed his head, whispering. "Bless me please, Father, as You always have."

As the sun set that night, he felt a familiar restless feeling. Patting his crotch, he said aloud, "Not this time, boy. Settle in. It's gonna be a long one." Looking around at his handiwork, he regretted tossing all the alcohol. *Damn. Big game on. Nothing to drink. Nothing to eat.*

He thought about trying a legit place tonight, a bar and grill, nothing with the words club or lounge in it. *No hostesses. Just friendly folks serving beer and whacking up some ribeye.*

It only took a few minutes to find a place. The sign said Rona's Bar and Grill. He took a picture to post to Facebook later. A red neon light flashed OPEN every two seconds. Another sign said home-cooked food. His stomach growled. He walked in and stopped short, as if he'd spotted a pit

bull—although what lay before him was uglier than any pit bull he'd
ever seen.

What he could only describe as three of the scariest, witchiest looking
hags he'd ever seen made a beeline for him, arms outstretched, saying lines
he'd only heard in bad Asian porn movies. He turned, quickly, retreating
out the door. Behind him, one of them cackled, "Come, honey, me make
you feel good." Another screeched, "You like good time?"

Maybe they weren't really cackling and screeching; maybe they weren't
witches sucking eyeballs out of a cauldron. But something scared him
enough to run full speed out into the parking lot. *Great Facebook caption
this will make*, he thought. The red neon OPEN sign screamed hostess bar,
but hunger overrode what common sense he had.

He slowed to a jog. Breathing hard, he turned. *Shit!*

They'd followed him out and were running toward him. *Crap, I'm
about to be kidnapped! They're gonna sell me off or eat me. They're even
uglier out here in the light! Are those broomsticks lined up outside the door?*

He pissed all pride to the wind and ran toward a fancy café next door.
At least that's what he thought it was. He burst through the door, nearly
stumbling, and stopped two steps in. The café's bar was at the front of the
house. He saw a dining room with orange, high-backed booths on the right
and a game room on the left. The only female there was the bartender, who
looked up with a welcoming smile. "Hello, love, have a seat."

Glenn stammered. "Not here to drink. Can I just . . . can I just hide
from the three ladies next door?"

Tia was unfazed. She'd seen it before. "Sit here, love. They won't bother
you anymore. What'll you have."

"Bud Light?" He was fishing in his pocket for money.

She watched him, a look of amusement on her face. "First time here?"

Still rattled, he kept fumbling in his pocket. "Yup."

She smiled. "First one's on the house, love." He smiled back, a little less
nervous, thinking he was gonna like this place.

He slid on to a comfortable bar stool with armrests at one corner
of the horseshoe-shaped bar. He felt like Norm from that *Cheers* sitcom.
There was a large mirror behind the bar, providing the backdrop for shelves
of whiskey and other liquors.

He took a long swallow. Ten steps away, right next to the restroom
and the kitchen entrance, was an open doorway to a game room. He saw
dartboards and some other standup game machines. Maybe poker, he
thought. Not wanting to look conspicuous or trying to look cool for Tia,
he stared into the mirror behind the bar to get a sense of what was behind

him. The orange booths filled the restaurant, and he thought he saw a chandelier. *Rather dark*, he thought, *maybe a romantic bistro.*

The place smelled fresh, not like some of the other bars he visited, and from the kitchen wafted aromas of either Korean or Vietnamese fare.

There were flatscreens in every direction showing different sports and games in progress. To his right, the stadium crowd suddenly roared as the Steelers scored to pull ahead. On the flatscreen straight ahead, there was Muay Thai boxing.

He did a quick visual sweep. There were only guys in there, and Tia was easy on the eyes. Ed Sheeran was singing in the background. He took it all in. *Did I finally find a bar to chill at?*

The guys were friendly enough. Retirees. Vets. Locals. Three older guys looked like they had been regulars for the last forty years. They warmed to him after he bought a round. Glenn settled into watching the game and small talk with Tia. She was gorgeous—Hispanic mixture, possibly Filipino Chinese Hawaiian—a fitness model who worked in real estate by day. He would have believed her if she said she was an NFL cheerleader.

She leaned forward, elbows on the faux marble counter. "You hungry, love?"

"I guess," he murmured, trying hard to keep his gaze above her neckline.

Her eyes twinkled, seeing him try so hard to be polite. She nodded over her shoulder. "There's food in the dart room. Help yourself. It's Mama's birthday."

"Mama?" Glenn was on alert as he walked to the buffet. He saw the spread. He hadn't seen food this tempting since the holidays. He forgot all about Mama as he retook his seat, loaded with food.

The food was delicious. The environment was welcoming. Tia was lovely to look at and even nicer to listen to.

Okay, I found the bar I want to die in.

A Vietnamese beauty walked in, trim body, in jeans and beige pullover sweater. She was ample on top and slim in the waist. Glenn thought she was in her thirties. Later he'd find out she was in her fifties.

Tia nodded to Glenn. "That's Mama Lynh."

He remembered what Tomo said. Even if it's not a hostess bar, always take care of the mama-san. "Hey Tia, can I buy Mama a birthday drink?"

"Sure, love. What do you want?"

"What can fifty dollars get?"

"Plenty enough. What's your name, love?"

"Glenn." He winced just a bit, unnoticeably. *I shoulda gave an alias, a bar name. Tomo always said, don't give your real name. They'll find you somehow.*

Tilting her head, she made a quick mental calculation. "Glenn, give me forty dollars, and I'll make sure she gets it."

"Thanks, Tia." Glenn tipped her the other ten dollars.

Class act, Tia thought, *haven't seen that lately.*

Ten minutes later, Mama came over with a glass of cognac. "Thank you honey for birthday drink." Her accent was heavy.

"Happy Birthday, Mama." They clinked cognac glass to beer bottle.

"You new here, honey?"

Glenn nodded. "I like this place, Mama. Good vibe. You have a great place here. Happy Birthday!"

Mama liked Glenn instantly. He had little boy looks, with a wrestler's body. Someone she'd want for her daughter and or even herself. "You married, honey?"

Glenn smiled. "Kinda personal, Mama, on our first date?" She hadn't blushed like that in a long time.

"No pressure, honey." She noticed no ring on his finger. It was on his key ring in his pocket. Mama thought he looked a little sad but didn't press it.

She tried again. "You want company, baby?"

Glenn nodded "no" so hard his neck cricked. "No need, Mama. You busy, but thank you."

Tia leaned over and explained. "Mama, he ran in off the street away from Rona's place."

"Ohhhh." Lynh smiled and laughed. Not the first time. Gently touching his forearm, she leaned over and whispered, "No worry, honey, this good bar. Just sit here, no one bother you, okay?"

Glenn nodded. Mama smiled. "I come back. Tia, you watch cherry boy. Make sure no one bother."

"Okay, Mama."

Around the same time, a group of very attractive women walked into the bar and crowded around Mama, wishing her happy birthday. Glenn thought they were her friends. Leaning over to the guy next to him, he commented. "Wow, looks like girls night out."

The guy peered at Glenn, wide-eyed. "You know this is a hostess bar, right?"

Glenn took a second to look around, and it came to him. He didn't think about it because the sign above the door said Cafe. He didn't see

"And Lounge." Too busy running from the three witches.

He let out a sigh of relief. The three women that came in earlier settled down with a group of men, and they were off into the other room with booths.

Earlier, Glenn had thought the booths were the restaurant section of the cafe. It could have been because there were some people eating. But mostly booths with tables, in a dimly lit room that provided more privacy for couples. Mentally, he named it the booth room.

But the front bar area was brightly lit and lively, and that was fine by Glenn. He decided to stay.

Other women came in and drifted off as well, some with the old guys Glenn had been at the bar with. Both stools next to him were now empty. He reassured himself. *Not to worry, right? Mama had said so.*

Glenn was having a rocking time just listening to the piped-in music. Despacito was playing. Tia was as sweet as can be. "Another Bud Light, love?" she cooed, wiping up the bar area in front of Glenn.

"Sure," Glenn said. She put down new coasters and was off to the other side. Business was picking up as men looking for company started coming in the door. Regular customers were met by their regular girls. Others hung about or sat in booths. Eventually, someone would go ask to sit with them. *Not me*, Glenn thought, *been there, done that. I just want to chill.*

The bar got lively. Two barbacks joined Tia, and servers were hustling drinks between the bar, the dart room, and the booth room. Any people watcher would be fascinated by the interactions between the girls and customers. Somewhere in the booth room, someone was belting out a karaoke version of "Achy Breaky Heart."

Glenn felt a tap on his shoulder and turned to his left. It was Mama Lynh. "Honey, my birthday, do me favor? I know you not lonely, honey, but you can help one of my girls. She shy too. You nice guy and she need nice guy to be with tonight. No pressure, no need buy drinks. Just sit. See how you like."

This was different from the high-pressure tactics in other bars. Very delicately and respectfully, he started to respond. "No, Mama, no need. I'm good."

She didn't wait for Glenn to answer. Nor did she hear him, or so it seemed. "You try. She here." Glenn turned to his right and saw the most gorgeous woman he'd ever seen. Gorgeous not in a heavy makeup sort of way, just gorgeous, whatever that meant to Glenn. He swallowed hard, wondering, *What was she doing in a place like this?*

Mama continued. "This my friend Maya. She shy and not want to work tonight. You just let her sit with you. No pressure, no drinks, no touch. Just sit. Okay? No need to talk. Just sit." Glenn looked one way at Lynh, and turned the other way, staring at the most beautiful girl he had ever encountered.

She was Asian for sure, but he couldn't place exactly where. With the other girls, you could always tell whether they were Vietnamese, Korean, Filipina or local. This one was petite, just a little over five feet tall. Straight dark brown hair barely covering her shoulders, parted slightly off the middle with just the right amount of highlights. She wore makeup, but not a lot. Smoky eyes, long thick lashes, and just the right amount of reddish-pink to her lips. Almond eyes and alabaster complexion—a line from some cheesy novel he'd read.

Underneath an oversized flannel shirt, she had on a blue bare shoulder cocktail dress that ended mid-thigh. Her legs looked longer than what they should have been for her height. Where Glenn could see, she was tan—not a dark, forced tan but the color you'd expect from someone who liked to be outdoors.

"Hello." She put her hand out to shake his hand. Glenn just stared. Maya looked at Mama. "It's okay, Mama. He nice guy, let's not bother."

Mama put her arm around Maya. "Just sit, Honey. He shy, you shy, keep each other company. Keep eye on each other so Mama can get back to work."

The look on Glenn's face was comical, contorted between bliss and agony. Maya laughed softly. Mama smiled triumphantly, then left in a hurry, jabbering orders to the barbacks and other girls.

"Are you okay?" Maya asked.

To Glenn, her voice sounded like an angel speaking, though he would hardly know what an angel sounded like. If asked, he'd say like wind chimes blowing gently in the night air. It touched his soul. He wanted to say something eloquent, to make an impression. He opened his mouth and said, "Huh?"

"Are you okay?" She laughed again. This time the wind chimes sounded even louder as she took in the embarrassment on his face. And she laughed even more. He was *not* like the other grabby customers in the joint, she thought. He was like a lost little boy.

She touched his arm lightly. He flinched, just slightly. She said reassuringly, "Don't worry, I will not hurt you." Irony in a hostess bar.

It was an accent he'd never heard before. "I'm sorry," he said, "I don't usually get rattled like this. I mean, I can hold my own in a place like this. I mean, I'm not scared." A winning record in over a hundred court cases, numerous multi-million-dollar negotiations, and never a moment like this. *I can't believe I'm stammering. She's going to see I'm a loser soon enough.*

He ruffled his hair like he was shampooing it. "I mean, um, so . . . shit, not making much of a first impression, am I? Sorry, I wish I was smoother."

She took in the embarrassed look on his face. She reached out and squeezed his arm, then quickly smoothed his hair. "No worries, you had me at 'Huh.'" She burst out laughing, encircling her arm in his, and put her head on his shoulder, just for a few seconds, and then let go. "You know, from the movie? Instead, you said 'Huh,' not 'Hello.'"

Glenn smiled, remembering the scene from *Jerry McGuire*. He felt more at ease. Beautiful and fun. Looking around, taking it in, he thought, *This is a hostess bar?*

Maya slid onto the stool next to Glenn and tried small talk. Glenn kept mostly quiet. After a bit, she seemed nervous, hurt maybe.

Tia came over to help. "Glenn, don't worry, you look like you're about to be eaten. Mama thinks you're classy because you bought her a birthday drink, and you hadn't even met her yet. I agree. You're safe here, love."

Glenn relaxed. He turned to Maya. "I'm sorry."

Maya touched his arm lightly. "No worries. We don't have to talk. Just sit. Chill."

And finally, he said it, what barreled around in his head since he saw her. "I'm not usually like this. But you're just drop-dead gorgeous, and I get nervous around women that beautiful . . . like you, you know?"

"Okay. Don't worry." A hint of blush on her cheek. Maya chuckled, looking downward. Then silence, for what seemed like minutes.

Tia thought, *uh oh*, and jumped in. Tia carried the conversation with Maya until the topic became fitness and bodybuilding, something near to Glenn's heart. The night took off at that point. The three shared fitness routines and what each was doing to get stronger and better. Tia was in training for the next Ms. Fitness, and Maya wanted to follow a year later. The conversation turned to workouts and progress made on abs showing and poundage and reps—all the usual chatter two women serious about weights and fitness training would have.

Glenn had no problem keeping up. He'd recently returned to the gym to get back into college shape. He'd lost fifty pounds and increased his bench press to 275 pounds. The girls wanted flat abs, and Maya showed Glenn pictures of her before and after shots. Maya whipped out her phone and showed Glenn a rear double bicep shoulder shot.

Glenn choked on his beer. She had her head turned in the picture, and so he knew it was her. Still, he blurted. "That's you?"

"Not believe?" She pretended to be hurt. Before he could react, the flannel shirt she used to keep warm came off, and she popped the same pose. Thoughts flooded Glenn's head. *Great body. Some tattoo, a phoenix. Smooth silky skin. Stunning physique. Disciplined.* The flannel shirt came back on. She turned to him, smiling. She knew by his expression she had impressed.

"Wow!" was all he could say out loud, as he asked himself, *I'm having a bodybuilding conversation in a hostess bar?*

The night wore on. The conversation turned from bodybuilding to what kind of place this was? *This is not where I've been the last two weeks,* he thought.

Tia explained. "Mama has a different philosophy. Family style hostess bar, if you could call it that." Glenn looked confused.

Tia continued. "No sex here." Maya nodded. "Just a sympathetic ear and companionship. We've had regulars going back twenty years. Younger guys come in on the weekend and try to have their way, but usually have a good time, and head off somewhere else for a nightcap, the climax of their evening, you might say." Tia searched Glenn's eyes, wondering if he was catching on, or if he really was that innocent?

Glenn just sat there. This is so the opposite of what Tomo had shown him, what he'd seen nearly everywhere else. He turned to Maya. "Um, aren't I supposed to be buying you a drink? It's been two hours." He hadn't been asked once.

Maya and Tia exchanged glances. Maya turned to Glenn. "Sure, if you want to. I not say no, but no need. You guest tonight."

Glenn put a Benjamin on the bar. "Whatever that will buy."

Maya stared at it. "How about twenty dollars for me, twenty dollars for Tia, forty dollars for Mama, and you keep twenty dollars for next time?"

Glenn hadn't even thought of next time. "Sure." The word slipped out of his mouth before he could think.

Last call at the bar came quickly. Tia moved away to close the register. Glenn looked at Maya. "Thank you for letting me sit with you Glenn." She stuck out her hand, and this time he welcomed her handshake. It was very natural for Glenn, like old friends.

"It was nice to meet you, Maya." He hugged her and walked out into the night, although still on the lookout for the three ladies from next door. He thought it had been a good clean evening.

From the doorway, Maya watched Glenn leave. *Nice. Hope he come back.* She knew the nice ones usually didn't.

She hated the bar. Mama sometimes made her sit with strange men.

They got to touch you just because they bought drinks and spent money at the bar. Glenn hadn't touched her once.

He turned and waved again. She waved back. *I hope he comes again.*

6

OUTFLANKED OUSTED

Seventh grade

Dear Mama,
I won first place boxing last night. I hate
Daddy. I showed him my trophy and he
stepped on it and threw it in the trash. He
said I don't deserve because all the time I
practice I can be doing chores at home.

I miss you Mommy. I wish you could hug me
right now. Billy's mommy still hugs him every
day and plays with him in the yard. I wish I
could get hugs from you. I don't remember
what it feels like.

He woke up thinking of her, reeking a little of alcohol but not of stale makeup and perfume. He recalled she didn't wear perfume, though her hair smelled nice. *She wasn't like all those other girls,* he thought. *It was like visiting someone you knew. A friend. No crotch grabbing. No regimented program of asking for drinks every ten minutes.*

He didn't hear the words "buy me drink" once all night. That was the kind of place he was looking to kick back in. He was about to enter negotiations to run a major political campaign to take back City Hall. He could use a place to unwind from time to time.

Glenn remembered other things. She worked Tuesdays through Saturday nights. She had a day job from Monday to Saturday. The bar was closed Sundays. She didn't work on Monday nights because she had the night shift for her day job. He made a mental note to ask what she did during the day.

In his head, he calculated she put in thirty hours a week at the bar, and assuming forty hours a week for her day job, this girl was cranking seventy hours a week. *Not impossible*, he thought. He averaged that much at his old job. Her work ethic impressed him. *But why so much? What did she do in her spare time? Is there a significant other?*

She also told him he'd missed her thirtieth birthday by a week. He thought she looked mid-twenties but was never good at guessing age. At some point in the evening, he told her he was forty-five, not fifty-three. She feigned surprise and told him she thought he was late thirties and didn't realize she was with an old man. He faked being hurt—though he wasn't sure why he felt a little irritated—but she squeezed his arm ever so slightly and said, "No worries, I have daddy issues—we're perfect together!"

The last three words wiped out any issues in his mind. He smiled. *This girl really knew how to make a guy feel good.*

And he needed to feel good. He lay back on his bed, forearm on his head. *How did I let it get to this?*

Half sleeping, have awake, he relived what had led to his demise.

Two quick buzzes. Glenn opened his eyes. It was 9:00 a.m. on a Friday morning—a holiday. At this hour he was usually in cabinet fighting with Clifford.

Two more quick buzzes. Glenn's brain clicked on. He reached over for his phone. Two quick buzzes meant it was the Admiral.

The Admiral was the de facto chair of an immensely powerful group, responsible for electing every governor and mayor in the state and county for the last forty years. He had a reach that touched every facet of business and politics. He had started the group to get influential people together to help less powerful people. Power and influence with a moral compass.

Glenn breathed in and composed himself. "Hello?"

"Get up, I'm already at the diner. Eggs, ham, hash browns for you. It'll be cold in twenty minutes." Click.

Shit, Glenn thought. *This guy always acted like he was in a John Grisham novel.*

No matter. For once, he'd called at a decent hour. The calls usually came at 6:00 a.m. or in the middle of the night. *Whatever*, he thought. Glenn would have swum halfway across the ocean at 3:00 a.m. for this man.

He ran into the diner ten minutes late. As promised, his food was cold. "Sit," said the Admiral. "I have an opportunity for you." It always started like this. Glenn sawed into cold ham and eggs and listened.

"The Senate Budget Subcommittee on Transportation and Housing has its final meeting on Tuesday. There's three-and-a-half billion dollars at stake for the state, split two billion dollars for the new rail project and one-and-a-half billion for an affordable housing project that will greatly curb homelessness."

"I'm familiar, Admiral. Both projects, heavily connected with the city."

"Yes, Glenn. It was your white paper that caused such a stir in Congress."

"*My* white paper? No, my staff did that." Glenn recalled that the plan formed the basis of a homelessness solution, linking a massive affordable housing project with economic revitalization measures to create much-needed jobs and training. The key was organizing a funding group to raise the money for the housing project. Private funding amounted to two billion dollars, short by one-and-a-half billion dollars. The federal funding covered the shortfall.

"Humble as always, Glenn, but that plan had your name all over it, even if you had your division chief sign off so the civil servant network would back it. Great ploy. We were impressed with how you shepherded the plan through the Council. A 9-0 vote on anything for the first time in two years."

"I think it's a safe bet that you made a few calls, sir. Pissed Clifford off though. And the developer mafia . . . well, they don't like me much, do they?"

Clifford had fought Glenn all the way. The local land developers didn't want a massive affordable housing project. They wanted to build smaller projects to keep the pricing high, essentially to line their pockets. Glenn was adamant that to have truly affordable housing, you had to flood the market. He was about to depress housing prices for a long, long time. Developers saw profit margins disappearing soon and blamed Clifford for not controlling Glenn.

The Admiral sipped his coffee. "Don't worry about the developers. The small-timers are the most vocal. We got the bigger developers covered. The way you weaved economic incentives into the plan was genius. They just don't want to get caught in between you and Clifford."

He slid an envelope to Glenn. "You leave for DC in four hours. Here's your ticket. The vote is split. Clifford and the mayor have done everything they could to tank the rail project so that this federal funding package dies."

The Admiral leaned forward. "As you know, the developers have promised Clifford and the mayor the next seats in City Hall and the Senate, respectively. We're fighting big money here, Glenn, and not just locally—real estate development is global. So it was a great idea of yours to put the white paper in the hands of a citizen group with very little say-so by the government."

Glenn let out a whistle. He reviewed the plan in his mind. The federal funding was sorely needed. If no funding, then no housing was built, and there would be no flooding the market. He sat back. One point he never made to anyone. With federal funding, the project would come with HUD oversight to ensure the project served the people HUD meant to serve. *It'll carry on long after I'm gone. The U.S. Department of Housing and Urban Development will make sure of that.*

The Admiral tapped the table. "The two Chinese firms are all over Congress to stop this. The Italian firm doing the rail is arguing for the full amount. Tons of after-hours happy ending parties going on right now in DC. The usual enticements. Be careful. Keep your penis in your pants."

Glenn wasn't sure what he meant. The Admiral noticed the confusion. "Just be careful. Spies everywhere. Check your human feelings and emotions at the door. Here's your itinerary. You're working with Andy and Betsy. Leave the elected guys out. They don't need to know."

Andy and Betsy were the chiefs of staff for the state's two US senators. Equal in stature to every other state's two senators and chiefs of staff. Each, in turn, spoke for the senators they served. Andy and Betsy had come up through the ranks of the group. They were groomed to be public servants first, everything else second. Glenn had worked on campaigns with each. They knew each other very well. Glenn had once crushed on Betsy.

The Admiral slid over a list of names. "Glenn, here's the game plan."

Looking at the list, Glenn saw that he would spend the entirety of Saturday, Sunday and Monday in meetings with various individuals on the Hill. The names of US senators were scarce on the list. The plan was to meet with those who influenced the senators who had a vote on the subcommittee.

The Admiral called for the check. "You remember Anya, my secretary? She'll have all the meetings laid out by the time you land." His name had that effect. Just a few chits out of his three lifetimes worth.

Almost as an afterthought, the Admiral casually said, "You know the story where someone starts off bartering with a paper clip and one day ends up with a car? Well, you're going to write your own story. You'll have three million dollars to come back with the votes for three-and-a-half billion dollars. You can go now, Glenn. And good luck." The Admiral shook Glenn's hand, internally sizing up his protégé. *We need more like him. No matter where he goes, he never shies away from even the toughest assignments. If people are involved and there's a chance to better people's lives, he'll get it done.*

Glenn landed back home on Monday morning on the first flight out of DC. He didn't have to stay for the hearing. He knew a two-vote margin would approve the federal funding. Andy and Betsy would ensure that their respective senators gave impassioned speeches on the Senate floor. The swing votes would credit such speeches as the turning point. It looked that way to the layperson watching CNN.

In reality, key voters were bombarded with enough calls on their private cells by influential constituents that they either abstained from a no vote, or outright reversed their earlier position and voted for the measure.

Meanwhile, the Chinese partying stopped on Friday night, spurred on by rumors of a corporate raid by a large multinational Japanese firm and new bids for the Chinese company's projects all over Asia—rumors all floated within a period of twenty-four hours.

Almost within minutes of the rumors hitting, the Chinese contractors and influence peddlers were on the first flight back to Beijing, leaving their key votes vulnerable to phone calls on Sunday.

Glenn came back with one hundred thirty-five thousand dollars in his bank account. He donated it to the homeless project.

He slept only four hours during the weekend and consumed massive amounts of beer, whiskey, wine and whatever the other side drank. His room at a four-star hotel was untouched except to store his duffel bag and to allow a shower before he checked out.

He slept all the way back on the plane. When he landed, a text was waiting for him from the Admiral. A smiley face emoji. *Geez*, he thought, *when did he learn to do that?*

He headed off to City Hall straight from the airport. Clifford was waiting for him—pissed.

The founding fathers built City Hall in the style of Spanish haciendas. Sound carried far in the great enclosed courtyard with a ceiling three stories high.

Clifford met Glenn halfway across the courtyard.

"Saw CNN this morning. You had anything to do with that?"

Glenn yawned. "No."

Clifford's eyes flashed with hate. "Great speeches by the senators. Sounded like the one you gave before the Council a few months ago."

Glenn stared off to the right, said "Hi" to a few people on the second floor. "Got mine off the internet. They must have too."

Clifford snapped, poking Glenn in the chest. "Bullshit."

Glenn stood his ground, his eyes narrowing. "Bullshit yourself. At least we're giving you credit for rail funding."

"Thanks Glenn, but that's not all. We're taking the rest of the money for rail too. Don't worry, we'll leave some in the pot for housing, and our friends have assured us homes will be affordable."

Glenn was tired of this shit and lost it. It'd been a slow decline since Katie left his life. She had always been his sounding board, patiently absorbing all his rage and angst.

Glenn poked his finger at Clifford and exploded in a voice that filled every inch of City Hall air. "You're a fuckin' retard!" Security looked the other way, rolling their eyes, having seen this before. The press started scribbling. The poke was followed by a shove, bouncing Clifford hard off a sandstone pillar.

Regaining composure, Glenn shot back. "Your developer friends like to say they're building affordable housing, but in what universe is half a million dollars affordable? The Admiral and group aren't gonna like this."

Clifford hissed back, "Fuck the Admiral. We're cousins, you know. But he always liked you better. You two and your Judeo-Christian shared ideology."

Glenn stared the deputy mayor down. *So the Admiral and I are Christian. I don't understand why Clifford always makes it sound like we're part of some medieval cult.* "This isn't over, Clifford."

"Yeah, it is Glenn. I talked it over with the mayor, and we need to discuss separation of employment. As you know, your position reports to me, not the mayor."

Glenn started to make an about-face and go see the mayor when Clifford caught his arm. "He's gone to Korea for a week. I'm the acting mayor, and you're fired. We can make this easy, or we can make this hard."

———————

That's how it ended, how he came to be where he was.

He flung the pillow off his face and punched at thin air. *Fuck you, Clifford! Just wait, union thugs owe me a favor.*

A small voice inside him whispered. *Vengeance is mine, Glenn, not yours.*

Glenn silently argued. *Really Father? Now You speak to me. Where were You the last three days?*

If he had had the eyes of a prophet, Glenn would have seen his Father by his side, not only those three days but all his life.

He sat up and buried his face in his hands. *Crap,* he thought, *I feel like shit. I gotta see her again. Tonight.*

7

SUDDENLY SMITTEN

Eighth grade

Dear Mama,

I hate girls. Nobody talks to me. I'm wearing hand-me-down clothes from the '70s from cousins in Missouri. Mama, I look like crap. Even I wouldn't talk to me.

I don't see Billy's mom hug him so much. He's way taller than her but she still gives him a quick hug and I see her ruffle his hair and as big as he is, he still breaks down and acts like a little boy sometimes. I try not to stare. My heart aches for you Mama. If I could just get one more hug from you. I hug my pillow but it's not the same.

"Hello, love," a familiar voice cooed, "we kept your seat warm for you." He thought Tia was even prettier tonight, imagining the most glam picture of Chloe Kim he'd ever seen.

She had a Bud Light before him even as he settled in at the bar. The place was bustling. It was later than the last time he stumbled in. All the girls were there with customers or looking for customers.

Off to the side, he spied the dart room with girls and guys playing for shots. The bar area was well lit, diluting the violet glow from the black lights above the bar. Behind him, he remembered the darker room of booths to which most of the girls retired to with their favorites, or was it the other way around?

The booth room, as he called it, had two large chandeliers that weren't lit, but the room was ringed with a neon light—purple, magenta, fuchsia? He wasn't sure what color that was, but it provided enough light to know you were getting back the right change, and it was dark enough to make everyone look good after a little alcohol.

Music with a Latin beat was playing. A lacrosse game was on one flatscreen, and the others beamed out assorted music videos. The place smelled like liquor and Febreze, a surprisingly pleasant, fresh smell. Servers were carrying drinks back and forth.

Maya peeked out from the dart room doorway and smiled. "Gleeenn!" she sang out, like clear chimes on a quiet windy night. Glenn had heard that in some movie—a bad movie, but shit, it described her voice perfectly.

Glenn did his best to look cool at the bar, but his heart started beating fast. "Easy boy," he heard Tia say under her breath, "let her come to you."

And there she was, by his side again. She wore shorts this time, olive green with a matching blouse. Same smoky eyes, pale red lips; Glenn never made his way past the other features.

"You like?" she said.

Something was different. Glenn searched his memory, trying to bring an image of her last night to compare. "I dunno, what . . ."

She ran her fingers through her hair, lifting the parts that used to be highlighted. "My hair . . . back to natural, black. You like?"

"I like." She could have been bald, and he still would have liked.

Glenn eyed the dart room. "You have customers tonight?"

"Just one," she said. Glenn looked disappointed, only for a second, before she poked his shoulder and said, "You!"

He nearly blushed. *Why do I get such a rush from that? I got so much more attention at the other places, but this is different.*

He downed his beer. After another beer and small talk about how she'd been, and how he'd been, and the weather, and Tia's dazzling dress, he ordered a third beer. Only then did he notice that she was drinking water. He cleared his throat and pointed to her glass. "Do you want something to drink?" The frustrations of the day were forgotten.

She smiled. "No need." She poured his beer into a frosted glass Tia brought over. "Here, try it this way." She clinked her glass to his. "Cheers! I'm just happy you here!"

Glenn found himself insisting. At the other places, he had to fight off girls who were too aggressive. Most asked for a drink as soon as they sat next to you. One drink later, they were asking for your phone number. Here he was on his third beer and not a peep.

Maya saw that he had the look of someone whose feelings were about to be hurt. "Okay, you win. What should I have?"

He felt another rush. "I have no idea—whatever you want." Glenn bit his tongue. The last girl he said that to ordered a $400 bottle of champagne.

Maya turned toward Tia. Tia already knew and brought a peach Ciroc with water back.

Lots of small talk followed. Then silence. He had grown quiet.

Concerned, Maya lightly touched his forearm. He didn't flinch this time. "What on your mind?"

She could tell he was struggling. She sat patiently, quietly. She kept her hand where it was. As if to say, take your time, it's okay.

He lifted his glass but then put it down without taking a sip. He took a breath. "Sorta wondering when you're going to ask me where I live, and what I do for a living, and what kind of car do I drive?" To the uninitiated, this was perfect small talk. Glenn knew it was standard procedure for every bargirl to inquire about such details to size up how cash-rich the customer was. That's when the "How much money can I get from you?" games began.

She smiled as if the answer should be obvious. "Why? You don't need to tell me anything."

This caught Glenn by surprise. "Really? Why not?"

She squeezed his hand and reached for her drink. "Most guys lie anyway, and the rich ones already tell me how rich they are."

He drained his beer glass. "So you think I'm poor?"

She filled his glass. "Do you want another?" He nodded. "No. I don't think you poor. Nice. Different. Interesting." She did have one question. "You married?"

Glenn fingered the ring in his pocket. "I don't have anyone waiting for me at home. All alone." She seemed okay with the answer.

Glenn took off his glasses and laid them on the counter. She picked them up right away. Looking like a lab tech, she held them up to the light. "Dirty." She started wiping.

He sat transfixed. *This is different*, he thought. *No one ever cleaned my glasses for me.*

She met his gaze then turned back to his glasses, breathing on the stubborn areas and polishing with a clean napkin. "I worked, um, eyeglass shop. Optho . . . " She was having a hard time. "Opto . . . opti . . . op . . ."

He jumped in. "Ophthalmologist?"

"Yes, yes. I work front counter, and I clean and fix glasses for customers." Her accent was exotic. She said customers with a silent S—"

"cu-tom-er." It was cute to him, evoking a smile. She cocked her head and smiled back. "Why smile?"

He wondered where he should start. The sexy shape of her eyes, the pout of her lips, the warmth of her smile, and the musicality of her voice. It was all spellbinding. "Nothing," was all he could muster, and trying to sound calm, "your accent . . . cute." He could feel his heart beat faster.

She put his glasses back on his face. "There. Perfect." She turned to him, her knee subtly touching his. "I know, cannot talk English good yet," she said in a self-conscious tone.

His eyebrows shot up. He smiled. Lifted his hands palm outward as if to say, whoa. "Oh no, you talk good. I'm always impressed by anyone who speaks English as a second language. I enjoy hearing your stories." He marveled at her command of the English language. He thought she spoke so much better than all those other girls, who only had a few choice words describing body parts, positions, and x-rated services.

Another two beers. Another peach whatever that was. It was midnight. His stomach gurgled.

As if signaled by his stomach, Mama Lynh appeared by his side. "You hungry, honey?" She had a knack for showing up at the right times to move things along. "Maya, tell uncle bring food." By now, Maya knew Glenn was on a low carb diet. Uncle was the bar's cook, and he brought a meat salad of sirloin cubes in some type of sauce. Glenn was wondering what kind of meat it was. Mama left with a smile, and Glenn smiled back.

He turned back to Maya. His lips bumped into beef cubes held out to him with chopsticks. "You eat," she said. He opened his mouth, without argument, and she deftly placed the food in his mouth. He started chewing. He swallowed, and she had another piece ready to go at his lips.

He pointed to the plate and then to her with a quizzical look.

She replied, "No, no need, my tummy too big."

You gotta be kidding, he thought. Glenn looked her over up and down. What she was wearing was tight, and though she was sitting, there was no tummy bulge to be seen.

She kept feeding him for the next few minutes. With a concerned look, she said, "I'm worried. You drink too much. You need to eat. Uncle meat salad, no drunk, get you sober, no hangover."

Glenn put both his hands up after half the plate was gone. "No more," he gurgled.

She got more concerned. Glenn was suddenly not smiling. She lightly grazed his forearm. "You okay? Why you look sad?"

Covering his mouth, Glenn blurted out, "Shame. I have meat in my teeth."

She laughed, nearly squealed, simultaneously delighted and relieved, knowing he was still happy. She reached up to his hand and ever so gently pushed it downward, uncovering his mouth. She reached back upward and squeezed his mouth between thumb and index finger like a mother does a child to see if he brushed. "Don't worry, cannot see." She lied and chuckled. He was cute. Like a little boy.

Last call. 1:30. He thought the bar was well lit before, but more lights came on.

She shifted in her seat. She'd maintained knee-to-knee contact with him all night. And he liked it. It was reassuring, as if she was saying I'm here and I'm not leaving. "Glenn, you can stay to closing, just no more alcohol."

He was the one that broke contact. "I should go. Early morning meeting."

Glenn got off his stool and she followed. She stuck her hand out. "Nice to see you again, Glenn."

He shook her hand. "Nice to see you again, Maya." He thought to himself. *A handshake? Really? Standard protocol at the other places was at least a hug—anything to get the customer to come back.* A nagging feeling came to him: Maybe she didn't want to see him.

No way, he realized. She was smiling, eyes almost twinkling. He was drunk, full, and feeling good. He hadn't felt like this since his and Katie's first date. That was when he thought he had found "the one."

She held his hand just a little long. "You going to be okay?"

He wanted to hold her hand forever. "I'll be okay. I promise." She walked him as far as the door. He took three steps out and turned. She was still there, and he waved. She waved back.

He took two more steps, and he was already missing her. He went back again the next night.

8

PRIDE STUNG

College freshman year

Dear Mama,
I met a nice girl and then I lost her. Why can't
I hold onto girls? I said don't go and she said
she wouldn't. She broke up with me the next
day. She said she couldn't take the pressure
of me not trusting her. Shit. Shit. Shit.

I'm heartbroken Mama. I miss you. I don't
understand girls Mama. I wish I had someone
explain to me. I'm all grown but would still
love a hug. BTW, Billy's mom died last month.
I guess all moms leave their sons sometime.

He walked in and headed for "his" seat. Tia had his beer open before he got there. "How ya doing love?" Between Mama's "honey" and Tia's "love," Glenn was subject to a lot of affection he just wasn't used to.

He took a swig straight from the bottle. "Great, Tia. How ya doing?" They made small talk while he wondered where Maya was. He heard her and turned toward the dart room. Another girl was with her, and four guys. She glanced his way and for a quick second, smiled. He was hoping she'd come soon.

He knew it was her job to entertain. Not much he could do.

It was different from the night before. Tia disappeared for a bit and left Glenn to his thoughts. He most always got what he wanted. And what he wanted wasn't available. He thought of the other clubs.

Tia slid into the chair next to him. "Maya said 'Hi.' She'll be here, but she needs to stay with the guy. He's been her only regular and treats her well."

Somehow that sounded cheap to Glenn. "Thanks, Tia." Tia was easy to talk to. Her voice was smooth as silk and a mix between cooing and purring. She wasn't aggressive. They talked about Tia's real estate work and her fitness dreams. Glenn had some ideas that Tia took to.

Maya came out of the dart room to order drinks at the bar. She looked taller than before. High heels. Black cocktail dress with spaghetti straps baring her tan shoulders. While waiting for her order, she walked over to Glenn and Tia. She rubbed his back while she explained, "Sorry, old customer, not see for long time."

He forced a smile. Trying to sound casual, he asked, "How long, Maya?"

She looked back to the room and then to him. "He usually stay all night. So sorry. Didn't know you were coming. I take care you though. Tia sit with you, okay?"

She turned to her friend. "Tia, can you take care Glenn tonight?"

Glenn stayed another hour, till Tia got called back behind the bar. He took one last look at the dart room. *Seems lively in there. No sign of letting up.* "Hey Tia, can you say goodbye to Maya for me?" He didn't wait for an answer.

Twenty-four hours ago, I was Jack from Titanic *singing "I'm the king of the world." Tonight, I might as well be Jack from* Titanic, *frozen carcass sinking into the Atlantic.*

Never a quitter, he went back the next night. A little on the late side, but he went back.

"Hiya love." *Must be serious*, Tia thought, *four nights in a row?* Ten p.m. The place was running full steam. Loud hip-hop music was pulsing on the jukebox, masking over the crowd noise of soccer and basketball games on the flatscreens. From the booth room, a male and female voice croaked out a tone-deaf rendition of "Summer Nights" from *Grease*.

By now, the regulars were snickering at this latest fly in the web. Glenn flashed them all a smile. "Hey guys, round of beers?" Instantly, he was their best friend.

From the dart room, he could hear her voice. Maya and the same girl from the night before. Same two girls. A different group of guys.

Tia texted Maya from behind the bar.

"Gleeenn!!" He heard heels clacking on the bar's wooden floor right before she slammed into his left side with a bear hug, laying kisses all over his forehead. All the hurt from the night before evaporated.

He sat at the bar. She stood by him with her arm around him, like someone was going to steal him. Emerald green dress describable only as a slinky fit, baring one beautifully defined shoulder, leaving the other shoulder to the imagination. She took his arm in hers and put her head on his shoulder. She'd had a few already. Her voice was a little breathy. "I thought I lost you after last night. Thought you don't come back. But now you heeeere!" Another round of kisses. The old-timers turned away, grinning.

For the next half hour, they recreated the vibe from Tuesday night. This time, Jimmy the manager got involved and made some exotic drinks for them. Glenn hadn't had liquor in twenty years. There was a green drink and a blue drink. They drank from the same glass. In thirty minutes, there were six empty glasses in front of them.

Feelings were running high. He had his arm around her waist, and she had her arm around his neck and was sitting on his knee. Sheeren was singing, "I'm into your body." Glenn couldn't agree more. Both were breathing heavily. The old-timers were grinning as if cheering Glenn on. He swore some were making bets on what was going on.

Out of the corner of his eye, he saw someone poke his head out of the dart room and for a long second, stare their way. He didn't care. He was king of the world again.

Then the iceberg hit. The other girl came out of the dart room and made a beeline to Maya. They exchanged some words in Thai.

"Everything okay?" he said to her, his eyes asking for reassurance.

She kissed his cheek. "Yes, but I have to say bye to customer. Baby, I will come right back, okay?" The night was young. Glenn was happy. He called Jimmy over for more of the green and blue stuff. He ordered for himself and Maya.

She never came back. He peeked into the dart room. None of them were there. Glenn felt his frozen carcass sink back into the Atlantic. By last call, he had downed all his drinks and all of Maya's. He tossed a twenty on the bar and zigzagged out the door. He felt no pain, just emptiness and a desire to fall asleep.

Just like all the rest, he thought. In his mind, he was hoping she'd come running out the door after him. Then he heard his name. He hoped it was Maya.

It was Tia. "Hey, Glenn." She ran out to him.

Tia had seen the hurt. Saw it many times before with others. This time it was different. Glenn was a nice guy. She hugged him. The kind of hug loved ones give at wakes. "It's okay, Glenn. She has a job to do, you know? Customers bring in money."

"I have money," Glenn said. "You guys take my money."

She made sure they had eye contact. She wanted this one for Maya. "I know, Glenn. But she's starting out and needs to build a clientele. She's dependent on other girls partnering with her. She can't leave them behind."

"Partnering?" Glenn never heard of it.

She glanced over her shoulder, making sure the bar was okay. "It's when a popular girl can bring in groups of guys. She needs a partner to help entertain them. See the other girl with darts. That's Chloe. She's got tons of customers. Sometimes she doubles up with clients in the dart room and the main room." The main room, also known as the booth room to Glenn.

One hand on his shoulder, she continued. "So if Chloe's got a big group, she needs help entertaining. And when she's got two groups simmering, she needs help keeping the first group entertained while she goes and visits the other group. Or else they all leave, with their money."

She heard Jimmy call her name. "Chloe and Maya, they're like sisters. Both from Thailand. When Maya first got here, Chloe took her under her wing. Brought her into the business, showed her the ropes."

The term "human trafficking" popped into his head. On cue, Tia said, "It's not what you think—none of that around here."

He ran his fingers through his hair. The bartenders at this bar seemed to be clairvoyant. "You know, Tia, I like Maya." He was slurring a bit but knew what he was saying. "How's a guy get to spend a little more time with her?"

She flashed a smile. Tia for the save. "Tuesdays. That's Chloe's off night. I'll let Maya know you'll be back next Tuesday, okay?"

The parking lot was spinning, but he was smiling. "Yes. Please."

9

FIRST TUESDAY

College senior year

Dear Mama,
It's over for me and Lila. I don't understand.
We knew each other five years. We were
supposed to move in together. She said she
wanted to marry me when she turned 28. I
thought we had chemistry. I thought we had
trust. The day before I was supposed to move
in with her, I went over and she wasn't there.
She was with some other guy.

I'm done with women. I think I'll just get rich
and live off hookers and escorts. Get a dog
for company. Mama how come I keep getting
all the losers. How come I'm always the loser?
What's wrong with me?

He walked in early. The blond behind the bar waved both hands. "Long time no see!" Marcie remembered Glenn from the first time he was there. A ten dollar tip for doing nothing. She was the early shift. Tia was going to be late. Glenn took a seat at the bar, back to the open door. A cool breeze drifted in. It was the last Tuesday in August.

The regulars were there. A motley crew. Most retired. Some toothless. There to nurse their beers as long as they could. Someone at the bar always made food around 8:00—mostly Vietnamese, with a fair amount of steaks and chickens and stews. The aroma was like home cooking.

The jukebox was silent, and every newscast on the flatscreens was about to sign off.

Was she going to show? Were there other customers? Did Tia talk to her? He was a little irritated Tia wasn't around to fill him in.

A pair of hands covered his eyes. *Soft. Hint of lilac. Probably hand lotion.* She made a play at disguising her voice and deeply said, "Guess who."

He reached up, took her hands in his, and brought them to his shoulders. "Ummm, soft hands, beautiful voice, can only be one person." He paused for effect. "Tia!"

She slapped his shoulder so hard he saw the mark when he went home that night.

"Naughty!" she scolded, and scooted on to the barstool next to him, wearing a velvet burgundy dress, long-sleeved, mid-thigh with plunging neckline, hugging her in all the right places. He barely noticed her Chanel earrings. Tia walked in just then. Glenn caught Tia's eye and put his finger to his lips. Tia looked confused. Glenn mock pleaded, in an overexaggerated whisper, "Don't tell Maya about the other night."

Oh, a game. Tia caught on. She smiled sweetly as she came around the bar, and whispered, rather loudly, "Don't worry, nothing to remember, already forgotten!" The peanut gallery roared, and Maya and Tia joined in. Glenn turned red but laughed along, even though he wasn't used to being laughed at. Maya gave him a hug and a kiss on the cheek, quickly wiping off her lipstick. All was good.

Jimmy came over. "Glad you still standing after all the blue and green you had last week." Jimmy and Tia filled Maya in on how much Glenn took in that night.

Glenn balked. "Are you kidding? No way my system can handle that."

Both Jimmy and Tia nodded.

Maya's face reflected concern. "You drove home?"

"No, taxi." The truth was he didn't know how he got home. He thought he walked the mile back to his condo. But he said taxi so she wouldn't worry.

Maya looked hurt, worried, scared, concerned, all of the above. She shot Jimmy a look that said, "No more." He grinned and shrugged.

She turned back to Glenn and said, "No more. That stuff dangerous. Hit you after, later, not during." She let it sink in and pressed further. "No more, okay? Only beer when I'm not around. You can have those drinks when I'm with you, so I can protect you."

He liked the sound of that. Something in his core stirred. His heart tightened. All sound and movement came to a stop. He thought of his mother and Billy's mother. His heartbeat sped up. Then he took a deep breath.

She saw him tense, then relax. She was about to say something when he cracked a joke. "I guess you better be around a lot because I very much liked that stuff."

She reached out and pinched his cheek, not hard, with considerable affection. "Don't worry. I will be here for you."

He glanced over at Jimmy. "What else you got? For my pretty friend here too."

When they were alone, or as alone as can be in a raucous bar, she reached over and squeezed his hand. "Sorry about the other night. My friend, too much drink, got sick. Had to take her home. I look for you but you was in bathroom." Glenn vaguely remembered getting up to pee.

She let go just as he tried to take her hand. Jimmy came over with a large shot glass. Brownish amber liquid. One ice cube. "Try."

Glenn eyed it suspiciously. "What's this?"

Jimmy gave him the thumbs up. "No worry. Good stuff. Japanese whiskey. Sip."

Glenn didn't hear sip and downed the liquid in one shot. Maya stared wide-eyed. Glenn smiled as the warmth spider-webbed through his veins.

She took the shot glass and sniffed. "You crazy. No more." She felt his face with the back of her hand. "Warm. No more, okay? Just beer."

He grinned. "Okay, just beer." At the touch of her hand on his face, he again sensed a tightness. It came and went, but it was like the lingering smell of lilac. Not obvious but . . . noticeable and pleasing.

He played with the empty shot glass. "Something for you?"

"No need," she replied. She took the empty glass from him. She replaced it with a frosted beer glass and poured his beer for him. He asked again. This time she nodded—peach Ciroc.

Mama Lynh came out of the back with a plate of what passed for chicken wings. "Ah, my favorite couple!"

Maya squealed disapproval. "Mommy!"

"No honey. He your man. You can tell. He hungry." On cue, Glenn's stomach growled. She handed the plate to Maya. "Here, Maya, take this."

Glenn looked over at the plate. *Curious. Not chicken wings.* "What's that?"

Lynh and Maya answered in unison. "Quail."

His mouth gaped slightly in surprise. "Quail? What hostess bar serves quail?"

Mama simply said, "This one, honey. This one do plenny things others don't do."

Mama left as quickly as she came. Her last words hung in the air long enough to make them both feel awkward. "Maya, take care your man. He good man. Take care."

Glenn didn't feel like he was at a hostess bar. He felt like he was on a date. The last date he'd had like this was in college, the first time he went over to Katie's house for dinner. Her mother had said the same things. Feed Glenn. Make him happy. All his life, people liked to feed Glenn. He had that kind of face.

Maya started stripping off quail meat from the tiny bones and feeding Glenn by hand. The barflies thought it was exotic. They'd never seen her do that before. One snickered to the other. "Like some harem girl!"

Glenn caught her hand. Mouth half full, he warbled, "What about you?"

She smiled mischievously as if to say, I can't wait to see your expression. "I eat bone." Glenn thought she was joking until she popped a tiny quail leg bone into her mouth. His jaw went slack as he gawked. The crunch sounded like she was eating pretzels. The bird was small enough so that the bones had been cooked through in the oven, and she relished eating them. Glenn marveled. He'd never seen anything like it. She kept feeding him the meat and ate the bones herself.

She waved a wing at Tia. "Hey girl, want some?" Tia came over and took a wingtip and popped the whole thing in her mouth.

He arched an eyebrow. "You too?" *Everyone in this place eats bones?*

Maya stuck a bone by his mouth, lightly grazing his lips. "You try."

Glenn begged off. "No, pass." He had a flash vision of bleeding to death while the bones tore up his colon. *Isn't this why we don't give chicken bones to dogs?*

Maya was adamant. "No, you try. You try. If not like, then no more. But you cannot say no if no try. *Try*, Glenn!" She didn't wait for an answer, nor was a protest even possible.

She stuck a small piece in front of his face. He couldn't say no and opened his mouth slowly. She put the bone on the tip of his tongue, and when he closed his mouth, he caught her finger as she pulled out. Her index finger lingered ever so slightly on his lower lip.

It was the most erotic experience he'd ever had. One quail bone, her fingers on his lips. He was mesmerized. Time moved in slow motion. She pushed his lower lip upward to close his mouth.

She was inches from his face. Her lips felt closer. "Chew." She said it softly, almost seductively.

He started chewing and expected to swallow grit with his beer. Such was not the case. It was like a pretzel.

She was beaming. "Good?"

He felt something he hadn't in a long time. Sheepishly, he softly echoed, "Good."

She tussled his hair. "Good," she repeated, then fed him more quail meat. Hand-stripped and hand-fed quail meat. She was happy to keep the bones for herself.

Somewhere during the night, she asked if he had someone waiting for him at home. *I guess she forgot she asked me already.* "No," he said, "not for a long time."

Turnabout was fair play. "What about you? Is there someone waiting at home for you?"

She took a sip of the Ciroc he'd ordered for her. "Yes."

Caught off guard, he blurted. "What?" *Okay, hands off then.*

She chuckled and slapped his thigh. "No, not like that." She laughed even more and finished her shot. Glenn waved Tia for one more.

She looked around. As if she was about to impart something personal. For his ears only. "I have dog. Divorced three years earlier. He kept everything. I got dog. All I wanted. I met him in Thailand. Military. Move to Wyoming. We divorce. He go Florida. I come here with cousin. Keep in touch sometimes. Keep in touch with mother-in-law. Still call me daughter."

She showed him a picture of a larger than average corgi. "Love my dog. My son. Six years old. Mommy's little boy. Cousin watch while I work."

He saw the opening to learn more. He waved Tia for a beer. "Where do you work?

She paused a bit, maybe to consider whether to tell him the truth or some lie, or simply change the subject. Other patrons had stalked her at work. "Not everybody here know, Glenn. I tell you. I dunno why but I trust you. I have a day job. Beauty consultant. Remember I told you last week? Work six days a week there. Five nights at bar. Day job not work on Tuesday. Bar not work on Sunday Monday. In between, work out and take care dog. Sleep. Send money home to mommy and sister."

He was taking it all in. By instinct memorizing her bio, profiling her out of habit. "So you had a day off today, but you came in?"

She wrapped up the last of the quail for him to take home. "Yes."

He frowned. "Sucks."

She shrugged, and half patted, half rubbed his chest. His rock-hard pecs did not go unnoticed. "It's okay. I get to see you now." She smiled. He smiled back.

Tia watched from the other side of the bar. Her only thought: *Awwww.*

This was like a first date. And he was working up the courage to ask her out again. But he wondered, *How do you do that?* He'd never had to ask about a second time. He went and whoever was available sat with him. This was different.

He was scratching his head, running his fingers through his hair. His expression was one of perplexity bordering on fear. He reminded Tia of a freshman asking a senior out to prom.

It was hard not to notice. One barfly whispered to the other, "Hey check it out, Jimmy Stewart asking out Donna Reed." The other barfly had no idea who the actors were but caught the gist.

She waited patiently. She got off her stool. Turned him to her and took one step between his legs. She put her hand on his shoulders. Just eighteen inches away. She gazed into his eyes. "Glenn, what on your mind?"

He cleared his throat, met her gaze, then looked away. She reached out and gently pulled his face back to face her. "What you want, Glenn?"

She was so close. He focused on her lips. Like delicate rose petals, pink rose petals. *Inviting. I so want to kiss her.* "So do you work here next Tuesday?"

She held steady. "I work every Tuesday." Inside, her heart was beating fast.

He took a deep breath. "So if I come and you're with another customer, I mean, it's okay . . ."

She patted his shoulders. "If I'm with another customer, I will come to you. You are my number one. I will come to you. I will wait for you. I will be here for you. I will not go away."

Somehow the last statement brought sadness and uncertainty to him. He shrugged it off. "Okay, next Tuesday?"

She felt something was wrong. *Maybe I said something?* "Okay. Thank you for tonight Glenn." She reached out and massaged his neck. "You come back, Glenn?"

He relished her affection. Any trepidation melted away. "Yes, for sure."

Tia watched. *What's going on here? These two act like he's going off to war or something.*

Last call came too quickly. Mama came running out. "Honey, you have good time tonight? How Maya, she take care you?"

Maya put on a happy face. "Yes, Mommy. I take care. He go home now. Early meeting tomorrow."

"What meeting for?" Lynh wanted to know.

Maya leaned lightly on him, yelling over his shoulder. Her hair smelled nice. "No, Mommy, he not say yet. Don't pressure."

Mama nodded. No need to know—yet.

Glenn wondered how clairvoyant Mama was. She always knew when he was coming and going. Maybe Jimmy or Tia called her. He didn't notice the surveillance cameras above the bar.

Mama walked off. "Good night, honey. Be careful going home." Glenn turned to Maya. This time they hugged, and she walked him to the door.

Divorced. Hard worker. Devoted daughter sending money home. He'd heard this version before. But somehow, he believed her. He was lost in thought, trying to hang on to all the pleasant memories the night produced.

He turned around. She was still at the door. She waved. He waved back. *I'm the king of the world . . .*

10

SEPTEMBER KARAOKE

College graduation

Dear Mama,
I think I met the girl I want to marry. I feel
safe with her Mama, like she never gonna
leave me.

And Mama, she introduced me to Jesus. She's
a good girl. I ask her what her superpower is.
How she can be so strong. She told me not to
worry. Love conquers all.

Are you still watching over me? I still feel like
it. I feel like you sent me her. She gives me
peace.

It was the first Tuesday in September, and Glenn had just started a new job at a low-level non-profit, the only one in town that wasn't somehow influenced by Clifford. He was a lowly bean counter with a storage closet for an office, dealing with the people you see yelling at invisible demons in the middle of the road or sitting in the gutter in their own piss, shit, vomit, or some combination.

His ego and id waged war with his sense of self-worth. *I guess it's a respectable enough title in a respectable enough non-profit run by respectable enough people.*

He paused, raked his hands through his hair. *Then why do I feel like shit? With Clifford putting this city on lockdown, it's at least a way to pay the bills. Nuff said. I just gotta keep convincing myself, that's all.*

By the end of the day, his ego had had enough. The place stank like homeless piss. There were never enough supplies, payroll was always two weeks behind, and in his mind, the CEO and COO were incompetent. *No wonder the accounting manager resigned. She waited long enough for them to hire another sucker—me. This was supposed to be a forty-hour-a-week job. She works sixty hours minimum, and now I have to cover her and me? I'm about to work the same hours as at the city, for half the pay.*

He sat at his desk, stewing, feeling empty, void, worthless, disrespected. He looked at his watch. 8:00 p.m. *I gotta go where I can feel good again. Good thing it's Tuesday. Back to my lifeline.* If he wasn't careful, she'd be more than that—an escape, a drug, an addictive opioid that he needed to handle with care. The problem was, he didn't care. He needed her to get through the week.

He got there first, met by the usual Tuesday night crowd—barflies, bargirls, and bar customers, with the usual sports and game shows on the flatscreens. The jukebox was revved up with dance club music, and somewhere in the booth room, a group of insurance sales types was reliving younger days.

She walked in right after him. She had on black shorts and a black bareback halter top. When her hair moved, he saw an amazing phoenix tattoo that stretched from shoulder to shoulder. He'd waited all week for this. Like a schoolboy waiting for prom day, with the cheerleader as his date. Only he didn't look happy.

She brushed his hair to one side. Stared at him, more like examined him visually. "You don't look okay. You look sad. Everything okay?"

Her concern flooded him with warmth. "I know. I'm tired is all. I upped my workouts to five a week. Two times on Saturday. I can barely drag myself out of bed."

Her expression questioned whether there was more. But she played along. "You take protein?"

He paused. "I eat enough." *She saw me eat meat last week. What an odd question. Where's this going?*

She was standing, hands on her hips, her lips a straight line manifesting a resolute seriousness. "No, you need protein. Not enough. I bring for you next week, okay?" She went on to tell him how the body needed protein for proper recovery.

He nodded every few seconds. *This is weird*, he thought. *I'm getting a nutrition lesson in a hostess bar.*

Subconsciously flexing his chest, he thought back to his early years pumping iron. *I've done this for years. I don't need her going about telling me how to do something I've done longer than she's been living. Still, gotta admit, she looks like she knows what she's doing, and at least knows the right people.*

He felt it best not to cause friction. "Yup, okay. I'll try whatever you bring." For the first time that night, she cracked a smile.

The night progressed to shots of blue and green, and the occasional messed-up purple. She observed him carefully to make sure he was okay.

He was supposed to leave at 11:00. The bar clock flashed midnight. Both drunk, both tired, neither wanted to leave.

She brought over a big black binder filled with song titles and numbers—a karaoke songbook. "You sing, Glenn?"

He turned his empty shot glass over on the counter with a clunk. "Sing what?"

She held out a wireless microphone. "Karaoke."

He smiled, wagging his head from side to side. "Uh-uh. No, no way. Too embarrassing. Bad experience as a kid."

She scrunched her face a bit, then softened. "Can I sing?"

That's different. "Sure!"

She sang "Impossible" by Shontelle, and the words were so haunting, he wondered if something had happened that day? He'd later download the song on YouTube to hear it again.

He reflected on her performance. *What happened in her life that put so much pain into this song? Was this one of those times her ex-husband had reached out to her? It must have been bad. Does she still have feelings?*

The lyrics played out on the karaoke screen and the words rolled by, telling a tale of love and heartbreak, of being cautious not to get hurt again and again, but finding it impossible. Finding that love always risks heartache, and heartache leaves scars that can be ripped off your heart, and so true love without heartache is impossible. *Whoever or whatever she's thinking of, lots of pain there.*

He swore she was nearly sobbing during the chorus. Then the performance was over. The barflies clapped. The customers clapped. The whole placed clapped. She could really belt it out. He'd never heard something so soulfully sung.

She held out the microphone again. "You ever sing? You try now?"

"Nope, and nope. But I love to hear you sing!" Inside his head, inhibition diminishing, Glenn was itching to sing, like he did so many times at home in front of *Karaoke on Demand.*

She observed him deep in thought, and could tell he wanted to sing. On the other nights, she saw him mouthing the words while she sang. She watched him mouth the words when other patrons sang. She had seen it.

He knew the words to all the Journey songs by heart. She leaned in closer as if readying to whisper a secret. "You like to sing, huh?"

He tilted his head, shrugged his shoulders as if to say I can't lie. "Yes."

Jimmy brought them two shots. Pink liquid. Looked like Pepto Bismol, smelled like bubble gum.

"Cheers." They clinked glasses. Down the hatch. His eyes went wide. Warmth radiated through his whole body. Even his pecker tingled. *Whooaaah! What is this shit!*

She leaned over and kissed his cheek. She left the lipstick. She felt bolder. "Why not sing?"

Glenn remembered the school kids, the ones that teased him in music class. "Nah, pass."

She glanced over at Tia and nodded.

She grabbed his face in her hands, pitching it side to side ever so slightly with each word, and just inches from his face whispering loudly, "Do. What. Make. You. *Happy*! No worry what others think!"

This line would stay with Glenn for the rest of his life.

Journey started piping in, and Glenn thought, *No way, not my anthem.* "Don't Stop Believin'." Microphone or no microphone, he was singing, doing his best Steve Perry, coming up on the chorus.

"You gotta believe!" She was nearly yelling, cheering him on now. She was singing with a mic in one hand, and with her other hand stuck another mic in his face. All his inhibition gone, he grabbed the mic and started belting it out. A star was born.

By the second chorus, he was on his feet playing air guitar and channeling Neal Schon. The whole bar was singing along. She was clapping, pumping the air, jumping, cheering him on, and singing with him during the slightly pitchy times, harmonizing.

In the end, the bar erupted in cheers. When it came to karaoke, it didn't matter if you were pitchy as long as you put your heart into it. And three hours of beer mixed with the blue and green, the pink bubble gum drink, and a beautiful woman found him lacking any inhibitions. Later the bar would name the drink Maya's Pretty Pinks.

She put her arms around him and hugged, squeezing him tight. "You did *goooood*!" She was feeling happy, much more than when she came in. It was so natural. They were cheek to cheek. He turned to her. She to him. He kissed her. She leaned back, arms still around his neck. He leaned in. Kissed her again. Not deep. A light kiss. They stood frozen. Eyes locked. Awkward. Now what? The question was on both their minds.

"Last call!" someone yelled, breaking the awkwardness. Elvis's "Can't

Help Falling in Love" started playing. The song was a shower number that Glenn had sung for many years. It was someone else's song, and Glenn began singing along without a mic. She slid off her chair and reached out for him.

He half-smiled. *Dance?* Most natural feeling in the world to go to her. They danced on a tiny floor in front of the bar. It was slow. She had heels on. A little taller than him. Didn't matter. She put her head on his shoulder, and they sang the chorus together. King of the world, and his queen. He kissed her again.

Tia watched wide-eyed. She'd never seen this before. Not in the bar. Sing. Dance. Kiss.

Do what make you happy . . . no worry what others think!

He went to sleep thinking about this, and it was the first thing that came to his mind when he woke up. Then he remembered the kiss—natural, soft, tender, sweet.

11

GROWING UP THAILAND

He touched his lips. *One week later, I can still feel her kiss. So soft, so sweet. Did I cross a line? Wonder what she's thinking. Must be okay.* He thought back to their last night together.

She walked him out. "Don't eat next week, okay? I will cook for you."

Glenn's eyes perked up then. He assumed she'd cook Thai. He never had Thai food. He didn't like to try new foods. He simply gurgled, "Okay."

One week later, he walked into the bar with one thought after another. *Should I say something about the kiss? Or just forget it? Was she really cooking something? Was this normal? Was she liking him?* Some in the bar were already calling them "the Tuesday couple."

It was a relatively quiet second Tuesday of September. Tia was stocking the bar. She nodded and gave a cheery "Hiya love." A sweet and sour aroma wafted from the kitchen. No music yet and only a few of the barflies were in, watching nothing in particular on the flatscreens.

Maya met him with open arms and a hug, wearing a beige cocktail dress. A jade pendant accented a deep V of cleavage. "I hope you like Thai food. Pad Thai—my family recipe." Simple dish, but it had been ages since anyone had cooked for Glenn. And he was nursing an after-workout hunger.

She smiled as if she'd waited for this all week. "Let's go to our spot."

He cocked his head. *We have a spot?*

She took his plate and went around the side of the bar. They sat, and she arranged the food in front of him, even placing a napkin on his lap.

He dug in. "Wow, this is great. I never had noodles taste this good! What's the secret?"

Maya watched Glenn eat. She giggled, thinking he looked just like her dog, Rusty, wolfing down his food at home. "No secret, just Thai fish sauce."

She filled her own plate and ate with him. Her eyes widened. *Finish already?* "Want more, Glenn?"

He nodded. She pushed her plate over. His eyes asked, what about her?

She lied, smiling warmly. "I eat some already while I cook. Don't worry."

He downed the second plate as fast as he finished the first plate. "Thank you, Maya. First time in a long time I had home-cooked food. It was *sooo* good." He gushed on and on, as if the food not only filled his inside but nourished his beaten soul. Reflexively he reached out and squeezed her hand.

She beamed. First time he reached out for her hand first.

Then it got quiet. From where she sat, he suddenly looked a little too serious. She could tell something was on his mind. She tapped the counter in front of him to snap him out of whatever funk he was in. "What you thinking?"

Glenn smiled unconvincingly. "Nothing. Just full now, tired."

She didn't buy the smile nor the answer. She was bracing herself. She had been here before. It was never good news when a customer went quiet and serious.

She took a napkin and began wiping the area in front of them. She stopped to get his attention. "Are we okay?"

He glanced away a little too long, before turning back to her. "Yes, of course, yes."

He wasn't convincing. She pressed her hand into his thigh, pumping twice for emphasis. "What, Glenn—*tell me already!*"

He raked his hand through his hair and cleared his throat. "Okay, then." He paused. With his hand, he covered her hand that was on his thigh. "Maya, it was wrong for me to kiss you the other night. I'm sorry. Forgive me. I crossed the line."

Maya felt a wave of relief so hard her knees went weak. *This guy for real? He know what other scumbags try? They come at me mouth open, tongue wagging. He is perfect gentleman.*

Glenn searched her face. *Was she pissed? Should they have just ignored it?*

Her smile reflected relief, frustration, and amazement, all at once. "Glenn, I kiss you too. Not mean sex. Mean I like you. I give you my friendship. It's okay."

He closed his eyes as if to absorb what he just heard, and just as quickly snapped them open. "You mean I can kiss you now, and it'd be okay with you?" He leaned in, and she leaned in. It was quick and felt more like how she'd kiss Rusty.

He pursed his lips, scrunched his face, conjuring up the courage to ask the next question. "Soooo, do you kiss others?"

She let go of his thigh and leaned back, her knee swiveling forward to make contact with his. "No. Only you." Her voice was slightly tinged with irritation.

He sat there, ever the lawyer, just one more question on his mind. He took a breath. "So what do you do when they try to kiss you?"

She retracted her knee. Her face showed displeasure bordering on frustration. Her brow tightened just a bit. She closed her eyes. One breath in, then exhale. Her brow relaxed. "Glenn, you know the guys come here they try anything. They try to kiss me. If I know they try kiss me, I turn and give cheek. Sometimes they surprise me. Quick kiss me on lips but I don't kiss back. I kiss you back. Remember? I know you lean in. Kiss me. I waited. Not turn away. Kiss you back."

Their eyes held during the silence that followed. He searched for a way into her soul. Instead, he let her into his. "I believe you. I absolutely believe you." Her face softened. He leaned in, and she met him more than halfway with a kiss.

She leaned back again, just slightly, and laid her palm to one side of his face. He turned and pressed his face into her hand, moving up and down, side to side, then kissing her palm. She felt something just then. A longing she couldn't explain.

The bar was getting busy. The barbacks and servers were hustling about. The jukebox was playing a Beyonce number, and guys and girls were filing in.

She was flushed and realized others were watching. "Glenn, want to sing?"

There was no hesitation this time. He was glad for the mood change. "Yup!"

They sang till their voices were hoarse. She put down the mic. "Need a break?"

Putting down his mic, he waved Tia over for drinks. "Okay. For sure."

She looked at him to make sure he wasn't getting bored. "You want to see pictures of my hometown?"

His smile could have lit up the booth room. "Sure!" *She must like me if she's showing me family pictures.*

She fumbled for her phone. "I come from Roi Et. You heard?"

He'd heard of Bangkok, Pattaya and Chiang Mai, but no Roi Et. "No.

Tell me." He made a mental note to google it later.

He recognized the gallery icon she pressed on her phone. *I'm about to see a lot of pictures.*

She started scrolling through pictures. "This is my town. Main street. Grandpa on the farm. Grandma helping on the farm. Grandma making food for dinner. See the kids in the rice field. That's how I used to look." Giggling now, she looked at the pictures wistfully.

He leaned over. "Looks like a great place. Where in Thailand?"

She showed him a map. "You come one day?" She was looking straight at him.

He looked back. "Me?"

Her eyes sparkled. "Yes, you. I will take you around."

He smiled, disbelief mixed with hope. "Sure!" *Was she serious?*

Head cocked and brow furrowed, she thought about what she wanted to say. "Glenn, I don't talk like this to anyone before. I feel like I can say anything. Trust you. One day you trust me?"

Whoa! Guilt hit hard. His face showed it. He reached for his pocket. Where her hand was. *Did she feel the ring?*

She drained her shot glass. He called for another. "I'm sorry, Glenn. Don't be mad. Take time. We okay? I don't get to talk, you know? Most time the customer only talk to me, all angry at wife or something. I gotta listen all night. But I get problem, you always listen to me. Thank you, Glenn."

He relaxed. She poured his beer. He took a sip. *This is getting heavy. Gotta lighten it up a bit.* "So tell me more about Thailand. What was it like growing up there?"

She swiveled toward him, making knee contact again. She held her phone in front of him. "I show you." Pictures of a farm field. "I grew up on Grandpa's rice farm in Thailand. We don't have money. I work hard. See?" Her hands still had scars from callouses she got working in the field.

She smiled sweetly, looking like she was playing home movies in her head. "Happy times, though. I remember Grandpa take me stream, we catch plenty catfish. Go town and trade for meat. I was just kid but haggle with shop owner."

She winked at him. "You know what happened?"

He nodded no, with a grin that said he'd bet on her.

"Give me extra please, I say, and pout and smile and make eyelashes at him, just like the bargirls in town. He give plenty extra! Me, Grandpa and Grandma eat meat, real meat, all week! It was best time of my life. Like dream!"

He could tell by her face. By the way she told the story. That it was something for her, and her family, to eat meat. He remembered growing up eating grass from the yard and three-day old hamburger that the mom and pop market sold illegally. He identified, and just then bonded with that little girl from Roi Et. "Where were your parents?"

Her shoulders suddenly drooped with her shining smile dimming right before his eyes. Her tone summarized all the sadness and hardship of her growing years. "They divorce. I was baby. Daddy alcoholic. Mommy stay city. Send me to farm to live. Visit once in a while. Grandpa and Grandma raise me. One day, maybe I was twelve, Mommy say I have sister, then say I have brother. I go live with Mommy in city with little sister and little brother. See?" Pictures of a young woman and young man, barely out of their teens. "That sister and brother. My babies. My kids. I take care. Send money. For car, school, rent. I'm oldest. In Thai culture, oldest take care of family. Karma."

He remembered having to do all the housework after his mom died but couldn't imagine caring for two babies. "What was it like for you, then?"

She picked up his beer bottle. Empty. She signaled to Tia for another, with a frosted glass. She took a breath. "Not enough food. I quit high school. I quit volleyball, basketball, and track teams. No time to practice. But you know what? I won English speaking contest in school. Then I went to work restaurant for tourists. I caddy golf on weekends. I learn. I learn if you want money, speak English, and be nice to tourists that look like they give big tip. Restaurant, golf, same thing. Be nice, get tip. Especially from old white guys."

Tia dropped off the beer and glass. Maya poured his beer, expertly wiping off the foam cap for him. "I work opti, optic, ummm . . ." Glenn cut in: "Optical? Yes. I work optic shop too. Remember I told you last time? I learn take care eyeglasses. Lotsa tourists."

Glenn was listening intently and licked his lips. She chuckled. *Just like Rusty,* she thought. She lifted his beer glass to his lips. He took a sip. She took a sip too. His eyes said tell me more. "One day, man from America come. I learn he was very important military man. He come to shop nineteen times. So persistent. I say excuse me sir, you try all glasses here. When you going buy something? I only know two men before that. A Thai man and an Australian man. I wasn't pretty. Tomboy farm girl grow up playing sports. No time make pretty or learn how."

Glenn wondered aloud. "So how'd you . . ." He didn't know how to ask. "How come so beautiful now?"

She blushed, just a bit, looked downward just for a second before looking up. "My friends at optical shop. I was youngest. I save all my money for Mommy, little sister and brother. Skip breakfast and lunch or bring something very small. We all eat together. I don't catch on till later. Someone always have too much food and ask me eat so not waste. They keep me from starving. I will not forget. And they show me how look pretty. Take me to club. Show me how to be around guys. My sisters. They raise me. So nice to me. Always going to remember. Karma. I will be nice to others, help others too. See? This them."

He was staring at pictures of five women in various poses, laughing, having fun, goofing around on a night out. Out of nowhere, a tear fell. She stopped talking. Her face almost a grimace, she took a few seconds to regain her composure. "My sisters, they take care of me so much. I will never forget. I will get rich. I will take care of them too."

He gave her a few minutes to collect herself. Then he had a thought. "So what happened with the guy from America?"

"I marry him."

12

COMING TO AMERICA

He shook his head slightly, disbelief and surprise on his face. "You're married?"

She held up her hand as if to say no, stop what you're thinking. "Remember I tell you? I'm divorced."

He let out a tortured breath, not knowing how long he held it. "Oh. Okay. That guy. So you married him. Then what?" He drained his beer. Then noted her shot glass had been empty for some time. He made eye contact with Tia. She was on it.

Maya called out, reminding Tia for a fresh frosted glass for him. "I move to America with him. Wyoming. NORAD. He nice back then. His mom still call me daughter. Work in America, make more money. Mommy need medicine. Little sister want college. Little brother need car."

She poured his beer for him. They clinked beer glass to shot glass. "He promise but after we come America, he not give me money to send home. He tell me make money on my own. My family my obligation, he say. I was sad. But marry is marry. So I do what I can."

He nodded as if to say go on. She rubbed her face. It was getting late. "Sad. He promise me and family he would take care of us. I send money home and I say from both of us so my family not worry. I was lonely too. He never home. Always at office or traveling the world."

Glenn peered into his beer, as if it was a crystal ball, before looking up again. "You worked on base?"

She shook her head. "I work Thai restaurant off base."

He looked skeptical. "A Thai restaurant. In Wyoming?"

She frowned as if to say, you should know this. "Glenn, Thai restaurant all over. Do google. Thai government had program. Long time ago send chefs all over America. Make sure Thai restaurant in every city. Make Thai food famous. Why you think more people eat Thai food than sushi? Thailand can send Thai people with workers green card to America. And Americans come Thailand for food and other stuff."

He reached for his bottle. She intercepted. While she poured his beer, he questioned her, half-joking, half-serious. "No way! More people eat Thai food than sushi?"

She nodded, pouring a little of his beer into her shot glass. "Yes, way. You see sushi on '*Big Bang Theory*?' Noooo. But nerds have Thai food night every week."

He snorted and grinned widely. "You watch '*Big Bang Theory*?'"

She shrugged. "Netflix. I like to laugh. Besides, help me understand nerds come to bar for good time."

He made a mental note to google Thai food government program. "Okay, so what else happened? You worked at the restaurant and then?"

She rubbed her temples as if she was reliving a painful moment. "Only one Thai restaurant. Small military town outside base. Dumbshit military guys eat there, treat me like bargirl. Say all kine things. Throw change at me. Tell me dance or ask me want drink?"

Glenn felt a surge of anger. "What'd you do?"

Her eyes flashed. "What you think? I need money. Mommy need medicine. I smile. Keep working. Not dance, not drink, but I pick up change they throw and keep. They think funny. Like I'm beggar or something. I don't care. Every little bit helps."

Her expression betrayed how demeaning the work had been. He reached out and rubbed her back, and she smiled as if to say thank you. "The people own the restaurant, they in America long time. I'm lucky they hire me, my country people. But I was like foreigner to them. Make me do all the things other employees not like. The restaurant was pub, open to 2:00 a.m. My job clean bathrooms before go home. Always on my knees. Military men not know how pee. Always miss the toilet. Disgusting."

She was rubbing her temples again. "One day husband come restaurant. I work late. He was deployed. I thought he come back next day. He come back one day early. He find me in toilet. He get mad. I don't want to embarrass him before so I say I wait tables. Not lie. I did but do all dirty work too. He drag me out of toilet. He was yelling 'Do you know who I am?' to owners. He was in full uniform."

She took a deep breath. Paused. Exhaled.

He reached over. "Hey, you don't have to do this. Sorry to press you."

She reached out with a quick caress. "It's okay. If you, I don't mind sharing. Anyway, restaurant owners don't want trouble with base people. He say I'm done working there. My country people, my brothers and sisters. All only look at me. Not help. Shake head. Tell me in Thai language, wish me well, call me sister but say please don't bring trouble on them, please stay away."

The look on her face said much. She was heartbroken then, and it still hurt. Her own people had tossed her aside.

She was nearly grimacing now. "He take me home. I try to make nice. Tell him welcome home. Make food. Want go bedroom? Sorry, thought come home next day. He hit me. Beat me. Again."

His fists clenched. "He beat you?" Glenn didn't know why he felt like he did. If he thought about it, he'd know he was feeling protective and threatened all at once.

She nodded slowly. "When first marry, everything okay. He go Iraq two time. Change. He beat me three years. See?" She maneuvered through her phone storage to a storage folder buried so deep it took seven clicks to get there.

Glenn's stomach wretched. He managed to keep the bile from coming up. *She kept pictures. He hit her where her clothes covered the bruises. The guy was like my old man. All these sick bastards knew just where to do their damage.*

She searched his face, wondering if he was judging. Seeing only understanding, she continued. "No one know. I didn't even tell family." She paused. Lightly brushed his forearm. "You don't say anything, right? I dunno why I'm telling you all this. I feel better though. Somebody listen. Somebody know."

He nodded. "We're good, Maya. He still threatens you?"

She shook her head. "No. He Germany now. Far away."

She played with her empty shot glass. "He beat me three years. I ask for divorce. He not know about pictures. He was going be promoted. He beg me stay. Promise he change. One day he say all this. In the morning before he go work. I say no. He yell again and I saw his eyes—snap!—like all the other times. I run outside to neighbor house. She nice. Alone. Husband deployment. He pound on door. She say she call police if he not go away."

Someone yelled, "Last call!" Glenn looked at his watch. *1:00 a.m.! Wow.*

She hugged his arm and put her head on his shoulder. "Oh Glenn, I spend your night just talking about me. So sorry."

He nuzzled her. Her hair smelled sweet. "No, Maya. It's okay. Thanks for sharing." Glenn lifted five fingers, and someone brought over five shots—three for her, two for him. "Go on, Maya. How'd you get from Wyoming to here, and then the bar?"

She kept her head on his shoulder. "I'm divorced. Give him everything. Keep dog. Move here to live with cousin and go beauty school."

Glenn saw their image reflected in the mirror behind the bar. He wished he could take a picture. She looked like she was sleeping. *She's had a hard life. And still so optimistic. I'm a wuss for giving up at the city so easy, when someone like her kept pushing forward.*

She was murmuring a bit. "I work all kine jobs to send money home. Thai restaurant. Thai massage." At this, Glenn's eyebrows kicked up.

She pulled back off his shoulder. He felt just a tinge of disappointment. "No, Glenn, not hoochie koochie massage with happy ending. Here I show you." She went behind Glenn and clamped on to his shoulders. He thought he was going to pass out. "Thai massage good. Work out all kinks, get circulation going again. You want I do some more?"

He wiped tears from his eyes. "Um, no, maybe next time."

She flashed a smile. Her eyes seem to say, point made. "Anyway, I work all kine jobs. Mommy more sick, and sister want go nursing school. If sister not go school and get good job, maybe bargirl like all the rest. No way!"

She slid back on to her stool and turned his way until their knees touched. "One day I have time off. I go to Thai festival at park. Meet Chloe. She was bargirl at a Thai hostess bar. Not Korean, Not Vietnamese, but Thai. I say, 'Me, bargirl?' All the bargirls back home take customers home for sex to make real money. I say not me, no way, I like you, Chloe, and respect your life but I cannot be like that."

She lifted her glass with a clink on his shot glass. "Chloe explain, 'No, here not like that. You sit, have drink, talk, make customer happy and get tips and cut from bar for each drink. Some girls let touch and do more, for more money, but not pushed. No pressure, you can just make money from drinks. Most local guys okay not like *faraangs* back home."

He'd heard about *faraangs* from Tomo. Thai slang for western transplants that move to Thailand to find whatever suits their fancy— adventure, girlfriends, wives.

They downed their shots. "Chloe tell me come see. I go. Not bad. Just like hanging out with friends. I go home with seventy-five dollars for two hours. I sit with old Japanese man who sat with old Chinese man was Chloe's regular. Lotsa girls make more money but I'm shy, you know already, to ask for drinks. Still, better than anything else. I was happy can help family and not lose pride."

Glenn looked around. Saw some old guys. Actually, he was one of the old guys. "So that was this bar?"

She read his mind. "No Glenn, old mean old. You not old—yet"

Her smile was teasing. "But your question. No, another bar. But once I'm regular, Mama there tell me sit this guy or that guy. If the guy too grabby I walk away and he get mad at Mama, and Mama get mad at me. She throw me out, and Chloe too. Chloe say she know somebody else and we go meet Lynh. Lynh already get chop suey selection girls but not have Thai. Now she have two."

She downed the next two shots one after another.

He was about to call Tia. "Want more, Maya?"

It was already last call. He must have forgotten. "No, Glenn. Save money. Next time."

He rubbed his eyes. Tomorrow was going to be a long day. "That is some story, Maya. You should write a book."

The lights came on. People started filing out. "Thank you for listen, Glenn. Thank you look my pictures. No one listen to me like that. I can tell you anything. Not like others. I say nothing to them." Glenn smiled. He reached out and squeezed her hand, just a bit. Then let go. It felt like she was trying to hang on.

She's hardworking, devoted to her family, and just trying to make a life for herself. I gotta give her credit. A few weeks ago, she was this exotic, gorgeous, sexy creature that gave me an ego boost. Can't see it like that no more. She's beyond gorgeous. She's beautiful, just as beautiful, more beautiful, on the inside.

Glenn had just met Maya, the person. It'd been a while since he'd fallen in love. But he wondered. *Did she feel the same?*

13

DESERTED

The following Tuesday, the third one of September, he walked in late, needing a beer badly after a long day at the non-profit. He was starting to feel homey about the bar. Looking around, he thought the bar looked the same as last Tuesday. Like he'd never left.

Tia and Jimmy were taking inventory before the night rush. The barflies were several beers in, chortling and ribbing over the same stories shared and forgotten every night. Somewhere to the right in the booth room, someone was singing a bad rendition of the *Titanic* song, with a heavy Chinese accent. There was a fight on the Tuesday night sports channel.

He saw his corner bar stool taken, then heard her voice.

"Glenn, over here." She waved. The bar was full except for two seats at the end. She walked over to get him. More than one barfly lingered over her as she passed, taking in how she looked. A fire engine-red cocktail dress with a scoop neck and hemline ending at mid-thigh.

She took his hand and led him to their seats. The click-clack of her high heels on the hardwood floor was audible above the din of the bar. "Sorry. Our spot gone when I come. I save these. Hope okay?"

He was beaming. *Geez, she looks hot. I'm with the girl the entire bar is ogling.* "No problem. Hope I didn't keep you waiting long." *I can't believe the stupid CEO wanted a briefing tonight.*

They slid onto their seats. She patted his thigh. "How was your week, Glenn?"

He looked around. Tia held up her index finger as if to say give her a minute.

He turned back to Maya. "Okay."

Her shoulders drooped a bit. She still managed a smile. *Again,* she thought, *always say okay. Nothing more about his life.*

She played with her earring. "What you do this weekend?"

He caught Tia's eye and nodded, holding up two fingers. Tia got to work.

"This weekend?" He scratched his head. "Umm, yeah, okay. I had to work. Boss lady was a bitch." Glenn turned it right around. "How's Rusty?" Last week was the first he'd ever heard of a dog with diabetes.

Tia dropped off their drinks.

Maya looked up. "Tia babe, Coke back this time and frosted glass for hard worker here." Tia was back in a second.

Maya took her Coke back and poured his beer. It was becoming a thing, her pouring his beer. "Rusty okay. Went beach Sunday. See?" She showed him pictures. "Doctor say his diabetes okay now. Under control. You help me, Glenn. I can buy better medicine for him now. My baby going to get better." She let his hesitancy to share go, again. More small talk followed. Her week at the beauty shop. The fight on TV. General bar gossip about this new girl or that new customer.

They were about three drinks in. "Glenn, you want to sing tonight? Last time not sing so much. Thank you for listen to me all night. No one ever listen to me like that before."

Tia brought another round and a fresh glass for him.

He scratched his head. *I should be thanking her for sharing like that. Does she do that with all her customers? She said no, but is that a ploy to make me feel special?* He drew a smiley face on his freshly frosted glass and turned it to her. "No problem, Maya."

She broke out in laughter, holding her hand to her mouth. Her knee pressed into his. "Glenn, you hungry? I didn't make for you today but uncle can make meat salad."

He cracked a smile, remembering the meat between the teeth incident from last time. "Sure thing. That was great the other night. This time let me go clean the bits and pieces, okay?"

She held back her laughter this time, turning away slightly, remembering how embarrassed he was last time. "Don't worry, Glenn, do what make you happy, remember?"

Her knee was in constant contact. Now and then, she reached out to massage his shoulder. They took turns feeding each other the meat cubes. One meat cube fell into his lap, and she instinctively reached to pick it up. He jumped out of his seat when her hand brushed against his crotch. They caught each other's eyes and laughed simultaneously like teenagers. Both blushed. There was no doubt he found her attractive.

He put down his fork. What a great night, as usual. "Hey, Maya, I gotta go wash up, okay?" He was making sucking sounds where the meat was stuck.

She started to clean up the plates. "You go, Glenn. I will be here. Make pretty for me, okay?" She laughed. The wind chimes were back. "We sing after, okay?"

Glenn nodded as he slid off his seat. Walking to the restroom, he didn't notice Chloe walking in with two men. When he came back, their plates were where he'd left them. Maya was in her seat, looking lost.

He stood in front of her, trying to catch her eye. "What's wrong, Maya?" *She looks like she's in a trance.*

She stared past him. Sliding off her stool, she kissed his cheek. "I have customer." She walked briskly toward the booth room. Glenn thought she was going to say hi and be right back. She had done that before.

Thirty minutes turned into one hour. One hour turned into two hours. She hadn't come back to check once. On occasion, he heard Chloe and her laughing along with two, maybe three male voices. Tia tried to make small talk several times, but Glenn's face said it all. Anger. Don't talk to me. No one speak to me. Then he heard her karaoke the *Titanic* song with the same crappy singer singing at the beginning of the night.

Neglected, abandoned, humiliated. The bar crowd went about their business. Every once in a while, someone glanced over at him. Glenn had had enough. It was 1:30 a.m. He'd waited for three hours. He threw a twenty on the bar and walked out the door. Tia called out to Lynh.

He heard stilettos on gravel. He turned. Tia.

There was no speech this time. No talk about how Chloe trolled for customers, and sometimes she brought two in and needed backup from Maya. No speech. Just a good long genuine feeling hug. She was taller by three inches. *Funny,* he thought, *she doesn't look that tall behind the bar. Then again, not always paying attention to her height.*

Lynh came running out with Maya. Tia backed off, standing ten feet outside of the door with enough neon to see the anger and sadness on Glenn's face.

Maya stood there, shoulders hunched, arms outstretched. Her expression one of sadness mixed with frustration, like a child upsetting her father. "Don't be mad."

His glare venomous, he lied. "I'm not."

She could see his jaw tighten. Reaching out and taking his hands, she said nothing, biting her lower lip. Her eyes said don't go.

He let go first, jerking her hands out of his. "Is the customer waiting for you?" He secretly hoped they were gone. Maybe they could spend a few minutes together. Disappointment came swooping in.

She reached out again, and he clenched his fists. She took a step back.

"Yes, they waiting. Glenn, please . . ."

Glenn cut her off, walking away. "I'll see you later." He lied again.

Her eyelid twitched at the corner as her lip tightened into a thin line. She stood there and watched him disappear around the corner. She wheeled about, took a deep breath, wiped something from her eyes, and walked back to the bar. Tia met her at the door and put her arm around her, drawing Maya into her for a hug. From behind it looked like Maya sobbed a couple of times.

———————

Two days later, Glenn returned to the bar, before Maya was to come in. He was with Tim Farber. Tim was a player, common knowledge among all the girls. Where Tim went, someone was sure to make a lot of coin. Old friends from the bank, the two bumped into each other two Tuesdays before and did the business card exchange thing.

That morning he punched in Tim's number. "Hey Tim, I'm done with that girl. Can you introduce me to someone else?"

Tim blinked. *Huh? He's with the best looking one of the lot. And I've never seen that kind of interaction—whatever they do—together before. Not the usual buy-drink-and-grab-ass situation.* "Wha . . . what? I thought you liked her? Swore off all the other places. Swore off all the girls. You told me you were a one bargirl man, remember? Tried to take you across the street?"

Glenn stared at his notepad. Two columns. One heading said "Stay," the other "Leave." Under the leave column, he doodled a stick figure with a stick knife in its back. That was as far as he got. "I remember Tim, but some developments occurred." Glenn spared no detail in his recollection of two nights before, with the F-word sprinkled liberally throughout his story.

Tim's brow furrowed. Not the kind of business call he expected when he gave Glenn his card. "Okay, I'll take you shopping but you know what, shouldn't you give her another chance?"

Glenn almost spit the words out. "Tim, the girl up and left me hanging dry. It was humiliating. All the barflies looked at me like I just sprouted pus all over me or something. They had that look, Tim—the 'I feel sorry for you' look. I waited for three hours. Not a word. I leave, and then she comes flying out, and says don't be mad?"

Glenn was seething, just recounting the story. Tim tried to diffuse the time bomb he had on the phone. "Okay, we'll go tonight but give Lynh some credit. Ask her for someone new. Let her save face. Girls come and go, but mama-sans stay."

Pinching his nose bridge, eyes closed, Glenn begged his voice to sound appreciative. "Yeah, okay Tim. Thanks much. Didn't mean to take this out on you."

It was early when Glenn and Tim walked in. Maya wouldn't be in for another hour. Glenn knew Lynh would be there early to cook dinner for one of her longtime customers. He found her in the kitchen. Lynh was happy that he was back. But Glenn wasn't back for Maya. He was never going to hurt like that again. "Hi Lynh. Favor, Mama? Can you introduce me to someone else here?"

She stopped chopping vegetables and turned to him, knife still in hand. "Why? Maya perfect for you."

He took a step back, out of range of the weapon in her hand. Tim smirked. It looked comical to him. "No, Lynh. Someone else. I don't want to see her. She hurt me. I'm the customer. What the hell? Someone else, Lynh? Or Tim is taking me to the other bars." This was no bluff. Lynh knew that. This guy was too green to bluff. Glenn sounded cold.

Her face screamed disappointment. She put the knife down and turned off the stove. "What wrong with you? She had customer. That's how bar is, Glenn. Sometimes she have other customers." Mama thought the devil had taken over Glenn. *All customers know this. What his problem?* She was almost right. He was hurting so bad. It'd be no problem in most cases, but right now he needed something, someone to fill the void. The emptiness was a raging fire, a black hole, heavy, cold, damp and life-sucking.

His eyes narrowed, jaw jutting. "No, Mama. Not where I come from. That was bad. Disrespect. I felt like shit for three hours. Everyone felt sorry for me. I don't need that. You help me or what?"

Her expression and voice softened as she wiped her hands on her apron. "Glenn, why you like this? We treat you good. She really care for you. I care for you. We don't make money from you."

His eyebrows arched. "What do you mean? I spent three hundred dollars the other night."

She walked past him grabbing his collar and pulled him along out of the kitchen past the bar and stopped at the booth room entrance. Tim followed along. "Glenn, look around. See him over there? Two champagne bottles, $300 each. Thirty minutes. Some buy me twenty shots at a time all water. No money, I take you ATM or take credit card. After all drunk, men do anything for pussy. We do that to you? You come in scared. Want only good time. You good guy. She never pressure you, Glenn. Three hundred dollars, that's cuz you wanted to make big shot and give out money. Three hundred dollars not big shot Glenn. Maybe for forty-five-year-old but not my girl. She care for you. I know. One month already. She not work you. She lose money, especially when she ignore other customers. They don't come for her anymore. These customers are thousand-dollar nights Glenn. You think she not care?"

He stood next to her, stone-faced and avoiding eye contact. She continued. "But that night, she had to take care someone else. She has to have business other nights too you know. She do wrong. She should have explained. Make you feel good first. Then go. But Chloe was pushing." Glenn made a mental note not to like Chloe.

Lynh rubbed his back. "She should have come back check on you. But she thought you were okay. I talk to her already. She sorry. She cry the other night. She think she lose you. She not do it again. She still learning. Not like the old days. We all take care customer. No moving around. But she new. Still learning. Never had more than one customer a night. Now she getting popular."

She led them to the nearest booth. Tim sat next to her. "Glenn, she good girl. Give one more try."

Lynh had a nose for good guys. Glenn was a good guy. And while a little mixed up, Maya was a good girl. They could make it she thought, and one less girl she had to worry about. "Glenn, she good girl." Lynh was perturbed. "All you men come here grab ass have fun. You think these girls not human? She have problems too you know."

Glenn pounded the table. "Mama, I do not grab ass."

Lynh pounded right back. "Shut up and listen to me, that not main point. She sick you know. Go hospital twice this year for sinus problems. You ask, she had nose job. Sinus not good since. Her mother sick. Her sister in school. No school no job, no job she become bargirl in Thailand. You know what that mean?"

Glenn knew the stories. Nodded.

She put her hand on his. "She has to make money for everybody. Drink every night. Exercise stay skinny to look good. She go hospital for ulcers. That night she still came to see you." Glenn remembered a night she was a half hour late and a little distracted.

She reached for a napkin. "Glenn, please." She was crying a bit now. "She good girl. Like my daughter. Give her chance." Glenn looked across the table at Tim.

Tim took it all in. He had a hunch. "Dude, give her another chance. If it doesn't work out, I know other girls like her."

Lynh looked up. "No, no other girls like her. Other girls fake, sweet talk. Not this one."

Glenn shifted in his seat. It was getting near showtime for Maya, and he wanted to be gone, with goodbyes done, when she got there.

Glenn glanced at Tim. "Let's go."

Lynh grabbed Glenn's hand. "Wait!"

Glenn got up, shrugging off her hand.

Lynh took a deep breath. She threw a Hail Mary. "God give all of us second chance, why you not?" Glenn's legs went weak and he sat, near collapsed, back into the booth. Lynh said it again. "God forgive all of us. You better than God?"

His hands were on the table before him, fingers laced, poised to pray. *Father, are You kidding? In a hostess bar? There's a Buddhist altar outside. From a bar mama? Are You talking to me?*

On cue, the small still voice sounded in his head. *Glenn, forgive as I have forgiven you.*

He heard it clear as day. *Shit! I got this from You all my life. And I've been a piece a crap and You still died for me. Yes, I know. You forgive so I should forgive.*

He bowed his head. The words sank in. He inhaled deeply, held, then exhaled. He didn't agree to see Maya again, but he didn't leave either. "Mama, I don't know where that came from, but I need time to think about this, even pray. Maybe pray and come back tomorrow." He glanced at his watch. It was nearly 9:00 p.m., and Maya was due in soon. He started scooting out of the booth.

Too late. Maya walked in, saw Lynh in the first booth, and headed that way. She stopped short when she heard Glenn's voice.

Lynh looked up and squealed, "Maya, my baby!" She wasn't about to let Maya run away. Jumping up and over Tim, she grabbed Maya by the arm, pulled, and sat Maya down next to Glenn, pushing Maya hard enough to bump Glenn deeper into the booth.

Lynh had the determined look of a real estate mogul closing a deal. "Maya, you not leave to till you apologize to Glenn." After that, up to you two. Lynh disappeared with Tim in tow. "I find you someone too, Tim, but you too cheap. Only Mama can afford you."

Lynh took one look back. She knew by the way they looked at each other that no one was leaving anyone that night.

It was the first time they sat in a booth together. She was wearing denim shorts and a plaid shirt knotted at the center like Daisy Duke, complete with a bare midriff. "Sorry I leave you that night. I don't do that no more. Don't be mad." She was almost pleading.

Glenn wanted to ask why, and who was so important to get her to leave him hanging like that. Gritting his teeth, he sat in silence. On the outside, he looked pissed. On the inside, he was that little boy who just found his mother dead. Tears streaming, not understanding why he was left alone, abandoned like garbage in a gutter.

Her arm was next to his, lightly touching. He could feel the warmth. She could too. Her calm exterior was made up to look like she ruled the Nile. On the inside, her heart was exploding. She wanted to cry out like a little girl, like the time she saw her father beat her mother to a pulp. Like the time she saw her father taken away by the cops.

She broke the ice, staring straight ahead, speaking in an almost dutiful whisper. "I don't blame you if you want sit with someone else. I appreciate all you did for me. We stay friends, say hi, okay?" He sat quiet, not moving except to blink. "Okay, no need to say hi. Thank you for everything Glenn." Years of hardship trained her to keep tears in check. They both sat in the booth, next to each other, close but not touching. She was inwardly imploring . . . *Glenn, don't be gone.*

The silence lasted ten minutes. Neither moved. Allie the server came over once, took one look, and left without a word. Regulars were coming in, but Lynh steered everyone clear of that one corner booth. Tia disappeared from behind the bar, and a moment later, "Don't Stop Believin'" started piping through the bar.

Maya gasped silently on hearing the song and took a deep breath. Her movement stirred him. He thought she was going to leave. Impulsively, he reached for her hand. Her hand reached out, meeting his halfway, and she turned to look at him, lacing her fingers through his. One single tear rolled out and down her cheek. So cliché, like the movies. But this was real life. This tear was real, not fantasy. He wiped it away with Steve Perry singing the woes of a young woman trying to make it in the solitary matrix of life. And he thought, *No way, you'll never be lonely again, not on my watch.*

They closed the bar down that night.

She saw him out the door. "You come back. I make curry for you next Tuesday." She pulled him close, gave him a goodnight kiss. It wasn't a peck on the lips like before. She lingered just a bit before she turned and whispered in his ear. "I make it up to you Glenn." He simply nodded. Two steps out the door, he turned. She was still there. He waved and was on his way.

Later he lay in bed. Eyes heavy. *What is going on? What is this feeling? Am I falling for her?*

He had forgotten Tomo's last words: "And one more thing—never, ever, fall in love in those places."

He sighed heavily. *I gotta talk to someone about this. But how do I explain what I'm doing?*

14

OCTOBER REBUKE

In a dojo with straw mats right out of a scene from *The Karate Kid*, he was practicing the ancient art of judo. It was traditional judo, not like the jiu-jitsu shops sprouting up all over the states. The club's lineage dated back to pre-World War II.

He and Brad Reynolds were the oldest of the bunch and could still give a considerable challenge to the younger *judoka*. Childhood friends, Brad was Glenn's best man when he married Katie.

It was after the first Monday night judo practice of October. They were shooting the breeze, each wearing a sweat-soaked *gi*. Brad wanted to change their workout to Tuesdays, but Glenn said, "No can do." Brad joked, "Why? You have a standing date with Anna?" Anna was their favorite bartender and longtime friend. It was the way Glenn hesitated that caused Brad to pursue the interrogation further, till Glenn gave some quick details. Too quick.

"A bargirl? You're seeing a bargirl?" Brad thought of all the bargirls he ever knew—in Thailand, Vietnam, Korea, the PI—and a teenaged, take-home golf caddy in Indonesia. He had a good time with them all. He even knew a few locally.

And they were all perfect for one thing: temporary distractions from life. You pay them money or buy them drinks, and they pretend to like you, make conversation with you, and for another wad of cash, they took you to a back room for sex. It was that simple for Brad.

His smirk could have spat disappointment. "Well, brother, I can understand an atheist heathen like me taking up with a bargirl, but you, my friend, are a self-professed child of God."

Glenn put on a dry t-shirt. "I've been trying to convert you since you were eight years old. Since that time you got caught after school by that gang." Brad winced for a split second. That incident drove him to earn black belts in several martial arts and work in an area where he killed for his country.

Glenn had found his friend, beaten unrecognizable after school. Every argument they ever had ended with Brad yelling, "If God loved me, where was he?" Glenn never had a good answer. Only words like trust, faith, hope. It was a standoff every time.

Brad stretched his hamstring. "Well, we're not here to discuss my pending date with hell. We're here so you can tell me how taking up with this bargirl is gonna take *you* down to hell."

Glenn ripped a bandage off his toe and flicked it at Brad. "She's not a bargirl. And I'm not taking up with her." No comment about hell.

Brad flicked the bandage right back. "Whaddya mean she's not a bargirl? Whaddya mean you're not taking up with her?" He counted out his reasons on his hand, one finger at a time. "One, you told me you met in a bar. Two, you keep meeting in a bar. Three, you buy her drinks, and she makes you happy in a bar. Four, you guys sing songs, get drunk, and she makes you food in a bar. And five, you only meet once a week in a bar." He paused for effect. "Man, did you hear me say 'in a bar' five times? She's a bargirl, and you're her regular once-a-week customer."

Glenn's eyes narrowed, ready to counter.

Brad continued stretching, pressing his chest to the mat. "What's wrong with you? You're like every wet-behind-the-ear pissant that goes off to these countries for the first time and gets all gaga goo-goo over these girls. You know they're trained from birth to psychologically manipulate guys like you?

Glenn shot back. "What do you mean, guys like me?"

Frustration crept into Brad's voice. "*Vulnerable*. You're vulnerable. You don't have Katie anymore and you're lonely, with needs. Here comes this girl and *boom*! You think that mama-san brought her over just so you could keep her company and away from the bad men? Are you that naive?"

His lips a tight line, Glenn's face demanded why his best friend wasn't supportive. "I was in a safe zone." *Why can't he see I'm happy?*

Brad pinched the bridge of his nose as if he had a headache; then his eyes flashed open. "Aw, screw that. There is no safe zone in those places. The girls are predators, and the guys are all prey. Look at the girls. Look at their eyes. Same predatory focus stock traders have when they're going after old people with money to invest or as a car salesman looking to saddle some young couple with a cheap car with high financing costs."

Glenn echoed his last talk with Lynh. "She's different. She can take me for a lot more, but she doesn't."

Skepticism was etched all over Brad's face. "Of course she can, but you're not a quick kill. You're a long-term bleed. It's like vampires keep humans alive forever. They bleed them but not till death. They harvest the blood as soon as the human can produce more. Same with you. You're a cash cow to her. If she tried to take you for more, she risks scaring you off. How much you give her anyway?"

Glenn scratched at his chin stubble. "Five hundred dollars a week. It's to help her mom and sister back home."

Brad's eyebrows arched wide. "What the fuck? You can get three nights a week for that and with fringes. Are you crazy? You've been abroad before, and I even took you out back in the day and showed you the ropes." His brow relaxed, leading into a disapproving head shake. "And she's from Thailand? Just google bargirl Thailand, and you'll get all the information you need."

An exasperated grunt rumbled out of Glenn as he protested. "She wasn't a bargirl in Thailand. Weren't you listening? She was working for an optometrist."

Cool downs over, Brad started packing his bag. "Is that what she said? Let me fill in the blanks, dumbass. Retail by day, bargirl by night. And how the fuck does she know English so well? I know girls been around the states for twenty years, and I still don't understand what they're saying." He looked up to make eye contact with his best bud. He wanted to make sure his next words hit hard. "Break it off man. She's using you. And by the way—*you're married!*"

Glenn slapped the mat hard. "We're not doing anything wrong!!! I wish you could understand us and what we have."

Brad heard "we" and "us," and he knew Glenn was over the edge on this girl. *Shit, I should have watched him closer. All this time I thought he was running off to Anna to cry on her shoulders and get the motherly affection he so needed. This is not good. I gotta take another tack—desperate times, desperate measures.*

Glenn looked around the dojo, half ignoring Brad's diatribe. Calligraphy adorned the place, spouting mottos like "Honor those that came before you," "Fight for the things you hold dear," and "Never say die." His attention turned back to Brad. *Man, this is going nowhere. It's not like I'm him and fucking every whore that opens her legs for him. Did he forget that I've been on those dates with him long ago? Always the third wheel or begging off some bargirl sister's advances? If he met Maya, he might understand.*

Brad was still going on. "And what the fuck is a family-style hostess bar? You make it sound like they have different standards."

Brad slipped on a dry shirt. "Listen, you meet, you drink, she drinks, you pay, you pay more, maybe you fuck or get a blow job, but if you have cash, they will tell you or do for you whatever you want, so you come back. Whether you call it—rough sex style or perverse taboo family style—it's still the same."

Glenn's face ticked with irritation. The edge he'd worked off over the last few hours slowly infected his id again. "But they treat me good."

Brad scooted closer. "And what are they supposed to do? Don't go into the jungle unless you know the rules. Five hundred dollars a week? And you're all proud because you're not getting anything physical? Do you at least get a hand job?"

That was it. Glenn lunged at Brad, fist cocked. Big mistake.

With a half roll, Brad had him in an armbar. He put just enough pressure to keep Glenn still until he calmed down. His voice was nearly taunting. "Yo, man, you've lost your cool. Look at this. You lost your cool. I touched a nerve. Now what, we fight? Go our separate ways? What? Your call, but I have your arm till you cool down.

Glenn turned his head. He needed breathing room. *I can't believe he's not backing me on this. I thought he'd be happy that I was happy.* Glenn winced. His arm was on fire. He could feel his tendons tearing. Still, he struggled.

Brad stayed on Glenn. "Calm down, bitch."

Glenn snarled. "*You* calm down." He thrust his legs up in the air and back rolled out of the armbar and was on top of Brad. Fist raised, Glenn had his bud by the throat. *What am I doing?* Glenn rolled off.

Both were breathing hard and sweating. They glared at each other as only childhood friends could.

Glenn thrust his finger at Brad. "Why can't you back me? Thought you'd be happy for me. I'm finally happy after all these years."

Brad leaned forward with a look like his friend lost his mind. He pointed at one of the scrolls. "What happened to *you*? Where's your honor? Where's your love for Katie? A bargirl? You're better than that." He pointed upward. "Where's your God? You're the Christian. What about your vows?"

Brad got up. "You keep seeing this girl, and I'll lose all respect for you. Don't even call me. Your choice." And he was gone.

Glenn watched his only childhood friend walk out of his life. *Is that it?* Abandoned again. He was missing Katie. He was missing Maya. He punched the mat till his knuckles bled.

15

LIKE A TATTOO

Glenn walked in a little early the following night. Still upset over his run-in with Brad, he was eager to be with Maya. He stared at his bruised knuckles, hoping the Nu Skin he'd applied and the bar's lighting would keep her from noticing. *Oh well, I'll tell her it was from punching the heavy bag, like the last time I came in with bruises.*

Reggae music floated in from the dart room. In the bar area, the hockey game was on. Two enforcers were wailing away, with the referees slowly circling. The barflies nodded his way, smiled, waved. He gave a salute. Over the sounds of hockey game, a newsflash on the other flatscreen cut in with a live shot of a fire in the industrial area. A bar like the one he was in had burned down.

He was sliding onto his stool at their spot when Verna walked up. Verna was a server, two years shy of Social Security. She was Lynh's longtime friend. They had been in this business together for more than forty years. Single, at one time extremely popular, but now single and lonely. She adored Maya and didn't want the same fate for her. Verna was also the designated karaoke DJ. You gave her money, and she put it in the machine and punched in your selection for you.

With a Vietnamese accent, Verna told Glenn, "Maya come late today. She call." Verna wondered why they hadn't exchanged numbers by now. Why they always communicated thru her or Jimmy.

He was playing with a coaster. "Okay, Verna." She gently took the coaster out of his hand. "And Maya say no bar tonight, sit booth." She grabbed his elbow and nudged him toward the first booth, just inside and to the right of the booth room doorway, right next to the karaoke machine.

Still early, the booth room was empty. He turned to her. "Are you sure, Verna? Maya always says she's not comfortable in the booth room, only the bar and dart room."

She waved off his concerns. "She say okay. Easier eat on table. After go bar and sing you like. What you want. Bud Light?" She sat him down and went to get his order.

Verna was also the self-designated chaperone when Lynh was not around. She made sure none of the other girls made a move on Glenn in Maya's absence. Word was getting around. Nice guy, with money, easy prey. Once when Maya had to go home early, he stayed and got milked for $500. Maya heard about this and vowed never to leave him alone again.

He had taken only two sips when he heard Maya's familiar voice up front. "Hello . . . *hello* . . . hope you hungry!" She came dressed in a shimmering black bodysuit with an open back, paired with a black leather skirt. She struggled, carrying a large pot with both hands, with a bag hung over her elbow with something bulky inside. She dropped everything on the table with a loud *ka-chunk*. Spoons and ladles came rolling out of the bag. Verna rushed over to help.

Glenn felt like the first time he went over to meet Katie's mom and was getting fussed over during dinner.

Between Verna and Maya's broken Vietnamese, Thai and English dialogue, Glenn got the feeling they'd never done this before. Not for a customer anyway. *Laverne and Shirley meet Lucy and Ethel.* He beamed. They were really giving it their all.

Verna dug through the bag. "Maya, what you bring? So much!"

Maya's eyes twinkled. She was not a bargirl tonight, but a dinner hostess. "Curry, Verna. Panang. Make plenty, feed everybody."

Verna shook her head but couldn't help smiling at Maya's generosity. Once Maya had fed the entire bar plus the homeless on the street outside. "Early, Maya. No one here. Feed homeless again tonight?"

Maya chuckled. "Maybe. Feed regulars first, Verna." She meant the barflies outside that nursed their beer for two hours while ogling Tia.

He was taking it all in. *Tomo oughta see this.*

She turned to Glenn. It was like calling Rusty for dinner. "Glenn, I ask you already. You hear me? You eat curry?"

He shook his head. "Oh, no. Not this kind." He'd never had Thai curry—only Indian and Japanese.

She was wiping the table. "You will like." Kiddingly, she shook her fist at him. "Eat or you gonna get it, mister!"

He smiled, holding up his hands, feigning fear. *She watches way too many American movies on Netflix.*

He imagined her doing this for him in a real home, and her beauty struck him out of the blue. Through her bodysuit's open back, the phoenix tattoo flitted about while she set the table. He was enjoying the show.

She was laughing and singing. When she sat down next to him, he could feel the warmth of her leg. She hummed an old Thai folk song as she served up the food for him. She reminisced. It was how Grandma used to serve Grandpa. "Glenn, this Thai rice. You call sticky rice. Eat with curry."

Like other curries, it was mustard yellow, but the smell was a notch above anything he ever had. There were bits of chicken and green peppers and red peppers and yellow peppers.

He started pushing aside the peppers when she stuck her finger in his face. "Uh-uh! No! You eat what Mommy make cuz Mommy work hard." She pinched his cheek and shook it twice.

He blushed and stared at her sheepishly.

She smiled back and pointed at the food. She was guessing another Rusty-like feeding frenzy.

He had an odd feeling he couldn't place. The feeling disappeared quickly once the food creamed in his mouth. All he could think of was having more.

Verna came back and started filling her plate. Outside there were oohs and aahs. Maya looked up. "Verna, you sit with us?" Verna took a seat across them.

Glenn brought his wallet out to buy the two ladies drinks.

Again, Maya uttered a loud "uh-uh!" and pushed his money back. With some authority, she pronounced, "No work right now. It's dinnertime."

Verna smiled. It was like having a family again. Though she wished Glenn had bought her a beer.

They were halfway through when Lynh plumped down by Verna. Jabbering something in Vietnamese, Verna rolled her eyes and smiled. Lynh turned back to her favorite couple. "Good? This good. Dinnertime. Quiet time. Talk. No drink, no sing. Just talk and enjoy. Like being home. This place Glenn your home okay? Maya honey your wife take care you." Lynh's eyes were twinkling.

Maya's mouth flared into an O. "Mommy! No! This only dinner!" Glenn was thinking. *Is she really protesting? This is more like the way Katie sounded when her mom teased her about learning how to cook so she could keep her man.*

Maya craned her neck to see over the booth, over Verna's head, checking on how the barflies were doing. Glenn tapped her shoulder. "I didn't know you could cook."

She turned to him. "What you mean. What about Pad Thai last time?"

His eyes rolled back in his head. He remembered how soul-satisfying that dish was. Under the table, she squeezed his hand. With her other hand, she fed him curry rice off his plate.

Lynh had seen enough. She and Verna jabbered something in Vietnamese. The tone was universal. Leave these kids alone and let whatever happens happen.

Glenn and Maya were finally alone. He glanced her way and broke out a wide smile. "This feels nice."

"You like?"

"Yes."

"I cook good?"

"Yes."

"I look good?"

"Yes."

"I sing good?"

"Yes."

Then she said something in Thai.

"Huh?" was all he said.

She was laughing. "Just testing. Maybe you autopilot say yes to everything."

He grinned. "Nope."

She giggled. Something about the meal made her happy. "You eat like my dog." She made a snorting sound and laughed even more. Then she grabbed his face and brought it to hers, and kissed him once, twice, five times, in rapid succession. "I save one more for you later for say good night. We sing now?"

Drinks started flowing. She hand-fed him the rest of his dinner then cleaned up. She cleaned his glasses. Then poured his beer and followed up with a back massage. She was strong. It was not a sensual massage but a real one that made him wince and took out knots that had been there since his teen years.

Other customers came in for her. Verna inquired. She waved them off, saying busy tonight, tomorrow. Verna wouldn't let any approach. She was like a bailiff in court. He asked Maya, "Are they telling customers to go away?"

She shifted. Her knee pressed to his. "Yes, they know, Glenn, you here first. I take care you."

He paused slightly as if bracing for bad news. "And what if I wasn't here first?"

She cocked her head to one side. "Of course, you here first. I will come find you make sure you first."

He shook his head. He had to know. "But what if I come late? Would you turn me away? Tell me come back tomorrow?"

She was getting exasperated. *He like little boy sometimes.* "Then don't worry, I still come to you. Don't worry. I don't leave you. Always with you." She brushed the side of his face with her palm. Instinctively he turned and buried his face up and down in her palm.

Eyebrows raised a bit, she caught on and wiped his face with her palm. *He like it. He just like Rusty, my little four-legged boy back home.*

He forgot all about the other guys. "Thank you, Maya."

She held his face in her hand. "You are welcome, Glenn. I promise you I would make it up to you. I sing special song for you now."

Glenn reached up to her hand. She took his hand and with the other hand, lifted a mic to her lips. She started singing as Jordan Sparks' hit "Tattoo" came on.

Some of the lines stuck in his head, and he wondered if there was a hidden message. To him the songwriter loved someone deeply yet desired to move on, but not without professing an endless love for the other. It was the ultimate "I'm breaking up with you but will think of you always" kind of song.

It just looked like she enjoyed singing the song. She gazed at him intently when she sang the last line. Somehow, he felt this was not a normal bargirl-bar customer relationship. *True. No matter what, she'll always be a part of me and forever have me, like love branded on our souls, two spirits entwined as one.*

The last line stayed with him even after they said good night. He could hear her singing it all the way home. It felt like something special was happening. *Best night ever.*

16

FAMILY TIME

The following week, she was waiting at the bar when he walked in. It was the second Tuesday of October. She wore a red lace sleeveless top with a front zipper extending from a deep V neck of cleavage to her exposed waist. He noticed right away the belly button ornament crowning her well-developed abs. Pinstripe black stretch pants that hugged in all the right places. *Damn, she looks stunning.*

She slid off her stool and reached out for his hand and led him around the side to what was quickly becoming their booth.

Maya wrapped her arm around his as they walked ten steps to their booth. Her fingers laced his. She squeezed a bit, as if to say hello, I missed you. "I come early today. Lynh let me use kitchen. I make pork larb for you. Thai specialty my part of Thailand—Isaan food." They sat down.

On cue, Verna appeared with a tray of food. Maya had come early to cook in the bar's small kitchen. Earlier, Verna pulled Maya aside. "You take care him when he come. No worry I bring food."

Maya began prepping the food. "How your day?" She poured the beer Verna had brought.

The booth room was empty except for one other couple several booths away. All but one of the flatscreens in the place were turned off. The one closest to them displayed a karaoke screen. The room was a little darker than the bar area, but his eyes could see clearly after a few minutes. The booths were more comfortable than the barstools and allowed them to sit closer. They held hands under the table like school kids.

He squeezed her hand, wanting to hold on forever. "It was okay." His new boss was getting on his nerves. They were side by side. He turned to her. Her hair was up in a French braid, eyes smoky. Was that red eyeshadow? Her lips were in a perpetual pout, like looking at sweet, luscious strawberries. *Damn, she's so fine, so stunning.* "What about you?

How was your day? Your week?"

She was focused on the larb, didn't see how intently he was staring. "After we eat." She wrapped the pork dish with sticky rice and papaya salad in a lettuce leaf and lifted it to his mouth. "Bite," she coaxed.

He was trying to taste the food to see if he liked it—half swirling, half ready to spit.

She wasn't having any of that. "Now Glenn, chew," she softly said. "It's good, I made it for you." She squeezed his cheeks and jaw like she got Rusty to take pills from the vet, keeping eye contact all along.

He chewed while getting lost in her eyes. Then the pork, spices from the papaya salad and basil mixed to provide a unique taste that wasn't hard to acquire. The culinary part of his brain was spitfiring. He forgot all about how great she looked.

He was amazed at how she could feed him and, at the same time, feed herself. At one point, there were pieces of food on the side of his mouth, and she deftly dipped his napkin in the water glass and wiped the food away. He felt like a little kid, and oddly wasn't embarrassed.

They were midway through when Lynh appeared. "Ahh my daughter and her man."

"Mommy!" Maya feigned embarrassment. "Mommy you want?"

Lynh shook her head. "No honey, Mama ate already."

Maya tried to look disappointed. "Not try, Mommy? I make."

Lynh winked. "No honey. Save it for your man." No protest this time.

Lynh lightly slapped Glenn on his wrist. "You lucky, eh Glenn? Pretty, funny, sing good and cook! Why you not marry her right now?" Glenn choked on a piece of larb and started coughing. Maya lifted his beer to his lips, and he drank.

Still coughing a bit, Glenn tried to reply. "Mama . . ."

Lynh cut him off. "You know, Glenn, I know you were coming. I told Maya you give her second chance because God give us all second chance." She turned to Maya. "Maya, I told you God send good man to bar. I told you God send good man for you. One week before he come remember?"

Maya sighed. She remembered. "Mommy, don't embarrass Glenn. Let him enjoy food, be happy, not stressed."

Lynh took a seat. "Look he stress, Maya. Because he not have good woman like you to take care him. Not just once a week in dark bar. Should be at home, in front TV, maybe kids next year. You bring to Mama and I babysit."

Glenn coughed up another chunk of larb. "Whoa, Mama! Where's this going?"

Lynh laughed. "I see all the time. My girls find good man in bar. Gone. One year later, come show me baby. I only want you to be happy, okay? Okay, no rush. But this month we make like family. Okay? Glenn you come, Maya you cook and you feed. No bar party. Just relax every Tuesday for you Glenn, okay?"

He was perplexed, and his face showed it.

This was not on the list of approved "How to make a bar patron feel special" bargirl gimmicks. Lynh waved. "You okay, Glenn? Just relax my girl every Tuesday, okay?

He nodded, in a trance almost. "Okay, Mama."

Maya had the look of a daughter whose mother just hijacked her boyfriend. She eyed Verna imploringly in the distance. "Mommy, I think Jimmy need you."

Verna came over and rapped out some Vietnamese to Lynh, and Lynh jabbered back. Glenn swore Verna's tone was along the lines of *Good grief, old woman, let the kids alone.*

Lynh turned to Glenn and Maya and winked. "I go make sure other girls not stealing from me."

Glenn held up two fingers for Verna. A minute later, Maya had a shot of peach Ciroc in front of her and was pouring his beer into a newly frosted glass. They clinked. "Cheers!" She raised her glass, and he replied, "Happy Tuesday!"

He took a big swig then let slip a burp. Smiling sheepishly, he looked up to see her amused, smiling, and then she burst out laughing. "You so cute! No need to hide burp. Only natural. Just let it out!" Then she let out a belch so loud that Tia yelled "Ewww" from the bar. Maya was snorting so hard, she fell out of the booth.

He couldn't help joining in. He pulled her back up.

They both wiped tears from their eyes.

She squeezed his hand. "I don't laugh like that long time. You so fun Glenn. Like having real friend." She stopped. "I mean . . . you are friend . . ."

"I know. You're a real friend too. Only thing is you only have free time Tuesdays, so I gotta come see you at work." He gave her a look that asked *do I have it right?*

She nodded. "Thankful you come see me." She hugged him, leaving a kiss on his cheek.

Her tone changed for the serious. "You help me, Glenn? I have money question."

He took a sip of his beer. Rubbed his face. "Sure."

She showed him a wad of money. "This $5,000, Glenn. You help me open bank account?"

He was bug-eyed. "What are you doing with so much cash?"

She nodded. "I save long time. I have account with ex-husband credit union but now I know he check up on me with his friend. I don't deposit last two months."

He searched his phone for a number. "Call this guy. He'll help you."

She typed the number into her phone and lifted the phone to her forehead, her gesture of thanks. "Thank you. I need bank account I can send Mommy money. I put in and she use ATM card to take out."

Then she had a sneezing and coughing fit. He thought she'd sounded congested when she first came. "You getting sick?" He rubbed her back, remembering what Lynh had said about Maya's sinuses and ulcers.

She wiped her nose, tenderly, dabbing not rubbing. "Just little bit. Don't worry. Nothing stop me from being with you."

Concern etched his face. "You really work hard for your money. I know—your mom, your sister, your dog. But you need time to yourself. Don't work so much. You're pushing your body. Get sick. I can help, you know?" He bit his tongue. *Most girls would work me on this, maybe ask for a condo or a car or an allowance. Brad can think I'm a dumbass, but whatever it takes. I believe her. Whatever she needs.*

Her thigh was up against his, lightly, as if joining their souls. She rested her hand on his forearm. "You help enough already."

A bit surprised, real respect for her eased into his spirit. He gently lay his hand on her hand. "I can come more, or I can bring more money for you." *She can take a night off if I give her enough money on Tuesdays.*

She poured his beer. While he was sipping, she explained. "No, Glenn. You do too much already. You too nice. You come. You take care me. You take care of other girls. I know you buy other girls' dinner. And you give Mei money for ice cream for her kids. She told me."

Verna looked busy, so he signaled Allie, the other server, for another round. "But these are your friends. Why wouldn't I take care of them? I want to take care of you. I miss you when you're not around. At least I'll know you're okay, money-wise. I worry you'll get sick working so hard."

He had her at "worry." Her features softened, and she put her head on his shoulder. She reached up, cupped his chin, brought him closer and kissed him. The first kiss was tender. She lingered, then reached around the back of his neck and drew him closer. Her lips parted, and she gave him a second, longer kiss. Their tongues were an inch apart.

Allie wasn't paying attention when she brought the next round. "Oops, sorry, guys." Hand on her mouth, she left in a hurry without a tip. She made a beeline to Tia waving her arms.

Both glad for the interruption, each sat there with hearts beating fast, faces slightly flushed.

She broke the ice. "Lynh take care of me too. You know I was at other Thai bar but there too much drama. Chloe say come here and I meet Mama and she like me and now she like my Mama here. Little too much. She always want find me good man but here not many."

Glenn wondered if there were others. "I date last year one guy but he text me fifteen times during day and was crazy. Mama kick him out. I tell her stop. I don't need . . . not want. Remember I told you I was divorced. The guy he beat me, remember? I tell you about other guys. I don't want no more. I do myself, Glenn. Remember? I take care of myself. Thankful for your help though."

Glenn nodded. One of the other girls walked in, saying "Hi" to Maya. Distracted, he looked around, past her at the other girls coming in.

She saw the concern on his face. "What wrong?"

He brought the bottle to his head to cool. "You have other customers?" *I'm having a good time, just like the other night. Can't help feeling an iceberg dead ahead again.*

She caught on. "No, only you tonight." Reading his mind. "Don't worry. Chloe not here. Not take me away." She wiped at his face. She remembered. It put him at ease. "From now on, Tuesdays for you. Only you Tuesdays."

He sandwiched her hands in his. "I do want to help you. What can I do?"

She kissed his palm. "It's okay. I do okay, you know me. Remember? I don't have father growing up. Grandpa, Grandma raise me on farm." She fished around on her phone for pics to show. "Mama work in the city, leave us on farm. Hard work. I take care of myself, and later sister and brother. I'm okay. I do myself. You help enough already."

She was insistent. Glenn felt a pushback vibe and didn't want to ruin the night. "Okay, okay. Just remember it's there, okay?" *She's so damn independent. Just like me. Gotta prove to the world she can do it on her own. Gotta love her for that. Brad, you got it all wrong.*

She nodded as if to prod the conversation elsewhere. "Okay. We sing now?"

He finished his beer. "Okay. Another round? How about Crown Reserve, the expensive stuff?" *She can make more money on the expensive stuff. It's only tea with droplets of alcohol anyway.*

Glenn had brought five large bills to spend tonight. And she saw his wad and knew what he was doing.

She kissed his forehead, her way of saying, I know what you're doing. "You know, Glenn, you don't have to always buy me drinks or keep giving money. Make budget. Don't go broke. Want to see you regular. Not want you tell me you broke-ass one day and not come long time. If no money don't worry, I stay with you all night no matter what. Remember first night?" He nodded.

Her expression changed to worry, just a bit. "But tomorrow night if you come . . . I have customer." She searched his face. *Is he okay?*

He shrugged and smiled. "No worries. I won't bother. I have to share you with the world, right?"

Her face reflected relief. "He longtime friend. We bet football together. Not like us. I tell you things I don't tell anyone else. I'm comfortable with you."

He fiddled with the karaoke mic Verna had brought over earlier. "Okay. By the way, do you have customers on Thursday?"

She signaled Verna for the songbook. "No. Only random. First come first serve. Ha ha. Like Jack in Box." She started looking through the book for some new songs to sing.

He continued. "I gotta go to a meeting that night. Lots of wine. I'm probably gonna get shit faced. I was hoping I could get dropped off here to chill. No worries if you have a customer. Just roll me into a corner. That okay?"

She dropped the page she was looking at. Her face looked troubled, worried. *Where he going end up that night?* "You come here and I will take care of you. Don't go nowhere get in trouble. Come here. okay?"

He felt her concern. It felt good. "Okay." He thought of Billy's mom.

She gave Verna a song list. "We sing now? I pick all your favorites. Mr. Glenn, may I make you happy now?"

He flashed a smile. "You had me happy when you walked in."

The night wore on with song and drink. A perfect night. Songs he'd never heard before. By now, the servers left them alone unless called. Closing time came quickly. She usually waved goodbye from the door then went back to settle her account with Jimmy. This time she asked him to stay, and when done with her account, they walked out together, arm in arm. A good night kiss in the parking lot.

Two nights later, Glenn stumbled into the bar and fell on his face. Drunk as shit. "Maya!" He was yelling for her. She wasn't there.

17

SISTER BRUDDER

Glenn got back on his feet and dragged himself to the bar. "Aaaay Jimmy! Jimmy boy!" Jimmy sized him up—this guy was passed out walking, or close enough. Glenn had killed two bottles of wine in two hours, after closing the deal for God and country per the Admiral's orders. He looked around. Things were a little blurry. "Is Maya here, Jimmy?" It was 9:30 and the bar was in full swing.

"Glenn, she late, but she coming soon. Have a seat. You want something." Jimmy put some green tea in front of Glenn, hoping he'd not want any alcohol. "You hungry, Glenn? Tia, go tell Uncle get pho for Glenn.

Glenn had had Uncle's pho before. "Oh yeah, that'd be perfect." He envisioned sharing it with Maya. Jimmy wanted Uncle to make a special pho with spices and herbs to counter alcohol poisoning. Jimmy texted Maya. *Where you? You late. Glenn here.*

The pho got cold. Glenn finished it off. It was an hour later, and the room was spinning. "Jimmy, she's not coming, is she?"

Jimmy feigned ignorance. "I don't know Glenn. Maybe traffic."

Rolling his eyes, Glenn replied, "Jimmy, it's 10:30 at night." Jimmy moved off.

Tia was texting hard. *Where are you? Didn't you promise?* She read Maya's response and went over to Glenn. "Hi love, how you doing?" Happy for the company, Glenn slurred something. Ten minutes later, her own regular came in, and she rushed off.

Amber, the other barback, was watching all this unfold. She'd noticed Glenn a month before. She was a Chinita. Classic white skin and exotic mix of Filipina and Chinese blood. Behind the bar in a skimpy red nightie, her shtick, she caught the eye of every barfly, including Glenn. She wasn't shy and often put on quite a show of dancing behind the bar for those with a view. If you were sitting at the bar, it was the same as being front row in a strip club.

Her smile was sweet and seductive. "How you Glenn? You miss Maya? Want company?" Glenn nodded her over. Amber came out from behind the bar and got the party started. "Dance with me, Glenn." She held out her hands. He got to her just as she swung her backside to him. She took his hands and put them around her waist. She didn't waste time and ground into him while feeding him shots over her shoulder.

Tia watched helplessly but couldn't leave her customer. Glenn fed Amber shots, and his hands got tighter around her waist, with a bit of wanderlust coming on. Tia was a little taken aback. She saw a different kind of Glenn. *Then again,* she thought, *Amber could probably turn on a dead parish priest in his grave.*

Jimmy slammed the registrar drawer hard and whipped around. "Amber, time close bar! Leave Glenn alone. Let him chill."

Glenn nuzzled Amber's neck before turning his head. "Dass 'K, Jimmy." He was slurring, half leaning on Amber, half against the bar, unable to hoist himself two inches onto a barstool.

Amber wrapped her arms around his neck. "Good night, Glenn." With a generous fake boob-crushing hug, she kissed him on his cheek and before heading off, breathed huskily in his ear, "Anytime you need me baby, I'm here."

Chloe witnessed all of this from the dart room. Seeing her chance, she whispered some illusory promise in her customer's ear, kissed his bald forehead, and ushered him out the door. Glenn's eye caught Chloe's eye as she said goodnight to her customer. Never dropping eye contact, he dropped a twenty on the bar, hoping she'd take a hint. She did. He'd never liked Chloe much, because she was always doing things to take Maya away from him. *Let's bury the hatchet tonight,* he thought. Looking on, Tia furiously texted. Chloe's phone buzzed, but she ignored it.

Swaying from all the booze, he could barely make sentences. "About time I said hi to you, Chloe?"

She leaned against the bar, showing ample cleavage. "Yeah, Glenn. Where Maya tonight? You being bad boy without her?"

Okay, she's pretty and got big tits, but she's a bitch. I don't need this. I'm out of here. Glenn nearly stumbled as he got off his stool.

"Hey, where you going? Just kidding." Chloe caught him and steadied him. "Sorry, Glenn. Not know you so sensitive." He smiled. Something in the way she talked reminded him of his favorite cousin—how she was like a sister to him.

She felt him buckle a bit. *This guy gonna get mugged he walk out now.* Her brow furrowed, trying to come up with something. "Glenn, do me favor? Some bad guys out there waiting for me. Can you sit with me in booth room till Jimmy chase them away?"

He was on autopilot now. "Yeah, okay."

An Elvis song came on right before last call. Glenn took Chloe's hand and swung her around. They danced where he and Maya first danced. Tia was throwing glasses in the sink without caring. Her face flushed, her eyes spewed daggers at Chloe as she yelled last call. The jukebox went silent. Glenn didn't notice.

Chloe took his hand. "Come, Glenn." Chloe led him to the booth room.

They sat next to each other, her purse in between them. She spoke first. "I thought you just one more guy using my sister like a toy. I guess you okay. You all right. Kinda bus' up now though, huh?"

The room started a slow spin. He willed it to stop. "Yeah, and I thought you were another sleaze whore pimping out your sister to pad your wallet."

Chloe's mouth slacked open a bit, eyes betraying surprise. Maya hadn't said anything about this.

In a moment of clarity, he got it, turning fully to her. "But you care for her, don't you?"

She nodded. "Yeah, you too huh? Not bad for loser bar guy." She squeezed his forearm, being careful not to linger. At that moment, they both came to understand how much the other cared for Maya and warmed to each other. It was after closing time. The lights came on. The bad guys were gone.

Chloe was feeling tipsy but hadn't made her quota yet. There was an all-night bar next door. Lots of suckers landed there after most bars close. She studied him. *Not meet customer like him. I was going to work him next door tonight. Maybe make him mine? But he sweet. I see why sister like him. I should get him home.*

He leaned back against the booth and turned to her. "Hey Chloe, you ever been next door? The place with the all-night license? I heard it's raunchy but was always scared to go."

One eyebrow arched in surprise, she chewed at her thumbnail. "No, not scary, I go all the time. You really going?" Chloe wanted to make sure this guy was okay before she let him go home. Jimmy and Tia thought differently. They'd seen Chloe take other customers next door. There was a time when Chloe took one of Maya's customers for herself.

Jimmy walked over. "Hey Chloe, let Glenn go home already."

Glenn cut in. "That's okay, Jimmy. I always wanted to get know Chloe."

Jimmy was desperate now. "Glenn, you stay here then."

Eyes half shut, he shook his head. "Nah, that's okay, Jimmy."

In the back of Glenn's mind, he was miffed and wanted to send Maya a message. *So you fucking stood me up. Okay then, you lost me. Count it up, $300 for Amber and I got another $500 in my pocket for your sister here. You can be replaced, you know.*

He was about to get out of the booth when Verna blocked his way. She held out an ancient flip phone. "Mama on phone." It was Lynh's night off, but she was calling him at two o'clock in the morning.

He stared at the Nokia relic. *This is bizarre. What mama-san calls her bar patron after closing? Who uses phones like this anymore?* He heard her voice. "Glenn, I see you on camera with Chloe. You too close to her, and why you dance with her? Where you going now?"

Chloe pretended to fix her makeup. He pinched the bridge of his nose. "Next door, Mama. I have day off tomorrow and not done party yet."

"You done, Glenn. Go home. Jimmy call you taxi, okay?"

"No, Mama."

"Glenn, no good you with Chloe. Ditch her. Think of Maya."

With that Glenn said, "No worries Mama, I am thinking of her" and hung up. On the other end, Mama stared at the phone and hissed some choice words in Vietnamese. Something about his nads falling off painfully.

Glenn grabbed Chloe's hand. "Let's go." They slipped out the back way. Seeing this on her camera, Lynh scowled and turned off the monitor.

Next door, Chloe shooed away the servers squeezing Glenn for drinks. They were talking among themselves, with one wondering aloud, "Something wrong here, that bitch always work some sucker for $500 at least," and the other simply asking, "Who that guy with her?"

Chloe didn't care about the servers. She'd generated enough tips for them over the years. It felt refreshing to be with a real person. *This guy was real. And he really likes Maya. My sister so lucky.* "Glenn, you want to see pictures of Maya when we first met?" She pulled out her phone.

He was so thrilled; he didn't even notice the hugely endowed strippers dancing all around them.

Chloe continued. "You like her, huh?" He started to feel queasy but managed to nod. *Sweet,* she thought, *Maya's right—he so different.*

He reached into his pocket. "Want drinks, Chloe?"

She caught his wrist. His money never made it out of his pocket. "No, you save for Maya. I'm okay." Chloe had had a down night. She could have used the extra income, and she saw other fish at the adjacent table she could squeeze. But she couldn't leave Glenn alone with so many vultures around.

She patted his shoulder. "Brudder, you take care my sister, okay? She all I got."

Glenn nodded. *Brudder? No one called me that before.*

He was getting sicker by the second. *If I don't leave now, I'm gonna puke all over her.* "Chloe, I gotta go. Not feeling good."

"Okay, you go. Brudder, you take care, okay." She took a last look at him. He looked all right. Walked him to the door and hailed a taxi for him.

She ran back in. The fish were still there. She slid into a booth with two scuzzy looking gents with three rolls of twenties parked in front of them. She eyed the wads. "Champagne, please!" The servers were thinking, *Now that's more like her.*

On the ride back, Glenn thought about what had happened. *She knew I had a wad of money. She didn't even ask once, and she shooed the servers away. What gives? Maybe she was done for the night?*

When Glenn woke up the next morning, he wondered if Chloe had fished his pockets. He had taken five hundred dollars out of the ATM to take care of her; he came home with four hundred eighty. *She took care of me. Does she like me?*

Somewhere in his foggy memory, he remembered her saying, "Sisters forever, take care her for me, okay?" *I will, Chloe. I will.*

He forgot all about hanging up on Lynh.

18

TENSION TEMPEST

He spent every day after that night mulling over the same questions and thoughts. *Where was she? She promised she'd be there. She cutthroat me again. I'm done. But I want to see her again. I need to see her again. Is she all right? Maybe she's hurt? Maybe she's dead? Is she okay?*

The following Tuesday, he stood outside the bar, letting the neon sign wash over him. It was only a light, but he wished it was some kind of magic Star Trek transporter thing that would make everything fine. He was scheduled to go off to DC again—Admiral's orders—so this would be their last Tuesday together this month. It would be November before he saw her again.

He took a deep breath and walked in. Jimmy was making a last-minute incense offering to the Buddha statue. "She not here yet, Glenn. Late today."

He stood by his corner seat, rubbing the back of his neck. "That's what you said last week, Jimmy."

Jimmy produced a shot glass. "I know. This time I know she come soon. I make up for you. What you want? On the house."

Lynh stormed out of the back and took Glenn by the elbow, nearly dragging him into the booth room. To the first booth on the left, her booth. "Sit."

He stood his ground, arms folded. "Mama, what is this about?" *So much for my free Hennessey.*

She pointed to the booth. "Sit! She not here yet. I tell her come late. Want talk to you."

His lips tightened. Arms still crossed, he sat. *Let's get this over with.*

She sat only after he sat. "You want Chloe? I tell Maya stop seeing you. You can have Chloe. You want Amber? You can have two. You can have two on one, you like?"

He raised his palms to her. "Whoa Mama, where is this coming from?" He was getting used to saying this to Lynh.

She had a lighter in one hand and a cigarette in the other. "I told you no go with Chloe. Maya know. She cry last Friday all night. Come work. No work. Make customers sad and mad. Just cry all night. Her and Chloe fight all night too."

She lifted the cigarette to her mouth and left it there unlit. "This happen before, honey. One night Maya sick not show up and Chloe take customer to hotel. He never come back to Maya. But too much drama for him so not come back for Chloe either. I lose good customer." She spit out her cigarette. "I don't want to lose you, Glenn. You guys fuck that night? You want blow job in the car in the parking lot after? I fix for you. Who you want?" Lynh eyed his broad shoulders. It'd been a month for her since she'd had anyone.

Glenn felt his anger rising. "Fuck you, Mama. I'm the customer. You want to get in my face like that, I can leave." He licked his lips. "For the record, Chloe treated me good, and she only was protecting me for Maya. All she did was show me pictures of Maya and only took a twenty off me. What the fuck are you talking about?" *Why is she acting like this? All sweet and nice before. She's like a scorned bitch now.*

She lit her cigarette, took one puff and ground it out. Her way of getting around the health code. "Okay, honey. Sorry. Just worried about my girl. Chloe is bad, stay away from her. No hurt Maya. She not like the others."

He opened his mouth, then closed it, burying his face in his hands. *She cried? Over me?* He straightened up. Took a deep breath, held, and exhaled. He pictured Maya crying. His heart softened. "Okay, Mama. I hurt her. I screwed up. What do you want me to do?"

Lynh relaxed, leaned back, then leaned forward and took his hands in hers. "You come back from trip. Buy her champagne. Make her feel special. I set you two up. Okay?"

He pulled his hand away and shrugged. "Okay, Mama. Whatever you want."

Maya walked in. Tentatively, she came by their booth. "Hi Mama. What you doing?"

Lynh stood up and put both her hands on Maya's shoulders. "Just talking, honey. Here you sit with him."

There was no food. No family-style dinner. She wore jeans with slits ripped across her thighs and a red tank top, covered by a light green field jacket. He noticed the dress-down. She slid in next to him. The bar area was livening up. A dance beat pulsed from the jukebox, and the regular couples were filing into the booth room. But in that booth, they were tucked away from the bar, from the world, and from everything else. It was just him and her.

She was staring straight ahead. "I'm sorry not come last Thursday. Had to work late shift." Then she turned. The cloth of her jeans brushed up against his slacks. "I heard you had fun cut loose. You want cut loose I can cut loose with you too."

He turned slightly. Knees touching. Bodies and souls connecting again. "No need. Just blowing off steam." But in his head, he was screaming. *Tia and Jimmy both texted you all night! What happened?* He let it go.

Her hands were on the table, fingers laced together. "You want be with Chloe instead? It's okay with me. She beautiful, yes?"

He eyed her hands, wanting to reach out so bad. "No, I don't want Chloe. I want you. Just that . . . " He hesitated.

"Just what?"

"You weren't here. That's all."

She leaned into him, shoulder on shoulder. "I'm sorry, Glenn. I thought I could make it here. I have late shift and had inventory that night. I forgot. Sorry. But I hope you had fun."

Glenn was pensive. *I'm an accountant, certified, inactive but certified. Who does inventory in the middle of the month?*

Things were tense. No beer tonight. He was drinking shots of Hennessey. Three shots later, things loosened up.

They clinked glasses. "You know, Maya, Chloe really cares about you. All she did was talk about you all night. She showed me pictures of you."

Maya nodded. She waited for an explanation about Amber, but it didn't come.

He pressed. "Maya, you and Chloe okay?"

She stared into her shot glass for a few seconds. "We talk. We fight. Sometimes we don't talk for a while. But we sisters. Always make up. Chloe beautiful, I know. I'm not."

He cocked his head at her. A look of disbelief. "What do you mean?"

She raised her shot glass to him, her way of asking for another shot. "I never think me pretty. Brown, short, flat nose. I was tomboy, you know. No boys like me."

He signaled two fingers to Allie. "Hard to believe. Wow, is that why you're with an old guy like me?"

She smiled, the first one of the night. "No, I like older, not old, guys. Grandpa raise me, you know. Older men know more than younger men."

Glenn wasn't sure. He remembered from last summer that she hung out with a lot of young guys.

She turned to him, creating space between them. "Glenn, okay you have fun without me. Thursdays hard for me because late shift at day job. I'm not here this Thursday in case you come. Okay, you have fun though."

He was wondering where Allie was. "Okay." Glenn should have read between the lines. If he'd looked her way instead of looking for Allie, he would have noticed an edge to her look. She was distant the rest of the night, and as the evening came to an end, Glenn had an uneasy feeling.

He'd felt this before—when he was in the doghouse with Katie. She was mad. He could feel it. *What do they say? A woman scorned, something something . . . the guy is up shit creek and no sex for a month. Something like that. But this was a bargirl. Why so mad?* He wanted to ask but instead reminded her: "You remember I'm not here next week?" It would be two weeks before they saw each other again.

She got up out of the booth. "Yes. I see you later."

He stopped in front of her, desperately wanting to hold her hand. "The week after, yes. Don't forget me."

She hugged him and walked him to the door. She didn't go outside with him. She dodged his goodnight kiss and offered her cheek instead. *I guess I deserve this. Not the best night. Not the best timing. Is she still gonna be here when I get back?*

Two nights later, Glenn walked into the bar. Same sounds. Same barflies. No Maya. Tia looked up. "Hi love, keep me company?" She shot off a couple of texts as she came around the bar.

Amber was there to cover the bar. "Hi Glenn." She winked at him.

He smiled. "Hi, Amber. Thanks for the other night." He slid a twenty her way. Amber made eye contact with Tia. Ever so casually, she pushed the twenty back. "No problem, Glenn. Just taking care of you for Maya."

Glenn was confused. *What's going on?*

Tia jumped in. "How's business in the dark secret world of politics?" Then she started talking about real estate. *These girls really know how to control the conversation,* he thought. Tia was easy to look at. It was easy to forget little things like bargirls giving money back.

Chloe came out from the dart room. "Hi, brudder."

He got up and hugged her. "Hi, sister."

Tia squinted as if doing that would explain what was going on.

Brother? Sister? Odd. Never heard Chloe call anyone brudder before.

He nodded toward the dart room. "You alone, Chloe?"

"Not for long, brudder." She smiled then went back.

Tia's voice cut in. "My fitness contest is just two months away, Glenn." She told him how she was cutting back on carbs. Again, easy to look at, easy to get sucked in.

Tia lifted her phone to him. "Maya says hi." Tia showed him Maya's texts. "She said to take care of you." Tia had babysat Glenn during the first week they met.

His shoulders hunched, just a bit. "Nah, Tia, you don't have to."

She lightly touched his forearm. "No worries Glenn. I got you. We haven't talked in a long time."

He held up two fingers at Amber, then pointed to himself and Tia. *Dammit. I feel marked, kept—like inventory on a shelf. Like being a branded bull. Can't blow Tia off. Nice to have her company though.*

Amber served up the shots, and he and Tia clinked glasses. As Tia rattled on, Glenn's eyes made contact with Chloe in the dart room. *Tia's fine but I want to go hear more about Maya. If I can't be with her, I wanna be with the next best thing.*

Lynh came out from the back, spying Tia and Glenn and following Glenn's sight path. "Tia, honey, stock more Seagram's please."

"I'll be right back, Glenn." Tia hurried to the storage room.

Lynh came around and grabbed Glenn's beer. "Come."

He raked his hands through his hair. "What?"

She gave his sleeve a sharp tug. "Just come." Glenn followed Lynh into the dart room. Chloe was sitting alone, fiddling with her cell phone.

Lynh nudged Glenn toward Chloe. "You want Chloe, I give you Chloe!"

Chloe looked up, eyes darting back and forth between Lynh and Glenn, "Mama, what you doing?"

Lynh pushed Glenn toward Chloe. "Never mind honey. He customer. You sit with him."

Chloe didn't budge. "My other customer coming, Mama."

Lynh's voice reflected she was the boss. "It's okay—till your other customer come then." Chloe moved over.

Tia came back to find Glenn gone then looked in the dart room. She started texting.

Lynh walked off after pushing Glenn into the booth with Chloe.

Glenn watched Lynh walk off. The expression on his face was pure *what the fuck.* He whispered to Chloe. "What's going on? Are you and Maya okay?"

She nodded, an equally *what the fuck* look on her face. "Yeah, yeah. We talk. We fight. We sisters. We okay." Then her phone buzzed. "It's her." She rambled on in Thai. He heard his name twice. "Maya said do what you want."

Glenn buried his head in hands then jerked his head up. He had enough. "Hey Chloe, can you go get Tia?" Chloe went out and brought Tia back in.

They sat across him. "Guys, I don't know what's going on, but this doesn't feel right. I'm going home." Chloe and Glenn described to Tia what happened. Eyebrows raised, Tia pursed her lips and let out a silent whistle. *Drama. Again.*

Chloe and Tia agreed, nodding and mouthing, "You go home" in unison.

He finished his beer; the same one he started the night with. "Can you guys square things with Maya? I knew she wasn't going to be here. I just was stopping by to chill."

Tia and Chloe looked united now. "Yeah, yeah, Glenn, no worries."

"Sorry about taking you away from your customers." Glenn tried to buy each a drink.

Both pushed back. "No, Glenn, don't worry."

Glenn did his own pushing. "No, business is business. Lucky shots. Sorry for the drama." Glenn was getting an uneasy feeling about Lynh. *What's her problem?*

Tia and Chloe weren't letting on. "So sorry, Glenn. We take care."

"Okay." He hugged both and left.

It would be two weeks before he saw Maya again. He was hoping everything was okay.

Across town, Maya stared at her phone. *He like all the others. All men the same.* She frowned and sighed, holding back tears. The last five texts she got were from Lynh.

19

NOVEMBER FEELINGS

He was off to DC and back with no hitches. It was a minor skirmish. An uncooperative senator here, an unsupportive HUD director there, but with the right dialogue Glenn was able to get all on the same page with workforce improvements, not only back home but across the nation.

DC was easy, he thought as he entered the bar. *Got a feeling tonight's not gonna be as easy. Hope Tia and Chloe were able to fix things with Maya.*

It was the first Tuesday of November. The bar was quiet, with only a few regulars in the front. He noticed one guy sitting alone in the dart room. The music was turned down low, and the flatscreens were off.

Jimmy greeted him. "Long time, Glenn. She not here yet. Running late."

"Okay, Jimmy." Glenn took a seat at the bar. Back to the door. Jimmy came around to join him. *Well that's a switch*, Glenn mused.

Jimmy slid onto the seat next to him. "You want a shot Glenn? On the house. Anything you want."

"Hennessey, Jimmy." Jimmy took the same. They sat there, sipping. A Hispanic beat started up and kept them company. Jimmy leaned slightly toward him. "You happy, Glenn?"

Glenn caught Jimmy's eye in the mirror behind the bar. "What do you mean?"

"With Maya. She not what you think. I can get you better. Let me know okay?"

She walked in before he could answer. Black leather mini skirt with halter top to match. Her makeup looked darker and heavier than usual. He saw her reflection in the mirror behind the bar. He could see her stopping short very briefly, then taking a quick left into the dart room. Glenn waited. She came out to get a peach Ciroc for her and a Heineken Light. Jimmy turned to her. "Hey Maya, look who here."

She feigned surprise. "I didn't see him." She spoke directly to Jimmy, never making eye contact with Glenn. To Glenn, the term "cold shoulder" didn't explain how shunned and in the doghouse he felt. *What's going on here? She knew I was coming back today. She said she'd miss me. Now this? So much for Tia and Chloe fixing things.*

He leaned back, peered over Jimmy's shoulder to make eye contact. "Hi Maya, do you have time tonight?" Awkward . . . removed . . . demeaned—that's how he felt having to ask for time after months of her saying Tuesdays were for him.

Her eyes narrowed, her lips a tight frown. Like she just saw a pile of shit. "I have customer tonight. I will come back. I didn't know you come back tonight so when he ask last Friday, I say okay for tonight. I have to work you know." Her voice was so cold he swore he saw her breathing frost.

He turned back to his drink. "Yeah, okay." *Wasn't this the night I'm supposed to buy her champagne? Where's Lynh?*

Kimmie pushed Jimmy off his stool and took his place next to Glenn. "Hiya, Glenn! How you doing tonight?" Kimmie was the second mama of the place. She'd never bothered with Glenn except for the infrequent karaoke rescue mission. Twice before, Glenn had come in early before Maya arrived just to sing a few songs or practice the songs he'd wanted to sing with Maya. Whenever he got a little pitchy, Kimmie came running down between the booths with another microphone to help with the notes and harmony. He always bought her a glass of red cabernet to say thank you.

But tonight, all she saw was a nice guy hurting. He was brooding and staring straight ahead. Didn't notice she'd taken Jimmy's place. She tried again and nudged him back to reality. "Hiya, sailor, buy a girl a drink?"

He let out a slight smile.

She pressed on. "Or at least sit here and pretend I'm desirable?"

This time he laughed. The ice was broken. She was the only person in the joint that drank wine. He nodded to Tia.

Kimmie held out a microphone. "Thanks, Glenn. Want to sing?"

He finished his scotch. "Nah, but thanks for being here."

She patted his shoulder. "No problem, my dear." She whipped out her phone and started playing Candy Crush, her favorite phone game. When Lynh was in the back, Kimmie was in the front coordinating the girls. And as they filed in, she doled out assignments like some police desk sergeant. He watched the whole thing go down, amazed. *She runs this place with military precision. The result? Every guy thinks it's a relaxation palace, a fun factory for lonely guys.*

Kimmie was Vietnamese like Lynh. Unlike Lynh, she was locally raised, so she was bicultural and bilingual. Ten years older than Maya, ten years younger than Lynh. She still had her looks and, with the right outfits covering a growing pudginess, still had her share of regulars from her days as a bargirl. It was rumored that she tried her hand at owning a bar across the street and that she'd run the place into the ground to the tune of a million dollars.

Maya's dart room customer left an hour later. She came out and spotted Glenn sharing a laugh with Kimmie. She walked right past them into the booth room to another customer waiting. Glenn saw this in the mirror. Confused didn't begin to explain the emotions welling up in him.

"That's it, I'm done," he muttered.

Lynh's voice snapped him out of it. "What you doing here alone?" It didn't matter to Lynh that Kimmie had sat with Glenn all night. Kimmie was a nonentity. Lynh demanded, "Where Maya?"

Glenn nodded toward the booth room. It was already midnight. Lynh jabbered something in Vietnamese to Kimmie, and Kimmie was gone, like a wisp of smoke. *Poof*, Glenn thought.

Lynh was quickly in the booth room jabbering away at Maya. Glenn was watching, almost horrified as he saw Lynh reach into the booth and drag Maya away from her customer and point to another girl to take her place. The guy didn't seem to mind.

Maya slid in next to Glenn at the bar. She stared straight ahead. Lynh was behind them. "Glenn, you buy champagne for Maya. okay?"

Maya protested. "No, Mama. No need." In the trade, champagne always came with extras.

Lynh had her hands on her hips. "Yes, Maya. He treat you special tonight, okay? Mama have room ready for you." By room, Lynh meant the ones to the side where couples enter and come out thirty minutes later with the guy looking goo goo-eyed. Glenn had seen lots of this action at other places. It was the kind of thing he wanted to get away from. Maya knew this but Mama did not.

Maya tried to explain. "Mama he not like that. Don't make him. I'm not like that."

Mama shot back. "Maya I don't say do anything bad. Just have private time." *What is wrong with this girl tonight?*

Glenn stepped in. "Mama, just bring the champagne. We can have private time out here. Shit, the bar's almost empty anyway."

Lynh shook her head and left. *After all I did for you two?*

Maya glared at Glenn. "You know I really thought you come back next week so I have other customers tonight."

"I know. No problem." He lied.

"Why you look like that then?"

"I'm tired." *I can play this game too. Better go home. This is going nowhere. It's like being married or something.*

Tia came around with two mini bottles of champagne that were already open. She poured out what looked like fruit juice into brandy snifters.

He pushed the snifters away. "Um, Tia, what is this?"

Tia pushed them back. "House champagne Glenn. Three hundred dollars each." He nearly fell off his chair. "So, I'm being worked?"

Maya stared at him like he was an idiot. "I told you."

Lynh came over to check. He turned on her. "Lynh, what is this? You working me now? Thought I was special. Thought you guys cared about me? This is bullshit!"

Hands on hips, Lynh retook her mama-san stance. "Honey, you a jerk. My bar. You like see my girl, you treat them good." Maya sat still, very still. Her eyelid twitched for a quick second. She breathed through her nose. *Time to go. Bad night. At least made some money off those two guys.*

Before Maya could act, Glenn threw six large ones on the counter, then pushed the snifters away as far as he could. Tia reached out thinking they were going to slide off the bar. "This is bullshit, Lynh. I'm coming back next week." He turned to Maya. "Be here next week, okay?"

He spun back to Lynh. "You want me to treat her good? Watch me. Let's do it for real. Not this cheap gimmick bullshit. I'm bringing my own champagne. I'll pay your corkage. I guess three hundred dollars for each bottle I bring. Now, can we have some privacy? Your bar, but I'm still the customer. Unless you are kicking me out?"

Lynh broke a smile. *So he have balls.* "Okay, honey, see you next week."

He turned to Maya. "If you're not here next week, or don't have time for me, I understand. I've been a jerk. Sorry."

She softened, but only a bit. *I thought he was like Darren, not come back, maybe move on. Meet Chloe someplace else? But he come back. This night is shit.*

They both stared at the fruit juice in front of them and decided to pass. Glenn was out six hundred dollars. He wasn't happy. Maya still wasn't happy. There was an edge to the night. Five minutes of discomfort passed. "Glenn, I have to go." She kissed him on the cheek and walked out without clearing her account, leaving him sulking. It was the first time she'd left first.

He raked his hair and turned his shot glass upside down. *Is she going to be here next week? Maybe I should run after her?*

He gathered his glasses and wallet off the counter when Kimmie's hand landed on his forearm. Her fingers said stay. "Last call, Glenn. Let her go. She'll come around." Retaking her seat, she brought out her cigarettes. After hours, smoking was allowed. She started playing her Candy Crush. "What's bothering you, Glenn?"

He slumped over onto the bar, catching Tia's eye for a beer to end the night. "I dunno, Kimmie. She lies to me, treats me like shit, and I'm the bad guy?" He still hadn't forgotten she said she'd be there for him when he got shitfaced and she wasn't. *She was gone. She promised she'd be there but she wasn't.* "Just like all the rest," he mumbled. "I'm so outta here."

Kimmie heard him. *The rest? He's got issues.*

She put down her Candy Crush. As she turned to him, she rested her elbow on his shoulder very lightly but clearly communicating that he wasn't going anywhere. Glenn didn't pull away. He sat staring at his drink. He felt a lecture from Number Two Mama coming on.

Tia put an ashtray in front of Kimmie, who continued her lecture. "Glenn, she's scared. She's been hurt by regulars before. It's easier for her to jump from booth to booth, room to room, customer to customer, an hour at a time." She lit her cigarette. "Whole nights with one customer? It's hard for any girl because it gets personal for both sides. These girls, they have emotions too, you know. They develop feelings."

He fully turned to her. "Feelings? What are you saying?"

She blew a puff of smoke, careful to make sure it was away from him. "Not saying anything, Glenn, but before you storm out of here pouting because she's giving you the cold shoulder, try to see it from her point of view."

He took a long swallow. "I'm listening."

She stubbed out her cig. "There was this guy Darren. He came here every night. He must have spent $5,000 a week. After a while, it wasn't the money for her. They settled into a routine like you two. A lot of girls would put out for something like that. Shit, they'd put out twice a night and let themselves get slapped around."

She lit another cigarette. "Maya doesn't have that advantage. She's got her pride. She calls it her pride."

Glenn tilted his head. "What do you mean, pride?"

Kimmie's face knotted up in thought. "It means not letting her body be used like a toy. She makes up for it. She sings, she flirts, she listens. She knows all the other ways to make men feel good. And so Mama picks her customers with care. They knew you weren't looking for physical. More emotional, right?"

Glenn nodded. *These women know more about the male psyche than all the psychology experts I know combined.*

Kimmie swirled her wine. "It's simple. Men tick by what's between their legs or what's between their ears. And she's good at getting at what's between someone's ears."

Glenn nodded. "So this guy Darren?"

Kimmie sipped her wine. "She goes home to Thailand once a year to celebrate Thai New Year. She left for only three weeks. I guess Darren got lonely. One night he comes in, and Chloe sits with him. Maya trusted Chloe to take care of her guy. They have a few drinks. Chloe can be cool when she wants, but get enough alcohol in her and smelling money, she'll be all over the guy no matter who he is."

Glenn massaged his neck. The kink had been there all night. "But she wasn't like that with me."

Kimmie reached for him. "Honey, let me get that for you. Turn around." No pushback. He did as he was told.

She started to work on his knot. "You were lucky. Darren wasn't. They ended up in a hotel that night. Chloe didn't come back for three nights. She made a wad of cash, and it wasn't for pleasant pillow talk conversation."

She finished up with one last squeeze.

He rubbed his neck. No knot. "Wow, that feels great. Thanks." He turned around. "But I wouldn't do that. What Darren did."

She lit another cigarette. "Really, Glenn? No one is that strong. And so when Mama saw you getting too cozy with Chloe, she stepped in. Verna stepped in. Jimmy stepped in. We saw this before. Didn't want it to happen with you."

She took a long drag, held it in, and exhaled. It was as if she was recounting her own disappointments. "You know she's thinking you guys ended up fucking that night, and Chloe was telling a story. Chloe denied everything about Darren when Maya came back from Thailand. But women know. They smell the scent of another woman on their man. It was all over for them. Darren would come in, and Maya wouldn't even acknowledge him. Eventually, he had girls crawling all over him. He stopped coming about a month before you showed up. That's why she was so man shy back then."

Jimmy brought over some water. Kimmie gave him the eye. He replaced her water with wine.

Jimmy turned to Glenn. "You want a beer?" The doors were closed. It was a private party now.

Glenn shook his head. "No thanks, Jimmy." *So she was man shy. She didn't want to get hurt again. I got it. Now I'm an asshole who's hurting her?*

Kimmie took another drag and continued. "You know, back then she cried every night for over a month? Two weeks ago, she started crying again."

She peeked at her phone, the third text in five minutes. "So if she's a little icy, don't hold it against her. Truth is that most men are dumb fucks when it comes to women. Whether she's a bargirl or not, she's still a woman."

She paused to be sure she had his attention. "Don't be one of the dumb fucks, Glenn. Give her a chance to come around. If you leave, it ain't gonna happen. Tuck your pride between your legs and be a real man."

She stubbed out her cigarette and took a sip of wine. "You know, she heard what a great time you had with Amber that night? The girls talk. It took all of us by surprise. We thought you were gonna doggie her right on the bar counter."

He rubbed his chin. "I was that bad?"

She gawked at him as if to say, really? "Glenn you were cupping her tits from behind! You were pretty much riding her against the bar!"

He poked his forehead with his thumb. "No way, I had my hands around her waist."

She couldn't help cracking a smile. Never saw someone poke their forehead. "No Glenn, those were her tits. And then you started dancing with Chloe and nuzzling her neck? You were hot for something." She nodded as if to make him agree, or at least remember.

She kept nodding. "And then she tells you she's not here on Thursday, but you come anyway. Clear signal Glenn to a bargirl that she's not why you come. That you come for any action."

"But . . ."

"No buts, Glenn, that's the way she's looking at it right now. And she's thinking maybe she should move on before she gets hurt like Darren hurt her."

He sat still. Anger fought remorse within his soul. *Where's my buzz? How did I become the bad guy tonight?*

Kimmie had a real big sister way of putting things straight. He looked up and simply nodded. *Me? She cried over me? I thought this was all fantasy.*

His face was contorted, the picture of perplexity. *She wants to move on before she gets hurt. What about me?*

Kimmie finished her wine. She stared at Glenn. *I think I got through to him. Hope so. They're good together.* Another text buzzed on her phone. "Gotta go, Glenn, I'm due next door." And she was gone.

Glenn sat outside the bar, thinking about what Kimmie said. *Why did I go crazy that Thursday? And why did I go back the following Thursday?*

He couldn't shake the vision of her crying. Of how it hurt when Darren betrayed her. And how hurt she was these past few times with him. Any hurt or betrayal he was feeling was taking a deep back seat to his not being able to stand hurting her. His heart ached, knowing she was hurt, and ached even more, knowing he caused the pain. *I wasn't thinking. I never meant to hurt her.*

He found his way to the beach. Watched the sunrise, hearing the waves crashing above the cacophony of the seagulls. The salt sea air cleared his mind, or so he thought.

He reached out to an old friend. *Hey Father, it's been a while. What am I doing here? I've hurt someone. Someone I really care about. Why do I do these things? Wasn't I the same with Katie? How could she stand me? I guess now she doesn't have to.*

He continued his half prayer, half rant. *What should I do? Maybe she's better off without me, You know? But shit, I need her. She's what keeps me going. She's the reason my confidence is returning. She makes me feel I'm worth something. Oh man, Father. Help me please?*

He heard it. Faintly. Over the sound of crashing waves. *For I know the plans I have for you. My grace will be sufficient.*

He fell backward on the sand. *What plans? What grace?*

20

ISSUES OVERFLOW

He woke on the sand to the sound of seagulls and a couple jogging by. The sun was just coming up. The sea air filled his nostrils, and he surmised that the other gamey smell was coming from him. His lips were parched and his tongue fuzzy. He dusted the sand from his hair and clothes and made a beeline for the public restroom to relieve himself. *This is gonna be a hell of day.*

He went straight from the beach to his office, which resembled a converted storage room—a ten-by-ten walled space with a desk, file cabinets and a computer that was over ten years old. *I didn't expect luxury here, but this looks like the janitor's closet.*

A woman young enough to be his daughter greeted him. "Good morning, boss." Danielle was only twenty-eight years old but smart in school and in life. He had promoted her from an accounting clerk to the supervisor position after the previous one quit. He needed someone hungry enough to work hard, but green enough not to find another job right away.

He rubbed his unshaven face. "Morning, Danielle." *Good thing I have Danielle. I can't believe Samantha quit two weeks after I got here. She interviewed me. Told me don't worry. She'd get all the accounting stuff done and I just needed to do the finance stuff. I asked her point blank whether she was looking for another job. I guess she wasn't lying; she quit to have a third kid. Bet she only wanted a way out.*

He visually spit at the mound of work in his office. *Now I'm stuck with the accounting stuff. I told all of them I don't do accounting. And now? Data entry, check signing, and all other drudgery accounting, workday after workday, hour after hour.*

His head was pounding as he flopped onto his ancient office chair. *Tuesdays and Maya—only things getting me from one bloodsucking, mind-numbing week to the next.*

Danielle followed him into his office with a stack of paper. "You look tired." She sniffed. "You smell. And that's the shirt you had on yesterday?" She came around the desk. "Same pants too!"

He leaned back in his chair, laying his forearm over his eyes. "Danielle, enough. Long night."

Danielle's eyes widened. "Uh oh."

He leaned forward. "Not what you're thinking. What do you need?"

Danielle produced a stack of paper eight inches thick. "These have to be input by 10:00 a.m., then proofed and reviewed, and approved by you."

He perused the top inch of papers with boredom and disdain painted on his face. "Why me?"

She adjusted her glasses, the ones that made her look like a cute owl. "You're the boss, and Joyce hasn't approved me to review yet."

He raised his eyebrows as if to say really? *Joyce. Our CEO. She told me at the interview that I'd be going home at 4:00 p.m. Every day go home at 4. Bullshit. I'm here till past 6:00 p.m. most nights and now the weekends? Because it takes all of us to do our job and make up for the things Samantha left behind. They won't even let me hire another person. Shit.*

He exhaled forcefully through puffed cheeks and threw what he picked up back on the pile. "Okay, Danielle. Close the door on your way out." He felt tired suddenly. He locked the door, lay on the floor and nodded off.

He got up an hour later. *Amazing . . . alarm apps for Android phones these days. No sound, just vibration.* He took Danielle's stack of paper, walked across the hall to her office, and dropped it on her desk. "Approved." He trudged back to his office.

She scratched her head. Danielle wanted him to sign each page. He'd initialed only the top page with today's date. She knew that's all she was going to get out of him. She did like Glenn, though, because he was able to solve all the complicated problems with ease. *Supposed to have been some bigwig for the mayor and now . . . this? Small time nonprofit controller.*

Glenn closed his door. He thought about what Kimmie had said the night before. It bothered him that he'd hurt Maya. Leaning against the door, he looked upward.

You know, Father, I don't know what I'm doing here. Technically, I'm still married, but it's been really lonely without Katie, You know? I can use some affection sometimes. Maya dishes it out pretty good.

He closed his eyes. He and Maya were singing, dancing, hugging, and kissing again.

Then she goes on these psycho trips. I don't know what the shit is going on. Like walking out on me last month. Leaving me hanging in the front bar. She's in the booth room with other customers. She didn't even tell me what was going on—just left me to rot.

He walked over to his desk. With glazed eyes, he started shuffling paperwork that was three months old.

She said she wouldn't do it again. I believed her. I trusted her. I gave her a second chance. Then she bullshits me about being there for me, and what? She's a no-show again. Again more bullshit about getting stuck at work, but no calls, no nothing. Left me hanging.

He slumped back in his chair. *And then I come back from my trip, and she snubs me. Lynh has to pry her away from other customers . . . on our night? Screw this. I don't need it.*

As if to call timeout, the phone buzzed. Joyce. He ignored it.

He sat quietly. Time ticked on. A familiar feeling. He'd been here before. The Father was touching his heart. His expression softened. Anger turned to regret. *Oh Father. What I did. I was wrong, wasn't I? I guess so. I wanted to send her a message. I knew Tia would tell her about Amber. I know she's jealous of Amber—her white skin, curves, how men flock to her like flies. I knew the dance with Chloe would get back to her. I wanted her to hurt, Father. I really did.*

Somewhere in his murky head—a vision of her, crying and cursing some guy named Darren. Cursing some guy named Glenn.

Are You telling me I acted out because she hurt me, and she acted out because I hurt her? So I'm ground zero for all this drama? But she was the no-show

He was arguing with an omnipotent God. He wasn't afraid. It had been like this all his life. His Christian upbringing was kicking in. Then he heard it. *Forgive as I have forgiven you.*

Seriously? Why do I always have to be the one to forgive, to turn the other cheek? This time I got it shoved right up between my cheeks! I hate this. You're always telling me do the right thing. The whole What-Would-Jesus-Do thing.

He'd been hardwired from childhood to do that. The feeling was getting stronger. He tapped his fist against his forehead. It was unmistakable. He heard it again, as he'd heard it all his life. He knew it was coming. The voice of truth.

Love conquers all.
Love as I have loved you.

"Shit." He closed up shop and went home to sleep off his hangover.

He got up at 8:00 that night, took a shower, then had his usual hangover cure, a Diet Coke and a burrito. He thought about her. *Can't take it no more. Gotta go say sorry. Be the bigger person. If she kicks me to the curb, so be it.*

He walked in and acknowledged the barflies. The flatscreens were a blur, and the music muffled, with only finding her on his mind. She wasn't at the bar area. Not in the dart room.

"Hi, Glenn." Jimmy waved, nodding to the booth room.

He took eight steps in before he saw that she was with a customer. She eyed him with a grimace. He held up his hand and mouthed, "Not here for you." That was a lie.

He turned around and smacked right into Lynh. She took him by the arm and led him to a semi-private room, which was basically a private room with no door.

She sat him down. "What you want, Glenn?"

He leaned forward, palms together. "Lynh, I'm sorry for the way I've been acting. Not right. I know. If you want me to stop coming here, I will. Just wanted to say sorry. Can you say sorry to Maya for me?"

Lynh suppressed a smile. *He's caving in. Men weak. Pussy desire always wins.* "Glenn, you be a man. Have some balls. Tell her yourself."

He lifted his hands in protest. "But Lynh, I don't want to bother the guy."

She shook her head. "You worry too much about other people. No worry. She can take break. He longtime customer. He not like you. He can take it." She smirked just a bit. "I talk little while with him. No be long with Maya, but." And she left.

It took but a few minutes, and Maya came around the corner. Maroon full-length evening dress with an open back and high slits running up each side to her waist. High heels and ornate earrings. Hair and makeup like she was headed to a high society fundraiser. *Just a friend on Wednesday nights, my ass. Even so, wow, she looks great.* She stared at him, appearing upset and concerned at the same time. "Are you all right?"

"Hey Maya," He paused. She stood there. "Hey Maya, I wanted to . . . "

"Glenn, this going take long?"

He shrugged. "I don't know."

She fidgeted with her earring. "Wait here." She turned and left and was back in two minutes. She sat down next to him.

He turned to her. "What did you do?"

She smoothed her dress, adjusting her hemline. "I told him go home.

Something came up."

His eyes followed her hands to her hemline. *She sent a customer home for me?*

She took his hand. Massaged it a bit, then let go. "What's going on?"

He took a deep breath. "Maya, I'm really sorry for the way I mistreated you."

She straightened up, eyes wide, rubbing her forearms. "You . . . mistreated me? I thought you mad I had customers yesterday."

He raked his hair, stopping to rub the back of his neck. "No, not what I'm talking about. Before I left on the trip. Amber, Chloe and the last Thursday." *How do I explain? I was hurt. Felt abandoned and rejected. Just lashing out and acting up like some prepubescent adolescent. Can she understand?*

Silence. Lips pursed. Face tight. She was gritting her teeth so hard he could see her jaw muscles flexing. She was holding back screaming as she recalled, and quickly dispensed, memories—all the memories of men hurting her, including him last week. "Don't worry, Glenn. I move on."

He blinked hard. *I don't think she's convinced.*

Hands clasped, he readied himself for the next round. "I need to explain. I might do it again."

Her face flushed. She scowled. He could've sworn her nostrils flared. She was done hiding feelings. Perturbed, she snapped. "What you mean?" She looked like she was about to get up and go.

His heart was fluttering. He reached for her hand. "You can leave me if you want. I'll understand. But please, hear me out."

She let his hand drop out of hers. Glared at him as if to say, I've heard it all, but try me anyway.

He clenched his fist, holding it to his chest. He spoke softly. "I'm not good with relationships. You need to know. My mom. She killed herself."

The words hung in the air. She felt her heart pierced. Anger started to subside. Still not convinced of his sincerity, she thought, *Darren was good actor too.*

He rested his elbows on his knees and bowed his head as if to hide the tears if they came. "When I was a kid, a little boy. I begged her, don't go." She could see his body move. His breathing was shaky. He continued, head still down. "She killed herself anyway."

His head buried in his hands, his voice sounded far off, like he was reliving so many hurts. "I don't trust women. I always get hurt. I know I'm going to get hurt. I get close to anyone, and if I feel they're going to bail on me, I act out, like a little boy, push them away, make them leave . . . kill off the relationship before it hurts me. Make her go away. Hurt her before she hurts me."

He looked up. "So you were a no-show, and I acted up . . . showing you I don't need you . . . pushing you away . . . so I don't get hurt again."

She saw the tears pooling in his eyes. She wanted to reach out but kept still. "Glenn, you . . . you hurt?"

He clasped his hands. "Yeah, I hurt. I don't have my head on straight. Every time something like this happens, I feel it all over again. My mom. If any trouble I push back and run . . . Right now, I feel like running, away from you, and to you. I like you, but I'm scared too. Don't know when you'll be gone, and I get hurt."

Head down again. Hands still clasped, he brought them to his forehead, eyes closed, as if in prayer. She saw the tears drop. A couple of tears landing between his feet on the whiskey-stained rug. It took all she had to stay still. Her heart ached.

He didn't see her reaction. Her own hands were clasped. Her eyes closed for a long second. Her lips parted, then closed. Her face wrinkled as if about to cry. Her lips trembled. She reached out without touching him, then brought her hand to her heart. She swayed. She willed herself. *Steady, Maya. Get control. He need you.*

He raised his eyes to hers. "I'm sorry, Maya. I came here to say goodbye . . . but I don't want to say goodbye."

She drew closer, leaning forward, placing her hands on his knees. Forehead to forehead, she whispered, "Then don't."

Silence.

She breathed in and leaned back. She wanted to see his face. So she lifted his chin and brushed his hair back. She searched his face. *He for real?* He was older in age, but at that moment, he sounded like a little boy. Uncertain. Frantic. Scared. She took it all in. She held his gaze. She felt her soul reaching out to him. *I protect you, Glenn. Don't worry. I watch over you. Nothing hurt you again. I take care of you.*

She took his hands in hers. She was done being mad. "I will always be here for you. If I'm with customer, I will come to you. Sorry about that Thursday, cannot help. But if I can, I will always be here for you."

She read his mind. "I really thought you were going to be gone for two weeks so I said okay to those guys coming. By the time I saw you, they were here waiting already. I couldn't send them home. If I knew you were coming home already, I tell them I was busy."

He scanned the room. "But you sent the guy home tonight? For me?"

She squeezed his hands. "This is real important. I saw your face. I know when important. I don't lose you."

He brought her hands to his lips. "Maya, I never told anyone this, but I really am a little boy inside. Little things can set me off. You'll think I'm stupid, but it can set me off and I end up acting out. Can you handle?"

It was her turn. She brought his hands to her lips. "I dunno. I can try. At least now I know what going on." She held his hands to her cheeks. *My little boy.*

He wanted her to say she acted out too. But she didn't. He let it go.

Verna came and whispered in her ear. He stared at her, eyes asking what's going on? She turned back to him. "Customer not go home. Still here waiting."

He got up. "I should go."

She held on. Pulled him back down to sit again. "No, you can stay. But I have to go be with him eventually. I will be with you little more. You want a beer? My treat." Glenn returned the favor. Bought her a shot.

He finished his beer. "So next Tuesday?"

Twinkle in her eyes, she nodded. "Yes, and every Tuesday after, okay?"

His eyes were glazed. Deep in thought. "Want to do something different?"

She peered over his shoulder. Verna was signaling. Customer waiting. "What, Glenn?"

He saw her look. "I'll make this quick. Not sure where Lynh was going with the whole champagne thing . . ."

She palmed his chest, gently. "Was Lynh idea?"

"Yes."

Her frown reflected both disappointment and suspicion. "She told me was yours!?"

Glenn bit his lip. "No. Was hers. I said no, but she pushed it."

A scowl replaced her frown. "Glenn, I make more money with shots. Bar make more money with champagne. Why she do that?"

He shrugged. "I dunno." *I stepped into something here. She's pissed.*

She was in a rush. Half standing, half still sitting. "She wanted me go to the private room. You know I don't do that. She know too. You don't do that you told me . . . not anymore. You lie?"

He got up to hurry her along. "No." He took her hand, changing the subject. "Let me give you a real champagne date next week."

She squeezed his hand. "What you thinking?"

He squeezed back. "Don't worry. Just meet me here same time?"

She glanced back at the dart room, then to him. "Okay." She was still thinking. Her nose wrinkling. Something else on her mind. Trying to decide. "Glenn?"

"Yes?" He wondered, *Did she forget her customer?*

She sat back down. "No more message you talk Lynh and she talk to me, or you talk Jimmy and he talk to me. You have problem, you talk to me?"

He let go of her hand. "Okay, but I only see you here."

Brow furrowed. Lips pursed. She thought for a second. "You have Instagram?"

"No, what is that?"

She held out her hand. "Gimme phone." He gave her his phone, and she loaded Instagram for him and connected him to her account. "Now you can DM, direct message, me. If something happen and you not sure about us, message me. Don't wait till Tuesday."

He nodded. "Okay." *Feels like she finally let me behind her wall.* "You better go to your customer before he acts out."

She stood up. He was sitting. She wrapped her arms around him, drawing his head to her bosom, rocking back and forth. "No Glenn, you only little boy around here." She offered her cheek, pointing. He stood and laid a kiss right on the X. She tussled his hair, and quickly gave him a real kiss, a goodnight kiss. She leaned back and grinned widely at what she saw.

His hair was a mess, and with a dopey expression, he truly did have a little boy look. Chuckling, she touched up what hair she messed, and straightened his collar for good measure. She leaned back again and took a look. Giving an approving nod, she drew him near for one last hug. "Be safe going home. Gotta run. Have to give last half hour to customer wait all night." He nodded and gently pushed her off. She blew him a kiss, turned and trotted toward the dart room.

As he walked out of the bar, he faced upwards and mouthed, *Thank you.* He felt like doing a victory lap around the parking lot. Billy's mom kept coming to his mind. *Odd. Why now? Why not? I just want someone to care about me. No way I'm having mommy issues with someone half my age?*

Walking past a car, he saw his image in the window. *Dang, I got a stupid smile on my face.* He couldn't stop smiling and he didn't care.

He did have one small care. *What the hell is a champagne date? I better come up with something—fast.*

21

CHAMPAGNE DATE

For the next week, he was like a high school kid getting ready for prom. Only he didn't know what going to prom felt like. It was the second Tuesday of November, and the temperature outside was cooling. Glenn didn't notice. He walked in extra early and sweating, carrying two bottles of Dom Perignon, a dozen Godiva chocolate-dipped strawberries, and assorted cheese and other fruits. As he wiped his brow, he thought back over the last week. *Amazing what you can learn on YouTube these days.*

Jimmy took the bottles from him and let out a whistle. The Dom cost $500, and Mama's corkage was $600. *This guy was laying out eleven hundred dollars to begin with. For her?* "I chill now, Glenn."

Glenn had his hands on his hips, just a little anxious. "Jimmy, you know what to do? You have a bucket?"

Jimmy let out a slight chuckle. "Yes, Glenn."

Leaning on the bar, watching Jimmy, Glenn asked, "You have champagne glasses? Not the snifters you all tried to pass on me last week?"

Jimmy wheeled around, with a big patient grin on his face. "I know, Glenn, I know. I work hotel fifteen years Hong Kong. No worry. I bring when you ready."

Verna took charge of the foodstuffs, grabbing the Godiva bag out of Glenn's hand. "I bring when you ready."

Glenn let out a big sigh of relief. "Thanks, folks." He took his corner seat at the bar just as Maya walked in. He nearly gasped. *She is stunning!*

She wore a bright blue strapless cocktail dress, with the right amount of tight and stretch to highlight her figure without imagination, and a hem ending right above her knees. Her makeup was light, with smoky, alluring eyes and full lashes, and pink inviting lips.

She walked in like she was on a fashion runway, then twirled around, not too slow, not too fast. "You like?"

He was mesmerized. "Huh?"

They laughed at their inside joke.

He looked toward the booth room. "Mama said we can have the first room." That was the private room with no door.

The room resembled the kind of private rooms found in a karaoke bar. It had a sofa lined up against the far wall, opposite another wall—the near wall— with a flatscreen TV. There was a low coffee table. Lighting was optional. Glenn turned it all the way up.

Maya followed and turned it down to a comfortable darkness that matched the booth room's mood. Couples that desired sleaze never opted for this room—too easy for someone to wander in.

Glenn thought it provided the right amount of privacy.

She sat first and patted the space next to her. "Sit, Glenn. I don't bite you know." Her eyes twinkled, curious with anticipation, amused at his nervousness. *This like a date.*

He was scratching his head, right above his ear. "I know. You okay with this?"

She pulled at his hand. "Yes. It not private room. I'm okay. Sit. You make me nervous." *He keep scratching there he go bald like Rusty*, she thought. *I gotta calm him down.*

Verna stepped around the corner carrying a silver platter arranged elegantly with the Godiva strawberries, fruits and cheese. He stared at Verna. *This lady is so talented. Where did they get a silver platter in this place?*

Jimmy came in next with the Dom in a champagne bucket. It was perfectly chilled, and he popped the cork expertly. He produced two champagne glasses and poured out the bubbly nectar. He handed one to Maya and the other to Glenn. Jimmy stood by with a towel over his arm like a waiter in a five-star restaurant

Maya marveled at what she saw. She'd only seen something like this on TV and in the movies, when fancy rich people had parties.

"Cheers." They toasted.

Maya took a sip and smacked her lips. "Nice. Sweet. I had before. Not like. Dry. This not dry. I like."

Glenn smiled and took a sip of his. "Did you ever have chocolate strawberries before?"

She shook her head. "How you eat?"

Glenn picked one up and took a bite, the part where the chocolate covered the strawberry bottom. She did the same. Her eyes widened.

He sipped. She sipped. The taste combination hit her, and her eyes widened even more. She wore a big smile like a child at Christmas.

Verna pulled at Jimmy's arm. Time to leave the kids alone. Jimmy reminded Glenn before leaving, "Have one more chilling. You call when you want?"

"Thanks, Jimmy. Thanks, Verna."

Maya gave Glenn a hug and held on. "You do all this for me?

He gazed into her eyes. "Just enjoy, Maya. This is champagne. This is a champagne date." It sounded to him like the right thing to say, like he did this many times before. In fact, it was a first-time experience for both.

She took a picture of the spread, the strawberries, the champagne on ice, the fancy glasses. Her Instagram account would be flooded tonight. Her eyes were wide in amazement, mouth slightly agape. She knew he spent a lot of money. She had customers bring that Dom stuff once. They let her taste but only bought her cheap drinks the rest of the night.

They were getting comfortable when Lynh walked in. She pointed at the Dom. "Why you bring that, Glenn? We have, you know. I give you good price last week."

He barely looked her way. "No Mama, that was shit. I'll pay you three hundred dollars for each bottle, but for the bottles I bring, not the ones from your stock. So you'll still make your money."

Lynh was almost drooling. "No Glenn, for this stuff fifteen hundred dollars per bottle."

"Mama!" Maya protested. The mood suddenly got tense. Maya's eyes narrowed. From somewhere, some protective instinct kicked in. He squeezed her hand as if to say I got this.

Glenn stood up. "Lynh, you know I'm helping Jimmy with your lease negotiation. Free! Of! Charge! And you got big problems with parking. With no parking for customers, that's gonna kill your business. I'm trying to help with that, you know."

He took one step towards Lynh. "So if you want to pull this business shit on me, then fine. Charge me the fifteen hundred dollars."

Maya reached out for his arm. "No, Glenn."

He knew what he was doing. He turned to Maya, away from Lynh, and winked reassuringly.

He turned back to Lynh, held eye contact, taking in ticks and facial tells. He had her. "So Lynh, charge me. And I'll charge you. All the advice and the letter I wrote for you all comes out to about five thousand dollars. The way I see it, you owe me another thirty-five hundred dollars."

Lynh changed tact. "Why you mad, Glenn?" Her confused face

foretold trouble for Jimmy, who'd forgotten to explain all the work Glenn was doing for the bar. "Why you mad? I only tell you what we charge other customers. You special. Mama not do that to you. okay? Mama take glass and leave you alone."

He wagged his index finger. "Oh, no. No, Mama, you have your own stock remember?" Maya kicked him lightly. "Nah, just kidding Mama. Let me pour for you." Faking a smile, he poured a glass, not a full glass, just below the halfway mark.

He raised his glass. Maya raised hers. "Cheers, Mama." Lynh got the message. They raised their glasses with a nice clink. Mama Lynh left in a huff. No goodbyes. Just a jerk of her head. Glenn could have sworn he heard *hmph*, or something like that. No matter. He and Maya were alone again.

Glenn sat down.

"Turn around, Glenn." Maya started a back massage. "You okay?" She'd never seen a customer one-up Lynh before.

He chuckled. "Yeah, no problem. She's a piece of work, isn't she?"

Maya nodded. "Bar not doing too good with new landlord. She always worried about money." Her hands rested on his shoulders. *So tight. So solid. This old guy more built than any young guy come here.*

He took her hands in his and turned to her. "Let's just have fun tonight. Okay?"

She nodded heartily, smiling appreciatively. "Okay, we have fun!"

They got cozy on the sofa, sitting close. They sipped champagne and ate strawberries and fruit. She put them to his lips, and he bit and ate. He did the same for her. They joked around, once toasting as they crossed arms to drink from their glasses.

The bubbly was having its effect on Maya. She was leaning on him. They were holding hands. He liked it. Then she let go. *Oh, well, that was nice while it lasted*, he thought.

She brought back a piece of cheese for him. Then reached for his hand again. She wrapped her arm around his, her head gently on his shoulder. She was humming.

He looked down at her. "What's on your mind?"

She was stroking his thigh, lightly, almost doodling. "I don't want this place no more Glenn. Start my own business one day."

His heart beat faster. Getting aroused, he reached for her hand, locking his fingers with hers. "What do you want to do?"

She raised her face to him, eyes glowing, excitement in her voice. "Beauty consultant. I do makeup for weddings. I know someone she do hair, I do makeup."

His face brightened. "That's great!"

Her chin dropped to her chest. She fiddled with her hemline. "You think I can do it, Glenn?"

He lifted her face to his. "I know you can do it! I know you can do even more! You're going to make so many people feel more beautiful—it's going to make the world that much more beautiful."

Her cheeks turned red. "Really?" She said it softly.

His eyes gleamed. His voice an octave higher. "Yesss! I know. I believe. I believe in you. I believe in your dreams. Watch. I'll be there with you."

She saw the look in his eyes. Whatever she was feeling, she closed her eyes as if to memorize it for life. She leaned into him, wrapped both her arms around him, and leaned her head on his shoulder. He kissed the top of her head, and she stirred, murmured something in Thai, and held him even tighter.

They stayed that way for a long time. Not moving, almost as if any slight move would break the spell.

She spoke first. "What you do Halloween, Glenn?"

"I was in DC remember?" He paused. "What you do?"

She looked up and pushed her hair back. "I help my police friend with homeless kids. I take them store to store at mall for candy."

He poured more champagne for them. "Is that what you did on the Tuesday I was gone?"

She nodded. "Uh-huh. Lynh not happy I don't come work."

Glenn pictured her herding a bunch of kids through a mall. The kids were dressed in various costumes, but he could only picture her in a cocktail dress. "How did you dress?"

She stood up and struck a pose. "I was zombie nurse."

He had a hard time picturing it but somehow managed to get aroused.

He took a sip. "Well I'll be. I thought you made some other guy happy that night."

She chuckled and bit into another strawberry. "I did! I made six little guys happy, and three little girls too." She turned to him and smiled.

He returned her gaze. "Wow. You like kids?"

She nodded.

He lifted her glass to her. "Are you going to have kids?"

She took a sip. Then reached for a strawberry. "I dunno. I don't have guy, don't want guy so maybe I gotta adopt or do the surgery, do that –"

"You mean artificial insemination."

She nodded, biting into her strawberry. "Yes. Doctor put seed in me, and I grow baby. You give me seed Glenn?" She giggled. "If I adopt, you be Godfather?"

He finished his glass. "Sure. All I ask is my godson get his finance degree from Harvard—my dream. And his law degree from Harvard too. I guess Yale would be okay too."

She wrinkled her nose. "You don't ask much, Glenn."

He chuckled, then got a little serious. Leaning forward, his knee touched hers. "No, not much, because I know you'd make a great mother, and would raise a good son—smart, hardworking, with a love for the world."

In her mind, she could see it, and at the same time, not see it. She stared off into the distance.

He said it again. "I think you would be a good mother." She didn't respond. She let go of his hand and sat up. "Maya, you okay?"

She played with her necklace. "I'm okay, Glenn." She reached into her purse and brought out a tissue, crumpled it up, took a deep breath, then put it back in. Her wet eyes told him something was wrong. *Shit, what did I do now?*

Jimmy came in and replaced the empty bottle of Dom with the second.

She licked her lips. "I have so easy time talking to you. Feel like I can tell you anything." The champagne was real. Not the watered-down booze she usually drank.

Head on his shoulders, hand in his hand, she started talking in a wistful, nostalgic and sad tone. "I had baby once. I had Thai boyfriend. In Roi Et. He not good. He beat me and fool around. I run away. Go to city. Bangkok. I meet new boyfriend. Dino. Australian. He live Thailand."

She lifted a strawberry to his lips. "He was good guy. At first. Then I got pregnant. I was twenty years old. He was twenty-nine."

She closed her eyes, slightly wincing. "I tell him sorry. He mad. I tell him no need stay. I have baby. He said no. Abort. He wasn't going to be father and stuck with kid. I say don't worry. I take care. I still want him be my boyfriend. But we only fight about kid. He say he love me. We can have when we ready."

She put down her glass. Her face twisted sorrow at first, then remorse. "So I went to clinic. Mother before lunch. After lunch, not mother. At least I still have boyfriend I thought. But he go back Australia. Not call again. His friend tell me he get married over there. Men pigs. I still feel my little boy."

Throat parched, he tried to swallow. He reached for her hand. "You knew he was a boy?"

Her voice cracked. She cleared her throat. "Nurse tell me. She ask me if I was sure. He was living. He had heartbeat. He was breathing inside. He cry too. It was hard but I thought Dino was going to be my husband and so I obey."

Her lips quivered. "I still feel my little boy in me." She went silent. He squeezed her hand. Then let go and pulled her to him in a hug. She buried her face in his chest. Whispering, "My little boy . . ." her voice trailing off into a sob.

He held her for what seemed an eternity. One sob, two sobs. Then quiet. He felt her lashes flicker against his chest, then wetness from the tears. He heard it again. Her whispering, "My little boy."

She sat up and took a long shaky breath. She dabbed at her eyes and fixed her makeup, then kissed his cheek. "Glenn, don't get scared. But my boy visit me after. You know I live with my cousin? I live upstairs. She live downstairs with husband. My boy come to me every night in dream." She smiled as if recounting pleasant memories. "I thought only dream. One night my cousin husband scream. He brush teeth before bed and he look mirror and he see little boy. He scream. I have to tell him about my little boy."

She examined Glenn's face. Making sure he wasn't freaking out. "Every night he come visit me. We play. We talk. I say sorry. He say, 'Okay, Mommy. Don't worry.'"

Her eyes searching for acceptance, she asked, "You think I'm crazy, Glenn?"

Glenn shook his head. *What I woulda given for my mom to come back and play with me in my dreams.*

He leaned closer. "He still come play with you?"

"No." Quiet again. She inhaled, then exhaled. "Two year ago. He come visit me. I'm happy. He tell me, 'I have to go now, Mommy. I love you, Mommy. I wait for you.' I wake up, Glenn. My pillow all soak. I cry in my sleep."

She sniffed a bit and brought out the tissue again. Just in case. "My little boy. I know he wait for me. In heaven. I will be with him one day. I miss him every day. Halloween I pretend one little boy was mine. So hard he go home later. He hug me. I cry little bit."

Her throat tightened. Tears pooled in her eyes. "Now all I have is Rusty. He my son now. He my boy. He sick, Glenn. What will I do if I lose him?"

"What do you mean? Isn't he still young?"

She dug into his arm. "He have diabetes for dogs." He remembered.

Canine diabetes. Lots of complications for dogs. Death was painful. His cheeks flushed; his own eyes turned hot. He recalled putting down his own dog.

She stroked his arm where her nails dug in. "I spend thousand dollars every month on his medicine. I must wake up 7:30 every morning and give him shot. But doctor say he still getting fat. I don't want Rusty in a dream, want him stay with me."

Glenn wasn't sure if this was some bullshit bargirl story. It sounded like the champagne kicked in, and she finally let her guard down. He could see the pain in her eyes.

He turned her to him. He put his hand on her shoulder and squeezed slightly. "Maya, love has no boundaries. Your boy lives on in your heart. He exists because you exist. Live for him and carry him with you always. He loved you enough to visit you all those years. But heaven called finally, you know?"

He paused. She looked like she was sleeping. Eyes closed; she was trying hard not to cry.

He continued. "Love conquers all, near or far, now and in the future. Love connects us all. If you have love for your boy, he is still with you, in spirit, in your heart. Just close your eyes. You can feel him. He is with you. The same for Rusty. Don't worry about the future. Make your memories now."

Her face peaceful, composure regained, she smiled suddenly. She opened her eyes and looked up. They were just a bit wet. She reached up, cupped his chin, and brought his lips to hers. "Thank you, Glenn. You sweet. You don't go away, okay?" She leaned into him again. Her head lay on his shoulder. He kissed her forehead.

There was good music piping in. "Despacito." "Perfect." "Into Your Body." Someone had a great playlist. They sipped champagne, holding hands, just listening to the music. A couple walked in. "Oops," the girl said. She slapped the guy. "Why don't you ever treat me like that." Then she looked their way. "Have a great night, Maya, you so lucky. Be good, Glenn." Nicole was the most popular girl there. A former auto show model and at 24, she had at least three guys waiting for her every night.

This lightened the mood a bit. Glenn turned to Maya. "Want to know something?"

"Yes? Tell me?"

He whispered in her ear. "It was my birthday yesterday." He smiled. He wanted to say something corny like she was the best present he ever got.

She leaned backward, to get a full view of his face. Her eyes widened, and she beamed. "Happy Birthday!" She pinched his cheek. "How old?"

He hesitated. "I'll tell you later."

She frowned. "You know I like old guys. I don't care you sixty-five years old."

"What? Serious? You think I'm sixty-five?"

She wagged her finger at him. "You don't tell me then I can think what I want, yes?" She got up suddenly.

He opened his arms wide. "Hey. Where you going?"

She took one of his hands and kissed his palm. "Too much champagne. I have to pee. I be right back."

"Okay." Glenn leaned back. *This was a dream date with a beautiful woman. Awesome night. And she's telling me real personal things. Maybe we're connecting?*

More than a few minutes passed. *That must be a lot of piss. Maybe there was a line.* He turned a blind eye, but sometimes the girls spent some time in the bathroom doing lines of coke. *No way. Not my Ms. Fitness.*

Then a nagging feeling. *Did she take off on me again? Did a customer come steal her? Dammit!*

Before he could overthink further, the lights went dark.

22

FAIRYTALE DREAM

He fumbled for his phone to get some light. *Shit, it's dark,* he thought, *what's going on?* Just then, a flickering light appeared around the corner. Maya was carrying a piece of cake festooned with a single candle. She'd brought all the other girls with her, and they were singing "Happy Birthday."

Glenn had helped all of these girls from time to time. Sometimes he'd brought dinner for all—pizza, Chinese, whatever they wanted, even pastries. When the girls had no customers, he'd slip them money for lunch the next day. Once he'd given Mei, a part-time hostess, money for her kids to spend on ice cream.

His jaw dropped, watching Maya walk in carrying the cake. He'd grown up watching so many movies and TV shows where the mom came in with a cake for her kid, singing "Happy Birthday." *It's really happening! For the first time ever! The old man never gave a rip about my birthday. Always crude. Like the time he gave me a pack of condoms when I turned sixteen. He'd wrapped them in the Sunday comics. The asshole even took one rubber for himself!*

She set the cake in front of him. "Make a wish, Glenn! Blow! Blow harder!"

He was like a kid, taking in a large breath. *What more could I wish for? My dream just came true.*

After hugs and wishes from each of the girls, he and Maya settled in again. She took a fork and hand-fed him a couple bites of cake. He took the fork from her and brought some to her lips. "What about you?" She ate, wiping the frosting from around her mouth. With the same napkin, she reached out and wiped frosting off his cheek.

His hand on her thigh, he asked, "What did you do? I thought you went to pee?"

She giggled. "I did! Then I tell Tia watch you and I run across the street to snack café and buy cake. They almost close but I know them, and they bring out from back. They remember you help them with lease too."

She was all smiles. "Verna find candle for me and Tia was telling all the girls get ready. You happy?"

He pulled her into a hug and rocked her a couple of times. "I'm happy. I'm so happy." He wondered, *Do bargirls do this?*

As if she read his mind, she poked his chest. "Only you, you know? I do this. You had me at 'Huh'. I buy you cake." She didn't know this was the first time that anyone had ever brought him cake and sang "Happy Birthday" to him. Even Katie didn't do this. His wife's family celebrated birthdays on family Fridays. No fanfare. No singing. There were cake and candles, but no procession with someone dear to your heart singing to you.

He had taken a picture of the cake. He whipped out his phone to make sure he still had it. It would be something he treasured for the rest of his life. *I remember when Billy's mom used to invite us over for his birthday.* The thought was too painful. He shut the memory out again.

The champagne was gone. Verna came and wrapped up the leftover strawberries for Maya to take home. It was nearing 1:00 a.m. Time flew. So much excitement. No time for singing tonight. "I have to go, Maya. Thank you for everything tonight."

She gave him a double kiss. "No Glenn, thank *you*."

It was a champagne date that crossed over into a birthday celebration. In between, there was a sharing of something so very personal of hers. There was a connection all around. He felt something he'd never felt before—warm, kind, loving. In his mind flashed a letter: *Dear Mama, I met someone tonight. She brought me cake, like all the TV moms I used to watch. Like Billy's mom. . .*

"Good night Glenn." She was walking him out, arm in arm. "See you next Tuesday?" It was unspoken that Tuesdays were his, but she always asked, maybe out of some insecurity on her part.

He was like an excited little boy. "*Yes!*"

She smiled warmly. "Message me when you get home?"

"Huh?"

She explained. "Send me message on Instagram. Let me know you okay."

He nodded. *This was new. Does she really care about me enough to want to know I make it home okay?* "Okay. You too. Oh, I'll be here this Thursday to help Jimmy with the lease. Don't worry about me I know you have customers that night. I won't bother."

She was glad he understood she had other customers. They were nice, but thinking of tonight, she thought, *Not this nice.*

Later they exchanged DMs.

Home safe. Thank you for everything tonight. I will always remember you bringing in the cake.

I home too. Happy Birthday again. Good night. Sweet dreams. ☺

He gawked. *Wow. This was more than a "good night I'm safe" kind of text.* The first thing he did was post a meme that said, "Bless friends that ask you to text after you get home safe."

She hearted the post right away. He stared at the heart. He always thought hearts and likes on social media were silly. No more. His soul was on fire. The happy chemicals in his brain were going haywire. He even giggled a bit.

He lay in bed for two hours without sleep, thinking if this was a fairy tale, this is where they'd live happily ever after.

Life, however, is not a fairy tale.

23

VALIDATION'S UGLY HEAD

The following Thursday, Glenn stopped by the bar early in the evening to help Jimmy with some legal business. He sat in their booth with a laptop grinding out a demand letter to the bar's landlord.

Maya walked in with Chloe at 8:00. They were a matched set, wearing mid-length burgundy and silver cocktail dresses with plunging necklines, a strap over one shoulder, a bra cup exposed under the other, and sexy side slits. He couldn't help but notice that Chloe had a serpent tattoo that started at her shoulder blade and disappeared under her boob.

Maya peered over his laptop. "I have customers. They go by 11:00. You still stay?"

He peered back. "I dunno. The letter might take me till 12:00 to finish. I could stay a while after that."

She reached over, put her arms around him, hugged and kissed his forehead. "Ooookaaay!"

He finished work a little before 11:00. "Hey Verna, can you let Maya know I'm done?" A few minutes later, Maya appeared at the booth, flushed. She slumped down next to him and put her head on his shoulder. They were in their favorite booth. She held his hand.

He looked her over. These longtime customers were assholes that knew the tricks and had her drinking the real stuff. "You okay? How many real drinks you had?" She held up ten fingers and then two more. Just then, Chloe burst in front of them and chattered something in Thai. Maya perked up. "Police customers come. They always watch over us. I go say hi little while?" She saw his concerned look. "Don't worry, I leave my bag with you. I will be back soon." That was enough for Glenn.

He watched her sashay around the corner. From where he sat, it looked like a group of six men. Tall and broad-shouldered with that certain haircut, whether cops or military. After a half-hour passed, Maya's voice came over the karaoke system, singing her favorite songs. He rubbed his eyes. *Shit, is this going to happen again?*

He peeked around the corner. The guys were gathered around her treating her like she was Beyoncé, clapping and urging her on. She saw him from the corner of her eye and looked away to the karaoke screen. She had the look of a child surrounded by her adoring uncles at Christmas.

Glenn called Verna over and gave her Maya's bag. *Okay, it's not my night. Can't be mad if other customers come in. But if she wanted to be with these guys, why not let me go home?*

Maya came back with Verna, looking agitated; Lynh had forced her to leave the group. One hand on her hip, the other rubbing her neck, she stared down at him and scolded. "Why you going? Only little while, they my friends, I don't disrespect." Her English was breaking up with no punctuating pauses. She was lit.

He glanced at his watch. *A little while? It's been an hour with no signs of letting up.*

He was tired after a long day with Joyce, plus dealing with the bar's legal problems. "Go back to your friends. I'm going home."

She took off, nearly running.

What the fuck? His only thought.

Lynh stopped her. Maya whispered, "No Mama, he said okay. Besides, not his night."

He took it in for a few seconds before he left. *They've got her surrounded, swooning and dancing to Aerosmith. Seems like a pattern was evolving here. Good times followed by bad. Just like my childhood, just like my life. Guess the champagne date was all an act. Screw this. I'm coming next Tuesday to say goodbye in person. And she's gonna regret it.*

24

DEMON NEEDS UNMET

Their night started off tense the following week. There was a mid-November cool in the air on this third Tuesday of the month, but nothing to match the arctic atmosphere between the two. Sitting at the bar, she was quiet. Her makeup was simple, hair in a ponytail, and she wore worn jeans and a plain white tank top. They exchanged single words and short sentences, without really listening and with lots of dead air in between. Tia kept her distance.

He fingered the folded piece of paper in his pocket. *I just need the right time. Short goodbye. Seventeen words to say grow up and get help. And my final payment. One George Washington.* He was upset, acting out, and wanted to end with a message.

Without looking at him, she deadpanned. "I told you I would be back."

His fists clenched, eyes blazing, he spoke choking with disgust. "Yeah. You said you'd be back soon. What does soon mean? I couldn't even go piss 'cause I had to watch your bag. If you wanted to be with them the rest of the night, you shoulda let me know and I would have left."

She glared at his image in the mirror behind the bar. "I go pee." She stomped off, leaving her bag.

He leaned back, arms folded. "Shit, she's gone again, isn't she, Tia?"

Tia tried to explain. "Glenn –"

"And what's with the bag again?"

She waved her hand past his face. "Glenn!" It was the loudest she ever cooed. "Glenn, listen to me."

He shrugged half-heartedly. Looked at her as if to say, *Okay, hit me with your best shot.*

Tia put a beer in front of him. "Glenn, in the bar world, holding the bargirl's bag means something. It means you're her man."

He froze. Opened his mouth. Nothing came out. Cocked his head to one side. Closed his mouth. Straightened up and leaned forward, both palms on the counter. "What?!"

"Glenn . . ."

He drilled his temple with his index finger. "That doesn't make sense. Other guys get to have fun with her, and I get to sit in a booth by myself with Louis Vuitton?"

Shaking his head, he reached for the bottle and took a long hard swallow. "Tia, I know the bag also means I'm marked territory—so I'm also without company while she's gone. Like I said, she could just let me go home. Like now."

Tia leaned forward, ready to grab his sleeve. "Glenn, don't go. Please hear me out. She's gonna be a while."

His brow furrowed. Mouth open again.

She shook her head. "No, not drugs. She's in there crying because she thinks she's lost you. She's giving you just enough time to leave. Happened before."

His shoulders hunched; his sunken eyes explained the rest of what he was feeling. *I'm here. How can she think that? She's the one bullshitting me. Jerking me. And I'm still here.*

Tia laid her hand on his forearm. "Glenn, a lot of bargirls are . . . well . . . broken."

He looked up, not wanting an answer but asking anyway. "Even you?"

She poured herself a shot. "Yes. Even me. But I got a stable guy at home. I grew up in a stable home. I do this . . . well . . . because it's good money, and I jumped behind the bar as soon as I could. Not as much tips but I keep my pride. And I can take care of my two kids while I find another line of work."

He was drumming his fingers on the counter. He glanced back toward the ladies' room. "And Maya?"

Tia didn't know how to start or whether to start at all, considering she was betraying a friend's confidence. "Think about it. She's told you. Her father split when she was twelve. Mother was a bargirl. No man of the house. She's begging on the street, raising her sister and brother, and keeping them fed. Meanwhile she's watching all the other girls with fathers taking care of them. She's lost her childhood. She's lost having a father. What did she have? Her mother's one-night-stands who sometimes took advantage of her."

The last part pierced his heart. He went limp inside. "She got abused by them? She told you that?"

She saw his face go pale. She poured him a whiskey, then confessed. "No, Chloe told me." She waited till he downed the shot. "Glenn, she craves male attention. The more the better. We've seen it. I saw a documentary about it—unmet needs."

He plopped backward and, leaning his head back, rubbed his forehead. "A what-the who-the needs?"

Tia wiped off the counter in front of him. "Google it: 'unmet needs.'"

She held up the empty beer bottle. "Want another, love?" He snapped forward and nodded.

The bartender-turned-big-sister continued. "Her need for attention drives everything she does. Getting attention validates her worth in her eyes."

His mouth agape, palms up. "Why does she need to validate her worth?"

She spied over his shoulder towards the restroom. "She'll kill me if she finds out I told you about this. But think about it. She's not a university graduate, not even a high school graduate. She quit to raise the kids. Her brother and sister finished high school. How do you think she afforded it?"

He showed no reaction.

She continued, voice slightly rising, not cooing. "Not begging. What do you think she did in Thailand? Where did she pick up English? And where did she meet her ex-husband? Know a lot of expats or GIs that cruise the shopping malls?"

He crossed his arms, just for a bit. "Actually, I do."

Her voice could have sanded wood. "Yeah, but how successful are they with the shopgirls when they only have two weeks shore leave?"

He leaned back. *What happen to the cooing? Where's the sweetness? She's got issues too. And she knows her stuff.*

Tia poured herself a second shot. "So she hopped the first *faraang*, Westerner, out of Dodge. She married and moved here, where there's ample opportunity for real money, US dollars, without the requisite sex that Bangkok or Pattaya require."

He was mesmerized. *I read about this in a book. But she sounds like she lived it.*

She offered him some chips. "Now Maya keeps her pride and her legs closed while being admired by all these men. Men buy her drinks, gifts, fall all over, and she feels attractive, wanted and desired. She's treated like a queen by all the court jesters who think they're knights."

The barflies were thirsty and called for another round. It took all of ten seconds for her to lay out the five beers before returning.

His lawyer instinct to argue was stirring. "She really likes this stuff? Seems creepy to me. Like some vampire queen wanting her minion zombies to worship her. She's gotta know it's all sweet talk."

She reached over and put one finger lightly, but forcefully, on his chest. "And . . . aren't you all sweet talk?"

Checkmate. He slid her a Jackson.

Tia poured two shots, this time taking down the Hennessy reserve from the top shelf. *He's so nice, so sweet, but still a guy.* "That's right. She doesn't give sex. Nothing between your legs. But she knows how to get between your ears. She gives companionship. In her customers' lives, she is the sad story listener, the anger diffuser, the problem solver, and the soul soother."

Glenn recalled one of their first Tuesdays. Maya explained her boundaries:

> *I don't do sex. I'm here to listen, be your friend, help*
> *you relax, make you happy. I'm not whore like other*
> *girls, other bars. You know, one guy think money*
> *can buy me. He put five grand on table to go hotel*
> *and fuck. You know what I do? I take money.*
>
> *I take money, stand up, and throw in his face.*
> *He mad. Leave quickly. Yell at me, yell at Mama.*
> *Mama had to fix. She was mad at me. I don't do*
> *dates. Only meet customers here at bar. One time*
> *man put thousand dollars on table to have dinner*
> *with nephew outside of bar. I say no. Work for*
> *Mama, and busy outside worktime.*

The sound of Tia dropping a longneck in front of him whipped him back to the present. "And the more attention she gets, the better. A group of four customers trumps a twosome anytime."

He shifted. Understanding began to shadow his face.

She saw she was getting to him. "And young handsome guys trump all others. She needs young good-looking guys to see her as desirable, to want her. She needs to see the lust in their eyes to validate herself as an attractive woman . . ."

He cut in. "But why? She's beautiful enough!"

Tia held up her hand. "Not enough. She grew up thinking she was ugly, teased by her friends. Tomboy. Brown skin. You know what brown skin means in Thailand? Her mom had porcelain skin. The guys the mom brought home either put her down or molested her or both. If there ever was an unmet need for her, it was being special to these young guys she so adored and couldn't have."

She coughed and took a sip of soda. "In the last six months, she's become that popular. So we're all surprised she's still with you. I mean, well, we thought you'd be one of the guys waiting his turn all night or just leave. Instead, you two are still exclusive, all night on Tuesdays. I see guys come in those nights and she doesn't even make eye contact. The message is clear for them: not tonight, not on a Tuesday."

She stopped. She wanted his attention. "Glenn, hear this. If anything, hear this. Given her needs, it must be hard for her to sit only with you all night, and not all the guys that show up. I swear I see her working the phone telling regulars to come on Monday, Wednesday, or any other day but Tuesday. She lines up her whole week schedule around Tuesday. Only you, Glenn. Only you, the whole night."

Tia let it sink in and made sure she had his eyes and his ears. "Who does that?"

Glenn shifted in his seat. It was time to be a lawyer again. "But that's because I give her good money. Don't I make it worth her while?"

She popped a beer and served it to the customer two stools down and came back. She shook her head, half frustrated, half hanging onto hope. *Doesn't he get it? It's not the money.*

"Glenn, if she runs three groups all night, she can make double, triple what you give her. But that's not the point. What she's giving up for you is all the other men she could be with. It's like she gave up the buffet for a one entrée meal. You must be one special entrée."

Glenn sat transfixed. *How does she know so much?*

The bar was getting busy. An older patron walked in, and she pointed him to the end of the bar, calling out, "Nicole! Russell's here! She's in the back, Russell, chill for a while. She'll be—oh, here she is."

Tia's attention pivoted back to Glenn. "Even for Darren, $5,000 a week Darren, she didn't clear the night. She always had a second customer waiting. You heard about how Chloe gets when drunk?"

Glenn nodded, remembering his talk with Kimmie.

Tia continued. "Well, Chloe has her demons. So does Maya. So do we all."

Glenn was skeptical and raised the timeout sign. "You sure Tia?" *Sounds to me like one bargirl covering another. I'm basically an ATM to them. They don't give a shit, and they butterfly whenever the money looked better with someone else. Unmet needs? Never heard of it.*

She recognized the expression, the disbelief. Now she was the lawyer, making her closing statement. She wiped the bar in front of him clean. Then leaned over for emphasis. He focused on keeping eye contact, and not the ample amount of cleavage she always seemed to hoist in front of him at inopportune moments.

She put one finger under his chin, lightly, as if to say focus on what I'm saying. "I've seen it over and over. Whenever she downs enough Crown, something primal kicks in. Like an addict to crack, she craves attention."

He unhooked his chin from Tia's finger and leaned back, arms folded. He peered back over his shoulder. *Is Maya coming back?*

Tia reached out, hand gently to the side of his face, and slowly brought him back to face her. "Just like the other night. If she saw a group of young men, she was drawn. And if she was in the midst of it, she was lost, soaking up all the adoration, affection, and encouragement a group of thirty- to forty-somethings would give a karaoke queen. Like pushers throwing crack at an addict."

She let go of him and pushed off the bar. "Since then, we've been watching out for her. Like I said, Chloe has her demons. So does Maya."

His expression bordered on confusion. "How do I fit in?" *I'm not the young good-looking guy Maya would crave. This is not making sense.*

Tia chuckled slightly, covering her true thoughts. *I really don't want to tell him. He's not her type, but she gives it all for him, like he was something she's been looking for all her life. Something different from those other guys.*

She gave it a try, to let Glenn know where he stood. "You're the old guy that doesn't look that old with little boy looks. You're the nice guy we're all waiting for." Cocking her head to one side, she continued. "Yeah, you're a dirty old man in the other bars. But here? You're different here. All of us, for the first few months, wondered when you'd give up or even start. Why are you different with her, Glenn? For all the shit you say she gives you, why are you still with her?"

He raked his hair one way, then the other, then tugged at it. "I dunno. Maybe I was looking for something that day . . . and I found it. Maybe I prayed to God and He answered, and I don't want to screw with something God gave me."

"Hmm. Never heard it like that before." She put away their shot glasses. "So, is God the only reason you with her?"

He rubbed his chin. "Guess not. She just makes me feel so good when I'm with her. I had a shitty summer. I get chased in here by the man-eating witches next door and meet her. That morning I asked God for help. She's been through so much and still fighting, for her, for her family." He was on a roll now. "She inspires me. She makes me want to live. She makes me want to be more."

Tia saw Maya coming. "You should tell her, Glenn. But about the stuff I told you—just between us, okay? And try to see things from her side. She doesn't know where you fit either."

"Tia, no bullshit, right?"

"I don't bullshit, Glenn. I don't need to, love."

———

Ten minutes earlier, Maya sat sobbing quietly in the bathroom. She knew she'd messed up—again. She didn't understand. *All I'm doing is respecting customers, make them happy. Good business. Why he not understand? Not even his night.*

Remembering several customers that walked out of her life, she asked again to no one in particular, *Why they—all the others—not understand?*

She looked in the mirror, shrugged and reapplied her makeup. *Might as well look good. I know he gone. Look good, snag a random. Still early, maybe text Sean or Reyn or Sonny.*

With one last dab at her eyes, she blew her nose then stepped back into the dank air of the bar, expecting nothing, and everything. She turned the corner into the bar. He was still there. Before she could feel any joy, he opened his mouth, without thinking, as all men do.

"Wow, you're back?" It was like throwing gasoline on fire.

25

WISE MEN SAY

Her eyes narrowed, she hissed, "I said I would be back. Just like that night. Why don't you trust me? Why you not be patient? Why you have to act like that?" She forgot about the little boy.

She leaned her head back and inhaled deeply, then sighed forcefully, bringing her back face to face with him. "Let's move on, please. I won't do it again."

Lips curling, Glenn glared at her, thoughts exploding in his head. *Why can't you understand? Why did you have to act like that? Do you need validation that bad? Am I not enough? I guess not.* He saw she was edgy, and he bit his tongue. *Gotta let this shit go,* he thought. With a great draw on willpower, he simply replied, "Okay."

Tia thought to say something but saw Verna coming down the aisle with the songbook. A few beers and vodkas later, Glenn and Maya were singing, trying to make the best of what was left of the night. For the first time since they met, they didn't sing their song, "Can't Help Falling in Love."

He rubbed his face. "Want to call it an early night?"

She faked a yawn. "I guess so. Sorry. So tired."

Tia watched this kabuki show. *Oh what the shit . . . they're pissed at each other but being polite? Like they're scared to make a mistake. Geez you two . . . show your passion.*

Glenn headed off to the bathroom.

Maya picked up on Tia being a little noisier than usual washing glasses behind the bar. "Tia babe, everything okay?"

Tia looked up, wiping her brow with her sleeve. "Yes, hun. You and Glenn okay?"

Glenn was making his way back. Maya didn't say anything. Her expression hinted *I don't know.*

The night ended without a real good night kiss, just a peck on the cheek.

Later at home, she hugged Rusty, then thought of her boy she'd left behind in Thailand. *I miss you, my little boy.* She replayed all her dreams as she often did. But this time, her thoughts ended with Glenn. Her heart ached for the little boy she'd left behind at the bar.

Meanwhile, he was at the condo, nursing an old beer he found in the fridge. The note from his pocket lay crumpled and torn on the coffee table in front of him. His Instagram chimed a message notification. He knew it was her. She was the only one following him.

Glenn. So sorry 😔 I so sorry for the way I treated you. I will never do it again. I will always be by your side, Tuesday or any other night.

Glenn was getting used to this kind of sweet talk but had his doubts after tonight. He wrote back.

all good see you next Tuesday ☺

She replied instantly.

Then she shut off her YouTube as the last notes and words of the Elvis song, their song, faded out.

Glenn stared at his phone. *What's this? Never got this before. Smiley emojis, maybe, but a heart? Doesn't that mean she's got feelings for me?* He wrestled with this thought, plus what Tia said. *Only you, Glenn.*

Whatever negative he brought home was quickly melting away.

The heart emoji and Tia's talk haunted him the rest of the week and into the weekend. The internal conversation was always the same. *How real is this? How about the vibe during the champagne date? My birthday cake? We got so close. Was it an act? So she's got problems. So do I. So do we all. Isn't that what Tia said? Love conquers all, conquers anything. Love can conquer her problems, my problems, our problems.*

The non-profit's CEO called him in on the weekend, demanding that 2,000 checks be signed by hand. He brooded in his broom closet office. *What's the deal with being so hung up on signature stamps? Noooooo. It had to be actual signatures.*

Danielle kept putting blank checks in front of him. His pen automatically looped and swirled his signature on each blank line he saw. He didn't see the checks in front of him. His thoughts were on Maya. Pelican-sized butterflies kept fluttering back and forth between his heart and stomach.

He could still hear Tia:

> *Why are you different with her, Glenn? For*
> *all the shit you say she gives you, why are*
> *you still with her?"*

He could still hear Lynh:

> *Maya, I told you God send good man to*
> *bar. I told you God send good man for you*

He sat staring at the blank wall opposite his desk. *Am I that good man? Damn, it started out as just fun and companionship. But now she was more than fun. More than a once-a-week companion. In mind, spirit and heart, she's with me every day. She's with me now. Telling me it's okay. Don't give in. Don't give up. I can do it.*

He rested his chin on steepled fingers. *She's been through so much. But always positive. So devoted to her family. So head-on-straight in a dumbass industry that peddles drugs and sex. She makes me kick myself for being such a whiny sorry ass. So. . . so positive. Just being around her uplifts me. Recharges me for the week. Makes me want to do more with myself. I can feel it. She makes me want to get back in the fight again.*

He leaned back in his chair, then sat up with a snap. *Okay, she's broken. Tia's broken. So am I. But I'll be damned. She's healed parts of my heart I never knew were broken. She's met needs in my life I never knew existed. And yeah, we had a couple of bumps, but she sure has a way of making me feel she'd be there for me no matter what.*

He recalled Maya's mantra.

Glenn, I will be there for you.
I will come back to you.
I don't leave you.

He paced in his office, stopping to stare out his tiny window. *Empty words lately, but the way Tia explained it, I can understand. And when she utters them, I believe her. So sincere. She plugs the hole Mommy left behind. Who needs Billy's mom? I got Maya.*

He signed the last of the checks. *It's more than fun and games now. It's not what Brad went off on—she's not just a bargirl. I need her. I love her –*

He caught himself. *Did I just say I love her? Do I really?*

Yes.

He flopped into his chair and rubbed his face. *Okay, I know she once told me this relationship was all make-believe, but I can't stop thinking about her. And maybe it's different. Maybe I am special to her. Only me. That's what Tia said. I have to tell her. It might be the last conversation we have but I got nothing to lose if it's playacting, and everything to gain if it's for real.*

26

HEART'S CONFESSION

The following Tuesday, they sat at the bar, not the booth, neither hungry for food. She wore a hot pink sequin dress with a plunging neckline. Jimmy and Tia were fiddling, arguing, over the prior night's receipts, while Verna ran beer and whiskey and microphones, to an early evening party in the booth room.

The flatscreens and jukebox were silent, deferring to the karaoke music drifting from the booth room. The smell of Uncle's garlic chicken with hoisin sauce saturated the bar area nearest the kitchen. The barflies mumbled and settled in for the latest weekly installment of the Glenn and Maya drama.

The couple sat side by side, scrutinizing each other's reflections in the mirror behind the bar. The first five minutes sounded more like ritualistic utterances than any form of conversation. "How was your week?" "Good. Busy. Yours?" "Good. Busy."

Then silence.

She swung her chair to face him fully. "What is it, Glenn?" She knew the look. She knew he was about to talk—a lot. "Can we get something to drink first?"

Nodding, he said, "Good idea," and held up two fingers for Verna.

She shifted, letting her knee lightly touch on his. "Okay, what you thinking?"

Glenn laid it all out, ending with "I think I love you."

Glenn searched her face. *She's thinking, processing. That's good, I hope.*

She stared at her drink. She closed her eyes, took a deep breath, and exhaled.

She took his hands in hers. "I'm so sorry, I lead you on. I like you. You good friend and customer."

She massaged his hands, almost apologetically. She spent a little more time on his ring finger, caressing the slight indentation left by the ring he always took off. "I told you I'm not looking for anyone. I'm hurt by too many already. I'm good with me, being with me. And having friends like you. But nothing more serious."

She looked up. Her eyes were begging for him to understand. "I have to concentrate on making money for mommy illness, and sister school. And she getting married after that. And then they need house."

He bit his lip, which quivered slightly.

Her heart broke just seeing his face. Like a little boy at his mother's funeral.

She hugged herself, rubbing her arms. Her knee pressed harder against his. "Don't be mad, Glenn. Please don't be mad. You nice person. I like you. You wonderful. Don't be mad."

He pulled back his knee, breaking contact with hers. "How am I going to do this. You do this for a living. How do I do this and not go crazy?"

Her mouth fell open slightly. She didn't like the "do it for a living" comment but let it go. "Don't be mad, Glenn. You make separate world, how they say, compartmentalize."

He broke eye contact, suddenly interested in his beer's calorie count. *Such a big word—compartmentalize. She must have used it lot in her life. Probably with all the other saps wanting to carry her off like knights in shining armor.*

She took hold of his armrest and pulled, bringing his knee to hers, his face to hers. "Tuesday nights still ours. I will be here for you, with you. When you leave, don't take me with you. Just come back. In the time we have, when we are together, my heart is yours. You are my world. Here in this place, this will be our world."

He sat silent.

She searched his face, his eyes. His jaw was clenched and his lips a thin line. He couldn't meet her gaze.

She knew he was hurt.

He turned his eyes to hers and tried a smile.

She rubbed his face, the way he liked it, and he pressed her palm to his cheek. She said softly, "Don't be mad. I want you to be happy."

He took a deep breath. She could see his body shudder as he exhaled.

He took another deep breath and exhaled with confidence. "Okay. I'm a big boy. Let's move on." He took a page from her coping strategy.

She noticed the change. A few weeks earlier, he might have sulked the rest of the night.

Verna walked over with the karaoke songbook and microphones.

Tia had cued up Journey. It was hard not to stop believing. But he sang the song anyway. They lined up the shots, and he had as good a time as any rejected person experiencing addiction withdrawal can have. *I said I was a big boy. I said let's move on. But it's not happening. If she feels so indifferent, why does she look as miserable as I do? So happy just to be here with her. But there's a hole in my heart that just won't mend. Two more shots oughta numb me enough to get me through tonight.*

At the end of the night, she walked him out. A kiss goodnight and a long hug. "Message me when you get home?"

"Okay. You too."

She returned to the bar, sat down in front of Tia and buried her head in her hands.

27

LOVE HURTS

It was five minutes before last call. Jimmy already left for the night, leaving Tia to close the bar. The place was empty except for some of the other girls, and one patron slumped in the corner waiting for a taxi. Roberta Flack's voice floated from the jukebox singing, "Killing Me Softly."

Tia walked over and put a shot of peach Ciroc in front of her. "Everything okay, love?"

Maya knocked back the shot. "Oh Tia, that was hard to do. He such a great guy. I didn't want to lie, but not sure you know, about telling him everything?"

Tia nodded, the same thing with her regulars. "What did he say?"

"He said he love me."

Tia dropped the glass she was drying. Inspecting the glass for cracks, she pressed Maya. "But you've heard this before, right, from the others?"

Maya had seen a lot in the past two years. "Men strange. They say I love you sometimes first time meet, sometimes after a while, sometimes smooth and classy, but most times clumsy . . . crude."

Tia nodded. *Been there, done that.*

It was 1:29 a.m. Maya held up two fingers, pointing to Tia then back at herself. "Hard us girls with pride Tia."

Tia poured two shots. "Got it, Maya. The no-sex rule. Makes us that much more wanted because men are pigs. Our pussy is like a trophy to them. Bed us, then brag, like the jocks in high school."

They clinked glasses. Tia smacked her lips, relishing her shot.

Maya held off downing her shot. "Yes, sis. Everything here no different from Thailand. Girls want love, guys want pussy. All guys basic dirtbags wanting pussy, power, and position."

Maya knocked back her shot, then looked at Tia as if to say, isn't it still 1:29?

Tia nodded and reached for the bottle.

Maya leaned forward. "But Tia, he different. Not super handsome, but I think lots about him. When shit go down in my life, I hear him say 'It's okay, everything will be okay.' That's what he always say, and things work out okay."

Hand on her heart, she shared further. "He not only help me. He help so much people. He work hard. Help homeless, old folks, people no money. He help all. I look up to him. Respect. I want to be with him every Tuesday. Sometime I want to take off. Tell him no money. Just go someplace. Talk. He listen to me all the time. He like a daddy, a papa, and sometimes he like a little boy."

Tia's eyebrows arched. "A little boy?" *That's different.*

Maya's face lit up, her lips curving into a smile. "Yass. I like to ruffle his hair. And he look at me so adoring when I walk in the door. No lust like other guys. More like . . . little boy when mommy come home from the market or work. Sometime, he like Rusty . . . so happy just be with me."

Tia grinned widely at Maya describing Glenn. Tia's reaction could have been the result of double shots in five minutes, or because she had seen the game they played, the cute one where Maya would tap her cheek or chin or forehead for a kiss. Tia even thought she heard a "woof" sometimes.

Tia poured another round. "Which one do you like, the daddy or the little boy?"

Maya giggled, paused in thought, then confessed. "I dunno. I like both. He my babypapa." She laughed. "He so genuine. But cannot tell him how I feel."

Tia pressed. "Why not?"

Maya took a slow look around. The other girls were knocking back real shots. Last call was only for customers. Once the bar closed, it was another scene altogether. For some girls, it was time to medicate, forget, and mentally wipe all the filth off them. On Tuesdays, Maya did the opposite and tried to hang on to the feelings as best as she could. "You know, Tia, here we build fantasy. Some stuff true, some stuff not. I wish I can start all over but cannot. He tell me he not like bullshitters. He value honesty. He tell me thank you for being honest. He say he can forgive liars, but never trust again."

Tia started working the register. "So what did you tell him?"

"I told him only friends. He look so hurt. Maybe one day, I can tell him truth? Tell him I had to lie . . . to make wall . . . so not get hurt. But maybe one day, we still together, and he can forgive and still trust?"

Tia blinked. "Anything can happen, love." Tia understood. *Gotta keep the guy on the hook. Make yourself interesting.*

Maya dug out her car keys. She had twenty minutes before the shots hit her system. "Good night, Tia. Rusty waiting."

Tia was already dialing up Uber. "Good night, Maya." *Please God, let them find each other.*

––––––––––

Glenn lay on his couch. The room was spinning. *Those last two shots were stupid. I feel so dumb. I think I love you. What did I expect? For her to run into my arms and kiss me and say the same thing? I guess that's what I was hoping for. The bitch led me on. Wait, that's not fair. She did tell me it was a fantasy business. She did tell me she wasn't looking. I'm hurt and I'm defending her?*

He sat up and reached for the TV control. *Why did it feel so real? A couple bumps for sure. Man crazy, huh? But the dinners, dancing, singing, kissing, the champagne date, the birthday thing, sending the customer home for me. All that could not have been make believe. If it is, she needs to be in the movies. And what about what Tia said? Only me.*

He mindlessly clicked through the late-night syndicated reruns and shopping channels. *But who am I kidding? Katie always said I was handsome in a rough sort of way. Not sure what that means still today, but I'm pretty sure not comparable to Brad Pitt. So she's so way out of my league in the real world.*

He set down on a rerun of *Friends*, another episode with Ross chasing Rachel. *Plus I don't know her that well. Is she really man crazy like Tia lets on? She's already torched me a couple of times. And that's me as a customer. What if I was a real guy? What would she do? Do I wanna get hurt again? Maybe I should throw in the towel. Is she worth it? Why do I care for her so much?*

And technically, I'm still married. So it's a no-no.

He turned off the TV. The room stopped spinning, and he craved for something to soak up the alcohol. As he nuked a burrito, he lost himself internally. *Maybe she likes me but she's not telling the truth, doesn't want to get hurt. After all, does she really know me? Maybe one day? I guess for now I'll chill. For our three hours every week, we can be anything we want. And well, love conquers all, and love can turn fantasy to reality. Fairy tales do come true. Saw that on the Instagram thing she set up for me.*

Burrito eaten, he sent her a DM, and she replied immediately.

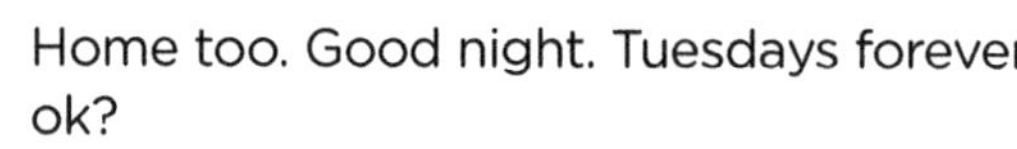

At least we understand each other now.

He rubbed his chin. *Things should be smoother with less drama from now.*

He coughed. *Yeah, that's what they always say in the movies before shit happens.* His gut told him something was about to happen. Ever since he was a kid, he'd always looked for the other shoe to fall.

28

HOLIDAYS

It was late November, and the holidays were around the corner. This would be the third season without Katie, and he did miss her. Having Maya on Tuesdays lessened the impact somewhat, but not all of it.

He sat in his office, reviewing invoice payments. His phone sounded a familiar ringtone he hadn't heard in a while. "Hi Mom."

"Hi Glenn. Are you coming over for Thanksgiving? It's tomorrow you know."

"Not sure."

"I'm sure she'd want you to. The kids are all looking forward to seeing you. It's been a long time. You don't come on Fridays anymore."

"Been pretty preoccupied, Mom."

"Okay, well, you know where we are."

"Thanks, Mom."

He wasn't lying. He was preoccupied with Maya. He recalled their conversation the night before.

"Hey Maya, what are you doing on Thanksgiving?"

She blinked twice and cocked her head. "My cousin invite all Thai friends their house and we have turkey and watch football. Mostly gamble. What you do?"

Glenn hadn't told her about Katie yet. "Family." *I hope she doesn't ask for more.*

She didn't press. "Okay." After several months of Tuesdays, she still hadn't gotten a lot of details about him, but she did notice the tan line on his ring finger.

Thanksgiving came and went, and so did the Tuesdays after. More of the same, though she started acting a little distant, and the "home safe" texts were less lovey-dovey. Next was the Christmas holiday.

———————

It was the third Tuesday in December. From the jukebox, Bing Crosby was crooning "White Christmas." The Grinch attacked Whoville on one flatscreen, and Charlie Brown killed a tree on another. He looked around. A Christmas tree was up next to the Buddhist altar. Stockings with each girl's name adorned the mirror behind the bar. Cheap Christmas lights hung from the ceiling. He smiled. *This is going to be my Christmas this year?*

So close to the holiday, the bar was nearly empty. Only Jimmy was behind the counter. Tia had gone back home to Cali to visit family.

Maya sat waiting for him, texting on her phone, next to his corner seat at the bar. She wore a dark green club minidress with a V neckline, bare back and bare shoulder, accented with long sleeves, with hemming that hugged her hips in just the right way.

She put her phone down as he took his seat. He flashed two fingers to Jimmy, who already had their drinks ready. Verna followed with the songbook and microphones. The place was all theirs.

After a couple of hours of Jimmy's concoctions and five straight renditions of "Baby, It's Cold Outside," he leaned over to her. She met him halfway, and for a few seconds, they were forehead to forehead, simply enjoying their time.

He could smell the rum on her breath. He asked, "What happens at Christmas for you?"

She leaned back and chuckled. "You don't know?"

"Know? *No*, I don't know!"

She laughed even more. "We get super drunk and you give me expensive present."

She saw his mouth drop. Then patted his knee to calm him. "No, only kidding. What you do Glenn?"

He thought for a few seconds. Wondering whether to bring it up or not. "I thank God."

She had an "uh oh" look on her face. Last year a customer went on and on about the Jesus story one night. She was too glad that the customer bought her shots all night to feel like he was converting her. She felt uncomfortable around Christians. Her Australian boyfriend had been a Christian, the one that made her kill her baby boy.

He turned to her. *Okay God, here goes.* "I thank God. He didn't have to, but he came and became one of us, then died for us. That's what all the Christmas songs are about, you know."

She gazed into her shot glass like it was a crystal ball. "Really?"

He held up two fingers for Jimmy. "Yes."

She nodded a thank you for her shot. "All the Christmas songs?"

"Yes."

Her eyes twinkled with mischief. "Even Frosty Snowman?"

He cracked a smile and flicked her forehead. He meant the hymns and carols. The sermon was over. "Let's just have fun, shall we?"

She flicked him back. "Okay. Don't forget Maya Christmas mean Maya present . . . " Her voice softened, she almost sounded tentative. "I buy yours already."

His lips parted slightly. He was touched. *She got me a present? Dammit, I didn't get anything for anyone yet. Katie used to do all this, and she always bought something for herself and let me know how much it was.*

Christmas Day came and went. He did put in an appearance at his in-laws'. Not knowing what to do, he shelled out $500 for a gift card at a Chanel store for Maya's present. He made sure to get a gift box and a Chanel bag. He gave it to her the Tuesday before Christmas.

"*Ooohh . . . myyy . . . God . . . Buddha . . . whatever . . .* Glenn, what did you do?"

"Something small. Don't open till Christmas, okay?"

She made a pouty face. "Okay."

She lied. She posted a picture of her present on Instagram the next day. He knew a lot of her customers were followers, and that the picture suddenly set the bar high.

On Christmas morning, alone in the condo, he opened the present she'd given him. *She's been talking about a special present since October, but I never took her seriously. Wonder what she got me?*

It was a necktie. He frowned. *A tie. A Calvin Klein tie. This is the special present? Geez, maybe in Thailand it's a big thing.* He turned it over. *A military exchange tag, so she bought it on base. Cheap stuff they sell there.* He remembered—her cousin's husband was in the military.

To show his appreciation, he put it on with a coat and took a selfie showing between the waist and neck, highlighting the tie, and posted it as his profile on Instagram. After that, he added it to the other twenty ties he had hanging in the closet. *A tie? Really?*

He messaged her.

> Merry Christmas. Thank you for the tie.
> Did you see my profile?

Merry Christmas. Thank you for my
present. Your body look handsome.
Where your head Ha ha

Cant wait to sing with you tomorrow

The next morning, bad news.

I so sorry I got fever and not feeling
well going emergency might not make
it tonight. Please don't be mad 😔

It was the first time she ever canceled. *Odd*, he thought. *She posted that video this morning of her pounding that punching bag. Garage setup. Georgia flag in the background. Her cousin's husband a Bulldog? She looked healthy to me. Really now? She's healthy enough to be whacking a heavy bag and all of sudden she's sick? Did she get another customer?*

> Ok. Next Tuesday?

Ok. But we have New Year's party at
bar this Friday. Can you come?

> I try. No guarantees.

Ok. Hope to see you 😊

He sat on his couch, fingers raking through his hair, cheeks puffed. *Geez. She knows I hate Friday nights. That's when all the young punks show up. But there was that one time I went on a Friday and she blew off all the young guys to be with me. Real ego boost. Silverback over young bucks, 1-0.*
He slapped his thighs and laughed, shaking his head. *Great way to*

start the new year. Maybe she feels bad about blowing me off and wants to make it up to me. It's Friday night. Usually get together with Mom at Katie's. I'll go see the family, then make my way to the bar.

29

DARK SIDE

He walked in about 10:00 p.m. The place was in full swing. Not like their Tuesday nights. The jukebox playlist was going full steam in the dart room with hip-hop music blasting F- and N-bombs every half-dozen words. All four dartboards were in play.

There were two NBA Friday night basketball games on the bar area flatscreens, with the regular barflies joined by the weekend barflies.

Karaoke was at an epic level in the booth room. All three private rooms were full. There were twelve girls working the rooms. Verna and Allie and two weekend servers worked at a trot, serving drinks. This was a $20,000-night for Lynh. "Hey Glenn!" Jimmy and Tia chimed in unison.

Tia pointed to one empty seat at the end of the bar, where she met him with a cold one. "Happy New Year, love. Didn't expect you here."

Jimmy came over to offer his hand. "Thank you, Glenn. Landlord pay for all our customer parking."

He took Jimmy's hand, quickly scanning the dart room. "No problem, Jimmy. Maya here?"

"Not yet, Glenn. Think pretty soon."

Glenn gave him a raised eyebrow.

Jimmy shook his head. "I don't know that girl sometimes. Plenty other girls here tonight, Glenn. You pick. One, two. I bring. No worry. I take care you." One of the weekend girls casually walked over. Clearly Asian, possibly Korean or Vietnamese. Gold satin full length evening gown, spaghetti straps barely covering her tan shoulders, with slits up to her waist.

She stood idly by with a microphone. "I heard you like to sing?"

Over her shoulder, Glenn spied Kimmie with one of her regulars, glancing up with a look that said go have some fun.

He gave the girl with the microphone the once over. *Wow, the pick of the lot.*

He slipped her a Jackson, and she smiled her thanks. "Thanks, but I'm here for only a while. But can you let Kimmie know I appreciated the thought?" He signaled to Tia to send Kimmie a glass of Mondavi.

Jimmy came up behind him. "Why you do that? Not like? I find you more. Someone here look like Maya. Sing better. I get for you." Jimmy motioned to two girls, stunners, at the other end of the bar.

Glenn waved off the girls and patted Jimmy on the shoulder. "No girls, Jimmy, I'll chill here. If she doesn't come soon. I'll leave." Glenn made sure he said it loud enough for Tia to hear. Tia was texting as they spoke.

He surveyed his surroundings like he'd been trained in the military. *I'm trapped. I'm at the end of the bar. It's a dead end. One way in, and one way out. And here comes trouble.* Lynh was casually making her way to him, saying "Hi" to everyone at the bar on the way. They had not seen each other since the champagne date.

She had a cigarette and lighter in one hand. With the other hand, she patted his shoulder, working her way up to massaging his neck. "What you doing here, honey? Finally dump Maya? Plenty girls here tonight. I find you another. Good girl, treat you good."

He swiveled to her, causing her hand to slip. "Happy New Year, Mama. What do you mean? You said Maya was a good girl when you introduced first time."

Her face puckered in disgust. "Yeah, yeah, but you spoil her, Glenn. Now she ruined. She think she Chloe. Have all kine customers. Young punks. Only like flash. Money, money, money. She brag, you know. All customers worship her. She mean you too Glenn."

His jaw dropped slightly. *She said she only had random customers on the weekend nights. That's why I gave her more money.*

Lynh's voice cut into his memory, sweeping her hand around the room. "You see her here? I need her and Chloe but not here. I bring in other girls work Friday nights. I don't need them. They do their own thing. They bring dates here Friday. They bring their own booze. At least you pay me off the last time."

He stiffened. "Dates?" *I thought she didn't date customers.*

Lynh rolled her eyes. Her voice tinged with derision. "What you stupid Glenn? Dates. Expensive dinner, and after come here drink. Young guys. Plenty money. Act like Hollywood. Sometime $10,000 on the table."

He signaled to Verna for a beer. He tried to act casual. A prickly sensation was building on the back of his neck. "But Mama. Here? Hollywood? I can think of lots of other places these crumbs could show off at."

Chin jutting, she crossed her arms, walking away sullen. "You watch, Glenn. She come here with dates tonight. Last few weeks same thing."

Verna came by with his beer. "Your booth open, Glenn. Come sit. Wait for Maya." Verna was hoping Maya would drop the gangster wannabes she and Chloe hung out with on Friday nights.

A while later, sitting in the booth, he heard Maya out in the bar area greeting everyone as she walked in. From what he could see, it was Maya, Chloe and two guys sporting clothes out of some lousy hip-hop video of triad society rappers. Young guys. Bad boys.

She was strutting in the bar area, saying "Hi" to regulars waiting for her in the highest heels he'd ever seen. The heels matched her two-piece black lace short skirt and bra top. *What to do? Go see her? Wonder if she's going to look for me? After all, she said to come.*

Five minutes later, she walked by on her way to the girls' room in the booth room. She stopped short when she saw him. The look on her face said *Oh shit.* "What you doing here?"

He cocked his head, raised his eyebrows. An edge to his voice. "You said to come."

She looked back, then sat down. Her forced smile didn't match the apprehension in her eyes. "Buy me drink?"

He waved for Verna. *Wow, what happened to the Tuesday charm. She sounds so cheap.*

She sat on the edge of the booth. Two feet of space between them. She licked her lips. "Hundred dollar shot?"

He played with his napkin. "No. Let's start with the usual." He wanted to know where her dates were and glanced toward the dart room, not seeing her eyes narrow. He turned back to her. "Where's Chloe?"

She fidgeted with her earrings—her lucky Chanel earrings. "Dart room." She craned her neck over the booth back, looking for Verna.

Careful to control his tone, he tapped the table in front of her to get her attention. "You sit with me tonight?

She nearly snapped out her answer. "Okay. But later. I have customer waiting." Verna brought her shot and she downed it without even a clink or cheers. "I have to go. They buy us dinner. We play Thai High Card. Gamble. They go after." She didn't say what the stakes were. In the past, losing hands led to all four leaving the bar together for the night.

His jaw tensed, signaling he was pissed. *I guess she forgot—again. I thought she didn't date customers.*

She saw his anger rising. A cheek peck, and she was gone. She didn't leave her bag.

Lynh came around the corner with a smirk. "Honey, she not coming back. See those guys at the bar. They here to see her too."

Their dates left an hour later. Maya and Chloe proceeded to work the customers at the bar. Glenn saw a side he didn't see before.

He watched her like he was viewing a nature channel documentary. *She's lit. Moves like a shark after prey. Looks like a game—of what she can do to get the guy to buy her a drink. She gets her jollies over the guy buying her a drink. She is man crazy. This is her validating her worth?*

She was in the bar area. Watching from the booth room, what Glenn saw was disappointingly familiar. One fellow played hard to get. She was working hard to get his approval. She hooked his arm in hers, then put her head on his shoulder. She sang for him and gave him a back rub.

After all this, he finally ordered five shots, at which she squealed and kissed his forehead. He tried for more and she pointed to her cheek, and he gave her a sloppy one while trying to maneuver his lips to hers. Meanwhile, his hand traced her figure down to her backside, and she deftly took his hand in hers.

She caught Glenn watching out of the corner of her eye. She whispered something to the guy, and both went to the other end of the bar where a wall blocked Glenn's view. *You're kidding? Shit.*

Back in the booth room, a group of thugs was holding court in the semi-private room with one doling out Benjamins left and right. The leader was a scrawny looking fellow. He demanded Mama send girls to do stripteases and lap dances. The braver girls visited the girls' room first, and high as a kite, walked in with house champagne bottles in each hand. Mama kept sending girls and champagne bottles. Glenn counted six girls and twelve bottles so far.

Verna took in a round of tequila and let out a scream. Glenn saw the scrawny guy hoist Verna onto his shoulders. Glenn reacted instinctively. In seconds, he was standing in the doorway, bellowing in his military voice. "Is everything all right here?"

The guy put Verna down and took a step towards Glenn. "Fuck you. Who are you?"

Glenn had his hands up in front of him, palms forward. "I'm a nobody, friend." He sized up the room. *One drunk guy in front. Kick to the crotch would have him down. Two guys next to the punk drinking Cokes, so bodyguards. Not sure if packing heat. The other four are dumb shit lackeys. Just worry about the bodyguards.*

The scrawny guy was getting louder. "I said whaddya want?"

Verna jumped in. "This my brother's son. He okay. No hurt."

Eyes narrowed into slits, swaying a little, the scrawny leader slurred loudly. "Yeah, well he should have thought better."

Glenn never backed down from a fight he believed in. And helping Verna was something he believed in greatly at the time. He took one step back with his right leg and shoved his hand in his back pocket. His feet were in a classic shooter's stance. Anyone with experience would see it.

He nodded at the two bodyguards. "I think we can all be friends. Verna looks okay. My mistake. I'm backing off. Hey Verna, Jimmy's calling you." He wasn't leaving till Verna left that den of jackasses.

From their viewpoint, the bodyguards saw a guy with a cop's haircut in a shooter's stance about to draw. Their job was to bring the young boss back home alive and not in jail. The big boss would skin them alive if anything else happened.

The young punk took another step forward. Glenn assessed. *Keep cool, Glenn. One more step buddy, then you're in range for a front kick. Just one more step, go ahead, make my night.*

The younger bodyguard stood up and looked like a referee extending his arm between two combatants. He gingerly placed his palm on the young boss's chest, nodding to Glenn. "No problem, friend. We go way back with Verna and just having fun. Got carried away, that's all. Didn't know she had family."

Glenn knew he didn't look Vietnamese, so he replied, "Calabash."

The young punk leader glared. "This isn't finished, old man."

Glenn met the stare. *One word and a dozen union pipefitters would find this guy in a bloody pulp tomorrow.* Diplomacy kicked in. "It is over, son. My apologies for getting a little overprotective. Want no trouble. I know you can kick my ass. But hey, you woulda stepped up for Verna too, right?"

The kid muttered, "Fuck, yeah" and sat down. His bodyguard still had his arm outstretched as a barrier between the two.

Glenn turned his attention to the arm-extended bodyguard, who gave a slight nod. Glenn nodded back and said, "Good night, all. Sorry to jump in." Glenn backed out so they wouldn't see that his hand was shoved into an empty back pocket. *Well, that was stupid of me. I could be in a gutter right about now.*

Glenn went back to his booth. Somewhere Maya was singing "Impossible" by Shontelle, and he could tell that she was lit, more than he'd ever seen or heard.

Amber came over, dressed in her usual red lace nightie. Through the sheer fabric, he saw her panties were also red lace. Something was wrong. Her face was white, and her lips trembled a bit. "Glenn, can I sit with you?

Mama want me go into the super private room but I don't want. I buy my own drinks and yours too." She leaned over and whispered, pleaded, almost begged. "Please, Glenn."

Glenn witnessed the terror in her eyes. A mother of three, Amber didn't self-medicate.

He patted the seat next to him. "Sure." He tried to smile reassuringly.

She grabbed a mic. "I tell Mama I was backing you up? She like you. If not for you she make me go there."

They started singing some Jim Croce song he ordered. After the song, Mama came over and sized up the situation. Instead of fighting, she sat down across Glenn and started complaining about Maya. "That girl no good. She out there acting like slut. Hanging on every guy. I not run a bar like that."

Glenn looked at her quizzically and shot a look at the private rooms.

Lynh retorted, "That different Glenn. Customers paying big money. She out there giving it for free."

Amber sat quietly.

Glenn leaned forward, elbows on the table, propping his chin in his hands. "Giving what for free Mama?"

Just then, Maya stumbled past the booth. Taking a step back, she stared at Glenn.

She was swaying. Her voice was gravelly like she sang too many songs. You could smell the Crown from two feet away. She peered at him, trying to focus. "You still here?"

Glenn snapped calmly. "You said to wait. You'd be back you said. Are you back?"

She focused and realized Amber was sitting right next to him. Amber wore a red lace nightie right out of a sex catalog. Maya frowned. She announced, "I go pee," and hobbled off.

Glenn turned to Mama. "Nuff already. Send her home."

Lynh waved her cigarette and lighter in the air. "We tried half hour ago. She no want. There's guys enjoy this shit, Glenn. They use her like toy. This where grab ass happen."

Glenn started to get up. "I'm gonna have a word with them."

Amber grabbed his shoulder. "No, Glenn. She'll raise a scene. We're watching her. We have to do this every Friday. By closing we put her in a taxi and send her home. Sometimes one of us go with her. We'll take care of her." He turned to Amber and sized up the situation. With no alcohol on her breath, he surmised this was not the Amber that had worked him a month ago.

Maya came back. "I'm bus' up." She was swaying even more like she was about to pass out. "Glenn, you have money? No money tonight? Amber don't waste time on him. He broke-ass have no money." She stopped. Thinking. "You always have money." She dove under the table and started searching through his socks. She took his shoes off and turned them upside down, shaking them for good measure. She pulled herself up and exclaimed, "See, no money."

Then, swaying and slurring, she looked at Amber and pointed to Glenn. "That my cut-o-mer. He *my* cut-to-mer." She leaned over Amber to grab at Glenn, pressing Amber onto Glenn. With one hand on his neck, she pulled herself to him over Amber, her face to his, and kissed him. Open-mouthed. Soft. Sweet, with the taste of Crown on her tongue. Glenn felt flushed, aroused, excited. Then she pulled back. Eyes locked. As if to say you're mine.

She stumbled off. Glenn was in shock. Lynh made a sound like she was disgusted and left. Amber turned. "Thank you, Glenn. I need to close now. Anything I can do for you?" She waited.

He gazed at the doorway through which Maya disappeared. Barely turning to Amber, he murmured, "No. Glad to help."

Amber leaned in, and he shifted enough to turn what might have been a goodnight kiss into a hug. She whispered in his ear. "You're a great guy. I would treat you better. Thank you for tonight." She patted his back, kissed his cheek, and was off.

He hurried out of the booth and walked out to the bar area looking for Maya. Tia saw the worried look on his face and called him over. "We packed her up and put her in a taxi. We know the driver. He'll make sure she gets home okay."

He rubbed his face with both hands, raking his hair afterward. *What a night.* "Thanks Tia." He headed home. *Wow, this girl has issues. Man crazy, huh? Somehow, it made him feel closer to her. Like he really wanted to be there for her, maybe show her a better life?*

Two hours later, he got a DM:

> Sorry I did not say goodnight to you and spend more time with you. Thank you for coming. It meant a lot. I glad Amber was able to keep you company. I hope you had fun with her.

Geez. She was that hammered and now she can go on Instagram and put together logical sentences? This girl is amazing. But she sounded a little not so happy. He replied

Good night. Hope you get some rest

Across town, she threw the phone on the bathroom floor and with a mighty retch, started heaving into the toilet again.

He sent a couple more DMs that weekend and posted several pictures. For the first time since hooking up on Instagram, there was no response from her. *What the hell? She mad at me maybe? Amber piss her off? I was only trying to help. She always hearted me or responded on DM. Now nothing? Crap, never knew how rejected Instagram can make you feel.*

Sitting on the couch, nursing a beer, he wondered what was next for them. *Shit. The first Tuesday of the new year is not shaping up too good. Am I getting another message saying no can do? Is she even going to show up?*

He offered up a prayer.

"Father, I know I'm not supposed to pray for this kind of stuff but I really could use Your presence Tuesday night, and give us some quality time to connect. No drama, no Lynh, no other men. Just me and her. Thanks."

30

JANUARY LETTER

*E*erie. That was his first thought entering the bar a few days later. It was his only thought as he looked around. It was after the holidays, the first Tuesday of the new year. Only Jimmy was behind the bar. A soft country playlist emanated from the jukebox. The Christmas stockings were taken down. The cheap lights still hung.

The dart room was empty, and the booth room was dark, except for the purplish neon string lighting along the perimeter. One flatscreen showed college football highlights and the other had "Wheel of Fortune," America's favorite game show. After a raucous weekend, the air in the bar was a mix of musk and Febreze.

He strode up to his seat at the bar, looking around. "Hey, Jimmy. Where is everybody?"

Jimmy put out a Bud Light. "Always like this, Glenn. Everyone tired. Everyone broke."

Glenn grabbed his longneck and took a long swallow. *Dang. Even the barflies are gone. And no other girls. We'll have the place all to ourselves. If she comes. No response to any of my Insta-shit all weekend. But she had time to post all her New Year's Eve pics, especially the one where she's carrying a bottle of Grey Goose around that party all night.*

He heard her heels on the asphalt outside and turned as she came in. She was dressed in Daisy Duke shorts and a simple long-sleeve green stretch top. Her simple makeup and ponytail matched what she wore. He pointed with his bottle. "You showed up!"

She stopped in the doorway, hands on her hips. She noticed his face was flushed as if he'd been pouting. "Why not? Not get message that you don't come, so I come."

His eyebrows arched, just for a second. *So you do see my posts.*

Only then he noticed she was limping. "What happened?" *The*

Instagram thing will have to wait.

She half-hopped over to him and scooted onto her seat. "Stubbed my toe, hurt my foot on kitchen table. Not sure—just happened."

He stared at her foot. *Here's a bona fide excuse to skip and she's here. I'm an idiot. Do something. Take her mind off the foot.* "How's things?"

Well, brilliant with words, me.

She turned to him, wincing at her foot. "Not good. Mommy gambling again. She take all my money and gamble and lose. So frustrated."

He couldn't tell. *Was her grimace because of the foot or the mother?*

He kept a steady rhythm, nodding. *She's in a talkative mood again. Does she do this with everyone? No, she said she only confides in me.*

He felt a warmth bubble up inside, overlapping any insecurities felt over the weekend.

He pointed two fingers at Jimmy.

She stabbed at a napkin with a straw; her frustration came out high pitched. "She drive me crazy. Sister get married soon. You know, yeah? Mommy wants to do wedding her way. I say no way, you had your chance. Let my sister do whatever. Her wedding, you know?"

She leaned back in silence, taking the shot Jimmy brought over in one gulp.

He drank likewise. *Easy boy. She's got more to say. Let her regroup and go again.*

He rubbed her back as if to say go on.

She turned toward him and pulled at his barstool to bring him closer. Knees touching, she continued. "My mother sick. Dementia. Gambling problems too. Don't mind me. She make me sad. But she my mother. I must help. Thank you for helping me help her. She keep asking for more money. My cousin say enough already. I dunno what to do."

He pulled her against his shoulder and kissed her head. "Follow your heart. She's your mother. If she's ever gone you don't want to have any regrets."

She nodded, nuzzling his neck. "I know. Thank you." She leaned back. "Glenn, my sister get married. I help plan. Go back Thailand in March. Okay with you? Gone long time. Three Tuesdays. You still here when I get back?"

He raked his hair back and forth. *Wonder if she's thinking about Darren, the guy that disappeared the last time she went back home. Darren, the guy that took up with Chloe while she was gone.* "Of course, I'll be here." *March is a couple of months away. Not worried. Why should I be?*

The shot was taking effect on her. "Okay, I Instagram you, okay? I post pictures for you. You can come with me, you know. Heehee."

He squinted through his glasses. *Is she joking?* "Nah, I'll be right here waiting on you," croaking out the line from the Richard Marx song.

She let out a fake shudder. "Ugh, need put on music for you." They both laughed.

She got up to get the karaoke books.

"Wait." He wasn't done talking yet. "Since we're on a roll here, can I ask you a question?"

She spun around. Leaned over, palms flat on his armrests. "Yes?"

He stared wide-eyed. *Geez, never noticed her cleavage before.*

She caught him looking and stood back up. With one hand on her hip, the other hand wagged a finger. "Naughty!" Her wide smile betrayed her pride in his attraction. His eyes stayed glued to her chest. "Ahem." She tucked a finger under his chin and brought his eyes to her. "What question?"

He asked, "What are your dreams?"

She smiled politely. "Huh? I don't remember when I sleep."

He twisted his lips into a duckbill. "No, what are your dreams, what do you want to do in life?"

"Oh . . ." Her face thoughtful, her eyes staring somewhere in the distance, beyond the current time. "Makeup and beauty, world famous, New York."

He cocked his head, nodding with approval. "Yep, I can see it. I believe it. When you meet J-Lo, you introduce me, right?"

She laughed. "Sure."

He laughed too, then turned serious. "Don't laugh, Maya. If you believe, it will happen. I believe in you." Her cheeks flushed as she bowed her head.

She turned to him, stroked his cheek. "What about you? What your dreams?"

He laid his hand lightly on her hip, grinning. "To drink and sing with a beautiful woman."

She blushed even more.

He grinned. "No seriously. I'm serious. I already did everything else."

She laid her hand on his, the one on her hip. "Must be more Glenn. You such a good guy. Not waste life. Do more. Make life good for others. Find people to help. Rest when you die." With the other hand she picked up the shot glass. "Cheers." He paused for thought, then lifted his glass. "To greater dreams. Rest when we die."

They sat holding hands, dancing in their seats, listening to "Into Your Body" by Ed Sheeran. He saw her face clouding over. "Everything okay?"

She was fighting a frown. "I'm so worried, Glenn."

"About what?"

She wrinkled her nose. "Rusty. He my one and only. What will I do if he die? He diabetes. I'm going broke. Thank you for your help. If no Rusty I will go crazy. He my safe zone. He keep me from crazy. What will I do if he die? Please be there for me, Glenn?"

He rubbed her back. "Yes, of course. Don't worry, you got a way to go. Okay?"

She smiled. Reassured, she laid her head on his shoulder.

His turn. He had his own questions. "Maya?"

"Yes?"

He was staring at their reflection in the mirror behind the bar. "Why do you care about me?"

She lifted her head. "Huh?" Her expression asked, *Isn't it obvious*? "Comfortable. I'm comfortable with you. What other customer I come with hurt foot and can rub in front of him?"

Just then, a customer came in. She got up and met him several feet away. Glenn watched as the customer tried to put his arms around her, and she diplomatically deflected him. She put her hands on the guy's shoulders and whispered something to him. He shook his head disappointedly and left.

She came back to him. Glenn's adrenaline was in rush mode. "You did that for me?"

She smiled sweetly. "Yes, of course. Tuesdays are for you."

He smiled so wide and looked so happy, she thought he was like the little kids on American Christmas shows—the ones that wake up to presents from Santa.

He jumped off his stool and swooped her up in his arms and twirled her around. She giggled like a teenager. "Down boy, down." She used both hands to ruffle his hair. He let her slide down till her lips met his.

Jimmy couldn't take much more, rolling his eyes and walking out the door for a smoke.

Glenn held out her bar stool, more like swiveled it outward, so she'd have an easier time scooting on, even with her foot.

With her fingers, she raked his hair backward, fixing the mess she made. "You need haircut soon."

He was transfixed. *I haven't been this comfortable—yeah, that's the word she used—with anyone since Katie. And I was worried that this was doomsday after no direct messages all weekend? Maybe she's making it up to me. I mean, she invites me, but is on a date, gets hammered, sticks her tongue in my mouth, and calls me a loser, all in a very frickin' drunken inebriated state.*

He tried to picture the girl in front of him and the girl on Friday being the same. "I still can't believe how hammered you were, and you direct messaged me at 3:30 in the morning? Wow."

She reached for the songbook. "No worries. I'm usually okay after shower. But head hurt anyway after sleep."

He called for more rounds from Jimmy. *Seriously? I wonder if I mean that much to her? Like maybe she understood she screwed up and was making amends? There definitely was a pattern. Bad . . . good . . . bad . . . good. She screws up, and makes amends, and so on. Just like a real relationship.* Now he was lost in thought.

She nudged his shoulder. "What on your mind? Glenn, hey, what on your mind?"

He looked up, caressed her face, and held her gaze for what seemed like an eternity. "If I could, I'd like to see you forever. I don't want to stop seeing you."

"Then don't." Her answer was quick. She wasn't pleading, nor was it self-interested, but matter of fact in her do-what-make-you-happy tone. "If you don't want to stop seeing me, then don't."

He loved the way she simplified things for him. "I have something for you."

She pushed the songbook aside. "What?"

He brought out a letter. "I wasn't sure what you were gonna be like tonight because you didn't respond to my direct messages and posts. I thought you were mad, or you were gonna dump me."

She bit her knuckle. "Glenn! How many times do I have to . . . " She caught herself, remembering the little boy. "I said I wouldn't leave. I was just so busy this weekend."

He reached out, squeezed her hand, and kissed her knuckle. "Okay, anyway, I wrote you a letter because I wanted you to know how I felt. Here."

She gently unfolded it, liking the font immediately.

> Maya,
>
> I wish I could have said this to you in person, but I couldn't let the year end without thanking you one more time. This past year, you were the greatest impact on my life. Not sure if you understand, and I don't expect you to understand, but you've greatly changed my life, and I really wanted to tell you how . . .
>
> I cannot believe it, but I sing karaoke now because someone pushed me and said, "No worry what others think and to do what you like" And now I sing in the shower, at work, at the beach . . . it's been a great stress

relief, and sneaking away to Jimmy's once in a while to sing a few has gotten me through the day/night. Yeah, I still sing like a toad at times but whatever, right? If I enjoy it, go for it! Not worrying about what others think has prepared me to make some critical life decisions next month.

Not sure if you can understand this, but I'm a better person. I learned to forgive. I learned to be patient. I learned to be humble. I learned that if I want something in a relationship and I'm not getting it, I have to ask respectfully and nicely, and sometimes explain why. But I have to ask and not sit there and sulk. I was heading down a bad path a few months ago. Maybe it was a midlife crisis, and before it got too bad, I met you folks. You all provided a safety zone while I found myself.

I believe I have a God that loves me, and He wanted me to meet you, so I can learn the things you taught me. When you told me what your name meant, then it made sense to me. You really are an angel sent from above.

I learned a lot about myself. I have daddy issues as well as mommy issues. Didn't really know this for sure till I tried to figure out why I got so upset a couple of times during the summer. Thank you for being kind, understanding, and patient with the little boy in me. You've helped him grow up a lot.

You're truly a wonderful person. I know you more than you think I know. Everyone that has you in their life behind that wall of yours is truly blessed to have you in their lives because in you, they have someone they can count on to support their dreams and fulfill their desires. Your heart is all about making others happy. My only wish is that you do something all for yourself. Don't wait till you are 60 years old to act out on things you've missed out on in life.

Fondly,
Glenn

Silent tears pooled in her eyes. With one blink, two rivulets streaked down her cheek. "I never got a letter like this, Glenn. Do you mean it? I really change your life?"

"Yes." It was her turn to say wow. She stared at him, then looked at the letter. She carefully folded it, kissed it and held it to her forehead. Reverently, she opened her purse and put it in a side pocket. From where he was sitting, there were some jade pieces in there and a tiny Buddha statue. She looked up. "My treasure chest. I will keep forever."

Last call came too soon. They had talked story for four straight hours. The karaoke system was never turned on. She walked him out, holding hands, and kissed him goodnight several times. "Let me know when you get home safe." They were the only two people in the bar the whole night.

Home safe.

Me too. Thank you again for letter ☺

He blinked for a bit. *I started the night wrestling with every disaster scenario from her not showing up, to her entertaining other customers. Neither happened, she showed up and we spent the entire night talking like long lost friends. That kiss in the parking lot was classic prom night stuff.*

Back at the bar, Jimmy padlocked the front door and headed for his car. Across the street, a 730i metal chrome green BMW roared to life and peeled off. An empty Crown bottle flew out the window, spewing shards of glass on impact with the pavement. Jimmy watched the uniquely colored car disappear around the corner. *Young punk asshole. Leave Maya alone.*

31

ENTER GOD

The following week, on the second Tuesday of the new year, an overcast sky and drizzling rain covered the whole town with a damp chill. Glenn left the office early for the bar, wanting to warm up with something stronger than a beer.

He got there before her. All the holiday decorations were down. A faint trace of Buddhist incense lingered in the air. The flatscreens were both turned to a mixed martial arts event featuring a local product. The barflies were back and cheering on the local fighter. A construction crew just off duty was getting started in the darts room, with Tia and Amber as company, subbing in for the other girls who hadn't yet arrived.

The jukebox was pulsing with electronic dance music, and from time to time, Amber got up to dance in her trademark red nightie and was rewarded with a shower of dollar bills.

Glenn scooted onto his corner seat. "Hey Jimmy. What you got to warm me up?"

Jimmy leaned on the bar. "Want try something new?" He was already pouring. "Korean soju with plum juice. You try."

Glenn sniffed and tasted a bit.

Jimmy's face soured. "No Glenn, take all one time. Let soak mouth and throat all one time."

Glenn complied. Every taste bud came alive and an intense warmth flushed his chest. *Yikes, a few more of these and I'm toast. She's not even here yet.*

Jimmy plunked a beer in front of him. "You relax now." A car screeched outside. Jimmy grabbed a bulky fanny bag from under the register. "Watch bar. I be right back, okay?"

Still enjoying the warmth, Glenn didn't think anything. "Yeah, sure."

Jimmy took two steps outside, hand buried inside his fanny bag. He saw the same chrome green BMW from the week before and started to make his way toward it. The car sped off, leaving Jimmy with clenched fists. *Fucking asshole.*

Maya came walking around the corner. She spied the fanny bag. "What wrong, Jimmy?"

His expression cold and disapproving, he growled, "Nothing. No worry. Mistake. Old age. Glenn waiting for you."

Back inside, Glenn peeked over the bar.

Wonder what I'd do if someone came in? Can I play bartender? Still feeling good from that stuff. What's tonight gonna be like? When we started it was party city. Drink, sing, raise hell. Then for a month it was family time, small talk, home cooking, pretending to be domestic. Now? Two friends? It was so like a real thing last week.

Jimmy walked in with Maya following. Glenn swiveled in time to catch her fixing her hair. She blushed, smiled, wearing jeans and a plain red wrap over a crop top with ample cleavage. *She's been showing more cleavage lately, or did I just not notice before?*

She draped her arm over his shoulders. "Can we go our booth? I need to talk. Let me vent, we play after, okay?"

Concern etched his face as he nodded. "Yeah, sure." *Must be some heavy stuff going on.*

He raised three fingers to Jimmy, pointing to her then himself. Three shots for each.

She tried small talk. "How you, Glenn? How was your weekend?"

He gently put his finger on her lips. "No small talk. We've been together too long for that shit. Tell me what's going on. Let it out."

She reached for his hand like it was a lifeline. "Thank you, Glenn. I feel bad. You the customer. I promise I will not do this all the time."

They did three shots each, while she vented her frustrations. "Sometime I feel like you my only friend. I wait all week to talk to you."

She read his thoughts. "I could text but not same. I need to see you. Feel you next to me. I wait till our Tuesday." She put his hand to her face. "I'm comfortable. I tell you things I don't tell anybody. Thank you for listen Glenn."

He rubbed her back. "Go on. I'm here."

She turned her back to him, rubbing the back of her neck. "I still stress about my mother. Doctor say not live long. Five years. But not remember us pretty soon."

His hands massaged her neck gently. "Love conquers all Maya. You will remember her. She will live on in your heart. How's Rusty?"

She searched her phone and lifted it in front of her for him to see.

He leaned forward for a better view, his chest leaning into her back. He breathed in a slight trace of perfume, his brain synapsing with happy chemicals.

She could feel him breathing faster on her neck, his pecs pulsating on her shoulder blades. "See? Still fat. My baby. He mad at me. Doctor say lose weight. Every morning I poke him, give shot."

The dog was as big as her. "He not like the shot," she said sadly.

He absorbed the video. The dog clearly didn't care for the shot. *Geez, never saw such a guilt-shooting stink eye from a family pet.*

She turned to him, hand on her chest. "I read your letter plenty Glenn. Thank you. No one write to me like that before. It make me feel special."

He leaned forward, his eyes caressing her soul. "You're a beautiful person. I just wanted you to know."

She felt a thickness in her throat. "You think I'm beautiful?"

He took her hand, played with her fingers. "Yes, outside and inside. With makeup and no makeup."

Her eyes popped wide. "How you know no makeup?"

Catching Jimmy's eye, he held up two fingers. "Your Instagram . . . last September's workout pic. I see all your pics. You should make a calendar. I would buy."

She laughed. "I don't think I'm pretty."

He grinned, face wrinkling in confusion. *Huh? How can someone so pretty think she's not? False modesty here? Tell me more,* his eyes implored.

She paused, eyes clouding dark as if remembering something humiliating. "I was ugly growing up. All kids tease me. I was tomboy from farm. Hands callous. Play volleyball, basketball, soccer. Walk like boy all the time. Short, brown skin, short hair. Ugly. I hate how I look."

Done with the construction guys, Tia brought over scotch for Glenn and Ciroc for Maya. A timely break. He stared into his shot as the two girls exchanged idle chit-chat. *Lots of stuff online. Thailand, where white skin good, dark skin bad.* He recalled the one forum where an expatriate explained the life of Isaan province girls.

Brown skinned farm workers. Third class
in a third-class country. Only the fucking
assholes from abroad looking for pussy
went after them, feeding the local sex
industry. Whites, Indians, Japs. All assholes
preying on these kids.

Glenn flinched upon remembering. *I hope God damns all these pricks to hell.*

Tia went off to the other end, and Glenn and Maya clinked glasses. Letting the warmth radiate through to his chest, he held her hands and saw the callous scars. *Did having callouses from working on the farm make her more untouchable? Maybe that's why she took up with an Aussie?*

Clearing her throat, she pulled out a picture of her sister. "See? She beautiful. I hate her. I love her but I hate her. Long legs. White skin." Glenn had seen Maya pose for pics with white skin from time to time. There were products on the market for such a purpose. The first time she didn't wear heavy makeup was the first time he saw her natural tan. He thought back, *Beautiful. Healthy.* He shook his head.

She turned to him, concern on her face. "What wrong?"

He scratched his head. "I don't understand. Western women, white, tan all the time. Eastern women, dark, make themselves white with chemicals." He raked his hair, leaning on the bar, voicing his next thought with some exasperation. "People just need to search inside."

She rubbed his shoulder. "Hard Glenn, when so much people only look outside." She thought of so many of her customers who only cared about how pretty she looked and how much cleavage and leg she showed. One brought a picture of an Asian porn star to show her how he wanted her makeup.

Maya worked on his neck next. From afar, Tia could see his tension melt.

His mood easing up, Glenn wondered aloud. "So what do you think of me?"

Maya finished with a back rub. "You nice, all that matter. After nice, cannot tell what you look like. First time I saw, I thought nice, little scared looking, like little boy. When you say how old I don't believe."

He cocked his head, rolling his eyes to the right. "Hey, you want to see something?" He searched for an old picture on his phone. An early picture of him over a hot rod, mirror glasses, a sleeveless cutoff jeans vest, and a red bandana. His wild days. Biceps still ruggedly cut a year out of high school.

She squealed. "Woooow! Hansum!" She jumped and went to show the other girls, including Lynh. He heard over the din. "Dis myyyy boyfriend!"

Tia walked over. "Glenn, you faker. What a stud. What happened?" She laughed.

Over the years his wardrobe consisted mainly of unexciting banker garb. "We all grow up, Tia."

Tia licked her lips, flashing a grin. "Hey, maybe you should grow *down* next time. You got her hugely excited."

He pushed two shot glasses to her. "Yep, she likes the bad boys, doesn't she?"

Maya came back with his phone. "You send me? I print at home. Put on my pillow, kiss before go sleep."

He grimaced comically. *Geez I have all this competition at the bar and now my chief competition is my picture from a stupid wild time?* "Yeah okay, but you know you can't take the pic into the shower, right?" Glen gestured, outlining a long cylindrical object.

She laughed and hit him on the shoulder. "Uh-uh-uh! Naughty!" Then she laughed some more, ending with a saucy, "We see heehee."

They did the next round. Compliments of Jimmy. Maya's Pretty Pinks, the deadly bubblegum drinks.

She dropped her glass in front of her and turned to him. Her cheeks were flushed. "You want to sing or talk story?"

A relaxed smile crossed his face. Maybe it was the pink drink or his desire to connect. "Talk story, please."

She smiled and motioned with her hand as if to say proceed.

He tapped his shot glass on the table. "Lynh said I changed you."

Her eyebrows arched. "You think? Mama think I change because I'm more independent now. I don't do what she want all the time. She mad."

He nodded. He saw she was deep in thought. *Let her think. Let her ask.* He raised one eyebrow as if to say ready when you are.

"Glenn, what you think of me first time?"

His brow furrowed, mouth pursed. He took a deep breath. "I thought, wow, gorgeous." He followed up quickly. "Then I got to know you and thought kind, caring, genuine."

She was thoughtful, taking it in.

He raised two fingers at Tia and made an eating motion. "Why do you ask, Maya?" *Where is she going with this?*

Maya opened her mouth just as Tia brought over the next round. She paused long enough for him to notice. "No, nothing" was all she said. All guys know not to press when the girl says *no nothing.*

I'll let it go. She's chatty again anyway. More intel.

She laughed softly, then whispered as if sharing some medieval secret. "You know I went to church once?"

Shock registered then turned to joy on his face, his heart churning some twenty beats faster. *Whoa! Whoa! Now this is different. Is this God giving me the chance to share? All Christians need to share. Never was much good at it. Katie was the expert.*

"Wow! Tell me everything!"

She noticed how excited he got. Liked making him happy that way. "My friend take me. Go church, sing, man talk about God, splash water from bowl. That's it. We eat with others. Go home after. Eat was good." Pensive. She decided to tell him. "My sister, she marries Christian."

He was caught off guard. "You mean a white guy?"

She showed him a picture. "No. Thai."

He rubbed the stubble on his chin. What did Pastor Ronan say about Thai missions? Only 4 percent of the country was Christian. This was a big thing for the families. She didn't seem stressed.

Something stirred inside him. *Share my love.*

He turned to face her. "You ever thought of being Christian?"

It looked like she winced to him.

"Hard Glenn. I went to temple with Grandma when I was kid. Family and culture pray Buddha, not your God you know?"

"Maya, you know that the real Buddha, Gautama, didn't believe in being a god?"

She looked confused. He didn't want to press. It was always like this.

"Maya, I believe you can live Buddhist and worship God."

Okay, I need to stop short of saying real Buddhism has no Buddha as a god. But dang it. The world is filled with Buddhist monks who hold themselves out like demigods, handing out blessings or merit for monetary favor. My side of the house is no different. Look at the pope and the rich evangelicals. I wish more people would simply understand that it's a matter of the heart. This was what got me kicked out of church.

He remembered his split from the church. Remembered beefing with the new pastor.

> *It's a relationship, not a religion. It's my relationship with God, not my bowing to you as God's rep. Bullshit. Glenn out.*

He was lost up somewhere in another part of the universe.

She nudged his shoulder. "Glenn, you okay?"

He nodded. "Yes, Maya. Do me a favor. Promise one day you'll think about checking out my God, okay? Your family, culture, temple, God, Jesus, all can co-exist." He left out the part about praying to Buddha.

Her body rigid, she held up two fingers for Tia, and one beer for him. "How you know can co-exist?"

He tugged at his hair. She reached up and took hold of his trembling hand. Her confused expression begged *why so nervous?*

He took her hand. Kissed her palm. "Okay, this might sound crazy." He took a swig of his beer. "My mom introduced me to God. Been talking to him ever since."

She squeezed his hand. "I know, I think you told me once."

"Okay, but I didn't tell you she was also village high priestess of their Buddhist sect."

Her eyes went wide. The look on her face said *What the fuck.*

He rubbed his face. "I know, right? I remember going to prayer with her. She'd take me to a temple with a large Buddhist goddess statue. I'd sit on the side while she sat, knees tucked in, in front of the statue chanting and clanging and swaying and sweating and almost swooning."

He finished his beer, set the bottle down, and took a deep breath. "The Buddha statue was scary. It wasn't the fat happy kind, but the standing-up-looking-down-at-you kind. Scared, bored, stink. I waited patiently because Mama always bought ice cream for me after."

Tia brought another round. He reached for his bottle. *Man, it took years to figure it out, till the religion prof turned me on to that book about Gautama. But good values are taught by the real Buddhists. Judo sensei was one of them.*

She shifted in her seat. Her eyelids were heavy. It was either call it a night or switch topics. Bargirl 101 basics. "Okay, Glenn, one day I try."

He did a doubletake. *Really? Here's where I'm supposed to invite her to a service. Talk about no follow up. I got no service to take her to.*

He looked up briefly. *Your call, Father.*

He waited. *No answer. Seriously?*

She steered the conversation back to her mother and dog. "I'm so worried. Glenn, you be there if something happen to them?"

Something stirred strongly and deep inside him. *For real? You want me to witness to her? Now? Here in a bar?*

The feeling got stronger. It never went away. *It's now or the buzzing gets stronger tomorrow. I'll go crazy by next Tuesday. Here goes. Father, You're gonna help me right?*

A voice. *My grace is sufficient for you.*

He took her hands in his. "Maya, can I pray for you?"

She looked at her empty shot glass blankly.

He squeezed an imaginary stress ball. *Oh crap. I spooked her.* "It's okay if you're not okay."

She turned to him, her knee against his as if to say we're connected—you and I are in this, all of this, together. "No Glenn, I trust you. Please pray for me." She placed her hands in his.

He looked down at her hands. *So natural. She's done this before.*

> *Father, I lift Maya up to You into Your*
> *warm embrace and love. Please take care of*
> *her mother and Rusty and bless her sister's*
> *marriage. Continue to bring happiness and*
> *joy to Maya, give her strength when she*
> *needs it. And bless her love for Rusty and*
> *her mom, and may they be together in body*
> *and spirit no matter what happens. Amen.*

She said amen, then reached out and caressed his cheek. "Thank you, Glenn. No one ever pray for me like that before. You are good at it. Thank you. I will pray to Buddha for you."

Last call came soon after. It was back to goodnight kisses outside, and home safe DMs. Jimmy insisted on walking both out. Maya noticed the fanny pack again.

An hour later, he lay in bed. Another sleepless night. *Seed planted maybe? Who knows? Father, was this Your plan? Can it truly be? Not while I'm still married though, right? Only friends? For now, I guess. Love conquers all right?*

Across town, the chrome green BMW stopped in front of her house. She got out. Walking up her driveway, she did a half turn, and blew a kiss before going in.

32

CALM BEFORE STORM

Their third Tuesday that month was uneventful to Glenn and Maya, mainly because they couldn't remember a thing about that night, other than him remembering what she wore. With a winter chill in the air, she wore designer jeans and a faded green field jacket over a silver satin spaghetti strap camisole. He remembered thinking only she could make surplus military wear ooze with sex. The booth room was closed for renovations, so they sat in their spot in the bar area. They ate Uncle's meat salad, sang songs, and got drunk on whatever Jimmy was experimenting with that night. After ten songs straight, they put their microphones down in unison. Glenn ordered ten shots for him and Maya, the real stuff, all of it gone in thirty minutes. Jimmy swore he never saw two people enjoy playing a sword fight with microphones more than they had.

For the fourth Tuesday of the new year, Glenn and Maya agreed to limit the alcohol intake. They were having dinner in their booth. Between bites of Thai fried chicken, he soaked in how she looked. A simple purple crop top with a plunging V neckline with white capris. *Hmm. What happened to all the fancy cocktail dresses? I guess she's getting more comfortable with me and her being us, not having to impress the other customers. Is this good or bad? Still looks great though.*

After some small talk, she got a phone call and jabbered for a few minutes in Thai. Her eyes widened, and she was bouncing up and down where she sat. "Glenn, lucky me! I will go to Vegas next week for Super Bowl. Lucky me. Chloe customer taking Chloe and I go too. He pay for plane and room. I will stay with Chloe. I will be third wheel but that's okay, I'm fine being alone. Don't worry I leave tomorrow and come home next Tuesday in time be with you Tuesday night. So don't make other plans, okay? You be good and Tuesdays as usual for us, okay?"

Before he could react, her expression morphed from excitement to worry. "We go to dinner when I come back?"

He picked at his food. "What do you mean? We always have dinner."

She lifted the chicken to his mouth. "No, not at bar. Not me bring food. We go out someplace nice. Ruth Chris?"

He chewed and swallowed. "I thought you had a rule about being with customers outside of the bar."

She nodded. A little more concerned. *Why is he not happy?* "Still rule. But with you not like being with customer. And want to thank you for all your support."

He was staring at her mouth, how fast she was talking and how she trembled with excitement. She wasn't giving him a chance to react. *She hits me with this shit about Vegas, then this dinner thing. It's like she'd got a playbook on how to make me feel special. Same playbook for most lonely schmucks that go to these bars. Yeah, real special.*

He faked a smile.

Biting her lip, she pushed his phone toward him. "Glenn, you make reservations for us." Looking at her phone, she said she was open the Monday after she returned from Vegas. He made the reservations right then. *Wonder why she can't make the reservations?*

Chloe walked in. They locked eyes for an instant, and Chloe went the other way. "I be right back Glenn." Glenn held up five fingers to Verna, and with the other hand pointed one finger to Verna, who smiled a thank you for her tip.

Verna brought the rounds, followed by Maya in a huff. Without a clink or cheers, she downed two shots. "I fight with Chloe. Someone told her I was stuck up, and she didn't fight for me. She supposed to be family but not fight for me." She slumped down into the booth, blowing the hair out of her face.

Brushing her hair back, he intoned soothingly, "Hey, you're a good person. Don't let what other people say get to you." He patted her back. "Assholes put others down to make themselves feel good because they have such a shitty life. They pick on the people they think have a better life than them. Whatever they say is their problem, not yours."

She nodded, the anger on her face softening. "Make sense. Thank you. I'm better now."

This time they clinked glasses: her third, his first. The conversation turned to her mother and Rusty again. She was still worried. Glenn thought this was the right time to give her a letter he wrote. He had worried about her all week. "I put it on paper so you can read it over and over, and whenever you need to."

"Another letter?"

"Here, just read it." He knew it would take a while for her to absorb.

She started reading. Holding the letter with one hand, she reached for him with her other hand. By mid-letter, their fingers were interlocked, united in each other's fear of losing all they hold dear.

Dear Maya,

You are a dear, sweet, wonderful, special person. I feel your pain when we talk about Rusty and your mom, and what the future holds. I see the sadness in your eyes and the uncertainty in your voice. You have questions and at the same time don't want to deal with it. You're not alone.

When you asked if I'd be there for you, I was touched beyond words. In my mind, I'm already there . . . holding you . . . letting you cry. I'm telling you it'll be okay . . . because love conquers all, even death. Death is simply physical separation . . . temporary. Love is forever. Those that we love are ours forever, if not in this life, then in the next. And while separated by here and there, we are still connected by the memories and feelings we have in our hearts.

Enjoy every second, minute, hour, and day you have with them. Find a way to love each day, and build a treasure chest of memories, sights, sounds, smells, touches, and tastes to keep you going until you're together again. When the time comes, your treasure chest, your love for each other, and the experiences that you've had . . . all of this will keep you moving forward.

And some parts of your loved ones will still be with you. You will find them in your heart. You will feel their spirit and sense their presence, like the warmth from a fire. You will hear their voices (or bark), faintly but clearly. You will feel their touch (or nuzzle), softly, like the wind. In time, you will remember the good times fondly, the tears will stop, and you will smile. And you will know that you will be together again.

I'm not going to lie to you . . . it's not going to be easy at first. Just getting out of bed will be difficult. But if our loved one means that much to us, we have to find a way to continue living, and honor and cherish all the memories made and love you shared. You must remember this, to keep living, for Rusty, for your mom, for whoever you shared life here with. They would want you to.

And in time, it will get better . . . not easier, just better, and until then, you will have the support of those that love you to get you through. They will be there for you because you were there for them. They will call you to make sure you are okay. They will bring you food. They will come clean your house. They will do your laundry. They will sit with you quietly.

And when tears roll up in your eyes, and your breathing gets hard, they will hold you and let you cry. My advice—let the tears flow. I'm already there, telling you it'll be okay. In time, the sadness clouding your heart will be replaced by the joy that comes from remembering the good times.

Yes, love has a stiff price to pay at the end. Love anyway. No matter the cost or price, love with all your heart! It's worth it.

Trust God. Trust me. You will not be alone. You will make it through. And you will smile again. I promise.

Keeping you in prayer,
Glenn

She read it all the way through. She sat in silence.

He searched her face. "You understand?"

She reached over, cupped her hand under his chin, gently pulled him to her, and kissed him. A soft kiss. So natural, soft, loving, engaging, exploring, so communicative of so many emotions. She let go and looked into his eyes. "I understand. Thank you." She put her head on his shoulder. He put his arm around her like he wanted to protect her from the world. They stayed like that for what seemed a long time. And they didn't care.

They drank and sang the rest of the night. "Tattoo." A new song—"Everytime." And a little after 1:00 a.m., they ended with a duet—"Need You Now." He smiled as the words he sang jibed exactly with the bar's clock showing a quarter past one.

Tia watched on. *I swear, these two have more* awww *moments than anyone else I know, including me.*

Maya held him tight before he walked into the night. "Good night, Glenn. Message me? If I win in Vegas I will give you half, okay?"

It was a nice night for a walk. *Still not sure how she can go to Vegas and be by herself? There's gonna be guys crawling all over her. Can't shake this nagging feeling. Only three of them going to Vegas?*

Around the corner, car tires squealed.

33

FEBRUARY CAVE IN

Glenn headed to the gym after the first Monday night judo session of February. He was finishing up his last set of bench presses when his phone pinged a tone that could only mean one thing. He shook his head as he clicked his Instagram icon. *Again? Another post? This is crazy, posting ten times a day?*

It had been a long five days for him, absorbing post after post of her winning cash vouchers, of her and Chloe in different poses, and her in various casinos. *If she's with someone, she's being careful not to show it.*

He sat on the weight bench, alone in the gym, perusing her latest social media offering with some irritation. At an oyster buffet, she scanned two tables with ten place settings each, then her table with food in front of her. The videos she posted were usually overlaid with hip-hop or rap songs, but this time, there were only voices, so he turned the volume up.

He heard a male voice ask her if she ever had oysters and another male voice snidely commenting, "Of course, she needs her strength to keep us all happy!" The video cut off shakily with a slapping sound and her laughing and saying, "Fuck you."

Confused, he recalled Maya saying the trip was only with Chloe and her customer. But the video gave him pause. *This is a party, not a threesome.*

The oyster party video rolled over onto another one showing her running through the halls of the Venetian hotel with Chloe and three guys that looked like the Friday night dates he'd seen them with a month before.

She lied. It's not just the three of them up there. Pretty stupid leaving the sound on. Man crazy again? The Crown must have been flowing. And snubbing my DMs now? I sent three. No reply. None. Zilch. Fuck this. She said we're friends. This is not friends. Maybe it's a fantasy game for her. Do I even want to see her tomorrow?

Tomorrow came and it was not pretty. The first Tuesday she was back started off rocky. She sent him a DM.

☺ I running late. Just a little. Wait for me ok?

He waited for her in their booth. She was an hour late. "Sorry my cousin needed help with work," she said as she slipped in next to him.

He addressed her without eye contact. "You hungry?"

She recoiled a bit. "No. I eat at home with cousin."

His brow furrowed. Sensing he made her uneasy, he relaxed and forced a smile. "You look really nice. Like you went to fancy dinner place." He was fishing. *Was there someone else? Did she honestly eat at home with her cousin?*

Relieved at his smile, she waved her hands over her dress, a stunning burgundy velvet maxi with a sexy high slit showing leg up to her waist and a laced back closure showing off her phoenix tattoo. "No, I wear this for you."

He sucked in his cheeks for an instant. *Spidey sense tingling. She never wore anything like that before. Shit, during the last month all I saw was jeans and comfort tops most of the time. No biggie. She said she felt comfortable with me. That's what she said.*

He played with his beer label, peeling it off the bottle in one piece. *Shit, but we ate dinner together every week in January, dressed in comfortable clothes, and the first Tuesday she's back, she's dressed to the nines, and not hungry because she had dinner with her "cousin." Not feeling good about this at all. Is there someone else?*

He called Tia over, asking for the entire bottle of Hennessey. *It's going to take all I got not to snarl at her. I need to medicate and start feeling better . . . now.*

He woke up the next morning with a massive hangover. He texted Joyce to say he wasn't coming in. *Damn, my head! What the hell? Last I remember . . . the dress. She got mad. Asked me what I was mad about. I said nothing. I think I said nothing. We drank a lot. Somebody put me in a cab.*

He sat on his couch, rubbing his neck with an icepack. *Still bothering me. Did she come late because she had a dinner date with someone else? This cousin comes up at the most interesting times. Is her cousin's husband for real? Found pics of him on her Instagram and asked her, but she took the pictures off, saying the cousin asked her to.*

He rubbed his face. *Here I go overthinking again. No matter. We still got the dinner date next Monday, then our regular Tuesday. Maybe the excitement of Vegas hadn't worn off yet. No biggie. We'll get back in our groove next week.*

No biggie, he thought. But by the weekend, her lateness the prior week bordered on an obsession. *Why? This rejection and abandonment thing has got to go. Nothing's going to happen. Everything's okay. It's my imagination. She can be trusted. We've been through so much. She's not gonna hurt me. Can't wait for our dinner date.*

Sunday night, she messaged him.

😔 Glenn, so so sorry. I try all day to get someone take my late shift Monday night but no one help. Have to cancel so sorry. See you Tuesday?

He slammed shut the book he was reading and gritted his teeth. *What the hell? Why set up a dinner for Monday night if you know you have a late shift? And I thought she didn't work on Mondays? Man, that's rubbing salt into the wound, making me cancel the reservations.*

Ok

😊 Thank you. See you Tuesday ok?

Monday morning, he got another message from her. His hopes jump-started. Maybe she got someone to cover?

😊 Hope you have a good day

😊 Hope you have a good day too

Okay. We're back on track.
A few minutes later.

 Sorry cannot make it tomorrow night. Glenn, so so sorry but my friend husband in hospital and I have to babysit her kids tomorrow while she go hospital. He have burns all over and she need to take care him. The kids have no one else and she has no one else.

Glenn was seething inside. Something took over him. *You got to be kidding? She doesn't have any other friends that can help? I mean who was doing the babysitting while she was working the Monday late shift? And we were supposed to meet at 9:00. But visiting hours are over at 8:30 in the evening so why couldn't we meet? Ever since the Vegas trip, she's distant and its seriously feeling like there's someone out there demanding time on Tuesdays . . . our Tuesdays. And what hospital in the states has family members come and tend to the patient? This isn't Thailand.*

A few minutes later.

 Don't be mad Glenn. I need to help my friend.

Okay.

Can you do me favor? Mama Lynh been talking shit about me. If you go tonight and she say something, can you let me know?

Okay. Take care of your friends husband!

He waited for ten minutes. No answer.

On top of canceling dinner, then canceling Tuesday, she's giving me orders to relay back to her something Mama Lynh says about her? This is fucked. Who does she think she is?

<hr>

He walked into the bar, knowing he was going to be alone. *Maybe a couple of beers and some songs? Catch up with Tia?*

Lynh was waiting. "Glenn honey Maya late tonight. You stay with Mama."

Rolling his eyes, he smirked out his answer. "Mama, she's not coming tonight. Her friend needs help."

Mama looked at him like he was an idiot. She took his arm and nearly dragged him into a booth. "Honey she spoiled. Not good for you. You think she with her friend? Yeah, she with boyfriend. Dump her Glenn. She use you. Mama find you someone else."

He shook his head, abruptly holding up his hands. "Whoa, Mama. Where's this coming from?"

She reached up for his hands, bringing them down to waist level. Her voice softened. "You nice guy. I take care of you. You know she married?"

"How do you know, Mama?" *So this is the shit Maya was talking about?*

She reached behind her, grasping for something. On the counter lay her lighter and cigs, next to two empty seats. "She know too much about football for bargirl. Must be someone she learn from."

He took two steps to the bar and slid onto one seat, signaling Jimmy for a beer. "I thought she learned from you guys. From Jimmy?"

She took the other seat. "No honey. How come Atlanta her team? All the other girls pick West Coast teams."

Jimmy brought his beer, cognac for Mama.

He tossed two Jacksons to Jimmy for Mama's drink. "I don't know, Mama. One video I saw on Instagram had the Georgia flag in the garage. I think her cousin . . . husband . . . from Georgia. Maybe she learned from him." *Maya wants me to report all this back to her?*

Lynh's eyes squinted. "Cousin . . . husband. You think cousin is husband?"

Glenn shrugged, raising his palms. "I don't know, Mama. What do you think?"

She flinched, sneering a bit. Her voice oozed exasperation. "She married, honey. Waiting for divorce. Get half pension." She leaned back, smirking as if to say you're a jackass for not knowing. But Glenn had heard about this. Brad had said it.

> *Bargirl from overseas marries a service guy,*
> *wait ten years, then get divorced. The prize?*
> *Half the guy's pension for life. Most guys*

*don't see it coming. Maybe it happens to
their friend, but never them, because they
found the right one.*

Glenn cracked his knuckles and waved Jimmy over. "Hey Jimmy, got a few minutes?" A question was on his mind since before she left. "Lynh said Maya is sweet on some guy. True? Not true?"

Jimmy sized it up, while also thinking about the green BMW. He knew Glenn was in love with Maya, but Maya was no good. For the guy he considered the bar's free lawyer and a friend, Jimmy couldn't hold back. "Yes, Glenn, she has boyfriend. The construction group, he not even the rich one. Just eye candy. She always take care of him. Take money from bosses. They all go Vegas. Super Bowl."

Glenn's mouth tightened. Jimmy didn't like causing strife, but now he was all in. "She no good, Glenn, I find you someone else."

Glenn clenched his fists hard and then pounded the counter. Tia could hear the dull thuds ten feet away. Glenn felt that familiar wrenching in his heart. He couldn't breathe. The last thing he remembered was asking Jimmy for a triple-pour Black Label—twice.

He woke up early the next morning. Adrenaline masked his raging hangover.

I went bar last night. Talked to Lynh and Jimmy. We need to talk. What I heard broke my heart and I'm trying hard not to believe.

She was waiting.

You see Mama? Yes. What she say?

I want to talk about this guy. Hear it from her. See her face when we do.

Not over social media. Bad karma. Can we meet?

No cannot. Gotta work. Tell me.

No, bad karma. What about after work?

No. why you not tell me?

I told you bad karma. Not good to talk like this on social media.

You know me. Mama talk shit about me. Why you believe her?

I didn't say I believed her. I just don't want to talk about it on social media.

I don't think I can be friends on Instagram with someone not tell me what Mama said.

What, she's threatening me now?

If you don't believe me no need sit with me.

I didn't say I didn't believe you. Just want to talk face to face.

No need already. I have to go work. Why you don't believe me? You know me!

Yeah, I know you. I know you lie.

Just meet me. We'll talk.

No I go work now. bye.

Why won't she meet with me? He started typing . . .

Why you don't let me go? What do
you want now?

When are you coming back to the bar?

I'm not. I told Mama already I quit.

So no more bar?

No

No more Tuesdays?

I guess. No more bar so no more
Tuesdays.

Ok

If you don't believe me, no need to sit
with me.

Are we done?

I told you. no more bar. I don't work
there no more.

Okay. Thank you for everything. I'm going to shut down Instagram tonight

???? Why? Why you do that? If you believe me why you do that?

If I can't see u no more, I can't handle seeing you on IG. It hurts too much.

I don't think I want to be friends with you on IG

I understand. Thank you for everything.

Me too. I appreciate you all you do for me.

She sent a picture of her wearing the Falcons hat he'd given her a while back, the one with the quarterback's autograph signature. It said it all—*nice to meet you, thank you, I still care for you, take care . . .*

He worked all day, then went home. His account was still active. She was active and hadn't cut him off yet. He sent a DM.

Just wanted to send one last time. Home safe. Thank you for everything. Will miss you.

He saw "seen" under his message. She saw what he'd written. He waited ten minutes. No reply. He deleted his account. That was that. It was over. In forty-eight hours, twenty-three Tuesdays evaporated into memory.

PART TWO

34

INSTAGONE

She sat on her bed, staring at the message on her phone.

> *Just wanted to send one last time.*
> *Home safe. Thank you for everything.*
> *Will miss you.*

Ten minutes had already passed. *Why is this so difficult? Why does he not believe me?*

She had his letters in front of her. She read them over and over and over the last three hours. *He was so genuine. I was so happy. Mama caused me shit. Why does he not back me up? They always side with the Mama.*

She traced his name with her finger. *We should talk. We can work things out. We work things out before. Huh??*

All trace of him disappeared. She knew. It had happened before. It's what happens when an account is deleted on Instagram. All his goodnights, his take-cares, his *I'm here for you's*, his sweet dreams. All the DMs she looked over every night were gone.

She buried her head in her pillow with a muffled wail. Rusty felt her pain and crawled into her lap. "Oh Rusty, my baby. I only have you now. Glenn good guy you know?" Rusty barked loudly at the sound of Glenn's name.

She thought back to the young guy on the Vegas trip. *Eddie. Bad boy. Handsome. When he come bar with friends, I always give him special attention. Being with him make me feel special. Like those boys never look at me in high school. Nice car. BMW. Always burning rubber. Exciting.*

But then she squeezed her eyes shut tight. *But he so insecure. Macho outside and nothing inside. Still easy on the eyes. And better sit with him than the other old or fat guys from the construction company.*

She sighed. *Eddie. Playboy. Only go after bargirls because he have money. He low level worker but gambling make him rich. He only marry bargirl down the street because she wanted green card. Tia say girl parents rich from Korea and buy house for them. Always telling me his problems. His wife this. His wife that. Can't wait to get divorced.*

She lifted the last letter Glenn wrote to her heart. *Eddie just a boy. Glenn, a little boy inside, but all man outside. Sincere. Always listen to me. Always there for me. Till now.*

Her tears hadn't soaked her pillow since the night her little boy left her. Rusty kissed her face, lapping at her salty tears. She buried her face in his neck and hugged. Wailing. Heaving. Sobbing.

Just then a buzz on her phone. *Maybe Instagram. He find me and ask to follow again?*
It was a text from Lynh.

She took a deep breath. *Better wash up. Mommy need money. Sister need money. Rusty need money. Construction company bring in lots of money. Time go to work. Showtime.*

Showtime. Since her teens, she said this each time she needed to do something she did not want to do, everything she had to do to earn money for her family.

She stopped, reached down to her phone, and deleted her Instagram account. She didn't want anything to do with Instagram ever again.

———————————

Across town, Glenn had second thoughts. *This is stupid. We can work it out. We've been through rough patches before. I gotta get back to her. I'll let her know. Reach out when she's ready.*

He created another account and typed her name in the search function. *She doesn't have to accept my follow request. I can still message her.*

Huh? He typed her name in again. She was gone. He felt something squeeze his heart so hard he couldn't breathe.

He did it again. He pushed, and they left. They left him, alone, again.

35

CATASTROPHIC CRISIS

The condo was trashed two days later, much like the summer before, with empty beer bottles and pizza boxes strewn across his glass-topped coffee table. During that time, the curtains hadn't been opened, and the air was dank and musky.

He called in sick at the non-profit for two days, drinking several bottles of whiskey, including the bottle of Johnny Walker Blue that Lynh had given him for Christmas. It was Thursday, two days since he and Maya spoke, and the day before Valentine's Day. He lay on the couch, forearm shielding his eyes from whatever sunlight crept into the condo. *I hadn't even thought of what I was going to do for her. Guess I don't have to worry about that anymore. Hope whoever this guy is, she and he have a great life.*

He tried to sit up but collapsed back onto the couch. *Wasn't thinking straight. I'll go tonight. She'll see me. See I'm hurting. Tell whoever she's with to come back tomorrow. Like the last time. We can get through this.*

His couch collapse triggered massive waves of nausea. He ran to the bathroom and had his head in the toilet for an hour. Afterwards, he dragged himself into the shower. He spent the day fading in and out on the couch. Daylight turned to dark. He woke. He warmed up a burrito and had a Diet Coke. Feeling better, he stepped into the evening. It was 8:00 p.m. She was going to be there at 8:30, and he wanted to be waiting.

Verna was waiting. "Glenn, you see Maya tonight?" It wasn't a question. It was more like a directive.

He peeked into the darts room, where Maya sometimes waited. "Yes Verna. She here? How was business last night?" What he really meant was who was she with?

Verna's head shook with disappointment. "She not come last night. Mama piss off. Large group come. No Maya. They like Maya. Chloe come and Tia and Mei had to cover. No barbacks. Mama and Jimmy had to work bar."

He blinked hard. "She coming tonight?" He tried to sound casual. He looked and sounded far from casual. Almost frantic.

Verna pulled out an Egg McMuffin from her oversized purse. "Here Glenn. You hungry?" She knew he always came hungry. Pointed to the booth room. "You sit Glenn. I bring beer for you."

He nodded a quick no, wanting to be clear-headed.

She made a gesture with both hands as to say, sit down. "Yes Glenn, only one. No more. No drunk tonight."

That, he agreed with. *Never could say no to Verna.* He saw pain etched into her face. *She miss Maya too?* Verna was remembering someone she'd once had in her life. For a split second, she wondered where he was. Then she thought of Maya, not wanting her to be old and lonely.

Lynh dropped in. "Glenn what you do to my girl? She not come last night. Group leave early. I lose money, plenty money. What you do? What you say?" She wasn't letting him answer. She didn't care about rules. She lit up a cigarette and blew smoke at him. "You say shit about me? She send me text this morning. She say you talk and then she mad at me. What you say?"

His face tightened with anger. "Mama, I didn't say anything."

She pointed the firestick at him. "Bullshit, Glenn. You owe me all money I lose she not here."

He was past anger. Rage, the quiet kind, was setting in. "Lynh, respectfully, fuck you. You want me out now, I'll leave." Verna's head snapped toward Lynh. She rapped out something in Vietnamese. Lynh let out what sounded like a bear growling in disgust. She left in a huff, waving her arms and yelling Vietnamese obscenities to no one in particular.

Verna never spoke more than three sentences. It was always making sure Maya and Glenn had drinks, had snacks and had songs. That was the priority. It didn't matter who was waiting. Her children were grown and long-gone out of the house. She looked forward to Tuesdays because it felt right with those two. And they always asked her to join them. She did, but always for just a while. She knew to leave them to their own time together.

Verna sat with Glenn, across him like she always did. This time she spoke more than three sentences. "Maya good girl Glenn. She like you. You like her. Try again. She young. She learn. You like her, you be man and apologize."

His blood pressure shot up. His face contorted in protest. "What? Verna, me apologize?! What did *I* do?"

She folded her arms, looking intently at him like she used to talk to her son. "No matter what you do. Say sorry. Make her feel special. Forget.

Move on." Glenn would later learn that this was the Thai way of keeping peace in relationships, of allowing others to save face. *Sabai*, they called it. "You try, Glenn?"

It was one thing to tell Lynh to fuck off. It was another thing to deny Verna. "Okay, Verna, I'll try. She's coming, right?"

A smile burst on her face. "I call now."

Verna and Glenn sat together for three hours. Maya never came. It was midnight. He nursed the same beer all night. "G'night Verna." His heart hurt. His head was dizzy. And his limbs felt like jelly. *I wonder if this is how suicides feel the day before they off themselves.*

He heard the voice of truth inside his head. *I am with you always.* The pain lessened a bit.

Slowly shaking her head, Verna wore an expression that declared her heart a pain zone. "Glenn, you come next Tuesday. Yes?" She was almost pleading.

His lips quivered. "I'll try, Verna."

Tears pooled in her eyes. "No, you come. Okay?" Her voice trembled.

He turned, avoiding her eyes. "I'll try, Verna." He left before she could say anything more.

Glenn returned the next Tuesday. He made a beeline to their booth, where Verna joined him. "Hi, Verna."

She sat across him, arms folded. "Glenn, she not come."

He rubbed his chin, slowly, not understanding what Verna was trying to say. "What do you mean? Not come tonight?"

Her face twisted in frustration. She was having a hard time translating what she wanted to say. "Not come last week. Not come this week. Call her. Leave message. She call say she come but she not come. Lynh text her tell her no come. Then call her tell her come."

Glenn tried to play it cool. He'd been hoping this was Tuesday, and she'd have a change of heart. She always did. "Verna, can I get a scotch and beer back?" A heavy fog descended around his heart. "Verna, same thing and a shot of Crown?"

Verna brought what he wanted. She laid her hand on his shoulder and went to work behind the bar. He sat alone for two hours. After the first scotch, Verna brought him a beer every fifteen minutes, just to be sure he was okay. Sometimes she sat with him; most times she had to run back and help Jimmy.

He didn't drink the Crown, choosing to gaze at it. He sang too, songs like "Everytime," "Tattoo," "Impossible," "Need You Now." All of Maya's favorite karaoke songs. The whole bar felt it. This guy was hurting.

Jimmy brought Nicole over. "Here, you sit Glenn. Make him happy."

Eyes withdrawn; he managed a weak smile. "Hi, Nicole." She smiled. Hispanic, Chinese and Hawaiian. An exotic blend. A popular auto show model. She was fine company, but she was not Maya.

Nicole's regular came in thirty minutes later. Glenn knew Denny from other nights. Denny always flirted with Nicole, throwing out one marriage proposal after another. Nicole once called Denny's bluff and told Denny she would be his. Glenn cracked a grin remembering Denny's panicked face, explaining to Glenn on the side that he was married.

Nicole was worried about leaving Glenn. "Glenn, you going to be okay?" All the other girls were with others.

"No, cool, Nicole. Go, I see Denny's waiting." Even Denny was cool about it. The bar was a small community. Denny had heard and gave Nicole hand signals to stay with Glenn.

Glenn peered out of the booth and gave Denny a salute. "Nah, Nicole, he waited long enough. I'm good." She squeezed his hand and was off.

The Crown had not been touched. The room was spinning. Jimmy came over. "You want another girl, Glenn?"

Glenn's shoulders slumped; eyes sagged. "Nah, Jimmy." *Shit, like a two-ton yoke on my back. Wonder what she's doing? On our night?*

Jimmy asked the question the whole bar was asking. "You come back?"

Glenn took a good look around. "Maybe." *This is it. I can't come back here. I love everyone like family but it's too painful. I gotta find another place.* "Hey Jimmy, you take care." He left Verna his number in case Maya needed it and stumbled out of the bar.

Verna's heart was breaking. She went back to the booth and downed the Crown that was leftover. She looked at her phone. She had texted Maya six times and left three messages. She shook her head.

That girl.

36

MARCH TAILSPIN

In his janitor's closet of an office, filled with the smell of the homeless circulated by a broken-down air system, he was rushing to finalize a ninety-page report to the feds to justify a $25,000 grant. It was the fourth deadline in the last ten days. *Why does Joyce do forty small grants a year, instead of ten large ones? Each of these small grants takes just as much work as the big ones.*

He slammed his mouse down. *Why? Because she doesn't want to be political. Didn't want me to use my contacts. Didn't want me to be the star. So me, Danielle, and Penny, we're working sixty hours a week on accounting and putting together these stupid expenditure reports. So she looks good to the board?*

He leaned back in a donated chair he'd stolen from the warehouse. Just as he was about to doze off, his phone buzzed, startling him out of the chair. A Google reminder. She was going to be in Thailand for the whole month, helping with her sister's engagement.

It was the first Tuesday in March. It had been a month since the breakup, as he called it. It had been two weeks since he last was at the bar. Verna left a couple of messages. Always starting with, "She not come." The last text said Maya had only been to the bar one Friday out of the entire month. And only an hour to see a long-time customer.

She must be with that young guy. Maybe he's rich. She doesn't have to work anymore. Maybe he's going to Thailand with her. Who cares? I do. I care. Pain welled up again.

Glenn had his demons. His imagination was going wild. His mind was blistered with images of her with the young construction worker, flirting, holding his hand under the table, putting off advances, letting him touch her thighs, singing for him, his arm around her, breathing on her neck while he complained about his shitty life, and tons of money on the table put there by some rich fat guy.

It affected his work. His staff, by now keen to his outgoing and warm-hearted personality, covered for him on bad days like this.

He leaned back in his chair again. *How did I get here? Dead end job? There must be more. I wish she was back. When I was with her, I felt like I could fly to the moon. Like I could do anything. Like Katie made me feel. I still hear her telling me I can do it. Do what makes me happy. Do what's right. Don't think about what others think. That's why I committed to the next mayor's race. The Admiral asked. She convinced. Can I do it without her?*

Three hard knocks at his door. He straightened up. His email program flashed. From Danielle. Subject line: JOYCE OUTSIDE.

His boss yelled through the door. "Glenn, you better not be sleeping. I'm coming in!" She was ten years younger but acted like she was thirty years his senior. No real experience in leading organizations, she was a walking book of quotes from the entire business book section of Barnes & Noble. Portly. Not attractive. He never looked directly at her.

He was almost sneering. "And what can I do for you today, Joyce?"

She sneered right back. "This is the fourth month in a row that the financial statements weren't prepped on time for the board meeting. No more. It has to be done on time next month. Failure is not an option. We have to maximize efficiency, problem-solve obstacles, and course correct to deliver promised results."

He gave her the Vulcan sign. "And resistance is futile, but we shall live long and prosper." In his mind, he slowly rotated his hand into the bird. "Hey Joyce, I told you this department is so understaffed that the financials will be late till we can add staff." His stress level was rising. In his mind, he was with Maya. *I really need you. I wish you were here to make this go away. If only I knew you were right around the corner, I can get through this.*

Hands on her hips, the stout woman in front of him was in executive lecture mode. "Glenn, your predecessor had no problem. What's your problem?"

His sneer morphed into a snarl. "Excuse me, I had two predecessors. A CFO and an accounting manager. I'm doing the job of both. I'm doing the job of the accounting manager, the one that left because she was so stressed, she was working seventy hours a week!" He was feeling stressed and wanted to be with the one person that could take that stress away. *Where are you when I need you, Maya?*

Joyce's face was blank. "Well, Glenn, that's what you gotta do."

Blood shot to his head, his face flushed and the vein in his forehead popped. "Bullshit, Joyce." He thought she was green as a CEO, but this was stupid to him. "You know that at seventy hours a week, I'm earning just over minimum wage. I can get ten times that. In fact, everyone around here is exploited." *Come back to the bar, Maya. Come back to me.*

"Exploited!" The young CEO pushed back, her own vein popping. "Glenn, you knew this was the situation when you came on board . . ."

He cut her off. "Bullshit, you said I'd be leaving at 4:30 every day. The only reason I took a fifty percent cut from what I was getting at the city was that I had a contract to run a political campaign, which I could fulfill every evening, but not if I worked seventy hours a week."

He started his history lesson before she could cut in. "Do you remember? This wasn't supposed to be an accounting job. You wanted a bona fide CFO!" *I was supposed to take the nonprofit to a higher level. She knows this. She said she needed me to leverage the land the non-profit owned to build a high-rise affordable housing and office project.*

He stood up and leaned forward on his desk. "Do you remember at the interview I laid out a vision to redevelop this entire block because of the rail transit coming through? And do you remember my proposing a forty-story affordable housing complex with the first three floors housing our offices?" He let it sink in. "You know what I remember? I remember you telling the board it was your idea, and you were glad that I embraced *your* idea." *That was so much bullshit, but I let her get away with it. We used to be friends. Not anymore.*

She glared at him, at a loss for words. He glared back with sullen, dead, angry eyes. "You said I didn't have to worry about the accounting. I told you I hated accounting. You said don't worry. That Samantha would take care of it. But Samantha quit! No wonder! You guys had her working sixty hours a week." He clutched his stomach. *Why does it hurt so much? Each day I'm counting beans. And with each bean, a little bit of my inside dies. Only Tuesdays kept me going from week to week. And now it's gone.*

Impasse was the best way to describe it as the CEO left, slamming his door in the process.

He stared at his closed door. *Dammit, I believe in this agency and what it does, could do, for the homeless.*

He stood silent. His fists opening and closing, jaw clenched, and his back tight. He had a buzzing in his ears. *Am I having a stroke? I might as well. I'm letting Joyce and the agency down. And it looks like failure for the Admiral is imminent. I gotta get the new guy elected so things can be fixed at City Hall. It's my fault. I got the current guy elected. I gotta help put someone in there to fix it all. And I'll be damned if Clifford will get another chance to pillage the city coffers.*

It was too heavy a yoke. He crashed that night, just like the summer before. He lost Katie. He crashed. He met Maya. He recovered. He lost Maya. He crashed.

He spent the rest of the month and much of the next month visiting all the bars again, though he purposely avoided Lynh's bar. He kept himself constantly medicated with booze. There were many girls this time, and he didn't care. Candy, Ivanka, Tricia, Penny, Min, Laney, Cherish, Cherry and some other girls whose names he never bothered to learn. Some nights, he had two or three at a time. His investment portfolio took a huge hit.

Every afternoon he walked the mall or the beach. To no one in particular, he asked *Why? Why is it when you break up with someone, every girl you see looks like her? She's everywhere. Reminders keep popping up. The mall plays songs we sang. I go to the basketball game. What do they play at halftime? "Don't Stop Believin'."*

Every night started the same. He'd head off to a watering hole. There he spent a good long time staring at the picture she sent. The one that said it all—*thank you, take care, wish you the best*. Somehow, he thought she still felt something for him. *Wishful thinking*, he admitted.

Then the demon construction worker returned. Taunting him. Teasing him. Making him feel worthless, like grade school again. After a couple of whiskies, he saw Maya in his head, turning on him like the girls he'd known as a teen. *Sorry Glenn, you're not invited to the party. Sorry Glenn, I don't think my parents would approve. Sorry Glenn, you're just . . . Not. Good. Enough.*

Around the middle of March, he had an entire bottle of whiskey at a bar next to Lynh's bar. He stumbled into Lynh's bar just as they were closing. Jimmy saw his eyes and knew Glenn was ripped, not knowing where he was.

Chloe was on her way out. "Jimmy, you want I take care of him? Brudder, you okay?"

Lynh shooed Chloe off and took Glenn by his arm. Verna was right behind. Glenn put four large bills on the counter. "Can I have some water?" Lynh told Jimmy to put together some pho. They'd need to get him a little more sober before putting him in a taxi. Lynh took the bills and tucked them into her pocket.

Most expensive pho ever, Verna thought, scowling at her old friend.

Chloe stood outside of the doorway, watching. Lynh came over and said, "Good night honey, see you tomorrow," then closed the door.

Glenn woke up the next morning and checked his pockets. There were four ATM receipts for $500 each. His CPA was not going to like this. Over the next month, he went on an $18,000 rampage.

One night, he cried himself to sleep and, in his dream, saw his mother. *Help me, Mama, please. Hug me. I hate girls, so mean. Can you wipe my face for me?*

After a month, the endless sex just didn't provide the ego boost he craved. It was the same as before, but this time there was no Maya to stop it all.

He got pounced on at every bar. At the last one, he got drugged at 3:00 a.m. and ended up in a bad situation with three girls. Cocaine was everywhere.

One evening, he looked at himself in the mirror. *Why did I let her go? There's nobody like her. I don't even know what I'm looking for.* He looked upwards. *Help me. This has to stop. I gotta go back home.*

Hands in his pockets, he slowly, tentatively, shuffled into the only place he felt safe.

37

UNMET NEEDS

Tia's eyes widened as she spied him walking in. "Hi Tia, is she back yet?"

The bar still looked the same to him. The dart room had a mix of sales types and construction workers mingling with three new girls Glenn hadn't seen before. NCAA March Madness basketball was in full swing on the flatscreens, with the barflies doing side bets. Only Nicole and her longtime customer occupied the booth room. Two more customers waited for her at the bar.

Tia set down the Saint Patrick's Day flyers and decorations she was hanging up and turned her attention to Glenn. "No love. Maya's not back yet. You know she's in Thailand, right? I heard she's back next week. Not sure when she's coming back here though."

Tia was on high alert, hoping Glenn would go get smashed elsewhere. It was a close-knit industry, and it was known up and down the bars that this high roller was making the rounds. All the girls knew who he was, and all knew he was on the prowl. Maya no longer had her stamp on him.

He rubbed his eyes. Lips pursed. He stepped forward. "Okay. Need to chill somewhere, Tia. Tired of getting in trouble."

She saw him under the light. *Good grief, he looks so tired. Not upbeat. Even his slouch looks unhealthy.*

She got closer. *He's stopped working out, and (sniff) he smells like the barflies that come in here every night.* "Sit, love. I got you." Tia put her phone away. No texting tonight. She strode over to the end of the bar and whispered to the man sitting there.

Glenn pulled out his phone and sat staring at his pictures of Maya. *Why am I so into her?*

A big bulky figure sat down next to him with some effort and a grunt that announced his presence. "Hey Glenn, how ya doing." It was Crazy

Tom, chief barfly and crazy man.

Glenn's gaze was fixed on the screen in front of him. State led by 14. "Hey Tom." He looked up for help. *Where'd Tia go? Oh, with Paul, her regular. Guess I'm stuck with Tom.*

Tom's eyes fixed on the side of Glenn's head, ready to lock in eye contact. "What's ailing you, my fine friend?"

Glenn squinted. *Who talks like this? I've sunk this low. I'm doing bro-talk with a crazy guy who looks like Wilson from* Home Improvement. *Okay, I'll bite. If it gets annoying, I'll leave.*

His head turned halfway. "Well you know Maya, right?"

Tom swept the room with a wave of his hand, like some medieval troubadour. "Indeed, your fair maiden, the Princess Maya—she who sings like the nightingale."

Tia came over to check on them. Glenn held up two fingers then pointed one finger to Tom. "Yeah . . . um . . . right. So, I don't know why I'm so into her."

Tom exaggerated a doubletake. "What do you mean? Look at her. What guy wouldn't be into her?"

Tia delivered their drinks. Both their eyes lingered over her as she went back to Paul. Glenn took a long swallow. "Yeah, but there's lots of pretty ones out there you know, and I've been looking. Why am I not satisfied with them?"

Tom held up his shot glass to Glenn in thanks. "Well, Glenn, for sure it's not sex. Heard you're the high roller getting all kinds of poon up and down the street?" Glenn didn't answer. "And you pick the one girl here that has a bona fide iron chastity belt. Yeah, so what does she do for you?"

Rubbing his temples, Glenn asked, "Wasn't that my question for you?"

Tom leaned on the bar sideways, drink in his hand. "Humor me. What does she do for you?"

Glenn went through a mental rolodex of all their nights together. "We sing, drink, whatever."

Tom leaned forward toward Glenn, closing the personal space between them. "Yeah, but lots of girls out there do that too."

Glenn's eyes went dead. He was off his stool, looking for Tia to close the tab. "Um, okay, yeah, Tom. Thanks for the talk." *This guy is batshit crazy. I'm done here.*

Tom hauled himself off his stool and made ready to grab at Glenn. "Hold on now, Glenn. I'm not done."

Tia was off to the side, watching with interest. *Guess Glenn's about to find how I knew so much about unmet needs.* She admired Crazy Tom, a.k.a.

Dr. Tom Emerson, former eminent state psychiatrist, practicing until he went to Iraq with the reserves and suffered trauma himself.

Tom cleared his throat. "You ever heard of unmet needs?"

Glenn recoiled slightly but sat back down. *Sounds like the stuff Tia told me about. Maya's unmet needs—the adoration of men. How does this guy know?* He played dumb. "Yeah, needs that are not met?"

Tom caught Glenn's sarcasm. Eyes narrowed, he glanced at Tia. She waved him on as if to say keep going. He turned his head, muttering, "Must be a lawyer" under his breath. He put on a smile. "Okay. There are different kinds, and they affect how you live. Grow up without money, and you're ambitious for money in the future." Glenn agreed with that. Being poor drove him toward success. He knew that. "For most of the customers here, it's something else. They get an ego boost from being with the girls here. These girls meet some unmet need. Usually, by how they look. Maya look like anyone from your past?"

Glenn held up his hand. He'd had his share of head shrinking in his life. "Wait, I thought we were going to talk about Maya's unmet needs?"

Tom's eye contact and tone were firm. "Your question was why *you* were into *her*, not the other way around. I think we all know around here that she has an uncontrollable obsession with men. Again, Maya look like anyone from your past?" Tom then let the silent pause work its magic.

Glenn peeled the label off his beer. *This is such a weird conversation. This crazy man makes sense, but Maya doesn't look like anyone I knew. She's exotic looking—wait, her smoky eyes and pouty lips, her drinking and partying—a lot like Darlene. She cheated on her boyfriend with me and used me to get her boyfriend jealous.*

Glenn thought further. *Gina's brown skin and pouty lips are like Maya's, but her personality was the ringer—her erratic off-again, on-again behavior was spot on.*

And then his eyes widened as understanding seeped into his brain. *And Lila! I had such a connection with her. We were supposed to get married. In the end she was so fake and everything she said and did was lies, deception and manipulation. But she did have great lips for kissing.*

He mentally compared the three. *Yeah, they all ground me into the dirt. So disappointed. They killed me. All of them—just wasn't in their league.*

Tom was watching. He could hear the gears turning in Glenn's head.

Glenn turned to Tom. "You know there are these three girls, put them together and it's Maya, I think." *Maybe this guy knows what he's talking about.*

Tom almost had him. "And do you feel you had unfinished business with these three?"

Glenn half frowned, his brow furrowed. "Sort of. I don't think I got a fair chance with them."

Tom held up two fingers for Tia, then pointed to himself and Glenn. "Go on."

Cocking his head to one side, Glenn looked upward at nothing in particular. "Actually, I think I never had a chance. Just out of my league."

Tom tented his hands in front of him and leaned back. "You're a lawyer, Glenn. Given the evidence, what do you conclude?" Again, he let the silence do its work.

Glenn raked both hands through his hair, tugging at the ends. *Maya had her demons. She wanted validation with men she couldn't have. Is it the same with me?* "So, combined, they're an unmet need that Maya fills?"

Tom smiled genuinely for the first time that night. "Not combined, Glenn. Your negative experience with each of those girls, and any other negative experience, is an unmet need. Just so happens that it looks like Maya is filling all of them one by one."

Tom looked at Glenn's eyes. *He's getting it. But this guy's on dangerous ground. All his needs filled by one person. That is a powerful emotional attachment, like being hooked on meth, alcohol and sex, and getting all three from one source. There's nothing the addict wouldn't do for that source.* Tom nodded at Tia, as if to say we're done here.

Tia sauntered over. "Refill, guys?" *Gosh, he looks so much better.*

Tom lifted his empty glass.

Glenn shook his head no. "I'm good, Tia. Think I'm heading home. Go for a run. Take a shower. Find my head and screw it back on." He pointed to Tom. "His night is on me. You have my card, right?" Tom wasn't arguing and nodded his thanks. Tia came around the bar and gave Glenn a hug and a cheek peck. "Come back soon, Glenn. Our Glenn okay?" He smiled and turned to Tom. "I don't know who you are, but you can be on my team anytime." Tom saluted with his whiskey glass. "Anytime Glenn, anytime. You know where to find me."

Coming out of the shower after a one-hour run was different from staggering home after a night of booze and sex. He parked himself on the couch, Jimmy Fallon's monologue in the background, nursing green tea on ice.

Unmet needs. My unmet needs. Women that I never had a chance with. I guess so. But I dated them. Even bedded them. Always the same end. Did they leave on their own, or did I push them away? But why Katie? She filled all my needs. Not a beauty queen. But she made me feel like I was the only one in her world. And that made me feel special.

Leaning back on the couch, he spoke. "Father, I could use some guidance here. And yes, thanks for sending Crazy Tom my way."

He turned off Fallon. Needed quiet time. *It's not only looks. It's how she makes me feel. Gotta think. Loved, secure, special. Lila made me feel like that too. Loved, secure, special.*

He grabbed his head. *Something's happening. Feel like blacking out.* He blinked rapidly, a buzzing sound in his head, his heart aching, and he squeezed his eyes shut till he finally blurted out loud, "I miss my mommy."

Crap, I miss my mommy? She's a mommy figure? Does this make sense? She's twenty years younger than me. I'd understand a daughter fetish, ewww, but a mommy figure? She's a mommy to me? How could I miss it? Is that why I never made a play for her?

He paced the length of the room. *What is it that I always want from her? I want her to hold my hand. I want her to tell me everything's okay. I want her to tell me she's proud of me. I hear her telling me I can do things if I want. I want goodnight kisses. Not French kisses, just lip kisses, like . . . the kind Billy's mom used to give him. That's it! I want her to be Billy's mom! I want her to be my mommy! Ohhhh shit! I have mommy issues. All those jokes by Brad and Anna. This can't be!*

Something popped in the back of his mind. Years before, a CEO he worked for had sighed the same way his father did in childhood. The CEO was an insecure self-made failure like his dad. Condescending. Ridiculing. The CEO had two senior vice-presidents reporting to him. He had gone through seventeen senior VPs in five years. Glenn was the latest senior VP hire. Something in Glenn snapped. He was sent to therapy.

He dug up an old psych report done on him. At the time, the focus was on issues related to rejection/approval by an authority. He seemed to remember something about his mother.

He found the report:

> *From the history with his mother, patient exhibits*
> *symptoms commonly found in those that had a*
> *non-nurturing environment as child, and as result,*
> *is constantly seeking motherly affection. This has led*
> *to his behavior of seeking the attention of women*
> *in various forms. While currently satisfied with his*
> *marriage, he has a history of not trusting women in*

*his relationships and admits to possibly torpedoing
several preemptively to avoid potential rejection/
abandonment.*

He beheld the words like they were ancient scripture.

constantly seeking motherly affection.

He was starting to understand. Mommy issues. He thought of Katie. He thought of the last time Maya kissed him, ruffled his hair. The little boy in him responded.

His need for beautiful women to pay attention to him, and his need for motherly affection, led to a loss of emotional control in stressful times—in other words, tailspin.

He tapped his head with the remote control. *Shit, this gets me no closer to Maya. Maybe I need to advertise on Craigslist. Grown man willing to pay for beautiful woman to party with, but also act like his mother. Extreme patience a must. This is gross. Like some sick porn flick plot.*

He tossed the remote. *I'm a loser like all the other guys in the bar. I need to call Uncle Howard.*

38

MOMMY DEAREST

Howard Forrester leaned back in his easy chair. He hadn't seen his nephew in years, not since that episode with the CEO.

They were sitting in his den, which doubled as a home office. Its four pastel blue walls enclosed a large physician's desk, a wall unit with four shelves of medical books, an easy chair, a couch and a coffee table. A coffee maker, minus the coffee, provided the hot water for afternoon tea.

Howard leaned forward, chuckling. "You're not a loser. And let's not get judgmental. Neither are your colleagues."

Glenn laughed along, though he didn't quite see what was so funny. *Did my uncle, the eminent psychologist, the guy who got me through my childhood and my nervous breakdown ten years ago, just defend the other lecherous losers in the bar? Colleagues? Wonder if he's ever been in one of these places? Still glad he and Aunty Lani watched over me after Mommy— well, after Mommy was gone.*

Howard poured tea from what looked like an antique teapot into two cups, equally antique. They'd done this since Glenn was a kid. Anytime Glenn had problems, it was teatime in the den. "Hey kiddo, it's quite common among men to have mommy issues."

The easy chair absorbed him as Howard leaned back to take his tea. "I was wondering when this was going to manifest. Most of your life has been dominated by your daddy issues—the need for approval. It drove your ambition. Not to mention how cash poor you grew up. It's the same for a lot of people. You had unmet needs—authoritarian approval and financial security—and this served you well."

Howard leaned forward, placing his empty cup on the table. "Served you well, except when you took on unhealthy risks and endeavors to meet these needs. Remember, you were going to stick it out with the CEO even though it was making you sick?"

Glenn suddenly felt queasy and a head rush. "Yeah, and I remember like a good third base coach, you got me out of that bind. Since then I've been able to watch myself."

Elbows on his knees, hands steepled, almost in prayer, Howard got to work. "Right, on the approval issues. And for now, let's leave the other female rejection issues aside. It looks like Crazy Tom got that right. Now you need to be aware of your mommy issues."

Glenn poured tea for both. Gave a look like, I'm ready.

Howard continued. "This is a little different. You're not ever going to have a mother again, Glenn. That has passed. You can receive affection but need to understand the limitations that come with having a mother no longer with you. If it's the affection you crave, that is possible, though not healthy. But if you crave your mom, then it's not possible and needs to be managed."

Howard sipped his tea. "Recognizing you have unmet needs is the start and the key. If you get frustrated or angry and feel any other negative emotion, it can usually be traced back to an unmet need and managed. Anytime these emotions arise, do a gut check."

Glenn looked around his uncle's office-slash-den. Nothing on the walls. Nothing but books on the shelves. *So private. Where are all the awards and diplomas that Aunty always talked about?* "So what about the other grab-ass guys in the bar? Is ass an unmet need? I can't believe they turned out that way because they didn't have ass grabbing as a child."

Howard smiled, and shook his head. *My nephew the snark.* "No, but they did lack other validation or esteem-building opportunities. Their ass-grabbing is an ego boost measure. That is, female allows touching, therefore male feels desirable or special. Of course, there are other ways of feeling special. But that is a whole other learning process."

Howard got up, came around, and sat next to Glenn on the office couch. Glenn scooched over to give him room. Every sense came alive. *Uh oh. Here comes the teaching moment. The bonding moment. Every time he does this, my life changes. Thank God for him.*

Howard sat down and filled their cups with the last of the tea. "Look Glenn, just remember part of mommy issues is that there is a mother figure showing affection and making you feel special. In this case, you found a person that fulfills two unmet needs. One to take the place of the disappointments you've had with women. Not just those three, but all that you experienced rejection with. And two, to take the place of all things you craved from a mother growing up. Like the things you like from your mom that stopped abruptly, and the things you witness other kids get growing up, like your friend Billy. Remember how you used to cry to me about Billy?"

Glenn drained his tea. "Got it, Uncle Howard." *Maya is my mother substitute.*

———————————

Later that day, Glenn sat poolside after working out. He saw a little boy hug his mother and felt emotions—frustration, bitterness and anger.

He heard his uncle's voice. *Anytime these emotions arise, do a gut check.*

Not taking his eyes from the boy and his mother, he did the check. *I get it. I'm jealous. I want that. Got it. Doesn't take away the desire, but at least I know what's causing it. This is why I'm so frustrated when other guys are in the picture. Geez, seeing her interact with so many on Instagram is killer.*

He saw the little boy climb into his mother's lap, looking serene and safe. *I'm a little boy inside, wanting to crawl onto a lap that's gone, poof, nonexistent. Maya my pseudo mother gave me back that lap, the serenity and safety. If she even hints of another customer or even hearts someone on Instagram, the brain kicks in and says it is another man about to take Mommy away. The threat is real to the little boy in me. The threats are real to me.*

He exhaled and managed a smile and happiness for the little boy by the pool. *There's so much crap to sort out and deal with. But at least I know how to deal with it. Too bad Maya and I are over.*

He rubbed the back of his neck. *Maybe I'll have Uncle Howard screen the next mommy figure I come across.*

39

APRIL RECKONING

A month after seeing his uncle, Glenn pulled into the non-profit's parking lot at his usual 7:45 a.m., aware that Joyce was at her office window watching for tardy employees who'd be docked their first hour's pay.

He walked in past all the homeless sitting in the lobby, waiting to see their caseworkers or health specialists. Unlocking the door to his office, he heard Danielle behind him cheerfully say, "Good morning, boss!" This always started his day right. But not for long.

After that, it was another typical morning battling Joyce over underfunded staff, unreasonable deadlines, and consolidating collections into his area. *So they cut two collections staff in the operations area, tell me it's my job now, but no funding nor extra staff. What bullshit. I gotta blow off steam tonight. Haven't done shit the last two weeks. Just working out and drinking beers watching Fallon at home.*

It was also tax filing day—April 20. He pulled the 1040 out of his pocket, planning to spend the morning behind closed doors filling out the form. Right then his phone buzzed. Randall Borncamp was a real estate developer, self-proclaimed midlife bucket lister and womanizer. Glenn and Randall had become bar buddies over the past two months—self-appointed wingmen for each other, both disappearing as soon as any girl could pull them into a back room. Karaoke was always the official reason for barhopping.

Randall's voice had that familiar "blue balls I'm horny" tone to it. "Dude, I don't have the kids tonight. Let's hit the town." Silence. "Dude?"

Leaning against his desk, Glenn gazed blankly out his window, his gut spasming. "Man, I think I gotta pass. The funds are getting low and the women thing . . . getting old. I've been shirking my nightly thing, so I'm gonna get back to that."

Randall heard this before. "I know, but this is Tuesday, your off night, right?"

Glenn felt his guard slipping. He rubbed his forehead. "Bro, low funds tonight. How about singing only?"

Randall could tell there was a mood change. He welcomed it. "Man, we always say that." His blue balls normalized. "Okay, let's chill tonight. Tell you what, we'll just go to your old bar. The safe zone."

Glenn rubbed his forearm like he had an allergy. "I dunno. That girl I was telling you about. She might be there. Real awkward buzzkill." The bar was one place he didn't want to be. And all the other bars still had predators waiting for his return. *I'm not strong enough yet.*

His phone buzzed again. A text from Verna. *Why'd I give her my number?* Verna wrote, "She come back. Work Wednesdays Fridays. No Tuesdays You come tomorrow Wednesday?" It was the second to the last Tuesday of the month. *So she's not going to be there tonight?*

His heart beat faster. "Hey Randall, I'll see you there."

The night started early, and it didn't take the two too long to get sauced. They hit a couple of other places before heading to Mama Lynh's. Tia and Jimmy were behind the bar. "Hey Glenn!" both sounded off. The two guys stepped up to the bar like they were in a western saloon.

Tia cleared two spaces. "Who's your friend, love?"

Glenn pointed to Randall like he was a PowerPoint slide. "This is Randall. He is rich and he wants to sing tonight." Glenn said it loudly. A couple of the girls' heads turned slightly, resulting in frowns from their customers.

Randall shrugged it off. He liked what he saw in front of him and put on his sweetest country drawl. "Miz Tia got time to sing with us?"

Tia smiled demurely. "No love, sorry." She said it so sweetly it made you feel good to be turned down. "We're busy behind here, and Paul's on his way. And looks like you're about to get something better anyway."

Kimmie walked up and squeezed herself between the two. "Who's your handsome friend, Glenn?"

Glenn feigned humiliation and hurt. "Geez Kimmie, handsome? Him? When did you ever call me handsome?"

Kimmie reached under his chin with her index finger and flicked his head up, lightly but with a message. "Lots of times kiddo, but hard for you to hear with your female bodyguard always at your side. You know, your eyes and ears, and whatever else was always planted on one person. No worries. We thought it was cute. She's not here tonight, you know."

He smirked so hard he almost winked. "Yeah, I know." *Where's Kimmie been? Doesn't she know?*

Kimmie seized her opportunity. "Not here for her. Seriously?" She had her hands on both their shoulders. "Well, buy me a drink, let's get the microphones and get this party started." She sized up the room to see who she could peel off their customer to give them a good time.

Glenn read her mind. "I'm here solo, Kimmie. Nothing for me tonight."

She poked him in the chest. "Geez Glenn you're like . . . like a cute loyal puppy dog. Like a buff corgi on steroids. *Sooooo* loyal." She poked his pecs again. *Yum! No wonder Maya liked hugging him good night.*

Glenn wagged his finger at her. "No, not so Kimmie." *She doesn't know we split up?* He faked a yawn. "Just tired. Just wanna give Randall a happy time tonight. He got the pass, you know. Someone else watching the kids and all."

She turned to Randall. "You have kids?"

Randall stared dreamily at Kimmie. "Yeah, three. You?"

Her eyes brightened. "Just one." Suddenly the bar turned into a PTA meeting with two parents showing digital pictures of their kids.

Glenn turned to Tia and shrugged his shoulders. "I guess I'm truly solo now."

Tia chuckled and slid him a Bud Light.

Out of the corner of his eye, he saw Chloe, alone in the darts room, fixing her makeup. *Probably waiting on her next customer.* "Guys, I'll be right back." Kimmie and Randall didn't notice him leaving. Tia did, frowning. She picked up her phone to text. It was reflex. She put it back down.

Glenn called out to Tia. "Can you bring something for Chloe?" Walking into the darts room, he smiled broadly with his arms outstretched. "Hey Chloe, long time no see!"

Chloe jumped up. "Brudder!" She gave him a hug. Little longer than customary. Rubbing his back for a few seconds. "How you been?" She leaned back, arms resting on his shoulders. "You okay?"

He nodded. It was like being with family. "You?"

She sat back down, pointing to the seat across her. "Okay. Business slow." She paused, searching his face, the same thing Maya used to do. "She not here you know. She only work Wednesdays Fridays." Sitting across her, he wanted to ask why. Maybe she was with her boyfriend the other nights.

Had he asked, Chloe would have told him Maya shied away from the bar because those were his nights, and she just wasn't ready to bump into him. But he didn't ask, and Chloe didn't tell.

Tia brought a shot for Chloe and a beer for him. "I know she's not here. I'm here solo with my friend." Randall's voice came over the speakers just then, crooning out a country song. Kimmie harmonized the duet. "I heard you went to Thailand too?"

They clinked bottle to shot glass. "Cheers." She answered his question. "Yeah. Everyone go. Thai New Year. We all go home to family."

He deadpanned. "I thought the bar was family." Took a swig to hide his smirk.

She gave him a look like *you kidding?* Then smiled.

"Well, nice seeing you, Chloe."

"Nice seeing you, Glenn. Thank you for lucky shot." She took him all in. The expression on his face said sad, covered by fake casual happiness. His posture said he was empty. His longer than usual hair was unkept. And his wrinkled shirt said he no longer gave a shit about how he looked because there was no one to look good for.

He made ready to stand, and she reached out, laid her hand on his forearm. "Wait, *you* miss Maya, huh?"

He turned back into the booth. "What?" His heart beat fast, keeping pace with the electronic Latin beat pulsating from the jukebox. He said it again. "What?"

She patted his forearm. Her smile bordered on pity, with empathy at its core. "I can tell, brudder. You miss her, huh?"

He closed his eyes hard, then opened and looked straight at her. He opened his mouth, and nothing came out. Then "Y-yes."

She swallowed the lump in her throat. Parched, she sucked on an ice cube. *He* is *like a little boy. Sister was right. He gets you in your heart. When he like this, you want to hold him and make everything all right.* She fought an impulse to reach out and fix his hair.

She cleared her throat and summoned her self-control. "Then come back. Maya miss you too."

Somewhat composed, his cheeks flushed a bit, "Then she should call me. I left my number here."

Chloe crossed her arms and set her jaw. "She not call you, brudder. I know her. She my sister. You call her. Then apologize."

His cheeks flushed fully. "*What*, me apologize? Why! I didn't do anything." *Why does everyone want me to apologize?* A familiar song came on. *Great . . . who's playing that Richard Marx song. Am I going to wait right here for her?*

She got up. "Stay here." It wasn't a request. She was back before he could decide to leave.

She slid a beer to him. "You need this." Then she downed the shot she was carrying.

He glugged half the bottle. She tapped her shot glass in front of him and leaned back, crossing her arms. "Brudder, be the man. IF you think you did wrong, come back, apologize, start again."

He brought his bottle to his head, hoping the coolness would ease the heat in his veins. "What makes you think I did wrong?"

She uncrossed her arms and pointed to him. "She hurt. *You* must have done something."

He thought of many things. The way he acted. The way he shut down Instagram. But he also thought of things she did, including the Vegas trip. "So she really was with a young guy?"

She lifted her hand in the air as if to say, What am I going to do with this guy? "Does it matter, brudder? So long as you want her and she want you? I know her. She my sister. She stubborn. Not going to apologize first. All I say. You want her. You man up and come see her. You do that she appreciate. Know you care."

He started pulling at his hair and leaned against the booth.

She thought he might slide under the table.

She leaned forward, reached out to comfort him, then thought better. She placed both hands palm down in front of her. "I know you miss her. Verna tell me you come almost every afternoon. Wednesday Friday you come early and sneak out before Maya come work. I know. Verna know. You miss her."

He shook his head weakly. "Nah, I just want to sing."

She cocked her head, half frowned and brought her eyes to his level. "That how it is? You too proud to admit?"

Glenn recalled Wednesday and Friday afternoons always ended with Verna begging Glenn to come back or stay and see Maya. He always begged off. He could keep Verna hanging forever. Chloe was different. He was afraid he couldn't say no.

Kimmie and Randall were into their third song.

Glenn sat up and finished his beer. "I work out Wednesday nights. I don't want to come stink."

She flashed her teeth with a smile. "They have shower there, right?" She knew she had him.

He rubbed his face, massaged the back of his neck. "Yeah, okay, if I come, I come. We'll see." He was not used to losing negotiations. *Checkmate, Chloe. Checkmate.*

She got up. Her customer had checked on her twice already. She left Glenn sitting, giving him a quick cheek peck. "Attaboy, brudder. Nothing fancy. Just come. See her. Say sorry. See what happen. Okay? We see." She walked briskly to the booth room. He could hear her tell her waiting customer, "Daddy! Your baby so *soooo* sorry . . . and thirsty!"

He left Randall with Kimmie and called it a night. He had time to think, walking back home. Strange feeling to be sober on a Tuesday night, or any night these days.

Am I really going back there tomorrow?

40

ORDER RESTORED REUNITED

He went to the bar after his Wednesday night workout. *Why do I have to say sorry?* He recalled Chloe's words. *Just come. See her. Say sorry.* He kept saying the words over and over. He got out of the car and headed for the open door.

He had showered after his workout. *Don't have long to stay. Must do my other thing.* He pretended to wipe his brow with his forearm and took a quick sniff of his underarm. *Smells okay.*

He stopped right before the door, the neon sign flashing and beating on him. *Is she there? Does she know I'm coming? Did Chloe prep her? Is she with a regular customer or random customers? Will she leave them to see me? Will she even want to see me? What if she tells me beat it? What do I say? Do I just walk up to her and say hello? What's the plan?*

He took a deep breath in, and with one strong exhale, he walked in.

Tia froze. The look on her face said, "Uh oh, drama." By instinct, he went to his stool at the corner of the bar. It was empty, like a long-lost friend waiting for him. It was a Wednesday night crowd, a mix of construction workers, auto salesmen, and insurance types.

Some of the barflies gave a shout out to him. Lively chatter and reggae music floated out of the darts room. The flatscreens showed mixed martial arts on one and world soccer on the other. In the booth room, a bad rendition of "Bohemian Rhapsody" fought gamely with Kimmie's attempt at harmony.

Tia walked over. "Hi Glenn. Still with the Bud Light, love?"

He hesitated, scanning her face. *Friend or foe?* He nodded yes without a sound. She plunked the bottle before him, on a coaster with a napkin.

He opened his wallet. She wiped the area in front of him, then flashed the warm smile he remembered. "No Glenn, first one."

"Thanks, Tia." He stared into the mirror behind the bar, trying to gauge who was in the darts room. His ears strained, listening for Maya's voice. Like part of a script, Verna appeared beaming. "I go get her, you buy drink." It wasn't a request. She took off toward the darts room.

Mei was working the barback, stocking beer into the ice well below the bar counter. "Hi, Glenn" she smiled.

He smiled back. "How's the kids, Mei?" *I guess I'm still welcome here.*

Mei stopped stocking beer long enough to blow him a kiss. "Good. Still remember the ice cream you bought them." He smiled.

Verna was back with Maya in tow, hand clamped around Maya's wrist. Glenn turned. "Hi, Maya."

No hi. No greeting. This was not a joyful reunion. The look on her face went from seeing a ghost to *what the fuck.* As she glared, she growled, "What you doing here? I have customer waiting."

He took a slow breath in. A tinge of regret crept across his face. "I know." An awkward silence followed. The barflies pretended not to care, but there were side-eyes and furtive glances all around. Mei was pleading with her eyes for Maya to give him another chance.

Verna could almost sense Lynh coming around the corner. She held on to Maya's wrist and tugged. To Glenn she motioned her head toward the booth room. Then she was gone with Maya in tow. Glenn slid off the stool and gave a nod to Tia. She mouthed "good luck" and smiled. Mei blew another kiss.

They sat at their booth, across from each other, not next to. Verna had sat here every Tuesday night for the last ten weeks, never allowing anyone to sit in their place. Maya patted Verna's hand. "Verna, that's okay. You don't have to watch me. I don't run away. You tell my customer I will be right there five, ten minutes?"

Verna scanned Maya's eyes. "Okay." She glanced at Glenn. Gave him a quick, tight smile and was gone. She was beaming. Her kids were back together again.

Verna came right back, put a Bud Light in front of him, and asked, "Drink for Maya?"

Maya had no intention to stay long. "No Verna, it's okay, I . . . " Verna cut her off.

Her gaze never left her adopted son. "Drink for Maya, Glenn, okay?"

He wiped his mouth to hide his smile. *She is trying so hard.* He nodded. "Okay."

Verna didn't wait for payment. She was off and running.

He turned to Maya. She was wearing a red midlength strapless cocktail dress that revealed her tanned bare shoulders. Her makeup was perfect as usual, though her hair was a bit longer than he remembered. He was almost ogling. *I forgot how attractive she is.*

She thrust her chin out. Her voice was defiant but softening. "What you staring?" She straightened her hair and adjusted her dress. Reflex actions. She was wondering how her lipstick was.

He slowly released a deep breath. "Nothing. Haven't seen you in a long time. You're still gorgeous, that's all." She could feel color in her cheeks. She hoped he didn't notice. The blush didn't show through her foundation. Her heart beat fast, and she swallowed hard. Her lips suddenly parched, screaming for her shot. *Where is Verna?*

Verna was back with the drinks and snacks. Like some magician on stage, she emptied a plastic grocery bag she was carrying on their table. In an endless torrent, snack-size bags of candy, nuts, peanuts, chips and some exotic cuttlefish chews came pouring out. She smiled, then sat in the adjoining booth.

Maya suppressed her smile. Verna was pulling out all the stops. Suddenly not as angry as she was ten minutes ago, Maya's eyes went from glaring to inquiring. "How you been, Glenn?"

He rubbed his temple. "Okay. I've been better. But I'm okay."

She knew he was lying. She heard all the stories. The bar industry had its own grapevine.

He pointed his bottle neck at her. "You?"

She took his bottle from his hand and poured some into her empty shot glass. Then poured the rest into a glass Verna brought. Reflexively, they clinked. "I only work Wednesday Fridays now. Mommy work part-time to help so I don't need to work too much." Now she was the one lying.

She searched his face like she always did, her attention landing on his glasses. "Ugh. Dirty." She took his glasses and started cleaning. It was habit for her. She asked again. "You sure you okay?"

He thought for a few seconds. "No."

She stopped cleaning. "What on your mind?"

He took a deep breath. "Maya, I'm sorry. I'm sorry for hurting you. I don't know what I did but I want to tell you whatever I did, I'm sorry." She put down his glasses as he was speaking, and focused on his face, his lips, his hands. She wanted to know if he was sincere.

Her expression showed a hint of annoyance, wondering why he didn't know what he did. But the annoyance morphed into something short of admiration, a look of appreciation for someone manning up and coming in to see her. *He got guts. I knew he come.*

Feeling giddy and nostalgic, her first instinct was to tell her customer to go home. But he read her mind.

He massaged the back of his neck. "Maya, I can't stay long. I have someplace else to be."

Her head jerked. "Huh? You have another girl?"

He blinked rapidly and waved his hands in front of him like he was waving down a charging bull. "No. No, Maya. No other bar. No . . . No other girl. Family stuff. And I don't want you telling your customer to go home."

A slight smile crossed her lips. "Why I do that? Not for you." She was half kidding, half serious. She put aside what "family stuff" meant. *Wife?*

He couldn't tell. *Is she serious? I better lay it all out now.* "Maya, I'm sorry. I can be a real jerk. You know that. I don't know what happened, but I feel like we're not done."

Her eyes were smiling, and her lips were pulling upward at the corners. "Okay, Glenn. We okay. We move on."

He wrinkled his nose and pushed up his glasses. He needed to know. "But Maya, what did I do?"

She shut her eyes hard like she was purging a memory. "I dunno. I forget what we fight about already. So long time." She lied. She didn't want this moment to turn ugly. "We talk next time?"

He did a doubletake, wondering if he heard right. "Next time? You . . . see me again?"

She gave one nod, tilting her head and raising her eyebrows. "Maybe, up to you."

She licked her lips. Her heart fluttering. She was hoping she looked casual, mildly interested. "Glenn, I ask how you are and you only tell me sorry. That not tell me how you are. Don't lie to me. How are you?" She almost reached across the table. He eyed her hands, palms down halfway between them. Beautiful slender fingers. Nails painted pink to match her dress.

He felt lightheaded, like he was about to do something stupid. He shoved his own hands in his lap, interlocking his fingers.

He looked upwards, inhaled then exhaled sharply. Something bad was about to be spoken. "Not good, Maya. Remember last summer? Before I met you? How I made friends all over the place? Not good. Bad karma. Sin. I wanted to stop. You said you would help. My safe zone." She was listening and nodding.

He shook his head. Broke eye contact. Scanned the room. "I messed up all over again. Up and down the street. All kinds of girls. Couldn't keep it in my pants. Almost lost my job. One night, three girls, cocaine all over."

She winced. It was worse than she heard. He looked like shit, like he'd aged ten years. Bags under his eyes. Skin pale. He got fat. Her heart hurt for him. She tried to tell herself it was only pity, and not real hurt. She was lying to herself now.

Verna beckoned. The customer asked for Maya twice already. She and Glenn had been together thirty minutes. She cut to the chase. "Glenn, you want do Tuesdays again?"

Color flushed his cheeks. "You would do that?"

She retracted her hands, dropped them into her lap. "Yes, I don't do anything on Tuesdays anyway." Again, she lied, but she would figure something out.

He nodded appreciatively. "Okay. I have Instagram --"

She cut him off. "I don't. No more Instagram." She lied again. Didn't want him to see some of the stuff she had on there. "Gimme phone." He gave his phone to her. She punched in her number. "Text me when you ready."

He scratched at his cheek. "Text? I thought you don't give out your number to customers?"

She gave him back his phone. Skin touched skin as she placed the phone in his hand. Warmth crept up her arms. Electricity shot through her spine. She steadied herself with a deep breath. "I don't. You not customer. You friend."

He rubbed his cheek, his face a mixture of hope and confusion. "What do you mean?"

She saw Verna with the now or never look. "Glenn, you go now. Text me okay?" Glenn knew forty-five minutes away from the other guy was pushing it.

He rubbed his face. "Okay, you go first. I talk to Verna really quick."

"Okay." She was gone.

Glenn walked over to Verna. He took his hand in hers. Squeezed. "Thank you, Verna."

She looked up. "I see you next Tuesday?"

He was grinning ear to ear. "I think so Verna. I think so." She smiled. Her shoulders slumped, then she sat straight up. Relief followed by mission accomplished.

Maya was by the jukebox. He walked up to her. "Goodnight, Maya. Thank you." She was fiddling with the playlist selections but looked up and offered her cheek, pointing to it. He kissed. And barked, "Woof!" She grinned and was off back to the darts room.

The first song on the list started playing—"Reunited," by Peaches and Herb. Desire and a long-forgotten warmth crept back into his soul. *Class act,* he thought.

41

TOGETHER AGAIN

G lenn didn't waste any time. He texted her from the car.

First Tuesday in May okay?

Staring at his phone, he thought, *probably won't answer for a while. Making up time with the customer.* He was wrong.

Ok ☺

His smile was wider than the one on the emoji she sent.

That first Tuesday of May came the way Christmas morning comes to children anxiously waiting for Santa Claus. Time moved slowly. Minutes were like hours. Hours were like days. And days . . . *eternity* was the word.

He walked in early. The flatscreens were tuned to music video channels. Two construction workers were playing in the darts room. Otherwise, the jukebox was silent, and the place was empty except for Verna and Marcie. "Hi Verna! Hey Marcie!"

Marcie was the first shift barback, just finishing up, taking closing inventory. She had brown chestnut hair and the natural build and golden tan of an outdoor hiker. "Glenn, long time no see!" She reached for his favorite. "Bud Light with a bucket of ice, right?"

He licked his lips like a hungry dog sensing dinnertime. "Thanks, Marcie!" *She remembered. After all this time she remembered I like that setup.* Glenn stood there, not sure if he should sit at the bar or at the booth.

Verna nudged him to the booth room. "Your table ready." He sat down, and she sat across from him. She wasn't going to let him run away.

She'd already texted Maya.

Verna turned over a plastic grocery bag and dumped out chips, crackers, candy, and some other edibles he didn't recognize. She pushed over the Doritos, his favorite. "No eat too much. She bring food."

Glenn leaned forward, tearing open the Doritos, and offering up the open bag. "How you been?"

She took one chip, nibbling on the corners, then popping the whole thing in her mouth. "Okay. Business slow. Last night, no customers. Close early. Tuesday always slow. After you gone, no business. You sing now?"

He toasted her with his beer. "No, Verna. I'll wait."

A heavy Latin beat kicked up from the jukebox. Maya came dancing into the booth room. He saw her come into view, wearing green shorts and a long-sleeved green stretch top that was generous with the cleavage. She had her hair up in a French braid, exposing Chanel earrings. Her lucky earrings.

She bebopped up to the table, stopping only to dance in place to the music. Her smiling face said she hadn't a care in the world. "How you doing?" The sound of her voice was like hearing a favorite song he hadn't heard in ages. He was sitting on the edge of the booth. She feigned a frown, wrinkling her nose. "You move over or you like me sit on floor?"

He broke open a grin. He missed the sass. The ice was breaking. He moved over slightly. With an affectionately determined look, she slid in with some force and nudged right up against him, pushing him deep into the booth.

Verna beamed. "I go now."

He eyed the bag she was holding. He smelled something spicy, not pungent but clearly spicy. "What you got?" He pulled at the bag.

She opened the top for him to see, and smell. "Panang curry. Know you like."

He whiffed in deep just as his stomach growled. "Any Pad Thai?"

She smiled in amazement. *Six months ago, he didn't know how say Pad Thai. Now he want everything Thai.* "Maybe. You eat curry first. Verna tell you don't eat?" She noticed the half-open bag of Doritos.

He folded the bag closed and pushed it aside. "Yeah, she did. Only ate a few chips."

She nodded her approval. "Okay." She laid out some sticky rice on a plate and poured curry over it, still warm. There were chunks of chicken. She touched the food with her pinky. Not too hot. Not too cold. Scooped up rice and curry with a spoon and lifted to his mouth. By reflex, he opened, and she deposited. He closed and chewed. His eyes smiled.

Awesome taste!

He opened his mouth again, and she fed him again, before sticking the spoon in his hand. He was three spoons in before noticing her watching him, a look of amusement on her face. He asked, "You having some too?"

Her face radiant, she was bouncing slightly where she sat. "Of course. It's *our* dinnertime. We talk, then we sing, okay?"

He broke out laughing. She was silly and giddy, childlike, in the most charming way. After small talk and more of the panang, they were done, the Pad Thai left uncovered between them. She started wrapping up the noodle dish in front of him. "I put away for you. Take home tonight."

He pushed it to her. "No, you take home."

She pushed back. "No, I'm training fitness now. Too much carb."

He shrugged. *Enough being polite. I love this shit, especially how she makes it.* "Okay, you win. Thank you. I'll think of you when I eat tomorrow."

She whacked his arm, letting out a loud chortle. "You need Pad Thai to think of me. Not think of me every day jus cuz me?" He joined her in laughter.

Tia came on shift and peeked in quickly. *Wow. Love does conquer all. That's what he said when I shared my boyfriend troubles with him,* she recalled.

Maya finished cleaning off the table, then slid back in across from him, not next to him. "Need to talk serious first."

His left eye twitched twice. *Uh oh. This can't be good. Definite mood change. Happy Maya was gone. Mad Maya in the house. How the shit does this happen so fast?*

42

DOGHOUSE IN MAY

Arms crossed, she stared straight ahead, not at him but somewhere over his shoulders. Her mind was in a different space-time continuum.

He studied her, still shocked by the mood change. *Man, it's like sunny Bahamas to dark Antarctica. She's got that wife look, like the time I came home drunk and puked all over the shower.*

Arms still crossed, one knee over the other, bouncing steadily. She started the interrogation. "How many girls?"

With eyebrows raised, he asked with some confusion, "How many girls what?" *What's going on here?*

Her eyes narrowed a bit. "How many you fuck?"

He leaned forward, mouth open, shaking his head. "You want to hear only about fuck or other stuff?"

She focused on his face. Looking for tells, signs, that he was lying. "Jus' fuck."

Irritation began to etch on his face. "Ten, twelve, fifteen . . . something like that. No more than twenty." *She looks like she could knife me. What has she been hearing? Lynh must be filling her with all kinds of shit.*

Her lips flatlined, features cold, and almost dead, she monotoned. "What about other stuff?"

He wagged his head. "Blow jobs, hand jobs, I dunno. Ten times? I wasn't counting." *Seriously, you're doing this the first time we're back together? What does she want? What's she getting at?*

Her nostrils flared, just a trace.

Interrogation training taught him well. *Here it comes. The others were softeners. What comes next is the main event.*

She repeated herself. "You sing?"

He rubbed his face. "Couple times."

Her nostrils flared even more. She growled, "Dance?" *Now how did she hear about that?*

Glenn recalled, he got friendly one night with Miki, an older barback at another club. They danced *caliente* to a saucy Latin number with lots of dipping and twirling. *We were the show of the night there.*

She knocked on the table, hard. "Hello? You dance?"

He raked his hair and sighed hard. "Yes. I danced. Once." *Serious? Is this what's bothering her? I fuck all over creation and she's mad I danced with someone? Someone ratted on me. I saw him, Sean, her customer in the corner. He must've ratted. Fricking flying monkey. Probably thought he was breaking us up. Didn't know we were on break.*

Her expression turned borderline hostile, tinged with fear and some hurt. She tried to sound strong, but it came out timid, almost scared. "You like?"

He shrugged. "It was fun. I was drunk. She was there." He winced with regret. *Shouldn't have said that.*

Her lips tightened. Under the table, her fists clenched. In her head, she gave him the finger. *Screw you,* she thought, *I was here, waiting for you to be a man.*

The edge in her voice was clear now. "When you fuck, get blow job. You use protection?"

He leaned back, thinking through a fog of memory.

Her impatience was off the charts. "Glenn! Always protection. These girls you don't know."

He saw her face contort with what he thought was anger, hurt, concern, all of the above. *Like she really cares. Like I could ever pass something on to her? Is that what she's thinking?*

He cocked his head to think. "I'm pretty sure the girl always had protection."

She was rubbing her leg like it itched. "You mean girl condom you use?"

He nodded like it was obvious. "Yeah."

Her nose wrinkled; eyes narrowed again. She pointed her finger at him. "You sure condom okay? No pinhole. Now, maybe you daddy. They come to you child support after DNA test."

Glenn never thought of that. *What crazy skank would do that?* For an instant, he thought of her aborted son. He looked around. *Where's Verna? Did she tell Verna not to bother?*

She wasn't letting up, crossing her arms again. "Tell me everything Glenn. Every detail."

It was his turn to cross his arms. *How kinky is this? She went to bitch school while I was gone?*

His ears were ringing, and his blood pressure was building up above the neck. "No, Maya, I'm not going to tell you everything. I don't remember everything. I was in pain, okay? I missed you. My world ended. I left you a note. I left you my number. And you didn't call. I walked beaches. I walked malls. Every pretty girl I saw turned into you. Every song I heard was something we sang."

He was on a roll. "You wanna know what? Every girl I bedded looked like you, or I wanted them to look like you. Heck, I don't know. Half the time, I closed my eyes thinking it was you, and the other half I just wanted to forget the pain. So, no. A fuck is fuck. A blow job is a blow job. No, I didn't go down on any. I averaged five to ten minutes without breaking a sweat, and once I did a mama-san at four in the afternoon for an hour and a half."

His eyebrows twitched a bit. "And last, a threesome is a logistical nightmare. I twisted my back using my dick and two hands at once."

She jerked suddenly, stifling a laugh, hand covering her mouth. She wanted to laugh badly. He could always make her laugh, even when she was mad.

Thirsty, he stood up, turned around and yelled, "Verna!" She came running. He ordered double beers and five shots. Then he sat down and faced Maya. "Why you so interested?" *Is she jealous?*

Her expression was still edgy, as was her voice. "I don't go to those places. Just wanted to know what went on. That's all."

He finished his beer. "Seriously? Never been? Chloe practically has a VIP card next door. Same shit goes on here. C'mon!"

Without answering, she looked off to her right, staring at a blank flatscreen. Knee on knee again, bouncing her leg harder than ever. Verna brought three more shots.

He let her brood. *At this point I'm ready for anything. Please God, give us a break here.*

After a long few minutes, she knocked back a shot, swallowing hard. It was the real stuff. Her voice was less edgy. "Glenn, sorry I was not there for you."

He sipped his second beer. "Me too, Maya. I wish we never . . . "

"Never what, Glenn?"

He shook his head. "I don't even know what to call it."

She took another shot. "Breakup, Glenn. We break up."

He rubbed his forehead. "What did we break up?"

She stared blankly over his shoulder. In the bar area, customers and bargirls were having a good time. She faced him. "Us. We broke up us."

Elbows on the table, he half-buried his face in his hands, then looked up. "Us? What is us? Customer, bargirl? Boyfriend, girlfriend? Bar wife, bar husband? What?"

She was silent, pensive, thoughtful. "Just us, Glenn."

He examined her body language. *It's not over yet. Now she's got the "next item on my list" look.*

She downed two shots, one after the other. Warm courage crept through her veins. "You know why I was so mad, Glenn?"

He swallowed hard. "I said in the letter it didn't matter and I didn't care what Lynh and Jimmy said."

She blinked rapidly, then closed her eyes, seemingly recounting something terrible. "That's what you wrote, but I didn't like letter. I want to see face emotion when someone say sorry."

He rolled his shoulders, trying to release the tension building up. "But I don't care what Lynh and Jimmy say."

Her whole body went rigid, her voice frosty. "You don't care. That's just it. You don't defend me, Glenn! They say I have boyfriend and you don't defend me! You heard my story. I'm divorced. I get beaten. I don't want nobody. Okay, yeah, I went with big group. Yeah, one of them like me. Yeah, I hang with him. He give me money to gamble. Of course, I hang with him. But no, I don't like him like that, and you know my story. Should know I wasn't going to fall for him. So why broken heart?"

He rewound what she said. "So . . . you're saying you lied to me on all points except the guy wasn't your boyfriend. That's from your perspective. But he thought you were his girlfriend."

She fidgeted with her cell phone, scrolling nothing in particular. "I cannot have boyfriend, Glenn. I cannot be married. What husband let his wife work bar. And I cannot have boyfriend. If I have boyfriend all customer leave cuz no chance with me."

He leaned back, shoulders slumping just a bit. *Ahhh, there's the rub. That's the angle. She needs people to think she's single so they think they have a chance with her. That's why the pissing match with Lynh telling people she's married. That's why the pissing match with Jimmy over this young guy.*

Glenn held on to his best poker face. *And you're pissed at me for not defending you? I have to defend you? You break my heart and I have to defend you?*

Somewhere in the back of his mind, he remembered a sermon about keeping peace and being careful with words that couldn't be taken back. He gritted his teeth. "I'm sorry you felt that way." *This is not going well. What else does she want? She's been saving all this shit up for three months. Never mind me. I've only been walking the industrial area every lunchtime, thinking about what a low-level scumbag she took up with, and why I wasn't good enough. It fucking hurt, bitch, and I'm supposed to* defend *you?*

She continued, oblivious to the tempest in his head. "You know I'm divorced. Not final yet. So separated. He give me GI Bill for beauty school. I wait ten years. Get half pension. He not want divorce yet. Want make more rank. But Lynh tell all my customers I'm married. Good thing they believe me. I have to explain one by one. But they all come back to me. They still think they have chance with me. You believe Lynh or me?"

His voice turned one octave higher and louder. "I already told you, in the letter."

She jabbed a finger at him like she was scolding a dog. "You tell me now. To my face. Who you believe?"

He grabbed his wrist, twisting to generate some distraction. "*You.*"

He bluffed through it. He was sure she was married. But didn't know to what extent. He wondered whether to tear her a new one. A little voice inside kept saying, *forgive.*

He turned away, pretending to watch a college lacrosse game on the flatscreen facing him. He didn't notice her eyes moisten.

After a few minutes, she spoke. "Glenn." Her voice was softer. She uncrossed her arms, and placed her palms face down on the table in front of her. He almost wanted to reach out and take her hands in his.

Her voice was smoother, less rage, sweeter, less dark, lighter. It was another mood swing. "Glenn, I miss you." With a start, she corrected herself quickly. "I mean . . . I mean I miss singing with you. Not sing since you left. Tuesdays always for you. Not work. No other customers. Still for you if you want." *Just like that, mad Maya is gone,* he thought, *and happy Maya is back.*

He felt a thickness in his throat. *She missed me or missed singing with me? Doesn't matter. She missed something about me.*

At first elated, his face turned down into a frown. He'd put all his money in investments leaving only his small non-profit salary as ready income, a safety measure to cut himself off from the debauchery. He regretted it, not knowing if he could come back every week. "Maya, money locked up. Not sure if I can come back every week. Maybe twice a month. Sorry. Be okay in six months."

She placed her hand on his forearm like the first time they met. "Just come, Glenn. I have customer. You wait. I will come to you. No one come after midnight anyway. We sing then. No need money."

He shook his head. "No, Maya. It's okay."

She scrunched her nose and squeezed his forearm. "Why?"

He put his hand on hers. "Habit, Maya. If I'm seeing you, I want to make sure I treat you right." *Plus, I'm not sure what I'd do if saw you with another guy.*

She lightly caressed his forearm. "That's okay, Glenn. We can stay in touch by text if you want."

He frowned. "Hard, Maya. I don't do well if I text and get no response. You know that already."

She squeezed his hand. "I will always respond, Glenn. If I get text I will always reply." She remembered how upset he'd been last Christmas. He messaged her. She was mad about something and didn't respond. The little boy came out the following week.

They agreed to see each other again in June, almost a month away.

They held on to each other for what seemed like hours, but in those few seconds, the storm passed for both of them. The air felt lighter and tight muscles unwound.

She came around to his side of the booth. It was time to change the subject. "I get citizenship."

His mouth dropped. "Really? When?"

Her eyes twinkled; her knees swiveled to touch his. "I mean I apply. Hope six months. I take test. Pass. Oath. Then US citizen. Nobody deport me. Study hard. You help me, Glenn?"

Warmth crept upward, radiating from where their knees were locked. "Okay."

They were two hours in. A small nod from him and Verna showed up. "Another shot, Maya? Maybe two?"

She nodded happily. "Yes. Bud Light for you?"

He grinned. "After. I'll do the two shots with you first. We okay, Maya?"

She reached for his hand under the table. "We all good, Glenn. Let's move on." Somewhere out there, Glenn knew there was a handbook that said when a woman declared all good, it meant that your transgression was noted and tucked away in a database for easy retrieval the next time you screwed up. To himself he said, *That's when she'd roll out all your past screw-ups after pounding you on the latest mess.*

She leaned her head on his shoulder. "I go pee now."

She came back with microphones and slid in next to him. "We sing now? You sing "Kawaipunahele" for me?"

He took a microphone. "Sure." *The girl still knows how to make me feel special.* They ran through all the old songs. Last call came quickly.

She rubbed his back. "Glenn, one more."

He caressed her cheek. "Okay."

She sat there looking at him admiringly like she'd found a long lost love. "Let's sing *our* song."

He felt alive again. *She said* our *song.*

They sang, holding hands. In the end, he leaned over for a kiss, and she offered her cheek. He took it. *Maybe too soon. Maybe new rules. A little disappointing, but I'll take it.*

They walked out into the night together. She turned left to her car, a little white Audi TT coupe. Lately, white Audis like this showed up every time he had any negatives going thru his head about them. For some, white doves signal everything's okay. For him, it was white Audis.

He turned to leave, then heard her call his name, and her footsteps running to him. She came right up to him, tenderly grabbed his face and kissed him. "Good night, Glenn. Text me you okay home." There were knowing glances between all the regulars hanging around outside the door. *Lucky guy.*

Glenn turned and saw the guys, gave a quick salute, then stretched out his arms and leaned his head back. Once again, king of the world.

He didn't see the massive iceberg over the horizon.

43

WHITE AUDI, WHITE LIES

The following Tuesday, Glenn walked into the S&B Karaoke Bar with only $150 in his pocket and a ton of regrets in his heart. *I can't believe I socked away all my money like that. I didn't know we'd get back together.*

The S&B wasn't so much a bar as a collection of private karaoke rooms rentable by the hour. For an additional cost, food and drink were served in the rooms. Now in the middle of May, the place was packed with the local college crowd just finished with final exams, and ready to belt out some tunes.

He saw two familiar faces waiting for him, though his thoughts were firmly on Maya. *She said I could still see her, no money needed, if she had no customers. But since when does she have no customers? Besides, seeing her with another guy? No way.*

They'd agreed to see each other in June, texting to stay in touch till then.

Two spitballs splat the side of his head, loads of laughter followed. Across the floor, Randall Borncamp and Jason Reynolds were loading their straws for another round of fire. Before they could send another spitball round his way, Glenn picked up a stray menu to use as a shield and rushed across the floor to smack each of them on their heads.

The group hugged, followed by the usual how-you-doing, more for Jason's sake since Randall had just seen Glenn. Already a few beers in, Randall and Jason pushed Glenn into the nearest karaoke room. Singing with Randall and Jason was fun, but his thoughts ran to her all night. He couldn't shake it.

Jason was a Christian buddy and asked Glenn, "Where you been hiding, man?" Glenn gave a quick rundown. Jason's face showed disapproval. For a few minutes, he launched into a morality sermon. "Hey man, I been there. You don't want this. You don't want to get involved with one of those girls."

Glenn took a step back, jerking his head as if to say are you kidding? "Kinda judgmental, don't you think, Jason? What did you think Randall— not a bad place, right?"

Randall knew better than to get involved between the two holy rollers. "What do I know? I'm the heathen. I'm gonna go talk to Donna at the bar."

Jason was the city's former Housing Director and had served alongside Glenn in the mayor's cabinet helping the homeless. Korean born, American adopted and raised, he stood over six feet tall. Pushing forty years of age, he still had the youthful look of a K-pop singing star.

Jason stared disapprovingly at Glenn. "Lotta people would be disappointed in you, Glenn, if they found out what you were doing and who you're doing it with. And what about Katie?"

Glenn's eyes flashed, just for a second. "And what about Katie, Jason? I don't think she's in a position to care. Besides, didn't Jesus want us to be among the tax collectors, whores and thieves?"

Jason faced his old friend; inside his head, he heard, *judgment is mine alone, not yours.* He softened. "Jus' saying, Glenn."

Glenn raised his palms. "I get it Jason. I'll pray on it." *Are You trying to tell me something, Father? Jason always was the perfect Burning Bush. Do You want me to call it quits with Maya? Then why the reunion? The enemy caused it or You? What do You want me to do?*

The threesome called it quits around 11:00. Glenn wondered if she was even at the bar. Jason walked out with Glenn. "You're going, aren't you?"

Glenn pulled his pockets inside out for emphasis. "No, got no funds." He had one Benjamin left in his wallet to cover lunch for the rest of the week.

Standing on the sidewalk, Jason asked, "Hey brother, can I pray for you?"

Glenn closed his eyes and held his palms up. "Sure. Appreciate it, brother."

Jason lay a hand on Glenn's shoulder. "Father, I pray strength for my brother here. Please be with him on this journey. Anoint him with what is important to You. And we ask for wisdom and guidance on what he needs to do. Amen."

Glenn opened his eyes and gasped. A white Audi TT coupe pulled up to the sidewalk where they were standing. Glenn stared wide-eyed, his mouth hanging for just a bit. It wasn't her driving, but it was a white Audi like the one she drove. *Dang,* he thought, *right after Jason asks for guidance on what I need to do. Right after I ask.*

Jason noticed Glenn's bewilderment. "Anything wrong, Glenn?"

His mind was a swirl. "No, Jason. It's all good." *What are you telling me, God?*

Jason gave him a bro hug. "Good night, brother."

Glenn rubbed his face. "Goodnight, old friend." He watched Jason walk down the street to his car.

He turned his attention to the white Audi. *Father, You trying to tell me something?*

The urge to go was swelling up in him. The feeling came from deep in his gut and not his crotch. *I've had feelings like this before, in prayer groups.* The guy in the white Audi sat, checking Google Maps on his phone. Found what he needed and drove off.

Glenn watched the white Audi turn the corner and disappear. *Just like that. I'm thinking about going. We ask for guidance, and a white Audi like hers pulls up. Is this You talking to me, Father?* He couldn't resist anymore. He ran to his car. *If her car is in the parking lot, I go in. If not, I leave.*

He pulled up in the bar's parking lot. *There's her car. She's here. I thought she didn't work Tuesdays—only for me? Maybe I should have called. Am I going to walk in on her and another guy? Tuesdays only for me, my ass.*

He walked in. She was sitting with her back to the wall, in the corner nearest the darts room, with a view of the booth room and anyone entering the bar. She was dressed in a plain white cocktail dress with mid sleeves and covered cleavage, fiddling with her phone, not paying attention to anything else.

He paused just inside the doorway. *Well at least she's not with anyone. And she looks good. She could be going to church or afternoon tea, the way she's looking.*

Their eyes connected. Giving him a look like it's about time, she opened her arms and beckoned to him. Two steps in, across the bar floor, and he was in her arms giving her a hug. Tia was already pulling a Bud Light.

She leaned back. Searched his face. "You okay? What you doing here? What you do tonight?"

He searched her face. *She looks genuinely worried.* "Karaoke night with the boys. You're not going to believe." He told the white Audi story. "I had to come. What are you doing here?"

She brushed his hair. "I had hunch. You go out. Get drunk. Come here. Wanted to make sure I was here. Make sure you okay. Not get into trouble." She looked around. "Lotsa new girls. Jimmy spread word. They come from Korea, Japan, PI."

He took a pull on his beer. *She shoulda been a poker player. Can't tell anything from her face. Did something happen between her and the young guy? Maybe she didn't have side action anymore and needs to make money. But she looks genuinely happy to see me and was happy to see me walk thru the door, and happy that I'm here.*

He fished in his pocket and brought out the Benjamin onto the counter, his lunch money for the week. "Here, this is all I got. I can get you five shots."

She took his hand, wrapped it around the bill, and placed his hand in his lap, near the pocket the money came from. "Don't worry Glenn. I'm off duty now. I buy you beer tonight. Only little while more anyway."

"But . . . "

She put her finger on his lips and said softly but firmly. "No. Save money. Eat lunch. Okay?"

He nodded, eyes moistening.

She wiped his tear away and kissed his cheek where the tear had fallen.

He took a deep breath and exhaled. Cheerfully, he asked, "What are you looking up on your phone?"

She showed him her phone. "You." She started scrolling. "You famous. You nice guy help all kine people. They all like you. Say plenty nice things about you."

There was page after web page of stuff on him or things he'd gotten done. She bookmarked two he'd long forgotten about.

Star-Gazette
January 14, page B-3

State University recognizes its outstanding graduating student for fall 1988

Mr. Glenn Forrester graduates with a dual degree in finance and economics, with honors. He served admirably as the University's student body president and president of its freshman honor society, and received the College of Business Outstanding Student award, along with both Dean's Service and Professional Development Awards. He will be the College of Business's graduation marshal at commencement.

Forrester has accepted an offer to join State Bank in its executive management training program.

Star-Gazette
January 14, page A-2

Mayor Names Forrester to Cabinet

Mayor Harris appointed Glenn Forrester to run his Department of Community Affairs, which oversees community welfare matters, including all homeless initiatives in addressing a largely looming problem for the state and county. Prior to his appointment, Forrester was Chief Strategy Officer for State Bank and was rumored to be on the fast track to CEO. When asked about this, he said, "If the mayor calls you to serve, what are you going to do?" In a statement, State Bank's chairman of the board said the bank supports the move and with current management solidly in place for the next decade, would welcome Forrester back in a key role in the future. This fuels speculation that Forrester already has a job ready for him after serving the mayor.

Forrester is a graduate of State University College of Business with a degree in finance. He graduated with honors from State Law School, where he was editor in chief of the law review, Order of the Coif and Barristers. He served for 20 years as an intelligence officer in the Air Force Reserve and was also the mayor's chief strategist in the last election.

Other headlines followed.

Homeless applaud their champion, only city official to visit encampment

HUD cites city community director with outstanding rental programs

Police thank city community affairs office for supportive partnership

Homeless navigation center created by city community affairs already a national model

AARP commends city director of elderly services for commitment to senior-friendly community

New administration builds multiple elderly housing projects after years of stagnation

He handed back the phone. "Did you really spend all night waiting for me and Googling me?" *No way.*

She continued scrolling. "I had one customer. He surprised see me on Tuesday. But he go home right before you came." She yawned. "Glenn, I have to go soon. Wake up early tomorrow. We sing little bit?"

They didn't go to a booth but stayed where he'd found her. She stayed by his side for the rest of the night. She went behind him once, to give him a massage, and she sang for him at the same time. *Wow,* he thought, *how does someone massage with one hand and sing with the other?* They sang. They joked and talked about her citizenship test. They high-fived, then locked fingers, holding tight for a bit after each song.

She acted as if her whole world and purpose in life were to make him happy and make sure he was okay. At least, that's how she made him feel. He looked at her reflection in the mirror behind the bar—beautiful, uplifting, positive, energetic.

She poured his beer for him like she used to. "Glenn, you have time next week? No need spend money. I take you dinner. Ruth Chris. Like we supposed to before we break up." She bit her lip. They weren't supposed to bring it up again.

She started to apologize. He cut her off. "Yeah, okay, I'd like that. Meet there? 8:30? I'll make the reservations." *Wow. Is it really going to happen?*

She lifted his beer to his lips. "This not date Glenn, okay? My way thank you for coming back. Not date. Okay?"

He drank. "Okay."

Suddenly, they heard shouting, glass breaking, and furniture being overturned. A small fight erupted in the booth room. Two insurance guys fighting over one bargirl. Jimmy flew by with a baseball bat. Glenn reacted, about to stand. She reached for his hand. Gripped it tight. As if to say, protect me, stay here, stay with me, don't do anything, don't worry, we're together.

The night ended with a kiss. Right there where they started. Nothing sexual or arousing. But almost to simply say, I care, I love you, be well. It was something he always longed for, that feeling when he used to see Billy coming home to his mom.

44

NOT A DATE

They met at the restaurant. He wore a coat and the tie she'd given him for Christmas. She saw it and was delighted. "You soooo handsum!" She wore a pantsuit—black pants with a black blazer over a lime green blouse. She wore her hair up and her makeup demure, perfect for a night out.

He held the door open for her. She stood on the inside and waited as he took the lead, following their hostess to their table. Together they killed two bottles of Stag's Leap and shared a filet mignon, lamb chops and a silver-rated sirloin between them.

As was customary whenever he drank wine, he took a few seconds before his first sip to acknowledge his faith, first taking a bit of bread followed by a sip of wine and a quick prayer under his breath.

She watched curiously. *Praying? Never had customer like that before.*

Midway thru the meal, she toasted him. "Welcome back, Glenn!" He thought the glassware would shatter, she pinged it so hard. She was stunningly beautiful. The manager came by to check this scene out. An old guy with a young girl. The manager pressed. "What's the occasion?"

Glenn took over and explained that it was a reunion of sorts between old friends. Small talk followed with him putting the manager at ease. The manager took a liking to Glenn and arranged for dessert on the house. Maya wondered, *how he did that? So smooth. Manager trust him right away. Just like Mama that first night. Just like me.*

Maya's eyes flashed and twinkled as she squeezed his hand. "I apply for citizenship today, Glenn. Here, picture of application." She handed her phone to him.

He took her phone. *She's trusting me with her unlocked phone?* He gave it back before he saw something he shouldn't.

She swirled her wine, taking a sip. "Mommy still sick. I'm still worried." She paused. "You know I used to be lesbian?"

Glenn's eyebrows arched. *Too much information, but happy she's sharing. I guess being outside of a bar let's her talk more.* Then he smirked like he had a secret too. He took a breath and declared, "You know I had a boyfriend?"

Her jaw dropped.

He explained the one-time affair, right out of puberty and experimenting.

Both the wine and conversation flowed freely. She peered at him over her wine glass. "You know group I went to Vegas with? The one guy, he want exclusive. I said no. He gone. He so jealous all the time."

He answered sarcastically, with a touch of glee. "Sorry to hear, Maya."

She rolled her eyes, flicking a bread crumb at him. "You not."

He returned a wry smile. "Yeah, you're right, I'm not."

She pinged his glass. "You tell me more about night job?"

When they first met, he explained the things he did for the Admiral as his night job, the real job, compared to what humdrum things he did during the day.

She swirled her wine, lifting it to the light. "Maybe I can do politics like you? Glenn, what you really do?"

He took some wine, swirling it in his mouth, coating his entire tongue. *Hmm. She was an expert at working people. With her charm, she'd be able work a lot of these shmucks. At least the lower level ones.* "I fix things, Maya. I call it a night job, remember, because I do it at night, after my day job is done."

Her eyes were blinking, her head trying to process. "What you mean you fix?"

He looked around quickly, and lowered his voice, leaning closer to her. "When things happen that could make the governor or mayor look bad or could hurt people—you, me, this town—I get the call. Someone tells me the problem, I make it go away."

It sounded to her like something from *The Godfather*. Her eyes widened. "You . . . you kill people?"

He shook his hand, waving off the notion. "No, no . . . never, but sometimes that would be easier. No, people live. But sometimes, what I do, maybe they feel like they woulda been better off dead, you know?"

She knew. Grandpa was part of the underworld back home. She knew.

She was talking again about all the stuff she found on him on the internet.

He nodded slowly. "Yeah, there's a lot on me out there." The Group controlled everything on the internet about him and made sure he looked like a saint. He wanted to get off the subject but she wouldn't let go.

She was almost gushing. "You know, I find book with you inside. You supposed to take over politics one day?" The Admiral had written a book. In it he named Glenn as one of the few in the upcoming generation that had what it took to keep the wheels turning.

Her voice was filled with wonder, speaking excitedly. "So much nice stuff about you. People say nice things. You know so much people. You meet people and they automatic like you. How you do that? Maybe I can?"

It was like getting a dozen fastballs thrown at you. And the matter was hard to explain. Especially after a bottle of wine and good red meat chunked down in your gullet. "I'll tell you more later, Maya. I promise."

She frowned, then seemingly pouted.

He paused. "I have to think about this. I never had to talk about it. Can you give me some time? If I explain, I want to do it right."

She evened out her frown. "Sure, okay."

He leaned back, shifted in his seat, then leaned toward her again. Subject change. "Hey Maya—"

She was ready. "Yes?"

His face went from serious to beaming. "Finances looking better. I think I can stop by next Tuesday. Okay with you? If you have someone, no worries, I leave and come back. I don't want you to make them mad."

She winced as if something rotten just popped. "Glenn, I tell you already Tuesdays for you, for us. Why don't you believe?"

He held up his palms. "Okay. I'll stop by. I think we're okay for weeklies again. You like that?"

Her face mirrored his beaming. "I like. I like very much."

She grew quiet. He noticed. "What's on your mind, Maya?"

She shook it off. "Nothing. How was your day? Your weekend? We don't talk yet."

He recognized the ploy. "Everything okay." He pressed. "What's on your mind?"

She studied his face. *Will he get mad?* "What about Thursdays?"

His eyes narrowed a bit. "What about Thursdays?" He knew what she was asking but needed to buy time to process and come up with an answer.

She tilted her head. "Thursdays, instead of Tuesdays?"

He sucked on his lips. *She's asked this several times lately. Something wrong with Tuesdays. And she's always leaving early. But my schedule's set.* "No Maya. Cannot. Family stuff." In the time they'd known each other, he was steadfast. It was always only Tuesdays. All other days same answer— family stuff.

Her brow furrowed just for a bit. *Family? Maybe he married?*

It was near midnight. The restaurant had transformed into an after-hours bistro. They called it a night. She explained, "I have to do inventory tomorrow for cosmetics store."

He rubbed his chin. *Again, like last time. Can't believe this store does inventory in the middle of the month. Really? Or does she have someone waiting for her? Ever since she admitted to lying about the Vegas trip, the excuses she made here and there sound hollow.*

He took his last swallow. *Never mind. Easy, cowboy. Don't push. Keep showing belief and trust in her. Love others unconditionally, the Good Book says. Love will conquer all in time.*

He brushed what bad thoughts he had aside. They walked out arm in arm to her car, the white Audi, and his good luck omen. He held her door open for her. She got in, and he leaned in after her for a kiss good night. On the lips this time. No turning the cheek. At first, it was light. Then they lingered, softly grazing each other, mouth open. She reached around and pulled him in, and with her lips drew him in deeper, their tongues introducing themselves like long lost friends.

He was somewhere in the clouds and barely heard her last words. "Don't forget, you tell me about night job next time!"

He watched her drive off. Then went back to his car. Had he not been put in a trance by her kiss, he would have heard tires squealing in the distance.

45

GAME ON

The following Tuesday afternoon, he sat in his office, self-sequestered from Joyce and Sherry, reviewing the non-profit's cashflow plan. In his mind, the CEO and COO were clearly out of their league, and he'd just found out they responded to the board's questions by blaming him for the non-profit's devastating cash flow problems.

He laid out his objections in his head: (1) the line of credit was maxed out before he came on board, (2) the deficit-creating government contracts were signed before he came on board, and (3) the decision to do away with the annual fundraising gala was made before he came on board.

He shook his head. *Idiot board of directors didn't even question these decisions. Of course, Joyce made sure the minutes reflected their approval of these decisions. Now it's my fault the company can't dig itself out just because I'm the CFO?*

He slammed his mouse down so hard the batteries flew out. *Can't believe Joyce denied me when I told her this place is headed for bankruptcy, and the board needed to do some fundraising fast. Can't believe she chose not to tell them. And now I'm shut out of the board meetings. We're done for today.*

With a huge sigh, he closed his eyes and imagined himself a few hours into the future. *How do I explain the night job to Maya without blowing my cover? I already told her too much. But the way they make me look in the papers has me taking on legendary, googleable, status.*

He signed off on the non-profit's cashflow plan, tossing it in the out tray. *How do I tell her I'm the youngest member of a group rivaling the Illuminati or the Knights Templar? I mean, these people elected every governor and mayor in the state and county for the last forty years. I guess I can say it like that.*

He opened an encrypted file on his phone that listed every group member and their contact info. The file listed law firms, architects, CPAs, marketing and public relations firms, engineers, labor unions, government unions, public safety unions, construction groups, general contractors and developers, and every other group that sought influence in government to help business revenue flow their way.

He went down the list. *Funny how they're simply called "the Group." But all the power players know about it and know a little about who is on it.*

He reminisced. *I remember someone telling me when I started in law that being part of this group would assure me success in life. If you're a political monkey, this was the holy grail. I like that the goal is to elect candidates to Congress, the governorship and key county mayor seats that sought only to serve the people.*

He looked around at his storage closet of an office. *How can this rathole be where I spend my last years? No—no way! All those nights as a political operative got me somewhere, just sidetracked is all. So I got burned by Clifford. It's time to get back in the game. And I have the Admiral to thank. Oh, and God.*

46

THE ADMIRAL

Over the years and various political campaigns, Glenn's resume had grown into an eleven-page dossier that landed on the Admiral's desk a few years prior. The Admiral was the Group's de facto chair. No one questioned his decisions, and the newest Group recruit was about to go through final review. The Admiral already knew Glenn by name and face, and only skimmed the dossier's highlights.

- *Campaign experience*
    - ☐ *1998 – Congressman Wilkinson. Website content research and production.*
    - ☐ *1999 – Senior Senator Aoki. Coordinated statewide young leaders conference resulting in next generation of political operatives (fourteen group operatives were recruited out of this conference)*
    - ☐ *2000 – Mayor Edwards. With two months left before election day and fourteen points behind, took over field operations, implementing efficiency and accountability measures. Pollsters credited the grassroots effort with the mayor's come-from-behind win. Rising star. Speaks to mayor on first name basis.*
    - ☐ *2002 – Mayor Edwards' gubernatorial strategy team. Appointed to run all cyber and electronic campaigning, including opposition research. Pollsters credited the electronic campaigning for the new governor's decisive win. Governor Edwards personally recognized him as the most critical strategic operative for the digital campaigning age.*

Shadow policy maker through governor's two terms.

☐ *2012 - Mayor Harris strategy team. Managed all operations including headquarters, field operations, public relations, and communications. Official title was deputy campaign manager of operations. People in the campaign simply called him boss.*

• *General comments:*

☐ *Over ten years in the reserves (Air Force Intelligence). Served military weekends every month while holding two jobs to support self through college.*

☐ *Known at the bank as the financial wizard, nicknamed by the bank CEO after he found nearly $10 million in loose change unaccounted for in bank's own ledgers.*

☐ *Street smarts off the charts. Hardened operatives and others close to him say one thing he can do better than anyone is see through agendas and lies, allowing him to diffuse situations before they became situations.*

The Admiral saw enough. *He reminds me of me. A fixer and doer. I saw him everywhere during the last campaign for Harris. Pretty sure he was a key factor in those other campaigns. Damned multitalented but best working with people. Over and over, reportedly diffused catastrophic situations. Creative head, calm mind, quick mouth, and true heart.*

The Admiral leaned back in his chair, staring out his corner office window on the thirtieth floor. *The guy has enough soft skills to demand a seven-digit income in Silicon Valley. Only thing, he once told me that saving the world was more important than money. Lucky for our fair state. All the information provided points to two things. The guy is a shitstorm-ender and a clusterfuck-fixer.*

The Admiral called his assistant in. "Anya, put this on the next agenda. Invite the mayor and Clifford too."

Clifford Schumaker was the deputy mayor. "Absolutely not! Speaking for the mayor now." Clifford blurted, "We were okay with him taking the Community Affairs office because that really doesn't affect the city's brick and mortar infrastructure, so how much harm can he do?"

The Admiral looked his cousin in the eye. "Look Clifford, cut the bullshit. You know we considered him for your job. You undercut him. Yeah, you and the mayor there grew up together. You guys had pillow talk. Some bullshit about him taking credit from you for the Edwards campaign?"

Clifford's face oozed smug. "You were there. He was a young punk. I mentored him. But he tried to take the credit and, furthermore . . ."

The Admiral cut in. "Bullshit again. Field ops was your baby. You ran it into the ground. Key people quit on you. We were fourteen points behind because of *you*. I give you credit. You brought him in. Then you disappeared. You planted your lips on the mayor's ass as his personal driver. Glenn carried the ball himself."

Clifford showed his fangs. "No, you're wrong. I gave him a shot at learning campaign . . ."

The Admiral cut in again. "What do *you* know about campaigning? Even at the bank, your expertise was bringing in number two's and taking credit for everything they did. That got you promoted, and these number two types always went along because with you out of the way, they got to be the number one. Really smart. Is that what Harvard taught you?"

The Admiral continued his interrogation. "Edwards told me Glenn did all he did at your direction."

Again with the smugness. Clifford nodded.

The sound of the Admiral's palm slamming his desktop reverberated out to Anya's desk. "Wrong! And we all know it. And when Edwards found out . . . well, that's why you weren't asked back on the team the second time right? Edwards found out the detailed stats you provided regarding your efforts and results were actually based on a report Glenn gave you at the end."

The current mayor cocked his head. His eyebrows showed his surprise, but he kept his mouth shut.

Sleaze replaced smug on Clifford's face, as he said, "Water under the bridge. Again, we let you dictate him being in the cabinet, but the Group, *no*."

The Admiral leaned back, steepling his hands. "This is not a vote Clifford. This is a courtesy update to the mayor and the deputy mayor. Case closed. He's in. I'm giving him his first assignment tomorrow morning."

As Clifford stormed out of his office, the Admiral recalled the day he notified Glenn about the change to his cabinet placement. It was rumored he'd be deputy mayor. "Sorry Glenn, we thought we had the votes for deputy mayor, but at least you're in somewhere—the start of a great career for you."

Glenn spoke from the hip. "That's okay Admiral. Actually, this works out well."

The Admiral rarely got caught off guard. "How so?"

Glenn thought about the crucifix he carried in his wallet. A keepsake from his mother. "Think about it. You and I have had God talks. I'm in charge of community affairs, dealing with homeless and aging issues. Deep in my heart, I think this is where God wants me to be. I wanna make the world a better place, starting with my own backyard."

The Admiral thought back to his own past, his hardships, his own desires to make the world a better place. With all his soft and hard skills, the one thing that kept driving him was making the world a better place to live. *Just like me. I can understand him. We need more like him.*

The Admiral's reach ran deep into every sector the Group dealt with. He had more chits than Glenn could use in three lifetimes. And he had even more gratitude and loyalty from the people he had helped. The Group was his concept—to get influential people together to help the less powerful people. Power and influence with a moral compass.

The Admiral smiled. *He does have a strong moral compass. Saw his raw potential during Senator Aoki's young leaders conference. So much drive. Natural leader. The irony of it all—me asking Clifford to bring Glenn aboard the Edwards campaign to see what he could do—to see if he was worthy of grooming and one day, tapping.*

The day had come. From that day on, Glenn was on call to liaise between all the power players in the state to get things done.

47

POLITICAL CAREER

It was the last week of May and summer was coming on fast, promising record heat in the next few months. Jimmy had the air conditioners on full blast. The regular girls were filing in, some taking their seats at the bar to wait for customers, others being greeted by their regular customers already waiting.

The jukebox bellowed out classic '90s rock music, no doubt requested by a bunch of sales types reliving their youth in the darts room. The flatscreens were tuned to soccer and cricket. Glenn wondered who controlled the channels in the bar. *What happened to the American sports?* The barflies were digging into the beef brisket that Uncle had whipped up that afternoon. Jimmy and Tia were arguing over her spending too much time with Paul.

Maya was waiting for him right by the entrance, sitting at the same "against the wall" corner seat where she sat the night a random white Audi called him to the bar. He gazed adoringly at her, dressed in a royal blue open-back velvet party dress with just enough hem stretched to cover her shapely behind and provide ample view of her gorgeous, tanned legs, fresh from a weekend hike in the woods.

She led him to their booth and sat him down. "Glenn, you hungry?"

He gave a little burp. "Little bit." She ran off to get some food for him and brought back some of Uncle's beef brisket. Verna brought a double round for them and a beer for her. As always, she sat in the adjoining booth, but not before dumping an assortment of chips in front of them.

There was the usual, "How are you" and, "Fine" between them, and the first clinking of glasses for the night, and more small talk about dogs, mothers, stupid CEOs, bargirl gossip, stupid COOs, grouchy mama-sans, as Verna continuing to dote over them.

Then a new subject from her. Her eyes sparkled as she babbled.

"Glenn, you know I live with my cousin and her husband? She work defense department. He work Navy."

His tone was hesitant and deliberate. "Oh, what do they do?" *Where is she going with this? The phantom cousin?*

She shrugged. "Computers. I dunno. I'm not supposed to know. They travel a lot. Plenty times I'm home alone. Only me and Rusty."

He nodded. *Where's this going?*

She turned to him, their knees touching. "I show them the book. The one you in. They ask, who you?"

Suspicion crept into his gaze. "Why?" *And who are they? And why show them the book?*

She held her glass to the light, studying the amber liquid it contained. "Dunno. Never met someone like you."

He got concerned. "Did you tell them about the night job?"

"No, Glenn, no. Not say anything. But they know you high up. Want to know more. I want to hear more. You promise last time you tell me more. If not like, then okay. You go back to sweet little boy Glenn, okay?" She held her shot glass up.

He raised his bottle. Cheers. Clink. He took a long swallow. *I did promise to tell her more. Big quandary here. The Group's work was done in the shadows. How could I tell her more and not break confidences? How?*

Deep down, he also fought the urge, the desire, the need, to impress her. *Maybe I can give out just a little more than what's in the Admiral's book and on the internet.*

He thought it through in his mind. *This is going to take a while.* He raised five fingers to Verna. "Okay. So sit back. This might be boring." She vigorously shook her head no.

He scratched his ear. "You know I never wanted to get into this line of work."

Her eyes widened. "For real? You so good at it."

He shook his head, finishing his first beer. "Yeah, but I thought politicians and elected officials were out for themselves. And I wanted to stay far away from them."

She blinked once, twice. "So what happened. Why . . ."

He cut in. "A senior partner at my first law firm changed my mind. He said, for me to be a top lawyer and make lots of money, I had to know people that can give me business—big business. And the best way was to dive into politics because that's where all the money-makers were."

Verna brought their drinks. They waved off the microphones she brought.

She poured his beer. "Why money so important? Lawyer already make good money. Why more?"

He shredded the beef brisket and made nachos with Verna's Doritos. "Money was important to me back then. I was hungry and ambitious. Didn't own a house yet. I grew up poor. My dad spent his money on beer and cigarettes. We ate grass and potatoes from the yard. We had rats in the house. I vowed as a kid that I would never have to eat grass from the yard when I grew up. I would have clothes without holes, the roof wouldn't leak, and we'd have air conditioning during the summer."

She saw by his face that he was sad and lost back in time.

"Maya, I ate grass from the yard. I needed to get somewhere rich fast."

She nodded. Like she been there.

He saw her wince. Remembered the story of how she traded fish for meat at market as a kid and how eating meat for a week was a dream come true for her.

He made a plate of nachos for her. His mouth full, he drained half his beer to wash down his improvised nachos. "I worked hard at becoming a lawyer. But even though I was a lawyer from a large firm, I started at the bottom in politics. It was hard and humbling. By then, I'd been president of this and that organization, including advising commanders in the military."

He smiled at the next memory. "Then, suddenly, I was a worker at various events passing out walkie-talkies, prepping food and chopping vegetables, and cleaning up garbage and rubbish after functions. At one point, they put me in charge of the bar at a high money function. Even if not glorious, I worked hard at doing the best job I could at every assignment, in addition to working at the law firm sixteen hours a day."

She imagined everything he was saying. She couldn't get over the image of a little boy eating grass from the yard for dinner. *At least you had grass,* she thought. She remembered nights in her village going to sleep hungry, then waking up and going hungry.

Once, she was so hungry that she stole from a neighboring farm. The neighbor caught and beat her. Her grandpa came to get her, took her home, and beat her some more. She vowed she'd do anything to eat well all the time. Mommy was a whore. Sister was only two years old. She would make sure Sister never got beaten like her. She would go to America, make money, and come home rich.

His face replayed his childhood torment. She stroked his forearm, a gesture of comfort, nothing more.

He watched her face—how intently she was absorbing not only his words but his emotion. He could feel the connection.

He continued. "Someone in campaign leadership noticed me hustling all over the place. He oversaw all field operations and knew my background as a good leader. He brought me on as co-director, so I could do all the work, and he could take all the credit. I didn't care. This put me in campaign management and was my lucky break. If I did good, I was on my way. If I did bad, I was toast."

He took a long pull from his longneck. "For four months I was all over the place, putting the mayor in front of people, and was with campaign leadership every night. I got noticed by the right people. I oversaw my own area and helped others in their areas. We won. And that was the beginning."

He was careful not to mention getting recruited by the Group because of that win, and the current struggle for power between the deputy mayor and the Admiral.

All her attention was on him. "And you powerful ever since?"

"No, not really." He said it matter-of-factly.

She brought out the book from her purse. "No, you wrong, Glenn. So how you become powerful now?"

He stared at the book. *She carries it with her?*

He took the book from her. "Where I am now took a while. Every few years, influential people in this town go to war with each other to elect their candidate. When you get a reputation for getting results, you get drafted to be on one team or the other."

He flipped to the chapter that discussed him and took a second to reflect. "Since then, I got drafted to be part of this campaign or that campaign, and over time, I got bigger and bigger roles. I ended up with a real reputation for running computer operations, and with each campaign, I kept meeting new people that turned into relationships."

He was getting more sober by the minute but kept going. *Never met someone so interested in this stuff.*

He sipped his beer. "During the last big campaign, I got to prove myself running bigger campaign operations. Again, someone took all the credit after I did all the work. It was a great experience, and I made sure the right people knew I was doing all the work. In twenty years of campaigning, I built up a reputation: hard worker, smart leader, good guy, has integrity, gets things done. The right people backed me, and I ended up in the mayor's cabinet. Mostly to take over a tough department, and to get the guy re-elected."

He sighed a happy sigh. "Twenty years of hard work, running campaigns and getting people elected. You get to meet a lot of people in twenty years. In twenty years, a lot of people come to know you, your reputation, and also come to trust you."

Her expression was a combination of surprise and deflated hope. "Twenty years! I will be too old by then."

He shook his head, waving his hand for emphasis. "You're thinking like a millennial, Maya. You saying I'm too old now?"

She smiled. "No, guess not. You maybe live two more years. Ha ha." He flicked a nacho chip at her.

He finished his nachos, still looking hungry. "Well, that's pretty much it."

She slid some of her nachos his way and refilled his beer glass. "That's all huh? Twenty years bust ass."

He bowed his head, then looked up suddenly. "Yup, that's all. Same as in anything else, Maya. Overnight success sometimes takes twenty years. You think Beyoncé or J.Lo were overnight?"

She understood when he said J-Lo. She'd seen the documentary on TV. "So, I just help campaigns?"

He yawned. *This interests her for real? Katie never could last more than a minute of me talking politics. She only wanted me to come home.*

To her question, he answered, "No, not just help campaigns. Relationships are also important. I've been through political campaigns year after year, and it's brutal without knowing how the game is played and who your friends are, who can be trusted or not trusted, and what skills people truly have."

He watched her nod. *Seems like she's getting it.*

He continued. "This game never stops. Once you win or lose, it's on to the next one. What's made me successful is the bonds and relationships I've created and maintained year after year. And that's why twenty years."

She sipped water. The first two shots were real. Couldn't afford to get drunk. "You just make friends? Like Thailand. Make friends. Give money."

He bit his lip. "Not really, Maya. A relationship goes beyond trust. It's a bond created by trust, created by having gone through tough times together. Always deliver first, then you can ask for help later. Give with no expectation. But the first time you ask for a return favor and the other person does not respond without good reason, either cut them off the list or drop them to the bottom of the list."

He hoped he was getting through to her. She kept nodding. She was absorbing. She raised her finger to her lips as if she was about to make a solid point. "In Thailand, politicians corrupt. I don't like. Bad people."

He rubbed his eyes. "Yeah, you meet a lot of real sleazy people that make you want to puke. Being around them makes you feel slimy, and you ask yourself why you do this. Just remember, politics isn't always a bad thing—there are good people doing good things, and those are the people I associate with. We want to make the world a better place, you know?"

She nodded. She wanted to make Thailand a better place for young girls.

He finished off his beer. "Focusing on the end goal is important here, and I always think of the many people I can help by stomaching some of the people I have to deal with. Working out helps—the gym is my sanctuary, so is God."

She leaned back. "You for real?"

He chuckled. "Yes. Maya this is between you and me, okay? I think you would do okay in politics. You're good with people and you hustle like the wind. If you like I can teach you more."

He was wondering what he was doing. *I make it sound like it was all me, but it was actually divine intervention. God brought the Admiral into my life and it took off from there.*

And of course I couldn't have done it without Katie, he reminded himself. *She didn't understand everything that went on, but she understood it was important to me and let me do what I needed to do. I regret going whole months without seeing her—no dinners, no hellos, no goodbyes. I sure put her through some crap—home after she slept and gone before she woke up.*

Remorse etched into his heart. *I remember hugging her when I got home but she never quite remembered the hug. The last few years were painful for her, seeing me put in so much effort sometimes only to have someone knife me in the back. It got to be too much for her at times.*

She saw him deep in thought. Any deeper and he'd be asleep. She nudged him back to the present. "Glenn, we sing now? Sorry make you talk so long."

"Yeah." Talking about politics wound him up. "I think tonight I need to do shots."

She ran off and brought back Hennessey for him and watered-down versions for her. "Glenn, I have to leave early tonight. Stay to midnight is okay? Wake up early tomorrow. Make extra money beauty store I do month-end sales reports for manager."

He wondered how his face looked, hoping for a poker face. "Really? Interesting. Tell me more." What he wanted to say was, *early again? How does an entry-level counter worker rate doing sales reports for the manager?*

She yawned this time. Looked a little fake to him. "No Glenn, boring. Enter numbers all morning. Manager press button. Report come out."

He leaned back. *Oh, data entry. Makes sense. Except it's retail. All these numbers should have been captured at the point of sale—at the register—and tied into the inventory database. Was she lying? Three Tuesdays in a row she had to leave early.*

This train of thought nagged him. *Is she meeting someone after or is there someone at home that wants her home early?*

The night ended in the usual way. Laughter, joking, the walk to the car, and a goodnight kiss. He caressed her cheek and whispered, "Are you always going to be leaving early?"

She held his hand to her cheek. "No Glenn, I promise I stay with you all the way next Tuesday. Okay?"

He nodded and smiled and stole another kiss. "Okay. Goodnight."

She drove off just as an app on Glenn's phone lit up. Black ops stuff. An alert that someone was digging up online info on him. It had happened all the time when he was with the city, but it hadn't happened for a while. *Curious. I'll take care of it tomorrow. Call Mike on it.*

He got home.

Home safe. Had a great time.

Me too. Good night. Sweet dreams. ☺

She waited to see if he'd respond. None. She smiled and took a few seconds to commit the night to memory, then fixed her makeup. She got out of the car, careful not to nick the chrome green BMW in the next stall. Two steps later, she walked into a restaurant pub on the other side of town called Thai Garden.

Thai Garden was a Thai restaurant and sports bar in an industrial part of town. A converted hostess bar, it still had the look and feel of one. You walked into a bar area. To the right lay two rows of booths, beyond that dartboards and pool tables and a dance floor.

It was one of three Thai restaurants owned by Joy. The other two restaurants, Siam Eastern and Siam Heaven, had stellar reputations for authentic Thai food. This restaurant was no exception, but memories were long in this part of town, and many had not forgotten the illegal gambling, floating brothel, drugs, and gun and knife fights that had pockmarked the former Candy's Place.

Joy had spent the last two years fighting the stigma. This restaurant stayed open till 2:00 a.m. It was an after-hours haven for her Thai employees from the other two restaurants, which closed at 10:00 p.m. These employees showed up soon after work to drink, cavort, and sing Thai songs. Boyfriends, girlfriends, wives and husbands, and other friends and acquaintances usually filtered in around the same time.

On occasion, the joint was closed for "private events"—code for gambling. Eddie, the young fellow Maya went to Vegas with, was one of the key organizers and acted like it. He looked like a lackey outside Thai Garden, but he was a known international gambler who liked to take big risks. He often played the part of the house with great luck and results.

When they first met, she thought he was an easy-on-the-eyes bad boy who came to the bar with his construction buddies, most of them old, fat and balding. He told her he was married to a bargirl down the street, strictly for her green card.

Eddie's flair and their shared interest in high stakes gambling initially attracted Maya, but their relationship had run hot and cold since the Vegas trip. Coincidentally, Tuesday night gambling started in May, about the same time Eddie found out Maya was seeing Glenn again. Once Glenn came back into the picture, she hinted that she was only there to help the house, not be Eddie's girl like before.

But she had run up some gambling debts with Eddie. Playing hostess on Tuesday nights, sometimes personally to him, allowed her to work off the debt and avoid interest.

Chloe greeted her. "He's been waiting for you since 11:00. Midnight already." Maya frowned. *Still think I'm his girl. Showtime.*

Somewhere back on base, the man she called her cousin's husband put down his own copy of the Admiral's book and googled Glenn and every other name he could extract from the book, and the websites that mentioned Glenn.

There was no stone unturned—Facebook, Instagram and LinkedIn for starters. Then the various websites that provided anonymous background checks. He wanted to know who this guy was who impressed Maya so much that she fawned over him like a little girl at a rock star concert.

She had come to him. "See, he famous. He do so much. Why you not?"

The last three words irked him. In his opinion, someone living in a house his sweat paid for should have a little more respect. *Who was this guy? He wasn't the usual shmuck she usually picked up on—the cops, fire fighters, construction workers, insurance salesmen, real estate guys, car salesmen, even respectable bankers.*

To him, Glenn smelled like a bona fide power player but didn't look like it. *She's so into him. Like a kid with a favorite teacher.*

He was poring over all the online background checks. He glanced at his watch and realized it was midnight, time to turn in—reveille at 8:00 a.m. He thought it would be another two hours before she finished at the bar, and with Glenn. He noticed she usually got home around 2:30, but lately she'd been coming home later, saying she spent time with the other girls afterwards.

Who is this guy my wife is so fucking enamored with?

48

CRICKETS IN JUNE

It was the third Tuesday in June. They'd been back together, as she called it, for a little over a month. It was a happy time. No drama. Every week: Dinner. Talk. Drink. Sing. Kiss goodnight. Both happy. Both reset. Back to reality for a week. Repeat.

The one nagging thing was that they'd closed down the bar only once since they'd gotten back together. It was always the same story. Trying to get promoted to assistant manager. Helping with inventory reports. Helping with sales reports. Once, she had to wake up early for a dental appointment. Another time, she had to take Rusty for an early vet appointment.

The sun just started to set. The barflies were yelling at World Cup soccer on the flatscreens. It was still early, with no other girls or guys around. The jukebox was silent, as was the darts room. The booth room was dark, except for the area near Mama Lynh's booth, where she and Jimmy were going over inventory purchases.

Maya was waiting at the end of the bar, making small talk with Tia, dressed to kill in a black stretch mesh dress with off-the-shoulder sleeves and laced backing, and a generously short hemline designed to arouse.

Smiling, she waved him over excitedly. "I bring surprise for your dinner." From a tote bag, she brought out a burrito-shaped object wrapped in tinfoil. Unwrapping the foil, she produced a Ziploc bag to reveal what she'd brought for dinner—a special surprise. At first, he thought it was boiled peanuts.

His reaction was mixed at best. "Crickets? You brought crickets for dinner?"

She scrunched her nose and pursed her lips. Her eyes were a bit agitated. "Why you say like that? It's good. My country everyone like."

He smiled, tipping an imaginary cowboy hat and did his best cowboy accent. "Sweetheart, this is America. We eat steak and fried chicken here. Burgers. Hot dogs. Apple pie."

She stuck her tongue at him. "American okay. Not better than Thai food." Her eyes twinkled. She knew how he'd react. It was hard enough to get him to try panang curry with squid. But he tried it and was okay with it. "Okay, okay." She smiled. *Such a little boy sometimes.* She reached into her bag again and brought out panang curry with chicken, sticky rice and Pad Thai. His favorites. "You like now?"

"Yes." He reached out.

She pulled the bag away. "Uh-uh-uh, uh-uh." She wagged her finger. "You try crickets first."

His entire body language signaled panic. "Why?" A bead of sweat formed on his left temple.

She stood hands on her hips, with an encouraging smile. "Chloe make. Special order. I bring for you. Just try. New thing. You ever go wrong new thing with me?"

Never, he thought. *But crickets?*

He stared at his dish. In the dim bar light, they looked like little brown Cheetos. These were *big* crickets. *Big* Thai crunchy crickets.

"Here I eat." She popped them in her mouth like candy.

He heard the scrunching like she was eating a can of Pringles.

He looked down. Jiminy Cricket stared back up at him. "You gotta be kidding. Dear, I love you but . . . "

She covered his mouth and started humming. Then she wiped his face. "Shhhh—be calm."

She covered his eyes with one hand. In a soft voice, she coaxed, "Just try . . . one." With the other hand, she opened his mouth, thumb on his lower lip, and placed one cricket on his tongue. She lifted his jaw. "Now, chew."

She took her hands away and saw the look in his eyes. She knew he liked it but wasn't going to admit it.

He expected it to taste like dirt or crap or whatever insect guts tasted like. *Damn,* he thought, *like eating pistachio-flavored Wheat Thins.*

She held his gaze, hand on the side of his face. "Sooo, what you think?"

He chewed slowly, mesmerized by her eyes. "It's okay."

She caressed his cheek with the back of her hand. She was seducing him to eat. "You want more?"

The impasse. *If I say yes, I'm admitting I like it. Her win. If I say no, well that's that.* "If you want me to."

She pinched his cheek, softly but firmly. "No Glenn, not mind game. You want. You know you want. If you want just ask. Just say. Don't think what I think or what others think. This not win loss game, Glenn. It simple. You want noddah cricket, yes no?"

How can someone know me so well? "Yes." She dumped a handful on his plate. They were great with beer, a smoky barbecue taste on top of the pistachio flavor. *So sorry, Jiminy. Welcome to the food chain. Maya 1, Glenn 0.*

Verna walked by. Saw the crickets, grimaced, shook her head and kept walking. He grinned. *Guess crickets weren't that big in Vietnam?*

Trying to change the subject, he pulled out his phone and punched on the citizenship test app. "So how's the studying going?"

She tussled with her hair, tugging at the ends. "So hard. Why your country so screwed up." Maya wanted to become a US citizen. Hubby was threatening to deport her. She was glad Glenn never asked why.

He scolded softly. "Dear, don't forget it was your decision to become a citizen of this screwed-up country. Screwed-up or not, it's still the greatest country in the world." Glenn had once worn a uniform and never stopped defending the flag ever since. "So I downloaded an app. I ask you questions, you answer. I'll help you."

She took his hand and swung it back and forth like a child. "Oh Glenn, why study. Tonight fun night. We have fun. No more studying."

He peeled his hand from hers with a stern expression and picked up his phone. "Bullshit, Maya. I'll help you." *God it hurts to do that. But I want to make sure this citizenship kick isn't another failed plan. Like how she was supposed to quit the bar last year to do beauty gigs. Or how she was supposed to start beauty school earlier in the month, but never did. I gotta know she's for real this time.*

She pouted, arms crossed, looking away.

Aw c'mon. Grow up, won't you? he thought and waved his hand in front of her face. "Make you a deal. Only ten questions. We have fun after. Any night you go ten for ten, I buy you five shots. Deal?"

Trying hard to feign anger, her eyes gave away her amusement. "No, ten shots, I pick first five songs too."

He exaggerated a wince and turned away so she wouldn't see him rolling his eyes. *This is hard. Fighting over five songs.*

With an exasperated sigh, he gave in. "Okay."

He rattled off ten questions. She got seven right.

She sulked, not happy about losing.

He relented. "Not bad. Here's your consolation prize—two shots of Crown Reserve and the first two songs." The night took off after that. Then crashed. The karaoke machine broke down. It was only 11:00.

They adapted. The jukebox playlist was still good, and so was the vibe—

some parts '90s rock, some parts Latin, rounded off by contemporary feel-good music. They talked story for the rest of the night. "I ever tell you about optical shop?" She poured his beer, then lifted the glass to his lips.

He peered over the top of his glass, eyebrows raised, as if to say go on.

She fumbled on her phone. "See my pictures." Glenn recalled all the bargirls he ever met. They all had a *huge* inventory of pictures to show customers. It was a way to keep them interested and occupied, and to find out what interested them. He went along and was glad he did.

It was a picture of five Thai girls, with a young Maya in the middle. "My sisters. I was youngest. All money go to Mommy and Sister. No money for lunch. I starve. Every day someone have extra food, bring too much. Give me. Ask me favor. Eat food or waste. I party with them every time I go back." She sniffed. "See this girl. She my favorite. She crying here. I was leaving. I'm only one outside of Thailand. One day I will be rich. I will go back take care all of them. They save my life, Glenn."

That was about all she wanted to share. Her sisters took her in. It was more than feeding her. They literally saved her life one night. One day she'd share but not yet. Too painful to even think. She blocked it out.

He wiped a tear from her cheek. "That's great, Maya. Nice to have friends. Love conquers all, you know, near or far."

She seemed at a loss. Karaoke had always been their mainstay. Over the time they'd spent with each other, she'd shown him all the pictures and told him all the stories. Sometimes she showed him the same pictures, slightly different stories. She was searching for a way to keep him occupied. She didn't want him to start asking tough questions. She remembered Darren asking hard questions.

Suddenly she snapped her fingers, eyes wide open. "You want to play cards?" The expression on her face was a mixture of relief and joy.

He replied hesitantly. "What kind?" *Never been much of a card player. This could be embarrassing. Her teaching me, a guy, card playing.*

She noticed he looked shy about it. "Thai High Card. Like poker. You know poker? I teach you." She was patient—teaching, coaching, coaxing, encouraging. At one point, he wasn't sure what he had. She leaned over, took his cards, and laid them out. "You okay. See? Here." She moved the cards around. Giving him a winning hand. "You win!" She had Tia bring over a beer and some snacks. Poured his beer and popped a few chips in his mouth. She laughed when he caught them midair. She thought, *Like my boy back home.*

In his mind, they weren't in a bar anymore. *Weird feeling*, he thought. *Is this what it's like to come home to a mom, and she feeds you and the two of you talk story and play parlor games afterward?*

To him, it was like some Mother's Day commercial. *Is this what it's like?* He looked over at her. In that moment, she was so nurturing. He felt like an eleven year old. He remembered Billy's mom, and wanting his own mama home again.

She noticed the stare. "What? You okay?"

He whispered like he was holding back a secret. "Yeah."

She leaned closer. Brushed his hair back. "What on mind?"

He took a breath, then another breath. "I don't want to be weird, but I feel like you're my mommy playing cards with me after dinner. It feels good."

She leaned back, eyes widening a bit, careful not to show any other emotion. Deep in thought, she remembered the little boy. She wanted him to be happy. No judging. "Uh-hmm. Maybe noddah life?" She took both his hands in hers.

He held on like he wanted it to last forever. "Maybe."

Time stood still. It was like they were in a freeze-frame. They stared into each other's eyes, gazed into the other's soul, things a poet might say. Yet this was real life, not a poem. In both of their heads nothing was registering except this unexplainable need to be with each other and make each other happy.

Allie broke them out of their trance. "Hi guys, what you doing?" It was like in the movies where the action and sound start up again with a blur and whir, the bar sights and sounds came back to them. Giggling, they let go of each other. "Whose deal?"

Then it got serious. He was down five hands. He raised the stakes. "Next hand double or nothing."

She fired back. "Higher stakes?"

"Like what?"

She smiled like she had him. "Dinner. You and me, dinner my choice?"

He broke open a broad smile. Ear to ear, some would say. "Seriously? Seems like I win either way. Hmmm. Let me think."

She puffed her cheeks and poofed at him. "Deal anyway. Play first. Prize later."

His expression said, are you shitting me? "What?"

Now she was teasing, her voice coy. "Don't worry. I will be fair. You scared?"

He leaned back. He took in her mesh dress, his eyes lingering near her hemline. Tapping his fingers, she could see he was thinking. Then he leaned forward. "What if I win?"

Without hesitation, her voice reached out and caressed him. "*Big* kiss from me."

The only encouragement he needed. "You're on!"

He was dealt a winning hand. Only two combinations could beat him. He sat back smugly. Her eyes gleamed with determination. He could almost smell the adrenaline coursing through her veins. She turned over her cards.

He lost. Tried to look upset. He couldn't control a weird grin. "Okay. Where do you want to go?" *Easiest loss ever!*

She feigned her most compassionate "I'll let you off easy" look. "Hmmm. Not go anywhere. Eat here bar."

He did a double-take. "For real?" *Getting off easy here.* "Okay, anything Uncle makes."

His stomach lurched at the playful look on her face, and as he heard her say, "No. You make dinner for me."

He shook his head in denial. "What?! No way. *No way.*"

Her lip curled slightly, morphing into a triumphant smile. She knew she had him. "Yes way. And not burger or sandwich or anything easy. You make Thai food for me. From scratch."

His mouth dropped in protest, his eyes wide and staring. *What the hell? Is she serious?* "I can't do that. You're asking for the impossible."

She leaned over and whispered, eyes twinkling, mischief in her voice. "But you night job man, you fix anything . . . right?"

Riiiight. He rolled his eyes. *I'd rather take on the national security advisor than do this.* "Okay. Next week come hungry." *She better be hungry to choke down whatever I come up with.*

She stuck out her pinky. Pinky swearing (crossing pinky fingers and pulling) was a big thing for them now. He called for Verna, lifting five fingers. Maya inquired with her eyes. "Three for me, two for you. Yes, I need a shot, two shots, not a beer." She wiped his face, giggling.

The picture show and storytelling continued. Some new pics. "This my grandpa . . . how you say . . . gangster. He kill people. Then monk ten years to clear karma . . . make right, so can marry Grandma. She wait ten years for him. He mean man. One time kill my cat. Throw against wall. I cried. I was a kid."

Another picture. A young man. "This my brother. So nice. Him monk. Make merit. Bring good karma to family. Help Mommy get better. After monk, join Thai navy. My baby. Twelve years younger. Not looking for anyone. Him not good. He get money, he give away. Give money to anyone that need. He not eat sometimes. I always make sure he eat."

A guy came in. They made eye contact. She frowned and looked away. Glenn asked, "Hey, what's wrong?"

The guy went to the booth room. "That's my . . . was my . . . customer. Over year. I ask him last week come same time Friday. One year he come every Friday. Last time, he tell me oh yeah you just want to make money off me." Glenn thought, *Hello, that's what this is all about.*

She brushed back her hair. "He apologize later and I'm okay now."

He was taking in her expression. *Funny, she doesn't look okay. She looks sad or upset or something.*

She stared off into the distance, almost like she didn't want eye contact. "I have pride, not here only for money. Not like the other girls. You see me pushing for money?"

He didn't know what that meant and wasn't about to argue. "No."

They finished their shots. "He not have to sit with me if not want to. I told him. He mad. Over year he come. No date yet. Not like us last week."

Glenn was wide-eyed. "Really? Why?"

"I dunno. Not feel like."

He paused, staring at his empty shot glass. Then looked up. "Why me? Why dinner outside with me?"

She made eye contact with him for the first time in a long while. Her voice flowed sweetly, softly. "You do plenty for me. Just say thank you. Oh, not date okay?" Their hands touched. Fingers automatically intertwined. "I don't care if he come back to me again."

Glenn swiveled his stool around. Caught the guy staring. Held the gaze till the guy looked away. Lynh took another girl to the guy. He noticed there were several guys he recognized from her Instagram account. *They're all waiting for her.*

She let go. Poured the beer Allie brought them. Then reached for his hand again. "Glenn, you know my birthday pretty soon?" He knew the exact date, but it was more than a month away. She asked him, "You come?"

"I dunno. Friday night, right? Yeah, I have family on Friday."

She wanted to ask what family.

He continued. "You know. Mom's house." It was ironic. She had the same birthday weekend as Katie. *Mom would want me at their house. The kids too.*

She scrolled through her phone, masking her disappointment. He could tell. It made his heart hurt. She wasn't going to pry. She held onto his hand. "You come help decorate? Afternoon. Last year all my customers come help me."

He saw a chance to make it up. "Maybe I can." She stuck out her pinky. He took her pinky with caution. "Maybe, I said. I try."

She perked up. "Okay." Then last call. She promised the week before. They'd close down the bar.

He finished his beer. *Wow. That was fast.*

She gave him a back rub. "Glenn, I go now. Walk me to my car?" The white Audi. His lucky omen. He opened the door for her. She got in, and he leaned in after her. She kissed him, then pulled him back and kissed him again. "That for being good listener."

She shifted and leaned backward on her seat, and pulling him down with her, they kissed again. Their mouths lingered, open, hungry, each feeling the other's breath on their lips. Her mouth parted to welcome him in, and for a split second, their tongues touched. Just the tips. But enough for him to react below his beltline.

Somewhere in the back of his head, he wondered about all the guys that he thought were waiting for her.

She was still holding him close. "Don't forget you cook me Thai food next week okay? Text me when you get home."

He gave her another quick kiss. Their usual quick, soft, no tongue, closed mouth good night kiss. "Okay."

She let him go. "You don't be worry. I always respond yes?" She said it proudly.

"Yes, you do." He leaned in and gave her another kiss. Her tender lips were quickly becoming a tender addiction.

Later.

Home safe. You're awesome and the best ☺ ☺ ☺

Me too thank you for everything ☺

She pulled up to Thai Garden. There were five texts on her phone. She had ignored them all.

49

CHICKEN FEET

On the weekends, Chinatown was a bustling, four-block sea of Chinese, Vietnamese, Laotian, Thai and other far eastern cultures. Shopkeepers and customers yelled at each other, mixing in their dialects and mangling the English language, haggling over foodstuffs, housewares, medicines, and hard-to-find items from their home countries. Somewhere in the distance, Glenn heard the drumming sounds of a lion dance put on by one of the many kung fu societies that ran that part of town. Every step brought new smells—sweet, acidic, sour, some good, some not so good.

It was Saturday. He parked his car and walked out of the municipal parking lot and headed over to a familiar shop. He heard someone calling his name as he got closer. He waved to the woman standing by the doorway. "Thanks so much for meeting me. I have no fricking clue what I'm doing."

Minh laughed as they hugged. "What's the big emergency, Glenn?"

He remembered long ago Maya saying her favorite food was chicken feet. He googled chicken feet and Thai and found some how-to videos on YouTube. *This stuff is easier said than done. Easier watched than done. So much crap about the sauce and presentation but no nothing about how to cook chicken feet. Where do I even get chicken feet?*

He finally tracked down chicken feet in Chinatown and was trying to tell Minh what he wanted to do.

Minh laughed again. "*You* talking to a Vietnamese shopgirl selling produce in Chinatown about how to make chicken feet for a Thai bargirl. That's what I'm getting. Correct?"

Minh was second-generation Vietnamese American, a former Miss Vietnamese Chinatown. They had been management trainees together. The shop belonged to her parents and she helped on Saturdays. *Shopgirl, my ass. She's a vice president and business banker at State Bank.* He pleaded. "Aw, c'mon—help me out."

She teased. "Why not a good Vietnamese girl? We're easy. Just make instant pho." She bent over laughing. "Nah, nah, Glenn. Do you even eat Thai food? Last time we all tried to get you to eat even ethnic Chinese, you wrinkled your nose."

He gave her the stink eye. *Mental note. Destroy her career when I become CEO at State Bank.*

He shoved his phone at her. "Look at this YouTube video. I follow this and I should be okay, right? But they don't tell me how to cook the chicken feet."

Minh thought about it. "Glenn, have you tried going to a Thai restaurant and asking?"

He tried to picture it. *Not a bad idea.* "Thanks, Minh. Remember me when you hit the corner office." She turned her attention to other customers, firing away in rapid Mandarin.

By the time he entered Siam Eastern, he'd been to four Thai restaurants, with major language problems encountered at each one. They kept saying that chicken feet was not on the menu.

He had a panicked look when he entered. The place had an excellent reputation, and the décor matched what one found in most Thai restaurants—pictures of Thailand and its royal family, temples, and Buddha statues. Thai music played softly in the background.

The waitress thought he wanted to use the restroom. "No public restroom," she began.

A different tack this time. Glenn put down a fifty dollar bill. "Can I get one order Pad Thai? The rest is a tip if someone can help me."

The waitress called back to the kitchen in Thai. It sounded like she was saying, we got a live one out here. Business was slow—somewhere between the lunch and dinner crowd. Noi came over. "How help?" She tucked Ulysses Grant into her pocket.

Glenn pulled out his phone and showed her his YouTube video. "I'm making chicken feet but don't know how to cook." Noi looked at him, thinking about how he was acting like her little boy back home with a science project. She smiled. She chattered something in Thai at the kitchen. Malee came over, and they rattled back and forth. Noi went in the back. Malee looked at him, amused. "Who this for? Why? What occasion?"

Glenn raked his hair. "My friend. I lost a bet." *Geez*, he thought, *so many questions about who gets to eat chicken feet.*

Noi came back with the chef. "You want us make for you? Not on menu. Usually Thai family only make."

He leaned on the bar. "No. I have to make it myself."

Noi and Malee translated for the chef. "Boil in salt. Not too much salt."

Glenn was taking notes on his phone, looking up. "How much salt?"

Noi fired off some quick Thai, and the chef answered, shrugging and giggling. "Don't know. Just enough." Noi giggled as well.

Glenn's face looked like he had to pee. "What is enough?" *This is not going well. I feel like I'm in some weird M.A.S.H. episode.*

Malee jumped in. "Enough to make taste." She said it like it was the most natural thing.

His frustration was boiling over. He looked like someone who had to take a crap and the nearest shithole a mile away. Both girls laughed. "No worry. Only little bit. Pretend making soup. Not too salty, just enough."

He nodded. *That sounded better. Why didn't they just say that?*

Chef said something, then Malee explained. "Then boil till feet tender."

Glenn gave the time-out sign. "What does that mean? Do you mean . . ."

Noi cut in. "See chopstick? Poke feet. If chopstick go through easy then okay. No stop boiling till chopstick poke through. Else cannot eat."

He was typing in notes with gusto. "Okay. That's doable."

Chef asked a question, Malee translated. "You da one come every week here buy Pad Thai. You like Thai food?"

Glenn nodded. "I make friend lately and she help me learn all kinds of Thai food. Crickets too."

They laughed. *Looked at each other. Could be? No.* Noi asked, "How you know this girl?"

Glenn got a puzzled look on his face. "Oh, just a friend." *Getting kinda personal.* They caught the hint.

Chef went back to the kitchen. Malee was curious to learn more. "You need more help you come back tomorrow. When this for?"

He was going over his notes, licking his lips. "Tuesday."

Again, they looked at each other. Noi turned to him. "You mess up, you can always buy Pad Thai for her."

Glenn laughed. "I wish."

Noi brought him a glass of water. "Maybe next time you bet expensive restaurant instead."

He drained the glass in a second. "I tried. She said I have to make."

Noi nodded. "This girl smart. You marry by year end I think."

He lifted his hand as if to say stop, waving for good measure. "I don't think so. Only friends." *Getting real personal, aren't we?*

He thanked them, and as he walked out, Malee took another stab. "I think this husband test. Good luck."

Glenn walked out. *A husband test? Seriously?* The fantasy suddenly got a little real.

The following Tuesday he brought some of his dish to work and made some plates for Danielle and Penny, and for Jensen, the resident food connoisseur. Danielle was Filipina, Jensen was Chinese, and Penny was a good ol' girl from Texarkana.

Jensen and Danielle were all over the feet, expertly popping them into their mouths and spitting out bits of bone. He turned to his clerk from Texas, "What about you, Penny?"

Penny exclaimed, "Hell no!"

He was enjoying watching them eat. "Good thing I added in some breast fillets for you all."

Penny was perplexed. "Look boss, I don't even do gizzards back home. Why would I eat something that's been tramping around in mud and hen guano for the last year?"

Glenn nodded, feeling a bit queasy at the last comment. "Fair enough." He turned to Danielle and Jensen. "Taste okay?"

Danielle answered first. "Sure."

Jensen was a little hesitant. "I think you coulda boiled the feet a bit more."

Glenn did a head tilt. "Really? I poked it with the chopstick."

Jensen kicked into expert cook mode. "Show me how."

Glenn speared imaginary chicken feet in an imaginary pot.

Jensen took over the imaginary pot. "No, boss. It should be a slow gentle poke and it should slide right in."

Danielle blushed. "That sounds like a porn flick, Jensen."

Jensen didn't hear her. "No, No. You can't just spear it. That means it's not soft enough."

Glenn was hoping warming up the dish later would soften it up enough for consumption. *Shit, she's lucky she didn't get burgers covered in Thai chili sauce.* He was still thinking about the husband test remark.

He'd sent her a text the day before with a picture of the raw chicken feet.

Wish me luck.

OMG 😊 😊 can't wait!

Maya felt warmth gush through her heart. *For me? This guy is special. How is that he's not married? Or is he? Can't believe he remembered.*

Noi and Malee saw Maya Saturday night at Thai Garden. "Oh sis, this guy come in Siam Eastern all panic how cook chicken feet." Maya giggled at how they described him.

They asked her, "Your crush? You second wife?"

Maya was coy. They were like three schoolgirls talking boyfriends at recess. "Maybe, what name?"

They wrote his name down from the debit card he used, and she pointed to it with glee, a hint of pride in her voice. "Yep, that's him." She stared at the name. *No Thai man do this. Shit, no man do this period. He actually bought chicken feet? Where he find chicken feet?*

Noi nudged Maya. "I tell him about the husband test. Look like he sweat."

They all giggled. Maya quizzed the two Thai women. "Oh no, what you guys do? He overthinks you know. Now he think I'm after him." *Who not marry guy with that much money backed by so much thoughtfulness?*

Malee was curious. "Really Maya, you second wife?" In Thai culture, many women resigned themselves to being second wives—called "mistresses" in the States—to men who would care for them for life, instead of being primary wives to assholes.

One alternative was to marry an ugly Westerner who, grateful for the submissive attention of an Asian wife, treated her like a queen. Some of these *faraangs* found happiness. Most found themselves on the short end of a divorce proceeding. The military guys usually lost half their pensions.

Maya was smiling, though shaking her head. "Not second wife. You know I'm already married." She thought, *technically anyway.* When Maya married Caleb, she was in it for life. Then things changed a few years after they married. She recalled with a shudder his uncontrolled rage and the beating that followed. He was not the same after seeing combat in the Middle East.

Glenn walked into the bar with a pot of Thai Chicken Feet à la Glenn. He bought some sticky rice from Siam Eastern. Noi and Malee were chattering in Thai as he left. Both chef and Joy, the owner, came out to check out this guy who makes Chicken Feet for a bargirl. Apart from Siam Eastern, Joy owned two other restaurants, including Thai Garden.

Tia's eyebrows arched. She usually kept her cool on most things, but this was different, a customer bringing food for his girl.

He took his seat and settled in on the boxing match on the flatscreen in front of him. The bar was empty except for a few barflies. The jukebox was quiet, and there was no one singing karaoke yet.

He didn't have to wait long. He'd seen her beautiful before, but never like this. She walked in, looking different from her usual dress and makeup. She wore traditional Thai clothing, gold in color. Her hair was tied in a bun in the back. And her makeup was simple with pinkish eyeshadow and lipstick lightly applied to match. Natural nails. Natural color.

She rubbed his back. "Hi, Glenn. I come from funeral. Friend's boyfriend mother die. Laotian funeral. Like Thai all week long. I help friend. Make food. Family friends come all week long, eat, drink, gamble. To show dead person everything okay. Can go heaven now."

His ears heard her words. His eyes soaked in her beauty. She gently grazed his forearm. "I go back tonight midnight help. You okay with that?"

He was still taking in how she looked. "Okay, yeah, gotta help your friend." His overthink process kicked into second gear. *Another early exit? Seems legit though. Or would she go through all this getup just to get away early, like all the other times? No way. No way she's splitting time between me and someone else. She said Tuesdays are for us.*

She smiled. "So, where my food?"

He brought out the pot, and she opened the cover. She breathed it all in. "Smell so good!" She went back and made bowls for both and came out. She ate. The feet were not so soft. "Next time boil ten more minutes, then perfect. But I like. I eat." She ate it all.

Glenn sat there, watching in admiration. *This shit came out like shit, and she's eating it all. Every bite. Every bone.*

He reminisced. The last time he saw something like this was in the third grade. *I made breakfast for Mommy. Boiled an egg, and a wiener. They were kinda raw. I burned the toast. But Mommy ate it all, kept telling me it was so good. Next time boil longer, but it was good. She told me she was so proud of me, her little boy. I felt so good, so . . . special. Like how I feel now.*

He reached out and touched her hand, pushed it down, letting the food slip back into the bowl. "Maya, you don't have to finish it."

She popped the chicken feet back into her mouth. "No, it's okay. I'm so proud of you. You make from scratch? Not buy from some restaurant?"

He shook his head no.

Her face beamed with admiration. "Good boy." She reached over and kissed his cheek. Wiping some sauce she left behind.

She thought it wasn't bad. She had eaten at the funeral. She was tired. The celebration of life started two days before. She'd only slept two-to-three hours a night. The gambling and eating was nonstop. Some of the men were also nonstop. She detested them. Grabby types. At a funeral of all places. She left Chloe and the others behind. They couldn't believe she'd step out for a customer? Chloe defended her. This guy was special. Noi and Malee filled in the rest.

Even though full, she was determined to finish the food. She wanted to show appreciation. *This more than anyone ever did for me here. He good guy.* "Next week I make something for you, okay?"

The karaoke machine was broken again. "Glenn, you want to play darts?"

Glenn had never been in the darts room. In his mind, it was where she met her other customers. "I'm no good."

Maya winked. "I teach you." Unbeknownst to Glenn, she had a reputation as a darts shark. Five shots for every win. Free company for the night if she lost. Sucker bet all the time.

She watched him play. He was having fun, and it made her happy. *He suck at this. He lucky he mine or the other girls would work him. I would work him. He work too much all these years. Never had time for fun. I'm glad I came.*

Midnight came quickly. He turned to her. "I think I want to stay for one more beer. Why don't you go help your friend?"

She put away the darts. "No, no. I stay with you."

His brow furrowed. "Now you're making me feel guilty." Allie put down his beer. Maya paid for it. By now, their arrangement had boiled down to he paid for her drinks, and she paid for his. "Go, Maya."

Her shoulders drooped a bit. "No! Don't be mad, Glenn. I'm tired." Her voice softened. "I stay with you, okay?" She was worried. *I was not here to protect you last time. I'm here now. Don't worry, Glenn.* "Glenn, finish your beer and we can both go. I worry you stay here by yourself. I can still help friend, don't worry."

He pursed his lips. He didn't know whether to be happy or mad. "Okay. 12:30 a.m., no later."

She nodded and caressed his cheek in appreciation.

A few minutes later, he bottomed up his beer. "Okay, let's go."

She saw what he did for her. She closed her account, gathered up all the stuff he brought and gave it to him. "Walk me my car?" This was becoming a regular thing.

She slid in behind the wheel. He stood there. *Should I, or shouldn't I? After all these times, it should be automatic. Always feels like the first time.*

She wondered, *Why he just standing there?* She waved at him to lean in with a come here kind of wave. He leaned in, and they kissed goodnight.

He didn't linger like the last time. "Don't work too hard at your friend's."

She blew him a kiss. "Text me, okay? Next week no inventory. Holiday next day. We close down bar, okay?" She was gone.

Got home safe. Thank you for tonight. You did good. Get your stomach empty for next week. ☺

Me home safe too. Thank you for staying longer it meant a lot to me. ☺ ☺

Looking forward to next week ☺

She smiled. *He appreciate me staying longer. I'm so happy he happy. And he do emojis now? Cute.*

The glow of the texts fell on her face in her Audi, parked at Thai Garden, next to the green BMW.

Eddie was watching, waiting at the door. "What took you so long? We got a lot of action tonight."

She snapped her response. "He didn't want to leave. What you want me do?"

He puffed his chest. "Dump him! You make tons of money here already. I don't give you ten percent of the cut to come late. You shake your ass, giggle, make the old farts feel wanted, and they gamble more. So what they rub you sometimes. Just keep them excited."

Maya and the other girls circulated the room. Maya was the best at keeping the patrons excited. She'd sing at times. Dance at others. Just entertainment. Mostly she was ignored until she served drinks to one patron or another that wanted to rub her ass for luck.

Eddie always gave her enough tip and the last hour off to gamble for herself. Most times, she lost the allowance and racked up more debt to the house—him. On more than one occasion, she'd text home and say she'd be late—having breakfast with the girls after work. She'd text some picture taken weeks before at some after-hours eatery. She had a stock of pics at various late-night places. The other girls had the same stock, and they all vouched for each other.

Eddie still had the hots for her. He decided that next time she'd be his personal hostess. Or pay off the twenty grand she owed him, with interest.

50

JULY FIREWORKS

It was the first Tuesday in July, Independence Day eve. They had traded texts the night before.

I got real bad allergy I might not make it tomorrow. I go doctor tell you later how I feel 😿

Oh no. Please take care, do what doctor says. Let me know if you need anything 🙂

Ok thank you 🙏

He was overthinking again. *So, you're setting me up for the big fall tomorrow? Holiday the next day. Figure you got some real plans tomorrow night. Friends? Husband? Boyfriend? Wherever you run off to all those nights?*

She sniffed. It wasn't a lie. Her allergy was acting up. *Can't believe Eddie such a jerk. Want me there from 6:00? Big night. Next day holiday. But he give me double allowance. I can win all. Pay him off. After that Tuesdays normal again.*

Glenn's demons plagued him all night and into the next day. Waiting for the hammer to drop, but determined to be a nice guy, the cool guy, not the temperamental little boy. At least not on the outside.

On Tuesday, the texts came as he wrapped things up at the non-profit.

Damn. She's actually going to make it. I thought for sure she was setting me up for the no-show.

She was sitting at Thai Garden's bar counter. As she looked up from her phone, she turned to Eddie. "Baby, I have to take break tonight. Little while. Leave 9:00. Back midnight. Okay?" She turned on the charm. Rubbed up against his arm. She was in a maroon cheongsam with gold and blue chrysanthemums. The dress was down to her ankles, with side slits up to her waist. Her hair French braided.

He sneered, just enough to let her know he wasn't happy. "Him again?"

She leaned up against him. "I'll treat you good after, Eddie." She almost purred. Inside she felt a little sick. She let him run his hand down her backside, for just a bit, then she spun out very slowly, like a dance, and ran her hand across his face. "I go distract all these guys now. Make excited. Drink and gamble more. Okay, honey?" *Oh shit, I'm starting to sound like Mama Lynh.*

She smiled demurely, telling Eddie, "Save energy for me, we have fun after." As she turned back to the room, her smile faded for an instant as she felt the queasiness. Then she straightened up and put on a smile.

Chloe was watching from across the room, feeling equally nauseous at the sight. The other girls were filing in. Maya took one last check of the pot

in the kitchen, her chicken feet soup, then went out to the main floor.
Showtime.

————————

Across town at Lynh's bar, the mood was festive, the atmosphere
raucous. The next day was the Fourth of July. It was like a Friday night.
Everybody was at the bar—barflies, bargirls, and bar customers. The
jukebox was pulsating with electronic dance music. The darts room was
overflowing with construction workers. The booth room was filling up
fast. Jimmy and Tia were behind the counter, with Mei and Amber acting
as servers, barbacks and whatever else customers wanted. Verna and Allie
were literally at a trot taking trays of drinks back and forth between the bar,
the darts room and the booth room.

There were lots of randoms milling about. Randoms—that's what you
called the guys that weren't regulars with certain girls. They came in and
took what was there, usually five shots, and they were out, on to the next
bar. Some girls liked it that way—no fuss, no muss, just a lot of horseplay,
and on to the next shmuck.

The good ones could do four rounds of five shots in two hours and
be home in time to watch Jimmy Fallon with $300. Others could stay all
night and graduate to champagne bottles or $40 drinks and go home with a
thousand dollars. It was get-what-you-can when the construction industry
was in full bloom.

He walked in at 9:30, remembering what she had texted, and never
asking what a little bit late was. She was there already, with another
customer. "When did you get here?" Glenn said, staring at the elderly
man with a bad toupee. He noticed the thousand-dollar suit the guy was
wearing.

She teased Glenn. "Ten minutes ago. You late. I go already."

She said bye to the guy, but he wouldn't let her go. "One more," he
said, almost pleading. She looked toward Glenn and turned back. She
whispered in the man's ear, and he looked up at Glenn. Glenn nodded,
and the guy nodded back and gave Maya a hug. As Maya made her way to
Glenn, Chloe walked in and took Maya's place with the gentleman.

Maya gave Glenn a hug hello. "Chloe's customer. I was keeping
company."

Glenn's stern one-word reply matched his expression. "Okay." *Really?
Why would the guy beg her to stay if Chloe was coming? Early customer? Did
she give me the running late story to get me to come late?*

Her face evinced surprise and disappointment. "You mad? Don't tell me you mad?" *How he mad? I'm just being nice. Keeping company. He overthinking again.*

His face contorted slightly with annoyance. "No, no, not at all." *I'm in a frickin' mood and don't know how to snap out of it. Maybe I should leave. I swear she was going to bail with the whole allergy story last night.* He eyed the booth room. It was packed. "What's going on in there?"

She followed his stare. "Birthday party. Mama rent out all night. Look like a $30,000 night. That's why all the girls here."

His voice got even edgier. "You too?" *So that's why you look so nice? Either for the old guy before me or for that party.*

She lowered her eyes and her voice. "I might have to help." *Little boy here again. Why does he have to be like this? My little boy. I'm here for you!*

His stony expression faded to wistful sadness, with some resignation. "You have customers here?"

She nodded. "Yes."

He was looking over her shoulder. "Who?"

"You!" She poked him in the chest, playfully till it hurt. He had no choice but to reach out and take her hand. On contact, some anger dissipated.

She took a deep breath, puffed her cheeks and exhaled like a deflating balloon. "You know it's Tuesday . . . only you my customer!" Inside she was a little hurt. *We do this almost one year. He still not believe me? He not understand how hard this is? I wish he knew.*

She turned on the affection, lifting his palm to her lips, kissing it twice, then laying her cheek on his shoulder. "Glenn, we stay out here tonight, okay? Our booth taken. Okay?"

"Sure." He was still edgy. The allergy texts the night before had started him on a downward spiral.

She started massaging him. "Glenn, you need to chill. You want beer?"

He nodded.

She went to get his beer. *I don't understand. I'm here. I leave Eddie. I'm here and he still upset?*

Two beers in, he relaxed. She lifted his face to her and looked in his eyes. "I talk to Mama. Enough girls. I stay with you. You happy?"

He nodded. Just a little sheepish. "Sorry about before."

She mussed his hair, then combed it back again. "Don't worry, Glenn. You hungry?"

He nodded. She ran off and came back with her chicken feet soup. They sat and ate together.

The fatty skin and cartilage slid off the bones in his mouth. *So, this is what it's supposed to taste like? This is awesome.* They took turns spitting into a bowl, like watermelon seeds.

Tia came over and wrinkled her nose. "Ewww." She watched in fascination. *Amazing how two people spitting chicken feet bones into a shared side bowl could make it look so romantic—like Lady and the Tramp. Leave it to these two.* She remembered back to last summer. *Never would have thought. Enjoy, loves.*

They finished up and ordered shots. He was glowing, the downward spiral forgotten. "That was great! You're such a great cook. I could learn from you."

She wiped the area in front of him. "No, only difference I boil feet for ten more minutes. Yours was good too."

He gave her an adoring look. *She'll never admit she had to choke that crap down, but she did it. Gotta love her, and I do. Too bad it's one way only*

Fed and a bit drunk, he took a hard look at her. "Wow. You really look nice tonight."

Hands on her hips, she feigned irritation. "Only now you notice?" She waved her hand in front of her like a model displaying the dress. "Chicken feet soup turn you on more than this?" She knew she looked good. She had Ubered directly from Thai Garden and kept her hair up. She'd told Tia to make sure the drinks she got tonight were extra watered down. It was going to be a long night, and she didn't want to let her guard down. But first, she wanted to make sure Glenn was okay.

She sat him in his chair, swiveled him toward her, and stepped in between his legs. He could smell the Crown on her breath. "Cannot sing tonight, Glenn. Mama give party karaoke machine. We just sing what they sing, okay?" She was taking shot after shot but she seemed pretty alert to him. He lost track at eight drinks. *She sure can down the stuff.*

They were singing along with whatever the partygoers were singing. Aerosmith, Bon Jovi, Van Halen. She stood next to him, leaning against him, sitting on the stool. He had his arm around her waist. The feel of the silk dress was smooth, and he could feel the contours of her shape against his arm as she moved back and forth to the music.

It was a great night. The booth room party brought enough birthday party cake for everyone. Tia put one in front of them.

Maya smiled with a twinkle in her eye "Glenn, you want cake?" Before he could say anything, she scooped up a piece with her finger, her beautifully nailed finger, and stuck it in his mouth. She left that finger in there for what seemed like an eternity. He sucked hard, using quick hard swirling strokes of his tongue off her finger.

Then she pulled out her finger and looked at it. "Missed a few." She stuck her finger in her mouth and pulled on it with a pop, all the while holding his gaze. He felt his crotch tighten and swallowed.

She giggled, leaned forward, and hugged him. She put on fresh lipstick and reached for a napkin, kissed it, leaving her lip prints on it. She carefully folded the napkin and stuck it in his pocket. She whispered in his ear, "Souvenir," and kissed him, open-mouthed. They could taste the cake inside each other's mouth.

She looked over at the party. "You wait here, okay?"

He sat up straight. *Uh oh. A customer?*

He was getting a little nervous. Then she came back with two microphones. "One song, Glenn. Birthday boy say one song. I ask special for you. We sing?" Elvis' song came on and they sang their song.

She reached for his hand just as a certain refrain came across the screen, and as he took her hand, she did a little pirouette as well. The birthday boy's wife cheered and slapped her husband. "Why can't you treat me like that?" When the song was done, the birthday room erupted in a cheer. Someone yelled, Happy Birthday! A twinkle in her eye, Maya leaned over and said, "I told them your birthday too today. Ha ha."

He kissed her cheek. "*Kab koom krub,*" he said nodding. She was touched. *When he learn say thank you in Thai?* Verna came to get the microphones.

Tia came over with two Crowns, laughing. "I think you two need this. Jimmy's about to firehose you two."

With a knowing glance to Glenn, Maya turned to Tia and said, "Join us, Sis." Tia was right back, and the threesome toasted.

Glenn had both hands on Maya's waist and said, "Tomorrow's a holiday. Maybe we can visit Kimmie next door?" It was midnight. The birthday party was winding down.

"Okay, Glenn." She seemed happy, warmed and primed. Two minutes later, she leaned on him a little.

He held her shoulders. "You okay?"

"Yes, okay." She leaned on the bar. "No, I'm drunk. Glenn so sorry. I call Uber. I think I need to go."

His face showed concern. *I guess she drank a little too quickly. It's hitting now.*

She had one hand on his shoulder. "Glenn, can you walk me outside wait for Uber?"

He was puzzled. He'd seen her when she was crocked. She seemed to be okay here. *But who knows?*

She leaned forward, nuzzled his neck. "I'm so sorry."

He stroked her hair. "No worries."

The Uber came and picked her up. They were on a side street in the back of the bar. *Why here? No wonder she wanted an escort.*

She hugged him. No kiss. Sat in the car and waved. He waved. She was gone.

Ten minutes later, she walked into Thai Garden. It was in full swing. A DJ was playing club music. The pool tables had been converted to baccarat, roulette, blackjack and craps tables. There was a high stakes poker game in the back room.

Eight girls in very skimpy clothing circulated with drinks, lingering with each gambler. More often than not, the girls accepted invitations to take a break with one gambler or another. Towards the back, there were several couches. A group of men were having a semi-private party with three topless girls. Lines of cocaine were laid on the table in front of them.

Eddie walked up to Maya yelling, "You're late!" He put his arm around her waist and tried to pull a kiss from her. She gave him her cheek. His breath was heavy with scotch.

She surveyed the room. Lots of money walking around. "Where you want me, Eddie?"

He pulled her into him harder. "Right here, baby." And he licked her cheek.

She managed a smile. "Hey, there's Uncle Bo. I go say hi."

"No way." He grabbed her hand and pulled her back. "You're mine."

"Okay, baby." She said it oh so sweetly. "You come take a pee with me too?" She pushed at his chest. Leaned in for a kiss, then pulled back. "Psyche," she poked his nose. "I'll be right back, honey."

Eddie held on as long as he could. "Remember you said you'd take care of me tonight!" He'd been waiting for this all evening.

51

DRAMA NEXT DOOR

Maya made eye contact with Vey behind the bar, thinking she had to do something, or this was going to end badly. Vey followed Maya into the bathroom with a bottle of Crown. Eddie was screaming at the baccarat dealer.

Chloe watched Eddie, disgust written all over her face. She had sweet, docile Uncle Jimmy to take care of tonight. She stood next to him as he sat at the roulette table, sipping expensive whiskey. He only wanted to touch her ass all night. Chloe used to tell Maya, "For four thousand dollars, he can touch my boobs too." Uncle Jimmy never did.

Maya finished gargling and rinsing with the Crown, spritzing herself with it afterward. Given the right act, anybody would think she was toasted. Vey drew close to Maya, sniffed, gave Maya the once-over, nodded and walked out. Maya followed and half-staggered to Eddie. He pulled her to him. "About time!" Vey was right there with a tray of shots, yelling, "*Toast* to the boss!"

Maya pushed Eddie back and slurred to Vey. "No, no, I'm drunk already."

Leaning against Maya on the table, Eddie was a bit horny. He could smell the Crown all over and regarded her as easy prey. In his mind, he was bedding her in a few hours.

Vey seemingly took control of the situation, turning to Maya. "Just one, honey." Vey winked at Eddie and put down the tray of three regular pours, not the small lady drinks the girls usually got. Vey shouted, "Down the hatch! Be a man!" and held a shot glass to Eddie's lips.

He drank the shot in one gulp. Then Vey downed hers. Maya protested, but Vey put the last glass to Maya's mouth while Eddie laughed. "C'mon baby!" It took three gulps, but Maya drank it all. *Ugh. Crown good but not when all tea and one drop Crown.*

Maya made a show of glaring at Vey. Vey winked and went off. Vey was back thirty minutes later and did the same thing, yelling, "Happy Fourth!" This went on every half hour for the rest of the night. By 4:00 a.m., Eddie was in the bathroom puking. He came out, smelling like Crown mixed with stomach bile. "Where's Maya?"

Vey was wiping down tables. "She in the ladies room puking. Why you two cannot handle tonight? Sit down, I go get her."

Maya came out, and fake stumbled to him. "I hungry. You hungry?"

The burning sensation in his stomach trumped the flaccid numb feeling in his crotch. "Yeah. Let's go eat." They went to a breakfast joint until the sun came up. He was harmless. She sat next to him, squeezed his thigh, and whispered in his ear. "I had a wonderful time." He stared at her, and in his mind, he pictured himself a stud. To everyone else, he looked like a wet stink sloth that needed to be put down.

She yawned and shook her head slowly. *Men. Stupid creatures with stupid dicks. Only thing he remember tomorrow I squeeze his thigh and I say had great time.*

Glenn walked into her mind. *Well, most men stupid dicks. I hope Glenn okay I leave early. Couldn't help. Make up to him next week.*

Eddie puked into his breakfast. Maya gave the waitress a Benjamin. She got him into an Uber, then crawled into another one. She got home just as Caleb was leaving for work. "Got an 8:00 a.m. Fourth of July ceremony aboard ship. Can you at least make an appearance tonight at the fireworks? To the captain you're still Mrs. Finnegan, you know."

She suppressed a sneer. "Yeah, I can. Don't touch me, though."

He didn't hide his own sneer. "We'll see."

She crawled into bed. Saw Glenn's text, but the phone dropped from her hand. She was fast asleep.

The night before, he left right after she left. He pulled into his garage, took out his phone, and texted.

> Home safe. Hope you're ok. Happy 4th of July! ☺

He waited. No response. *Oh well. Maybe passed out.* He took out his lipstick souvenir and held it for a while. *Wow. Greatest present ever.*

It was only 12:30. The night was young. He still had money. Allie told him Kimmie was the new mama-san at the all-night club next to Lynh's bar. Divided into two bars, the club had a bad side that was more like a strip club brothel. The runway doubled as the product display line for patrons that wanted some private backroom action. The good side was a regular hostess bar.

Kimmie was trying to cultivate a family-style atmosphere like Lynh's. Trouble is, she catered to girls who worked at hostess bars closing at 2:00 a.m. who hadn't made enough money yet. Some of them were looking for a drug fix. They'd start on the good side and lure patrons to the bad side. Kimmie didn't fight it. It was business.

He was tapping his steering wheel. It'd be great to visit Kimmie. He still remembered her helping him sing and her sisterly talks explaining how bargirls think.

He parked on an off-street and walked into the place, well before the 2:00 a.m. hour when all the girls from the other places arrived to try their luck. They were usually followed by all the guys who thought they'd snag some desperate girl who'd put out for cheap. Kimmie kept a watchful eye. She once pulled a guy out of the booth by his ear, telling him to go next door.

Kimmie spotted Glenn walking in. A little surprised, she waved her hand with the cigarette in it. "Hiya, sailor!"

He smirked. "Airman, actually."

She crushed out her cig. "Shut up and buy me a cabernet."

He feigned shock. "No singing first?"

She cleared her throat and rasped out. "No karaoke here, Glenn."

In some dramatic fashion, he drawled. "Well that sucks. What am I going to do?"

She got off her stool, took two steps and grabbed his ear, dragging him to the bar. "Darling, this is a hostess bar, not Dave & Buster's. Take your pick." Six gorgeous women sat in two booths looking at him. They knew who he was. Most of them had circulated through Lynh's bar before, like piranhas waiting for someone to step into the water.

All he could see was sharp fanged teeth about to sacrifice him to the ATM god. "Naw, Kimmie. Can I just hang out here by the bar? Safe zone, right?"

She rolled her eyes and shuddered. "Glenn, I'm not going to promise anything like that. You don't have Tia protecting you here and you certainly don't have Maya to beat off the hyenas."

He let out a chortle. "That's what you call them?" He thought some of them did look like that, the way they put their makeup on.

She let out an exasperated sigh, thinking Maya had this guy trained like a puppy dog. "Just say no, Glenn. No offense taken if you don't buy drinks. Oops, gotta go." Her syndicate boyfriend walked in. She pointed to the private room that doubled as her office, where she had his dinner waiting. 2:00 a.m.—the place was starting to fill up. All the girls from the other bars were filing in, with the guys who still had any money left following them over.

He sat alone at the bar. *Where is Chloe? I thought for sure she'd be here. I had a blast last time. The stories. The pictures.*

Now it was past 2:00 and still no Chloe. He didn't know she was at Thai Garden. Meanwhile, he watched a customer getting worked by one of the girls. *Oh well, it was fun watching this guy spend three hundred bucks or so in thirty minutes so he could make out with some hostess. Poor shmuck. Talk about leaving with empty pockets and a frustrated crotch.*

He continued to watch the hostess as she hustled the empty-pocketed customer out the door. *She's pretty, though. Never seen her before.*

He thought the girl was Asian, maybe Korean. He noticed her bouncy, shoulder length, brownish-black hair with highlights, the kind of hair surfer girls get from the sun. And even in that lighting, he noticed how tan she was. When she got off her stool, he reckoned she was about Maya's height, dressed all in a black cocktail dress with ample cleavage. *Show's over. Guess I better get going.*

He turned to go, then heard a rough, sultry voice yell, "Give that man a shot." He looked over and suntan girl was staring at him, half-smiling with a look that aroused him. He waved no, and she mouthed, "Don't be shy." The bartender slid a shot over to him. He smelled it. Sweet. Some kind of liquor. Had Maya been there, she would have taken the drink from him. Teenage girls are warned not to take drinks from anyone they don't know; the same should go for middle-aged men in after hours hostess bars.

Seems harmless enough. It's coming from the bartender. "Cheers." He downed it. "Okay, gotta . . ." Too late. She was sitting on his lap, grinding and rubbing. *Where the heck did she come from?*

She blew a kiss looking back over her shoulder at him. "You going already? I bought you one. You buy me one?"

So, he thought, *this was the game.* "Okay." He nodded at the bartender. "I really gotta go." But now he was feeling warm and a little horny. She asked for another drink, and he nodded. She took both his hands and put them on her ample boobs. He could feel the hardness of her nipples as he pinched them between his index and middle fingers. She moaned slightly. Just enough so he would hear and react.

She whispered in his ear, breathing heavy warm air in his ear and down his neck. "Do a shot with me?" By this time his instincts had taken over, and he nodded yes. Three hundred dollars was gone in forty-five minutes. She took his hand. "Let's go, babe."

He slurred, "Where?" Something wasn't right. He could barely see. Things were blurry. And he wasn't able to think. "Maya?"

"No Maya here babe." She took him by the hand to the other side—the bad side. First stop—the ATM.

The ATM only gave him a thousand dollars. He was in a private room, making it with her and two other girls. The first girl left to find more meat. The other two girls took a break and took him to the ATM again. No money this time. He'd reached the withdrawal limit. They zoned in on the MasterCard in his wallet and tapped it with their glittered nails.

A hand reached in between them, grabbed his elbow, and yanked. "Hey!" Both girls yelled.

In broken English and with a strong Vietnamese accent, Candy said, "Enough already. Go find someone else." She had seen Glenn from a distance and saw he was out of it and didn't even know where he was. The girls started yelling in Vietnamese and giving her the finger.

The bouncer took one step closer before Candy waved him off, yelling, "My customer. Why he here with them?" The two girls were pissed but had made some money, so they laughed and went off to prey on others.

She took him to a booth. "Glenn, you okay? You remember me?" A server brought water. Candy dipped her handkerchief and wiped his face. Candy was one of the good ones during his summer of sin. If he didn't meet Maya that night, he'd plan to go back and explain the situation to Candy. She thought he was nice, out of his element, and didn't know why he was in the badlands.

He called out, "Maya?"

Candy leaned back. *Maya? Oh, he get girlfriend now? His wife? No, must be girlfriend.* "No Maya here." She'd seen this before. He'd been drugged. "Glenn, where you live? I call taxi." She reached for his wallet—his ID would show his address.

He snatched it back, thinking he was getting rolled. He called again, "Maya?"

"Glenn, no Maya here." It was 4:00 a.m. The bouncers came, pushed Candy aside, and got him on his feet. They pushed him towards the door and closed it behind him. He was on a public sidewalk now. Candy ran out the back but couldn't find him.

He knew his eyes were open, but he couldn't see a thing. His last thought: *I'm in trouble.*

In the park across from his condo, some kid exploded a Fourth of July pipe bomb large enough to set off the building's fire alarm. With the explosion and the alarm going off, Glenn groggily regained consciousness. He was in bed. Naked. His clothes were in the shower. His head hurt immensely. He felt sick.

He ran to the toilet and let loose. *Never had a hangover like this before. What was in that shot?* He remembered the black cocktail dress girl coming over. *Shit. I got taken.* The rest of the night was a blur. *Two girls. ATM. Some girl wiping his face with a towel. Not Maya.* Then getting pushed out the door. Then nothing.

He thought about Maya. The night. It was great. Then—panic attack. *Is it still there?*

He ran to the shower to find his shirt soaked. *Shit.*

He dug in the pocket. *It's not there!* He dug through his pants pockets. *Not there. Crap.*

He sat on the toilet, moping like a kid who'd lost his favorite toy. On a hunch, he asked himself, *where would I put something that important?* He snapped his fingers. *That's right, my wallet.*

He peeked into the pocket where he kept his mother's crucifix. There, neatly folded and tucked into the same pocket—his lipstick souvenir. Everything was right with the world again.

He searched the rest of his wallet. *Everything there. ATM receipts up to $4,000.* He logged online to his accounts; no more money taken. *Whew!*

He'd heard stories of people having their credit cards maxed out in these places. *Who was the girl with the cool face towel? A dream?*

His keys were in the toilet. He fished them out. *I drove back?* He stumbled to the garage. The car was there, parked at a crooked angle. *Thank you, God—I didn't kill anyone or kill myself. Imagine detectives knocking on my door to show me photos of crime scenes.* He circled the car. No scratches, no bits of flesh.

He went back inside. The building alarm was finally silent. He stood in the shower till the water ran cold, then stood there for another half hour. He got out, dry heaving. Kept drinking water and heaving. His body wanted whatever was in him to get out. *Funny, why didn't I throw up last night?* He peeked hesitantly over the side of the bed. The stench was noticeable. He went and got the baking soda. It was going to be a long holiday spent cleaning the carpet.

He picked up his phone. He remembered texting her. No reply.

Wonder if she got home okay? He texted her

R u ok?

Two hours later, he had cleaned the carpet by his bed as best as possible, but a big wet spot remained and a stench clinged to the inside of his nose. He checked his phone. Still no answer. He began to worry. *The Uber driver didn't look too cool. I shoulda gone and checked him out. Now all these grisly thoughts.*

Gathering his cleaning supplies, his mind was on Maya. *I'm overthinking. I still remember the time Katie didn't answer for four hours, and driving across town to her workplace thinking she was abducted. Not cool barging into that workplace safety meeting. At least they thought it was great timing and part of the presentation. Really embarrassed her, though. She was pissed and touched. She found an app that let her text back "okay" at the touch of a button anytime I texted. She had always replied ever since.* He sighed. Lately there were no texts between them.

He thought about calling Maya, but she texted first. Maya lay on her bed, staring at her phone and the texts Glenn had sent her.

Home safe. Hope you're ok. Happy 4th of July! ☺

R u ok?

I ok. Thanks for checking. Just woke up. Guess I drank too much ☺

She stared at what she wrote. *Not lie. I did drink too much. I feel so bad I keep running out early on him. He had time to stay out late last night because of holiday. And he went home? Most jerks would go next door.*

She continued to text.

Happy 4th. Thank you for last night I had fun ☺

 Sorry I left you last night ☺

Happy 4th to you too. No worries no sorries needed. Ur always awesome to me ☺

Rusty crawled into her lap. She needed to get to the gym and detox and get the smell of the previous night off her. And there were the July Fourth fireworks at her husband's ship that night. She'd promised to keep up the pretense of their marriage in front of his superiors. Though some suspected, they didn't press. It was part of the way of life in this part of the military.

What a night. Eddie texted too.

Thanks much for taking care of me last night/this morning. I had a great time with you. I guess I drank a little much. Sorry I was a jerk. I'll quit the macho shit from now. Maybe we can just be friends again?

Sure ☺

This was the Eddie she liked in the beginning.

52

BUSTED

Monday night. A week after the July Fourth holiday. Her off night, when she would spend hours on social media catching up with kin and friends in Thailand. The last text for the night was for Glenn.

She wanted to make it up to him. She stared at his text. *He nice guy. Most men jerks. If still early, go another club look for more action. He said he loyal and he prove it now. I will make him something special. Same thing catch Caleb. Catch a man by his penis, stay for the night. Catch a man with his stomach, stay for life.*

It was time for bed. "Rusty! Time for bed." Rusty came running in and onto her lap.

Caleb Finnegan followed and hung by her door. Rusty ran up to him, begging for a pat on the head. "Texting your Tuesday night john?"

She looked up, hate in her eyes. "Screw you, my dearest husband. You owe me." She had put together an act for Caleb's superiors on the Fourth of July that left them beaming.

The captain summed it up. "Caleb, you two make a great couple. It's amazing how much she knows about naval operations, then she tells us about her brother, an officer in the Thai Royal Navy."

She had stood there, smiling as sweet as any Southern belle. *Suckers, like bar customers. Upload random pictures of Thai navy officer and say my brother.*

Her real brother was an entry level mechanic recently enlisted in the Thai navy. She said it again, "You owe me for July Fourth, husband."

He half sneered, half drooled. "Babe, it wasn't hard to pay you back with a good time before. How about it. Old times sake?"

She shuddered, a little more exaggerated than needed. "Good night, Caleb. You owe me." She turned away. "Here, Rusty. Time for bed."

Caleb Finnegan stalked back to the guest room, his room for the past three years, muttering to no one in particular. "Owe her, my ass. I got her out of that third world country. She gets free rent and medical. Don't understand why she has to work these bars." He slammed the door. Then got into bed and opened his laptop onto his favorite porn site and settled back to do his deed, still muttering, "At least in Wyoming there were no bars, but she still had guys from the base thinking she was single and buying her drinks, hosted drinks, at the restaurant. Any fucking Thai restaurant in Anytown USA can double for a hostess bar. It's like one huge worldwide franchise. But geez, she was a great fuck."

Tuesday night couldn't have come any quicker for Glenn. She was waiting. She wore a bright red sleeveless strapless mid-length cocktail dress that was held up by her bosom. Classic A-frame highlighted her hourglass figure perfectly.

He walked in, and she sauntered up to him and hugged him. "I will get our food. Come." She took his hand and led him to the booth. "Hungry?"

There were no weird texts the night before and she was on time. If there was a word meaning the opposite of tailspin, that would describe his mood. "Yep."

She made a simple dish, a Thai omelet. He'd never tasted anything like it. "What is this? It's just an omelet, but why so delicious?"

Her face was pure delight. She sat across from him because she wanted to see him eat. He was like Rusty, the way he ate. It made you feel special. Like he truly appreciated the food. She imagined him growing up eating grass from the yard and fighting for rice with his brothers. How he must have wanted decent food. "You like?"

His mouth full. "Uh-huh."

She had made Caleb some before she left the house and took some for Eddie as well. "Eddie, can I skip the rest of tonight? My customer. I need to take care of him."

Eddie threw up his hands. Remembered his promise to be less of a jerk. "Okay, if Grandpa needs you that bad."

She offered a pained look. "He's not that old, Eddie, and what Americans say? He can do circles around you in gym." Her eyes flashed. "You being a dumbass again, huh?"

He sighed. "Okay, okay. Go."

Her eyes widened. "Really? Just like that?"

He laid his hand on her arm, gently, lightly. "Have dinner with me first, though?" It was slow. There were girls available for the other men. And most were just having dinner themselves.

She tilted her head from side to side and nodded her okay. Eddie gestured to Vey. "You take care?"

"Yes, boss." Vey raised an eyebrow at Maya. Maya shot a look back as if to say she knew what she was doing.

Eddie was amazed. "Wow, this is great stuff. You made this or did Aunty in the back?"

She dumped a little more on his plate, at the same time glancing at her watch. "I made it."

He took a swig of soda. She noticed no liquor. "Wow. Remember that buffet in Vegas where the guy flipped omelets in the air?"

"Yeah." She chuckled, remembering how amazed Eddie was at some guy flipping eggs in the air. They talked about nothing for a half hour. No complaints about the wife. "Still separate rooms, Eddie?"

He wiped his mouth and burped. "Always been like that. She does her thing, I do mine. I thought it'd take only a year. Gets her green card. Gets citizenship. We divorce and her parents take care of their former son-in-law. I'm thinking of divorcing her and moving on."

She raised an eyebrow. "Moving on?"

He nodded. "Yeah."

She licked her lips. "With who?"

He shrugged. "I don't know."

She was surprised he wasn't more aggressive. *A new leaf?*

It was hard for him to keep it under wraps. Maya always had an easy way of listening to him. His boss at the flooring company was married to a Thai woman. He thought back to that afternoon his boss gave him advice. *The way to their heart is patience, Eddie. Show patience. And be supportive.*

He folded his hands in front of him, thinking he wished his hands were on her. "Hey Maya, just wanted to say sorry I've been a jerk . . ."

She cut him off. "Eddie, you apologized already. You texted. We're done. Move on."

He blinked hard for a few seconds and made a big show of appreciation. "Thank you. Hey, time for you to go? If you can, make it back, but if you want to go home after 2:00, then go."

She gathered her phone and keys in seconds and got up. "Thanks, Eddie." She gave him a peck on the cheek and was off. *Hmm. Didn't even try to steal kiss.*

An hour later, she was with Glenn.

She watched with joy as Glenn finished the last of the omelet. She took a picture of him. *This the happiest face I see long time. He happy I'm happy.*

He ate so fast he had to gulp air between bites. "So what's the secret? Why so tasty?"

She giggled. "Fish sauce, Glenn. Fish sauce."

His face said, *eww.* His stomach growled approval. "Great, I wish I didn't ask . . . gross . . . but so good."

She shook her head. *Westerners, unless ketchup mustard salt or pepper, they say exotic and foreign.* "You like? Next week I bring Thai fried pork, okay?"

He high-fived her as he finished his plate, and hers.

She was cleaning up the table, humming. She was reminiscing about the great times they'd had, when they first started seeing each other, including the family dinner nights, when Lynh tried to set them up as a couple. *Nice,* she thought, *really nice do that again.* She asked him, "What want do now? Let's sing later. Drink shots now? Play cards?"

He was wondering if he could stay awake. His belt was straining. "Okay and . . . okay."

An hour later, five drinks in, and after a nine-hand losing streak, she called Verna for the karaoke books. "Let's sing, Glenn."

Then she walked in—the suntan girl from the other night. Glenn glanced up with a start. Eye contact. Just a nanosecond. *She saw me. What the hell?*

Maya followed his stare. "Glenn, what wrong? Who's that?"

"Shit. Maya, that girl."

Her face said to go on. His brain should've said caution, danger ahead.

He rubbed his face. "You know the other night? I went home. Then went out again. I went next door to visit Kimmie. Got drugged. That girl. Pulled me to the bad side." Glenn explained the whole episode.

Maya sat there and absorbed. Shocked at first, anger and hurt came soon after. *Stupid. Ass. Men. Pig. All the same. Just like Darren. I knew it. Can't be trusted. Fake. Liar. He say he went home. He texted me—home safe. Better off with Eddie. At least I know he's a shit.* She was livid inside.

She didn't hear the rest of his explanation. She didn't hear the part about looking for Chloe to hear more about her. Anger, hurt, disappointment started to drill into her heart. But she kept her cool on the outside. *After everything I did. I only left a little early. And him . . . with her?* Maya had seen her before. *Pushy bitch. LA Vietnamese. Kimmie's friend.*

She turned suddenly. "I go pee. I will be right back." She came right back.

Glenn looked up. "Ready to sing?"

She was holding her phone. Looked like she was crying. He sensed something. "Glenn, I have to go. My cousin called. Rusty, my dog, sick, threw up. I need to leave now." She was all packed up.

Cousin? His antennae stuck right out. "Um, okay."

"Don't be mad, Glenn. You can stay if you want." Verna was already sitting in the booth. This was not ending the way he wanted.

He was blinking more rapidly than usual, trying to process what was going on. Every nerve of his brain said something was going on. "Okay. You take care of Rusty."

"Bye, Glenn." A peck on the cheek and she was gone.

He sat down. "Just you and me, Verna?" Verna smiled. "I go home early too." The bar was dead at that point. "I guess me too." Next door crossed his mind. *No way. Learned my lesson.*

Tia walked by. "What's Maya so mad about?"

Glenn looked up. "Mad? No, she's upset. Her dog is sick."

Tia did her best thinker pose, eyes almost rolling back into her head. "No, she's pretty pissed. You could hear her car door slam, and she peeled out of the parking lot. Yep, she's pissed." She took one look at his face and realized she'd said too much. "Maybe you're right. After all, you know her better than we do now."

Glenn walked into the apartment. Put the sixpack from 7-Eleven on the counter, then turned Jimmy Fallon on. He texted.

Home safe. Hope Rusty ok.

Me too. Goodnight

Something triggered as soon as he typed home safe. *Shit! I told her I went home that night. She thinks I went home. Then I hit her tonight about going next door. Not only that, all the crap that happened. I was home, then I changed my mind. No, I think she sees it different. Shit, Shit. SHIT.*

She walked into Thai Garden, surprising both Chloe and Eddie. Chloe had a look like what about Glenn? Eddie just smirked. "Put the old man to bed early?"

She poked his chest. "Shut up, Eddie. Are you going to buy me a drink? This my night off. We have fun now."

"Glad to oblige, babe!"

Chloe almost spat. *Glad to oblige. What Asian guy says that?*

Maya was with Eddie till the wee hours.

Caleb Finnegan stared up at the ceiling, spent. He looked at his watch. 2:00 a.m. He knew he had another two hours before Maya got home but thought it was better to wrap things up. "Sweetheart, you need to go. I need to sleep."

The buxom blonde he was with was in cuddle mode. She was from another ship. He'd met her at the All Hands Club two weeks before. They'd fucked on three prior nights. She called them dates. He called it military mentoring. A fuck was a fuck to him. He'd be on deployment soon. A fuck toy in every port and several more back on ship.

He licked his lips at the site of her bosom, wondering if they had time for one more go. *Good thing the wife and I have separate rooms. Not the submissive kind of Asian sex but being from Kentucky, good old-fashioned howling, grinding, three-orgasm sex.* The young girl kissed his dick goodnight and yanked it for good measure. He stifled a howl. "G'night, sailor." She knew her way out, and also knew she needed to be gone by 3:00 a.m. Duty called in five hours.

He thought it was a great thing, a matter of pride, that this lass was all of twenty-two years old, the same age as Maya ten years ago.

He thought Maya still held together well but was getting rounder in certain places. Thinking of their first time always made his dick hard, and he headed off to the shower to relieve himself. If there was one thing Caleb was known for in every port, it was that he was always ready for more.

A few hours later, he heard Maya come in. The front door slammed. Then her bedroom door slammed. Then he heard crying. *Crap*, he thought, *she's pissed at something. Maybe I can get consoling sex.* He picked up his dick. Too raw. *Sorry babe, you're on your own.* The last thing he heard before falling asleep was her bathroom door slam. *Yep, she's pissed.*

53

RETRIBUTION

She had several days to fume about it. She and Chloe met for dinner at Thai Garden, loading up before a busy Friday night with the off-duty cops. Chloe's look was somewhere between frustration and confusion as she pulled at her hair. "Why you mad? He said he was home."

Maya's eyes narrowed. "Liar. Big fucking liar." She didn't catch the fact that he changed his mind after he texted. "And he went out to Saigon Lounge. You know? Where Kimmie mama-san now." Saigon Lounge, also known by its short name—Saigon—where Glenn had been drugged.

Chloe nearly pulled out some hair. "To Saigon? I thought he was scared that place. That's why I went with him. I guess not scared this time."

Maya stabbed at her Thai fried shrimp. "He was with a girl."

Chloe stopped cold. "He went to see Nina again?"

Maya's fork fell to the floor. "What you mean *again*?"

Chloe sat quietly, hiding behind a menu she knew by heart. "Nothing. No matter. Move on."

Maya pulled at the menu to make eye contact. "No, Chloe. What you mean Nina *again*. This wasn't Nina. I saw her the other night. The Viet bitch."

Chloe tugged at the menu, desperately wanting to shield herself. "Oh."

Maya yanked the menu from Chloe and tossed it back over her shoulder. Her gaze could have cut wood. "Just oh? Sister, what you not telling me. Tell me *now*, Chloe!" Anyone close to her knew that Maya could be so demure in conversation and so loud and dirty-mouthed when pissed. She was pissed.

Chloe sighed, grabbing a nearby bottle of Crown Royal. "Okay. Take a shot." She poured one for Maya. A real shot.

Maya downed the amber liquid, bringing the shot glass down hard, with a distinct glass-on-wood sound. "Make it two."

Chloe wrung her hands, then took a deep breath. "When he stopped coming around. Your breakup . . ."

Maya winced. She hated that word and never wanted to talk about it.

Chloe continued. "He came to find you one night. You not here. You was with Eddie."

Maya gritted her teeth. "I know who I was with. Get on with it."

Chloe played with her shot glass. "He and Tim showed up next door. I jumped Tim. Glenn was okay only watching, I guess. We were having fun. Then Nina went and sat on Glenn lap."

Maya's look was pure disgust. "You mean plastic ass, plastic tits, plastic lips Nina?"

Chloe nodded. "Yeah, 2:30 in the morning—must've felt pretty horny. He bent her over on the bar and started humping her there. Your man is wild man, Maya. He ever do that with you?"

Maya responded softly. "No."

Chloe slid the bottle of Crown to Maya. "You lucky, you know? He respect you. He nice to you."

Maya wondered about so many things. *Was it really respect? He never touch me. I always have to make first move. Even with Amber—that night, he was grinding her from behind. Something wrong with me?*

Chloe knew her sister well. "Stop overthinking. He not Darren." Chloe bit her lip, thinking, *wrong example.*

Maya leaned forward, both hands on the table. "How you know, Chloe? You sleep with both?" It was Maya's turn to bite her lip. The silence lasted five minutes. Vey saw the impasse and came over with the expensive stuff. Another shot poured for both.

Chloe pushed forward. "You know, Maya. I think he like you. Respect you. Not want to treat you like meat, like all the rest. Something about you. Like he treasures you. But man is man, okay? They all horny. Need to blow off steam sometime. You ever think do it for him? Yes, you have pride. Maybe hand job? Happy ending? Nothing wrong with that."

Maya fiddled with her phone. *Ugh.* "No. The smell. Not come off for days." At least that's what it seemed like to her.

Chloe made a motion like she was slipping something over her fingers. "That's why the girls use rubbers even for hand jobs."

Maya's face looked like she'd seen a sewer rat. "Eww. Chloe, change subject."

Chloe's confidence grew. She leaned back, arms crossed. "Okay. We good. Let him go, Maya. Only a man. Don't forget, last time he and I went, he only talk about you. All *goo goo ga ga* over you. I coulda been naked and he only think of you."

The ice broke. Maya snickered. "Shut up, sister." She'd seen Chloe naked. It would take some iron will to think of someone else. The memory of Chloe naked brought back a smile and fond memories of her early nights getting to know her, when Chloe lived with her during Caleb's first deployment out of their current port.

Chloe smiled back, then leaned over and kissed Maya. Good times back then. Now in the present, they were tipsy and horny. Their cop friends were about to have a memorable night.

She was still upset the following Tuesday. Sitting in her kitchen feeding Rusty, she couldn't get the image of the Viet bitch having her way with him. *Her? How many times I have to tell him don't hang with girls he don't know when I'm not around? No self-control. Cannot say no? Be a man. Free drink and you cave? Yeah the bartender was in on it.*

She sat on the floor, hugging Rusty, telepathically spilling her guts to her dog. *That late, he should know better. Stupid. Ass. And plastic Nina too? He like a dog. Smell pussy and all over. I don't care if dry hump or real thing. I bet he still come in his pants.*

The anger came in waves. So did her affection. She softened. *I should have stayed. I promised I would protect him always. Hard to believe. He like a little innocent boy sometimes. Maybe my fault.*

She let up. But only for a second. *But what the fuck. I treat him so well that night. That was such a good night. I was so happy. I thought maybe not just customer anymore.*

She frowned, shaking her head slowly. *And I got night off for him last week. I made food. And for what? He ruined it all! Better to settle for Eddie. Still a macho jerk but he has good side too.*

She looked at the text he had sent her that night. She saw the 12:15 time stamp and saw "Home safe" next to it. *Liar. Was at Saigon already.*

The phone buzzed. He was texting her.

We on for tonight? Thai fried pork ribs?

yeah

The ribs were cooling on a rack on the stove. In a fit of anger and frustration, she took the whole bunch and swept them into the garbage. *Ass. Fucker. All men same. Shoulda stayed lesbian. Maybe Chloe my dream man.*

He looked at his phone. *Yeah? Just yeah?* He had an uneasy feeling. *With Katie it was always Yes this, no that. When Yeah shows up, it's never good news for the guy. Hmm . . . interesting Instagram meme this would make.*

———————————

He walked into the bar at nine, right as she was coming out of the kitchen. "What's up?"

She had a glazed look. "Sorry, no fried pork. I didn't have time." She was carrying something and walked to the booth room. He followed. *This feels like I forgot to take out the garbage and am about to eat a tuna sandwich for dinner.*

She sat across from him, not next to him, laying out papaya salad, cabbage leaves, beef cubes, and crickets. She wrapped the papaya salad in the cabbage leaves and ate. The crickets followed.

He kept quiet and made do with the beef cubes. A man knows when the woman is pissed.

She ate the cabbage like it was potato chips. "My friends come tonight little while. You okay? She DJ. Plan for my party." Verna came and chattered something, and Maya translated. "Oh, they here." And she was gone.

Maya walked back with two gorgeous ladies, a mother and daughter pair. Maya introduced them to Glenn, who found the mother was his age.

Glenn sat in the booth while the women spent a good chunk of time mapping out the dance floor, where the DJ station would be, how the lighting would be set up, and where the speakers would be blasting. He watched it all. *Dang, she's gonna spend a good chunk of money.*

Mother, daughter and Maya, joined by Chloe, were at the bar talking and laughing. The bar never heard the Thai language tossed about so liberally. Maya came back to the booth. "Want to join me and my friends at the bar?"

She spent the rest of the night with her friends. He bought five rounds of drinks for all of them. There was some singing. Towards the end, he felt a little neglected but was glad she invited him to be part of the group. *Maybe I'm making inroads. Not every customer gets mixed in with the bargirl's friends. Why does she have to be over there, between mother and daughter, instead of by me? She still pissed? Is this her version of the cold shoulder? No matter, mother's a hoot. Great time chatting with her.*

The daughter chortled. "Hey, Mom, maybe you and Glenn can go date." He thought Maya nudged the daughter a little hard.

To the experienced eye, it seemed Glenn was just bankrolling a girls night out for Maya and her friends, with very little return.

Her friends left at the end of the night, and Maya came to give him a hug. "Glenn, walk me car. I work early tomorrow."

He sat expressionless. "Okay." *Are we back to doing this again? Not much us time tonight. Hope this means I'm forgiven. Get back to normal next week.*

As she unlocked her car door, she turned to face him. "Gimme kiss." He leaned in and she gave him a quick peck on the lips, like how she'd kiss her dog. "Text me, okay?" She was gone.

Cruising down the freeway in her Audi, she glanced at her phone. Eddie had buzzed her twice already. Some heavy hitters were asking for the song girl, but Eddie had said she could take her time. *Geez,* she thought, *he turning into real gentleman. Last two Tuesdays only listen to me complain about Glenn. What a switch.*

The Thai Garden casino closed early that night. Eddie came up beside her, placing his hand lightly on the small of her back. "Hey Maya, nightcap?"

She didn't mind his touch and quickly replied, "Sure."

He brought out a bottle of Crown Reserve. The real stuff. "You feeling up to it?"

Maya nodded yes. *Hmm, three months ago he wouldn't have cared. Try to get me drunk, not ask me if I can handle. Maybe he change.*

In his head, Eddie heard his boss say, "Patience, Eddie."

After three rounds, she was talking freely. "So, why all you men pigs?"

He brought up the subject first. "You still upset, Maya?" Every time it seemed like she was ready to move on, he reminded her how Glenn lied to her about being home safe.

He filled her shot glass. "I'd never do that. I'd be too scared you'd cut my nuts off or something."

She poked his chest. "That's right," she slurred. The heavy hitters were keen on her downing the real thing with them, not the watered-down stuff. Then there was the nightcap with Eddie.

She slurred on. "Why gotta lie? You think I'm bad, Eddie? I shoulda stayed with him. Your fault, you know. You said come so I come."

He put his arm around her. "Sorry, babe. If I'd known I woulda let you stay."

She reached out and ruffled his hair. "You so sweet. I misjudge you."

They were in a booth. He wanted to take her right there. "Easy, Eddie," he heard his boss say in his head.

Her expression was pure pout. "He lie. That's all. Tonight, I make him pay for my party night with Rona and her mother. I teach him."

Eddie's eyes glinted. "So it worked?"

She rambled on. "Yeah, thank you for idea. You think he learn his lesson? I hope so. I think he was hitting on Rona mother. Maybe he not know. He mad little bit though. I say I make food for him. Ribs. Give him cabbage and crickets. He look like he was going to cry."

They both laughed. Inside she felt something. How a mother would feel right after she slaps her baby boy. Remorse. She shrugged it off, looking at her watch—4:00 a.m. *One more shot. I will go home before Navy wives across street wake up and see me come in.*

Eddie put on his best helpful tone. "Hey, maybe next time you have another customer drop by, just for a bit. So he'd appreciate these exclusive nights you're giving him."

She wrinkled her nose. "Not good idea. I promise him Tuesdays for him. Still for him."

He shrugged. "No biggie. Only a thought. Just so he knows. You have a choice, and you choose him."

She tilted her head back. The room spun a little. "Maybe. I will think about it."

They called it a night. Eddie reached out for a hug and a kiss. She gave him her cheek. Eddie scowled. His patience was wearing thin. *Fuck, seriously? Well, at least another seed planted.*

Glenn was still up. He texted four hours ago that he was home safe. No reply.

Across town, she saw his text as she pulled up. She thought if she answered now, it wouldn't look good. *I will say I fall asleep again.* She yawned. *Tomorrow high intensity workout day. Need my rest.* Rusty came running to the door to greet her. *You never lie to me, yeah boy?*

54

DETH MONK

The last Tuesday of July found him at the office, cleaning up for the day, hoping to get a workout in before he headed to the bar. His phone buzzed.

> **M** I running late tonight. Can you pick up food for us?

> What you want?

> **M** Anything. I have late shift. Need to close store. Come about ten

> How about Mexican. You eat Mexican?

> **M** Anything okay

> okay

He'd gone by the beauty store that morning. He brought flowers to say sorry about Saigon. The front clerk never heard of her. An older employee said she hadn't been around for months. He was pissed. *Late shift . . . right. Plus now I have to pick up food? Who was hosting who? Maybe she should buy me drinks at exaggerated prices.*

He was in a mood. The little boy was in full bloom. The cold shoulder last week was wearing on him, like sunburn that hurts the day after the beach. At first, it was just a warm feeling, then an itching, then a howling, screaming pain.

He was somewhere between the itch and the pain, closer to the pain. *I spent $900 to sit there and watch her party with her friends? I feel like a sucker. I can't even remember her spending any time with me. Don't remember her even being next to me. I guess I was too fixed on her being irked. But what a bitch. That was supposed to be my night and she invited her friends. This is how it's gonna be?*

Sitting in his car outside of the beauty store, he continued to sulk. *Now she's gonna be late but for what. She hasn't worked here since last year. Inventory, sales reports and late shifts, my ass. What is going on?*

He got to the bar early. There was no room at the bar area, which was packed with the barflies plus a group of out-of-staters in town for a sales convention. His corner seat taken; Glenn went straight to the booth room. Verna followed with his beer.

Maya walked in looking casual, wearing Daisy Duke shorts and the green long-sleeve stretch top she'd worn a couple of months ago. She had her hair done up in a ponytail. *She could have been doing spring cleaning,* he thought. She had an edgy tone to her voice. "I'm hungry, you have food?" He laid out kalua pork quesadillas and goat cheese pizza. *She's on edge. Why?*

He tested the waters. "You look starved. No food at the beauty store?"

She ignored the question. "You eat too." She sat down across him and slid a plate of food to him.

He cocked his head. *Why sitting over there, across from me?*

She took a bite of pizza. "Birthday next week. Can you come?"

He hesitated. "No, Maya. Family, remember?"

She suppressed a frown. "Okay. I know." *Can't he drop the family thing just once?*

He saw her disappointment. *I feel bad, but I don't want to deal with all her other customers. Especially on the Friday night punk-a-thon. And I gotta do my thing.*

She changed the subject. "I went to temple last Thursday. Make merit. See brother from another mother. He monk you know. He take us all expensive sushi that night."

Glenn did his best to smile and seem interested. "Wow." *A monk, in a hostess bar?*

She did her best to sound enthused. "Yeah, we friends long time. Good guy. We had fun. He take care all of us that night."

He finished his pizza. "Wow. Sounds like a great guy. Maybe I meet him one day?" *Where's this going? Never understood a religion where the founder himself disclaimed any notion of deity, then was revered as a fat little god by half the world. Last I heard, Siddhartha Gautama was in pretty good shape, not a roly-poly guy with a belly people like to rub at casinos all over Asia.*

She started cleaning up the food.

She suddenly looked up and jumped up out of the booth.

Glenn would later think there was something weird about the way she acted surprised. *She's never this surprised. Something fishy here.*

An Asian man, about fifty, bald, came strolling in. He was in a t-shirt, shorts and slippers. They said something in Thai or Laotian, and she turned to Glenn. "This my brother from another mother."

Glenn did a quick assessment. *Monk? Brother? Looked like another customer to me. This why she's been so edgy?*

She pointed to the booth and the space across Glenn. "Can he join us?"

Glenn nodded. "Sure." Still sitting across of her, he thought, *at least she has to come sit by me now.*

The man sat across from Glenn, and she slid in next to him.

Glenn's jaw dropped. *What the fuck? I thought she was coming over to sit with me?*

Verna arrived with a Heineken Light, and the guy bought Glenn a beer. Maya and the guy were talking in a mix of Thai and Laotian. Half an hour in, Maya got up. "I go pee now." The two customers were alone.

Glenn did his best to sound friendly, like a newfound bro. "So, your name again?"

The new guy looked around to see where Maya was. "Deth."

Glenn half-smiled. *His name is Death? Yeah, might as well be. Killed the night.*

Glenn took a pull on his beer. *I gotta know more. What is this guy to her?* "So you from Laos?"

The man grinned. "I go high school here. Know Maya long time."

It was getting hard for Glenn not to cross-examine the guy. "Really? Wow? How?"

The guy had a one-word answer. "Temple."

Maya came back, and the foreign conversation started up again.

Glenn fiddled with his phone, Googling nothing in particular, looking up Laos on Wikipedia. *Shit, the least they can do is speak English.* Glenn continued to surf his phone, catching up on today's news. The mood was pressurizing by the minute. Glenn got up to take a pee and to find Verna.

He found her at the bar well. "Verna, how long is this guy going to stay?"

Verna looked nervous. "Not know, Glenn." Allie came over. "Glenn, the guy came last Thursday and took Mama, Chloe and Maya to sushi, then came back and spent a lot of money. I think he's staying the night."

Glenn was fuming. It was no little-boy kind of fuming. It was a solid full-grown man, bull in a china shop, ready to kill fuming. And Maya could tell even from twenty feet away. Glenn came back to the booth, their booth. The guy was coolly sipping his beer with a look that said I'm here to take over, buddy. Maya saw the look. A tantrum was brewing. She edged outward, creating space between her and Deth. Deth relaxed and spread his legs a bit, covering the empty space between them.

Glenn texted.

Should I leave?

He looked on his side of the booth. *I don't see her bag so I'm not the guy, according to bargirl custom. If this is gonna go all night, I'll leave. Start again next week. Still early. Other places came to his mind.* For some reason, he thought of Candy.

Why you acting like that?

He sat glaring at her. She saw. It was too late. He was over the edge. She blamed the beer. He texted back.

I thought this was our night.

She stayed put. A few minutes later, she got up and announced. "I have to go."

Glenn got up as well. "Wait, can I just have a moment with you over there."

She frowned. "Why?" She didn't want a scolding. From her perspective, Glenn had spent the night glaring at her. "Why you mad? Why acting like that?" *I just want him appreciate exclusive nights. Oh, why I listen to Eddie.* Deth was supposed to leave early on, but he didn't. She couldn't tell a high-ranking monk to leave either. It was bad karma.

Deth sat still. Monk or not, he wanted Maya. Last Thursday was the most fun he had had with any girl. It was amazing. Outside of the temple, he was a mid-level warehouse manager. At the temple, he was God to all of these women.

Glenn was still standing, hands on hips. "Okay. We'll do it here." He heard a voice say, *restraint.* His own voice drowned it out. He was growling, almost roaring. "You gotta be fucking kidding me. This guy appears out of nowhere, surprise, like he owns you and plops down. Did he know you were going to be here? Didn't he know you had a customer tonight? Either you didn't tell him, or he didn't hear."

True, all she said was she worked on Tuesdays too. She'd hoped Chloe would be here to run interference, but Chloe got stuck at Thai Garden. She just wanted Deth to stay a little while, not stay as long as he did.

He pointed at her, accusing, blaming. "Then you don't sit with me, but you sit next to him, but I had to buy drinks for you and bring you dinner?"

She felt her chest tighten with remorse. She held out her hands. "Glenn, can we do this later?"

He was beyond stopping. "No. You hear it now." She slumped back into the booth.

Verna ran to get Lynh.

His face and body language spit forth all the frustration pent up in him the last week. "I ask you if I should leave and you give me that 'why you act like that?' speech, so I stay.

"Then, I sat here for two hours listening to you two talking in Thai or Laotian or whatever it was. Ever think of talking English and letting me join in? Do you know how ignored I felt? This was worse than the last time you did this."

She felt panic. She understood now. *I don't go away this time. I stay here. Maybe worse this way. Other customers don't mind sharing. I thought he was getting better.*

Lynh came barreling into the booth room, followed closely by Verna, chattering what must've been some update in Vietnamese. "Honey, what wrong? Customers can hear you!"

He didn't turn to Lynh and kept staring at Maya in the booth. "I don't care, Lynh. You said last year give her a second chance. Well I did." Maya sucked in a quick breath. *Second chance?* She forgot.

He glared at Lynh. "Honey . . . " she touched his arm. He shrugged it off. Lynh walked off in a huff. Verna followed but stopped a few feet away.

He turned back to Maya. "So what. You mad at me? Is that what this is about. Me going to Saigon?"

At that, she let loose. Patrons would later say it was like a husband and wife fighting. Deth was uncomfortable. He wondered what he'd gotten himself into. He thought these two fought like a married couple, not like the casual bargirl and customer she said they were. He decided Tuesdays with Maya were not for him.

It was her turn to spit a month's frustration. "Well, fuck you! Why you had to go there? I'm not good enough?"

His voice rose another octave. "I went there to talk to Kimmie about you!" He meant Chloe. "I mean Chloe."

She matched his higher octave. "Well Chloe not there huh? And why you gotta talk to Kimmie about me?"

He pointed at her again. "Didn't you hear me? I meant Chloe. But she wasn't there."

Deth reached out to calm her. Mistake. She slapped his hand away. She swung her legs off the booth seat and crossed her arms, one leg bouncing on the other. Her eyes flashed white-hot anger. "I know she wasn't there. But you found another bitch. Why don't you go be with her?"

Glenn's eyes closed, then opened. One trembling hand up reached up and pinched his nose bridge. He took a breath, tried to lower his voice, but it didn't help. He met her gaze, hissed so loud the barflies heard it. "You really want that?" She glared at him. He glared back. Tia tried to help. Verna waved her back. These two need to get this out.

His hiss turned to an angry howl. "*You . . . really . . . want . . . that?*"

Her expression turned blank, shoulders drooped, and her voice flattened. Her spirit deflated. "Up to you already. I do plenty for you." She got up. "I go now." She had to get to Thai Garden. She was late. She heard her phone buzz three times. *This loser situation. Liar. Let him go Saigon. I don't care anymore.*

She got up and walked past him. Deth followed. She made a point of saying quite loudly, "You take me home" to Deth, although she'd actually driven her own car. Deth decided he wasn't ever coming back.

Glenn flopped into the booth and took a bite of cold quesadilla. Lynh came over. She was fuming. "What you doing? Get control. You drink too much."

His look said, are you kidding? "Lynh, I had four beers."

Sitting across him, she leaned forward, in his face. "You spoil her. Why you not share tonight?"

He rolled his eyes, sneering a bit. "Sick, Lynh. If that's what this place is about, I'm out."

She leaned back, flicked a balled-up napkin at him. "Go. Fuck you. We don't need you."

He tried to recall what the jail time was for hitting old Vietnamese women. "Get outta my sight, Lynh."

Jimmy came over and rattled some words to Lynh, convincing her to leave. "Everything okay, Glenn?"

"Yeah, Jimmy."

Jimmy surveyed the slaughter, deciding he couldn't let Glenn go home in that condition. "Stay, Glenn. Cool off."

Glenn took a deep breath and exhaled with a whooshing sound. *Sounds right. None of the beers tonight night tasted good. I just want one good one.*

Then he spied a familiar face at the bar. A beautiful face.

55

KRENG JAI

There was only one seat left at the bar, and it was next to her. *Lucky me,* thought Glenn.

For half past midnight on a weeknight, the bar area was packed and thriving. CNN was on one flatscreen and ESPN SportsCenter on the other. The jukebox played an upbeat contemporary Hispanic beat.

In her usual red nightie, Amber flirted with four business types at one end of the bar. The other end of the bar was a mixture of randoms looking for company.

That left Julie and Glenn in the middle with the late-night barflies. "Hi, Julie. Long time no see. Mind if I sit?"

She looked up from her empty glass. "No problem, Glenn. Tough night?"

He climbed onto the seat next to her. "Yeah. What are you doing here, Julie? I thought you were in school."

She poked at the ice in her glass with her stirrer. "On break, Glenn. Making some extra cash. Med school not cheap."

Julie Santana had worked at Lynh's bar through community college, then undergrad at State University, and was recently accepted to the local university's school of medicine. One of the success stories he enjoyed meeting last summer. With the right touch, she could pass for Ariana Grande. She was also the mother of an eight-year old.

He brushed back his hair. "How long is your break?"

She popped an ice cube in her mouth. "Just finishing up."

He nodded approvingly. "So you working tonight or visiting?"

She signaled Tia for another scotch with ice. Glenn called for a beer. "I was working earlier. I guess this is the visiting part." Tia brought their drinks and handed Julie a microphone. The two girls sang a heartbreaking country song, something about a rodeo star leaving town with the girl singing pregnant and alone. Glenn sang along to the chorus. The whole bar clapped after. Glenn clapped the hardest, feeling the edge he felt earlier slip away.

Julie didn't forget the hundred-dollar tip Glenn had given her last summer. She was able to take her son to Chuck E. Cheese with that. He didn't even sit with her. He just put it in front of her on his way back to Maya from taking a pee. It was one of the few nice things she cared to remember about working for Lynh.

She swiveled her seat to face him. "What's happening, Glenn?" She didn't need to ask. Anyone within a hundred feet of the couple didn't have to ask. But she wanted to hear his side.

His face was half frown, half pout. "Naw. I don't want to bother."

Years as a bargirl gave her an instinct. She knew he was itching to unload, and it was payback time for his kindness last summer. "No Glenn, tell me. These guys here are boring." The barflies snickered. Inquiring minds of the barflies wanted to hear from Glenn as well.

Glenn unloaded his side of the story, or stories, in lawyerly fashion. Much like an opening statement, he laid out his version of the facts, arguing for his innocence against the charge of being a jerk. He laid out the Saigon drugging, much like he had explained to Maya. He talked about paying for Maya's night out last week with the mother-daughter pair, and what happened with the monk tonight.

She patted his forearm, lingering on the last pat for a few seconds. "You and Maya got a lot closer since last summer. Last I saw, you two were playing Connect Four in the corner."

He shook his head. "I don't get it, Julie. I think she's lying to me. She's always coming late or leaving early. She mentions her cousin a lot, but sometimes she messes up and says her husband, then says she meant her cousin's husband."

He lifted a finger to Tia and pointed to Julie. Tia refreshed Julie's drink and got Glenn a Bud Light. "She told me she works at the beauty store and I went by with flowers yesterday, and they said she hadn't been there since April. And even tonight, she made it sound like a surprise the guy stopped by, but it seemed so arranged."

Julie waited, thinking no sense jumping in because they always had one more thing.

"And you know what? About a month ago I wanted to stop by on a Thursday and she was excited. Than an hour before we were supposed to meet, she texted and said it was a no go, that she had to work late. So I came here solo and cooled my heels with Verna because no other girl will sit with me without feeling uncomfortable."

She touched his shoulder. "Wait Glenn, should I feel uncomfortable? What do you mean?" Her knee was inches from his. She pulled back a few inches.

He rubbed the back of his neck. "Well, there was this thing with Amber, and well –"

"Oh, I heard. Are you a regular now? I remember that night I met you, you were going from girl to girl. Usually the girl goes from customer to customer. I guess you're tied to one now. Maya?"

Still rubbing his neck, twisting side to side like he had a kink. "Yeah, I guess."

She sipped her scotch. "It happens, Glenn. It's called a bar marriage."

His face looked like someone dropped a bowling ball in his crotch. "What?"

She burst out laughing. "So sorry. I'm not making fun of you." *This guy—all the girls say he's so cute and cuddly. Now I know what they mean.*

She patted his shoulder reassuringly. "No worries. There's also bar divorces or separations. The good news is, no alimony. But there's a commitment till separation do you part, and all the girls have a code, you know. Especially in this bar. We don't steal from each other."

He looked around as if to spot spies that would report back to Maya. "Are you okay with us sitting together, Julie?"

She nodded, eyes sparkling. "Sure. I'm buying you a drink here too. It's reciprocal." Tia put down another Bud Light. "And all I'm doing is letting an old friend cry on me."

He took a long pull of his beer. "Thanks, Julie. Anyway, that Thursday night. She said she couldn't come by, but she did text me all night long. At one point I got up and drove across town to this restaurant. Thai Garden. I know that's where they hang out sometimes. Her car was there. A lot of cars were there. I was in the parking lot when she texted me and said she was at home and had to turn in for early inventory at the beauty store. By her count, that makeup store does inventory at least twice a month."

She sipped her scotch on ice. The look in her eyes said go on.

He tapped his forehead with the longneck. "So I'm tired of all the lying, Julie. I wanna call her on it. I can't stand liars."

Julie gave it some thought. "Glenn, did you know I'm part Thai?"

With eyes wide, he asked, "Really?" *Sooo what? She changing the subject?*

She showed him a picture of her mother. "Yes, on my mother's side. Have you ever heard of *kreng jai*?"

He smacked his lips. "No. Sounds delicious."

She chuckled. "No silly, not food. It's a lifestyle, a way of thinking. Westerners have a hard time with it. You can google it but it's basically being aware of other people's feelings and showing politeness, respect and consideration. It's telling you what you want to hear or what will help you save face. Some call it white lies on steroids for the duped person's benefit."

He opened his mouth. *Where is she going with this?*

She reached out and put her fingers to his lips. "Give me a chance, Glenn. All this time she's been meeting you on Tuesdays. You know it's very hard to be with anybody for more than an hour. The conversation stalls. People get too familiar. It gets boring. Have you ever tried entertaining a child for two to three hours straight? Even the quiet customers get bored, and there's only so much TV you can watch here—and the customer figures out he can do that at home."

She brought her hands back, then took a sip of her scotch. "And there are a lot of customers to juggle. Not everyone has set days and times. Most only know their plans that night. I'm sure she's had to turn away a lot for you."

He rubbed his chin. "Okay, Julie. I get it. I owe her." *But she has fun with me. Or does she? Telling me she's bored?*

She ordered another beer for him. "No, not at all, Glenn. You don't owe her. And maybe she does have a good time with you." She let it sink in. "But just letting you know that she does have to juggle. Maybe sometimes see them before you get together. And maybe sometimes after. Or maybe she has a boyfriend, a husband, a female partner, kids, or she waits tables at Denny's. I don't know for sure. But the Thai way, Glenn, she'll always tell you what she thinks will be best for you, what will best save face for you."

She surveyed his expression and saw that he was absorbing. "So, if another customer is waiting for her she's not going to tell you that, after saying Tuesdays are for you. She wants to maintain the façade of exclusivity so you'll feel special. To tell you there's another customer would be a lose-face situation for you. She hasn't delivered your fantasy, your special arrangement. So for whatever reason she has to run off early, she'll tell you what is most save-face for you. In your case she probably thinks a business reason is the most believable for you."

She could tell he was struggling with the concept. "Don't focus on the lie, Glenn. Focus on her intent—to save face for you so you won't be embarrassed, so your fantasy remains intact. Can you understand? If you were hungry and I wanted to give you food, I'd say I had too much, and could you help me or my food would go to waste. The intent is good though the words may be false." This reminded Glenn of Maya's optical shop story.

She reached for his hand, only to reassure. "That night she got pulled to Thai Garden, I'm sure there was a good reason. I'm sure it wasn't to go eat Pad Thai with her friends. Whatever the reason was is not important. *If* she could have been with you, she would have. Otherwise, she lied to save face for you. Let you keep your peace and not get mad. You can always google it to learn more." She wrote it on a napkin—kreng jai.

He took the napkin. "So what about tonight?"

She shrugged. "I don't know the facts, Glenn, but I'm sure she was dealing with the situation as best as she could. The guy looked high up in the community by the way Verna was hustling around getting his beer. Those communities are tight-knit. Irk one of the community bosses and you'd get shunned by the others. Not saying it's right, but it seems if she could have done something about it, she would have. And instead of telling you not to come tonight because he was coming, she thought she might try to make it work. And telling you the old friend and brother from another mother is another way to make you feel less displaced—save face."

He finished his beer and signaled Tia for another round for them. "But why keep me in the dark by talking their language?"

She shrugged again. "I don't know about that. Seems odd, but maybe the guy wanted it that way. Again, sounds like she was caught in a situation and she couldn't say no to either of you and was trying to make things work out. Not a malicious intent, Glenn."

She gave his shoulder a quick rub, again to reassure. "I can see how she could've done things better. Especially having both of you in the same booth together. But I heard she had another customer before and you walked out? Maybe she thought if she stayed close to you, you'd be okay?"

It was his turn to shrug.

She continued. "Just remember. The Thai way is to help the other person save face, even to the point of telling a white lie. Sometimes the white lie is on steroids. For the other person's part, it's important to understand, and if it doesn't kill you, to accept the proffered situation as reality, and together continue to walk in harmony."

He gave a small chuckle. "Geez, Julie. Do bargirls really talk like you?"

She let out a chortle. "No, I guess not. But who says I'm a bargirl? Tonight I'm just your friend. Passing on cultural knowledge."

He patted her hand. "Thanks Julie. Helps a lot. Are you going to be here the rest of the week too?"

She lifted both palms as if to say, what can I do? "I go back to school Monday. I'll work every night here. Pick something up here and there. Pays for food when I get back to school."

Glenn fished in his pocket. He still had most of his budget left. Feeling a little conflicted, he thought, *I was gonna blow it on Candy, but there will be other nights.* "Here Julie. A gift. Can you take a night off with this?"

She stared at the money. To her, it was equal to a Friday night take. It meant she could go out with her family and not worry about hustling back to a bar filled with thugs. She pushed his hand away. "No, Glenn. Not necessary."

He pushed back, dumping the cash on the counter. "No, Julie. Take it. Just take a night off. If you do that, it will make me feel good. You're also saving my ass. If you let me keep it, I'll probably go blow it next door."

Julie smiled and batted her eyelashes. "Are you doing kreng jai on me, Glenn?"

He thought about it. "Oh, I get it now. No, I'm not lying. But I can see how I'm trying to make it easier for you to take the money. How about I just say please and thank you from a friend?"

She took the money and slid a twenty to Tia. "His beer's mine. Thank you, Glenn. Good luck. You're sweet."

She got up to leave and gave him a hug. He hugged her back. "Good night, Doctor." She smiled, said bye to Tia and left. He finished his beer and walked off into the night. He texted Maya when he got home.

> Home safe. And staying home. Good night.

 Me too good night

Finally! She was outside Thai Garden in her Audi. She'd sat there for an hour. The glow of the phone reflected off her anxious face. She stared at his text. *I so mad at him but so mad at me. I shouldn't have tried this. I knew little boy was going to come out. I broke my promise to him. He still mad but he text me.*

She bit her nail. *He sulk over hour. At least not like last time. Last time he left me. He shut down Instagram. Not this time. He texted. This his way to say we still together. Still so mad. But happy too. Possible? I guess. Next week try again.*

She went into Thai Garden. Eddie came over. "So how'd it go?"

She was glad to see him, forgetting it had been his idea to invite another customer. "C'mon. Let's have some fun." She grabbed his arm and pulled him toward the baccarat table.

Back at Lynh's bar, Lynh's nephew was fiddling with the surveillance camera footage. Lynh made sure she had four clips on camera—Glenn sitting next to Julie, Julie holding his hand, Julie rubbing his back, and him giving a wad of money to Julie.

Lynh's face was pure hate, mumbling, "I show her tomorrow."

56

CAVE IN

Glenn went to bed early Wednesday night, thinking of Maya and hoping she was having a good night. Suddenly at midnight, his phone started buzzing crazy. The last time it was like that was during a false missile crisis.

I heard you give away money to Julie you know what stop the bullshit to me I done!!!!

Hope you find someone better than me !!

I don't wanna see you anymore you're so bull shit just like another guy that I knew

Stop texting me no more this shit for me!!

I bought her a couple of drinks why so mad?

You think I dunno shit? I'm not stupid stop texting me

What are you hearing? From who?

What the fuck is going on now?

He dialed her number. *"Hello . . . this is Maya,"* he heard. *"Please leave your name and number and I'll call you right back."*

He hung up. *I don't think she's gonna call me back if I leave a message. It went straight to voicemail. Am I blocked already?*

He threw on a t-shirt and ran out the door to his car. *I can't believe this is happening. I should be the one pissed. Who told her? What did they tell her? I didn't do anything.*

He gassed it, running two yellow lights on the way. *I gave Julie my leftover wad. Did she think it was her money? Is she really pissed about the money? Or that I sat with Julie? No, it's the money. She was clear about that.*

He stopped at a red light and looked at her text again. *Yup, it's the money. How is this bullshit? It's my money.*

The light turned green, and he floored it. *Hope I find someone better than her? You mean someone that doesn't lie? Doesn't play games? Damn right I can. Can she find someone better than me?*

He pulled up to the bar with a screech. *Never seen her this mad. Why is she taking it so personal?*

It was Wednesday night, so he knew she'd be with her regular in the darts room. He walked in and looked left. She noticed him right away and glared at him, giving him the double thumbs down.

He mouthed, "What's going on?" She turned her back on him. Her customer stepped into his line of view with a look that said, "Dude, go home." As odd as the situation was, Glenn still noticed how gorgeous she looked, with her hair up, in a gold cocktail dress with spaghetti straps. It was the sexiest double thumbs down he'd ever seen.

Lynh grabbed his elbow and had him outside before he could shrug her off. "What do you want, Lynh?"

Lynh tried to catch his eye. "She mad, honey!"

He heard enough. "What did you tell her, Lynh?"

"Nothing. What you two fight about?"

He shoved his phone at her so she'd see the texts. "Someone told her about me giving Julie money. Did you Lynh?"

She spoke without looking at the texts on his phone, lighting a cigarette. She took a puff. "That what you two fight about?" He was getting nowhere.

In his mind, he pictured Lynh talking to Maya. *He no good, Maya. He womanizer. Girlfriends all over. You leave he find new girl. Maybe go next door after. You not want that. Dump him.* It was something easily imaginable.

She struck a casual pose puffing a second cigarette, as if bargirls going nuts was commonplace. Three barflies sat outside, enjoying the show. "Come back tomorrow, honey, everything be okay." Bile came up his throat. It was a long day, and he was grouchy as shit. He glared enough to piss her off. His look sent chills down her spine.

Her fear quickly turned to anger. "Oh screw this. Go home. You a stupid cowardly dog. Wrong girl. What, you lap her pussy, like the taste now? No other girl good enough?"

The barflies sat bug-eyed, having never seen Mama like this.

She sounded like a jealous schoolgirl. "You can do better but *noooo.* You like her. You take her shit. I tell you over and over she not the nice girl you think. She like young wild boys. Make her feel young again."

Again, he wondered what the jail time was for hitting an old woman. He walked away. "Go back inside, Lynh. I'm going home." *Don't look like you all are gonna see me again anyway.*

Back home, he wondered about calling or sending another text. He read her text again. *Nope. Sounds final. Didn't expect it to end like this. At least the last time she sent a nice picture—kinda romantic actually—as if to say thanks and take care. This time it's one big middle finger. Can't believe she gave me the double thumbs down.*

He got ready for bed for the second time that night. *Well, that's that. I'm tired of this shit anyway. To think I spent a day convincing myself to forgive her for the stupid stunt she pulled on Tuesday. After Julie gives me this kreng jai lesson, I even texted her to show we were okay. Still pissed about the other night. Trying to deal with it, and she does this? How psychotic is this girl? I don't even know her. Maybe it's better this way. She might drug me one night and take my kidney or something.*

It was getting late. He had a 6:00 a.m. meeting with the Admiral. What started out as a chance for a decent night's sleep turned into a two-hour nap. Last thoughts as he dozed off. *Fuck this shit. Man, I use the F-word a lot since meeting this girl.*

———————————

The next day was an exercise on how to stay awake doing accounting data entry, and more importantly, how to look like you cared to an otherwise incompetent CEO ranting about late financial statement preparation again.

He threw his financial statements binder at his boss' feet. "Look, Joyce, I've been here almost a year. I told you I'm a finance guy, not a bean counter. You didn't replace Samantha yet. Did you know she was going to quit two weeks after I came on board?"

The non-profit CEO stood stone-faced.

He continued. "I've resigned three times and you asked me to stay three times. But now you don't let me run the show the way I want, you don't give me the staffing I need, and now you give me the collections function? Get a grip. It's me and two clerks doing everything. I'm only a glorified accounting supervisor."

Her face was beet red. "What are you trying to tell me, Glenn? I promised the board the financials by this week. Maybe you should have talked to me first?"

They were at an impasse. He softened and thought to himself, *She's green, has her own demons, and deserves patience.* Agape, *as they say.* "Joyce, we'll do what we can."

She pointed her finger in his face. "No Glenn, get it done. No excuses."

He raised an eyebrow. *Aw, screw* agape. "Get out of my office, Joyce. In fact, get out of my face. Ask me anytime you want me to resign. But till then, stay out of my face."

She made a hmmph sound, did an about face, slammed his door and skulked down the hall.

He massaged his nose bridge, the part between his eyes. *Okay, God, I blew it again, huh? I got bitched at by three women in the last twelve hours. Gotta be a personal best.*

Danielle carefully opened the door and poked her head in. "You okay, boss?"

Glenn forced a smile. "Yes, Danielle, don't worry about it."

She saw the binder on the floor. "Don't quit, okay? We need you."

He nodded at her. "Who's *we*?"

Like something out of a "Brady Bunch" episode, Penny poked her head in above Danielle's. "The two of us!" they said in unison.

He chuckled, shaking his head. These two were the only reason he hadn't quit months ago.

He spent the rest of the day in his office. He put the reports aside and went over the events of the past week. The past month. The past year. *It was a good run. She was good for me. I hope I was good for her. I'm never having a regular girl again. Indiscriminate sex doesn't sound so bad.*

He wavered between melancholy, being pissed, and missing her. *Yeah, it was a good run.*

Quitting time came and his door was still closed with a Do Not Disturb sign. *Wonder if I should drop in tonight? Maybe she's in a better mood. Nah, family obligations. And I missed a couple already. And judo practice too. Time to get life back on track again. Maybe tonight is the night for a good night's sleep.*

He had a hard time drifting off that Thursday night. *Geez,* he thought, *I haven't been this pissed in a while. She does a "bullshit bring-a-monk-to-our-Tuesday-night" stunt, followed by an "ignore-the-crap-out-of-me-by-talking-a-third-world-language-all-night" stunt, followed by a "walk-out-like-a-crazy-bitch" stunt while I'm asking to talk. Stunt, stunt, stunt. Three strikes, baby.*

He was now arguing into thin air, muttering, "So *you* leave me there with all these girls and with a wad of cash unspent, and *you* think what? I was going to curl up and go home?" *And it wasn't even anything bad,* he thought. *I didn't go next door. For Pete's sake, it was Julie! Everyone's sister.*

Internally he continued, arguing, *So what if I gave Julie money? She's going to school. What the shit are you doing with the money I give you? Some bullshit about buying brain medicine for your mother. You told me last year she only had one more year to live. I guess the brain medicine worked. Should get the FDA to approve it for US consumption.*

He rolled into his pillow. *And you give me so much bullshit about going to beauty school. You said you'd start last month. Nothing. Not a peep. You only talk about what a great birthday party you're gonna have next week.*

He sat up, suddenly remembering, *the birthday party . . . hmm. I promised her I'd help decorate. I promised her a present. And I promised her Dom.*

Shit, he thought, *a promise is a promise. I'll show and if she doesn't want me to stay, I'll leave. Somewhere in the back of his mind, he pictured a tearful reunion.* Not gonna happen, his ego said.

He woke in the dark. *Morning already?* It wasn't the alarm clock buzzing. It was five o'clock Friday morning. His phone was buzzing. One long buzz. A text. The Admiral?

I don't wanna feel awkward on Tuesday cuz I still have to work if you still stopping by at the bar let me know you want to sit with somebody else so I wont bother

He rubbed his eyes, trying to focus. *What is this? She just got more psychotic. Who the fuck gives someone a big middle finger, then turns around with a text like this?*

He did the time analysis. *It's 5:00 a.m. She works till 2:00 a.m. Either she's up early or she's been up all night thinking about this. Maybe her Thursday was a bad night and she's come to appreciate me, and my money? Maybe someone at the bar pulled her aside and said, "Bitch! You're lucky Glenn's a great guy and you should take care of him."*

He got up to pee. *Maybe she had a bad night and is just getting her act together? Maybe the psych doctor got her to take her meds again?*

Back in bed, he stared at the text. *What is going on? I guess she didn't block me after all.*

Sunlight was starting to slice through the curtains. *This is really pissing me off.*

He started typing.

Fuck off. I'm blocking you now.

No. Erase

Beg me for mercy if you still want me.

No. Erase.

Go to hell, psycho bitch.

No. Erase.

He read her text again. *What does she want?*

He began composing again.

Don't worry I'm never going to that psyche ward of a bar again.

No. Erase

He threw his phone on the bed and went to wash up. *Sounds like she's saying if I don't want to sit with her anymore, let her know so she doesn't feel awkward. After all this, she wants me to worry about* her *feeling awkward?*

He stabbed his toothbrush in and out of his mouth, frothing with each stroke. *And how would she feel awkward if I'm dead to her? Just ignore me. The bar's a big place. Hide in the darts room while I'm in the front. Doesn't matter. Stay outta my face and I'll stay out of yours.*

He read her text again:

let me know you want to sit with somebody else so I won't bother.

Could it be? Sounds like she wants to sit with me again. Man, this sounds like the half-baked ice breakers my college girlfriends used to send me when they got pissed, kicked me to the curb, and came crawling back to me.

The whole "I'm free on Saturday night if you still want to go dancing with me, but if you don't want to go with me please don't ignore me at the club and make me feel bad."

He sat on the couch, turning on the TV for company. *Katie never played these bullshit Jedi mind tricks. It's been a while since I had to decipher girlspeak. What a bitch. She's like any other girl. Wait.*

He rocked back and forth on the couch. *Like any other girl . . . who has . . . feelings. If this was a bargirl thing, she'd just move on. Or let Lynh try to fix it like last time. Even the money thing with Julie. Something going on here. She . . . has . . . feelings.*

It'd been a half-hour since he got the text. Something was stirring in him. *Damn*, he thought, *she's got guts though. Gotta give her that. She's got real balls.* A small voice in him that sounded like Pastor Ronan kept bringing up one word—*forgive.*

He looked at his watch and thought, *Time to go to the most wonderful job in the world of non-profit accounting.* He texted back.

> If I stop by Id want to sit with you. Give me another chance?

ok

> See you next Tuesday?

ok

She fired back immediately with the okays. *I guess she was waiting.*

He reread his text. *Sounds weeny. I shoulda said give* us *another chance. Still, how's that for kreng jai?*

57

SISTERS

Maya sat in the dark on her bed, knees drawn up to her chest, with only the glow of her phone for light. Rusty snoozed in a ball at her feet, only looking each time she gasped.

For the last half-hour she'd seen *Glenn is typing* flash over and over without any text coming through. She imagined so many scenarios. But as long as he was typing something, she was hopeful. *Glenn, don't stop typing. Say something. I don't want you to go. I was stupid. Little girl got mad. Don't go.*

She thought back to a few hours before at the bar, a Thursday night spent chasing down randoms, pretending they were wealthy, handsome or jocks. It was a slow night. By midnight the place was empty, except for a couple of regulars and the few barflies that could still stand. Julie Santana sat at the bar area, chatting with Tia.

Maya had suppressed it till then, but she was still mad after what Lynh showed her the night before. *I will talk to Julie. Find out what really happened.*

She slid onto the stool next to Julie.

The atmosphere turned awkward, and more than one barfly raised an eyebrow. One of them turned to leave but chose to stay for another beer, and the show that was about to start.

Julie turned, holding her arms open for a hug. "Hi, Maya." They embraced like long-lost sisters. A trained eye would notice the tension between the two.

Maya released first. "Hi, Julie. You look beautiful, baby."

Julie smiled. "You too, girl. Thought I saw you with Glenn last night?"

Maya fiddled with her phone as if to show it meant nothing. "Oh, he come and he go." The way her voice trailed off betrayed her distress.

Julie asked the obvious. "Honey, you guys fight?"

Maya put down her phone. "No fight. No us anymore."

Julie waved Tia over and bought a drink for her former co-worker and sister bargirl. "Cheers!"

Maya's Crown felt warm going down. She recalled the last time she'd drunk Crown with Glenn. She breathed in, seeking courage, and spoke, "Julie, you sit with Glenn the other night?" She expected Julie to say mind your own business—the bargirl code.

Julie sipped her scotch. "Not really sit, Maya. He needed someone to talk to and bought me a couple of drinks. I bought his beer. Just two friends, you know?"

Maya clenched a napkin in her hand. "Allie say he give you lots of money. Why? He want chance with you? Dump me and be with you?" Maya didn't mention what Lynh showed her.

Julie turned fully, making eye contact. "Now Maya, you know I have pride. Like you. Even if he did that, I wouldn't have, you know?"

Maya leaned forward. "I know. But –"

"No buts, Maya. Not like that. I'm here on school break but working to pay bills. I told him and he gave me his whole wad and said take the night off so I can be with my family or do whatever without hustling. It was like a Friday night payoff, Maya."

Maya knew how much it was. She knew exactly how much money she'd left on the table.

She felt her heart tug at her. "He gave you money so you no need work?"

Julie's look said it all. *Forgive him girl. He's a good guy.* "Yes, he gave me money to take tomorrow night off."

Maya bit her lower lip. Her face contorted for a split second as if she was ready to burst into tears. She used a wad of napkins like a stress ball. She breathed in deep, leaning her head back. She suppressed all her emotions. On the outside, nothing. On the inside, her heart ached. It hurt a lot. *Oh Glenn, I bullshit you and hurt you with customer, then you turn around help Julie. Then I fuck you all over with text. Shit.*

Julie's voice brought Maya back. "He's a sweet guy, Maya. He doesn't belong here or any other place like this. If I was one of those girls next door, I would have worked him. We've all worked the occasional asshole that comes in here. But that's just assholes. He's not one of them."

Julie reached out and touched Maya's forearm. "Maya, he told me about Saigon."

Maya sat up straight. "Really?"

Nodding, Julie continued. "You know he went because he wanted to see Chloe?"

Maya cut in. "I knew it. He has hots for Chloe. Cannot believe . . ."

Julie squeezed Maya's arm. "No, you're wrong on that one." Julie was piecing it together. *What's wrong with these two? They're not the normal bar couple. They're more. Like they . . . love each other? And yet can't get beyond this bar. They care for each other but can't accept it.*

Julie explained. "He said the last time he was with Chloe she showed him pics of you and talked about you. He only wanted to hear more about you."

Maya's lips flatlined. Her heartache radiated to her stomach. Guilt started flowing through her veins. "He didn't tell me that. I ask him why he went. He didn't tell me that. I thought he went to be with her. I thought he went to . . ." She was silent. She didn't say it out loud. *I thought he went to spy on me . . . to dig up dirt on me . . . to chance Chloe.*

Julie saw the pain and rubbed Maya's shoulders. "He's very confused. He thinks you're mad because he said he was home safe then he went to Saigon."

Maya's eyes flashed suddenly. "Yeah, he lied."

Julie held her hand up. "Now, Maya. How many times did you say you did one thing but were doing something else?"

No answer.

Julie continued. "We all juggle. But we lie too. Why? Cuz we don't want the guy to get mad. We don't want the guy to get hurt. We don't want the guy to take off. Right? With him, he wasn't lying. He really was at home. Then he changed his mind. He simply forgot to tell you. Now he's all overthinking and thinks you think he's a liar. I can tell by your face that you actually thought that's what he did—that he lied. Maybe cuz we do it too."

Maya let the wad of napkins she was squeezing out of her death grip, then squeezed again. *Julie always the smart one. Sometimes tell us girls the hard truth. That's why soon she's gonna be Dr. Julie.*

Julie gingerly took the wad of paper out of Maya's hand and replaced it with her hand. "And he changed his mind because he wanted to find Chloe so he could hear more about you. He's not like the rest. He's like . . . I can't put my finger on it . . . He's like . . ."

Maya cut in. "A little boy."

Julie nodded, thinking about her own boy. "By the way, he's very smart. I know lawyers, but this guy is way smarter. He can pick up on a lot of things and Maya, he's picked up where your stories don't always match. But he lets it go you know? But not for long. He's getting frustrated."

Julie stopped briefly. She thought through what she was about to say, whether it was good or not. "I gotta tell you, don't tell him I told you, did you stand him up one night and tell him you were at home, but you were at Thai Garden?"

Maya leaned forward, about to protest, about to cover.

Julie shook her head. "Maya, don't answer. It's me you're talking to. You should know he took a ride down there. Saw your car. Texted good night to you from the parking lot. Is that when you said you were home all night?"

Maya wore a worried expression. "What you say when he told you this?"

Julie shrugged. "I told him we all juggle. I told him you probably didn't want to hurt his feelings, so you lied. Nothing mean intended. You had to take care of business and you lied and gave him the fantasy he wanted."

Maya stared past Julie into the empty dart room.

Julie continued. "Maya, most marriages would have ended right there. But he's still with you and never brought it up. He believes what you tell him because he wants to. Don't make him out to be weak, Maya. He knows when you're lying but he takes it, works with it. I don't think he's going to do this forever. Be careful."

Maya leaned back. She felt small. She felt like a piece of crap. Guilt consumed her. She had let him down.

Julie lightly squeezed her bar sister's hand to make sure she had her attention. "You know what he told me when I asked him why he was doing this? All he said was, love conquers all. Love conquers all. How's that?"

Maya nodded, her face contorted with grief, guilt, sadness and remorse. "I cannot face him now, Julie. He know I lie."

Julie lifted Maya's hands to her lips and kissed Maya's palms. "Of course you can face him. Tell him the truth from now. But if not, be smart about it. You know, if you can't be with him, tell him you can't be with him. No need for stories. He'll understand from now. I told him about kreng jai."

Startled, Maya asked Julie how she knew such a phrase.

Julie rattled off some Thai, explaining her mother's side of the family.

Maya flicked her own forehead. "I did not know. You are sister from another mother!" They laughed and hugged like long lost sisters.

Julie leaned back but kept her hands on Maya's shoulders. "And about your brother from another mother. The other night. That was hard for him to take. He stayed because he asked if he should leave and you didn't let him. As much as it hurt him, he stayed, Maya. He only wanted a few minutes with you at the end of the night. You know the rule, Maya. You never mix customers that don't know each other. I'm not going to ask you why you did that. You have your reasons. But put yourself in his place. How would you have felt?"

The look on Maya's face said it all. Regret and remorse were waging a battle with Maya's heart and conscience. *No more listen to Eddie.*

Julie caressed Maya's face. "I'm not gonna judge, Maya. Most girls know how to get another customer to leave or wait in another booth. I'm not sure why you couldn't sweet talk this guy to leave or have another girl sit with him. I mean I would have for you. And there were two other girls out here."

Maya took Julie's hand in hers. "I only want him to know I have other customers. That he appreciate I make time for him."

Julie nodded. "I think he knows, Maya. You don't have to do this. Did you set this up for real?"

Maya rubbed her nose. "No, not exactly." She lied. She had told Deth she worked Tuesdays, knowing he'd come. She didn't tell him she had a regular.

Julie cocked her head. The "not exactly" was a giveaway. "Bullshit, Maya. We've all done it. But only to the assholes. He's not an asshole, Maya. And he stayed. Most guys woulda said, screw this, and left, permanently."

Julie wasn't finished. "One more thing. Last night."

Maya's eyes widened. "You saw last night?"

Julie gave her a look like, *hellooo!* "Honey, the whole bar saw last night. You two are like a soap opera. You know Lynh dragged him outside and embarrassed him? Called him a cowardly stupid dog in the parking lot. In front of a bunch of guys. Something about lapping at your pussy and liking it. I couldn't hear much but Lynh was loud. Those guys outside heard it but we heard it all in here too."

Julie looked around carefully for Lynh. She lowered her voice to a whisper. "She humiliated him. Some other guy would have hit her. She taunted him. Told him to hit her and threatened to fire you. He sucked it in and left. What control. Pretty sure he didn't hit Lynh so you wouldn't get in trouble."

Julie looked at her watch and slipped off her stool. "I have to get going."

Maya hugged Julie hard. "Take care baby, call me next time come town okay?" Julie squeezed Maya's hand in response.

Several hours later, Maya was at home, freshly showered, makeup off, in bed with Rusty in her lap. She had stared at her phone all night, reading his text over and over, as if the words would change magically. He'd sent the text—home safe—right after she got in the Uber.

Her thoughts were many and came rapidly. *He not lying? Stupid. Why didn't you tell me? Maybe he did? I did not hear? Maybe I'm so mad I did not hear. Oh Glenn, Mama Lynh treat you like shit outside. If I knew I would have . . . I dunno. Not sure what I would have done. Why didn't you tell me why you go Saigon? Maybe you did. Why didn't you tell me why you give Julie money? Stupid Allie. Made it sound like Darren all over again. And stupid videos Lynh show me. He not Darren.*

At 5:00 a.m. she heard Caleb downstairs getting ready. Adrenaline had been coursing through her body for several hours. She took out her phone and unblocked him. *What to say? Hard to say sorry. Hope he can read between the lines. Did he block me? It's okay if he not want me no more. No, not okay. Glenn, hope you still there for me.* She sent a text.

I don't wanna feel awkward on Tuesday
cuz I still have to work if you still
stopping by at the bar let me know you
want to sit with somebody else so I
wont bother

Her heart beat faster each time she saw, *Glenn is typing.*

Then the message would go away, and there'd be no text. Then she saw it flash again, and again no text.

Finally. *A reply!* She read it three times to be sure. She smiled. *So sweet. Give him another chance? He should have been Thai. Better than any Thai man I know. Can't wait see him again.*

If I stop by Id want to sit with you. Give me another chance?

ok

See you next Tuesday?

ok

The words blurred as her eyes moistened. *Most beautiful text I ever got.* She went to sleep hugging her pillow, wishing it was him.

58

LOVE LIES MONEY

Twelve hours after trading texts with Maya, Glenn pulled into his condo parking lot. After a long Friday at the non-profit, all he wanted to do was detach from the world. He had been on autopilot for ten hours doing non-profit accounting. The bulk of his brain was stuck on one issue only. *Why her 180 degree change? Wednesday night she kicks me to the curb and thirty-six hours later on Friday morning, we're back on? What happened?*

He opened a beer from the fridge and plopped on the couch. He channel-surfed mindlessly while scrolling through her texts on Wednesday night.

I heard you give away money to Julie you know what stop the bullshit to me I done!!!!

Hope you find someone better than me !!

I don't wanna see you anymore you're so bullshit just like another guy that I knew

Stop texting me no more this shit for me!!

You think I dunno shit? I'm not stupid stop texting me

I blocking your number right now stop
texting me

M

It's only money. I have more if she wants. Why so mad that I gave it to Julie? They're friends. I gave money to other girls before. They all need help. Why not help? Pretty selfish if she wants all the money to herself. Bitch! Why so money hungry and territorial?

He continued scrolling to the text he got that morning.

I don't wanna feel awkward on Tuesday
cuz I still have to work if you still
stopping by at the bar let me know you
want to sit with somebody else so I
wont bother

M

Who does this? Gotta talk to someone about this. Either she's psycho or I got something wrong with me. And I think I know the right person to see.

The next night, he headed off to the bar on a hunch. He knew Maya wouldn't be around on her night off. The Saturday night crowd packed the place, and the jukebox and flatscreens were screaming to be heard above the crowd. There was only one seat open. Luckily, people didn't want to sit next to the crazy guy. "Hey, Dr. Emerson!" Glenn called out, sliding onto the empty stool.

"Just Tom, Glenn. Just Tom will do fine."

He reminded Glenn of the guy on that home improvement show, the guy who only showed parts of his face over the fence. Usually quiet, Tom was known to go off into rants and gestures at thin air, consequences of two tours in Iraq. Prior to seeing action, he'd been an eminent psychologist. He and Glenn had talked about Glenn's unmet needs before. So if anyone could give Glenn psychoanalysis about Maya, it was Tom.

Glenn drummed his fingers on the bar counter. "Hey doc, got a problem for you."

Tom swiveled to Glenn. "For me? It's never for me Glenn. For you, right? Hmm. And for me to figure out . . . for you?"

Glenn cricked his neck. *Uh oh. Is he gonna go crackers on me?* He tried a different tack. "Absolutely right, my good doctor." *Maybe talking like him will put him at ease.*

Tom's eyes shined. "Righto, Glenn. What's bothering you?"

Glenn did a mental high five. *Hot damn, it worked!* "It's Maya. It's about money." He ran down the entire fact sheet and his own conclusions. Tom kept up with a steady stream of *"Hmmm," "Uh huh," "Unnh," "Yes," "I see," "Go on,"* and one *"Oh really?"*

They were both three beers in by the end. Glenn asked, "Whaddya think doc? Is she certified crazy? Certified selfish? Certified money hungry?"

Tom rubbed his neck. "Glenn, how much do you know about Thai culture?"

Glenn reached for some peanuts. "I know about kreng jai. I eat Thai food. That's about it. Why?"

Tom replied, "Just gauging, Glenn."

Glenn pressed. "So your conclusion? Psycho, right?"

Tom's answer caught Glenn by surprise. "Not at all, Glenn. She's merely a Thai woman."

Glenn's twisted expression reflected absolute confusion. "She acted like that because she's a bargirl from Thailand?"

Tom shook his head. "No Glenn, I said Thai *woman*, not bargirl. She's a Thai woman, and she has feelings for you, or at least your relationship is something more than casual."

Glenn wanted more clarity when he walked in. Now he was afraid he was going to be more confused going out.

He gathered up the most emphatic "Huh?" he could muster. "What's being a Thai woman got to do with this? Feelings for me? More than casual? All I did was give money to Julie."

Tom twitched a bit. "If I'm right, you might as well have gotten down on your knees and asked Julie to marry you. You were basically transferring your love and affection for Maya to Julie in front of all to see, and to Maya's great embarrassment."

Again from Glenn: "Huh?"

Thinking this was going to be a long night, Tom called for two shots of bourbon. Tia obliged. Tom paid and slid one over to Glenn. "Cheers, Glenn."

Tom leaned on the bar and steepled his fingers. "Glenn, keep an open mind, okay? Eastern and Western cultures look at love and romance differently. Here in the quote-unquote *civilized* West, marriage or coupling is founded, at least currently, on notions of love, romance, good vibes and all the things that make Cupid and the turtledoves prance and fly about.

In the East, marriage or coupling is founded on more practical lines, like financial support and the sustainability of the bride and her family. That's why marrying a Thai girl involves a substantial dowry. Marrying off the girl takes her off the market. If you can't support her and them, the family wants a security deposit to fall back on."

Glenn crossed his arms and leaned on the bar as if absorbing some arcane legal principle.

Tom continued his lecture. "Not a crazy idea. Same way in this country until the 1900s. Marriages were often arranged for convenience, for one family to take care of another. Only after the Great War of 1914 did romantic love and marriage take root in Europe and then America. Sure, there were marriages based on love, but that was a luxury for rich folks. Farming families had to marry based on what the other side was bringing to the table—a strong back or a fat wallet with livestock and land to boot."

Glenn scratched his head.

Tom scratched too, somewhere below the beltline. "Are you sure you went to law school? Let me simplify. In the West, we marry for love. In the East, they marry for economic stability. And not merely for the sake of money; the number-one concern for every Thai woman is to make sure her parents are cared for, her kids are cared for, and her siblings are cared for. It was her job to go out and snag a man who could do all that. Looks, physique, intelligence, charm and dick size were secondary considerations to his ability to provide."

Tom signaled for another shot. "So the money you provide Maya to support her mother is something she considers akin to your affection for her. Your exclusive support for her family and thus your affection only for her."

Tom downed his shot. "By giving such a huge wad to Julie, you were telling her here's my affection for someone else. It might've been one time only, but akin to a one-night stand."

Glenn shifted on his stool. "And how am I supposed to know all this?"

Tom shrugged. "How are we men supposed to know anything that makes women tick? We don't. We utter the magic words I'm sorry, you're right, and I'm wrong and hope everything smooths over."

Glenn ordered another shot for Tom. "Thanks much, Doc." He turned to leave.

"Wait, Glenn, one more thing," Tom said, "You should know I'm married to a Thai woman. Twenty-seven years. I give her my paycheck every month. Whatever I need she provides. The rest for her family. I'm certified crazy. Can't work anymore. She's still with me, Glenn."

Glenn gave Tom a respectful nod.

Tom summarized. "Remember the next time you're buying drinks for her or providing support money, it's not an economic transaction to her. It's a relationship."

Glenn sat glued to his seat. "Tom," he said hesitantly, "one more question?"

Tom's eyebrows arched as if to say go on, ask me.

Glenn scrolled through his phone while he spoke. "So she kicked me to the curb on Wednesday night, and thirty-six hours later, like early Friday morning, this."

Tom blew out a sharp whistle. "That was fast!"

Glenn held his palms up as if to say, give me something here. "What do you mean?"

Tom rubbed the stubble on his chin. "As I said, it's a relationship thing, not only money. If it was about money, she could get that anywhere, considering how popular she is now." Tom paused. "It's about what comes with the money."

Glenn raked his hair back and forth. "What do you mean?"

Tom's reply was quick. "You. It's you, Glenn. You come with the money. The relationship she has with you comes with the money. She's trying to save the relationship."

Walking to his car, Glenn was in deep thought. *What rabbit hole have I gone down? It's crazy, but I can't do without her. Can this be more? Can love conquer all? We have a relationship? She said, friends. Fantasy. Tuesday only.*

Relationship. That word stuck with Glenn to the following Tuesday.

59

ENTER LOUIS VUITTON

Maya went to work at the bar on Friday night, still happy about Glenn's text that morning. Lynh greeted her. "Maya, my baby! How are you? You okay? Cop friends not here yet. Come. Sit with Mama."

Maya eyed Lynh warily. "Okay, Mama. Just little while. Sergeant Mike here already."

Lynh took Maya's hand and led her to the booth room. "Sergeant Mike can wait. I buy his first two rounds. He watching sports, and Amber." Lynh brought out a cigarette, looked around, and put it back. "You talk to Julie? What she say?"

Maya recalled the videos Lynh showed her and what Lynh said last Wednesday night. "Mama, all okay now. Julie explain to me. He wasn't chancing her. Just helping. It's okay. All okay."

Lynh scoffed. "No, honey. He not like I thought. Every time you not around, he go after other women. Amber, Chloe, now Julie. He not right for you, girl." Lynh puffed on the unlit cigarette. "You like, I send him away for you. Find another girl."

Shaking her head, Maya said "No Mama, I –"

"He married, Maya!"

Maya's jaw dropped.

Lynh reached for Maya's hand. "Just like Darren. Remember Darren?"

Maya remembered Jimmy breaking the news to her. Darren was married with two children. Another bar manager had told Jimmy. No wonder Darren could only see her certain nights, and never the weekends either. He always said, family, too. Not only did Darren cheat on Maya with Chloe, but he had been married all along. All the nights he confessed his love for her, that he would take care of her, that he would be there for her always. She was just a toy to him. All lies. No future. And it left a huge scar on her heart.

Even now, it hurt. She felt like Lynh had just ripped a giant scab off her heart.

Breathing hard, she gasped out, "What you mean, Mama? You know for sure? How you know?"

Lynh rubbed Maya's forearm. "I know, honey. Been in this business long time. I know. Only come weeknights. Never on weekends. He not even coming your birthday next week!"

Maya pulled her hand back, covering her mouth. Breathing deeply, she focused on keeping the tears from welling up and overflowing. "Mama, you know for sure like last time? Somebody know for sure and tell you? Tell Jimmy?

Lynh leaned back. "No, honey. But everything same as Darren. Must be married." She scanned Maya, satisfied the seed was planted. "Honey, you sit here for while, then come work, okay? Sorry Mama had to tell you, but I love you and want to make sure you not hurt again, okay?"

Maya nodded as Lynh got up to leave.

The rest of the night was a blur. Maya started with five straight tequila shots, the real stuff, and went home in a taxi. For a long time, her cop friends said it was the wildest Friday night ever.

For the rest of the weekend, one thought haunted her over and over. *Why he not coming to my birthday?* Overthinking pushed her from a state of confusion on Saturday to a downward spiral of anxiety by Tuesday.

On Tuesday evening, she was still anxious, unsure and unhappy about Glenn. *He married or not?*

She met Eddie for dinner at Thai Garden a few hours before she was to meet Glenn. They had started eating dinner together at Thai Garden a couple of times a week. He married his wife to get her a green card, but things weren't working out. His family was giving him gas about it. He needed to vent to someone, and she offered to listen. She liked that he depended on her. She held him sometimes while he groaned, "You're the only one I can say these things to." She bit. She felt special. This bad boy was like a little kid inside and he needed her.

It was almost 9:00 p.m., the time she usually met Glenn.

His mouth tight in a frown, Eddie's eyes screamed in frustration. "Can't you stay longer?" His boss coached him to beg her for a little more time so that she would be late and frustrate Glenn, driving the wedge deeper between Glenn and her.

"Wish I could." She meant it. She wasn't looking forward to seeing Glenn. Her feelings were mixed. Over the weekend, insecurity set in. Bad memories of Darren. How it hurt when he left. How it hurt to find out he was married. She wasn't sure about Glenn. She didn't want to get hurt again.

Eddie grabbed her wrist, then let go. "C'mon stay." He was pleading. *This,* Eddie thought deviously, *will frustrate the old man even more. Maybe cause another fight?*

She shifted in her seat. "Okay, maybe little while more." She texted Glenn—running late.

An hour later, happy he'd been able to spend more time with her, Eddie brought out a box brightly wrapped with a red bow. He'd planned to give it to her later that night but wanted her to think of him while she was with Glenn. "Before you go, early birthday present," he said.

She tore off the wrapping revealing a rustic orange-brown box. Inside she found a Louis Vuitton bucket bag. Retail $2200. She gasped, then squealed. Impulsively, she reached down, cupped his chin and drew him to her and kissed then hugged him. "See you later, baby."

It was the first time she'd called Eddie "baby." He smiled, thankful for his boss's coaching and for his advice that Thai girls go wild when given money or name-brand accessories.

He leaned back, licking his lips, watching her ass as she walked out of the restaurant. In his head, he was already having his way with her.

Driving over to the bar, she was perplexed, conflicted, frustrated. *Eddie not that bad. Not too smart getting involved with bargirl wanting green card. At least Caleb and me . . . the marriage real at first.*

She thought back to the charming, boyish American sailor she'd met at that bar in Pattaya, who had then tracked her down at her day job at the optical shop. *He so easy to please, and control. I could tell from start. My ticket to America.*

She stopped at a red light and checked her makeup in the mirror. *Eddie act tough outside but easy too. Lots of money from gambling. At least no kids. All the other guys that like me, all have kids. Kids take money first. Nothing left for me, mommy, sister, brother, grandparents. He said divorce in a year. I say take it easy till then. If Caleb find out, he can divorce me now. I lose pension.*

She was half a block from the bar. *Not sure I like Eddie anyway. Easy on the eyes though. He looked like Ken Wongpuapan, Thai movie star. Maybe not marry but good for fuck around with. Life short. Live love laugh now. Worry about future later. Rest when die.*

She pulled up to the bar. She frowned. *Glenn. Always family on other nights. Or quick in and out. All customers spend that much time with family gotta be married. Like Mama said. I think he married. Bastard. Same as Darren.*

She reached over and touched her new bag, breathing in, the smell of leather thick in her car. Eddie was looking good to her.

60

LIFE AFTER DETH

Glenn got to the bar early. He needed time to think. Tia and Jimmy were playing with their phones. The darts room was empty, and the booth room only had one couple. A construction crew was filling in a broken water main outside, killing the bar's business.

Glenn jumped on his corner seat, and Jimmy slid him a Bud Light. Glenn leaned on his elbows staring at his reflection in the mirror behind the bar. He thought about what Julie said about kreng jai, and what Tom said about marrying for money. *So . . . lies equal love. So . . . money equals love. What did that book say? The one on love languages—words of affirmation, quality time, receiving gifts, acts of service, and physical touch. I guess you can add white lies and money for the mother to the list.*

He took a long swallow of his beer. *Then all that talk with Tom about a relationship. Me and her? A relationship?*

He shook his head, recalling what she'd said the time he confessed his love for her:

> *Glenn, I'm so sorry, I lead you on.*
> *I like you. You good friend and customer.*

Hope crept into his heart. *Maybe she changed her mind since then? After all, love does conquer all.*

Just then, his phone buzzed. She texted.

Running late

Crap, he thought, *no sorry? No see you later? No have a good day? Only two words—running late. Where is she? Still mad? So much for a relationship.*

She walked in at 10:00 and hopped on the barstool next to him without mentioning sitting in their booth. He noticed but didn't push it. She was dressed all in black, like what you'd wear under the beauty store smocks. *An act*, he thought, *out since April.*

He turned to her; knee extended. "You hungry?"

She turned only slightly. "No, I ate with my cousin." She stared at his hand, trying to discern a tan line on his ring finger. "You hungry? I can have Uncle make for you."

He licked his lips. "Sure. That beef cube thing?" *Ate with her cousin, huh? I guess she forgot the fried pork ribs again. I don't blame her. Lots has happened since that promise.*

She went to order, taking her phone with her, and took a while to get back. As soon as she sat down, he spoke. "About last week, Maya." He wanted to know. *Why the mood swing? Was there a relationship?*

She crossed her arms. There was still an edge to her voice. "No last week, Glenn. I don't want to talk. Let's move on. Okay?"

The room was colder than a supermarket freezer.

Jimmy came over. "Karaoke broken. Sorry." The rest of the night was filled with shots and watching the Miss Vietnam rebroadcast. *How the hell does Jimmy rate a connection to Viet TV?* Most of the talk was between Jimmy, Tia and Maya. Occasionally, she turned and poured his beer for him. She only wanted to get through the night. So did he.

She softened a little towards the end of the night. Sometime after the ten Miss Vietnam finalists were announced, she spoke to him. "You come my party Friday?"

He wanted to tell her he was coming. But no, his obligations came first. "No, Maya. You know I told you already . . ."

"I know. Family." She played with her earring, wondering if she should ask the question that had been on her mind. "Tell me about family, Glenn," she said, but thinking, *Are you married, Glenn? Is Mama Lynh right?*

He rolled his shoulders and shrugged. "Maybe next time, Maya."

"Okay." She suppressed her frown. *Must be married. I'm so done here.*

There was an ache in his throat. *I don't want to hurt her like this. How would she understand? I barely understand. I gotta make it up to her.*

He sipped his beer. "How you doing with the party?"

She brought out a napkin with scribbles. "I think small party, Glenn. Mommy call this week. Need more money for medicine. I send this morning. Not much left for party. Cancel DJ too."

His mouth slightly open, he reached out and touched her forearm, lightly. "So how much are you short?"

She looked at her napkin, her original party plan. "For everything? Seven hundred dollars."

Without asking, he slid off his seat and went to the ATM, the first time he ever used the ATM in Lynh's bar.

She tried to stop him. "Wait, Glenn, what you doing?"

He was back already, placing thirty-five Jacksons in front of her. "Early birthday present."

She gasped. "No Glenn, I cannot –"

He put his finger to her lips. "No, no arguing. Just take it. It's okay. Have a great time. I'll go cheap on you next week, okay?"

She put the wad in her purse before anyone else saw what happened. "Thank you, Glenn," she said softly. She leaned over and gently kissed him.

She stared at the counter.

Glenn noticed the quiet. "What's on your mind?"

She turned to him. "Nothing, don't worry." *He still care for me. More than he give Julie last week. No need but he did. But same as Darren. Plenty from wallet. I appreciate but what about heart?*

He rubbed her shoulder. He saved a surprise for last. "One more thing, Maya. How about I come to help you set up?"

Her eyes lit up. "Really?"

He nodded.

Warmth flushed her cheeks. "Oh thank you, Glenn! No need. I know you work afternoon."

He winked at her. "No worries. I'll be here. Four o'clock okay?"

"Yass!" She perked up. She turned slightly; her knee pressed to his. *Oh, he care. Still wish he come party but he care.*

He wanted an excuse to bring her present anyway, and the Dom she wanted. It was going to be like a root canal asking Joyce for the time off, but it was worth it. "By the way, nice bag. Early present?"

She hugged it like it was a puppy. "Yass. From me to me!"

He eyed the bag, conjuring a million scenarios on how she got it. *Bullshit. One thing for sure, she didn't buy it with her own money.*

She cast a glance sideways. "Glenn, I have to get up early tomorrow. Dentist appointment."

One eyebrow arched. *What dentist takes appointments at 7:00 a.m.?* Hiding a sigh, he spoke. "Okay. Let's call it a night."

She smiled apologetically, her face a combination of regret and relief. "Okay. Walk me my car?"

She got in, and he leaned in, perhaps too quickly. All he got was her cheek to his lips. *I guess I'm in the doghouse.* She saw his look and blocked it out. Eddie was waiting.

She waved. "Text me, okay?" He watched her Audi speed off around the corner. He started texting as soon as she was out of sight.

Minutes later and across town, she breathed in deeply as she parked next to the green Beemer. The smell of the bag was thick in her Audi, almost hypnotizing. *I'm so lucky. He went out and bought it for me. And so expensive!*

She'd taken a picture earlier and posted it to Instagram.

She saw Glenn's text, quickly pounded out "Good night," then ran into the restaurant. Eddie came over. Same as last time. Lots of action at the baccarat table. "Here's five hundred dollars. Go have fun but be entertaining too, okay?" He played it cool.

Eddie came back two hours later. "Hungry?"

They went to the same eatery afterward. The waitress started calling them Mr. and Mrs. Pancakes. The normal conversation had her complaining about Glenn, and him jawing on about green card wife. But this night, they sat giggling, recounting the hilarity of two older gentlemen with very young girlfriends at the baccarat table. It wasn't that great a night, but alcohol, a full stomach, fatigue, and lots of jokes about Viagra caused non-stop giggling at the end, and that's what she remembered.

For the first time in a long time, she thought of someone other than Glenn before falling asleep. She fell asleep hugging the bag. *Eddie must really like me.*

61

AUGUST BIRTHDAY

Maya wasn't the only person Louis Vuitton impressed that day. The image of her hugging the bag stayed with Glenn all week. Friday afternoon found him on his laptop, searching the internet. *Twenty-two hundred dollars! Who the fuck has that much money to buy her a twenty-two hundred dollar bag? A gift to herself? No way. She barely spends any money on herself to eat.*

He scratched that itchy part of his scalp right above his left ear. *I'm starting to feel a little second string here. No wonder she's off and running every Tuesday night.*

He did some mental calculations. *Nope. At about $300 a week, she'd have to sit with me seven times to get that bag. And somebody just bought it for her? So much for the $400 Gucci gift card I got her for her birthday.*

He drummed his fingers on his laptop. *Second string. At least I'm still on the team. Maybe I'll make the starting team one day.*

———————

Two hours later, he walked into the bar with a bottle of Dom and her birthday card stuffed with a Gucci gift card. Not a twenty-two-hundred-dollar Louis Vuitton bag, but it would have to do. He promised he'd help her set up.

She spotted him as he peered into the booth room. "Glennnn!" She came running down the aisle and jumped him. He slammed back into the wall, and she bounced off, laughing. "You came! I didn't think you come." There were black and gold balloons, and same colored streamers hanging in weird fashion all over the booth room. There was a guy in the corner blowing up balloons. *Is he the major league player?*

He kissed her cheek. It was an odd feeling to see her during daylight.

"Where's the rest of your customers? I thought you were going to have a bunch of help?"

She kept blowing up balloons. "I know. I dunno. But Vic here. You here. You remember Vic?"

Oh yeah. The fisherman. One Saturday I came here to surprise her. He had brought Jimmy ten pounds of tuna ahi and Jimmy made some Hawaiian-style poke, sashimi on the side, and grilled the bones and belly. The guy was nice enough to offer me some.

I didn't know he was a customer waiting for Maya till Allie told me. I followed the bro code—didn't infringe on another customer's time with the girl—and cleared out. Didn't want to be a bother. Found out later, Wednesdays were for him. According to Allie, this guy was Maya's first customer. Over three years running—every Wednesday. Gotta give props.

"Hey Vic."

"Hey Glenn."

They shook hands. *Funny. This was not the guy that was here the night I came and she gave me the double thumbs down. That was a Wednesday. Does she double up on him too?*

It was an unusual sight for the bar at 4:00 in the afternoon—two guys blowing up balloons for a bargirl. She handed Vic stuff to do like he was the boyfriend. *Funny,* Glenn observed, *they seem cute together. Now that's the kind of guy she should settle down with, or me.*

After an hour, the place looked better. Cheeks ready to bust, Glenn called out to Maya, "I gotta go."

She didn't ask if he was coming back. She knew better. "Thank you, Glenn. It mean a lot you come." She walked him out. No kiss. It was broad daylight and some of the barflies were filing in. She gave him a hug.

He patted her head. "Have a good time tonight, Maya."

She almost curtsied. "Okay. Not same without you."

Half sweet talk, half genuine? She ran off waving as the mother-and-daughter DJ team pulled up.

Glenn watched her run back in. *Maybe I shoulda told her I fixed things so I could stop by tonight. Hope she likes that part of her present.*

Five hours after he left her at the bar, Glenn was ready to go back.

He waved at the hospital staff. They noticed he was leaving earlier than usual. "Good night, sir. Same time, same place tomorrow?"

He smiled. "Of course!"

He pulled up. The parking lot was full. He had to park on the street. It was the first Friday night of August, and a bargirl's birthday was a major event that added to the usual weekend crowd.

The bar clock showed 12:14, real-world time was 11:59. He wondered how she was doing. At last year's party, patrons had her drink eighty-one shots, and she'd taken home over ten grand. *Was she lit up like the other Friday night I came?*

He winced. His stomach turned. *I really don't want to see her like that again. Oh well. I've been looking forward to this surprise. Maybe this is a bad idea. How bad can it be? I saw her at her worst that night, pandering to all those guys. Part of the business. I can buy that now.*

He walked into the booth room. The crowded room smelled like stale cigarettes and tequila or whatever was spilled into the rug in various places. Empty shot glasses were everywhere. Verna and Allie were like roadrunners shuttling drinks in and empty glasses out as quick as they could. A heavy ghetto beat was pulsating from the DJ's special speakers. Through the crowd, he spied her. She was shaking a bottle and letting loose on those nearest her. People were drenched, and so was she. It resembled a wet t-shirt contest. She was in another world.

He decided to hang back in the rear and watch. *She's having fun. I'll make my way to her soon. She does have a lot of young guys around her. They look like jackals sizing up their next meal.*

She started dancing with several guys at once. *Tame*, he thought, *no touching. But what's this?* She backed into one young guy and pinned him against a wall with her ass. The guy put his hands on her waist, and the other guys started yelling, "Go Eddie, Go Eddie!" There were some "Yeah, Mayas" mixed into the cheering. *So this is Eddie. This is the young guy she was in Vegas with?*

She ground him into the next song, reaching upward behind her, and bringing his face to hers. He leaned in for a kiss right before she pulled away. His lips landed on her neck, and she arched her back. She spun around and was right back at it. Someone yelled, "*Tease!* Give it up already!" The crowd threw Jacksons at the couple as if they were at some primitive marriage ritual.

Glenn was getting aroused and pissed at the same time. He saw Eddie whisper something in her ear. She turned around, cupped his chin, and pushed lightly. It looked like a rebuff. Glenn felt relief. Then the iceberg hit. With both hands, she pushed him into the private room and followed. The door slammed shut, and the crowd went nuts. It was like the Patriots had scored a come-from-behind touchdown in the Super Bowl. The DJ turned the music louder.

He stood there, transfixed. He clocked the time. It was ten minutes before she came out, hands raised, walking and gyrating to the beat, like a ring girl holding up a card. The crowd cheered as he walked out. She turned and hugged him. He leaned down to kiss her and she stopped him with her finger on his lips and wiped sideways snapping his head to the side. He slapped her ass, and she moved off through the crowd. The guys surrounded him like he scored a touchdown. She wanted to get another bottle from the bar.

The crowd parted to let her through, and then she saw Glenn standing at the edge of the group. Startled, she yelled, "Glennnn!" and ran over to him. With stiletto heels adding seven inches to her height, she had to lean over to hug him. Heavy with the smell of Crown and tequila, she was breathing huskily. "What time you get here?" In the foggy dark matrix that was her mind at the moment, a little girl jumped up and down, clapping her hands, happy that he came.

He lied. "Just got here." He managed a smile. "Just wanted to say Happy Birthday."

"Thank you, Glenn." She was nearly out of it. Swooning. Breathing heavy. You could have lit up what she exhaled. "Buy me lucky shot?" Glenn pulled out a Benjamin while he took a good look at her, particularly her eyes. *Something not right here. She looks like she's out of it. Her pupils really dilated and uneven.* "Maya, are you all ri . . ."

"Thank you, Glenn!" She snatched the Benjamin from his hand, and with a smile, stuck it in her bra and went out to the bar.

He sat in the nearest booth. *I'll check her out when she gets back.*

Eddie spied them over the crowd across the floor and flung his shot glass at the opposite wall. *The old guy! Bastard, she's mine! Play it cool*, he heard his boss say. *Yeah, play it cool.* "She'll be mine soon," he muttered, shoving his hand in his pocket and fingering the pills he brought. He'd started with five. Only two were left.

The crowd started chanting, "Maya, Maya, Maya!" and one of the girls ran off to the bar to get her. They both came running back to even louder chanting. Carrying the bottle of Dom and a shot glass with whiskey, she jogged past his booth. Glenn knew the way it worked was someone buys you a shot, you at least come back to toast. He justified it internally, thinking she needed to drop the bottle off with the crowd.

She downed the shot, then ran to Eddie, climbed the table next to him, grabbed his hair, and tilted his head back. She took the bottle and poured it down his throat till he erupted, and the bottle contents spilled over. The crowd roared and laughed. Glenn wasn't laughing. *That was my $400 special edition Dom she just spilt all over the guy she said was crap. That was my Benjamin she took and never came back. This is worse than the last Friday I came.*

He clenched and unclenched his fists and cricked his neck. Anybody watching him would think this guy was about to blow. *She's a completely different person. Maybe this is the real her. Maybe Lynh was right. Tuesdays were a complete act. Fantasy. For my money only.*

He got up and left.

She took a belt of Dom straight from the bottle and smacked her lips. Only then she remembered who gave it to her. Something was foggy. She touched her bra. The Benjamin he gave her was still there. Eddie climbed up on the table and was holding on to her around the waist. She pried his fingers off and jumped off, then stumbled through the crowd and to the booth where she left him. Empty. She went out to the bar. Empty. To the darts room. Empty. Chloe was there with a customer. Glenn was gone.

62

DEVASTATION'S EDGE

Chloe looked up. She'd seen that look on Maya before. They started up in a high-pitched Thai staccato. The smiles on their faces and their pleasant happy tones were for customer appeasement only. The words were serious.

Maya's stomach started to churn. "Where is he?"

Chloe feigned ignorance. "Who?"

Maya read disgust in Chloe's eyes. "Shut up. You know. Glenn."

Chloe kept her emotional distance. "He not here?"

Inside, Maya started crumbling. Her reality was falling apart. "No, Chloe. He buy me shot and left. Not wait."

Chloe gritted her teeth, did her best to smile and whispered to her customer, kissing him goodnight. She took Maya by the elbow and moved to the booth farthest back in the darts room. She pushed Maya into one side of the booth and sat down across from her. Maya opened her mouth. Chloe cut her off. The Thai staccato octaved higher. "Shut up, Maya. You bullshit. I saw. You came to bar counter twenty minutes ago to get shot and bottle. He left five minutes ago. He waited fifteen minutes? What you do?"

Panic breaking out on her face, Maya fessed up. "I was excited. The crowd chanting. Got me excited. Vey came and got me. She said Eddie waiting. Didn't want to keep Eddie waiting." She was looking around, hoping by some miracle Glenn was casually sitting at one of the other booths, waiting for her.

Chloe waved her hand in front of Maya's face. "Focus, girl." She saw the Benjamin sticking out of Maya's bra. "So you went to Eddie with Glenn's hundred-dollar shot? You musta walked right by Glenn. You know he musta been watching! Oh Maya. What you doing?"

For Maya, the room started spinning. Maya had a look that said I don't want to hear this. "Fuck you, Chloe. You not my mother. You not even my real sister."

Chloe knew enough that this was Maya on defense. "Fuck you too, Maya. Not mean you not stupid tonight."

Maya tried to stand but couldn't. Her legs were numb. She rubbed her shoulders. The room got very cold suddenly. "What you mean stupid?"

Chloe's entire body language was screaming frustration, asking Maya where her common sense was. "Maya, the private room?"

Maya waved it off. "Don't worry he didn't see. He come right after. Good thing." She breathed easier. At least that wasn't a disaster. That's what she thought. The look on Chloe's face sent electric chills down Maya's spine. She brought her hand to her mouth and screamed, *"No! Noooo! Nooooooo!"*

Chloe crossed her arms. Her voice was matter of fact, low, tinged with anger. "No, Maya. He was here. I saw. He was in the back. He came right when you started dancing up against Eddie. I know. I was right behind him watching you dance."

Being drunk didn't prevent the sheer feeling of panic hitting Maya's gut. She started trembling uncontrollably. Chloe grabbed a small bucket next to a mop and jumped at her sister. Allie peeked in. Chloe smiled at Allie. "Sick. Be okay soon."

Allie ran back to Eddie, who was yelling for Maya. "Get that fucking bitch back here. I'm the king, and I earned this!" He was throwing money all over the place to the delight of all the girls. In his mind, he knew the pills would have taken effect by now.

Verna entered the darts room with a washrag and wiped Maya's face and neck while Chloe held her hair. Verna went to get a fresh wash towel from the kitchen. Tia called a cab.

Between heaving up tequila, Crown and champagne, she blurted out her confession. "I don't do anything, Chloe. I kiss him. Cuddle. That's all. Not even tongue. You know my story. I have pride. Still married."

Chloe was behind the birthday girl, holding her hair, talking in soothing tones. "I know, Sis. I got you." *So many times she do this for me too.*

In her messed-up state, Maya still had the strength to ball up her fist and pound the floor next to the bucket. "I miss Glenn, Chloe. Why he married? Why he cannot be Eddie?"

She heaved, and with bile running down her chin, she tried to look at Chloe. "I want to feel for Glenn. I want to want him, you know? I want to grind him like I did Eddie."

She continued pounding the floor. "But he married. I know he married! Like Darren. I don't want to get hurt again. I miss Glenn so much. Eddie just a toy."

Chloe wanted to tell Maya that Eddie was married too. The lecture could wait. Jimmy came and picked Maya up and carried her to a waiting cab. Maya reached out to the booth room. "I have to say goodbye."

Jimmy pretended not to hear. "Last call, Maya. Everyone going home." Chloe jumped in the cab with Maya.

The crowd had dwindled to the diehards of the Thai Garden casino crew. They brought their own booze, and Jimmy was a little pissed. He was going to enjoy what came next.

Jimmy had the DJ cut the music and turned on the lights. He stood in front of the booing crowd, hands on his hips. "I have announcement. Maya go home. Had good time. Last call is over. Bar closed. Thank you for coming. Please get the fuck out of my bar." He turned and started back to the bar.

Eddie yelled out. "Motherfucker! What?" He started towards Jimmy.

Jimmy turned around. "You like I call cops?" Two off-duties were already casually nursing beers at the bar—friends of Tia's.

Eddie had an arrest record and didn't want any more trouble. "No. Fuck you! I'm outta here." Picturing Glenn in his mind, he thought, *Fucking old man had something to do with this. I know.*

Eddie was beyond any advice from his boss, as he dialed Maya. He got her voicemail and started yelling, "Answer, bitch! Are you with him? Are you fucking him? About time you give me my fair share. And know this—I'm going home with three of your bar bitch hostess friends." Any recollection of his boss telling him to play it cool was gone. To make matters worse, the three girls he lined up had already slipped out the back, each pocketing $500 of Eddie's money.

———

In the cab, Chloe stared out the window with Maya's head on her lap. *This weird. I seen her handle lot more. And the private room. No way. Something wrong.*

Maya was murmuring and struggling with something.

Chloe looked down, wiping the sweat on her brow. *She not look drunk. She look—drugged. Someone drugged her. Ecstasy? Not sure. She might not remember tomorrow.*

Maya's demons came to visit. The dream was real to her. Eddie pinned her up against the wall. He looked so much like her first man. A Thai man. Everyone said she was too ugly to get a Thai man, especially one from Bangkok. She was too short, too brown. Her nose was too flat. She didn't know how to act like a woman. But he pinned her against the wall. "But you can fuck, huh? That you can do."

He pushed her down to his waist and forced him on her. She gagged. Then he pulled her back up and turned her around and pinned her to the wall again. Her face pressed against the wall, she could barely breathe. She heard him spit, and then he took her anally with one thrust. She screamed. It hurt. She was only seventeen. Pure. She cried out. Back then, it was for Daddy. This time she cried out, "Glenn!" He was standing there in the corner. Watching. "Why don't you do anything? Glenn!"

Chloe was watching. Tears were streaming down Maya's cheek while she thrashed to and fro. *What is she dreaming about?*

It was more nightmare than dream. The Thai man pushed her away. "Now you woman. But not good enough for me. You used. Take your shit and get out." She jumped at him, crying. She grabbed him around the leg. "No! I will be good to you. I will be good to you!" She clawed at his belt, fumbling with his zipper. This was man's clothes. She didn't know how to work it. Tried to suck his dick through his jeans. He slapped her. She wouldn't let go. Crying. "Let me stay! I don't have anyone! I don't have place to sleep. I only have you."

He slapped her again. And with the other hand, pushed against her face till her neck cricked. She let go for a split second, and he pushed her out the door into the hallway of the dingy apartment building. She gathered her clothes and was crawling away when she heard the door open. Hope came to her. *Maybe?* Short-lived.

He gave a swift kick rugby-style. She flew five feet forward. "Still here?! Get the fuck out of here before the neighbors see! No girl from Isaan for me! Why you even think that? I told everyone you my maid whore, not my girlfriend!" He made ready to kick again, and she yelped like a dog, taking off half-naked down the hall.

On the street, the shops were closed, at least to this half-naked waif. She passed an optical shop. The lights were out, the door locked. Then the lights came on. The door creaked open. Two girls barely older than she came out. "Stop, sister. Come here. It's cold." The taller one put a jacket around her. They both hugged her to get her warm and walked her into the store. No explanations spoken. A stray off the street needed caring for.

Chloe wiped her forehead. Stirring from her dream, Maya opened her eyes. "Glenn?"

Chloe covered Maya's eyes with her hand. "Go to sleep, Maya. Everything okay." She tapped the driver's headrest. "Driver, take us to hospital." *Better go pump stomach.*

———————

Back home, Glenn downed a pint of Johnny Walker Blue he'd been saving for a special occasion. *Well, this is a pretty freaking fuckin' fucked up special occasion isn't it? How could I have been so stupid? To think she was some kind of innocent girl working hard in a bar, the right way, to send money home to her family.*

The room started to spin. *I'm in love with someone, something, that doesn't exist! She's a wild caged animal. And I'm just feed.*

He was holding a picture of Katie. He instinctively took out his phone then remembered, phone calls were useless. *How could I think anyone could replace Katie? Fucking Academy Award-winning act.*

He fumbled with YouTube. *Where was that song she kept singing the first time?*

The song was "Take a Bow" by Rihanna. She sang the song a few times early on, an ode to cheaters and wannabes who are embarrassingly exposed as clowns and nothing more, then shown the side exit and kicked to the curb.

"Auuuuuuuwwwwffffffuck!" He muffled it with a pillow. The room was spinning. One just does not guzzle a pint of scotch. *Need to barf it out.*

He got up and fell over the coffee table, shattering the glass. *Dammit!*

The blood spurted a foot in the air before he covered it with his hand. According to the medical training he'd had in the military, he'd nicked an artery and would be dead in twenty minutes. *You're kidding?* For a split second he thought of lying there and dying. *That'll show her.*

He saw Katie's picture where it fell. *What the hell? No way I'm dying on you.* He flipped open his phone. Punched 911. "Uh yeah, I nicked my artery, and I'm bleeding out."

The operator saw the address. Former city director. Priority call. "We see you sir. We'll have someone there. Can you make it downstairs? Hello, sir?"

He leaned on the kitchen counter. "Yeah, I'm pretty lightheaded. Got a tourniquet on."

Emergency Medical Services found him in the hallway and rushed him to emergency.

They wheeled him in past the waiting room. Chloe looked up from the forms she was filling out and stared. *What the shit? If the stars weren't telling these two something then . . . then I don't know what. Meant to be together.*

She sneaked around the corner and saw that they were in adjoining units! Only the curtain separated them. *This like some Thai love comedy drama. Nothing funny here, but.* She walked into Maya's unit. "You okay?" Maya's eyes were open, ears listening.

A familiar voice next door. "I'm okay, doc. Just stitch me up."

An older voice. "Sir, how much did you have to drink? We're waiting on a psych eval."

There was thrashing about, like someone trying to get out of bed. "Are you kidding? You think I tried to kill myself? I fell. My coffee table. Arrest my coffee table for attempted assault. There's no crime story here."

Maya smiled. *Sounds like . . .* then she remembered the night, how she acted, how he left. She threw up. A dry heave and some spittle. Chloe wiped it up and said, "Wait, okay?"

Chloe peeked next door. Nobody from the hospital there. He was sitting on the gurney, waiting to go home. Looking like some game show model, Chloe grabbed the curtains separating the units and pulled them back with exaggerated, dramatic flair.

63

STAR CROSSED

He was more than a little startled. His eyes were open, but his brain wasn't registering. *Damn nurse looks like Chloe.* He squinted and opened his eyes wide, several times. *Chloe? Sister? I must be passed out. Realest dream I ever had. Drugged again maybe. Maybe I'm dead. Chloe an angel? No. Am I in hell?*

Chloe saw the look on his face, then looked the other way. He followed her gaze to the person in the other bed, covered by a bedsheet from neck down. *Who is that?*

She was facing him with tubes up her nose, makeup smeared, hair matted and tangled. She opened her eyes briefly before closing them again.

He caught his breath. *I'd recognize those eyes anywhere. The way they sparkled, twinkled.*

She opened her eyes again. *Another dream. Thank you, Buddha, or as Glenn would say, Jesus—same thing, right? My dream come true. He's here.* She smiled. She reached out to him, still thinking she was dreaming.

He jumped off the bed.

She saw the blood on his shirt and his arm. *Not dream.* "What going on? Where . . ."

Chloe stepped forward. "Maya, you in hospital. You drugged. That's why you stupid tonight." The explanation was more for Glenn than Maya. "Stomach pump. You rest. Doctor said go home tomorrow."

Chloe turned to Glenn. "What you doing here? Lose Maya. Kill self already? You give up too quick. Heehee." She tried some humor.

He rubbed his head, his voice sheepish. "No, got drunk. Fell. Broke my coffee table. It tried to kill me. I think I won."

Chloe tried to picture it and couldn't. "I bet on coffee table anytime."

Maya struggled to get up. She wanted to go to him. Chloe pushed her back down.

Suddenly, Glenn started swooning back and forth, and Chloe helped him to his bed.

Chloe glanced back and forth at the two. *Oh crap, tired already. I gotta take care two of them?*

A nurse came by. "What is going on here?" She closed the curtains. The last thing Glenn and Maya saw was each other's eyes.

The nurse motioned to Chloe. "Miss, you'll have to leave too if you're not family."

Chloe leaned back on the railings of Maya's bed. "She my sister. I stay or you arrest me." The nurse glared at her. She wondered about these foreigners, having had her share that night with first a Vietnamese family and then a group of Micronesians. It was her break time. She let it go. Chloe stayed.

Chloe tapped Maya on her shoulder. "I'm here, okay? Not leave you."

Unsure of what she saw, Maya looked up. "That Glenn?"

Chloe glanced over her shoulder. "Yeah, weird, huh? I think karma saying something."

Maya slumped back down. "Yeah, we both stupid, almost die."

Chloe nodded. "Yeah something like that. I agree. You both stupid."

Even weak, Maya had a look of concern. "Chloe, you check on him come back tell me?"

Chloe squeezed her hand. "Okay. Stay here."

Maya managed a weak smile. "Really? Maybe I run away now."

Chloe kissed her forehead. "Shut up, sister. Go sleep."

Chloe pushed aside Glenn's curtain. "How you doing, brudder?"

He was sitting up, looking like he was ready to keel over. Hangover plus blood loss was not a pleasant feeling. "I'm okay. What the hell, Chloe?"

Hands on her hips, she scolded him like some schoolmarm. "You answer me first, then I answer you. What the hell to you too, brudder?"

He touched his stitches. "I went home. Downed some scotch. You know the real stuff. I tripped. My coffee table. Glass top."

She winced. "Lucky you don't cut your face. Oh, maybe should. You get plastic surgery. Look twenty years younger. Look fifty again—"

"Ha ha, Chloe." He pointed over Chloe's shoulder. "So what's the deal there?"

Chloe gave him the whole story. "Only kisses and cuddles, Glenn. She not like that. Drugged. Go crazy. Not even go private room otherwise. You know her, Glenn. She not do that ever. She not good in the head tonight. She feel bad. You like her, huh? Why you tell her you don't see? I tell her. After that she got sick. Almost overdose I think." She exaggerated. "She forget your shot too, huh? She forget Glenn. Drug make her do that."

Maya was listening, thankful for Chloe. *Oh Buddha, you help me with this I will go temple make merit next week.*

Chloe observed his face and could tell emotions were at war within him—confusion, anger, sadness. If she could read his mind, she would have known it was one hundred percent fear.

He spoke with some hesitancy. "So Eddie—boyfriend?"

She leaned back on his bed, next to him, arms crossed. "You have to ask her, Glenn. You know her story. Not ready for anybody. You her boyfriend? You ready to say you her boyfriend? What stopping *you*?" *She don't ask. I ask.* "Glenn, you married?"

Maya was listening. *My business, Chloe. I get it. I won't ask either.* It took all her strength, but Maya called out to Chloe. "Enough already, let him rest."

He heard. *She's awake!* He jumped off. He opened her curtain, stepped in, and shut the curtain behind him in case the nurse came back.

He was by her side. He picked up her chart and nodded as he read. She half-rolled over to him. "You doctor, Glenn? I thought lawyer?"

Without looking up, he reached for her hand. "Not doctor, Maya, but I can read these charts."

Shift change. A different nurse walked in. "I'm sorry, sir, you'll have to leave." He turned to the voice. She recognized him immediately. "Oh, Glenn, what are you doing here?"

He tried to smile. "Visiting a friend, Marta. What are you doing here? I thought you were sixth floor?"

Perplexed, the nurse responded as if all was normal. "Just covering a shift." Then she saw the blood on his shirt and his patient's wrist bracelet. "Glenn, you really . . ."

"Marta, can I have a few minutes? My bed is right across the way. I know the doc's not around anymore. Just a few minutes." His face pleaded.

Marta looked at him, then at Maya. Saw how they were holding hands. She stepped out with a quick "Okay, Glenn."

Maya was drifting in and out but didn't let go of his hand, being more concerned for him than her. "You okay?" she asked.

This time he looked down at her, caught her look of concern, bordering on fear. "I'm okay, Maya. Takes more than blood loss to kill me."

She shook her head weakly. "No, you okay tonight? I'm sorry, Glenn. I promise I will not do that no more but I did. You can go away you want. I understand."

He was silent.

She brought his hand to her face. "No, I change my mind. Don't go, Glenn. Stay with me."

He scoured her face, trying to get a bead on what was in her head, with so many thoughts in his own head. *I got so many questions about Eddie. I'll let it go for now. Dr. Tom once said that the way of Thai man was sabai. If it doesn't kill you, let it go. Peace was the main objective for Buddhists. Or something like that.*

He closed his eyes and tried to recount scripture. *Jesus said forgive and love the unlovable. If it's okay with Buddha and Jesus, it's gotta be okay. Besides this is not the place. No matter, love conquers all. I gotta believe we love each other but just can't say it. That's that.*

He lifted her hand to his heart. She could feel it beating fast. "Go to sleep, Maya. I'm not going away. Tuesdays forever, right? I'll see you next Tuesday if you're up to it. Like that?" She nodded. He bent down and kissed her forehead.

She squeezed his hand. "Text me?" Then she relaxed. She was out. He laid her hand on her chest. She was breathing heavy. A deep sleep. A faint smile on her lips. That's what he thought anyway.

Marta came back. "Glenn, you'll have to leave now. Docs are making their morning rounds." It was 7:00 a.m. Chloe reached in and grabbed his arm. "C'mon, brudder. You get back to your own side. Mama Chloe here to watch both of you." She yawned.

He pivoted toward the nurse. "Marta, tell the doctor I feel fine. They know where to find me if they want to. Under law I'm under no obligation to stay unless someone wants me committed. I'll sign whatever."

The nurse produced a clipboard. "Okay, Glenn, you know the drill. I have the forms here. I knew you'd be anxious to leave."

While signing, he whispered, "Marta, can you make sure she's okay?" He nodded toward Maya's bed. Marta was a little confused, wondering who Maya was or what Maya was to Glenn. She'd never seen Maya before and took a shot. "Didn't know you had a daughter, Glenn."

Glenn thought, *Good try.* "I don't, Marta. Again, take care of her for me?"

Marta took the hint. "Sure, Glenn. Probably a day of observation then release this afternoon." Marta slid out through the curtain.

He turned his attention to Chloe. "Sis, you want me to stay?"

Chloe yawned and stretched her arms. "No, Glenn. Go home. You okay?"

He rubbed his face. "Yeah, called Uber already."

Chloe's face scrunched, deep in thought, just for a second. "Glenn?"

He turned to her. "Yes?"

She put one hand on his shoulder. "She confused. Give her time. All good men give their women time."

He yawned, covering his mouth with one hand, taking Chloe's hand with the other. "Okay, sis. I'll try." It sounded like Confucius to him. Or something that Oprah would say. He was tired. *No more wisdom from the universe, please.*

He cricked his neck. *Lots to sort out as soon as she's healthy.*

64

EBBING MARRIAGE

Caleb got the call at 7:00 a.m. It was Saturday morning. He usually slept in. "Sir, this is Blue Mountain Hospital. We have your wife here in ICU. You're listed as the emergency contact." He ran upstairs to her room. Not there.

He rubbed his eyes. "What happened?"

"We can explain more when you get here."

Then Chloe got on the call. "Hello, it's Chloe. Can you come? They not release her unless you here. I don't count—this not military hospital. Why take her to base hospital? This was closest one. Just come, okay? They need you to come."

He hung up the phone. *That's sweet. I'm still her emergency contact.* He got dressed.

Maya sat up. "What you mean they called him? I cannot go on my own?"

Chloe shrugged. "No, they call him. Want to talk to him."

Marta opened the curtain. "Ma'am, your husband is here." Marta was more confused, but she'd seen many things in this hospital and didn't think it was her business. She'd known Glenn for the last several years and thought he was a nice guy. She figured there must be trouble between the girl and the husband. She didn't sense the usual concern a husband would have when called to a hospital for his wife. And then she thought, *What about Katie?*

Soon Caleb strode in—all swag, self-centered, unconcerned. "Well bless your hearts, ladies, what trouble have you stirred up now?"

Maya's eyes shot daggers. "Bless your heart too, Caleb. Just sign the papers so I can go."

They both knew in Caleb's native Georgia, "bless your heart" meant *screw you very much* wrapped in a pleasant Southern drawl.

"Hey Maya, you're still my wife. And I still have some position in this place. So don't mind me if I'm a little concerned they might have to call the cops because you ingested some kind of drug."

Maya's whole body went rigid. "That what they find?"

Caleb snorted. "No, you must have puked up a whole lot. Barely found any traces. They might have to send to the FBI to analyze."

Maya looked at Chloe, who excused herself, poking at her phone as she left. One of their cop friends should be able to help.

Caleb looked at Maya. The last time he was in a hospital with her, she'd been dehydrated. That was only a few years ago. They were still in love and held hands. He regretted hitting her. "Hey Maya, not a great time but maybe there's still a chance for us? I can change."

She was exhausted. "You right."

He perked up. "Seriously?"

Rubbing the back of her neck, she replied, "You right, Caleb, this not a great time. Just get me out of here."

His face flushed with disappointment. "Um, okay, I'll swing the car around."

Maya shook her head. "No, just sign the papers. Chloe take me home. I Uber last night. Remember, my birthday?"

He signed the release and tossed it on the bed. "Yeah, I know." She had asked that he not do anything, so he just sent flowers to the house. She'd put them in a vase on the kitchen table—their neutral territory.

Back home, she rested all weekend. Caleb got into his computers—playing music, Xbox. Rusty was by her side constantly. Once in a while, he went to check on Daddy. His doggy parents had no reason to make him feel pulled apart, although Rusty seemed to know there weren't that many family outings anymore. Outside activities these days were Daddy-only or Mommy-only.

The vet told them that pets could sense things, and that stress was contributing to Rusty's diabetes. The pair agreed on a monthly outing for Rusty's sake. They both agreed that they loved their dog. When they'd gotten him as a puppy, they were still very much in love. But that had changed, and Rusty sensed it. And now Daddy was gone for nine months of every year.

On Sunday morning, the one-time loving husband reminded Maya about their upcoming annual vacation week at a pet-friendly resort. "It'll do you good to get away from the bar," he said. He was hoping their flame might rekindle outside of that environment. Meanwhile, their families knew nothing about the changes in the relationship. Her mother still called

Caleb her "number one son from the West," and his parents still doted on Maya via social media.

The monthly outings were useful. She'd take some pictures of the three of them and post them to her Facebook page, and everyone would think that all was hunky-dory—everyone including ICEM, the agency charged with enforcing and sniffing out false marriages in the military.

She couldn't yet bear to tell her family of the failed marriage. They adored Caleb. His Southern charm was infectious, and his mother flying over to Thailand for the wedding had made a great impression. At first, things were wonderful. Wyoming was the best place ever for a young military couple—and their little four-legged "son."

Things got rocky when her family started asking for more money.

"Caleb, we can send more money back home? Sister going to college and need car. Mommy need new moped. And still looking for house for all of them. And doctor say Mommy need new medicine for brain disease."

"Geez Maya, when does all this end? What about that hundred thousand dollar sin sod I paid before we got married? That dowry was my whole life savings. It was supposed to take care of your family up front, including the house. We need to save for our own house too. Unless you want to move back to Georgia and live with my folks? We're not gonna have base allowance forever."

"I know, Caleb, sorry. I can help. I'll go work at the restaurant off base. I'll make up the money somehow."

"I love your family, Maya, but Mom wants grandkids too. When's that going to happen?"

She didn't answer that night. But she did comfort him in other ways.

He'd been okay, sort of, with her working overtime at a Thai restaurant in Wyoming. But being a bargirl recently was getting under his skin. In particular, he was starting to wonder about these trips she took with Chloe and Chloe's customers, "just to keep Chloe company." Hacking into her

Instagram once, he freaked at a video taken at dinner at the Venetian, with multiple male voices in the background.

She'd explained it away as "Chloe's customer's friends from the convention," but he didn't buy it. Before his next deployment, he'd arranged with a friend to watch the house while he was gone. If something was happening, he needed to know before their tenth anniversary—he wasn't about to give up half his pension, especially since they were clearly on the rocks.

Then there was the beating—the last straw. Just once, he'd lost his cool. They'd gotten into an argument, and she'd wised off at him, even slapping his face with the flowers he'd brought home for her. She'd meant to hit his shoulder but caught him flush on the side of his face, thorns and all. He responded impulsively. It wasn't even a beating, but she still held it over his head.

One backhand sent her flying through the glass door into the patio furniture, resulting in a concussion, a broken wrist, and cracked ribs. She assumed it was PTSD from his tour in Iraq, but base counseling disagreed—he'd been shipboard in the Gulf and hadn't seen action. Still she held it over his head, delaying promotion once. His colleagues were all a step ahead of him in rank because of that incident.

The agreement was they'd stay married till he made rank, then make the divorce final. She would get the pension, GI Bill for school, and continued housing and medical. In return, he asked that she honor the marriage for his career's sake—and also because he still hoped for a reconciliation.

He hoped this trip to the resort would bring back old times. It's where they'd gone on their honeymoon.

———————

She was lost in thought. He asked her again about the vacation.

She smiled meekly. "Caleb, can we do the resort the week after?" She desperately wanted to make the next Tuesday with Glenn, and still didn't know what to do with Eddie. There were already eight voice messages from Eddie, and twenty-three texts. Pretty much all alternated between *I love you and worry about you* and *Where are you, bitch?* He was clearly losing it and getting worse.

Caleb ignored her question. "Hey, Maya, we haven't had Sunday brunch together with Rusty in a long time. How about it?"

"I cannot, Caleb. Vey needs me at the restaurant. Need to prep for lunch, and today there is also a baby shower. Two hundred guests."

She wasn't lying. But Vey didn't need the help. She always hired out additional kitchen staff from the other Thai restaurants for big parties. Still, she didn't object when Maya texted earlier about helping. Maya was going to make her famous beef basil.

Maya needed to be there. After Eddie texted her for the eighteenth time, she simply replied she'd be at Thai Garden at noon. She wanted to head off anything heavy Eddie might be considering after the private room thing. She couldn't recall. She only knew what Chloe had told her about that night.

Caleb rolled his eyes, his expression bordering on disgust. "Suit yourself. I'm off to the docks to fish. Remember catching your first fish there?"

She did. The $300 rod and reel he bought had been gathering dust in the garage for the last two years.

He continued. "And no, a deal is a deal. We're headed off to the resort Monday. I already have my time off. And you know the following week, I'm prepping for deployment. I'm gone in two weeks, but I'll be watching you. Stick to our vows, wife."

Ugh. Vows. She hated that word. "Only on paper, Caleb. Only on paper."

He was sneering now, almost leering. "Not really, dear. Remember our deal? The pension, GI Bill, rent and medical, time with Rusty every month, sex once a month, and a week of R&R before every deployment. So I can remember my dearest wife while I'm gone."

Ugh, again. She didn't know how she was going to be able to stand his skin against hers, much less him inside her. Still, somehow, she got excited thinking about it. He was still the only man she'd had in seven years and not about to get anything else for a while. Marriage vows were important to her. Her pride was based on that. It was too bad he didn't share the same values as her. *I'm the warmup*, she thought, *then sucky fucky in every port and more on the boat.*

Her expression was equal parts disgust, wiseass, and "fuck you." "Okay, lover boy. Once a night for four days. You'd better perform, and enough with the hour-long foreplay okay? I can play with myself to get wet. Only fuck and run. Okay?"

He smirked, even licked his lips. "Sassy. You're still the sassy one."

She wasn't being sassy. She meant it this time.

———————

Eddie was already at the restaurant when she walked in. He was sitting at the bar talking with Vey. High noon, but nursing a beer. They were holding hands across the bar. "Thanks, Vey, I needed that."

"What that about?" Maya asked, a tinge jealous.

He swiveled his barstool toward her, snapping his hands out of Vey's. "Nothing babe, just complaining about the wife. She's consoling me." He didn't notice Vey staring at her empty hands.

Maya stood her ground, crossing her arms. "Hmph. I thought I'm the only one you open up to?"

He beckoned. "Yeah, fully. But Vey's okay in a pinch." Vey walked away, clearly hurt. *What about all that time he and I spent together in his driveway,* she was thinking, *when I drove him home after Maya's party?*

Eddie thought he played it right, with a little bit of fire in him now. "Hey, babe." He said it with swag and held out his arms. "Come here, sweets." Lately, he had a dozen nicknames for her. She went over and gave him a hug, palms against his chest. He leaned in and got her cheek. He frowned. "What's the matter?"

She laid her head on his chest, mostly so he wouldn't see her expression. "Still not feeling that good, Eddie." Her expression was worried, confused—very confused.

He patted her head with one hand, sucked on his beer with the other. "Right—everything check out okay? You had me worried." His tone was more horny than sincere.

She leaned back, pushing on his chest. "Eddie, we need to talk about Friday night."

His hands slid down to her waist. He wanted to spin her around, get to her backside again. "Ummm . . . I knew you'd come around."

Taking a step back, she pushed him an arm's length away. "Wait. I didn't know what I doing that night."

He felt her waist slip from his hands. Frustration started to creep in. "What?" Sounded like backpedaling to him. "I thought . . . "

"No Eddie, don't think right now. We good friends. You know. Good times. Maybe things go better in a year. When you divorce your wife final?"

"In a year maybe." His voice was uncertain.

Her voice was not. "You sure? Long time together already, huh? You sure you not messing me? You say you don't like her, but you sure she not like you for real?"

His tone progressed from pleading to arguing. "Yeah, really. I think she got someone in LA. We got separate rooms, Maya." He didn't tell her that his wife insisted on separate rooms because of his late hours and snoring, and she needed to wake early on days she doubled as a golf caddy. He also didn't tell her booty calls were a regular thing between the two, especially when he came home frustrated after a night with Maya.

Anger crept into his voice. "Yeah, the stupid DUI she got on her moped messed up the green card application. Honest, nothing between us. It's a business deal. You should come over those weeks she goes to LA." *What the hell happened to her? I almost had her. What the fuck? Did the old guy get to her?*

She was clear in her head for once. "No, marry is marry, Eddie. You fix then maybe we chance okay? Keep clean till then. For now, friends. Good friends." Maya didn't think twice about her own marriage. She needed something to keep Eddie at bay.

The other night, at the hospital, she felt so warm with Glenn. *But a woman knows. He has someone at home. Never lets me take him home. Always family this or family that on the other nights, or in and out quickly on nights not Tuesday. Like someone waiting. At least Eddie tell me about his marriage. Maybe he telling the truth. Available in one year. Done with Caleb in one year. Maybe. Oh, but Glenn . . .*

Her thoughts kept whiplashing between Eddie and Glenn.

Eddie felt ignored. It was like she was on the moon, like some of those times when she came in on Tuesdays after being with that guy. "Aw, fuck this, Maya." He was pouting now. "I treat you good. I bought you a bag. I took you to Vegas last year. All I want is some time with you outside of the bar and this place. Either take me home or come home with me."

She put her hand to his heart. To the onlooker, it looked like a romantic gesture. To her, it was a defensive tactic to keep him at bay. "Soon, Eddie. This not okay? Vegas wasn't okay? We not going Vegas again next Super Bowl? If not okay, then no need." She put on the game face that kept him on his toes, followed by silence, then staring—a blinking contest.

Bluff taken, he sputtered. "Okay, okay. I got it, babe. I understand. I'm patient. You're worth it, you know. Let's not fight. We're here to party and celebrate Nat's baby."

She smiled on cue and gave him a hug and a peck on the cheek. "You here to celebrate. I'm here to work." She went into the kitchen. Chattering in Thai. Aunty, the kitchen mama, saying, "We got it in here. No worries. Go outside with your man. Enjoy party."

Maya frowned. Chattering back in Thai, she explained, "Not my man. I want to help. Let me help. I make beef basil." She was already pulling packages of raw beef, basil, and spices from her $2,200 LV bag.

Eddie watched. Somehow the tone between the two ladies felt more like one telling the other to go away, and the other asking to stay. Vey came over and started giving him a shoulder rub. He gave in to it for a bit, then shrugged it off when he thought Maya was looking. "Let's go see Natalie, okay, Vey?" Maya did see. Under her breath, she mouthed, "Thank you, Vey."

Two hours later, he was standing by Natalie looking at the baby. Maya came up from behind and hugged him. "I gotta go, Eddie."

He turned. "Already?"

She gave him her best *please forgive me* face. "I work tonight. Cover shift for friend. Sunday. They close in two hours. Inventory after baby. New manager. Everything all screwed up this week. Orders come in but no one input."

Eddie was a laborer and gambler. Dumb on retail, but still a little perplexed. Glenn wasn't the only guy who thought the cosmetics store took a lot of inventory.

Maya caressed his forearm. "And baby, no Thai Garden for me this Tuesday. Doctor say no alcohol all week and rest. I help Vey today and help store tonight. Rest this week till Friday. I will be at bar if you want to come? Bring the boys?"

Out of the corner of his eye, he observed Vey bending over cleaning up a table. "Okay, Maya. Yeah, you rest."

65

FAMILY VACATION

Two days later, on Monday morning, husband and wife packed Rusty in the back seat of her Audi and drove down the coast to the resort. Caleb drove. Rusty hopped in circles all the way, barking. You could imagine he was exclaiming, Mommy and Daddy, Mommy and Daddy, Mommy and Daddy! Yay!

At least that's what Maya thought. Her Thai upbringing kicked in. *Make the best of it. We are still family. We did have good times. If only things could unwind back to Wyoming, before the violence. He act nice now because divorce soon. What if get back together? No. Still young. Still future. For both of us.*

She adjusted her sunglasses. *And he not fooling anyone. I clean room for him after he deploy—those panties under his bed, disgusting! And other Navy wives tell me about bad boy club on ship. Fuck in each port when deploy. I endure like proper Thai wife. No more. Marry is marry.*

He broke the silence. "So, tell me how your customers are doing, Maya." When she started, she'd always tell him about them. He'd even coach her on how she could work with them. She never picked the greaseballs for regulars. Always the docile ones. The ones that don't touch, who were simply happy for the attention.

He tapped the GPS causing it to refresh with a new route. "It's been over a year. How's Vic?" He knew Vic the fisherman was her first customer ever, and that Vic had a kid and was head over heels in love with Maya. "Did you ever have the talk with him?"

She tossed Rusty a treat. "Yeah, we jus' friends. Caleb, you fishing again. This what caused fight last time, remember?"

He looked out the window, taking in the coastline. "No, only asking. No need to talk if you don't want." He changed the subject. "How's Mom?"

She reached for her phone, wanting to take a pic of the coastline. "She okay. She happy." *But I'm not happy. I send $2,000 home every month. He* *only give $200. Mom and sister think he give all amount. We discussed before marry. They think he the greatest thing ever happened to family. They think I'm saving all my bar money to buy house. I have nothing.*

He reached for her hand. "Maya, you want I give you more money?" He knew she was adding to the pot. *Maybe that would get her out of the bar,* he thought.

She made a fist, retracted it to her lap just out of reach. "No need, Caleb. I can handle." She knew what he was doing. *No, we talked it out. Fought it out. He not going to change.*

They were flying by some beautiful coastline. The surf was up that day. Rusty settled in for a nap. Doggy diabetes took its toll sometimes.

They pulled into the resort. She was taken by surprise when the bellman led them to the honeymoon suite they'd had eight years before.

Her hand to her mouth in awe. "How you do this?"

He put on his best aw-shucks look. "I asked." His tone betrayed his underlying smugness. "I asked nine months ago."

A bottle of champagne greeted them, and a plate of chocolate strawberries. She had told him about Glenn and the champagne date. *I know what he doing. He so competitive. No matter. Sabai. Make the best of it.* She took a glass and a strawberry and went out on the lanai. Rusty was running from room to room. The resort was pet friendly. He was smelling the last ten dogs that had been through the suite.

She told herself this was going to be hard. There were a lot of wonderful memories here. She remembered when they were young, twenty-four and twenty-seven. Life was good. She was leaving the land of smiles and poverty, entering the land of opportunity and riches. He was a nice guy. They were both musicians and liked to jam together, he on the drums and she on her guitar. She couldn't remember the last time they'd jammed together.

He came out to join her. "What do you want to do first?"

"Let's chill here first, baby." The words slipped out.

He smiled.

Her lips flatlined. *I just went through a talk with Eddie. Him too? Never mind. Just enjoy. Like old friends. For Rusty.* "Here boy. Come to Mommy." She was on the chaise lounge and the dog jumped up on her, taking a bite of the strawberry in her hand.

Caleb leaned on the railing, watching the surf. The sun was straight up. Their room had the best sunset view in the entire resort.

She played with Rusty on the lanai all afternoon. It was like any other weekend. Except there was no Xbox.

She went back inside, took her phone to the bathroom.

———————————

Glenn's phone buzzed.

I soooo sorry. Cant make it tomorrow
night. Still feeling bad. Doctor said don't
work whole week. Maybe Friday. Sorry
Glenn I make it up to you next week.
Cant wait to see you

Ok. Take care

Glenn stared at his phone. *She didn't look all there that morning. But all week?* He looked forward to continuing some of the feelings expressed in the ICU. The private room thing was all but forgotten. *Well, that's that. Till next Tuesday.*

———————————

Leaning against the sink in the bathroom, Maya's heart ached just a bit. She hated to lie to him. It didn't feel right to her. *I'm so in deep with my lies. One day I will tell him. One day.*

Rusty scratched at the door and yelped. She closed her phone. "Coming, baby." She opened the door, and he jumped on her. "Good boy, good boy. Let's go find Daddy."

The days were filled with golf in the morning, beaching it in the afternoon, and lunches and dinners at the resort's high-end restaurants. The nights were spent exploring with Rusty, and with what she called her "wifely duty." A few times, Caleb and Rusty raced up and down the hall with other dogs and their owners.

On the last night, walking the grounds with Rusty, their hands touched and he grabbed hers. She didn't flinch. She was feeling nostalgic. The love-making that night was almost genuine. She shut off all thoughts of the present and revisited the past. If only they could stay back there.

Eddie texted all week, and she had to hide in the bathroom to answer. He was getting to be a little much again. Yet, for some reason, his neediness made her feel special.

She and Caleb had a final breakfast before checking out. They had room service on the lanai, listened to the surf and watched the surfers and windsurfers do their thing.

He took a bite of sausage. "Did you enjoy the week, Mrs. Finnegan?"

She leaned back. "Yass, Mr. Finnegan."

Rusty circled the table begging for scraps. Caleb dropped a piece of link sausage. She reacted like any mother would. "Hon, no—bad for him." The honeys, dears and babies had been nonstop since yesterday morning.

He knew it. *Get her away from the bar, from all the guys, and it'd be okay.* In Pattaya, they had their bumps, but as soon as she gave up the clubbing things settled down. He'd noticed there was always trouble when guys were around.

Maya reached over to his plate. "Baby, you gonna eat your fruit?" She was already stabbing at the kiwi on his plate.

His eyes were smiling. "No, so I'm glad you ate it already."

She chuckled and flipped a piece at his head. It went over the railing. They looked at each other and laughed like two pranking teens. He launched an orange slice at her. She tried to duck, but it hit her squarely on the forehead. Rusty was barking, a happy bark. To Caleb, it felt right. Now was the time.

He came around the table to her side and got on one knee.

Her eyes went wide.

He took her hand. "Maya Finnegan, will you again be my wife?" With the other hand, he held out a ring box. It was open.

She gasped. *He remembered. The ring from the downtown jewelry store three years ago.* It was three times the size of the tiny ring she had on now. It must have cost at least $10,000. "How did you . . . ?"

"Baby, I saved up. I can help more with Mom and Sis now too. We can move back to Buford after my twenty years. Houses are cheap there. Not too late to start a family. Mom Finnegan would love to have you back. So would all the nieces and nephews. They keep asking for you."

She was tearing, hands trembling. "Oh, Caleb."

She hardly ever teared. He knew this. *Never saw her cry. Even that day. On the verge of a home run now*, he thought.

"Oh, Caleb." Her hand went to her heart. *I wish this could be true. But sweet talk. He will get violent again. Not want to go to anger management. And not keep dick in pants.*

As if he read her mind, he implored, "Baby, I'll go to anger management like you wanted. We'll work this out." He had no answer about his infidelity.

He didn't think she knew. To him, it was never part of the deal: It was his right, the Navy way, to enjoy all that life at sea could provide.

Her hand still on her heart, she spoke, her voice trembling. "Oh, Caleb. I'm still your wife. Maybe after you come back, we can talk." Like with Eddie, she was buying time again.

She had to think. *Chloe was married and had boyfriend. Bella soon divorce Army officer husband even though they have child. This is the path.*

Confusion set in again. *Maybe this my life. Settle down. Have kids with him.*

But she could not get how he looked that day he hit her out of her mind. *Like Grandpa looked when he killed my cat—those crazy eyes. Need to talk to my sisters.*

He was still on his knee. "Sure thing, hon." Then he took her finger and slipped the new ring on it, right over the old ring. He kissed her hand then looked up. She leaned in and kissed him, long and open-mouthed. Rusty barked. It almost sounded like a "yay."

He wanted her to see that ring every day while he was gone. The next deployment was five months. FaceTime wasn't going to cut it.

Driving home, the conversation turned to his next deployment. She half-turned to him. "When you leave?"

He turned off the GPS. "I'm on the ship two Wednesdays from now."

She gave him her full attention. "How long?"

He scratched his neck. "They don't say yet. Five months. Maybe six. If there's trouble in the region, there might be extended missions. Depends on the carrier command staff. The *Stennis* is looking to pull its weight in the region, and the *Winston* and other destroyers are needed to provide protection."

She nodded. "How many ports?" Now she was fishing.

He turned up the air conditioning. "I don't know. We'll know better when we get our printed orders." He knew she was fishing. *Does she know about my port calls?*

She was fixing her makeup. "I hope you get to sightsee."

His grin was peculiar. "Not much time for sightseeing. Lots of public relations work to do in each port."

Observing his face, she thought, *No one grin like that talking about work. Horny asshole.*

They came to a red light. "Hey, Maya, I know you got this Tuesday guy you're pretty devoted to. But any way to have a nice dinner the night before I leave?"

Without thinking, she answered. "Sure, Caleb. You got it. I'd love to.

How about I cook for you?"

He turned to her, wanting to look in her eyes. *She said it right off the back. Without even checking her calendar. Maybe this trip did a lot of healing.*

She was quite sure that was the week Glenn said he'd be out of town.

She adjusted her sunglasses. The universe was cooperating and helping. *Next Tuesday back to Glenn and Eddie. The following Tuesday no Glenn and dinner with Caleb. I will work out things with Eddie. At least we cool off little bit.*

She leaned back in her seat. *Then Caleb gone, but Glenn back. In between and the other nights, other regulars and randoms but we see who show up. Someone always show up.*

They got into the house and unpacked. Rusty ran up and down the stairs between their rooms as if to say, is this necessary? She laughed. "We're home, boy." She opened her phone. There were thirty-two text messages from Eddie. None from Glenn. One from Chloe that morning.

She picked up the LV bag, a little disappointed that Glenn hadn't texted. Then again, she thought, she hadn't either, and she was supposed to be sick.

Caleb called out. "Babe, I'm taking Rusty for a walk. Wanna come?"

She lay out on the couch and gave a big, fake yawn. "No, tired. You go."

He observed. *Hmm. Back to his-and-her activities with the dog. Well, maybe she is tired.*

As soon as Caleb was out the door, she texted Eddie.

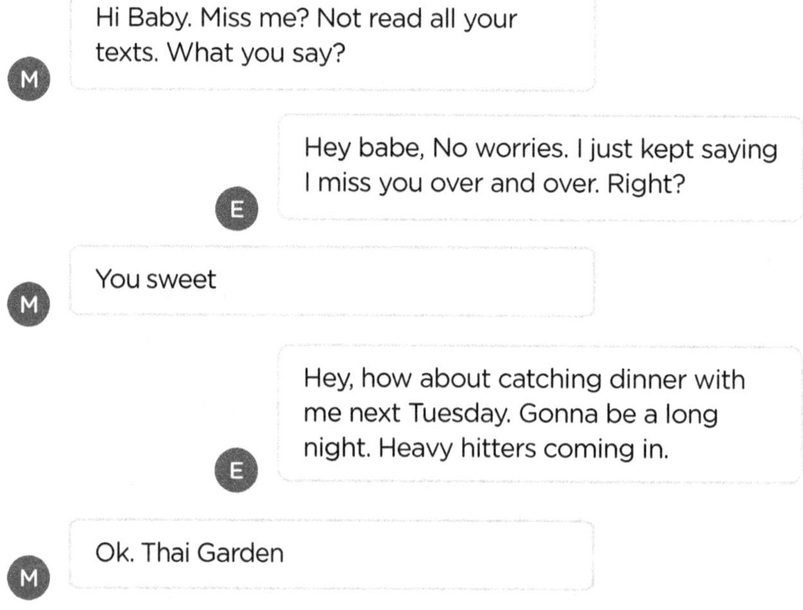

No. Can we do Korean. down the street.
Kal bi. Not a date. tired of Pad Thai and
panang curry

Ok. Kim Chee III across the street at
7:00. I gotta leave at 8:30

Yah I know. The guy

Eddie don't be mad

Not mad sorry we cool?

Yes. See you next Tuesday

She slowly put her phone aside. *This not date. Hope he not think date. But should do something for him. Should be fun. I like kal bi. Besides, good way to tell him no Thai Garden for me next Tuesday after dinner with Caleb.*

Her phone buzzed. *What Eddie want now? Oh Glenn.* She was pacing in the living room.

Hope ur feeling better. Have a good
weekend ok? Had an idea. Want to do
dinner next Tuesday? Since I'm gonna
be gone the week after, I thought Id
treat you to something nice. Yes, Yes.
Not a date. Its my evil way of making
sure you don't forget me. How bout it?

Her knees buckled. She fell into the couch.

He want same day same time. Not good. He will be mad. The little boy. What do? Already said yes to Eddie. Cancel Eddie? Maybe dinner at 9:00? Two dinners? Not want him mad right before he leaves.

Oh Glenn, so sorry. I have late shift.
Might come little late. But I stay all night
with you ok? Cant wait to sing our song
with you

k

She could tell Glenn was not happy. *At least we close down the bar. First time since . . . hmmm . . . when was last time?*

She gathered her thoughts. *I will make Eddie happy at dinner and tell him I come Thai Garden late. Not gonna be happy about next Tuesday—dinner with Caleb night.*

She scratched her hands and arms. *Itchy. So much stress now. Before easier. Just show up and hustle shots from whatever randoms there. Too grabby, move on.*

She thought about the last year. *Not so easy now. More bars open. More girls from out of town. Girls getting younger and prettier. Too hard to break in regulars. Better to keep what have now. Eddie's crew, Glenn, Vic. Plus gamble money from Eddie.*

She scratched even more. The back of her neck was burning. *Sister wedding cost plenty. Still need down payment for house.* She thought of the house she saw the last trip. *Six bedrooms. One for Mom, one for Sis and brother-to-be, one for her, and one for grandparents. One left for brother in navy and last for anybody else that need it.*

Bzzzt. Bzzzzt. Bzzzzt. *What now?* Chloe was texting.

Hey girl.

Fuck work tonight.

Its Friyay. Party??!!!

Maya texted Lynh.

Still sick mama. Come back next week
for sure.

66

FRIYAY FUNDAY

She met Chloe at the Mai Tai Bar, a well-known hangout in the world's largest outdoor shopping complex that attracted locals, military and tourists in equal numbers.

This was their thing. They gyrated, swooned and swayed to the live music. Dancing with each other, they put on a show primed for every set of male eyes in the place. The waitresses knew them and sometimes got caught up in the act. It was clear that they were there without dates.

As the night wore on, and the beat got heavier, the alcohol flow took its toll and men approached in consistent fashion.

After five minutes of chit-chat and flirting, the two would have their new friends jonesing to meet them at the bar the following Thursday or Friday. Sometimes, if the haul included groups of four or more, they'd set up Saturday night parties.

They called it at 1:00 a.m., their Instagram accounts filled with a dozen new followers. Maya took Chloe's hand. "Let's go eat, Chloe."

The guy with Chloe grabbed Chloe's elbow. "Darlin'—don't go!" In the worst broken English they could muster up, two Marines were trying to tell them they were going off to war in the morning. "We go bang bang America enemy tomorrow. Maybe die. Want happy happy one more night. You two make happy happy come home with us? We live hotel over there."

Chloe took the lead and lightly brushed the guy's crotch. "You like, sailor?"

He puffed out his chest, mouthing to his friend. "Stupid chick got it wrong."

He turned to Chloe, "Babe, I'm a Marine."

Toying with him, she rubbed his chest. "Don't get mad, soldier boy." She knew if there was one way to piss off a jarhead, it was to call him by another branch's nickname.

He sat straight up. "I'm a Marine, ma'am."

Chloe looked him in the eye. "I'm not your ma'am." She stood up, leaned over him, her bosom two inches from his face, and whispered in his ear. "I'm your fuckwhore fucky sucky—you like?"

He nearly fell off his seat. His Asian fetish porn dreams were about to come true. "Oh baby, Daddy like. You like Daddy?" As he reached for her, she facepalmed him hard. The waitresses stopped to watch. This part was always enjoyable.

Chloe straightened up, got right in his face, and snapped back in flawless Uncle Sam's English. "Look, jerk, I don't know where you think you are, but this isn't B-roll from *Good Morning, Vietnam*. Go fight your war tomorrow and if you get lucky and survive, come back and visit us here," she sneered, scrawling the bar's address on a napkin. "And bring money—we're not cheap."

His friend fell over laughing. Chloe and Maya stood up and walked off, whistling "The Marines' Hymn."

A twenty-minute drive later, they settled into their favorite booth at the Seoul Grill, a Korean barbecue restaurant open 24/7. It was a favorite after-hours hangout for bargirls and entertainers. Maya chuckled. "Chloe, how you talk so good?"

Chloe guffawed. "You know how. We get that act all the time. I rehearse all night."

Maya giggled. "You sound like some blonde outta the movies."

They laughed together. "You think they come see us, Maya?"

Maya laughed so much she was tearing. "Yeah. They always do. Watch tomorrow. Remember the time two construction guys come and fill up the bar with their whole crew?"

Chloe snorted, and they broke down in hilarious laughter again. "Yeah—a good night! We the queens, Maya."

"You the queen, Chloe. I'm your bitch remember."

Chloe hooked Maya under her chin for a second. Then caressed her cheek. "Nah. You grew up, sister. You doing okay. Don't do this all your life. I told you. The path. Find something you can do. Still thinking beauty school?"

Maya let out a soft, unconvincing "Yeah."

Chloe grew quiet.

Maya tilted her head. "What you thinking, Chloe?"

Chloe had been waiting to have a serious talk for a long time. Now was as good a time as any. "Sister, this game we play. I told you. Don't fall in love."

The waitress brought them five rounds of *soju*. Maya took one and clinked glasses with Chloe. Chloe looked over. "Well?"

Maya reached for another shot. "I'm not. I don't fall in love."

Chloe reached for her own second shot. "Really? What that ring on your finger?"

Maya played dumb. "What ring?"

Chloe pointed at the LV bag. "The one you put in your bag before Mai Tai tonight."

Maya brought out the ring Caleb gave her. "I had Cartier appraise. Eleven thousand dollars, Chloe! Maybe I should chance again?"

Chloe slapped her forehead and buried her face in her hands. "Hfffargngh!" She sounded like a cat with a hairball. "I was going to ask you tonight about Eddie and Glenn, and now Caleb? You in love with the wife beater again?"

Maya started rubbing the base of her neck. It was itchy but not itchy. She kept rubbing. "No. Maybe. I dunno, Chloe. I dunno."

Chloe downed her third shot. "Get your head straight, girl. You like me. Poor. Brown. Thailand not good to poor brown farm girls. Only the white city girls get the good Thai man. We get the brown Thai man punch us around and fuck around all they like while we clean house, raise kids, work extra jobs, and spread legs when his whores too busy."

They both paused long enough to order food. Chloe started in again. "We don't get rich in Thailand. Here in America can. Find the right guy. Save money. Send home. Buy house. Make savings account. Enough US dollars, retire rich in Thailand."

Chloe waved the waitress over. Thirsty again. "Me. Not lucky. My guy's a loser. Fifteen years Air Force and only four stripes? At least I getting half his pension. Making divorce now. At least he get me here, and I get citizenship. Maya, you need citizenship. What if Caleb dump you? You gone baby. Back to Thailand, no return ticket."

Maya shifted, and signaled for a beer from the waitress. "I know. What your plan after divorce, Chloe? Half pension and work bar?"

"No. Reyn."

Maya's eyes narrowed. "Reyn? Eddie boss?"

"Yeah."

Maya pointed at Chloe, grinning. "So when we went Vegas last year and you two disappear. We joke you two went Tahoe . . ."

"No Tahoe, Golden Nugget. Not leave room two days." Chloe broke into a lustful chortle.

Maya laughed along. "Happy for you, Chloe. He single, divorce, no baggage. Own his own company. Good man with son. Eight years old, right?"

Chloe smiled sweetly, like recalling something pleasant. "Son likes me. Call me Aunty. We have dinner every Thursday."

Maya's eyes widened. "What? You said you working out, so I don't call you!"

Chloe's smile had sex written all over it. "Heehee. I do my workouts with him Saturday afternoons."

Maya choked back a cackle.

Chloe continued. "But he mad. He want me quit bar. Okay, I help Thai Garden gamble, but in bar too many guys make like my boyfriend. Especially Allan."

Chloe sighed. Allan was special. He was there five nights a week. If she was busy, he waited. If she was busy all night, all he got was a goodnight hug. She made sure she had dinner with him at Thai Garden once a week. Never more than a goodnight peck on the cheek. Loyal as a dog. "I'm not sure what to tell him."

Maya signaled the waitress for a round of beers. "I think he know, Chloe. I saw sometimes Reyn come and Allan watch. A man know when another man more special."

Chloe was finally ready to ask the question of the night. "So Maya. Who more special? Glenn or Eddie? Or Caleb?"

Maya tried to make light of the situation. "You special, Chloe. You my honey. I will make you happy girl when old man Reyn retire!"

Chloe's grave expression let Maya know how serious her sister was. "Shut up, Maya. Don't run from this. I'm your friend. You need to figure this out. Get serious."

Maya frowned. "I'm not young anymore, Chloe. You know my story. Thai man break me. The optic shop girls they help me. I meet Dino. You remember Dino? Aussie boyfriend make me kill my little boy. He was the one Chloe. I was confused long time after. He used me but I didn't stop loving him."

The waitress put down two Heinekens. "Then I meet Caleb. Nice guy. American. Strong. Navy. Future. I meet his mother. So sweet. Loving. Not same as Dino but good enough. You know Thai style. I'm the oldest. I must take care family. Mommy, sister, brother, grandparents. Even aunty and cousin."

Maya took a long pull on her beer. "And now Daddy. He come back. Drunk bastard. Hurt his back. I must send back money to help him. Everybody come before me. You know. You the oldest too. Karma say our duty. My sister go school meet good man. Mommy go from man to man. Sick. Need expensive medicine. Brother not need much but he give all his money away. Monks do that. But he not eat so I send to sister for him and she buy him food and make him eat."

Maya's beer was half gone. She called for another. "I told Caleb all this. At first, he was, yeah yeah yeah, take care of family. And we married little while. After Wyoming he said, 'nuff send money to family. He want keep money for us. I say there is no us if I cannot take care family. We need house so everyone can live together. Even us. I say maybe we go back Thailand. I work my ass off right now to send money home. They all think Caleb send money. Sent from his account. Only his name on account because I'm not US citizen. They think he so good. They think we still happy. Every year, last three years I take pictures of us together and put on Facebook. Everybody think we happy married. I need to tell them Chloe but shame. Maybe I could be better wife and make marriage work?"

Chloe sat quietly and listened. She knew Maya was on a roll and needed to get it all out.

Maya fidgeted with her phone. "But that day he show true self. He get crazy eyes. He hit me, Chloe. I was scared. I thought was like Thai man again. I lock in room three days."

Chloe thought back. It was the first year she lived with them but was on her yearly Thailand home visit. "I'm so sorry, Maya. I should have been there for you."

"No sorry, Chloe. Good I found out true him. And he fuck around on me too. Even in Wyoming. Even in Pattaya. I found out all after we married. I stay devoted. Like many our sisters in Thailand. Hope he change. Maybe I'm first wife at least. Not mistress or like we say second wife. As long as I'm first wife I think maybe okay, but then he get crazy, like Thai man. No. Not want. He kill me maybe. Maybe I kill him." Caleb had taught Maya how to shoot in the mountains of Wyoming. They each owned their own Glock pistol.

Maya closed her eyes, took a deep breath, and exhaled. "He want to try again Chloe. He told me last week. Give me new ring. I told him we talk after he come back from deploy. Next year maybe. I have time to think. But I know cannot. Ten years next year. We made deal. We don't divorce till he make rank. I get pension, beauty school and live on base. I get Rusty too. I don't press wife beating charges. I kept all the pictures Bella took. Her attorney say I have good case. Call him if need."

Chloe finished her beer, put some kal bi on the grill at their table. "I didn't expect all this, Maya. I thought only Glenn or Eddie."

Maya stirred up some mushrooms and onions on the grill. "Chloe, not sure about both. At least no kids. I'm happy if can support family. Eddie so easy on the eyes. Underneath all that stupid he's good guy. Make plenty money. I can take care of family, but his money is stupid money. He make money doing wild gambling and wild investing. He throw money around. Sometime money come back. Most times no. All his friends, even Reyn, take his money and invest and lose. Cannot rely. Maybe ten year from now no money."

The waitress laid out more meat for them. "Glenn smart. He make money smart. Good businessman. He make his money make money for him. So talented. Everyone want him. He too nice too. He make Vey restaurant website for free. He help Mama Lynh with legal stuff no charge. But he not stupid with money. He make money and make more money. Even if no more money in bank, he talented. Can make more money. He generous too. He already give me money to help Mommy and sister. I send Glenn's money through Caleb's account. They think Caleb sending. I have to tell them everything. Caleb marriage not good. Money come from me and sometimes Glenn. Every time I need money he give me. One time last summer he didn't have enough to help me so he do extra job for governor and give extra money to me."

Chloe's brow furrowed skeptically. "No one that nice, sister. He told you this? He get second job to help you?"

Maya laid some meat and mushrooms on Chloe's plate. "Yeah but he tell me only after. I was mad. I wonder why he do that? I feel guilty. But also happy he do that for me."

Chloe crossed her arms, feeling protective. "You sure this guy for real? Seriously, no one that nice. All customers bullshit."

Maya sucked on her kal bi bone. "Glenn good man. You know what he do last five years? He the mayor's man. He help homeless, old people, people who need jobs. That was his job. Good karma that one. But he not good-looking like Eddie. And not that young. Not ugly, not old. Just not young, not handsome. In between. No matter. Caleb not good looking either. Main thing good heart. I know Glenn not hit me."

Then Maya leaned forward and whispered, "But, Chloe, Glenn married. I didn't ask him yet but one time I feel his pocket and I felt ring with his car keys. He must have someone at home. Always can come only Tuesdays because family the other nights."

Chloe played her trump card. "Eddie married too, Maya."

Maya's response was swift, repeating everything Eddie had told her. "Yeah but that not count. Business transaction. Marry for green card only. Like Bella, and Mint, and Vey. Separate bedrooms. No sex. She get boyfriend LA. They divorce soon. Same time mine and Caleb final too."

They quieted for a bit, each lost in their thoughts. Before Chloe could get a word in, Maya took a breath, then exhaled, as if making a final decision. "I think I stay with Eddie. Friends with Glenn. He married."

Chloe shook her head. "No, Maya. That not going to work. You always thinking of Glenn when you with Eddie."

Maya tilted her head, eyes narrowing a bit. "How you know?"

Chloe signaled for more beer. "I know you. You get blank look sometimes. I know you not thinking about Caleb or Rusty. You don't even know if Glenn married. Ask him."

Maya's face scrunched up a little, her nostrils flaring. "No. He only tell me no one at home. Feel like lie you know? Like he not telling me something."

Chloe sipped her beer. "Maybe separated? You need to ask. You cannot just say Glenn married so I pick Eddie. You don't even know."

Tears started to well up in Maya's eyes. "Why I cannot just meet good guy who take care me and my family?"

Chloe's lips twisted. "Where Maya? At bar? Not going to happen. Losers, you know?"

Maya slapped the table. "You found Reyn! I can get lucky too!"

Chloe scoffed. "You think I lucky? I have to send money home but now he tell me don't work bar. I work twice as much at restaurant for half money. He not helping me either, Maya. He say wait till we married. He paying alimony and his kid more important. Yeah, get money to blow on us if we fun good-looking bargirls. But once we future wife, things change."

Maya softened to her friend's plight, reaching for her hand. "So why you stay with him?"

Chloe's eyes glazed over. "The heart wants what the heart wants, Maya."

Maya gave a half-smile. Inside, joy for her friend started to percolate. "You love him? You love him over family?"

Chloe nodded. "Maybe. Other brothers and sisters help now. I'm not the oldest, Maya. Second oldest. Big brudder doing better now. He tell me thank you for helping last ten year. But now he take over and tell me go be happy."

Maya sighed with envy. "You lucky, Chloe. Your brothers and sisters almost same age?"

"Yeah."

Maya explained. "My sister and brother twelve and fifteen years younger. My babies. I take care when Mommy was in Bangkok, not on farm. They not settled yet. Cannot help. Cannot even help selves. Grandparents getting old too and need to come live with Mommy. But Mommy sick and not make enough money to help."

Maya's sigh sounded like a sudden gust of wind. "I have to buy Mommy moped again. Glenn help with that too. I don't need anyone, Chloe. I make it on my own."

Chloe's eyebrows hiked up. "Really? Sound like Glenn come along at right time. And he not just throw money at you. It's like he . . . that's how he show he love you?"

Maya cast her glance downward, playing with her phone, scrolling to her favorite picture of Glenn. "Feel like that sometime. I don't ask. He figure it out and always give me extra or early birthday present or some kind of holiday or tradition I don't understand. I ask Tia one day and she said no such holiday or tradition. He make up excuses, holidays, traditions, all to give me money so I don't lose face. Sometime he just give me and say don't argue."

The waitress brought over the check. Chloe took out her credit card. "Winner, Maya. Only place Eddie win is easy on eyes. Not easy on eyes twenty years from now. Glenn easy on eyes too. He rock hard body for his age. Not handsome like movie star but rugged sometimes, little boy sometimes."

Maya frowned. "You like Glenn, Chloe?"

Chloe threw her head back. "Yeah, but not like that. Maybe different if I met him first, I dunno. But no matter. You should find out, Maya. You should ask, know for sure."

Maya closed her eyes and leaned back. The food, *soju* and beer were having an effect. "I know. But right now I don't ask and he don't ask. What if I ask and then he ask? It does not feel good to lie. And if I lie, and he find out, I lose him. I can tell him later but then he will know I lied too. Hard to ask right now."

Chloe reached over and tapped Maya awake. "You can just tell him about Caleb."

Maya's eyes popped open. Her lids may have been heavy, but her mind was one hundred percent awake. "But I already told him we divorced and Caleb in Germany. He say honesty important to him. I tell him now, I can lose him. I need to find way to tell him and not lose him. And yeah, sometimes when he smile, when he eat, when he happy, he easy on the eyes like Eddie."

Chloe's brow furrowed. "So what you do?"

Maya shrugged. "Only friends. Both of them. For now. I figure something out. Family first. I choose family over love, always."

Chloe picked at her teeth with one hand and covered her mouth with the other. "You can have both, Maya. You gotta figure out who you love.

But you gotta choose first."

Maya hugged herself and rubbed her shoulders. "I know. Not now, Chloe."

On a roll, Chloe wanted to get it all out. "Soon, Maya. Glenn deserve to be happy too, you know? If you don't want him, let him go. Plenty girls want him. They think he easy on eyes too. No young guy get body like that. Respect you too, Maya. They think you lucky with Glenn. Not so much Eddie. They all know him up and down the street. Playboy."

Maya nodded. *Yeah. Exciting. When gambling with him all adrenaline. I like so much. How come I like that more than Glenn's generosity, reliability, faithfulness? He so faithful to me, not see other bargirls. But he faithful to his wife? Need to find out. Marry is marry.*

While Chloe signed her credit card slip, Maya lost herself in her thoughts. *I must be strong. Do whatever to help family. Caleb said he would help more. Maybe I stay with him? He said would do anger management. But cannot trust. He still screw around. At least Eddie said only me for him. Loyalty important too. For now, finish marry Caleb. Eddie finish marry. Then we can see.*

Chloe nodded to the door. Maya slid out of the booth. *Glenn?* She let out another long sigh. *Need to find out more. Just friends for now.*

The following Tuesday, at 6:30 p.m. Maya was looking forward to kal bi with Eddie. Then singing with Glenn. She texted Eddie.

> Hi baby. I hungry. 7:30. Kim Chee III.
> Cant wait to see you. You hungry baby?
> For me or for kal bi?

She looked at what she texted. She was being sassy again. *Hope it don't make him go all crazy again.*

She parked at the bar a little early. She wanted to talk story with Verna before heading to Kim Chee III.

She was thinking about sending something sassy to Glenn when her phone rang. Eddie? He always texted, not called. *Hope he not canceling.* "Hi baby. Why you calling, everything okay?"

"Hello *baby* . . . this is Eddie's wife. Who the fuck are you?"

67

BREAKTHROUGH

An hour earlier, Eddie came home to take a shower. Heejin was waiting, on his bed, naked, legs spread. "Yeobo, take me. I'm horny. Let's make-baby time." Eddie always found an excuse to spill outside. He jumped on her. She worked him hard. She rode his face like it was a saddle. She was a bargirl, or used to be. Since they'd married, she'd passed herself off as a golf pro and caddie at the country club.

They met four years ago at the bar next to Lynh's. She liked his white Asian looks right off the bat. Round eyes—the deal clincher in Korea. She'd seen this high roller several times. The other girl wasn't around. Her turn. She slid in next to him, her hand going right to his crotch. He liked her. She was wild in bed, but sweet and demure on the outside. His parents liked her. Her parents liked him, or what she told them about him—a successful contractor and entrepreneur.

The third time they were together, she asked while wiping him off after sex, "Yeobo, I need green card. You help me? My father send me ten thousand dollars. This enough?" She knew it was only a $500 deal. Her DUI complicated the green card process later. Eddie was irked, thinking she should have been naturalized by now. He was okay with the fake marriage but noticed she acted more and more like they were the real thing.

She fell in love with him as they spent more time together. She couldn't get enough of his looks and the adrenaline he produced when gambling and doing business. He didn't worry about losing money since her daddy always had more for his princess.

With a grunt, he pulled out and brought it to her mouth, like the porn movies. He kept his hand busy, making her come, and she grabbed greedily. She yanked at his penis. "Next time, Yeobo, remember we trying for baby too."

Breathing hard, he smiled and rolled over. "Gotta shower. Running late."

She propped herself on her elbow. "Where you go tonight?"

"Meeting Reyn at the job site. Behind schedule. Again."

She caressed his chest. "I wait for you?"

He rolled over. "No. Overnight. I see you tomorrow, okay?" He was off to shower.

In his hurry, he left his phone out, and she saw a text from Pete come across. She always wondered why she never met Pete when they all went drinking together. The phone notification said, "Hi baby can't" then was cut off. At first, she smiled, thinking it was a prank, but then her bargirl's sixth sense took over. She grabbed his phone and punched in 1-2-3-4. She read the text, then read all the other texts from the week before. He'd been careless. He usually deleted all the texts at least once a week.

She recalled that he'd kept screenshots of all the dirty talk texts she used to send him when they were dating. On a hunch, she tapped his picture gallery icon. Her jaw dropped as she read all the texts between him and Maya going back a year. *Pissed* only began to express what she felt.

He came out of the shower and saw her holding his phone. *Oh fuck*, was all he could think. He felt like he'd rolled the dice on an all-in bet—and lost.

———

Korean accent. Soft, silky, but hard, edgy, sarcastic, pissed off, ready to blow. "Hello *baby* . . . this is Eddie's wife. Who the fuck are you?"

It felt like electricity was shooting through Maya's brain. She stared at the phone. It said Eddie, but this was a woman's voice. The Korean accent was there, but the English was good enough. The woman's voice shrilled through the phone. "Answer me, bitch!"

Maya hung up. *Must be mistake.* On impulse, she punched Eddie's speed dial.

The Korean accent answered. "I'm still here, bitch. He's in the shower. Who the fuck are you! You're not Pete." Maya knew that Eddie had her in his phone as Pete because Heejin sometimes looked through his contacts.

Maya hung up. The phone buzzed again. She let it ring, then picked up, answering tentatively. "Hello?"

The Korean accent asked again, "Who are you?"

Maya pushed back. "Never mind. Where Eddie?"

The voice spoke back edgier. "It's where *is* Eddie. Speak proper English, cunt. I read all the texts between you and him. Now I know it's not a job he works on all night, you fucking cunt."

Maya's face flushed with anger now. "How can you say wife? You faking it for green card!"

The voice mocked Maya. "Is that what he said? You must be more stupid than you sound!"

Maya's self-esteem took a major hit. Like growing up with all those white Thai girls teasing her about the way she dressed and spoke. *Was he lying?* She felt like she was running down a hallway naked. She hung up again.

The phone buzzed again. Maya let it go to voicemail. Four minutes later the voicemail icon popped up. It was a long one.

Maya tapped the voicemail button and brought the phone up to her ear. Her hands trembled as she listened.

*Listen, you fucking cunt. I don't know what he
told you. Maybe he fucked you like a toy one-night
stand and now you think you're taking over. We're
married, you marriage wrecker. I hope you rot in
hell for this. Go find your own man. Karma will get
you for what you're doing to us.*

*Don't believe? I texted you links to our Facebook
and Instagram. Nothing fake here. By the way I just
had his cock in my mouth and if I find out he had it
in yours, it's coming off. Doesn't sound like you two
do much, but bitch, your days of calling my Yeobo
"baby" are over. Leave him alone. We're trying to
have a baby.*

*Don't you ever talk to him again or see him again.
I bet you're a bargirl. I know the mamas in this
town, and I'll get you. If you're illegal, I'll get you
deported, you shit.*

*I'm not that mean. I let him call you one more time
to say goodbye. I'll be right next to him, and I'll
have my hands wrapped around his dick.*

*He's not coming back to you. Unless your daddy can
bankroll all the shit he's doing. And if he bought you*

*anything with our money, I want it back. Oh fuck,
never mind. Keep it. It's soiled. Don't want it.
Why do people like you exist? Go die and make the
world a better place!*

Fuck you, marriage wrecker. I hope you die!

Maya went to the links. Nothing but happiness. Comments between his wife and her friends about making a baby. Their pictures together were the stuff of contemporary graphic artists. It didn't look like she had a boyfriend in LA or that she thought it was a sham. Maya thought of her own marriage and pictures on Facebook. The difference was she had his wife saying the marriage was still on.

She felt like she got punched in the stomach. *Trying to make a baby? Her father bankroll him?*

Sitting in the bar, she was mostly numb. It was past 7:30. She went over to the restaurant, hanging on to the notion that it was a crank call. She walked through the door, and the smell of kimchee and guttural Korean jabbering greeted her. *I know he is here.* She looked around twice. *Shit. Not here.* She waved off the Korean waitress.

Back at the bar, she dialed Chloe. No answer. *Must be with Reyn.* Her legs felt weak. She plopped down on the bench outside of the bar. *Should I call?* She sat looking at her phone. *The voice message said he would call. Today? When?*

She leaned against the bar's wall. *All that money. I thought was from business investments. From the girl's father? How I'm so stupid? He use me. All year long he use me.*

She scrolled on her phone. *He had two Facebook pages? He show me one that said no relationship. I thought it meant he didn't believe in the marriage. The Facebook page she sent said they married. I'm so stupid. A stupid bargirl.*

Glenn pulled up at 8:30. He wanted to practice some songs before Maya got there. *Funny, she's here already. What's she doing outside? She looks funny. Kinda pale. Is she okay? Still sick?*

He stepped out of his car. "Hey, I'm early. Wanted to practice singing a bit. You okay?"

She looked up. "Oh, I'm early too." She tried to smile.

He observed her blank expression, her posture slightly drooped, a defeated aura. "Maya, you okay? Still sick?" *Something wrong here. Boyfriend troubles? Tuesday night guy?*

She gave him a blank look. "Little bit, Glenn. I'm okay. I must take call. I will be in soon, okay?"

His expression reflected concern, and confusion topped with worry. "I can wait here with you." He felt a little uneasy.

She sniffed.

Allergy? he thought. *No way.*

Her face said, don't make me beg. "No, I'm okay. This is little private. Go Glenn. Please."

He glanced back at her as he entered the bar. *This is not good. Must be that Eddie guy. Pretty sure he's the reason she comes late and leaves early. I guess I am the second string. I got a lot of questions. Not sure if now is the time to ask. I'll get with her after the trip. I don't want a fight hanging over my head while I'm away.* "You sure?"

She turned back to him, holding her phone. "Yes, Glenn. I'll be in soon. Waiting on a call."

He got the hint. *I'll check on her in a half hour.* He didn't have to. She came in around ten minutes later. He didn't hear her talking outside.

She'd gotten a seven-word text instead.

Nothing else. She stared for a bit. Then blocked his number. No Thai Garden tonight.

Glenn was sitting at the bar. With construction on the street again, it was a slow night. There were only a few barflies. The darts room was empty, and only Tia was behind the bar. A bar regular was killing time in the booth room waiting for his girl. The muted flatscreens were turned to CNN and Fox. Roberta Flack was quietly singing "Killing Me Softly" from the jukebox.

She pulled up onto the seat next to him, wearing a pink business dress with bare shoulders and a hem to her knees. She could have come from a day at the office.

He turned to her. Something was not right. He could have made a list, and mentally he did. Upset. Distraught. Confused. Shock. Denial. She looked like she could burst into tears any second.

Pain crept into his heart. "Everything okay?"

She managed a smile. Her voice was soft, trying to sound cheerful. "No. Not really."

He was one hundred percent focused on her. "Want to talk about it?"

She took another look at her phone, then put it away. "No. Only some bad news. I will be okay."

He was thinking to himself. *What is it? Eddie? Husband/cousin? Never saw her like this. Are those tears?*

He reached for some napkins and put them in front of her. Everywhere Glenn worked, he was the resident chaplain. This was no different. He had an instinct. He switched into compassion mode.

She turned to him. "You hungry?" Their usual ice breaker. Amidst her chaos, she was trying to take care of him.

Truth is, he was starved. He thought better to lie. "No. I'm okay. You hungry?"

"No." All her appetite was gone.

She stared straight ahead blankly. Only her blinking said she was still functioning.

He laid his hand on her arm lightly. "Need a shot?"

She turned to him, reacted to his kindness. "Yes, can I?"

He looked toward the well. "Five shots, Tia, and a Hennessey for me, with a beer back."

Maya looked up, tears welling up in her eyes, voice trembling. "Tia, can you make those real shots?"

Glenn sat quietly. *I can feel her pain. This is serious. I'm gonna kill whoever did this to her. I wanna hold her so bad. Make it all go away. Best let her be, though, until she's ready. Best let her be, and just be here for her.*

She was still staring off into space. "Cheers, Glenn." She took two shots quick. They sat there quietly. No booth tonight.

She kept staring straight ahead, blankly watching the TV.

So did he. He could see her reflection in the mirror backing the bar.

"Cheers." She downed the third shot. That was three in five minutes. Her eyes were glassy and red and teary. The way they'd look if she'd been crying outside before coming in. The tears wouldn't stop. She kept dabbing at her eyes and sniffling, followed by some light heaving, suppressing her sobs.

He clasped his hands as if praying, laid them in front of him on the counter, and leaned ever so slightly. *Oh, Father. I didn't expect this. Tell me what do. Is there trouble she needs to take care of, and she's parked here because of some blind bargirl devotion? Best I can describe is she's weepy, like teardrops from a slow leaky faucet. One drip every minute. One drip, one tear, one dab, one sniff—every minute.*

Maya shook her head as if trying to snap out of a trance. "Tia, can you change TV to karaoke?"

"Sure, love." Tia looked at Glenn, and Glenn looked back. Silent agreement. *We're here for her.*

Jimmy came out of the back. "Hi, Glenn. Hi, Maya. Maya, what you look like shit for, make Glenn happy."

Tia reached out and palmed Jimmy in the chest and pushed him back into the kitchen. She came back a few minutes later. Jimmy made himself scarce the rest of the night.

Drip, tear, dab, sniff. With one long sigh and heave, she sniffled in a breath and exhaled. She turned to Glenn with a weak smile. "How was your day, Glenn?"

His soul had a meltdown. *She's trying one hundred percent. Something terrible has happened. Her world is upside down and she's trying to make me happy?*

He cleared his throat. "It was okay."

She said it almost absent-mindedly. "That's good." The TV turned to karaoke mode. "You want to sing, Glenn?"

He sensed she needed to sing more than him. "Not right now. You go ahead."

She put on some Thai videos.

He rubbed his chin, and left his hand covering his mouth. *Never did that before. They look like breakup videos. Some girl with a guy. Rural farm scene. They have a fight. Then the guy goes off with another girl on his moped. The first girl is crying. Lots of flashbacks.*

He snuck a look at her. *The faucet's leaking again. Drip, drip, drip, sniff, dab, dab. Like a song beat.*

Glenn turned back to the video. *Don't know what they're singing but the music rivals any late-night honky-tonk I've been in where some guy sings about losing some girl. I guess sorrow's the same musically the world over. Kinda like the songs Mommy used to listen to way back when.*

Glenn kept watch on her reflection in the mirror. *Whatever it is, she needs to deal with it. And she's here with me? Can't thank her enough, but I gotta be the bigger dog here. Let her do what she needs. Not about me tonight.* "Hey Maya."

Her voice was a raspy sweet whisper. "Yes, Glenn?"

He turned to her, their knees within inches of each other. "If you have to leave and take care of business, I'll understand. Don't worry about me. Take care of . . ."

"*No! Don't leave me!*" Reaching for his hand, she pleaded, "Don't leave me, please." Her voice was panicky, like a little lost girl. She squeezed hard for a minute and held on for a few minutes more. She stared straight ahead, trembling. The strains of the Thai video played on. Her weak smile flatlined. She was gritting, almost grinding, her teeth. The tears flowed faster. Maya was one step away from full breakdown.

Tia watched carefully from the side, making sure she was out of Maya's view. Staring at Glenn, Tia thought, *He's got this. He's like my man. Quiet—sometimes needy, like all guys—but strong when you need him.*

It was a few minutes, but later they would say it was like a thousand years, but also time standing still. *Is that,* he wondered, *even possible?*

She squeezed once more and dabbed her eyes with her free hand. Her voice softened. "Don't leave. Stay with me, Glenn. Tell me you'll always be here for me."

He squeezed back. A quick one. "Maya. I'll always be here for you. I'm not going anywhere. Okay?"

He leaned over and whispered in her ear, "Tonight I'm not your customer. I'm your friend, okay?" She nodded. He rubbed her back. He was protector, friend, man. She put her head on his shoulder and left it there. He savored the moment. Something very real was happening here. Tia turned away and wiped her eyes.

Maya saw their reflection in the bar mirror, her head on his strong shoulders. "Don't ever leave me, Glenn."

He returned her gaze. "I won't. I won't." He thought she meant don't leave her that night. She meant forever. "Do what you need to, Maya. I'll be right here."

She nuzzled his shoulder, hooked her arm around his. "You don't see me like this before, yes?" She sniffed, breathed in then exhaled.

He took a breath himself, calming his own emotions. "No, Maya. No."

She was desperately trying to pull herself together. "I just need . . . I just need to be like this . . . like this." She waved her free hand in front of her. "Like this tonight. Just tonight. I will get through this. I will get over this. Just tonight . . . let me be like this."

She repeated it. And again. He kept letting her say it. Her head never left his shoulder. He didn't move one bit. "Glenn, am I horrible person?"

His eyes sharpened. He cast a glance sideways at her. "No, Maya. Absolutely not. Who said that? I'll take care of them."

Arm still wrapped around his, she reached down, her fingers interlocked with his. "No, Glenn. No need. It's over now." She knew he wasn't kidding. Inside, it felt good that he cared that much.

A while passed. The Thai videos stopped, replaced by the jukebox emitting a steady Latin beat. She sniffed one more time, then lifted her head off his shoulder. "Tia, microphone?" Maya wanted to sing.

A good sign, he thought. He let go of her hand, thinking she'd need it to sing. She reached out and took his hand back and squeezed as if to say not yet.

Verna came by and took her song orders. Only then did Maya let go of his hand. His hand free, he rubbed her back and whispered, "Hey, do what you need to do. I'm gonna rub your back every now and then just to let you know I'm here, okay?" She nodded. He hardly touched her back that night. She reached for his hand again and held on for the rest of the night.

"Tattoo" by Jordin Sparks came on, followed by Britney Spears' "Everytime." They'd sung it together many times before. He turned off his mic. *I'll let her go solo. Definitely not dedicated to me or us this time.* Midway thru each song, her voice cracked, and stifling a sob, she handed her mic over to Glenn to finish. He put all the hurt he felt for her into it, resulting in applause from the booth room.

She smiled at him, a real smile. "They like you, Glenn. Everybody like you."

He smiled back. "You like me, Maya?"

She caressed his face. "I like you, Glenn."

He kissed her palm. "I like you too, Maya. That's all that counts." He was euphoric, suppressing what confusion was waiting around the corner. *What's happening here? Is this still fantasy? Is this real? Are we friends only? Is this love conquering all?*

She put her head on his shoulder again, for a minute. "I go bathroom. Be right back." There, she took out her phone, brought up her text thread with Eddie, including the last, and deleted all 983 text messages. She flushed the toilet. Symbolic. *Nothing in there*, she thought, *only memories.*

She turned to wash her face. Staring in the mirror, she thought, *Oh shit, I look like crap.* She chuckled. *This what he saw when he say he like me?* She smiled. Felt a little warmth creeping in. She was about to adjust her makeup, then wiped it all off. *He always wanted to see me without makeup.*

When she walked out, Tia was the first to see, bringing her hands to her mouth, she blew kisses. "Oh wow, Maya!"

Glenn turned. *She did it. She actually did it. Wow. So much natural beauty.* Glenn failed to see the symbolic act. She was baring her soul to him, making the ultimate sacrifice and denying her need to cover her insecurity with makeup. In front of him was that ugly, brown, flat-nosed girl she'd grown up as.

She stepped to the bar hesitantly, avoiding her reflection in the mirror. "You like?"

He almost stammered. "Like. Yes. Beautiful. Natural."

She laughed. "Joking, right?"

His face glowed with admiration. He was falling in love all over again. "Not joking, Maya."

One of the barflies piped in. "That you, Maya? You should be like that all the time. You cute like my daughter!" Maya laughed. Her spirit was rising. A fleeting thought crossed her mind: *All other guys bring me down, but Glenn always bring me up.*

She downed her last shot. "Cheers! Glenn, want another beer?"

He drained his current bottle. "Sure."

She reached for the microphone. "I sing song for you. Was my wedding song. I sing for you." She sang a soulful rendition of "A Thousand Years"—Cristina Perri and more recently, Taylor Swift.

He stroked his chin. *Not sure if this is good for her. Her wedding song. Hope she doesn't crack. I can't finish for her. I hope she knows. Whoa . . .* he got caught up in the song as she sang, looking into his eyes, reaching out for his hand.

The song was about love, about fearing to love, but also fearing not to love. Over the course of the song, the singer step-by-step chooses love, resolutely deciding to wait a thousand years for that love if necessary.

He felt flush. *She's singing this to me?* He thought back to the hospital. He took it all in.

They closed down the bar that night.

She held his hand in both of hers. "Text me from Vegas, okay?"

His heart ached with love. "You want me to cancel? I don't feel right leaving you like this." *A thousand years. It's gonna be like a thousand years before I see her again. I don't want this to end.*

So many thoughts swirled in her head. The night went from bad to good. From two choices to one. The universe was moving her along. "No. I'm okay now. I will be okay. Because of you." She thought back to the hospital, how she felt then, how she felt now.

He had to hear it. "See you Tuesday after I come back?"

She knew what he wanted. "Of course. Tuesdays are for us!" She kissed his hand.

He walked her to her car and was about to open her door for her. She turned. "Gimme kiss, Glenn!" He smiled. This night went from zero to sixty like nothing he ever saw before. It was like something out of a movie. He pictured Richard Gere in the role. *Whoa, too much grey hair!*

She'd never asked for it like that before. "Gimme kiss, Glenn." She cupped his chin and pulled him to her. Her lips lingered after, and she kissed him again. She drew him into her for what seemed like a blissful eternity to him. They were up against each other, her back on her car, his arms around her waist. *We fit good*, she thought. "Good night, Glenn."

He held tight. "Good night, Maya."

"Text me, okay?" With all her strength, she had to push him away—gently. With all his strength, he let go, understood, and was grateful.

She got in the car. "Good night, Glenn." He stood there. *Aw, hell.* He leaned in, put his hand around her neck, and pulled and kissed. This time, she took it all in. Wet, soft, he felt the tip of her tongue, tasted the Crown. Her tongue danced with his, and there was one last lingering parting kiss. The shots they'd had that night bore no contest to the intoxication they felt then.

He was trying not to breathe so heavy, and his legs felt weak. "Good night, Maya." He closed the door, keeping eye contact the whole time. She held his gaze, blew a kiss through the window, and was gone.

68

GAMECHANGER

The next morning, Glenn lay in bed staring at the alarm clock—6:45, still another fifteen minutes to go before it went off.

He'd already been awake for an hour, eyes wide open and thinking, *What was that last night? I went with so many questions, so many things I wanted to follow up on. I wanted to see if our vibe in the ICU was for real. Maybe she was drugged. But they say a person intoxicated shows best what's in their heart. And what about that Eddie guy? I understand. She was drugged. But what is he in all of this?*

He touched his lips and thought of their last kiss. *Now last night? Was it the Eddie guy? What does she mean by asking if she was horrible? And she said, "It's over now." What's over?*

He sat up and rubbed his eyes. *I was ready to just tell her, okay, go be with that guy. I'm second string. Got it. Customer only. Got it. Yeah, all a fantasy. Got that too.*

He could still feel her head on his shoulder. *Last night didn't feel like a fantasy. I didn't feel like a customer. And for sure, there's been a change in the depth chart. For once, I felt like I was the number-one draft pick. For the first time, this shit felt real. Very real.*

He stretched his arms, reached up. *Time to get up. Bad timing. Gotta go outta town. Screw Joyce. Didn't want me to go but the Admiral needed things fixed again in DC.*

Glenn learned the previous week that the Senate Defense Appropriations committee wanted to move a carrier group out of the state to another port, and the Admiral was having none of that. Glenn arranged to meet Tomo in Las Vegas to implement strategy with Tomo's contacts.

He lay back down. *Didn't want to lie to her but needed to keep the cover. Telling her I'm meeting an old friend wasn't lying. Tomo is an old friend. The less she knows about the Group, the better. Even Katie didn't know half the things I did. She thought I was on the international board for a non-profit revitalizing third world villages.*

He let out a sigh. *This is terrible timing. Wonder what the Admiral would do to me if I said can't go because I want to visit this bargirl next Tuesday? Something good happened last night. We got some momentum going. It could be gone next week. She could go back to that Eddie guy. I don't know. Whatever. Not sure where her head is at. Not sure what I'd do. I hate being second team at anything.*

He hit the snooze button a third time. *She must be up by now.* He sent a text.

> Hoping things are better for you today. Just want you to know you are a good person. Doesn't matter what others think. What matters is what you think. You taught me that. I believe in you. Stay positive. You will get through this.

She shot right back:

He grinned like a schoolboy. *Wow. That's a lot of smilies. Heart eyes too?*

Maya sat on her bed with Rusty curled up in her lap. She was on the phone with Chloe. "Yeah, he stayed with me all night. Not feel like work. It was like . . . like if you were there but . . . I dunno."

Chloe shook her head. "But but but! Girl, with you it's always, but this, but that. I told you Eddie not good. Now no decision, no need choose. Only Glenn left. I guess. Unless you still thinking about Caleb?"

Maya was nearly pouting. "No Chloe. But don't rush with Glenn, right? You always say don't rush. Make sure I feel good. Plus marry is marry. Even if Glenn not married, I still marry, technically. No nothing till I take care of that with Caleb."

Chloe's tone of voice said don't blow it girl. "He not wait forever.

Maybe you need to explain . . ."

"I know but then I gotta tell him I lie all this time. He was good to me and I needed someone with me, and I felt happy was him. But maybe I'm screwed up now. We see when he come back. Gotta keep my story, my pride, my wall. Then if serious I chance telling him. All-or-nothing roll dice."

Chloe gave the "shhh" signal to Reyn, who was lying next to her, bored. "Don't worry, sister. I think he listen to me. I help talk to him too."

Rusty was restless. Maya rubbed his belly. "I know, Chloe. He really think you sister, you know that? Wow. I second wife. You sister. Sound like some weird Thai drama. Or Thai porn movie."

Chloe guffawed over the phone. "Ewww, gross. You thinking the movie we saw last year?"

Maya covered her mouth. "No, what you mean?" Both laughed.

Maya wrapped her arm around the giant corgi. "Gotta go give Rusty medicine. See you work tonight?"

Chloe slapped Reyn's hand away from her ass. Then pulled it back, rubbing it on her nipple. She was horny again.

"Chloe?"

Chloe's eyes were already screwing Reyn. "Yeah, yeah. Work, yeah."

Maya stifled a giggle. "Oh shit, Reyn there, huh? You gonna fuck, huh?" She heard Chloe shriek, then go offline.

Maya shivered. *Reyn, seriously? Oh well, I only have dog.*

Maya tickled Rusty behind his ear. "C'mon boy. Don't look at me like that. Mommy pay thousand dollars a month for your medicine. Mommy do anything for you." *Glenn make it so easy to take care of Rusty.* "And he always ask about you, boy. One day you meet him, okay?" Rusty barked twice, then lowered his tail when he saw the syringe.

She kept Rusty's medicine near the plaque Glenn had bought for her. Caleb hated it.

> *Mommy works hard*
> *so she can give her*
> *dog everything*
> *he needs*

Next to the plaque was a chew toy Eddie had brought for Rusty. For a brief second, she thought of Eddie. Sadness flooded her heart. She was surprised by the sudden rush of feeling, like a heroin balloon bursting in her gut: Betrayed. Duped. Abandoned. Belittled. Spit on. Kicked.

She felt a wrenching in her stomach and collapsed.

69

CAN'T WAIT

It was almost quitting time at the non-profit, and Joyce was having a meltdown. "Glenn, I can't let you go next week. The auditors are here. You need to coordinate the audit."

Glenn rubbed his forehead. "Joyce, this is a personal emergency. Do you think I want to go? Danielle knows what she's doing. She knows where all the information is. And even though they're coming next week, I'm meeting with them tomorrow to square things away. I can take care of any issues when I come back."

"No, Glenn. You have to be here, otherwise I have to do it myself. When I did it last year, there were lots of questions I had to field."

They were in the hallway. His hand on his hips, he was smirking. *Right. I already talked to Wes, the lead auditor. He said you created most of the drama last year. Asking questions that didn't make sense, unless you were trying to throw the former CFO under the bus. I guess you did and that's why he left.*

"Joyce, that was last year. This is now. I don't know how you ran audits in years past, but I've run audits before, and I got this under control."

Her face was turning beet red. It was comical. "Glenn, don't make me pull rank on you."

"Go right ahead, Joyce." *This is getting old. Real playground acting.* "I got this. And I'm gone tomorrow after I meet with the audit team. I'll work with Danielle from abroad. Text me next week if you want me to come back or not." Like she did so often, she turned, made that hairball noise, and stomped back down the hall to her office.

Glenn head-butted his door. *Getting tired of this. Danielle's ready to take over. Taught her everything. Even my job. I'm so ready for the next job the Admiral's putting me in next month. Just gotta do this thing for him and help the non-profit through this audit.*

It was a long day. He didn't notice the Instagram notification. She posted a picture. *What is it this time? In the weight room? On a mountain top? At the beach? Maybe another picture of Rusty?*

His blood went cold when he saw a picture of her arm with an IV sticking out of it. It was too soon after being in the hospital with her. She captioned it. *Stomachache. What a pain. Emergency room base hospital sucks.* She'd posted it seven hours ago.

His mind played tricks on him. *She's hurting because she misses Eddie. She tried to kill herself because of Eddie. She's running a sympathy scam to get Eddie back.*

His demons were screaming. *She's doing this because she wants Eddie back. You mean nothing to her.* A bunch of comments followed the posting. Mostly from her bargirl friends, but some idiot customers had the balls to comment how sexy she looked in a hospital bed. *Losers. I gotta get her outta that business.*

He fired off a text. She responded quickly.

What happened. R u ok?

Pain. Stomach. At home now.

Ok praying for you.

Thank you

Lmk you need anything

Thank you

She smiled. Rusty lay at her feet. She never did tell him about her ulcers. Years of drinking and starving wreaked havoc on her insides. The doctor had prescribed bed rest for the rest of the week.

Chloe was at her bedside. "What he say?" Chloe could tell the text was from Glenn.

Maya lifted her phone to Chloe. "Nothing, praying for me."

Chloe gave the phone back. "He religious, huh? Allie said he pray for her at the bar last Christmas. What you going do about that?"

Maya thought back to the last time Glenn and she talked about God and Buddha. "We don't talk about it long time. He ask me what I think of being Christian and I say hard. Go temple with Grandma when I was kid. Family pray Buddha, not his God. He tell me real Buddha, the guy started Buddhism, not believe in being god. I promise one day I check out his God. He keep saying family, culture, temple, God, Jesus, all can co-exist."

Chloe smirked skeptically. "Real holy roller, huh?" Chloe thought back to Glenn's time with Nina at Saigon.

Maya missed the smirk. "Maybe. My sister marrying Christian. Thai wedding then Christian wedding. Caleb not care about ours. We had Thai wedding then judge over here. But sister marrying Christian. I should try . . ." She stopped abruptly, shaking her head. "Me and him, we fix when we get to it."

Chloe cocked her eyebrow.

Maya corrected herself. "I mean *if* we get that far."

Chloe grinned a mouth full of teeth. "Sounds like your heart already there."

Glenn read through the texts again, glad she was okay. He entered the meeting with the Admiral and the rest of the Group leadership with a clear head. This trip had its complexities.

He went to bed confident he could do what the Group wanted, but not so optimistic about Maya's physical condition. He decided not to bother her and let her rest. Images of Eddie by her bedside haunted him.

He woke up and had a text waiting for him from her.

I home today. Resting from the beauty store but going back to the bar tonight. Mama Lynh needs me. Hope you have a good weekend.

I was just thinking about you. Actually I dreamed about you all night. Glad you're better. I wish I could see you one more time before I go so I can see you're okay. Thank you for texting. Not so worried now. Be good to yourself ok? ☺

I will be ok. No worries. Have fun over there ☺ send me pictures.

She read his text and giggled at the sweet talk from him. She felt a glow, or was it a warmth? *Definitely something down there, moist. Not make me feel like this before. He really dream about me? Nice someone worry about me. He sound so real. I always feel like someone cares when I think about him. He said he visiting friends. Never mentioned friends before. Family trip? Take wife? Have a wife?*

———————————

He texted Saturday morning before he got on the plane.

Hope ur doing ok and having a great weekend. If I hit megabucks I'll send a plane back to get you 😍

See you when I get back. Text or call if you need a friend ☺

☺ ☺ ☺ ☺ ☺ ☺ ☺ ☺ ☺ ☺

Thank you have fun over there

Can't wait till you get back

He fixated on her texts. *Can't wait till you get back. This is turning into a real lovefest. Is it still a fantasy? Is it still friends only?*

Three miles away, still in her sleepwear, she held the phone to her heart. *Oh, Glenn. I wish you don't have to go. Come back soon. I wait for you.*

70

SEPTEMBER DEPLOYMENTS

The last Tuesday of September rolled around with Glenn out of town and Caleb about to leave town. She kept her promise to have dinner with Caleb the night before his deployment. Eager to please and impress, Caleb booked a table at the town's priciest restaurant, a five-star renowned for its seafood and steak.

Perched atop the highest hotel in the state, it was a slowly revolving structure with a view of the mountains on one side and the sea on the other, with full rotation taking an hour.

The seacoast was always her favorite view, and he made reservations at 7:00 p.m. so she could watch the autumn sunset over the first round of drinks. She wore his favorite red velvet sleeveless dress with a mid-thigh hem. More than one pair of eyes followed her across the floor to their table.

He was almost leering. "Nice, Maya. You never change. I know all the guys here are checking you out. Some of the girls too." Laughing, she always took his leering as a compliment. The optical shop girls always said there was something wrong with that, but she didn't mind, for some reason. He wore his Navy dress blues, knowing she liked men in uniform. The manager and staff lined up to thank him for his service after they were seated.

She took in the view then turned back to him. "Caleb, you ready?"

He placed his service cap on the seat next to his. "Yup. All packed. I got a full set on the ship. Not much else needed. I'll pick up clothes as we hit the ports. Even then, not much sightseeing. Lots of work to do."

She studied him, her head cocked slightly to one side. *Do you have to bullshit tonight? I know about your second wife in Indonesia. You left computer on last night and fall asleep. She waiting for you, huh? Best of luck, Caleb. I hope you find happiness with her. But for her, I pray Buddha either you change, or she find someone else.*

He set his menu aside. "Maya, you think about us?"

She peered over her menu, "Caleb, after you get back? Let's just enjoy tonight."

He stared at his menu without reading. "Okay, Maya. You know I'd wait for you a thousand years." *Visiting Mai in Indonesia. Pretty happy with her, but if Maya and I could get back to where we were . . . I'd drop the Indo whore in a flash.*

She swallowed. Confusion established a toehold in her heart.

Her purse vibrated unnoticed by Caleb. "I go pee, Caleb." She felt sure who the text was from. It was Tuesday after all.

Happy Tuesday!

Cheers . . . good luck. ☺

So sweet of him to remember.

Stuffed with five-star lobster and steak, they went home after dinner feeling nostalgic over their years together. They had shared so much in the early years, finding common ground in music, and overcoming prejudice on both sides of the ocean. Most important, he understood her culture.

Feeling good, they went straight to his room and made love to her wedding playlist, including "A Thousand Years." She felt it was the least she could do, her wifely duty. She was thankful for the opportunities he'd given her in America. They cuddled afterward, joined by Rusty. Instinctively, she took a picture of the three of them and posted it to her Facebook. She thought her mother would love this, lately complaining there were not enough pictures of her American son on Facebook.

Other pictures on the Facebook site and other Instagram accounts provided cover for INS and ICE to maintain the marriage façade. More importantly, it was to keep appearances up for the folks back home.

The next morning, they were up before the sun. Walking alongside him to the ship, she carried his duffel bag to the gangway. The command staff overlooking the boarding of the ship thought she was the most dedicated wife ever; you didn't usually see the wife carrying the sailor's bag. Caleb took his bag from Maya. "See ya, babe."

Her eyes were puffy behind her shades. "See ya, sailor. Take care." Deployment was never easy.

He pulled her shades down to see her eyes. "FaceTime as usual?"

She leaned back, pushing her shades back up. "Sunday mornings. Of course. Rusty wants to see Daddy."

He gazed intently. "Do you?"

"Yes, Caleb." She lied. Sabai.

He reached down, hugged her, and picked her up. She kissed him. Turned him around and patted his butt and pushed. He looked back with a smile and saluted. She waved, and waited till he was up at the top. Ready to board, he gave one last look behind. She waved again and blew him a kiss. He made like he caught it, kissed his hand, and stuffed into his pocket. Something they always did when he deployed. Then he was gone.

She was deep in thought, walking slowly back to the Audi. *If only it worked out. Maybe we should try again? No, he will not change. Oh, Caleb. Our future was set. Why?* She felt alone. No Eddie. Caleb gone. Glenn away. And not even sure if there was a future with Glenn.

She once heard a TV psychiatrist say life is like being on a beautiful luxury ship cruise, but if you don't have anyone to share it with, it's lonely and not so beautiful. She wondered, *Am I on* Queen Mary *or* Titanic?

It was a long drive home. Rusty was waiting. She crawled into bed and hugged him close. "Oh, Rusty, I only have you. Can't you stay with me forever? The doctor said maybe three more years. Don't go, Rusty. Don't go. I can't live without you." *What did Glenn say? Love conquers all. I hope so.* Her last thought before slumber took over.

71

COME BACK ALREADY

Several thousand miles away in Sin City, Glenn had spent several nights with Tomo in various gentleman's clubs. He was ready to be among people who didn't depend on peddling flesh for a living. They shook hands in the hotel lobby the morning Tomo was to leave.

Tomo slapped Glenn's chest. "Hey, good luck with your newfound friend. She sounds like a keeper. A little confused but a keeper. Judging by the latest texts, sounds like you da man. You sure you don't want me to get some of my intel guys to do a little digging and find out more about her?"

Glenn's face was one of resolve. "Nah, Tomo. I gotta ride or die on this one. Either I believe or not. If she's holding back from me, I want to find out from her. Else I woulda sicced my staff on her."

Tomo nodded his understanding. "Sounds good, Glenn. Till next time, then. Regards to the Admiral."

Glenn gave a half-ass salute. "Safe travels, Tomo. 'High winds' or 'choppy waters,' or whatever you Navy swabs say."

Tomo flashed him the finger. "It's 'fair winds and following seas,' ass wipe." Then with a smirk, he turned and left.

Glenn was left to himself in historic downtown Las Vegas. *Hmmm, one afternoon left before taking the red-eye tonight. Dinner at Main Street sounds good. Haven't been down Fremont Street in ages. Not since Katie and I used to do this every year. Those trips with Mom and Dad were sacred. Best times for me and Katie.*

He ambled down Fremont like a man without a care in the world. *Wow, some of the hotels have changed, even disappeared. But same old crazy-ass street performers. It's three in the afternoon. Great Friday crowd on the street.*

Then he heard something, jerking his head left and back forward. *What's that? Sounds like a cello . . . deep . . . soulful . . . playing . . . can it be? Seriously? "A Thousand Years." I gotta get a video of this. It's up ahead somewhere.*

He whipped out his phone and started recording. And as he walked through the crowd, there was a parting, and he saw an old gentleman straight ahead. A young lady was holding up an iPad. *The cellist doesn't know it by heart. Someone musta requested it. Amazing how you can look up sheet music online.*

He texted the video to her. *I hope you like it, Maya. Hmm. Five minutes. No reply. Maybe too personal. Maybe it didn't even go through.*

Several time zones away, Maya pulled over to the side of the road. She'd watched the video three times. Eyes blurry with tears, she couldn't trust her driving. And her heart hurt like someone had dug into it with two hands and pried the two halves apart. The kind of hurt when you miss someone so much you scream and nothing comes out.

Her hands trembled as she tried to steady them on the steering wheel. *Where these feelings come from?*

She thought back two weeks. They were just good friends, and he was only a good customer. In a world of jerks and assholes, he was someone that didn't belong. A nice guy. A generous man. Full of love—for someone lucky enough to connect.

She wiped her tears with her sleeve. *And we connect somehow. He need someone to care for him, to love him, to be there for him. I saw that. I was that. He was willing to be there for me too. He prove it the other night. He push aside all his needs that night—for me. This all start with him needing me because I lift his spirits. I see him come so strong now. He lift my spirits now. I need him more than he need me.*

She wiped away her makeup. *He likes me for me. For me he find the music. For me he push his way to front. For me he stood there. All this to get the recording for me.*

She was about to start the car but released the key and picked up her phone. *Sweet talk was one thing. Action was another. He not there with family? A wife? Look alone to me. I miss him so much. Ever since Caleb left, he the only one I think of. I miss his patience. His encouraging words. His everything-will-be-okay attitude. Oh, Glenn. Ten days already. I wish Tuesday already. I wish every day was Tuesday.*

Six words. She sent it out on impulse; never said it before.

Come back already I miss you

It was Glenn's turn to stand on the side, and as the Fremont crowd jostled past, his eyes were glued to the text from Maya. *This can't be a fantasy.*

Six words just changed the game for Glenn. Six words just changed the world.

I'm coming for you, Maya. Prophetic words.

PART THREE

72

SMOOTH SILKY SEX

Glenn entered Maya from behind. Her skin was smooth and silky, like the pink satin sheets on her bed. He thrust slowly back and forth, inserting just the tip and pulling out, over and over. He lingered at the mouth of her vagina, lubricating himself with her natural juices. Then he stopped, with just the head penetrating, and savored the moment.

He pushed a little more, moaning, and he felt his eyes roll backward. He felt the warmth, the moistness. He was lost in his own world and lost in her moaning. She pressed her face to her pillow and pushed backward and upward. He felt her positioning, and with one slow thrust, he was in deep. She gasped once and yelped into her pillow, breaking into a groan punctuated by lustful sobbing.

His right arm reached around her and held her, as if to protect her, as if to say, *I got you, I won't hurt you, this is for you.*

He cupped her breast and squeezed and pinched her nipple lightly. She shuddered, and he reached down and teased her button. She came immediately, shaking hard, almost collapsing into the sheets.

He cupped both breasts and kissed the back of her neck, then reached down and rubbed her button again, faster than before. With one hand on her stomach, he reached up with his other hand and grabbed her hair. He gently pulled her head towards his, arching her back, before he released her. Cradling her in both arms, he licked her spine and moved to her neck. Still moving together, she felt it build up.

Then she was on all fours, and with his hands on her hips, he was like a piston, hard, fast and driving. She started breathing faster, heavier, gasping, grabbing at the sheets. With his hot breath blowing on her neck, they moved together like their Latin dance the night before, like their tongues danced each time they kissed goodnight.

He could feel himself getting ready to explode. She whimpered, "Baby, stay with me." Both panting now, she cried out, "Fuck me, Glenn! Fuck me. Fuck me harder!" Her words came out in single syllables. "Fuck. Me. Good. Fast. Hard." With one final thrust, he drove her into the bed as she clutched her pillow and screamed out something so guttural that the sound alone made him come.

His chest heaving, he tried to catch his breath, and suddenly, his crotch felt wet and cold.

"Oh shit, shit, shit, *shit*!"

He laughed. Fully awake. It was a long time since he'd had a wet dream. It was so vivid. He lay there in his own pool. *Aw, shit. I guess laundry day came one day earlier. At least I'm seeing her tonight.*

73

AUTUMN BLISS

It had been several months of Tuesdays since he returned from Vegas. Six words bounced around in his head all the way back on the plane. *Come back already I miss you.* He stared at the text message through two inflight movies, as well as a rerun of *The Big Bang Theory*—an old episode about Leonard's first date with Penny. *I guess the nerd does get the girl sometimes.*

It had been a fun, romantically intoxicating two months. Their Tuesday nights were not like before. They were not a bargirl and her customer. It was just two friends enjoying each other's company. They traded texts during the week. Over the last month, her fondness grew for him.

The same thoughts ran through her head. *He always so positive, so confident things going to be okay. All action, no mouth. All walk, no talk. He not the same as last year. What they say? He back in the game again.*

There was no doubt in their minds, nor any other mind at the bar—Tuesdays were for Glenn, for them. They sang, danced, ate, drank, played cards, sat close, joked, mostly at their booth, and sometimes at the bar when they wanted Tia in on the party.

Each night ended with a quick but not so quick goodnight kiss. Sometimes Glenn leaned in, and sometimes she did. Always outside the bar, away from prying eyes. Most times, it happened when he walked her to her car, and she settled in, and right before he closed the door.

Glenn's reaction was always the same. Her lips were soft, always inviting more, sometimes lingering. And when their tongues did their dance, they lost track of time. Once, she reached down to feel his hardness, happy that he found her so exciting.

Others in the bar swore he had some kind of aura, and it kept getting brighter. Glenn always said it was God.

This Tuesday was an anniversary of sorts—one year since their champagne date. Too bad he was running late. He texted her.

Running late. New job. Briefing Council.
Srry

Take time papa. No rush. I wait. So
proud. You important again.

It had been a long day, with no lunch at a new job that kept him busy, happily busy. *Glad I told Joyce to go screw herself. Tired of her nagging. Insubordination, she called it. Free at last!*

He surveyed his office surroundings. *Two days later I'm the senior policy advisor for the City Council's Vice-chair. Cover by the Group so I can run the Vice-chair's mayoral campaign. The fallen angels want to support Clifford. So be it. The Admiral and I agree. This wasn't only about the mayor's seat. It was about who would run the Group afterwards. Many say it's going to be a bloodbath. It ain't going to be my blood.*

He rushed into the bar, out of breath. It was more crowded than usual, and he saw familiar faces, some old friends by now, he hadn't seen in a while. It was nice to see Mei, Amber and Nicole again. *Wow*, he thought, *Mama must have booked another party in the booth room tonight.*

Both flatscreens were flashing NFL Sunday and Monday football highlights. Jimmy held court in the darts room, peddling football gambling sheets and simultaneously arguing with his bookie over the phone for better odds on the upcoming weekend games.

The jukebox was pulsating '90s dance music, and Allie and Verna and Tia were hustling drinks between the darts room and the booth room.

Maya stood next to Glenn's corner seat, looking like a waitress wiping down the counter area in front of his bar stool.

She saw him jog in out of the corner of her eye and turned. "You late, baby," she teased. "Your food cold. I threw away."

He walked behind the bar and started rummaging through the trash.

She shouted, "Glenn! What you doing?!"

He continued rummaging, with a hint of a smile. "I'm hungry."

She threw a rag at him. "Stupid! Wash hand. Come eat. Your favorite. Pad Thai. Extra chicken. Extra tofu. Extra egg and peanut flakes. *No* vegetables, not even bean sprouts. You know, vegetables make the dish. This only noodles and meat with fish sauce."

"So?"

She playfully shook a fist at him. "So, you such a little boy. You lucky I lov . . ."

His eyebrow arched.

She caught herself. "You lucky I like little boys. You can have your dinner however you want."

She took the whole setup to their booth in the booth room.

He slid in and took a swallow of the beer Verna had waiting for him.

She wore white short shorts with a red halter top. When she ran over to the bar to get some plates and forks, she dropped the napkins and bent over to pick them up. He almost choked on his beer. She heard and came running back. "You okay?" Patting his back.

Still coughing, he managed to clear his lungs. He took her hand. "Um, yeah. Don't get me wrong, but you have an awesome hot ass!" Chloe overheard from two booths away and laughed. "Yeah, she work hard on that."

Maya was proud. No offense taken at all. "Yeah, I work over two years. Want see more?" She scooted in, whipped out her phone gallery and showed him a bunch of bikini pics that reflected all her hard work in the gym. He was quickly aroused. *I didn't need this. Gotta work out more. Can't be washing my sheets all the time.*

She kissed his cheek. "I made you garlic Thai shrimp too." He beamed. *Yes!*

She stuck a shrimp in his mouth. "Hurry up eat, Glenn. Lots to do tonight!" She was feeding him the Pad Thai with one hand and the garlic shrimp with the other. She wiped his mouth with a napkin and poured his beer, handing it to him after. "Almost done," she said. "Wait I be right back."

He took the time to check messages from the Vice-chair about tomorrow's budget meeting.

Suddenly the room went dark, and the first line of the Happy Birthday song pulled him back into the fantasy. *She remembered! My birthday tomorrow!* Maya walked in carrying a cake with two candles—it was the second birthday he'd had with her. Last year it was a slice she'd hurriedly bought from the café next door. This year it was a whole cake.

Except for Lynh, everyone in the bar was singing. Every bargirl hugged him. A couple of them had the night off but had come in just for the occasion. Kimmie walked in as the crowd sang the song's final line.

It was all white noise to Glenn. Like a dream, she was standing before him, singing, cake in her hands, for him, two candles flickering. In that light, she was beautiful. And as she sang, something unexpected.

Happy birthday to you
Happy birthday to you
Happy birthday dear
. . . my love!

He sat in the booth staring back and forth between her and the cake. *Did she say my love? It's a good thing I got it on my phone.* He cracked open the video while she cut and served the cake. He watched it seven times, and seven times he heard *my love*. Something stirred deep in his heart. *Couldn't remember this feeling ever. I thought last year was my best memory. This tops it and then some.*

Everybody got cake, even the barflies. Maya sat by Glenn, radiant, lifting pieces of cake to his mouth. Tia cranked up the karaoke and handed the microphone to Maya. "Glenn, I sing special for you, new song. Everybody quiet! I sing for Glenn. First time I'm singing this song." It was "In Case You Didn't Know" by Brett Young, and Glenn settled back into the booth as she sang.

As the words rolled off her tongue and he took in how she gazed at him, it was apparent that the song was about one person secretly having loved another for a while, and finally finding the courage to admit it.

She dropped the mic, walked over and hugged him. Applause, whoops and general cheering erupted for several minutes. The party was over with the mic drop, and people said their last words and filtered out. Jimmy and Verna were redirecting girls to their waiting customers.

Glenn sat back in the booth, his arm around Maya. "Thank you. That was great." He nuzzled her cheek and breathed in deeply.

She felt a shiver up and down her spine. *What? Was that Thai kiss? Only in the most intimate relationships.* She turned to him.

He looked at her and nodded once, as if to say, *Yes, I know what I did.* "How was that?"

She touched his face. *Was he real?* "Perfect, Mister, just perfect. Thank you." She leaned in, head on his shoulder.

"Glenn?"

"Yes?"

She took two steps to the booth directly behind them and was back. "Not finished yet."

He took another bite of cake. "What?"

She held out a bag with a package inside. "Here. Hope you like. You read card after, okay?"

It was a Coach wallet set for men—a combination wallet, ID holder, and key ring. "Maya, how much did this cost?"

She put her finger to his lips. "Shhh. My money, my present to you, okay?"

He nodded and hugged her. It was bittersweet, though. The tattered wallet he carried had been a gift from Katie on their tenth anniversary. Maya asked if it was okay to set up his new wallet, then gently transferred everything including his mother's crucifix.

She found something in his old wallet and squealed. "Ah! You keep?" It was the souvenir—the napkin with her lip prints from that great summer night. She lifted the new wallet to her cheek and swayed to and fro, like a little girl hugging a baby doll.

Then she put his old wallet into the Coach gift box; she sensed it had sentimental value and wanted to treat it with respect, as if respecting the person that gave it to him. She put the box back into the package and pulled out the card.

She took his hand and slipped the card into his palm. "Glenn, you have to read." She said it as if it was the most precious jewel one could ever give another. To her, it was.

The card was homemade, with a picture of Rusty on the front. Inside it said:

> *Happy Birthday, Glenn*
> *Thank you for everything*
> *you had done for me.*
> *I appreciate and thanks*
> *for always be here for me.*
> *Love Maya*

It was so simple, so straightforward. Every word, every sentence had meaning. And for the first time, she signed it with *Love*. Not friends, thank you, or always. She signed it with *Love*. He knew this was something he'd keep in a special place for a very long time.

He stared at it for a while. She took it from his hand, put it in the envelope, and put the envelope in the package. She knew it was what he wanted. It was exactly what she wanted to say. It was the perfect night for her little boy, her man child. She knew it.

She didn't want to ruin it, but she needed to let him know a few things. "Glenn, we sing now?"

He nodded, still admiring his new wallet.

She touched his forearm. "But I have to tell you something first."

A shadow of concern crossed his face. *Uh oh.*

She searched his face intently as she spoke, to gauge his real reaction. "Don't be mad, Glenn. Cannot help. Remember my father? He hurt himself. Fall off construction site two floors. Break back. Family no money. Need to put in government hospital for surgery."

Maya held her breath. *He going to pout? Get mad? Leave?*

He reached out, his hand lightly on her forearm. "Need money, Maya?"

A wave of relief rippled through her body. "No, we have enough. You help enough already. But I go back Thailand next month. Help take care. Not come back till after new year."

She could tell his gears were moving, making mental calculations.

He couldn't hide his dismay. "That's five Tuesdays, Maya."

Her face said it all—sorry, kill me, hurt me, but don't leave me. "I know Glenn, I know. Sorry, but my father . . ."

It was his turn to put his finger to her lips. "Shhh. No worries. Family first."

She kissed his finger. Searching his face, she thought, *He so different from before. I thought he would get mad. Pout. Like little boy. I can tell his face. He only worried about me. About my father.*

Kreng Jai. Sabai. Good stuff to know, he thought. "Good time to see your family too, huh Maya?"

She answered appreciatively. "Yes. Thank you for understanding."

He focused on a mental calendar in his head. *The politicals are gonna keep me busy so no problem. Either way, not worth stressing.*

Then he caught himself. *Huh? A year ago, I woulda gone ballistic, if not on the outside, on the inside. Crazy Tom would be proud.*

Maya nodded at Verna, who brought out the songbooks and microphones. Just before they started singing, Glenn saw Chloe and Mama arguing in hushed tones by the bar. Then he saw Chloe enter a side room, a private room. Mama followed with a bottle of champagne.

Six songs and several shots later, Chloe came out with a man. He looked rich, but greasy—Glenn had no other way to describe him.

Chloe turned to the man, facing away from Glenn. She laughed and hugged him, putting her arms around his neck. He tried to kiss her, but she turned her head. He grabbed her face and turned her to him and kissed her, hard. She laughed and said, "See you next time," and hugged him again.

He looked over her shoulder, saw Glenn, winked as if they were brothers, and squeezed Chloe's butt hard. Chloe giggled and pushed him away and said again, "See you next time."

When Chloe turned around, her expression had gone from smiling to disgusted. She looked sick, as if she were going to throw up. She walked quickly past Glenn toward the restroom, and another girl followed her with a bottle of water. Mama was with the man, who was handing her a wad of hundred-dollar bills.

All this happened quickly, and Maya saw Glenn taking it all in. She could see the sadness and anger on his face. His fists were clenched. He gritted his teeth, growling, "No one should have to do that."

Maya put her hand to the side of his face. Gently, she turned him to her, eye to eye, and said "Chloe okay. Sometimes must do what you have to do to help the bar."

Glenn whispered, 'You?" and braced himself.

She caressed his face, wanting to soothe his mind. "No, never. One night, customer throw five thousand dollars on the table and I threw it at him and walked out. Mama mad but found another girl. I didn't work for a week after that."

His eyes followed Chloe to the bathroom. Tia walked past with a bottle of water. Still staring at Chloe's direction, he murmured, "You need to go, Maya?"

She pulled his face, his eyes, back to her. "No. She's okay. I take care of her later. Tia know what to do." Maya kissed his forehead. "We still have one more Tuesday before I go. We have fun next week?"

He brightened a bit. "Yup! For sure!"

He was still concerned about Chloe. What he saw both angered and disturbed him. *This can't be happening in this day and age.*

Sadly, Maya knew that was not the case. She tried to explain. "Glenn, got teenage girls back in Thailand, they give sex to sixty-year-old man for iPhone. They don't think bad, no shame. Just want iPhone. Sometimes want money for weekend. Go old man office, blow job. Money for weekend. Freelance hookers. We call sideliners."

Flustered, Glenn slammed his fist down on the table. "This is bullshit. Women should be respected. They are precious gifts from God." He was getting visibly agitated. "I swear, Maya, I'm gonna do something to fix this." He stared again at the restroom where Chloe had gone.

Maya wiped his face with her hand, the way Glenn had told her his mom had done, and tried to calm him. "You wait, okay? I will go check." She ran off to the bathroom, not really for Chloe, but for him, to put him at ease. She knocked and went in.

Tia came out, with a weak smile. "She's okay, Glenn."

Maya followed, with Chloe.

Chloe managed a weak smile at Glenn and slurred, "I'm okay, brudder. No worries."

Chloe's knees looked weak; Maya was half carrying her. Turning to Glenn, Maya said, "Baby, I take Chloe to Uber. Be right back, okay?"

"Despacito" started on the jukebox, and she was back before the song ended. He felt better.

Maya gave him a quick kiss. "Sing now?"

He reached for the Johnny Walker Blue that Jimmy brought earlier. "Yes, time to sing and drink." He looked like he needed it.

She cracked a smile. Good thing she had Ubered.

Later, much later, he walked her out to her Uber. With the driver on the clock, there was no time to get hot and heavy. Leaning on the car, she pulled him to her, kissing him as hard as she could, running her hand through his hair. He thrust his tongue into her mouth, then ran it along her neck.

When he came back to her mouth for more, the driver revved the engine, breaking the spell. Glenn gave Maya one more quick kiss, closed the door, and gave the driver a thumbs-up. She blew a kiss as the car drove off. Apart from the incident with Chloe, it had been a fun birthday.

The Uber driver tried to make small talk, but Maya kept silent, staring out the window, as the lights flashed by on the freeway. She had told Glenn about the trip home, but not everything. Once again, she didn't have the courage to share certain things. *Would he even understand?* she wondered.

74

STRIKE THREE

Maya's weakness for gambling went back many years, and lately she'd gravitated to the Saturday night parties at Thai Garden. But she'd had a run of bad luck and was now trying to pay off her debts by spending time with Luke, the local thug who'd taken Eddie's place organizing the gambling. It had been innocent at first, but now Luke considered her his girl. She spent several nights a week with him, before or after working at the bar. As she stared out the car window, she wondered, *Why does this always happen to me?*

She hadn't given up her Tuesdays with Glenn, though, something Luke wasn't happy with.

So hard to keep life secret from mother and sister. Want to tell them about Caleb but they think he so wonderful. So shame if marriage not going good. Life is shit. Owe Luke so much now.

She scrolled through her phone to the last picture she'd taken of Glenn. *Good thing Tuesdays. My safe place. Funny, long time ago Glenn needed me to feel secure, to feel like life worth it. Now he stronger. What he say? Back in the game. Now I need him. He make my life worth it.*

She leaned back, hugging her phone. *He so positive. Like sun rise every Tuesday. What wrong with me? I need to get back in game too. Always ask him to text when home. Want to know he's okay but want to hear from him one more time too. I look his text every day till Saturday.*

She scrolled to the screenshots of Glenn's Saturday texts. Simple words of encouragement like have a great weekend or stay strong or don't stop believing. *I love Tuesday night text*, she mused, *but I love Saturday morning text more. Always something positive. Something give me hope. Something make me want to do more. Make me believe. If I have jerk customers on Friday, I read his text. I read his text again before Saturday night customers. Friday and Saturday night customers always assholes. Want to touch everything.*

The car came to a stop, the driver announcing, "We're here miss." She said good night to the driver and walked up to the house. She could hear Rusty at the door. She took a last look at her phone. *My heart sing when I see his texts. Feel like sun after storm. Like breathing after drowning. He give my pride, my dignity back to me. He help me refocus my family. I want to be like him. Make the world beautiful, one person at a time.*

She dropped into the couch, and Rusty came running, tail wagging. "Oh Rusty, you would like him." Rusty barked twice, sniffing the scent of the human who made Mommy happy. She patted Rusty's head. "I think so much of him. When I have to keep Luke happy, listen to his stupid jokes, take his macho crap, Glenn get me through. Good thing no more gambling, yeah boy?" Rusty barked his approval.

Now she sent all her money back home, where her sister put whatever was left over in a savings account in Maya's name. Two more weeks and the debt would be paid off.

She watched Rusty play with his chew toy. *Chloe said I need to tell him truth. My sham marriage, Caleb, Luke, gambling problem, Thailand, everything. But he going to know I lie to him all this time. What he do then?* She thought of one customer who had left and never come back.

She opened a cabernet and poured a glass. *If I knew this was going to happen to us from start, I would take chance back then. No, maybe not. No . . . I dunno. It hurts. I want him. So scared to lose him if I explain. So scared to lose him if I don't explain. Hurt to lie all the time. Just want to start over again. With truth. No can. Time machines don't exist.*

She posted a picture to the web before going to sleep.

Back in his apartment, Glenn saw the post. She took the selfie right before she met him that first night. Her lightly colored hair, broad smile, and the flannel shirt she popped off to show him her muscles. But it was the caption that got to him.

> *I wish I could go back in time. This smile will never*
> *be back. New Year please bring me happiness. I've*
> *been hurt enough.*

He studied the picture like it was a court exhibit. *This is so odd. I remember her. I remember the flannel jacket. That was the first night we met. She wants to go back in time. Why? Does she wish she didn't meet me? Why? It was a great night, but this is how she ends it? Did she forget I follow her? Does she want me to see this?*

———————

The next Tuesday, their night started like all the others. The only difference was they knew they wouldn't see each other for five weeks. Except for the barflies, it was a small crowd, with only Tia behind the bar. There was no one in the darts room and only a small group of construction workers in the booth room. It looked like Jimmy or Lynh had called three girls in just for this group. Reggae floated out of the jukebox, and college football highlights played out on the flatscreens.

She wore a bright yellow, off-the-shoulder, open-back cocktail dress. It was a figure hugging stretchy material kind of dress that ended a little above the knees. She brought Pad Thai for him and papaya salad for her. She stuck with water while she ordered his first beer. She poured his beer, asking, "How was your day? You never told me about new job."

No answer. She turned to him. *Uh oh. He got that look. Something bothering. How long already.* "What wrong, Glenn?"

He snapped out of his funk, glancing sideways. "Wrong? Huh?"

She took his chin and swiveled his face to hers. "No huh me Glenn. Your face not joke. Spit it out."

He took his glasses off. "The picture."

She sucked in her cheeks. "What picture?"

He scratched his head, tugging at his hair. "The one on Instagram last week?"

She picked up his glasses, started to clean. *I knew it. I knew he was going to ask.* "Last week? I don't even know what I post yesterday."

Glenn explained, but she barely listened. She needed him to keep talking. She was stalling, trying to buy time, still not knowing what to say. She only remembered he followed her after she posted the picture. She went to delete the image, but his avatar showed up in the first minute. He'd seen it. *I thought he not catch on. The picture so old. But he remembered how I look that night? That's why he good at night job.*

She put his glasses back on him. "I dunno, Glenn . . . that was the night we met? You sure?" She cocked her head like she was thinking. "Maybe. I like the smile. Just being stupid, I guess. Not remember what I was mad about. Maybe I miss you so much after you leave."

He caught the hint. No more interrogation. "Okay, got it."

She wiped his face. *It's okay, Glenn, let it go. He always know when to stop. He push just enough to let me know he know, but then back off, give me space. One day I let him know. Not now.*

She tried for a mood change. She dipped a napkin in her water glass, wet her hand and used her fingers to comb back the part of his hair he'd tugged at. "So you tell me. You don't tell me. How was day other than obsess my old picture?"

He grinned. "Well, it got better as soon as you walked in. How was your week?"

She sucked in her cheeks. *Always you say okay, same thing all the time. I get it. You don't want to talk about you.* "Oh Glenn, so excited. You stalk my old picture but don't say nothing about my citizenship post."

He feigned surprise. "Huh? Instagram musta screwed up. I didn't get that post."

She frowned, then puffed her cheeks. "You don't get off easy, mister! Not post Glenn. It was a story and I saw you saw!" The wonders of Instagram let the story poster know who exactly viewed their story posting.

He poked his temple, with great drama pretending to remember suddenly. "Oh, the test! Okay, I saw."

She whacked his shoulder and decided that wasn't enough. With crablike reflexes, she pinched the fatty fold right under his bicep. *Ooooowwwww!* He sounded like a third grader at recess. Tia and Verna came running and stopped short when they saw Maya had him in the death grip. She was in full mommy mode. "You going keep bullshitting me, mister??!"

He was tearing up. "Noooo! Sorry! Geez, let go."

It was her turn to smirk. "Wow, so much military and martial arts . . . but big wuss when little me pinch you like little girl." Verna rolled her eyes and walked off. Tia chuckled, lingered just a bit longer than Verna, then left too.

Maya let go with a giggle.

He rubbed the sore spot. "That . . . was . . . *not* . . . a little girl pinch." Years of massage gave her a strong grip that allowed her to pinch, then twist.

She swiped his face and playfully wiped away the tears. She pulled his head to her shoulder. "There, there, my little boy . . ." she cooed, patting him on the head." She was half-joking, but to him it felt good and unnatural at the same time.

He pulled away. "Okay. I'm sorry. Can we start again?"

"Yes we can, Mister Glenn."

He was excited, though a little sore. She was excited, and still very amused.

The big news was that Immigration had scheduled her citizenship test for the following month. Still rubbing his sore spot, he bubbled over. "Wow,

Maya, finally! You've been working so hard—I know you got this." He fired off five civics questions from an app on his phone, and she answered in rapid-fire response. "You're good. No more."

She reached for his hand. "You sure? Want to bet, Glenn? Remember card game? Make me chicken feet dinner again?"

He rolled his eyes. "Pass. Sucker bet."

She giggled. She thought back to how hard he'd worked to prep Thai chicken feet after losing that last bet playing cards. Her Thai sisters at the Siam Eastern restaurant still gossiped about him. "Okay, what do?"

He did a funny little dance, like a Teletubby on ecstasy. "Let's just have fun."

She mimicked him. No Teletubby ever looked that sexy. "Sounds *goood*, baby!"

The night progressed as it always did. Laughing and talking over dinner. The other girls called them Mr. and Mrs. Tuesday. Tia dropped in from time to time on the conversation. Mama watched from the back office. Unhappy. She wanted Glenn for herself. She tried to tell Glenn that Maya was no good, too young, too wild and boy crazy.

Glenn had never found Maya to be wild, and since that one night she'd left him alone for the cops, she had always stayed by his side.

Lynh knew this and also knew that Glenn once described that night as "strike two." She was about to set up a fastball for strike three. A former Vietnamese beauty queen, she was a fifty-something woman with a thirty-something body, though she also had the tight-skinned visage of someone who'd had more than one facial tuck.

Nearly as old as Glenn, she had gradually developed a fondness for him. During the first breakup, Glenn would still come to the bar, and it was Lynh who sat with him to "protect him from the other girls till Maya came back."

She liked his casual conversational style, his little-boy humility, and his executive presence honed from years of business and legal battles. He was a little short, but when she ran her hands around his shoulders and chest, she felt a sensation she experienced only a few times a month, and she liked it.

The group of thirty-to-forty-year-old guys in the booth room numbered five or six, depending on who was outside grabbing a smoke. They looked like construction workers—solidly built, tanned and looking to blow off steam. They were getting slowly primed, and Lynh had sent the three girls in to keep them occupied, happy and drinking.

Maya knew the group was there, and even knew a couple of the guys, but focused her attention on Glenn. It was easy if she didn't drink too much, and the bar made sure she kept getting what they called "lady pours"—virtually water or tea with an eyedrop of the real stuff. She didn't mind. A clear head allowed her to enjoy being with Glenn more and have something to remember the rest of the week.

Now Lynh sent Verna to pull back one of the girls. Verna brought back a drink order as well. When they were short-staffed like tonight, Lynh usually carried the drink orders in herself or had Verna do it. Casually, she walked over to Maya. "Honey, do mommy favor and take this to those boys, then come back right away for Glenn." Maya paused, glancing at Glenn. Glenn had heard "right away" and nodded. Faked a smile.

Maya took the drink order in, and when the guys got their shots, there was one shot glass left on the tray—hers. It was customary for the server to have a shot. They all clinked, and everyone went bottoms up. Maya immediately felt the warmth course through her body. It was Crown. It felt good. *But how come not lady pour shot? Someone at the bar got it wrong. New barback. Need to talk to her.*

The alcohol had its effect. Maya thought a couple of the boys were cute. All of them were looking her up and down. "Hey, aren't you the singer? Sing us a song, and we'll buy another round." Maya looked around for Verna. "I'll be right back."

Glenn saw her come back and brightened up, but from behind the bar Lynh asked Maya to take in one more tray of drinks. Glenn heard this and nodded, but this time no fake smile, only a concerned look. She walked over and kissed him on the cheek and said, "I be right back. Here, drink."

Pouring his beer, she looked at her empty shot glass in the middle of the tray and yelled out, "Mama, lady pour this time okay? Last time not!"

He drank down his beer, then stared into his empty glass. *Please come back, Maya, and pour me a beer.* He looked to see where Maya was.

One of the guys had his arm around Maya, and it looked like they were trading phone numbers. He could hear him asking loudly whether her phone display showed a Florida area code? She was giggling a bit now. Glenn could tell she was feeling the booze. She started walking away from the guy. Glenn felt relieved, thinking *that wasn't that long.* But then trouble.

The guy called out "Hey, can I get a picture?" She turned and seductively posed for a half dozen clicks. In the last pose, she bent over low, and Glenn could imagine the cleavage shot the guy got. Then she walked over and took a selfie with the guy and, at the last minute, planted a lingering kiss on his cheek. The guy turned to get more, but she pushed him away playfully. She walked back to the bar, and the guy followed. His eye caught Glenn's for a split second and he made a beeline to the restroom.

Glenn wanted to follow him in there for a private conversation when Maya walked over and asked for a shot. Then she was gone again. Lynh asked Maya to take another round of drinks to the boys. This time Maya avoided looking at Glenn. *Shit*, Glenn thought, *not again.*

Maya went back, and this time the guys surrounded her. As soon as she downed her drink, the real thing again, one of the guys refilled her shot glass from his own. She didn't flinch, and then another guy refilled her glass. Not wanting to be rude, she downed it and said she had to go. Lynh came over. "Maya, honey, can you stay with these studs five more minutes. Other girls take quick break. I ask Glenn, he say okay."

Meanwhile, Glenn was wondering what was going on. He swiveled his barstool around so she could see he was watching, concerned. She saw him sitting there, watching, and thought this meant, maybe drunkenly, that it was okay. After all, that's what Lynh had said.

Verna brought another round for the guys and a shot for Maya. A rap song came over the system, and two of the guys started beating it out. She started dancing to the beat, first with one guy, then another, and another. After all, she thought, it was her job to entertain till the other girls came back. Lynh had already deployed these other girls into the darts room. Maya was alone in this. Every time she twirled around, she made eye contact with Glenn and blew him a kiss.

Two rap songs later, she was still dancing and no longer blowing kisses at Glenn. The guys were getting touchy. She deftly fended them off. "Hotel California" came on, and she did a solo, surrounded by them, cheering. It was the cops all over again. She was swooning, taking it all in.

Lynh came by Glenn. Glenn asked if he should leave. Lynh leaned on him, her hand dropping between his legs. "No, honey. Almost over. Other girls coming back. But honey, you need to know, this is her, the other nights you not here, this is her."

Glenn swiveled his chair back around, almost breaking Lynh's wrist between his thighs. *Shit on this, I'm leaving.*

Then he heard Maya's voice over the karaoke system. "I sing this song for you." The first notes of their Elvis song came out. *I guess she feels bad. She's going to serenade me. Kinda hokey, but I'll take it.*

He swiveled back to her. *What the fuck?* Her back was still turned to him, and she was swaying in front of the whole group of guys. Then he heard, "This song is for you guys!" Plural—them, not him. His gut turned inside out. Our *song, my ass.*

She was on a high. Five Crowns in ten minutes had her flying. All these guys cheering her on, adoring her, giving her the affection she craved.

All the loneliness of childhood she carried, welled up inside her, somehow dissipated with the warm feeling she always got from performing like this.

This was the curse on most girls like Maya. He remembered what Tia had said: *I've seen it over and over. Whenever she downs enough Crown, something primal kicks in. Like an addict to crack, she craves it.*

Unmet needs—attention, appreciation, affection—encouraged girls like Maya to make all the wrong decisions. Add alcohol, and all control is lost. Some dance for others, some get pregnant. Maya had lost other good customers like this before, and she was on her way to losing another.

One guy took her hand and did a slow dance. She didn't know he was behind her until she felt his clasped hands on her tummy somewhere south of her belly button. He was pressed up against her back. She took his hand and inched it up near her chest. The man thought he was going to get lucky. At the last second, she twirled out of his embrace, a bargirl trick.

Glenn's fists clenched as he grit his teeth. He couldn't move. It was like seeing a bad accident happen and not being able to avert his eyes. It was like seeing his mother die all over again. Abandoned. Alone.

She was halfway through the song, and as she twirled, she stopped cold, looking in Glenn's direction. It was as if she suddenly remembered he was there, sucked back into the reality of their fantasy. For a brief second, she stopped singing.

She saw Glenn, sitting, staring, her little boy—hurt. His face was stoic, but she'd known him long enough. It was as if something snapped in her. This time her heart wrenched along with her gut. The alcohol was no longer there. She wanted to run to him like a mother to her child. The guy tried to embrace her again. This time she pushed his hand away gently, but with a message. And she took two steps forward to Glenn and started singing again. The look on her face said it all. *I'm sorry, baby. I'm coming, baby.*

Glenn saw her coming toward him. He was breathing heavily. He saw it in her eyes. *I'm sorry, baby. I'm coming, baby.* His fists unclenched. No thoughts of his mother. Only memories, good memories, of him and Maya these past few months. He wanted to run to her but sat glued to his seat.

The group somehow got the message; something was going on here. Most of them headed back to their table for more booze. Two still stood there in disbelief. Now she was singing this song to that old guy, walking toward him, like a cliché scene in an old movie.

She was two steps away and reached out. She felt Glenn's hand in hers and choked up singing the next line about giving her whole life to him. Gripping tightly, they stared into each other's eyes, professing in song what they couldn't yet say—that they couldn't help falling in love with one another.

They sang the rest of the song. The spell was broken. No strike three here. Love conquered her demon, her unmet need. She leaned over and kissed him, a long kiss, the tips of their tongues gently touching in front of all to see. He swiveled back to the bar, and she stood by him, leaning into him, half sitting on his seat, his arm around her waist.

She dropped the mic on the bar. Someone had set her up. Someone was in trouble. She poured his beer. "Drink, Glenn. I'm here now." She put her head on his shoulder. He didn't hear it, but she mouthed, "I love you." She didn't see it, but he mouthed the same three words.

75

HOLIDAY BLUR

They closed down the bar that night. Nerves were scraped raw, but disaster had been averted, and healing set in. After Jimmy locked the doors, they sat outside on an old couch Jimmy kept outside for smokers. More than one couple used it after hours for activities other than smoking.

It was nearly 2:30 a.m., with just the two of them on a couch in an empty parking lot, talking, not wanting the night to end because she was off to Thailand for five weeks. She took his hand. "You going miss me?"

"Yes."

She held up her phone. "We can FaceTime. I drink on my side, and you wire me money?" She managed a smile. "Text me, okay? Be good boy?"

He mirrored her smile, thinking, *She's still worried I'm like the other guy. That I'm not gonna be here when she gets back.*

He rubbed his face, suppressing a yawn. *The holiday season right around the corner. She's going to be with her family. And me . . . well, yeah, there's much work to do on the campaign.*

She caressed his cheek, then leaned in and nuzzled his neck. His hand traced the small of her back. She took his other hand and placed it on her breast. She wanted to make sure he remembered her. It was soft and ample like he dreamed. He felt her nipple harden between his fingers. Breathing heavy, her voice husky, she said, "Gimme kiss, Glenn."

Their tongues danced torridly. At one point, she popped her breast out of her dress and pushed his head down. He drank greedily, her head leaning back, eyes fluttering. A few minutes later, she pushed his hand down between her legs. Lust and morals were waging war in his soul. He was weakening and threw up a prayer. *Help me, God, and if not, forgive me, because I'm taking her home.*

Out of the blue, a security guard came by to shoo them away, off the premises. He shined his flashlight, more like a searchlight, on them. "Ya acting like high school kids! Thar's a hotel down a ways. Get a room, why don't ya?" Glenn studied the guy. *Is he from this place, or this planet? Who talks like that, like some Norwegian whaler out of* Moby-Dick?

Even in the softened light of the streetlamp twenty yards away, you could tell she was blushing. She put her hand to his face. "Text me, okay?" With a quick kiss, she got in her car and was gone. He didn't drive that night, having decided to walk home. If she knew, she'd panic. It was supposed to be a bad neighborhood. He never had any trouble. Always told her he parked around the corner.

The next day Glenn was sitting in his new office, a real office, eight times the size of his broom closet at the non-profit, complete with a conference table on one side, and a sofa and coffee table on the other, and his ten-foot long oak desk in the middle. The desk dwarfed his laptop and phone system and provided seating for four in front.

Outside his secretary, Debbie, acted as gatekeeper. The walls were bare except for his law school diploma, a flatscreen and a large whiteboard. Senior policy advisor to the Council Vice-chair by day, and his campaign manager by night. And though unsaid, but always understood—chief change agent for the Group.

He stared at the brass plate on his desk with his title. *Might as well change it to Chief Lovesick Fool. It's been only a day and I miss her already. I thought the first five months we knew each other were fast. But the last five weeks together were exponentially faster.*

He took up the remote and turned on the flatscreen on the wall opposite his desk. *Okay. She said this is all fantasy. She explained it a couple times. But I feel so—loved! Little things, like cleaning my glasses. Big things, like cooking for me. I get the no sex. Maybe even the no dates, nothing on the outside, everything at the bar philosophy. Okay, that means I'm only a customer. That's all, a customer.*

Like he did at home, he channel surfed, stopping at the closed circuit link to a council committee meeting in progress. *But what was that last night? What was that slow walk back to me? And there's a lot more head on shoulders and kisses than I imagine friends to have. And what about the way last night ended?*

He put his fingers to his lips. *They're still tingling from so much contact.*

He ran his tongue across his lips. *Still raw. Damn, the way she ran her tongue up and down my neck, doing circles around my tongue. And her nipple in my mouth. But I guess we were sitting outside of the bar, so it counts as happening at the bar. But still only a just-friends fantasy? This can't be a fantasy. Okay, maybe last night was physical. But the hearts and emojis in her texts?*

He felt his crotch tighten and got up to pace the room, hoping he could calm down. He thought about all her sentiments over the last few weeks:

When he was in Vegas:
Come back already I miss you

When she'd sung Happy Birthday to him:
Happy Birthday dear . . . my love

The way she'd signed his birthday card:
Love Maya

And the Brett Young song she'd sung—"In Case
You Didn't Know"—admitting her love for him

He plopped into his executive high-back chair and did a 360-degree swivel. *Is this still just a fantasy? Still friends? Do I continue to shield my heart? Tell myself it's all Disneyland. Enjoy Tuesday nights like some apple pie dessert, but go back to life's meat and potatoes the rest of the week?*

He turned off the flatscreen and opened a file on his desk. *Or do I risk asking again and get blown out of the water with her "I told you it was a fantasy" talk. Maybe not. Is this why Darren or the other guy left her? Did it get to the point of wanting reality and not fantasy, and she couldn't deliver? I have five weeks to think this out.*

He was startled out of his thoughts by his door flying open. Debbie walked in, and without saying a word, grabbed the remote and turned on the flatscreen. Clifford was on TV. His press conference was just starting.

"Thank you for coming," he intoned. "I'm speaking today on behalf of the mayor, to announce the administration's response to the City Council Vice-chair's new position on homelessness. We believe this measure to be fool's gold. It calls for a return to building more homes at considerably lower prices by flooding the market. This approach has proven dangerous in the past and has extremely damaging ramifications in many other sectors, including public safety. Only a fool would devise such a plan, and a greater fool would go along with it. To be truly effective, a leader cannot be a one-issue horse. One must consider how any plan would affect all sectors of city operations."

Glenn absorbed the performance, hands steepled in front of him. *Right, Clifford, you have no choice but to say this—considering it was a policy quashed by you and reluctantly by the mayor, when special interests like developers and powerful property owners fought the mayor's desire to introduce it.*

The Vice-chair was outraged that a plan so successful in other big cities failed to see a hint of daylight locally. Clifford said the plan was inept—a backhanded swipe at Glenn and at his opposition candidate. The war was on.

In the back of his mind, Glenn heard Maya: *Take this asshole down. You can do it. I believe in you. I got your back.*

He raked his hair and pinched the bridge of his nose. *I wish you were here, Maya. I wish I knew I was gonna see you next Tuesday, but it'll be another five Tuesdays before I see you again.*

He was lonely. He missed her. He longed for her. Turning back to the flatscreen, he glared at the smug, condescending look on Clifford's face. He furrowed his brow and willed himself to focus. Shaking off whatever was going on with Maya, he compartmentalized and stepped back into this reality bubble. The fantasy bubble would have to wait. Time to go to work.

He picked up his phone. "Mike, can you come in here?"

Glenn's power was that he knew everything about anything. He had his fingers on the pulse of every bit of intel in town that could sway votes to his candidate. Part of it was his solid team of intel experts, a team led by his old friend Mike, who had been with him through twenty major campaigns—for Congress, governor, mayor and one small state House race. Mike also doubled as the public relations and legislative lead for the Vice-chair. They were a package deal.

Glenn started as soon as his right-hand man dropped his six-foot five-inch, 420-pound frame onto the couch. When he stretched out, it made the couch look like a large easy chair. A former college football and basketball player, Mike had met Glenn in their school's weight room. Apart from Brad, he was Glenn's best friend; both Mike and Brad had been in Glenn's wedding party.

Glenn leaned forward onto his desk. "Did you see the press conference? Got our work cut out for us, Mike."

Mike shook his head. "You mean that?" he scoffed. "No traction, boss."

Glenn lifted his index finger to make a point. "Today yes, tomorrow I don't know, Mike. And I don't mean simply countering what the mayor's jester clowned around with today. I mean getting this initiative passed. The Group has the federal funding ready to go, but it has to look like there's local backing. Besides the Vice-chair, we need four more votes to get this plan passed—five to prevent a veto."

Mike counted to himself: *Mayor's got his three cronies. The Vice-chair and our two friends make three. That leaves the chair and the two crazy independents.* "Yup. Your call, boss."

Glenn got up and stepped over to the whiteboard that covered an entire wall of his office. Mike could feel his adrenaline surge. They were about to scrum with the deputy mayor. Glenn looked back at Mike. "This thing goes to full Council in five weeks. Let's see what we can do. Anything we need outside this city, let me know and I'll work it out."

Mike tapped the arm on his chair. "The Admiral?"

"Yeah, the Admiral is with us. After all, it's the last bit of his legacy."

Mike had to ask, "You sure not yours?"

Glenn shrugged. "Not sure. But does it matter? Helping the people is everybody's legacy."

Mike nodded. *Always for the people. That's why I'd take a bullet for this guy any day.*

It was a long five weeks. Glenn missed all the celebrations during the holidays, putting everything into the win. Amidst so many policy issues, he and Mike spent countless hours cultivating the three additional votes needed to pass without veto, including the council chair. They spent even more time working the landowners and developers.

Very influential, powerful and rich interests in and out of the state and county had profit margins tied to the housing development market. Millions were about to be lost over the next five years.

It came down to Glenn's textbook speech at a single meeting that Mike and Glenn called with the seventeen power brokers.

> *Folks, we have five votes. The two swing votes term*
> *out and don't need your money for a re-election*
> *that's not going to happen. The remaining three*
> *votes, including the Vice-chair, have never been on*
> *your happy list so we don't give a fuck if we piss you*
> *off. Maybe you should have considered playing ball*
> *with our team, and then maybe this plan wouldn't*
> *have been so hard on your wallets.*

He let the numbers sink in around the room.

> *Maybe we would have entertained a softer plan that*
> *would allow you to line those wallets, only not as*
> *much as the rape-and-pillage plan you had going*
> *with the executive branch. Please note that now that*
> *we have a voting bloc, we will decimate every plan*
> *the administration puts forth that even smells like*
> *you profiting and someone else going homeless.*

The private-schooled individuals had no idea that the person in front of them had spent a summer homeless on the beach.

> *You might be depending on the mayor's veto power,*
> *but that doesn't always pan out. Here's the deal.*
> *The chair is up for reelection. Back off on him this*
> *one time and let him vote yea to prevent a veto.*
> *We'll mark up the plan right now to provide for*
> *exceptions allowing a certain percentage of market*
> *priced homes that will provide you a competitive*
> *return, so long as those market priced homes are*
> *owner-occupied. Else, expect a very long fight*
> *on this and every other project you have in your*
> *current portfolio.*

He held up a large black binder marked BUDGET on the spine.

> *If you don't believe me, review the draft budget that*
> *came out this morning, and then read tomorrow's*
> *headlines about how, in a very crazy and irrational*
> *move, the Council majority gutted the planning and*
> *permitting department in favor of road repair and*
> *safety projects. This will garner public approval,*
> *but at the cost of permit processing that could*
> *delay your projects for several years. And tick-tock,*
> *folks—every day means more money pissed down*
> *the sewer for you all.*

Glenn had personally worked the numbers. The bags under his eyes showed it, and he was not in a diplomatic mood. There was hate in the eyes of everyone across the table, but in Mike's only wonderment. *Damn,* Mike thought, *best show yet this year.*

*My friend Mike and I are going to take a piss now.
While we're out of the room, consider this: There
are seventeen of you here. You are the mafiosos who
represent the developers bloc. We know you make
the decisions, and you can make them right here,
right now. The mayor and the deputy mayor are in
their offices. Feel free to run crying to them.*

He surveyed the room, deciding it was time to bring it home.

*If the chair feels inclined to vote with the minority,
the budget will pass as is. If the chair votes with us,
the Vice-chair will offer a friendly amendment on
the floor giving the Department of Permitting and
Planning back half its budget—for this year, enough
to keep your projects on track. When Mike and I
return, we expect to know whether we have a deal.
If you're still here, we'll take that as a good sign. If
you're not, you can prepare for a long winter.*

76

NEW YEAR VICTORY

At the first meeting of the new year, the Council voted 6-3 in favor of the plan. No veto possible. Later that night, Glenn and Mike headed to BJ's across the street to celebrate their victory. It was the first Tuesday night of the new year. Mike slid Glenn a longneck. "Hey, don't you have plans tonight?"

Glenn leaned back, recalling that Mike met Maya once and knew about the Tuesday nights. Like a cheap movie flashback, the night Mike met Maya rolled through his head.

Mike and Glenn needed to talk business and decided to meet at the bar—early, before any of the girls showed. They were still at it when Maya walked in. She hesitated, but Glenn waved her over. "Come meet my friend."

Mike looked up and saw someone his daughter's age.

"Hello." She put out her hand. "You hungry?" she asked Mike. She turned to Glenn, "You talk, I bring back food for all of us. In the car. I picked up." She surveyed the space in front of Mike. "Nothing to drink? How come no one help you? You talk business. Iced tea okay?" She hurried off.

In those few short minutes, she had Mike at ease very quickly. Mike gave a low whistle. "So this is where you disappear to on your off nights? Does Brad know? Does the family?"

"No, and I'd like you to keep it that way, Mike."

"Yeah, no problem. We're finished here anywa—ooof!"

She slid right into Mike, pushing him deeper into the booth. Mike's jaw dropped at such a small person moving him so easily. Glenn wasn't that surprised, knowing how her fitness program packed power into her petite frame.

Verna followed with iced tea and a package. By the smell, it was Thai curry. Maya looked disapprovingly at Glenn, then Mike. "You not finished yet. Eat, then talk business." She looked at Glenn. Not sure how much Mike should know about them. Her eyes asked, *act like nothing and just disappear?*

Glenn chuckled. "No worries, Maya. He's my best buddy. We do the night job together. Mike, this is Maya. Maya, this is Mike. And we're done talking business."

Her face beamed with pride. *He introduce me his family finally.* "Oh, okay. Hello." She moved around the table and sat next to Glenn.

Mike made a move to leave. His stomach growled.

She asked Glenn, "You feed him?"

Glenn licked his lips, his own stomach growling. "No. Why?"

She pointed a finger at Glenn, then at Mike. "You talk business. Not on empty stomach." *Grandpa always feed his people.*

Glenn tried to explain that Mike worked for him. "But—"

"No, no excuse." She turned to Mike. "Sit. Five minutes. Eat." She put a generous serving of sticky rice and panang curry on a plate and pushed it over to Mike. "Sorry I didn't cook. I pick up. Good thing I eat already so plenty enough." She was talking loud enough to cover the sound of her own stomach growling. She took a bit off Glenn's plate and ate. "Ummm. Just right." Satisfying her own hunger, at least for a bit. "You eat now, Glenn."

Glenn knew she was hungry. They were supposed to eat together, and she'd only brought enough for two. "I'm sorry, Maya but I ate lunch at Teddy's Big Burgers with a client. Couldn't help. Ate late, still full. Help me eat?" She remembered the optic shop and how they always made sure she ate. She remembered kind hearts, like Glenn. She also understood what Glenn was doing and smiled humbly. "Just a little please, Glenn."

Mike took it all in. He hadn't seen Glenn this happy since the tragedy. He saw the chemistry, and the kabuki show between Glenn and Maya. The threesome talked a bit. Both Mike and Maya had corgis at home, and both traded Instagram accounts because of that.

Glenn pointed at Mike. "You have a corgi?"

Mike fired back defensively. "Yeah, what's wrong with that?"

Glenn lifted his hands. "No, just didn't know. Figured you as more like a pit bull guy."

Mike drummed the table, inching his hand closer to the spoon she laid out. "You never asked. And corgis are just as fierce as pit bulls." He grabbed the spoon and dug in. The food was gone in seconds.

While Mike ate, Maya jumped in. "He your friend and not know about corgi?"

Glenn shrugged. "Yeah, only talk work, I guess."

She was scolding now. "Only talk work not good."

Mike liked her. He thought Maya was the same as someone else he knew and was pleased with the way the twosome clicked.

Glenn cut into Mike's thoughts. "Don't you have to be someplace?"

Maya again scolded, like they were at a dinner party and Mike, the guest. "Glenn, don't be rude."

Mike had seen enough. He was genuinely happy for his boss and friend. "No, he's not, Maya. Pleasure to meet you." He meant what he said when he said it was a pleasure to meet her, and never brought it up again, till now.

Mike flicked a peanut at Glenn, summoning his boss back out of his memories. They sat at their favorite booth at BJ's. Mike took a swig of beer. "It's Tuesday. What are you doing here?"

Glenn drained his mug in one try. "She's in Thailand."

"Really?"

Glenn flicked a balled-up napkin at his friend. "Whaddya mean, really? That's where she's from."

Mike flicked the napkin ball back. "I just figured she wouldn't want to leave her honeybunch, is all."

Glenn smirked. "Who says 'honeybunch' anymore?"

Mike poked his thumb into his chest. "I just did."

Glenn sighed. "She comes back tomorrow. But I have to wait till next Tuesday to see her."

Mike couldn't resist the urge to pry since they were on the subject. "So how're things going? Still enjoying the fantasy ride?"

Glenn stared into his mug. "Not really."

Mike did a double-take. "What?"

The waitress brought onion rings and a pitcher of beer. Glenn continued. "As a fantasy it's okay. She's a lot of fun. And if you don't overthink it, it's enough to get you by. But as soon as you want more . . . it's kinda hard right now. She's throwing out a lot of signals."

Mike filled both their mugs. "Well isn't that their job? Throw out the signals, keep you in the game?" He lifted his mug.

Glenn lifted his mug. "Yeah, but telling me she misses me. Love. All that stuff. She could be more subtle and not lead me on."

Mike took a jab at his boss. "But why take a chance? Handsome guy like you might bolt to another chick anytime."

Glenn retorted. "But I wouldn't."

Mike was a little disappointed. He wanted to irk his boss a little. "Yeah, but she don't know that. And sounds like she's been burned a few times, so why wouldn't she chum the water between your visits to keep your blood hot."

Glenn reached for the onion rings. "I don't know. You be the judge."

Mike drained his mug, anticipated that this would be a long night, and signaled for another pitcher.

Glenn showed Mike the texts for the past few weeks. The last one was especially sentimental. "This was the day after she left."

Have a good weekend

You too

Was nice to see you by video

I MISS YOU!!!!

Have a good night ☺

"This was the second week."

Hoping your trip everything you wanted it to be

> Awww thank you so much my mom was so happy and I so happy too. Thank you my trips will never be complete without you 💕

"And last week."

> I didn't think I would miss you this much, but I do. I didn't go to the bar last night because its not the same without you. Cant wait to see you again. Be good to yourself ok?

> I miss you too

> Almost done here

> Its gonna get better for us

> Are we gonna get rich together? ☺

You bet ☺

Glenn filled Mike's mug. "So what do you think? Just a show?"

Mike took Glenn's phone and scrolled through the texts a second time. "Just a show? Maybe. Kinda sentimental on your part that long whine last week about missing her."

Glenn nodded. "Yeah, I had a beer before working out and I was sitting in the parking lot thinking of her."

Mike got analytical. It was like they were assessing a piece of legislation. "The first night she tells you she misses you."

Glenn took his phone back and scrolled the texts again. "Yeah, kinda fake right?"

Mike made sucking sounds, his way of thinking. "No, I don't think so.

When you left Katie behind to go on trips, when was it hardest?"

Glenn thought back. "You know, it was the plane ride. As soon as I took off, I missed her."

"Yup," Mike concluded, "so, looks genuine. Her first day there she misses you and she comes right out with that cartoon girl crying and all. If all this is fake, she's some kinda dedicated bargirl and/or you must be something special. I don't think the money you put down is worth this treatment except . . ."

Mike's voice trailed off. He wanted to be careful about what he said next.

Glenn pressed. "Except what?"

Mike laid it out. "Maybe she thinks you want more and might go look for it, and since she won't give it up, that she has to do stuff like this to keep her top of your mind?"

Glenn raked his hair. "I dunno. That's what I'm asking you."

Mike arched his eyebrows. "Asking me what?"

Glenn lifted his mug. "What's going on? Is she for real? Are we actually an us?"

Mike punched his mug against Glenn's and chugged his beer. "Dude, *you* have to ask her that, you know. No matter what I say. It's what *she* says."

The beer was influencing Glenn. "Yeah. I think she's married, or she has a boyfriend or both."

Mike lifted his mug, then put it down. "What? Come again?"

Glenn took a swig. "Let me lay it out like a lawyer."

Mike feigned a yawn and stretched his arms, as if all lawyers were overpaid bores.

Glenn pointed at Mike. "C'mon man. You want to listen or not?"

Mike waved his hand as if shooing away a fly. "Yes, proceed, counsel."

Glenn took a deep breath. "Okay, first she tells me she lives on base with her cousin and her cousin's husband who's in the Navy. You and I both know only spouses and dependents can live on base, and cousins are not dependents. The only exception is a waiver from the base commander.

"Second, she says she is technically married but they're separated, waiting to divorce. But she's going through with citizenship. Those INS guys are sharp, if this was a sham marriage, they would have sniffed it out.

"Third, she's always jumbling up her words. Sometimes it's my cousin did this or I did this with my cousin's husband, and then sometimes it's my husband this or my husband that. Sometimes she catches herself and does the 'I mean my cousin/cousin's husband' thing.

"Fourth, she's going for her citizenship soon. How does she do that without proving cohabitation? He could not have been on constant deployment for three straight years?"

Mike held up his hand. A lot of information was getting dumped on him. His eyes rolled up as he tried to process the arguments. "Okay, go on."

Glenn finished his beer and called for another pitcher. "Does not add up. I asked her about it, and she gives me this thing about the marriage started out okay, but he beat on her three years ago. So she moved here with her cousin and cousin's husband, and her ex left for Germany. They remained technically married so she can retain medical benefits, obtain citizenship, and get half his pension. What swabbie gives up half his pension? I asked and she said it was in exchange for not throwing him under the bus for wife abuse."

The waitress brought their beer. Glenn asked for chicken wings and fries. "I can buy all this except the living on base with a cousin that I've never met. Weird, in the beginning, she showed me pictures of this girl in Instagram and said that was her cousin. A year later I meet that girl but it's a friend she goes to temple with, and she says her cousin is camera shy so there are no pictures. Clear inconsistency here."

Glenn leaned back. The place started to spin. "So, what do you think?"

Mike wanted to help, but it sounded like some bad teen movie. "I dunno. Hard. You've already asked her, and if you press she'll think you don't believe her."

The wings and fries came. It was that time where you drink enough beer, and you want something greasy going down your gullet. They ate in silence, concentrating on getting as much food into their stomachs as possible.

Mike blinked first. "Tell me, man. Any thoughts of Katie while all this is going on? If too personal, let me know and I'll shut up."

Glenn waved his hand as if to say it was okay. "I do think of Katie, but lately I've been thinking it might be best to move on. I haven't given up hope, but it doesn't look promising. She's in another world now."

Mike was sympathetic. "Yeah, I hear you, man."

Glenn knocked back the last of his beer. "Well, Maya's back tomorrow. I don't get to see her for another week but at least she'll be back."

Mike took another wing. "You going to see her tomorrow?"

Glenn wiped his mouth. "Nah, don't want to intrude on some other guy's time with her, you know? Kinda like bothering her at work. They don't bother us on Tuesday, and I don't bother them on the other days."

Mike picked at the last chicken wing. "You sure she has a regular the other days?"

Glenn rubbed his chin. "I know for sure Wednesday. I don't know what's going on the other days."

Something occurred to Mike. "Hey Glenn, you don't truly know anything about this girl except for Tuesday, huh?"

"Yeah, I guess so."

Mike was in interrogation mode. "And nothing outside of the bar?"

"Just a welcome back dinner once at Ruth's Chris."

Mike was suddenly concerned about his friend. "Then tread lightly, man. Tread lightly. One outing's not enough. It might just be a fantasy—a good one. Don't make it your world. Not yet, anyway. If she don't do things with you outside of the bar, it's a bar thing. Some girls, they go on dates outside the norm, and some even travel. This one, not sure. You don't even know if she's jetting off to Morocco on Wednesday and coming back on Monday or Tuesday afternoon even. My point—you don't know her well enough to call it real."

Glenn could have sworn he heard a gavel banging down on the last point. They called it a night. As they walked out the door, Mike slurred, "Hey Glenn, you want to walk me to my car and kiss me goodnight?"

Glenn gave him the one-finger salute. "Fuck you, ass."

They high fived and went their separate ways.

The alcohol numbed what Mike had said. Somewhere in the back of his head, Glenn was thinking. *Everything at the bar. Just friends. Just fantasy. At the bar.*

77

INCONSISTENCIES

Driving home, Mike was mildly happy for Glenn but also wondering about this relationship. In his mind, Maya did seem to be going off the deep end. He knew girls who carried multiple relationships and expertly kept their worlds separate. Just watch any season of *90 Day Fiancé*. It took a lot of work, understanding what buttons to push, and multiple phone lines.

But he was still Glenn's wingman, and his life mission was to protect his friend. Glenn didn't ask, but Mike did some background checking over the next few days.

Mike wasn't looking forward to telling Glenn what he found. Social media sites were easy to crack, and given bits and pieces of information, other information could be searched and found online.

Maya had an Instagram page that showed her to be single, a party girl, with a dog, and both day and night jobs. Maya gave access to her Instagram page to many bar patrons and other bargirls. This was no big bit of news to Glenn, since she gave him follower rights too.

In fact, she had given Mike follower rights the first time they met, so they could trade corgi pictures. Back then, Mike thought the Instagram page looked more like a client portfolio for her bargirl trade. But Glenn had disagreed, pointing out that a lot of young women fill their Instagram page with risqué selfies. No argument from Mike.

But now Mike had found something Glenn didn't know about—her Facebook page. At their first meeting, Mike had asked Maya if she had a Facebook page, and Maya acted as if that was old fashioned. She said, "Everything on Instagram now, no Facebook in Thailand." Glenn bought it. Mike did not.

Her Facebook page was private but easily cracked. Mike found pictures of her that were quite different from what she looked like now—

scrubbed, clean, no makeup. Lots of pictures of her dog.

There were also pictures and videos of her husband. These were recent photos, not of someone she'd divorced several years before. Maya had mentioned she lived on base with her cousin and her cousin's husband, but anyone in the military could tell you that wasn't allowed.

Senior Chief Petty Officer Caleb Finnegan was stationed aboard the USS *Winston*, deployed nine months out of every year, and currently out to sea. He was not due back for several more months. A confidential background check showed both he and Maya currently lived at the same address on base. They were on the lease together.

Mike surveyed the file he created. *This is not going to be easy. I'm about to burst his bubble.*

Mike and Glenn lifted weights together on Thursday nights. Glenn could tell Mike was distracted. They sat poolside after the workout, drinking Diet Cokes and assaulting the club's free supply of peanuts and chips. Glenn flicked a peanut at Mike. "What's with you?"

Mike stuffed a bunch of chips in his mouth, a delaying tactic.

Glenn rapped three times on the table between them. "Ahem, for Pete's sake, I said, what's . . . with . . . you! Geez, spill it!"

Mike washed the chips down with Diet Coke. "Okay, you asked for it. She's got a Facebook page."

"Okay, so she's on Facebook. So what"

"Don't you remember? She said she didn't do Facebook. Too old fashioned or some bullshit like that."

Glenn grimaced at Mike's tone. "I don't remember her saying that. Like I said, so what, so she has a Facebook page."

Mike could tell Glenn was curious. "You sure you want to hear this?"

Glenn popped a bunch of peanuts and thought, *Why do people that have something to say always say are you sure you want to hear this? And how can anybody be sure they want to hear something they know nothing about?* "Yes, I want to hear this. I want to hear every scandalous post and comment."

Mike ignored the sarcasm. A small part of him was now going to enjoy this. He described her personal Facebook page in detail. Scrubbed face, dogs, husband, Thailand, marriage, Navy sailor. "Here, look." He tossed his phone to Glenn.

Glenn scrolled through the Facebook account in disbelief. The language was Thai, but the pics were unmistakable. His brow furrowed. "This can't be. The guy must be her cousin's husband. Maya said her cousin's husband was in the Navy."

Mike shook his head. "Nope. Don't think so. Why so camera shy on her Instagram page, but tons of this guy on Facebook? And why tell us no Facebook?"

Mike shook his head again. "It's her husband. Keep scrolling. The pictorial history goes back nine years to their wedding ceremony in Thailand, up to a resort trip last fall." Glenn nodded. At the time, she had told him she was taking a family trip to the resort with her cousin and cousin's husband.

Glenn kept scrolling. There were pictures of the guy. *Her cousin's husband*, he thought, *or her husband?* There were pictures of her. There were no pictures of any cousin.

Mike was no longer enjoying this. It was time for a reality check. "Man, you know Facebook and Instagram are pretty much bullshit these days. It's whatever the person wants it to be. You know that, right?"

Glenn finished his Diet Coke. "So the Facebook page could be bullshit too. Maybe that's her way of showing INS they still have a good marriage so she can get her citizenship."

Mike smelled denial. "Yeah, maybe. Might be best to ask next time you see her. Get it over with."

Glenn glanced at his watch. It was Thursday. *I can't wait till next Tuesday. Maybe I'll stop by the bar a little while. It shouldn't be a bother. She said she had other customers, but longtime customers that wouldn't mind. Just a few drinks here and there to stay in touch.*

Glenn felt sure he wouldn't be intruding. *These customers never stayed the whole night, not like Tuesdays. Tuesdays for us, she called it.* "Okay pal, I'm going in. Wanna come?"

Mike waved him off. "Nah, I'm tired. Following your love life exhausts me."

Glenn shot him the bird. "Ass."

"Wipe." Mike responded in kind, watching his friend take off in a hurry.

78

INNOCENCE LOST

Glenn walked into the bar. The barflies were on one side of the bar, and a group of girls were waiting on randoms on the other. The flatscreens were tuned to sports highlights and the jukebox was playing some romantic ballad. Tia was taking down the holiday decorations. A Christmas tree stood in the corner, dried up, its use long past. Startled, Tia cooed. "Hi, love. Got your beer right here."

Glenn thought she sounded a little tense. *Maybe Jimmy's working her too hard.* "Hey Tia, where's Maya?"

Lynh suddenly appeared behind him, taking his arm in hers. "Come sit, honey, here at the bar, long time no talk with mama. Maya come soon. She with customer, I tell her already. She expecting you? This Thursday you know."

He gently extricated his arm from hers. "I know it's Thursday, Mama. I'm a big boy now. If she has customer, I can wait till done or maybe she takes a break. Only fifteen minutes. Can?"

Lynh exchanged glances with Tia. "Yes, no problem, honey."

Glenn cocked his head, confused. *Thought she'd go take a message to Maya. What's she doing just sitting here? Ahh. Probably worked it out already. She did say she told Maya I was here.*

Glenn sat with Mama, the usual small talk. First five minutes, then ten, then fifteen. He glanced up, catching Tia eyeing him a bit. *She looks nervous. Like a witness on the stand. What's going on? Feels like they're stalling. Wait, I don't hear anyone in the darts room. Shit!*

Glenn got up, shrugging off Lynh's pulling, and walked into the booth room. He took a few steps and scanned all the booths. *Well, I'm an idiot. Thought she was cozied up with a customer in one these booths. If Lynh tells her, I'm in the doghouse. I better cover with Lynh.*

He heard Lynh making her way back to him. *I better put on the apology face. Wait. But Lynh said she was with a customer. And if she wasn't in one of the booths then . . .*

Maya came out of the private room. She was adjusting her black leather skirt, a perfect match for her black lace long-sleeve scoop neck top with much of her back exposed. She was giggling that same fake giggle that Chloe had used the week before. The same guy Chloe had been with followed Maya and slapped her on the ass. She squealed and giggled some more. Glassy eyed. You could tell she'd had a few, and more.

Two other men followed. She gave each of them a hug too. They took their sweet time rubbing her ass.

She had just spent two hours being passed from one to another. And they made her drink till she didn't care. They touched, rubbed, and tugged whatever they pleased. Each time she squealed and giggled as if she liked it. She made sure she spent equal time with each. Exhausted, they finally decided to leave—after each one took a last turn at her.

They said their goodbyes, the lust still in their eyes. She patted each guy's crotch and squealed one last "Come again boys" before she turned away. The smile melted immediately—she was feeling sick, barely controlling the urge to throw up—but she plastered it back on again till they walked off with Lynh, who was now prattling away. Maya turned toward the restroom.

And saw Glenn.

He couldn't breathe. His pain was unbearable. It was as though someone had pried his chest cavity wide open—his bleeding heart laid bare and exposed, scarred and wounded. Everything started to go black. He turned to go. *I can't breathe. I need to get out, get away, not be here. What the fuck. So much pain. Can't see. Gotta get out of here.*

She stood still, her stilettos cemented to the floor. She reached out. The words came out soft, faint, weak, drained. "Don't . . . go . . . please . . ." She couldn't see. Her eyes filled with tears. Through the blur, she watched him move toward the exit.

Maya's wailing cry brought all the girls running into the booth room, where she had now crumpled to the floor. She beat the floor with her fists—some of her press-on nails had come loose. Her makeup was a mess. Lynh came back in, and Maya lunged at her screaming, "I hate you. I hate bar. I hate this place!"

Mama barked out something in Vietnamese, and Jimmy came in, swept Maya up and carried her into a side room. Tia followed with a bottle of water, a towel and a trash bag. Tia knew this was going to be a long night. Amber followed. They all knew. They'd been at this too long. Amber took the towel, water and bag from Tia. "I'll take care of Maya. You go after Glenn."

Chloe sat in a corner booth, taking it all in and weeping quietly. She was close to Maya. She knew what Glenn meant to her.

Lynh dispersed the other girls. "Go customer, drinks on house!" Allie kicked up the jukebox louder. Slowly the crowd returned to normal. Another hysterical hostess bar scene.

––––––––––––––

Glenn was already out the door and inside his car. He wiped his face, hyperventilating, and started the engine, heading nowhere in particular.

Tia appeared out of nowhere, pulled opened the door and yanked him out of the car. She slapped his face hard. The car rolled gently to a stop at the curb, the door still open. She checked the side of his face, bright red now from her stinging slap. *He'll survive*, she thought. Holding his hand, she led him to the curb and sat, pulling him down to sit with her. Still in shock, drained of self-direction, he followed her lead, no questions asked.

It was like a scene from a '30s movie, with Bacall about to lay some backstory on Bogart.

She turned to face him. "Glenn, those men. They're bad. The way you took off, I wasn't sure if you'd come back. Maya's my friend. I don't want that. Hear me out. If you don't like what I have to say, then go and don't come back. Up to you."

Glenn stared out at the street. A slight nod. His senses were coming back. *What is going on? Why hit* me? *Maya said she doesn't do this kind of stuff and I come on an off night and there she is. How do I know what I'm going to do? I feel like soiled laundry. Just wanna go somewhere and get drunk. I should leave.*

He made a move to get up. She clamped her hand down on his shoulder. "You said you'd hear me out, Glenn. Just listen, then do whatever you want."

Glenn could feel the tension in her grip and in her voice. He lay back flat on the sidewalk, his voice edgy, beaten. "Okay, what? Tell me."

Tia pulled him back up. "Glenn, those men are gangsters, and Mama owed them money. If she didn't pay, they were going to burn the bar down tonight with people inside. They've done it to other bars. Mama paid what she owed." Tia flashbacked the night's events for Glenn. It had all started a few hours earlier . . .

———————

The oldest thug pulled Lynh's hair, snapping her neck back. In broken English, heavy with a Chinese accent, "Where interest?"

Lynh shrieked, "What interest? I pay you all already. Leave me, my bar alone!"

The man slapped her. "Bitch, you owe interest for today. Pay or we burn!"

Lynh had no more money in the bank, in the till, or in her wallet. Jimmy had gone to an ATM and cleared out his account. They were still short. One of the men went outside and came back in with a gas can—then started fiddling with his lighter. Another brought out a kid's water gun. Mama had heard about this—they filled water guns with acid and sprayed the girls to ruin their faces.

Lynh was panicking. "What you want, boys? Fuck me, blow job, anal? I give you anything. Please . . ."

Their laughter cut her off. "Old lady, you no good!" Some of the girls knew what was going on and came over to offer themselves. Chloe saw it too. She took a deep breath and walked right up to the lead guy and rubbed his crotch.

He pushed Chloe away and laughed. "You!? You a used-up whore! We don't want skank like you! You smell like jizz all da time!!"

Chloe clenched her fists, tears welled up in her eyes. The guy with the acid gun pointed it at her. "Hey, you cunt, you want some of this?" Chloe turned away, covering her face with her arms. He squeezed the gun's trigger, just catching her legs. The acid started burning immediately, and Chloe screamed and ran into the restroom.

Lynh was frantic, yelling, "What you want!?"

The leader smiled lasciviously. "Yeah, I make you a deal." He pushed through all of them to get to the darts room, where Maya was with her regular Thursday customer—an older gentleman who had inherited his family's real estate business. The lead thug grabbed Maya by her hair, kicking the older man back into the booth when he tried to help.

With the help of his two accomplices, he now dragged Maya across the floor into the booth room. "This is what we want—*now*!" He was sneering, his heavy breathing signaling what was to come.

Maya was hysterical. "Mama! No! Bad men! You promised!" The thug kept his arm around Maya, squeezing her breast and reaching down to dig down under her dress, which was already pulled up to her waist.

Mama was face to face with Maya. "Please, Maya, for bar. It be over quick. They drunk. No can do anything. Have five shots. You won't think anything."

Maya was sobbing now. That thug still had his hands in her crotch, pretending he was making her wet, while another guy pawed at her breasts.

Mama implored. "For bar, Maya. Everyone's jobs."

Maya looked over at Tia, Chelsie, Amber, Mei, Chloe and the other girls Mama had taken in. Between Tia, Chelsie and Mei, they had seven kids.

The bar regulars were starting to peek around the corner to see what was going on. Maya knew a bar room brawl was about to start—her good friends would be hurt, the bar would be torched, lives would be ruined.

She closed her eyes and took a deep breath. At last she pushed the pawing hands away and walked, almost sauntered, ahead of the men into the bar's private room. *Showtime.*

No doubt Glenn wouldn't have believed it, but it was him she thought of as she endured what came next in that back room—transporting herself to a happy place where she had kicked back five Crowns and was laughing and dancing with him. As best she could, she kept her mind occupied that way as the men groped and pushed her down onto the sofa . . .

———————

Back on the curb, Tia recounted all of this through tears, knowing Maya was inside, probably a suicidal wreck. These gangsters had been after Maya for months, and she had managed to push them off over and over again. The last time, Chloe had even offered herself in place of Maya. After that, Lynh and the others had thought it was over with—until tonight.

Glenn sat silently. He didn't think he could hurt anymore. He was hurting for himself, but he was hurting for Maya too. *Tomorrow, I'm making some calls. This is war. The river's gonna stink with three slimy dead fish.*

Glenn got up. "I need to see her." He helped Tia up and headed back to the bar. It was past last call. The bar was empty. Lynh met him at the door. "We sorry, Glenn."

He shoved past her. Amber came up to him and hugged him. "She's not here, Glenn. Mei took her home. Mei will take care of her, first to check if she needs to see a doctor. We know some urgent care doctors that don't make a big thing out of this. She took in a whole bottle of Crown and the champagne they ordered."

Glenn slumped into a booth. Her legs burned by the acid, Chloe hobbled over. "I'm so sorry, brudder." He looked up. Opened his mouth.

Nothing came out. He started crying, and she took his head on her shoulders and let him cry.

She whispered in his ear. "I will have her at Thai Garden tomorrow night. You know where, right? Come visit. Talk. No bar tomorrow. Okay?"

He nodded and cried some more. She joined him.

79

WORKING IT OUT

Glenn had been to the Thai Garden restaurant before, but only to order takeout. He walked in at 9:00 p.m. and saw them both at the bar. It was different from Lynh's bar. Here the bar was to the left, the dining area to the right. With darker lighting, the dining booths could easily be a hostess bar booth room. Beyond the booths were several pool tables, which converted to game tables on gambling nights.

He didn't notice the closed sign. Chloe had ensured privacy for this meeting, coughing up $300 of her own money to cover the restaurant's lost profits for the night.

Chloe was facing him. Maya had her back to him. They were dressed casually—jeans and simple tops, hair tied up, minimal makeup. Chloe nodded toward Glenn, and Maya turned around. It was the first time Glenn had ever seen her this way—the empty eyes, clenched jaw, tired features and slumped shoulders all reflected hurt and anger mixed with sadness and terror.

He wanted to hug her bad feelings away. She got off her stool and walked toward him, and he toward her.

She met him halfway to the bar, and he reached out to her.

She slapped him across his face with everything she had. It was right on target and his neck cracked from the force, jerking his head to the side. Before he could think, she hit him again with her fist. This time he saw stars. He remembered all the kickboxing workout videos she had shown him and regretted the boxing lesson he'd given her. He was bent double, trying to regain his senses. *Dammit! Again? Two times in twenty-four hours. Why am I the bad guy?*

Sobbing heavily, she screamed. *"You left me! You asshole dick piece of shit support system! You left me! Fuck you!"*

Chloe edged toward the door. She knew what was coming next.

Maya stepped around Glenn and headed to the door, stopping when she saw Chloe blocking her way. "Go back Maya. Don't make this mistake again."

Glenn stood there, watching Maya and Chloe whispering.

Chloe took Maya by the shoulders, turned her around and pushed gently. Maya let out a wail and a loud heaving sob. Glenn stepped forward just as she fell into his arms. There was no comparing the sting on his face to how much his heart hurt hearing her cry.

She cried—wailed, really—for a very long time. She pounded on his back. She leaned back and pummeled his chest and shoulders. She reached up and grabbed his hair, jerking his head around. Like she wanted to snap it off like a chicken bone. She raked his face down the side for good measure. He began to bleed some.

Glenn endured it all. And never let go.

He kept whispering to her. "Baby, I'm so sorry . . . so, so sorry." *Guess the Facebook page has to wait.*

In time, her wails subsided to sobs. Chloe, who'd been sitting at the bar till Maya stopped crying, walked over and gently peeled her off of him. "Brudder, I clean her up little bit. Take her restroom. Then come back okay? You stay. Sit there. Dinner on me."

A waitress brought over some Pad Thai and Thai chicken wings, with iced tea on the side. Glenn's shoulders and chest were soaked. Faint traces of makeup stained his shirt. He caught Chloe's eye and mouthed, "Thank you."

Chloe nodded.

Maya looked back at him.

He gazed back. He wasn't sure what that look meant.

Maya wasn't sure either. Thoughts swirled in her mind. *I hate you, I hope you die, where were you? You same as all of them, fucking pig.* Then, *I love you, please be here when I come back.*

Maya slumped against the women's restroom wall. "Why you do this to me, Chloe? Tonight was supposed to be us and the girls. Get drunk. Forget men. Fuck men. No-good assholes. And him? He see me like that and he leave? That mean he believe I'm like that. He saw me hurt. He saw you last time. Real man would have stayed. Asshole!"

Chloe slapped her. Maya gasped, held her face, rubbing where it stung. Shocked, she dropped her hand, and Chloe slapped her again. Maya's eyes teared.

"Shut up, Maya. Enough already. He only a stupid man. They all stupid. They get mad, then leave. They all do that. But you blame him?"

Chloe let it soak in. "You put on show. You lie to him. You think he think everything okay the other nights you not with him. Other days, you let some guy rub your leg and your back. Sometimes if they fast enough they grab your tits. We all do that, so they think they get chance. Make more money. Guys I like, I have fun. You have pride. You stop at tease."

She took Maya over to the sink and helped her wash up. "They all go away, Maya, after they figure you out. No get, so no more they say. But he don't know better. He so new at this. Maybe but he always thinking, nightmare, you banging some guy maybe. Maybe he think that but he not ask."

Chloe handed Maya her makeup bag. "He believe in you. Keep coming back. He good man. Loving man. I see it. This guy. He not even touch you. You kiss and that's it. Yeah, he know how special that is. But last night his nightmare come true. Tia catch him. Talk to him. Explain. He came back. But you gone already. Amber and Mei take care of you. I stay behind make sure he not go away. That's why he here sister. I ask him come. If not, he gone forever. No way he come back after what he see."

She took both of Maya's hands in hers. "We all thankful, sister. What you do for us. Those guys. Hope they don't come back. Maybe time you get out. You don't need this. No need the money—you get house and medical. But we all same too. We like the attention, especially the young hot guys. But those guys always with the attitude and grabby hands. But nice to be wanted, yeah? But we getting old. The guys want the younger girls. We get stuck sometimes with the old ugly guys. Same with the hands all over. Just close eyes sometime. You know."

Chloe took a last look at Maya. *Okay, she look good.* "Maya, you said he like a little boy. He better now days but if he really that little boy, what he feel when he see you like that? How you feel you see him come out of private room?"

Maya was drained of emotion. She heard Chloe's words but couldn't absorb them.

Chloe brought it home. "Sister, I don't want you go out there do something stupid. Go out and be with him little while. Nothing need happen tonight. Only chill. Agree to get together next Tuesday. That's all. You want me sit with you guys?"

Maya shrugged. Her face still stung. It was red on one side, even with her makeup touched up.

Chloe came out with Maya. "Brudder, we don't talk tonight. Just sit. You both shock and don't want you or her say something stupid, then you break up and me and Verna gotta work hard for two months bring you guys together again, then beg you guys talk to each other. That bullshit. Before you do something stupid, stop. Just sit here. No need talk. But before leave, agree to try next Tuesday again."

Chloe forced a smile. "Me, I'm your what that tonight . . . chaperon . . . I'm your Verna tonight." Chloe called out to the waitress, chattering in Thai, calling for a double round of Cuervos, large pours, to be brought over. "Cheers!" For their own reasons, each pounded back the shots. The tequila took off some of the edge.

The sisters sat across from him. Quiet. Chloe played on her phone. Maya leaned against the wall and stared off to the side, avoiding eye contact with him. A playlist was going. Bon Jovi? Aerosmith? The song was "I Don't Want to Miss a Thing."

He had some Pad Thai left. He made plates for both and pushed them over. Chloe wrinkled her nose. She'd been eating Pad Thai her whole life. If she was lucky, her boyfriend was going to take her out for midnight sushi. She had a couple of hours to get Maya squared away.

Maya had a different reaction. This simple, kind gesture started her heart melting. The Cuervo helped. It was hard to square the bittersweet loving feelings she had for him, with countless abuse by men over the years, including what had happened last night. She tried to reconcile this in her head first. *Chloe right. Not his fault. Superman would have run too. But I don't feel good yet. Cannot even look at him. I don't feel good about me yet. Only wanted to get drunk tonight. Forget.*

She nudged Chloe. "Tequila?" Chloe trotted off.

His phone buzzed twice, sending vibrations throughout the wood top table. He didn't pick up. Didn't even look to see who it was. It buzzed again. This time she picked it up for him. One word: Governor. She handed it to him. "You have to answer, Glenn." He took the phone from her.

For the briefest amount of time, their hands touched. Electricity shot through them both. He tried to concentrate on the call. "Sir, yes, no, yes, yes. *Stop!* Sir, I'm busy. Your shit will be cleaned up by tomorrow end of day. Don't worry. Does the Admiral know you're calling me direct? Okay. Yes. You're welcome. Good night."

He put the phone down and looked her way. "Thanks."

She was still feeling the effect of their hands touching. She stared at the man across from her. *So different from first time. He walk in so needy last summer. Like lost little boy. Sometimes same. But now days, much stronger. Confident. Not take shit. Why he still want to be with me? Why he come tonight? Why he so nice to me? Last month, mom and sister needed new air conditioning. He give money no questions. I wire over but had to say from Caleb.*

Back with the tequila, Chloe could feel the vibe between the two. *Sushi gonna happen.* "I go pee now. Come back okay?" She left without an answer. Neither was one given.

They were still sitting across from each other. She cleared her throat. "Glenn?"

He looked up.

"Sorry you see me like that. I never do that before. But had to . . ."

He held up his hand. "Stop, Maya. Tia explained. Stop."

She shook her head. "No, I tell you myself. Mama never ask me do anything. I have trouble at other Thai club, and she help me out, no questions asked. Was my turn with these guys."

His brow wrinkled as he tried to understand. "What, what do you mean, your turn?"

Her cheeks burned with shame. Avoiding his eyes, she spoke softly. "Everybody else sacrifice one time or other."

His eyes blinked rapidly as he wrestled inwardly over human cruelty. "Maya, who are these guys? Tia never said." *I'm gonna kill these guys.*

She looked up at him, eyes red from crying. "I dunno. From Chinatown. Mafia. Not good. They run Chinatown. I know where office. They give me business cards."

His eyebrow arched. "You kept their business cards?" *I got them now!*

She showed him the cards. "I was going give one of our cop friends a call but Chloe said no, get cops involved not good."

"Yeah, not good Maya. What if the cops are on their payroll? You know, corrupt, work for them? Then they rat on you."

The cards had names and an address. She took them back. Tore them in half, crumpled into a ball, and launched at the rubbish bin. Three pointer.

He eyed the rubbish bin. "Karma's a bitch, Maya. These guys will get what's coming." He heard the voice in his head. *Vengeance is mine, Glenn.* He heard it, then ignored it.

She lightly caressed his arm. "Glenn, it's okay. Next time someone else turn. That's how it goes. Night still young, Glenn. Want to sing? This restaurant get karaoke. Not as good as bar but free."

His expression was one of surprise. *She's all beat up but still wants to take care of me?* "Maybe you should go home? Be with Rusty?"

He really wanted to be with her. She saw it. All she wanted was to go to bed, hug Rusty tight. Wash away again all the filth from the night before. But she saw how he looked. "I come right back. Fix face again. Stay little bit. Three songs one shot, Glenn." She managed a genuine smile.

He watched her walk away. *This girl is tough. All this crap and one smile from her and I'm flying through heaven again.*

She came back with Chloe five minutes later. Maya had changed into a dress that Chloe kept in the back for her customers who dropped by the restaurant to be with her—a sleeveless maroon number that hugged her in all the right places, ending mid-thigh. "You like, Glenn? I change for you."

For all he cared, she could have had a mudpack on, and he still would've thought her beautiful.

Then the party started, turning into a Thai fest right before his eyes. The restaurant staff came out to join them. Employees from Joy's other restaurants came too.

Noi and Malee from Siam Eastern walked in together. Malee saw Glenn first and elbowed Noi, nodding toward the two. They walked over. Glenn looked up surprised. Noi spoke first. "Hey Mr. Chicken Feet! Dis da girl you cook for? Look like you pass husband test!"

Malee jabbered something in Thai and from where Glenn stood, it sounded like three women at a bachelorette party, lots of giggling and shoulder slapping. There was some kind of denial from Maya, then the two ladies cross-examining and pointing to Glenn. At one point, Noi made a move like she was going to take Glenn, and Maya wagged her finger at her. Then Maya hooked Glenn's arm and laid her head on his shoulders.

Noi and Malee squealed "ooohhh oyyyyy" and all three women laughed. Malee turned to Glenn and said, "Okay, you suck at chicken feet, but you still pass husband test." At this Maya tried to kick Malee, who was already running to the other Thai employees, followed by Noi, jabbering away and pointing at Glenn. Off in the distance, there was one resounding "ooohhh oyyyyy!" Maya's face thoroughly flushed as her fingers found his.

So much going on led to so much in his head. *I'm in her world now. Is this still fantasy? Are we friends only? Would her friends make such a fuss over fake fantasy? Would she have been that hurt if it was someone else last night?*

The music was all Thai and Maya, Chloe and the other employees sang soulful renditions of Thai love songs. *Are these really love songs? The videos look like breakups. Shit, some of them look suicidal. One after another, so heart wrenching watching female after female abused and tossed by some seedy guy, while the nerdy guy watches from afar. Is Thailand that bad? Dang videos have one common theme—men are pigs.*

At one point, she reached for his hand again and squeezed tightly. She was in another world. It was a place she'd forgotten about—a happy place.

Tomorrow she'd have a headache, but she'd be on her way to moving on. Tonight, she wanted to forget, be in the happy place, and be with him. It still hurt inside but being with him was like a salve on a wound. Sabai—happen, be still, gone. Tomorrow will be another day.

In all the ruckus, he'd forgotten she'd just come back from Thailand. "How was it?"

"Oh plenty to tell you." She yawned.

He saw she was tired. "Hey Maya, maybe sing little bit more then you go home?"

"Okay, but I have something tell you. Come outside with me? More quiet."

80

AWAY FROM BAR

They sat out on a stone bench right by the entrance. Still holding hands. "Glenn, I'm not ready to go back bar next Tuesday."

Glenn let go. *Uh oh. There goes next week. Wait, I need to be the better man here.* "You want to take a break?"

She reached for his hand and kissed him deeply, tongue darting in and tickling his. She wanted him to know where her head was at. "No break. About that place you wanted to take me to? We talk couple months ago."

A few months back, he mentioned having dinner with her at the exclusive Paradise Club. Maya had begged off the outside dinner saying, "You know the rules, Glenn, but we can have Jimmy make garlic ribeye special for us next time here at bar?" They always sat together in the booth room for this, and to Glenn it wasn't that bad a place. Sitting across from her, he could get an eyeful of how beautiful she was.

When she brought up an outside dinner, he looked at her as if to say, "Really?" and she nodded. "Next Tuesday, I have night off. Told Mama already." She lied. She was going to call in sick. "I want to be someplace else with you. No need be that place. McDonalds okay." She winked, smiled and put her head on his shoulders again. He leaned down and snuck a kiss, biting her lower lip.

He wasn't sure how to take this. Early on in their relationship, Maya explained to him the golden rule. She was happy to make him happy, but it was a fantasy world, albeit their world at the bar every Tuesday. He recalled her words. *Glenn, every Tuesday I'm yours, and you mine. So long as at bar.*

They always had to meet at the bar. She had a no-outside-date rule. To make things different, they would bring different foods for dinner, and sometimes watch a video together. Some of the other girls thought it was a different vibe, cute, domestic, worthy of an *awwww* each time you saw them. It was the one night of the week Chloe left Maya alone.

She searched his eyes, telepathically sending her thoughts. *I want to go someplace. Not bar. No Mama always looking at us. I want people look at us like people, not bargirl and customer. I know how society think bargirls. So tired. I'm not a desperate skank. You not a lonely loser. I don't want you think us that, Glenn.*

She looked up. "I want to be away from bar. This okay, Glenn? I want to treat you to say thank you for staying with me all this time." She didn't tell him the real reasons. *I can't say it out loud. I want to be away from prying ears. I want to tell him how I feel, how special he is, how special he makes me feel.*

He looked down and snuck another kiss. This time, she bit his lip, almost suckling on it. He nuzzled her nose. "Absolutely okay. I'll let you know what time, all right?" So many questions running through his mind. *What's happening here? Go with the flow. Still fantasy? Just friends? Does she do this with all her customers? Is this a date? Or simply a venue change? And the Facebook stuff Mike told me about. Now's not the time, but someday we gotta clear the air.*

This time she leaned upward and stole her own kiss. She pulled him in hard, running her fingers through his hair. He drove his tongue inwards, and she pushed back with hers. All his questions faded away.

Noi stuck her head out the door. "Hey Mr. and Mrs. Chicken Feet, come back! Party getting started!" Along with the restaurant staff they drank and sang till the birds started chirping outside. He left Debbie a text—be in by noon. He sent another text to Mike—call gov's aide, mop up aisle 9, then call me at home.

They walked out arm in arm to her car. He kissed her goodnight, or rather good morning. "See you Tuesday, Maya."

"See you Tuesday, Glenn." She was gone, just as the sun started streaking the morning sky.

He climbed into the Uber he'd ordered. He didn't notice the car across the street.

Luke had been there all night. He'd seen them talking and kissing hours earlier. And he'd just watched the goodnight scene. "Fuckin' old man," he muttered. "Fuckin' bitch. Just wait." Then he burned rubber speeding away down the street.

81

JUSTICE

The next morning, Glenn woke to the ping and *bzzzt* of his phone.

Mike didn't wait for a hello. "Where are you? Never mind. Oh shit, are you with her? In her bed?"

Glenn rubbed his hungover head, then his bleary eyes. "No. By the way, I'm okay, thanks for asking. I don't have a contagious disease, wasn't probed by aliens or mugged. I got home safe and sound."

"What the shit?"

Glenn sat up straight. "Just shut up and listen. Did you take care of aisle 9?"

"Yes, boss!"

"Good."

Glenn grabbed the business cards on his end table. He'd fished them out of the rubbish while Chloe was cleaning Maya up in the restroom.

> *Baron Wu*
> *Secretary*
> *Chinatown Merchants Association*
>
> *Jermaine Shu*
> *Treasurer*
> *Chinatown Merchants Association*
>
> *Stuart Chow*
> *Executive Director*
> *Chinatown Merchants Association*

He read off what he saw on the cards. "What you got on these guys?"
Mike smelled something. "Why?"

Glenn filled him in in hushed tones, though he was the only one in the room.

"You gonna clear this with the Admiral?" Mike sounded almost panicky.

A few seconds of silence. "No." *He'd never okay it*, Glenn thought, *act now and ask forgiveness later, as they say.*

Glenn could only imagine the incredulous look on his friend's face. Mike cleared his throat. "Okay, it's your funeral."

The next Monday, the headlines in the morning paper were eye opening, to say the least. The Admiral put his paper down and dialed. Glenn's voice sounded a little tired. "Hello?"

"It's 6:00 a.m. You have to stop this habit of sleeping in so much."

"Good morning, Admiral." Glenn waited. Braced himself.

The Admiral's voice was calm, but it had a shut-up-and-listen tone. "Whatever your reason, I hope it was a sound one. And I hope it was good enough for not talking it over with me beforehand. Don't say a word. This call is one-directional. This is your one mulligan. Next time, you call me. This morning, all I want to hear you say is yes."

Glenn thanked God and with considerable conviction answered, "Yes."

<hr>

Star-Gazette
January 14

Feds Raid Longtime Chinatown Association, Executives Found Dead in Delta River
Special by the Star-Gazette staff

City police have announced that three suspected homicide victims were found Sunday evening in the Delta River. A police spokesman provided few details but identified the deceased as Chinatown Merchants Association (CMA) executives Baron Wu, secretary; Jermaine Shu, treasurer; and Stuart Chow, executive director. Police are initially investigating the deaths as a robbery gone bad, although sources close to the Chinatown criminal element suspect gangland retaliation as a possible motive. According to local crime expert Jesmond Barr, the deaths were clearly meant to "send a message," although no suspects have been identified.

In a related development, federal agents raided the CMA's offices yesterday in an early morning sweep. A joint task force of agents from the Internal Revenue Service; Immigration and Naturalization Services; Bureau of Alcohol, Tobacco and Firearms; and Department of Homeland Security confiscated all records on site. According to a confidential source, federal authorities are investigating the organization for alleged tax evasion, money laundering, illegal drugs and gambling, and human trafficking. The CMA reputedly has strong ties to organized crime figures controlling illegal activities both inside and outside Chinatown, particularly among local Vietnamese, Laotian and Thai communities.

See page A-3 for more.

Maya and Chloe hardly read the local English newspapers. Tia did. She stared wide-eyed at the article. *Glenn?*

82

BIG DATE

A few minutes after the Admiral's call, Glenn was sitting on his bed with the paper open in front of him. He read the article once more, folded the paper and tossed it onto the pile near his dresser. *Well, I guess Gotham is a little cleaner today. Vengeance is mine, sayeth God. Karma always says, let her be the bitch. But Kenny Rogers said, sometimes you have to fight to be a man. No matter. Done. Move on.*

Lying back in bed, he could hardly contain his excitement. *Tomorrow's our first Tuesday back together since she went to Thailand for the holidays. That crap that went down last week was horrible but brought us closer. I can understand why no bar tomorrow. She's not ready. She said so. I was ready to give her a break. But here we are. Going to the Paradise Club tomorrow night.*

He was a member of the most exclusive club in the state. He wasn't one of the silver spoons inheriting a seat at the table, but self-made, scratching and clawing his way in with reputation and merit. It was long past the day that he'd attained membership. No longer a bragging right, the club was a genuine place to go and pass the time.

Whether in the dining room with friends or in the gym, he was a familiar sight there and comfortable among his fellow movers and shakers. Glenn and Katie were known as the workout couple because they were in the gym five nights a week. The last time he was in the main dining room had been three years ago, the last time he had dinner with Katie there.

He texted Maya.

See you tomorrow?

YES ☺ ☺ ☺ ☺ ☺

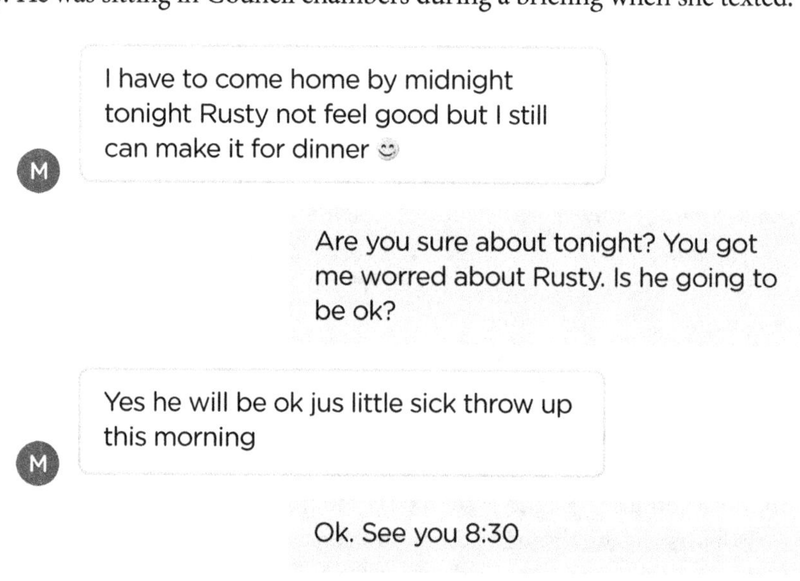

It was a dream come true, but reality hit the following day, in a very odd way. He was sitting in Council chambers during a briefing when she texted.

Back in his office, he examined her texts again. *Does she have to meet someone else at midnight? Are we doing this again? Is Eddie back? I guess her dog getting sick is believable.*
Then more texts.

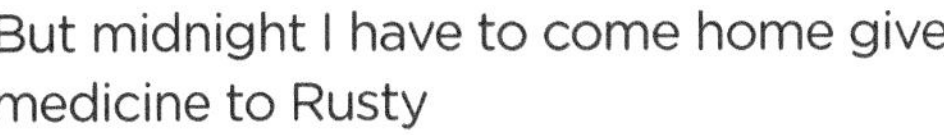

He rubbed the back of his neck, an uneasy tension building between his shoulders. *Could it really be she's meeting someone else at the bar so wants to avoid my being there? But she said she didn't want to go back to the bar.*

———————————

Maya looked forward to this dinner all week. Checking her makeup in the mirror, she thought of Luke. *He has nerve tell me see him tonight. He know Tuesdays special. I owe him money, but he not own me. But he can cut me off anytime. I have to stop this gambling shit.*

She could still hear Luke's voice, arguing. "Tuesdays end at midnight babe, so make an excuse for your special friend. Anyway, it's only one time, meet me at Thai Garden, I have clients to impress." Luke relished ruining their first Tuesday since she returned from Thailand.

For Glenn, Tuesday nights usually started off for him with a workout at the club and a shower, after which he'd speed off toward the bar. There was no speeding off this night, but some semi-nervous anticipation started to creep in. He felt like this was a first-time prom date, only he never could afford to go to the prom.

They had late reservations for 8:30. The dining room had once been a huge plantation entertainment room where state dinners and dances were held. The room still had that feeling. Dining tables were spaced apart to ensure privacy. High-backed rattan chairs and overhead rattan fans gave the place an exotic feel.

Paulo, the maître d', had known Glenn since Paulo had been a busboy. He'd last seen Glenn and Katie three years ago, before the tragedy. Back then, he was the chief sommelier and knew all their tastes and took care of them every weekend. And even now as the room's maître d', he insisted on overseeing table 65 himself tonight. This was one of only two tables (along with table 45) on the balcony overlooking the club pool, which was lit brightly for night swimming and glowed azure from a distance. It felt like they were overlooking a blue sea lit up by the moon.

Paulo canceled both reservations for table 45 that night, so that

Glenn could be alone with whomever he brought. He and the staff hoped it wasn't one of the high-profile politicians or power players he usually brought to lunch. Paulo also let Anna in the back bar know that Glenn was in the main dining room. In the past, Glenn had made it a habit to have a nightcap in the back bar anytime he had dinner at the club.

The staff committed to staying overtime as well. This was the first time Glenn had dined in the main room since he was with Katie. They knew this must be something special. He was returning to his old self, and the reservations were for two. All hoped his life was back together again.

Glenn paced out front and saw the white Audi pull in. He could barely hold back running to her. *I wonder how she'll look.* He swallowed hard as she got out of the car. She did not disappoint. She was stunning, pulling off a black jumpsuit in elegant fashion, light makeup and no accessories—just her favorite Chanel earrings.

He met her at her car and walked her into the dining room. Paulo was waiting. They shook hands like old friends, and Paulo led the way to table 65. Glenn took his usual seat while Paulo seated Maya. "Paulo, my old friend, this is Maya, a very dear friend of mine."

Beaming. Paulo thought Glenn's companion a little young and yet sensed the couple knew each other well. He surmised this wasn't their first date, and that something important was happening tonight. Paulo recalled the last evening Glenn had sat at table 65, with Katie. It was always with Katie, no other. *Yes,* Paulo thought, *tonight is special.* In addition to clearing out table 45, Paulo had cleared out the two other tables nearby. The whole middle section leading to the balcony was for Glenn and Maya.

Impressed, mouth slightly open, Maya scanned the room, taking in its austere, wood-paneled, Old World opulence. The place had entertained more than a hundred years of the state's most powerful people. Until just a decade earlier, club membership had been all male.

As Paulo held her chair out, Maya sat slowly, her hand to her mouth, disbelieving. It had been a long time since someone seated her, much less someone who was dressed like he owned the place.

The scent of the tropics was noticeable as she took in the wide-spreading plumeria tree right below the balcony. The view beyond was breathtaking. *How can pool look so blue, like daytime?* she wondered.

Above the pool, she could see the stars in the sky. It was like a perfect picture that an Instagram user would spend hours Photoshopping and filtering to get just the right effect. For a moment she felt something but wasn't sure what it was. This place was a long way from the bar.

Glenn took in how beautiful she was. She was staring off the balcony and turned to him. They were finally alone, together.

She gave her full attention to him. "What you looking at?"

His eyes reflected warmth, appreciation, desire. "You."

"Why?" The warm feeling fired her cheeks. *I hope I'm not blushing.*

He saw the color rise in her expression. "Beautiful."

Her tension melted away. The nervous line of her mouth morphed into a smile, a genuinely heartfelt, away-from-the-bar smile. She whispered a quiet "thank you."

Maya's heart was beating fast. She was thrilled. She had fretted all day over this like a schoolgirl on her first date. What she wore had to be perfect—elegantly casual, fitting for the club, but oozing sex in a very intimate and subtle way. She'd endured two hours to get her lashes done, the full lashes he liked. Her makeup was light but enough to take her natural beauty one step further. Her eyes captivated, and her lips invited trouble.

No perfume, but she washed her hair with the shampoo he liked. She kept her hair the usual way, nothing to show she went through any trouble for him. She touched up her nails with the emerald color he liked so much the week before. And she put on her lucky earrings from Chanel.

Maya put her hand to her chest. *This place so beautiful. I'm so happy. We are not at the bar. We can talk free here. No one listening or watching.* "How was your day?"

He gushed like a third grader coming home after school. "So many exciting things happening at City Hall. Campaign really shaping up. Great to be in the fight again!" Going to war always excited him. The adrenaline was infectious, and she was equally excited for him. He paused. "Maya?"

"Yes, Glenn?"

He avoided her eyes, looking somewhere off to the side. Someone was prepping a flaming dessert. He was almost stuttering. "If I win. I mean, if *we* win . . ."

"You will win, Glenn."

He breathed in as if filling himself with confidence. "Okay. When we win, will you come see me at the election night party?"

Her eyes twinkled. "Yes Glenn, I will." *How cute can he get? Like asking me to high school dance.*

"And if I lose?"

She said it firmly. "You will not lose." Then with mischief in her eyes.

"But if you do, you come see me and we get stinking drunk. My treat." She cleared her throat. "Ahem, okay. My treat first round, you pay rest." She laughed, and he joined in.

She took a piece of lavosh, thinking about what to say next. Her joy shifted to adoration.

"Glenn?"

"Yes, Maya?"

Her voice brimmed with assurance. "You will win. I know. You will win." The back of his neck tingled. Adrenaline rushed through his system as happy chemicals surged in his brain. For a split second, he had an image of himself giving his heart to her.

She said it while spreading a piece of lavosh with butter and chili mango aioli. He never liked such fancy things, having tried it just once and not really enjoying it.

She prepared the lavosh expertly. "I bet you never try like this, huh?"

He nodded no and grinned, knowing what was coming next.

She whispered loudly, "*Try it!*" She held the piece right in front of his nose. She'd made sure it was bite-size. He couldn't say no. He leaned forward and took it between his teeth as she pushed with her index finger to make sure he took it all in. Mouth full, his eyes went wide. She had mixed the butter and aioli just right.

Paulo waved off the wait help and brought over menus and the wine list himself. He addressed Glenn as "Monsieur Glenn" with deference and respect.

Maya's head cocked to one side as she recalled they had met in a bar only a year and a half before. This was a side of Glenn she'd only heard of. She was witnessing it firsthand tonight, and she was impressed.

The menu choices sounded sumptuous. She lost herself in thought, then looked up.

Glenn smiled at her tenderly. "Know what you want?"

"No. What good?"

Glenn gave a false grimace. "Everything but the elk. Seriously, don't order the elk."

Paulo stood by with the wine list. "Ever had wagyu beef?"

She found it on the menu and gasped. $140 for eight ounces! "I cannot . . ."

Glenn cut in. "Why not? You never do anything for yourself. You eat the same thing every day—papaya salad at Thai Garden. Sometimes you go out for sushi, but that's it. Let me spoil you tonight. Just a little."

She rubbed her nose. "Huh?" *Don't joke.* "I'm not spoiled."

Glenn held up both palms. "I didn't say you were spoiled. Opposite. Agreed. You are not spoiled. You do everything for everyone else. Tonight, let me do something special. Let me spoil someone who deserves to be spoiled just because she's not."

Her face softened. She got the gist. She swallowed hard. She spoke hesitantly, her tone bordering on embarrassment. "Glenn, I want to take care you tonight, but I don't have $140 for steak."

It was his turn to be confused. "No, this is my treat Maya. Let me treat you good tonight."

She stared at him like he was from a foreign land she never heard of. "You are too good for me." She searched her mind. *No one buy me something so expensive to eat. So touched. More than touched.*

He smiled and shook his head, his voice aiming to convince. "No, I'm not too good for you. We're both just right and perfectly good for each other." *I can't be the only one to take her out to someplace like this. No one's ever taken her to a high-class club like this?*

Paulo reappeared with the wine list. She caught Glenn's eye. "Order for us?"

He took the lead. "She'll have the wagyu beef, with the wasabi encrusted mashed potatoes." *She loves wasabi.* "Lamb chops for me." *The rack at Ruth's Chris was always her favorite. I hope Chef is up to taking on Ruth's Chris tonight.* "Paulo, would you pick a wine for us?"

More small talk and Paulo soon appeared with their entrees. "Monsieur Glenn, I took the liberty of picking out a Stags' Leap cabernet for you."

Glenn inspected the bottle and took a taste. "Perfect, my friend!"

She fed the first slice of wagyu to Glenn. He thought back to their many dinners. It was amazing how she could reach across the table and, with precision, place the food with her fork at the exact right place on his tongue. And for Glenn's part, it was the most natural feeling to open his mouth and know the food would be deposited at just the right spot. They'd done it so many times at the bar with quail, chicken elbows, chicken feet and crickets. A steak slice was no challenge at all.

The beef melted in his mouth. She took a bite herself and savored it like a child savors candy. She loved her steaks. Glenn put one of his chops on her plate. "You should try this too." She cut into the meat, perfectly done, brown on the outside surrounding increasingly pink hues and a juicy red at the center. Again, she savored her cut like a kid with a confection.

Glenn asked, "How is it? Like Ruth's Chris?"

She glowed with happiness. "Better." This was already the best night of her life.

Their small talk continued in leisurely fashion—the food half gone, the wine bottle nearly empty.

Paulo came back. "Would the couple like another bottle?" Their eyebrows arched, eyes sparkling, at the word "couple."

Glenn looked at Maya. "Lady's choice, Paulo." He watched as she interacted with Paulo, who was making small talk, asking where she came from, how she knew Glenn, about other wines she'd tried in the past, and what her dining pleasures were. Glenn took it all in. *She belongs here.*

She tasted the cabernet Paulo brought out. "Little dry for me. What else you recommend?"

Hand on chin, Paulo gave a "hmmm" and with a happy grin suggested a special grenache he had on hand. Maya glanced at Glenn. Glenn nodded his thanks to Paulo, who was already on his way to his reserve cellar. He was back quickly. Glenn nodded toward Maya, and on cue Paulo poured a taste for Maya. She took it expertly, first swirling and aerating the wine. Then a sip. "Ummm . . . thank you."

Paulo poured Maya a good fill and turned to Glenn. "Fill it, please, Paulo, new glass. No taste necessary. I trust her judgment."

She smiled, complimented, and sighed. "What a wonderful night. I don't want it to end." She was going on about her citizenship test coming up and beauty school after that, and it was almost as if he were in a trance, where all he could think was how beautiful she looked.

She prattled on about how nice it was to be away from the bar and be seen as "regular people," how she felt so comfortable and cared for by Glenn. Somewhere in the middle of it all, Glenn thought he heard "I love you," but she kept talking. *Whoa,* he thought, *was that my imagination?*

He decided to let it go. He'd brought it up once before, and she'd given him a long speech about not taking their world outside of the bar. But here they were, outside of the bar.

She took another savory bite of lamb, then fed him a bite. "You so nice to me. Thank you for everything."

"What do you mean?"

She was enjoying the grenache. "You help me care for my mother, sister, brother. I know you care about me. I know you worry about me. I appreciate you care for me. I post to Instagram my problems and the jerks I have to deal with, and you always respond first with 'r u ok?' That make me feel so special. I always think of you first when life gets hard. You make me positive."

She reached across the table and took his hands in hers. "Thank you, Glenn. Thank you always here for me. At least I know someone care so much about me. You give me confidence in life." *There, I say it. If people heard this at bar, word get around. Maya in love. Other customers fade out of my life.*

He was speechless. He held on to her hands like he'd lose her if he didn't. *It must be the wine talking. Did alcohol lower inhibitions and make people cough up the truth, or did excessive drinking lead to bullshit being thrown around?*

Glenn hadn't expected this. Their hands drifted apart, and they reached for their glasses in unison. He watched her sip her wine. *For someone who speaks English as a second language, she can be so eloquent and to the point.*

He was ready with his own little speech. "Not sure what I really do for you, but I know what you do for me." He reached into his pocket, carefully unfolded the note he'd spent all day composing and started reading.

> I've been trying to say something to you for a while, but I haven't been able to figure out what.
>
> You know I've changed a lot from when we met because of you.
>
> People come in and out of my life according to what God wants. I used to think He put me in your life to help you. But looking at how much better a person I've become this past year, it looks like God put you in my life to help me be a better person.
>
> I've been sad lately because I've gotten really good about how to deal with my attachment to you, and how to handle life in general, and I wonder if this means my learning is over, that God will take you out of my life. I want to stay friends with you. And I'm scared, because that's how life has been for me. I get close to someone, and then that chapter is over.
>
> No matter what, I will never ever forget you.
>
> It's you I run to in my mind when things get tough, when I want to give up, when I don't want to even start, or things don't seem worth it. I keep hearing you clap your hands and say 'You can do it.'
>
> Only you know my little boy problems. This past year, you've healed parts of my heart I didn't even know were broken and met needs in my life that I didn't even know existed.

You were friend, sister, mother, girlfriend, wife. Encourager, comforter, protector, teacher. Inspiration. You were sun and light when everything else was cold and damp.

I'm never going to forget the night you taught me to play cards. So patient. Maybe nothing to you. But sitting with you playing cards – I remember thinking, Is this what it's like being with a mom or big sister playing cards with me?

Thank you. Thank you.

One day, I don't know when, you will be gone from my world, but in my heart, in here, you will live and exist every second of every hour of every day and when I sleep there you will be smiling, laughing, singing.

I loved my mom very much, but she left way too soon. I wasn't ready to let go. I don't want to, and I hope it doesn't happen soon, but I am ready to let you go. And I've been so scared to realize this, because, maybe, when you realize it, you will want to leave too.

But before you go,

- *I'd tell you to remember you're a good person and don't let anyone tell you otherwise.*
- *I'd thank you for making the last year of my life my best and happiest.*
- *I'd bless you and let you know God loves you.*
- *I'd promise you I'll watch over you from wherever I am.*
- *I'd make you promise to make the best of life, take care of yourself, and be happy wherever you are, whatever you're doing and whoever you're with.*

So many words, and she only heard two of them—*I'm scared.* She wanted badly to comfort him.

She held out both hands across the table. "You scared?"

He put his hands in hers. "A little bit."

She squeezed. He was looking downward. She tugged, and his eyes lifted and met hers like a mother reassuring her little boy. "I told you I will always be here for you. And if I'm not, close your eyes. Find me in your heart. Love conquers all, Glenn, near or far, this life or next, you will always find me in your heart. And I will always find you in mine." *These are your words, Glenn. You taught me all this.*

Standing attentively just a few feet away, Paulo overheard this exchange, and he smiled and nodded approvingly. This was indeed a special night.

One question haunted her, but now was not the time. Not when things were so perfect. She wanted to remember the one perfect night in her life. But eventually, she needed to know. *What did family mean? Was he married?*

Caleb sent her a Facebook link. Glenn's Facebook. There was a woman on it. The postings stopped three years ago. *Divorced? If so, why not free the other nights? Why only Tuesday? But not ask tonight, not here.*

For dessert, Bananas Foster specially made for the occasion by Danny, the dessert chef. Danny made an appearance from the kitchen, was introduced to Maya, and recounted how he saved cans and bottles from the club all year long so he could go back home to Vietnam once a year and cook for an orphanage there. He was leaving the next day. Maya was overcome by all the humanity she'd experienced this night.

Glenn glanced at his watch. "Oh geez, it's late. Anna's waiting."

He and Maya said their goodbyes and thank-you's to Paulo and the wait help and made their way to Anna's, the club's secret bar. Danny led the way through the kitchen. Stepping through the double doors and around the kitchen staff trying to close up for the night—some spotted the couple and thought, *Ah, so that's who we were cooking for tonight*—they skirted the puddles by the dishwasher rack and passed through a pair of antique doors into a true speakeasy. There they were greeted by the sounds of cool jazz, and Danny announced Glenn and his "special guest."

Anna's secret back bar was by invitation only, and she ruled the roost lovingly from her perch behind the bar. A local woman who might be in her late thirties, Polynesian with a dash of Asia and maybe Scandinavia, Anna could easily pass for ten years younger and could hold an engaging conversation with any patron. She was Tia without the cooing "Hello, love."

Anna stepped out from behind her bar. "Well, hello stranger, long time!" Hugging Glenn, she spied Maya over his shoulder. "And who's this? I thought I was your only girl!"

Anna smiled warmly as she gave Maya a hug. Maya hugged back. *She just like Mama Lynh when she used to be nice.*

Anna pointed to the bar. "Come sit, come sit." There was only one table occupied that night—two women and a single guy, celebrating his birthday.

Anna had known Glenn for a long time. Part sister, part mother, she'd heard from him often during the tragedy. She had liked Katie, hoped they'd be around for a long time. "So Glenn, who is this really?"

Maya jumped in, smiling. "I'm his driver." Anna smiled back. She got it. A little too pressing for the first time.

Maya shivered. Glenn noticed, and put his coat around her shoulders. She looked tiny, as though the coat were a large sleeping bag. Anna took note. *He cares about her.*

Anna gave a sweeping gesture. "First drinks are on the house."

Glenn grinned. *For the fees I pay here, all the drinks should be on the house.*

Anna read his mind. They had this conversation before. "Okay, wise guy, rich guy, just order, and thank you so much for the crazy fees you shell out for my meager salary."

Glenn grinned even wider. *She should talk. She owns four rental properties. She doesn't need to do this. She does this for fun.*

Glenn ordered Dom Perignon, and Maya stuck to water. She really was the driver and was still working off the wine.

Small talk, catch-up talk, ensued. Anna learned that Maya was Thai. It was last call, and Glenn had two sips left. Just then, "Don't Stop Believin'" came over the music channel, and Glenn and Maya turned to each other. *Fate? Destiny?*

The people at the other table started singing softly. At the first chorus, Glenn caught Maya's eyes, and on cue, they both joined in. Softly at first, then louder till they were singing and rocking at the top of their voices, she drumming on the counter, and he on air guitar. Anna stood back and watched, thinking the two had known each other a while. The people at the table sang louder too, and for a brief few minutes, all five voices joined in staging a Journey resurrection.

When the song ended, Glenn and Maya high-fived each other and walked over to the other table for more high fives and a round of "Happy Birthdays" once they learned it was the gentlemen's fifty-fifth.

Glenn turned back to the bar. Anna was already into her closing routine. "Hey Anna, gotta go, goodnight!"

Anna waved. "Goodnight, sir. Come back soon or I'll hunt you down and kill you."

Glenn saluted.

Anna winked at Maya. "You too."

Maya nodded, smiled and said goodnight.

Anna watched them leave. *That girl has a smile that could melt the hearts of 300 Spartans.*

Glenn and Maya walked out into the clear night sky. Free of any incandescent lights, the stars shone perfectly outside the side entrance to the club. For a brief second, Glenn pictured Katie smiling.

Maya took his arm in hers. "Glenn, I feel better about bar now. Want to go sing songs? Visit Tia? She has new lashes."

He pictured Tia with large, exaggerated lashes. "Sounds good. Gimme a ride?" Glenn had Ubered to the club.

"Sure, I'm your driver, right?"

They drove up to the bar. No one knew about the dinner date. She had called Lynh and said she felt better and was coming in. Lynh told her she was lucky because Glenn wasn't there yet. They decided Glenn should walk in first.

Tia saw him walk in. "Hi love. She's running late but she just called. She'll be here soon."

Glenn tried to look disappointed. Tia noticed. *That was the happiest response I ever got to something that should have bad news. Maybe he's growing up?*

Maya walked in fifteen minutes later and sat down next to him. They stared at each other. A little longer than Tia was comfortable with. "Ahhh, you two okay?"

Maya broke the ice, smiling sweetly. "The usual for me, dear, and a beer for him."

Tia took only a minute to fill their order. *What's wrong here? Odd. It's like rainbows and unicorns just erupted all over the place. No small talk. Right into the songs. Maybe because it's late already.*

Maya earlier said she had to leave at midnight but after checking her text, let Glenn know she could stay longer because her cousin would give Rusty his midnight medicine.

Glenn pinched his knee to keep his mouth shut. *Her cousin?* Glenn didn't argue. He wanted to keep tonight's memory perfect.

Maya was having such a great time; she didn't want it to end. She texted Luke and said she had car trouble and would meet him as soon as she could. No response. *Perfect, he can wait.*

But one thought kept nagging her. She was in love. She just had to ask. Couldn't keep it in anymore.

She signaled for Tia. "One shot Crown, Tia? Up and up." Up and up—bar code for the real stuff. She knocked it back. And before she could chicken out, she touched his arm lightly. "Glenn?"

He turned to her. "Yes?"

The pictures from his Facebook page haunted her. The woman looked so sweet, so loving. They looked so happy. *How to ask?* She blurted it out. "You married?" She wanted a quick no. She only got silence. Worry erupted in her gut.

He played with the ring in his pocket. "It's complicated, Maya." *I'm getting this from a woman who says she's not married, but has married couple pics all over a Facebook page she says doesn't exist?*

She stared, almost glared. She had a panic look on her.

He grabbed her hand. "Come with me. Actually, you're driving."

"What? Where, Glenn?"

"I'll let you know."

She drove. It was only a few blocks away.

They entered the room. "Maya, meet Katie. Katie, this is Maya."

83

TRAGEDY

Three years before

It was like any other night that Glenn and Katie Forrester went to work out at the club. He wished her a good swim and trotted off to the gym next to the outdoor pool. Brightly lit, the pool looked like an azure sea beneath the dark blue, star-filled night. From the dining room, it appeared that you were overlooking a resort evening beachscape.

He smiled as he watched her walk off to the dressing room. Yelling after her, he challenged her to break her record of fifty laps. "How many laps tonight?" She glanced back with a wry "whatever" smile. But he knew her. *She's going to go for it tonight. Maybe we should celebrate with Mexican tonight? Maybe Anna will keep the bar open longer for us?*

Like many other Wednesday nights, they had the place all to themselves. The pool for her and the gym for him. A single attendant was in the kiosk folding towels.

Half an hour into his workout, arms and legs done, he went out for a drink of water before working on his chest. He saw Katie going at it strong. He called her the swim champ. Facebook peeps were getting tired of the same picture of her every week, mid-lap in the pool. But he didn't care. He was proud of her. She'd lost forty pounds in the last year doing this. She looked better than she had in college.

They were living the dream—house, career, status, club nights. They had eaten ramen and Spam their first ten years together, and their sacrifice had paid off. But a half hour later, Glenn's world turned, tragically, upside down.

He heard Alden, the attendant, scream "9-1-1!" and then heard a splash from the pool. Adrenaline shot through him. Running out of the gym, he already knew that his life had just changed. In the water Alden had almost reached Katie. Her body bobbed face down, arms outstretched as in those TV scenes where the camera pans the drowning victim.

A lifeguard by day, Alden turned her over and started mouth to mouth while pulling her poolside. Glenn's heart was rushing, the blood drained from his head and his legs felt weak. Everything seemed slow motion and fast all at once. Other employees were running down from the dining room to help Alden, who was now doing CPR.

Someone yelled, "How long was she under?" Alden shook his head. "Dunno." Sirens blared outside. The hospital was so close, they could almost carry her there faster, but the EMTs arrived in minutes and whisked her away. A police officer offered to drive Glenn over, but he said he'd walk.

Alden was shaken. Katie had always treated him kindly.

The attending intern on duty at Blue Mountain Hospital met Glenn as he walked in, gently guiding him to a corner of the waiting room. They sat in unison. "She's alive." That's all Glenn heard and the tears came, for just a bit.

Glenn was brought back to reality by a doctor's hand on his shoulder. "You need to know she's alive physically. But she had no oxygen for fifteen minutes. We don't know what caused the blackout in the first place."

Glenn's eyes narrowed. "What do you mean?"

The doctor stared downward for what seemed like a long time. He was bracing himself for what came next. It was never easy and never a calm response. "She might be brain dead. We don't know yet. We'll run tests. Do you have a friend that can be with you? It's going to be a long night."

Glenn sank into the chair, shaking his head. He didn't want to bother anyone. He was sure God wasn't going to get them through so much during their life and then end it like this, just when they were enjoying the reward of years of hard work and sacrifice.

As the doctor promised, it was a long night—but the next day was even longer. At 7:00 a.m. a nurse woke Glenn gently and escorted him to the doctor's office. "Can I see her?" he asked the nurse.

The nurse kindly patted his back. "It'd be best if you saw Dr. Heller first."

The same sick feeling he'd had poolside crept up in him. Glenn said a silent prayer, thinking back to his mother. *God, no, please no, bring her back to me. Don't punish me like this. Not her too.*

The doctor was somber and encouraging at the same time. It was a dry, matter-of-fact, one-sided discussion. "She's alive, but we had to place her on a resuscitator. Brain activity is almost undetectable. You need to consider your options, Mr. Forrester."

Options. At this word, Glenn lost his composure, stood up, fists clenched. *"What fucking options?! I'm not killing my wife!"*

Without saying a word, Dr. Heller leaned back in his chair, palms open and facing outward, the passive stance. It usually took a few moments for family members to regain composure. At last, Glenn unclenched his fists. Fatigue washed over him as he slumped back into the chair and asked the doctor to explain the options.

Heller stood, moved around the desk and sat next to Glenn. "I understand she doesn't have a DNR directive, so you could keep her on life support indefinitely. But of course cost will be a factor. I don't encourage hoping for miracles, but I can't say it's never happened. It's something you should talk over with your family, her family, and your spiritual advisor, if you have one."

The doctor rubbed his hands, assessing how Glenn was taking the news. "You can see her today. We've made her comfortable. We do have counselors on staff, so I suggest you get some rest and then contact one of them for next steps. Please don't do this alone."

The doctor stood up. "Do you have a friend or someone who can come be with you now? Otherwise, our policy is to have a counselor with you to make sure you're okay."

Brad was up watching the news when he got the call. He and Glenn were good friends, the kind that didn't see each other for months but would then pick up a conversation as if it had never stopped.

He called out on speakerphone "Yo!"

Glenn's voice on the other end. "Brad, it's me."

"Yo man, what's up!" There was a long silence. "Yo man, you there?"

"Brad, it's Katie. She's hurt. I'm at Blue Mountain." Glenn started choking up.

Brad knew something was very wrong. "Glenn, talk to me. What's going on?"

Then an unfamiliar voice. "Hello, this is Dr. Heller. I'm here with Mr. Forrester. His wife—I assume you know her?—is in our critical care unit, and we're concerned with your friend's mental state. We'd like family or friends to be here with him. Can you come?"

Brad was already out the door.

Inside Katie's room, a *whoosh-whoosh* sound filled the small space, and the buzz of a life support monitor was faintly discernible. A radio provided music for anyone close enough to hear. Apart from the tubes, she looked like she was taking a Sunday nap. Glenn brushed her hair back. *I love our naps. She on her end of the couch and me on mine, our toes barely touching. Knowing we were there, together.*

He held her hand. Tired and with no control over his impulses, he began to sob loudly, burying his head in her bosom. "Don't go. You promised. Always together to the end. You promised. We'd die together." Then he was whimpering, crying, "Don't go, don't go."

84

RECOVERY

Within the hour, Brad stood beside his friend, looking down at someone he thought of as a sister, but more than that. She was the one person who understood his good friend and brought him the love he needed. The doctor had explained the realities of the situation, and now Brad reached down and gripped Glenn's shoulder. "Pal, we got a lot of work to do. Let her rest. You need rest too. Let's go. We'll be back later. I promise."

Growing up on the same mean streets, they had joined the military together right after high school. Both served in intelligence and had each other's back through some dangerous situations.

After Glenn met Katie, Brad knew Glenn had found "the one" and reluctantly but happily convinced his brother from another mother to get out of intel and become an average person. They had only seen each other sporadically since then.

Brad called Command and used a long-burning chit to take a month off. There was a long to-do list: Call the family, console the family, make immediate arrangements and long-term plans and get Glenn moving again. And make sure his old friend didn't kill himself.

Strong Christians, her family hoped and prayed for a miracle and asked Glenn to keep her on life support. Glenn was all for it and welcomed any hope that she'd come back. He ignored the fact that she breathed only because the machine breathed for her. He ignored hushed conversations with doctors about low levels of brain activity. He read every Web article he could find about miracle cures and comebacks.

Brad got Glenn to return to work on a limited schedule. The bank had been understanding, of course. He was their chief strategy officer, after all, who had orchestrated their rise to a billion-dollar institution. He was owed time off, and then some. The CEO looked upon him as a son, the one to take over one day. He knew his boy would bounce back.

Glenn was at the hospital every night. Laptop open and phone at his side, he worked, texted, consulted, and laid out and executed plans while telling her anything that came to mind. He forced himself to believe that those little twitches he saw meant she was still in there, trying to reach out.

He never missed an evening, usually staying past midnight. Sometimes Marta, the night nurse, came in and pulled a blanket over him as he dozed. On occasion, Marta brought him home-cooked food; something about Glenn tugged at her maternal instincts.

Over time, Brad got Glenn to working out again, with some judo and mixed martial arts training on the side. Sometimes they had dinner together. But these evenings always ended with Glenn "going home" to Katie's bedside.

Two years later, Brad returned to the field. By now Glenn was a highly paid government operative. One who many felt was headed for a powerful position at City Hall. He continued the judo practice and gym workouts but always ended his evenings at Katie's side.

Her appearance had changed over two years. Glenn had pictures of her all around the bed that didn't fit with today's reality. Right after the tragedy, he had spoken directly to her, but he now found himself looking increasingly toward heaven when he addressed her, the way he'd once talked to his mother.

One day he sat next to her on the bed. *Did you check out?* he thought. *Are you really there in this bed? Or did you already leave to find a place for us in heaven?* For the first time in a long time, he prayed:

> *Father, if she's there with You, please take*
> *care of her and let her know I'll be coming*
> *one day. And if she's stuck here, and not*
> *coming back again, can you free her to*
> *come be with You?*

It was a heartbreaking prayer that he absolutely would not have uttered two years before. But like most people dealing with long-term death, he was ready to let her go, confident they'd be together again.

He touched her hand lightly. With a heavy heart, looking down at her, looking for any sign, he whispered in her ear. "If you're there, give me a sign, come back to me. But just so you know, I'm okay now, and it's okay if you need to leave." And then he looked up. "If you're there already, wait for me."

A year or so earlier, the nurses had noticed he was starting to leave before midnight, for the first time in two years. They'd seen it before. Life always moves on.

Except for Tuesdays, he still visited her every night. The family insisted he take a night off. He chose Tuesdays, the nights they used to have dinner at the club.

On the other nights, he had much to say. In the beginning, he told her he'd found a friend. *Don't worry. Nothing there. Too young. And just not available. More like a pretend friend. Just someone to pass the time with.*

And he'd told her about the karaoke. *Can you imagine? Want me to sing for you here?* He could almost see her wincing with a smile.

But lately, he was confused, unsure. *Is it possible to have two loves at once? Or do I love Katie, and merely in love with Maya?*

85

WORLDS COLLIDE

"Katie, this is Maya."

Glenn and Maya held hands as he explained it all. Maya looked at the waif of a person in the bed. Nothing like the vibrancy given off by the pictures around the bed.

Maya leaned on him. "Oh, Glenn, I'm so sorry." *So this where he go rest of week.*

"Don't be. I swear she was looking down on us and smiling tonight. I felt it, Maya. So good. I thought you should know. She's alive by machine only. Technically we're still married."

He thought he noticed a slight wince. "But marriage is marriage. I didn't want to cross the line anymore after last summer, and you helped me. I didn't count on falling for you."

Maya's brow furrowed. *I dunno how to feel. The night was so perfect, and now this. He married, but he not. He married, but care for me enough to show me. He married to her, but he love me. Just like me. I'm married to Caleb but love Glenn.*

Her knees felt weak. *We have future? Can we ever be together? Coma and life support can be forever. Not wake up for years. Sometimes they wake up. What would her family think of me?*

Sadness and frustration took turns tearing at her soul. *I give up. Cannot make Glenn be unfaithful. Never going marry. Not want to be second wife either. Cannot take care me and Mommy and sister and brother. Mother's doctor, sister's house and wedding, and brother's education still up to me. Always up to me. Nothing for me. Only Rusty. Karma. Oldest daughter duty.*

He was observing the turmoil and could tell she was thinking. "You okay, Maya?"

She shrugged off the sadness. Sabai. "Yes, Glenn. She's beautiful.

Thank you for sharing. Mean a lot to me." *Maybe we should talk it out, before I give up.*

Her phone suddenly buzzed. "Oh Glenn, my cousin." The voice was loud. "It's 1:30. *Where* the *fuck* are you?"

His eyes narrowed. *Her cousin?*

She slipped into the hallway to take the call. Luke was pissed. "*Where are you?* Baby, ditch the old guy and get your ass over here. We have business to discuss. Be here in ten or I call in your debt—all forty-three thousand dollars."

She ran back to Glenn. "So sorry but my dog. Sick. Vomited. Not right." *No time to talk future now.*

Glenn saw terror in her eyes. "Go, I can Uber home."

She gave him a look that said, *I don't want to leave you.*

Glenn got it. "I know, I know. We'll talk later. Just go."

Instinctively she leaned forward and kissed him and was gone.

Glenn sat back down with Katie. Marta came in with some coffee. "Thought you could use this."

He stared into the coffee like it would talk back to him. *Cousin? Didn't sound like a cousin. Sounded like some asshole customer wondering where she was. Perfect night. Even brought her here. I'm baring my soul. Perfect night. Fucked-up ending.*

He reached out and took his wife's hand. *Why'd you go Katie? Why? Can't you come back? Just for a while? I miss you.*

He lay his head down on her chest, like so many times, and cried himself to sleep.

86

TROUBLE BREWING

She walked into Thai Garden and was immediately overwhelmed by the smell of tobacco, tequila and cheap perfume. Semi-dark, with loud Laotian rock music playing, the place was filled with general raucousness and middle-aged southeast Asian men acting like frat boys.

Maya had quickly fallen into debt with Luke. Drafted into working the games, Maya played hostess and baccarat dealer. She vowed she wouldn't get messed up as she had with Eddie. But she also played hard to her addiction, falling into severe, five-figure debt with Luke over time.

Luke pointed to the first booth.

She didn't like the looks of the men that were there. They looked Chinese to her. Memories of the incident with the Chinese mafia induced a wave of nausea.

Luke pushed her toward the booth. "They're general contractors. Had a good year. Taking their crew to Vegas for a good time. All high rollers." He sneered. "You and Chloe are going to be hostesses every night. For free." He enjoyed saying the last part.

She turned and opened her mouth, and he slapped her lightly. The shock more than the pain silenced her. The old men chattered in Chinese and laughed.

Luke read Maya's mind. "No babe. Before you tell me to fuck off, think about it. What do you think I am? I'm not a pimp. You're not going to be bedding anyone." To this, one geezer with a heavy accent made a crude joke about side deals and pumped his fist. The three men laughed. Luke grabbed her wrist. "You go, you host, you make these guys happy, and the debt's off. All nights. You have the day to sleep and if you want, gamble. Your own money though."

Maya had heard enough. "Debt gone?"

"Yeah, everything, principal and interest."

Maya had her mental calendar up and running. "When?

Luke looked forward to this all night. "Next Tuesday to the following Tuesday."

Maya shivered. It suddenly felt cold. *Two Tuesdays in a row. Five Tuesdays gone during holidays. Now two more Tuesdays. Glenn going be okay?*

Luke sat there sneering. "Yeah, let sweety pie know he's out in the cold next week and the one after that too."

Maya wasn't sure what to tell Glenn. About the Vegas trip or their future.

87

DECEPTION

The next morning Maya was up at her usual 7:00 to give Rusty his diabetes shot. Afterward, while her four-legged son laid out on the kitchen floor, she sat at the dining table, sipping her morning coffee. She thought about last night—the club, the dinner, and Katie. And she thought about Luke and his Vegas deal. She decided what to do.

Sis you really going to lie?

No choice Chloe. I tell him one day maybe, one day he understand maybe. Jus not today

Jus tell him truth already. You two been through more than other married couples. If he not trust you now, then leave him. Or else . . .

I don't want hurt his feelings. I don't want the little boy hurt. I don't want fight before leave. Explain when I get back. Cannot tell him I leave him two Tuesdays for another customer. He already mad about Eddie. For now, keep peace. Let him save face.

She texted him.

Glenn, my cousin is going thru tough time with divorce. She cry all night last night. I taking her Vegas for a week to cheer up and forget. Only one week. I leave tomorrow, come back next Monday. I so sorry not going to see you tomorrow. I text you everyday and take you dinner when I get back. Hope you ok. My cousin very important. Family.

She lied about coming back next Monday, thinking she could blame a flight delay. She waited ten minutes with no reply. She sent another text.

If you go out, don't get too drunk ok? Tia will take care of you if you come to the bar

She kept staring at her phone. Waiting to see the *Glenn is typing* notification. *Glenn please answer me. Please be here when I get back. Don't be like Darren. Don't go be with someone else. Ten minutes already. You always answer quick. Where are you? Are you mad? Did you block me?*

Across town, Glenn was sitting in a negotiation session between the Council's budget committee and the executive branch's housing department. Mike led the discussion, leaving Glenn to drift in and out of his thoughts, thinking of last night. Mostly he wondered about what happened at the end. *What is going on? Who was calling her at the hospital? Why'd she have to leave all of a sudden? Her dog sick, seriously?*

Then he got her text. Stunned, he stared at the text on his phone between his legs, and squeezing his armrests, did his best to contain the rage rising. His overthink mechanism was going full blast. *She just got back! We had a great date! Well, I had a great date. Maybe she didn't. What's going on? Does she have a problem with Katie? At least I came clean. She's still making up stories about her cousin. Support her cousin, my ass.*

Back in his office, he picked up his phone, ready to reply, then tossed it on the couch. *Not yet.*

He flopped onto the couch. *That's a real screwed-up schedule. The last time she took a trip it was with Eddie and the flooring contractor to check out the Super Bowl in Vegas. But at least she left on Wednesday and came back home on Tuesday afternoon for me. This time, she was taking off on Tuesday afternoon. And there is no cousin. That night with those sleazebags, I was going to ask her about what Mike found on Facebook.*

His hands were shaking. Burying his face in his hands, his thoughts were all over the place. *Fucking, lying bitch. Things were going so well. Was that a fantasy date? Why so much emotion at Thai Garden? Split personality or what? Who the fuck are you going to Vegas with? Are you back with Eddie? Who or what are you?*

She waited all day. It was mid-afternoon. *Maybe he's busy.*

She scrolled through all their texts. He always answered within ten minutes. *Wait! One time he was stuck in meeting with boss. Maybe he's in a meeting.*

Then her phone buzzed. Her heart skipped. Happiness. Then sad. One word from him.

ok

Just ok? Asshole, he not understand family? He that much of an asshole not let me take care of my cousin? She bought into her own lie, basing what she thought of him on his response to her own fabrication.

Thirty minutes later, fear and worry pushed anger out of her mind. *Maybe I will call already. Not text. Need to hear his voice.*

Just then, her phone chimed. Another text. Her heart jumped.

Maya, family important. Take care of your cousin. I'll be here when you get back. Try to have fun. You are a good person.

She took a deep breath and exhaled with a whoosh. *Ahhh, okay he busy so he quick send okay. Second text better. One day, I will explain everything.*

Glenn gritted his teeth and had to take a deep breath before hitting send. He read his text over and over to make sure he said the right thing. It was a lie. But he was not going to get into it over a text. His mind was in a whirl. *What the hell is going on? Who is she going with?* Eddie kept haunting him. The private room thing kept haunting him. Her pushing Eddie into the private room kept playing over and over in his mind.

Maybe Mike was wrong. *Maybe there is a cousin? This is driving me crazy. I need to see her. Call her. Talk it out.*

He texted her.

Do you have time for lunch tomorrow?

She stared hard at the text. She wanted to see him again. Things weren't right between them since that time with the construction crew. It seemed he was distracted and distant, even after their big date, which ended so bittersweet for her.

But she needed to get ready for the trip—luggage. Luke wanted her and Chloe at their best.

The following day, she went to an eyelash salon, got a makeover, and bought two dresses on Luke's dime.

Glenn, I so sorry. no time for lunch. so much to do. need to get Rusty to sitter. still need to pack

She made the mistake of posting her makeover and dresses on Instagram. Given her need for validation, there was no second thought to the posting, so her regular peeps could send their hearts her way. She was making the same mistakes that cost her the other customers.

Glenn stared at the post. She modeled two new dresses and showed off her new lashes. *What the fuck? She has time for a makeover and dresses, but no lunch for me? Why the makeover for a trip with her cousin? Because there is* no *cousin.*

He texted back.

Ok, have fun over there

She saw his text, but somehow, she felt it wasn't okay. She fired off a smiley emoji, hoping it would help.

He saw the emoji. *Can I believe her anymore? Seen too many bargirls sitting at the bar texting customers, like robots sending sweet talk and emojis to give their customers the high, to keep them loyal, to keep them trapped in the fantasy. Shit. Always that empty look in their eyes, almost cold. These girls fabricate fantasy like some sweat shop apparatus pumping out fake love as a commodity.*

He touched the smiley face. He so wanted to connect with her. *I wonder what she looks like texting me? I'm such a sap. Like the Good Book says, the greatest of these is faith, hope and something else. I don't remember what, but hope springs eternal. She keeps saying I'm special. A support friend, not a customer.*

Over the next few days till Maya left, whatever was bothering Glenn burrowed into his soul like a tapeworm. Somehow, he suppressed all the doubt until now. Fierce imagination took over. The prowling lion mentioned in the Bible that devours all was in his face.

He saw some mystery customer, arms wrapped around her, his hand in her crotch on the plane while she giggled, and both of them laughed at what sweet shit and stupid emojis she was sending to this schmuck she'd left behind. He swallowed hard.

The following Tuesday, she texted before boarding.

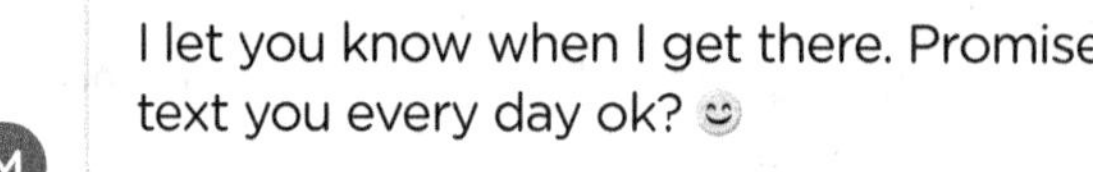

He paid her back with his own insincere emoji. This was his addiction, and only hope was keeping him sane. *Gotta put up a good front. It hurts so bad, but I don't wanna deal with this till we're face to face. We can still*

smooth things out.

But as the clocked ticked on that day, he felt the downward spiral he hadn't felt in a long time. He was in pain. *Can I get through this? Go back to see the shrink? Shrinks—know-it-alls who have issues themselves.*

He went to the gym to attack the iron, nearly running over people in crosswalks as he drove.

There was a church nearby. *Talk to God? Sit in the sanctuary? Soak up the spirit.*

He never made it into the church. Instead, he turned into a 7-Eleven, bought some scotch, went home, and drank till he passed out. He woke up a few hours later, his face planted in his pillow, smelling of vomit. *Stupid.* His only thought after slipping and cracking his head in the tub.

88

VEGAS IN FEBRUARY

"Flight attendants, prepare for landing," the captain intoned. Sitting next to the window, Maya watched the Luxor and the MGM and the other bright lights of Las Vegas coming into view. She checked her makeup, then fastened her seatbelt. The couple next to her was still sleeping, holding hands as they had since take-off. Maya daydreamed what it would be like for Glenn and her to hold hands on a flight like this.

Happy brain chemicals surged through her as she walked through the terminal, with the clanging of slot machines sounding from every direction. She was the last of her group to arrive, several hours before their initial gathering. She texted a picture of the terminal to Glenn, along with a message.

A private car whisked her to the Bellagio. It wasn't the penthouse suite, but she had a room all to herself and was met with champagne, flowers and a gift bag on the bed. She checked her phone. No reply from Glenn.

She called Chloe, and they burned through a thousand dollars each in an hour on *pai gow*, roulette and craps. An hour was all they had. It was time to go to work; soon they'd be driven to a very private party. Maya checked her phone. No reply from Glenn. *Where is he? He mad?*

A few hours later back home, Glenn wished he were dead.

Dry heaving next to the toilet, sitting on the tub, it took him ten minutes to compose a simple reply. *Need to sound like nothing's wrong. Stupid four leaf clover emojis so hard to find when you can't open your eyes.*

Good luck ☺ ❀

Maya saw the text. Finally! For one second, there was sunshine in her day. But it passed from her memory quickly. It was showtime, and things had taken a shitty turn.

She entered the backroom of a seedy Korean restaurant off the strip. The men's ages ranged from twenty-three to sixty-seven. They sat around three tables, with liquor and food set out on each of them. Off to the side were private gaming tables staffed by hired dealers. All the men had companions, except one.

Chloe was with a sixty-seven-year-old CEO who had long professed a fondness for her. Maya recognized him as Uncle Jimmy, a regular who always treated Maya and Chloe respectfully, though from time to time would playfully attempt to negotiate much more from them.

Once Uncle Jimmy had placed $5,000 on the table to finance a dinner date for Maya and his nephew Jae—with "dessert" afterward. That night her temper got the better of her as she grabbed the wad off the table and flung it back at Uncle Jimmy, who laughed, as did Jae. Lynh swooped in to make light of it, and Maya recovered quickly enough to notch up her party vibe with fake smiles and a double pour of Crown.

Tonight she recognized the one man without a companion. It was Jae, who patted the chair next to him. Uncle Jimmy was retiring, and this was his retirement party. This was also the time that the thirty-six-year-old Jae would be announced as the company's next CEO.

Maya also recognized girls from other clubs. Most of them put out. There were sure to be drug parties. Her eyes narrowed, and her lips flatlined. Luke caught her eye. His sneer said to suck it up and do what she must—and her debt would be paid. As she walked by him, he whispered that he'd tacked on $10,000 in interest that morning, plus she would owe him her trip expenses if his clients weren't satisfied.

She sauntered over to Jae. She was a smooth actor, and around the table the liquor was already flowing. She smiled seductively and yelled, "Let's get this party going!" She bottoms-upped the bottle of Crown, expertly spilling half the pour to the ground.

The men whistled and jeered like frat boys at their first bachelor party, while the girls clapped politely. The night was young and the girls were mostly lukewarm—none had yet had their first drink or snort.

But Maya felt the need to medicate immediately, and she bottoms-upped again. A girl she didn't know came up and pushed her onto Jae's lap. Maya scooted right off and sat in the chair next to him.

Her thoughts went to Glenn. It was, after all, Tuesday night. *I can get through this. I miss you Glenn. Hope you having a good night.*

Head pounding and still dry heaving, Glenn made his way to the bar—the best he could do to feel close to her. He was oblivious to his surroundings. Everything was a blur, he was both tearing up and still drunk. He sat at their regular booth, staring at a shot glass filled with Crown, drowning in loneliness.

Across the room sat Nicole, a twenty-four-year-old auto show model whose part-Asian, part-Hispanic heritage made for an exotic look that really slew. Men waited in line to sit with her, just so they could look at her up close. She wasn't much for conversation. She sat, vaped, drank and texted on her phone. She looked up occasionally to acknowledge what blabber the latest guy was gushing.

Glenn had sat with her once, and they'd had a lively conversation about something he no longer remembered. Since then, he had a tip for her whenever he saw her. Never sat with her again, but he'd always have a Jackson in front of her whenever he saw her, with a cheerful "Have a great night."

Tonight, it was her turn. She kissed her date on the cheek and sent him into the night, then walked over to Glenn and leaned over the table to be face to face. "Glenn, are you okay?" Nicole looked like she'd just come from a lingerie model shoot. He couldn't miss all the cleavage and quickly averted his eyes. She smiled. *Just like him . . . sweet and polite.* "Glenn, I have no plans tonight. If you need to talk, I can sit with you. No drinks, just company."

Glenn looked up. He was the envy of every barfly in the place. Tia was taking all this in, hoping Nicole wasn't making a move on Glenn. *Nah*, she thought, knowing Nicole wasn't like that. Nor was Glenn.

Nicole thought he looked miserable. Like a lost little boy.

He sipped his beer. "Naw, Nicole. You're sweet for asking, but it's okay. I'm okay. Really."

She started to offer herself again, edging closer to his side of the booth.

He cut her off. "Really Nicole, you're so sweet, thank you. I'm fine. I'll remember this though—how kind you've been."

She touched his arm ever so slightly and smiled as if to say, "You know where to find me." He tried to smile, hoping it conveyed what little gratitude he could muster over his heartache. With a last glance to be sure he was okay, she walked off. At least three guys wanted their turn with her.

He'd texted Maya twice since that morning and no response. He was hammered. Not a fan of Crown, he passed it off on Allie the server. He looked at his watch. *Three in the morning in Vegas. She's sleeping already. Text me every day, my ass.*

Maya had spent all night with Jae at the baccarat high roller table. Baccarat had always been her weakness. It was intoxicating for her. The lights. The action. The sounds. The high stakes. Girls in babydolls were serving her drinks. He slipped a wad of hundreds into her hand for her own gaming. It was 3:00 a.m., and there was no letting up.

Once she tried to answer her phone, but he gently put his hand over hers and said not on his time. And he gently guided her hand and phone back to her purse. She got the message, and the phone never came out again. She hoped Glenn would understand. This time her thoughts didn't linger on Glenn, though.

Jae was nearly six feet. Slim and slender with refined facial features and a fair complexion. *This guy,* she thought, *not look like other Korean guys.* To her, he looked like some of the more handsome Thai actors she followed on Instagram. Ken Wongpuapan and Mario Maurer were two of her favorites, and Jae could have been their brother or cousin. He had a swimmer's body that drew stares from other women floating around the room. He looked like her first Thai boyfriend.

At some points, she stood behind him, and at others, he stood behind her. They were always close enough for her to feel his warmth. Very briefly, he put his hands on her shoulders and leaned forward as if to see what she was doing. Before she could decide whether she liked it or not, he backed off. He was smooth. She felt it but wasn't sure what to think about it.

By 6:00 a.m., he was up $25,000, and she was up $10,000. They were on a high, but then had a couple of bad hands. They were the only ones on the table and wanted to keep playing with the same Thai dealer, but the girl was tired. Maya yawned. She turned to say she wanted to go to sleep, but he cut her off. "Are you hungry?" On cue, her stomach growled. He took her hand. "Let's go get something to eat then you're off to bed." She was too tired to fight and let him hold her hand for a bit longer as he pulled her up out of her chair.

They talked over breakfast. "My mother is Thai European and father Korean." He gave her the nickel-and-dime bio on his parents. "I grew up in LA's K-town but spent summers in Pattaya where my mother is from." They found a common interest in the sights and sounds of Pattaya.

She was an attentive listener, and he liked to talk. After eggs, hash, sausages and toast, it didn't matter how much coffee they drank. They were both ready for bed. He was in a different tower, so they parted ways at the restaurant. He leaned over to kiss her, and she offered her cheek, already taking a step back.

She got back to the room. Two early texts from Glenn and a goodnight one just a few hours ago. She felt good and guilty at the same time. She lay down on the king-size bed, phone in hand to text him. The last thing she remembered before the phone slipped from her hand was wondering whether to start with sorry or I miss you.

Glenn was up at 7:00 a.m. The messaging app indicated she'd read his texts but no response. *Really? Text every day, my ass.*

She woke to her phone buzzing. It was Jae. "Luke gave me your number. Are you doing anything today?" She was rubbing her eyes; the sun was streaming into her room. Jae continued. "Let's get out of the smoke and into nature. Red Rock Canyon." She had told him at breakfast that she liked hiking.

She nearly jumped when she realized she'd never replied to Glenn. "Ummm, can I take a raincheck? Maybe tomorrow? I'm not unpacked yet and I fell asleep no shower last night. My face a mess." She told it like it was.

Jae laughed. "Okay." He'd bailed from a golf game with his uncle. He'd bet Uncle Jimmy $10,000 that she'd spend the day with him. Uncle said they'd keep his place on the foursome and bring the $10,000 with him to the course. When he arrived, Uncle Jimmy simply said, "Happy Birthday, nephew" as he took the $10,000 wad. "I brought you on the hunt, but up to you to bag the trophy."

She hung up on Jae and started scrolling her texts. It was early afternoon in Vegas. Nothing from Glenn. He was already at work. She texted.

> Hi. Sorry I didn't text. Cousin and I had
> lotsa fun last night but too much drink.
> Fell asleep early. Just got up. Thank you
> for your understanding. It means lots.
> Cousin still sad. Gambling is good. You
> know me, once at tables, the phone
> stays in purse. Sorry not answer right
> away. Hope you had fun wherever you
> went last night ☺

She hated lying. *I rather do this than have Glenn lose face or have hurt feelings. "Kreng jai" in Thai. Most westerners not understand. Like white lie. Done with good intention.*

Glenn stared at her text. Each mention of the cousin caused his gut to wrench. She was five days from coming back. Part of him was mad, but most of him oozed "I miss you" from what felt like every orifice.

> Ok have fun

Maya saw a text from Tia.

> Love, wanted you know Glenn was here
> last night but he wasn't in good shape.
> All the girls respect you and no one
> made a move. But he stared at a shot
> glass of Crown all night. Lynh came
> in as he was leaving and tried to get
> him to stay and talk, but he was pretty
> hammered and his Uber was here. It
> was wierd Lynh came in since she took
> the night off. Hope you're doing ok.
> Don't let Jimmy pull one over on you

Maya wondered why Lynh's interest in Glenn. *Just five more days, Glenn.* She pictured him staring at the Crown shot. She saw her makeup-smeared face in the mirror and rushed herself into the shower. She wanted to go for a jog but not looking like this. A text from Luke said they'd meet for dinner at 6:00 p.m. in the hotel's five-star restaurant.

89

ENTER JAE

They followed a set pattern for the next five days—dinner at 6:00 followed by gaming all night at the high roller tables. A few excursions outside of the hotel to check out other casinos. Everything they did flowed with alcohol. Jae and Maya were inseparable. Each "day" ended with breakfast and more stories of Jae's childhood, high school, college, and what he'd been doing till now in anticipation of taking over his childless uncle's empire.

He was easy to listen to, with one funny or exciting or charming story after another. By now, for Maya, he was also easy to look at. She liked the vibe she got from the other girls as she was clearly with the best-looking guy in the pack.

She was down to one goodnight text to Glenn each day, and short ones at that. She made a mental note to make it up to him when she got back. But for now, she was in another universe, and at times caught herself imagining what being with Jae would be like.

Chloe caught Maya a couple of times in the bathroom, and they argued about Maya not falling for Jae. Maya laughed off Chloe and told her to go back to her sugar daddy. They didn't talk to each other for the rest of the trip. Chloe knew that Glenn was the real deal and Jae was a player, and she wasn't really sure who was falling under whose spell in Vegas.

They did go to Red Rock Canyon one gorgeous, blue-sky day. Jae was charming and fun to be around. There was a lot of handholding as he helped Maya scale the rocky terrain here and there. It wasn't lost on Maya that soon Jae would be rich enough to take care of her family ten times over. As for Jae, material girls were easy to charm. He'd had them all as a frat boy at UCLA.

Another day, Jae surprised Maya with lunch at a local Thai restaurant. Their favorite dealer met them there along with other Thai expats. It was a fun afternoon that rolled into the evening with karaoke, Thai style. Maya was impressed that Jae knew a bit of the language and could hold his own with some of the Thai songs. She let him buy shots for her all night at a hundred dollars each.

Maya also was feverish with the gambling bug. She was up $100,000 by the last night. A little more and she wouldn't need anyone. She could buy her own condo in the States or a house in Thailand. That night, Jae and Maya headed for their favorite table, but their usual dealer was nowhere in sight. The house brought in another dealer, and Jae gave a barely perceptible nod when the dealer looked his way.

It was high stakes time. Jae put thousands on the table, with an opening bet of $25,000. Uncharacteristically, Maya did the same and lost it. She chased the rest of the night and lost it all midway but felt she could turn it around. She hadn't seen Luke all week, but he was there for the final night, and she asked for a marker. She had succumbed to the bug by this time. By 3:00 a.m. she was into Luke for $98,000. And then he cut her off.

She felt ill. She had lost $100,000 and would have to go back home $98,000 in debt. Then she heard a heated exchange between Jae and Luke— Jae was accusing Luke of preying on her. The pit bosses told them to take it outside, and Uncle Jimmy moved quickly to intercede.

Maya walked over to Jae, who instinctively put his arm around her. She felt warm and protected. She gasped as Jae pulled out a fat roll of large bills and shoved it in Luke's chest. "Here, with interest!" Jae shouted. Maya's knees went weak, and Jae held on tight, glancing at Luke with a smile. Uncle Jimmy reached out to shake Luke's hand, and the two of them walked off for a "peace pipe" drink.

She looked up, took Jae's face in his hands, and kissed him. And he kissed back. Not aggressively. Lightly. He could sense it—he almost had her on the hook.

Still in his arms, she asked, "What can I do to repay? I'll pay you what I can every week."

"No problem." He smiled. "All debt paid if you do something for me."

She suddenly recoiled, but he immediately calmed her. "No, not like that. I need to run off to LA for a dinner meeting and was hoping you would keep me company." He held out his hands, palms facing up, a sign of peace. "Separate rooms, and a shopping trip on Rodeo Drive as part of the deal."

It was like something out of *Pretty Woman*, she thought.

"And don't worry, we have our way of getting our money back from Luke."

Unknown to Maya, the gambling operation was Uncle Jimmy's, and Luke worked for them. Maya was fully ensnared in a spider's web of duplicity. Still under his spell, she said yes to Jae.

In his mind's eye, Jae also saw the twisted face of Maya's Tuesday night customer, the guy he'd heard so much about from Lynh.

Five minutes after a heated Monday afternoon discussion with the mayor and deputy mayor over priorities the Council had disregarded, Glenn returned to his office to review legislation for the coming week. He stared at page 1 of his binder for ten minutes before yelling "Fuck!" and slamming the book closed.

It had been five days of once-daily short texts, sometimes without emojis, and Glenn was at a fever pitch with jealousy. Rejection and abandonment issues, mixed with feelings of disrespect, sent him on his greatest tailspin since he'd met Maya. Texts he sent went unanswered and unread for hours. In one case, two days.

Still, he was somewhat happy. She was due back today, and tomorrow would be another Tuesday. He was vacillating about whether they should have a talk about all this or just let it go and continue where they'd left off. Then his phone buzzed.

The text might as well have been a right cross. *Serious? Seriously? What is going on? Again, the cousin. The one that doesn't exist.* His reply was simple.

k

She expected as much. Felt some remorse. But felt euphoric with Jae. Her mantra regarding Glenn had quickly dissolved to halfhearted I'll-make-it-ups.

On Monday afternoon, Maya and Jae drove to LA, top down, in a rented Cadillac convertible. He conducted his dinner meeting quickly and with Maya in tow at one of the town's high-ticket restaurants.

Much of the conversation was in Korean, and had Maya understood the language, she'd have known it wasn't a high-level negotiation at all, but simply Jae giving orders to two of the company's LA employees who were surprised to get a last-minute dinner invite from the next big boss.

Jae made good on the separate rooms and the Rodeo Drive shopping spree. He shelled out $5,000 on Tuesday for a Dior purse for Maya. She couldn't resist and posted it on Instagram.

Several time zones away, Glenn was in his office poring over the binder he'd been trying to read the day before when the purse post popped up on his phone. A quick Google image search revealed she'd taken the picture at Dior on Rodeo Drive. He was livid. *Two more days in Vegas, my ass—it's over!*

It was more than a tailspin. It was a full-scale crash. Heartbreak combined with shortness of breath. He scratched DO NOT DISTURB! on a Post-it, stuck it on his office door, then closed and locked it.

He buried his face in his hands, whipped his head back and forth, ran his fingers through his hair. *How could this thing go so bad so quick?*

Evening came, and another Tuesday night went by without her. He spent it at Anna's this time. The song "A Thousand Years" came over the PA. He looked slowly up at the loudspeaker. *Really?*

It had been days since he'd last seen her, and it felt like he died a little every day that he waited. This was her wedding song—she'd sung it for him a few months back. *I can't get this song out of my head. It keeps popping up in the weirdest places. God, are you trying to tell me something? Like I should wait for her?*

Shit, one day I hear it in Nordstrom, then it's playing on Debbie's radio, then working out at the club, they do a wedding rehearsal with that song. It's everywhere. And I keep dying every day waiting for her. Every single minute of every single day, I die waiting for her.

Anna hadn't seen Glenn like this since the tragedy. She poured him something stiff, and he sat in silence for the rest of the night. She didn't even try small talk. "Don't Stop Believin'" came over the PA. *Serious?* "Bullshit, I'm done believing," he muttered, and walked out.

He looked up into the night sky—the same stars he'd seen at the end of their dinner date. He asked, "God, are you there? Why me, why her, why now? What's going on? I miss her so much." In the still of the night, he heard a small, still voice say, *Then tell her.*

He texted her.

> Hey, I didn't think I'd miss you this much but I do. Never thought I'd ever feel like this about anyone again. Hurry back. I miss you so much. I would wait a thousand years for you.

Jae was staying one more day in LA, so Maya flew back by herself on Wednesday. As the plane landed, she heard a passenger yell, "What happens in Vegas *stays* in Vegas." *I hope LA too,* she prayed. She could still smell Jae on her skin. He had knocked on her door at 2:00 a.m., and before she could ask what was wrong, he kissed her. She put up her hands to push him away but instead they went around his neck.

She's finally mine, Jae exulted.

An hour later, he stood in her shower, washing up. She sat on the bed, confused. Her phone buzzed. She read Glenn's text. And something inside melted, though not enough to erase what had happened just now, or during the past week. Jae pulled on his clothes and bent down to kiss her. He didn't notice she was a little cold, figuring she was just tired. And like most conquering frat turds, he could only think of his conquest.

He walked out. She closed the door behind him and leaned against it, then slumped to the floor, crying as she saw Glenn's face—with the same expression he'd worn weeks ago when she abandoned him at the bar.

Oh my baby. My baby. She was at a loss for words. Her reply was simple.

Several time zones away, Glenn took one look at the sparse reply to his heartfelt rendering and threw his phone against the wall.

90

NEED TO CHOOSE

On the plane ride heading home, Maya scrolled through every text she'd ever gotten from Glenn. First she went over all the *"goodnights"* and *"home safes"* and every sweet, Tuesday-ending nugget he'd ever sent. Then she looked up every "Saturday text." That's what she called the encouraging messages he sent her without fail on Saturdays, the midpoint between their Tuesday visits. She waited every Saturday for these texts. Some of her favorites were:

> *Keep going forward. Follow your heart. Believe*
> *in your dreams. Believe in yourself. The universe*
> *believes in you. I believe in you. Those that love you*
> *believe in you.*

> *Keep moving. I believe in you and all that you can*
> *do. The present and future is yours. Make it happen.*
> *The universe has your back. I got your back.*

> *Be passionate. Whatever is happening, believe . . .*
> *keep reaching . . . you can do it . . . and I'm with*
> *you all the way. Always praying God's best for you.*

Tears blurred her vision. She leaned her head on the window, closed her eyes, and let the tears roll down her cheeks. She fell into a light sleep, recalling her last conversation with Chloe. *Oh Chloe, he make me feel like someone care, like someone gonna be there always for me. When things get rough, I think of him first thing.*

Amidst her chaotic world, she read her favorite texts from him the way an evangelical sought Scripture. Words that gave hope, words that bolstered, words that expressed belief in her. Describing how she felt in Thai, she told Chloe the texts were like "sunrise after a dark night, like air keeping me from drowning." Chloe had never heard Maya talk like that.

Maya buried her face in her pillow. *Mommy sick, sister getting married, brother going college. Need money for all that. Need money for sister house after get married. And me. After Caleb divorce, not get pension for four years. No place to live. Need to pay rent and medical. All this take money. Who take care me, Mommy, sister and brother?*

She searched her purse for a tissue. *Glenn give me money but he have wife already. And he have to take care her. I'm not marriage wrecker.*

She remembered the stinging rebuke from Eddie's wife. *We stay friends but I'm not second wife. He good for me once a week, but I need someone 24/7 soon. Getting older and one day off market.*

Eyes dry, she took a deep breath. *Jae not married. We same age. He have lots of money. We wait till divorce final and see. He legitimate businessman. I saw in LA.*

Her eyes teared again. *If only Glenn not married, but his wife real sweet. How can I replace? Cannot. Sometimes hard to take care of the little boy. Jae is the other way. I feel protected all the time with him. With Glenn, sometimes I must protect him, take care him.*

She sighed. *I need to tell Glenn friends only. Tell him I led him on. Hope he understand.*

She fell asleep. Two texts chimed on landing. The first from Glenn. The second from Jae.

> I hope you have a safe flight. Cant wait to see you next Tuesday. Maybe lunch this Friday?

> Took an early flight out from LA

She wanted to wait on Glenn. She texted Jae, or she thought she texted Jae.

> See you soon?

Glenn sat in his office, watching the Council on his flatscreen as the members discussed the city budget. His phone buzzed. Glenn stared at it.

She wants to see me. Today? Tonight? What about her Wednesday regular? Nice guy. The bro code—don't infringe on another customer's time. I can't displace him. Maybe he canceled. Not sure. What do I say? Don't want to seem eager.

He texted back, trying to sound casual. Barely able to contain his excitement.

What do you have in mind?

After she got her bags, she opened the text from Glenn and froze. She got the texts sent wrong.

Glenn waited thirty minutes. *No answer? Maybe that text wasn't for me?* He wrote back

Not a problem if cannot. Take care of what you need to take care of. If Friday opens up let me know

Thank you Glenn. See you Tuesday?

He threw the phone at the wall again. *Dammit! She responded immediately. She was talking to someone else! And so what? She couldn't respond to my original text? And no time for even lunch this week after canceling last night? And that's it? Thank you and see you Tuesday? After all the sweet talk and great times the last few months, this is what it comes to?*

This is bullshit. Don't need this no more.

He leaned back in his chair. Interlocking his fingers, he covered his eyes. *Canceled last Tuesday to go on a shopping spree in LA. With who? Not with her "cousin."*

He rubbed his eyes. *Can't even text the right person after landing. Why not rub my face in it. See you soon? See who soon? Not me, that's for sure.*

He felt a familiar tug at this heart. Then he heard the voice. *Forgive.*

He sat up with start. *You're kidding? Father, I can't do this no more.*

Again, the voice. *She's only a child. See her through my eyes.*

Glenn half-rolled his eyes as he sighed. He pinched his nose bridge and asked, "Why?"

And he heard. *Because she's good for you. Because you love her. Because I love you. Love conquers all.*

Maya canceled her Wednesday night with one of her longest-running customers. Jae said he had a surprise and wanted to take her to dinner.

They met at a Korean BBQ house. He cooked for her. She'd never had kal bi before and liked it. She felt like a little girl having dinner made for her. Grandpa used to make dinner for her like this. She might've mentioned it to him at the Thai restaurant they went to. She took it all in—lots of chit-chat that night. They sat side by side, and he put his arm around her. She shifted a bit, creating space between them. "What's wrong, babe?"

"Nothing." *I'm babe now?* She put her head on his shoulder for a split second. "I go bathroom." She came right back and put her purse between them. He picked up on it but let it go.

After dinner, he reached for her hand. "Listen, I think we have a connection. I didn't intend to fall for you up there, but I did. You're different from anyone I've ever met. I know we should go slow, and we can. Just asking if there's any chance for us to try?"

He was smooth. He cooked for her like Grandpa did. He was easy on the eyes. He was unattached. With money. "I'm not trying to buy you or anything like that," Jae said. "I grew up poor. I want to make sure you get treated right, that's all. Can we just try and see where this goes?"

She reached around his arm with hers and put her head on his shoulder. Before she knew what she was saying, she said, "Okay." Only afterward, she remembered there was still Caleb and Glenn to deal with.

They had driven separately. "Can we do a nightcap?" he asked.

She shook her head. "No. I need to go to the bar."

"About that." He wanted to push. The surprise. "You don't have to do that anymore. I can take care of you and your family." He'd heard a little from her about her mother and sister.

She looked away, then back. "Not work tonight. See friends."

His smile tinged with disappointment. He expected some appreciation. "Oh, ahhhh, okay. But I hope you consider what I just said."

They walked out the door arm in arm to her car. She got in. He leaned in for a kiss, and she gave him a quick peck. He lingered while she pulled back slowly. Caressing his cheek, she meekly said, "Sorry Jae, tired." *Something not right,* she thought. *Kiss not feel right. This not feel right.*

91

HEART TO HEART

After leaving Jae, Maya spent a couple of hours driving around town with her sound system pulsating hip-hop love ballads. Deep in her soul, lust and greed beat up on her true passion. Jae was easy on the eyes, had available wealth, and was single. Glenn was married, not available, with wealth spoken for. Yet, his image tugged at her heart.

She walked into a near empty bar at midnight. Only Tia, the barflies and two girls were in the bar area. Two other girls were finishing up with their randoms in the booth room. Both flatscreens were tuned to late-night shows. The jukebox played reggae hits.

Chloe was sitting with a Jamaican fellow from the base, who'd been buying her a drink for every squeeze of her breast. He'd already bought ten rounds, and she was feeling a little sore.

Spying Maya entering the bar, she turned to him. "Honey, my friend come. I gotta go. See you next time?"

Before he could feel any disappointment, Amber appeared in her red nightie; boobs planted three inches from the fellow's face. Over his shoulder, Amber gave Chloe a wink and nodded backward to Maya.

Amber whispered, "Come with me?" in the guy's ear, and like a little dog, he followed Amber to the booth room without even a goodbye.

Maya dropped into the booth across Chloe. "Good night tonight?"

Earlier, Chloe had taken care of Maya's Wednesday night regular. He'd gone home right before the boob squeezer appeared. "Your customer Vic real pissed, Maya."

"I know. I got his texts"

Chloe rubbed her nose. "What happened?"

Maya explained the side trip with Jae.

Chloe nodded. "I know. I saw Dior purse you posted. Vic saw too. He say you went Rodeo Drive with your boyfriend and shaft him."

Maya pursed her lips. "How he know Rodeo Drive?"

"I dunno. I think Google or something."

Maya called for two shots of Cuervo. "Poor Vic. He has daughter, you know. Not good for marry. He will always take care daughter over me. He knows. He go Thailand next year, look for wife."

They clinked glasses. Chloe burped. "He told me. Cannot wait for you Maya. He say you always sweet talk, say you like him, but nothing. All show, no go. He say he catch the hint. He said if nothing happen, you should have said. Don't tell him I told you, okay?"

Maya frowned. Cash flow was about to take a hit. But she was happy for Vic. "Cool guy. Make someone happy."

Chloe pointed her finger at Maya. "How you know he not take care you too, and your family?"

Maya grimaced as she shook her head. "I know. They always choose their blood. You should know, Chloe. You think Reyn choose you over son?"

With a glance over her shoulder, Chloe put a finger to her lips. "Shhhh. Not so loud. His crew over there."

Maya looked at her sister, quizzically. "He came tonight too?"

Chloe nodded. "Yeah. But we don't sit. He make like bar customer. He not happy I sat with Vic." Chloe looked Maya over, took a deep breath and leaned over closer to Maya. "So did you guys fuck?"

"Chloe!"

Chloe leaned back, crossed her arms, and mouthed, "You guys fuck. Maya, how?"

Maya closed her eyes and inhaled, either trying to remember or forget. "I dunno, Chloe. It happen. Not have long time. He smell nice. He look good. The vibe was right. I was tired. Not fight no more. So much stress. I let go. He was there."

At first, filled with judgment, Chloe's eyes sparked with curiosity. "Was he good?"

"I don't remember. So I think . . . not sure." They giggled like schoolgirls.

Chloe answered a text. Reyn was texting from the other table. *Meet usual place after.* "Wanna come, Maya?"

"No. Tired."

Without looking up, Chloe asked, "You ate?"

"Yeah, with Jae."

Chloe's head jerked up. "What?! You just spend how many days with the guy and you land and have dinner with him? Good thing Vic not know." Chloe played with her napkin. "What about Glenn?" Her tone was serious.

Maya's chin jutted. "What about Glenn?"

Chloe signaled for two more Cuervos. It was serious talk time. "Yeah, Glenn. Brudder." Silence. Chloe shot a quick look at Reyn. He got it. Ordered another beer for himself. Dialed up the restaurant to say they were going to be late.

Maya let out a quick breath. Her turn. "Glenn married, Chloe."

"What? You only think . . ."

Maya raised her hand. "No, I saw. He took me to see." Maya explained about the hospital.

Chloe knocked back her Cuervo. "That not married. That more not married than you and Caleb. Why that stop you?"

Maya was almost glaring. *Why she had to bring up Caleb? Shit. No matter how you look at it, I cross line with Jae. Marry is marry. Now I'm unfaithful to Caleb. Karma will get me for this. Come back next life as goat!*

Maya played with an earring. "Chloe, brain dead or not, I'm not marriage wrecker. I don't take her place while she breathes, and I'm not going be second wife like lot of our sisters in Thailand. Wait around all week for scraps from husband? Everybody look down on us like whores anyway when second wife. No way."

Maya knocked back her shot. "And Jae, he make me feel like . . . I dunno . . ."

"I know, Maya. Like he your daddy."

"Yeah."

Chloe played with her empty shot glass. "But Glenn, he like that too?"

Reyn looked their way. Over Chloe's shoulder Maya mouthed her thanks. "Yeah, complicated. Sometime daddy, sometime little boy. But I need daddy all the time."

Chloe dropped her glass. "You sure? I see you with him. You like the little boy. Just like if—"

Maya cut in, fired up. "You think I miss my son and that's why I treat fifty-year-old man like little boy?" *How can she say that? So gross.* Maya's head was at war with her heart.

Chloe's phone buzzed. "Not like you breastfeed him. Not like that. But you mother him . . . and you like that. True? Not true?"

Maya didn't want to admit it. She did miss the little boy she'd lost. In some ways, Glenn pulled that maternal instinct out of her, like Rusty at home. *So weird I feel like that about Glenn.* She thought of all the times she'd bring food for Glenn and how she fed him. The time she played cards with him. At the back of her mind, she'd suppress the thought of doing these things with her little boy.

Chloe snapped her fingers to break the trance. "So you have choice. Full-time daddy or half-daddy, half-little boy. If you ask me, combo dinners always the best—two entrees in one."

Maya thought about it. She heard how Glenn protected Verna from the thugs. She wondered about how the Chinese mafia ended up in the river. He did have a way of protecting and caring for her. The reason why she started calling him Papa lately. But the little boy part. The look he sometimes had. She always thought it was a burden. Now, maybe not. That look always made her run to him, like the time she was singing with those guys, and his look snapped her spell. Burden? More like love.

Reyn walked past and out the door. Chloe's eyes followed him out. "I gotta go, Maya."

"Yeah, me too. Can't wait to see Rusty."

———————————

She walked into her house. "Where's my boy!" Rusty came bounding up and jumped in her arms, knocking her down. She was laughing. *This how I feel every time Glenn and me first meet for the night. Heart about to burst. Never felt like this with Jae. Maybe I only need another dog.*

Coming out of the shower, she lay in bed with Rusty in her lap. "Oh, Rusty. Mommy not a bad person, right? Mommy trying to take care of all of us, you know? Marry is marry. I was wrong in Vegas." Rusty nuzzled her as if to say everything was okay. "And I don't make Glenn unmarry his wife. I'm not a marriage wrecker." She remembered the sting of Eddie's wife's words. *We only friends. I need to cool it with all the love talk. Not want to lead Glenn on like Vic.*

Maya kept telling herself that she wasn't a marriage breaker. A trained ear would say that was her main reason for shying away from Glenn, not any lack of affection.

She played with her phone, scrolling through her Instagram account. *I don't want to break his marriage. No matter, I'm stupid man-crazy too. I don't want to hurt him again like that too.* She thought back to all the times she left him hanging when there were other men around, when she had a few too many. *Why I always do that? Even with Darren one time.*

She rubbed Rusty's tummy. *Feel so special when guys pay attention to me like that. The younger the better. The more good looking the better. The richer the better. And the more there are, the better. Every time so hard sitting with Glenn and got groups. But I see Glenn. So happy when I'm with him. So happy when I make him happy. Gotta control the Crown.*

She thought harder. She grimaced and winced, holding back tears when she came upon a realization. *Can I really control the Crown? One way to make sure never hurt Glenn like that again. Leave, not look back. I'm not good for him.*

92

MARCH DATE

"She's killing me, Father. How can she be good for me?" Glenn had just finished his weekly Tuesday briefing with the Vice-chair and returned to his office. He was getting ready for his workout before heading to the bar.

He shut down his computer and held his Bible while looking upward. "You gotta admit these past three weeks since she got back, it's been pretty lukewarm, and her head's been someplace else. She doesn't want to be with me. I can tell."

He raked his hair. *What's going on? Ever since Vegas, she either comes late or goes home early. That first Tuesday back, she had time only for dinner—an hour—then had to run home. She had to go to sleep early to pick up her cousin at the airport the next morning—5:30 a.m.? Bullshit. I checked the airport logs. The first flight came in at 7:00 a.m.*

He shook his head. *The next week she tells me her dog is sick, and the dog doctor says the dog has to take the pet meds at exactly midnight. Seriously?*

He breathed in deeply. *Then she's late last Tuesday. Why? Because her cousin was sick, and she had to make dinner for her cousin's husband. Geez,* he thought, *isn't there a McDonald's on base? Maybe her phantom cousin's husband needs to take the same antibiotics the dog was taking.*

It knotted up his stomach any time she mentioned the cousin. *Wish she'd come clean. Still haven't told her about what Mike found on Facebook. Probably thinks I'll drop her if she admits lying. Maybe I should tell her?*

Shit, his mind swirled, *this lady ought to write a book. She has the imagination for it. Maybe I ought to write a book about some poor schmuck falling in love with a bargirl.*

Late afternoon on the fourth Tuesday after Vegas, she texted Glenn.

Glenn so sorry I sick have to go
emergency got food poisoning hot
fever need antibiotics.

Glenn stared at the text. The overthink beast was in full control again. *What's going on? All these excuses the last three weeks, and tonight's a no-show based on food poisoning? I've seen her eat bugs and hot peppers. She has a cast iron stomach. What is going on?*

Feelings came rushing in like crashing surf. Anger. Hurt. Frustration. Rejection. Betrayal. Manipulation. And questions. Lots of questions. *Is there someone else? Why this behavior change since Vegas? Did she go up there with someone? Are they an item now? Is she using my money to fund their fun?*

He texted back.

Ok. Take care. I'll miss you tonight.

No reply. *You gotta be kidding? I tell her I miss her and nothing back?* She texted the following morning.

Let's go to Paradise Club again. I sorry
Glenn. I make so much trouble for you
since Vegas. Sorry I got sick last night. I
know first time I cancelled you. Let's go
have a quiet night next week. No bar.
only you and me. Maybe you can buy
me shots at Anna's ha ha

Glenn was still at home, getting ready for work. He stopped dressing and sat back on the bed. *She's trying to make up? Or she going to mess with me again? Seeing someone else but not hurting my feelings? Bullshit. My feelings are out the door. In a garbage heap somewhere. Is this really kreng jai? No wonder Thai guys are assholes and pissheads that abuse women. Abuse first or be abused.*

He let out a long exhaustive frustrated sigh. *But the first date went so well.* He lifted his voice upward. "Father, You always taught me love conquers all. If she is lying, she must be doing it to save my feelings, keep from hurting me. All the great times and warm feelings . . . that can't be fake, right? There's gotta be something there." He heard the voice. *Love conquers all.*

————————————

Across town at Jae's place, Maya was not as optimistic. She hated lying to Glenn.

She had tried to muster the courage every week to end their Tuesdays, but she could not, had not. Once, she told Glenn, "I will not forget you," and he jokingly replied, "Are you dumping me?" She thought of how hard it would be for him, clutched her stomach and ran to the bathroom to hide her crying. She explained, "ulcer" when she returned.

Food poisoning was the excuse last week. In reality, Jae had had a tantrum and hit her. She touched her eye. The color was returning to normal. She didn't want Glenn to see her black eye. *Why Jae like this? I must have done something. I wise off when he in bad mood. I remember next time. But lately he always in bad mood.*

Since returning from Vegas, the Tuesday nights were tension-filled, with Jae constantly texting and calling her to ask where she was. Yet, the goodnight kisses with Glenn were real, nothing less than the soft, warm and affectionate kisses they always shared.

She was thinking of their last kiss when suddenly Jae's palm rapped against her skull. She saw stars. He was standing over her holding her phone. "Why the fuck are you still seeing that old bastard?" Jae regularly checked her texts. She'd forgotten to delete the last text.

She grabbed the side of her head, glaring at him. "What your problem? I told you I love you. I choose you. You choose me? You still party with those girls from Starfall Lounge? What about those girls from Lucky Seven Lounge?" She didn't know for sure; heard it from some other girls that just started working for Lynh. On many late nights, Jae and Uncle Jimmy walked out of the Lucky Seven with several girls trying to pull them back in. It was a tug of war, and the girls always won.

She yelped when he raised his fist. "None of your business, bitch. It's business. They're with Uncle Jimmy. For him to relax. Get rid of the old guy."

She turned on the charm. "Why you worried about old guy? Let me treat him to one more night. We go public place, I let him down easy. No trouble. He famous. Powerful. He can make trouble. I do this for us, okay?" She was rubbing his crotch.

He threw her on the bed, pushing his pants down. "Yeah, whatever. It's over next week." He was on her. She turned to the mirror and through her tears, saw a vivid memory of a broken little girl raped by uncle after trusted uncle on many nights. Tears welled up and fell with each of Jae's thrusts. Was this all life was going to be? At least I can take care of Mommy and sister. She could hear Mommy. *Just close eyes. Go happy place.* She closed her eyes. She and Glenn were singing.

The morning of her second date with Glenn, she prayed to Buddha. *No let Glenn hurt too much. Give me strength to let Glenn go. I ask for Paradise Club. I tell him at Anna's. At least she will be there to help pick him up the pieces.* She was crying. Sobbing. She thought of all the times they'd had together. It was going to end tonight.

Glenn met her that night as she parked. Her hand covered her heart. "Awww you came to meet me?"

He put on his worst British accent and extended his arm. "I came to meet my lady."

She took his arm, and they walked across the lot to the club's main entrance. The valets noticed her first, wearing the same black jumpsuit she'd worn before.

Paulo met them at the door and led them to their table, above the azure pool that made it look like they were overlooking the sea, but under nighttime stars. Like the last time, the smell of plumeria was subtle yet mildly intoxicating.

Chef prepared a special three-course sampler of Kobe beef, lamb chops, and filet mignon. Glenn had had a rough day sparring with Clifford, and the wine flowed freely.

Maya pursed her lips. *He drinking too quick. Seen him drink more though. Maybe okay he numb when I tell him. Please Buddha, let it go well. No trouble. Let Glenn be okay.*

Reaching out for his hand, she sent her thoughts with her eyes. *I want you know I never forget you okay? Only you treat me high class, take me nice places, give me respect. Only you. I won't forget you, Glenn.*

Glenn gazed back. *Whatever was the problem this past month, it must be over. The way she's looking at me. Good times ahead. Maybe she's getting rid of her cousin or husband or whoever. One day we'll talk it out. Plenty of time in our future.*

Irony was about to bite him in the ass.

93

IRONY AVERTED

After dinner came complimentary *crème brûlée* and fruits. Then off to Anna's.

Glenn took his usual seat and asked for a double pour of cabernet for himself and grenache for Maya.

Maya could tell he was getting a little hammered and was looking for an opening. "I got call from Lynh the other night, Glenn."

"Really, what'd she say? Wait, tell me when I get back from the restroom." He knocked back his double pour of cab and scooted off his stool.

Anna overheard and piped in. "I know Lynh."

Maya's eyes went wide. "How you know?"

Anna grinned. "I used to work with her."

Maya leaned forward on the bar. "You were bargirl? Me too."

Anna's eyes showed surprise. She had wondered after the last time.

Maya took a tiny sip of her grenache, then asked for water. "I work for Lynh three years, come from Thailand, no friends, divorce from husband. He beat me, waiting for ten years, then divorce for pension. Already agreed. He in Germany. I live with my cousin and her husband. Work bar to help mother and sister. Glenn was customer, but now we friends. He help me with my mother and sister."

Anna started her closing routine. Drying glasses. "I worked for Lynh as one of the girls, then worked behind the bar."

Maya nodded. Like Tia and Amber. Just then, Glenn stumbled out of the bathroom. The wine had hit that part of his brain that caused blackouts. He was out on his feet.

Maya had seen this before. *He in no shape to hear bad news tonight. He not going to remember. Jae going be pissed. Fuck him. I take care Glenn first.* "Papa, we have to go now."

He was slurring now. "But you're not done with your grenache. Oh that's right, you're my driver." He reached out, and before she could say no, he downed her grenache. Her look of concern touched Anna. Maya brushed back his hair. She looked down at her watch, did the calculation in her head. *Twenty minutes. He drink half bottle wine then my wine. He smashed after dinner, coma now.*

Glenn climbed onto a stool. Anna decided to ask. "Where are you and he headed, dear?"

Maya examined Glenn. *He checked out?* She turned to Anna. "Home. I take him home."

"No dear, I mean the future. I mean, you do know about his wife?" Maya nodded. Anna continued. "He's still technically married, like you, I suppose."

Maya desperately wanted to say she dreamed of spending the rest of her life with Glenn, but after learning about Katie, she'd settled for Jae. Mommy, sister and brother were counting on her.

She took a deep breath and chose to lie to Anna, hoping the bar mama radar wouldn't kick in. "Glenn and I only customer and bargirl. I give him fantasy of young girl liking him, and he pay me good. Just business. Just fantasy."

Anna stared a bit at Maya. "Is that all, dear? You two look pretty comfortable together." Anna glanced over at Glenn, who was staring at the TV. She'd seen this before. He was out. Nothing being said was registering.

Maya hoped Glenn would hear so she could do the breakup scene. But it never happened. Like Anna, she saw what a wreck Glenn was. "Papa, we have to go now." She'd picked up the habit of calling him Papa. It felt good to her. A papa that protected and cared for her, but at the same she cared for as well.

Glenn almost fell off his chair. Maya scooped him up just in time. Anna dropped her towel. "Dear, are you sure you don't want us to call a cab for him?"

"No, no need. I know where he live. I take him home now." She had her arm under his to steady him. He was rocking front to back, and swaying side to side. She thought if she let go, he'd hurt himself.

It was a different exit from the last time. Maya was nearly carrying him, even in her high heels. Anna saw this. She'd seen many bargirls simply put drunk customers in cabs for the ride home. *Are they only customer and bargirl? Never saw one carry a customer out before, high heels and all.*

Anna thought there was something more here but went with what Maya told her, confirming for Anna that Maya was a gold digger—only after Glenn's money for as long as it lasted.

Outside, under the starry sky, it was anything but romantic.

"Be careful, Papa." She steered him clear of anything that could make him stumble. "Take your time, Papa. All okay. Lotsa time. I got you. Don't worry. I got you. I care you."

"Thank you, Maya. I had a great night. Sorry you have to take care of me." He said, "sorry" and "thank you" over and over.

She reclined the passenger seat and laid him down. "Papa you tell me if you sick and I pull over and let you puke, okay? Okay?" He was fast asleep. She took his coat and rolled it into a pillow for him. She placed it gently under his head. *Oh Buddha, help me get him home.*

She looked over at him. She ran her fingers through his hair, caressed his face, bent over and kissed his forehead.

There'd be no breakup tonight.

94

OVERNIGHT REVELATION

Glenn woke with a start. *Where am I? My bed. Foggy. Cobwebs. Dry mouth.* He staggered to the bathroom. Last night's steak and wine were all over the tub and sink. He'd somehow managed to puke over everything in the bathroom—everything *except* the toilet. His head was pounding. He heard her call out from the living room. "Good morning, Glenn."

He smelled the coffee she'd made. He was still fully clothed. He opened his mouth. Nothing came out. A slight croak. *Maya? She's here?*

He staggered out into the living room. She was drinking coffee, on the sofa, watching the morning news. "Good morning. There's coffee. I go now."

Still foggy, Glenn leaned on the wall in front of her. "Did we? Did I treat you with respect?"

She smiled, shook her head, eyes twinkled in amusement, "Glenn, no and yes. Nothing happened. We all good. You treat me good. We don't do it. No way you can. I don't let you, too. No trouble last night. I want make sure you okay and then you start puking. I stay make sure you okay. I'm not maid, but. You clean your own mess."

She gathered up her purse and put the coffee cup in the sink. "I go now. Not sleep yet." Glenn tried to give her money, but she pushed it back. "Last night enough. You keep for lunch this week." He leaned in to kiss her goodbye. "Ewww nooooo . . . You stink. I owe you double kiss next time, okay? You go brush teeth now."

She wanted to do one last check. "Glenn, I go. You okay?"

"I'm okay."

She blew him a kiss and slipped out the door.

He texted work. Sick today. Not coming in.

She sat in her car. Phone open. There were 14 missed calls, 12 voicemails, and 20 texts from Jae. *Where are you. You're dead. He's dead. Just come back. Tell me you're sorry and it's forgotten.* She ignored them all.

A few hours earlier, before the sun came up, she'd been alone in his apartment with only his steady breathing to keep her company. She'd had plenty of time to reflect. *Is there really future for us? Is Jae better choice?* She had seen his wife's pictures around the apartment and saw how happy they had been. She had looked through their wedding albums and all the photos they had kept over the years. She saw all the happiness. *Could I do that for him? Why even thinking about it?*

Maybe write him letter goodbye and leave? She found a pad and pen. Speaking English wasn't her strongest suit, but she excelled in writing, especially with the help of a translation app.

> *Dear Glenn,*
>
> *You make me so happy when I'm with you. This is not fantasy. For me, it's very real. But marriage is very important for me and I cannot be the one to come between you and your wife.*
>
> *As long as there is a chance that she will come back to you, we should remain friends only. I only want you to be happy and pray that one day you two will continue to make wonderful memories and keep adding to the pictures I found in your apartment. Maybe she will come back to you soon.*
>
> *But you already know I also have a problem. Crazy Tom and Tia tried to explain to me but no need since I've seen several times how I can get, but more important, how my actions or inability to control my actions hurt you.*
>
> *Please know I cried each time I hurt you. I don't know what is wrong with me, why I do it, or what I can do to stop it. You say love conquers all. I fear one day it will rip us apart.*
>
> *I love you so much. Tonight, I was going to leave you, but that is for another time. I'm watching you sleep now so peacefully. I'm glad you got drunk. It gave me a chance to come to your home and feel*

how happy she made you.

Glenn, in my wildest dreams, I don't think I can ever make you as happy as she did. I would love to try, but I fear the opposite, that my madness will take over one day again, and hurt you beyond the returning point. I cannot bear to hurt you anymore.

Don't worry about me. If I can care for my family, I will be okay. And you've helped so much. One day I will tell them about you and all you've done.

Please remember that first night I sang "Tattoo" for you.

I'll always love you Glenn. You'll always be a part of me.

Love, Maya

As she finished, she heard him murmuring and ran to his bedside. He was sweating. She wet a washcloth and wiped his face. He reached for her hand and cradled his head in it. *Mommy?* That's what it sounded like. She kissed his forehead. *Go to sleep, baby.*

After that, she went to sit next to him from time to time. Most times to make sure he didn't drown in his own puke. *He look just like baby. Like an angel. My angel.* He shivered once. She put a blanket on him. Caressed his face. He responded, even in sleep.

———————————

Sitting in her Audi, she had her eyes closed as if committing that moment to memory. Bzzzzzzt. Another text from Jae. She ignored it like the others.

She started the car. In her hand, she held the letter she wrote. *One day I give him.*

Driving back to her apartment, she wasn't sure how Jae was going to react. But for the first time in a month, she felt decent.

95

CONSOLATION

The bathroom sink, tub, floor and walls were splattered with regurgitated wine and steak. It looked like a giant purple brain had exploded in there. *Idiot! Why didn't I stick my head in the toilet and keep it there?*

By afternoon, the apartment was clean with an odd smell—Pine-sol overlaid on the putrid smell of last night's dinner. *Good grief,* he said to himself, *I better call a maid service or something to clean this place up right. Maybe a hazmat company.*

He sat in the living room with the only things he could hold down, a burrito and Diet Coke. He went through critical emails, called Debbie and Mike with instructions, and reassured them he'd be back the next day.

The room was still spinning, and the dry heaves kept coming. *I wish I could remember last night a little better. How'd she end up here? I remember going to the restroom at Anna's. Wait, she said something about Lynh, like Anna knew Lynh? How did she get me up here? Did I walk or did she carry me? What happened at Anna's?*

He leaned back on the couch and thought he smelled her just so slightly, before losing her scent to the Pine-sol. He suddenly felt tired and sleep crashed over him like a wave.

He woke up five hours later and drank a quart of water. Last night's events were still a blur. *I can't even be sure this morning wasn't a dream. Maybe it was? Oh, wait.*

He ran to the kitchen. *Yeah, the coffee cup she used is still there.* There was a trace of lipstick. The sight of it caused a wave of warmth to course through him. *Who would take care of their customer like this? Is this still a fantasy?*

I wonder what Anna thinks?

It was near closing time at Anna's back bar. It was empty, and Anna was into her closing routine. She'd already sent her barback home. It was just the two of them, like so many nights before. "Hi Anna! So what did you think of her?" He wanted a good opinion from Anna. *She's seen us together twice already. I know she saw the spark between us. She knows Maya took care of me, took me home.*

Anna came out from behind the bar and took a seat next to him. Her leg slightly touching his, she poured his beer for him. Then, she took a potato chip and popped it into his mouth, then took his glasses from him and started cleaning for him.

His eyes narrowed. "What the heck, Anna? What are you doing?"

She let her hand touch his. "What do you mean?"

He pulled his hand back. "Stop it, you're creeping me out. You're acting like—"

"Like a bargirl, Glenn? Your bargirl? Like Maya? Like someone who knows you have mommy issues and is using it to get to you and all your money?"

She got off the stool, standing in front of him with arms crossed. "What is wrong with you? If you needed someone to lean on, why didn't you come here?"

His eyes twitched. *She sounds like she's jealous. Is she?*

She could read his mind. "Don't get stupid. I'm too old to be jealous, and besides, darling, you're not my type." Then she slapped him across the face.

She let the sting settle in before she drilled into him. "Do you know what you're doing? Does she know you have mommy issues?"

He looked over her shoulder, at nothing in particular, to avoid eye contact. "Maybe. I told her about my mom."

"Stupid, you know they can smell it right away. Like sharks smelling blood in the water. They know how to twist you up to get money out of you."

He slid off his stool. This is starting to sound like a lecture. "I gotta go."

She pulled at his sleeve and pushed him back against his stool. "No, after all those nights you sat here crying into your drink, and all those nights I had to put you back together again, you owe me this. To hear me out."

He stood there, hands on his hips. "Okay, Anna. I know this is for my benefit because you care for me."

She rolled her eyes. "Oh, fuck you, you pompous, self-righteous, self-pitying ass. This is for Katie." Anna and Katie used to go shopping together.

Especially the yearly, what-to-do-about-Glenn's-wardrobe shopping weekends.

He'd never heard her swear before.

She sighed as only an old friend could. "Glenn, I know the industry. She doesn't care for you. It's business. It's money. I called around. She's got lots of men around her. You're just part of the stable. And she's using you. You think I'm dumb on this? Put it to the test, tell her no more money, only love. She'll dump you so fast."

He stared at the TV. Rejection settled in. The devil's voice said, "Fuck Anna, let her talk five more minutes and get out of there."

Anna went on. "Don't be a stupid dog, Glenn!"

At this, he turned to her. She sounded like Lynh. She knew it too.

He challenged her. "You called Lynh?!" Her denial couldn't come out fast enough. He exploded. "Aw, fuck this. All you bar bitches stick together, don't you." Years of friendship and crying at the bar evaporated. He stepped away from the bar, pushing her hand away.

She followed him with her eyes as he walked to the door. "Are *you* kidding me? I'm trying to knock some sense into you." She was yelling across the floor. "*What would Katie say?* What would she say, Glenn? She would say, you're still married to her, you worthless piece of shit who brought this bargirl to *our* place. That's what she would say!"

She wouldn't let up and walked halfway across the floor to make sure he was hearing her. "Don't bother bringing this girl back here again. And if you keep seeing her, don't bother coming back here, period. And when she takes you for all you got—your money, Katie's money, your house, your dignity, shit, your wedding ring too—*don't come crying to me!*"

He was angry. Red hot. Couldn't see straight. Clenched fists. Gritting his teeth. Breathing hard but not really breathing. He had nowhere else to go but out of there.

Anna was upset. *How could he do this? He's better than that.*

He was out the door before she could say she was sorry for saying all those things. But she wasn't. She had a feeling he wasn't coming back. *Oh Katie, if you're up there somewhere, look out for our boy.*

He turned to the only person he'd ever fully trusted. It was nearly 1:00 a.m.

He walked into her room. The smell of antiseptic mingled with the sweetness emanating from flowers around her bed. The familiar whooshing sound of the ventilator and low din of the radio in the background. The lights were down low.

Except for the ventilation tube, she looked like she had so many nights when he came home late. She always woke with outstretched arms, and they'd hug and kiss goodnight.

He was by her side. No outstretched arms. No hug. No kiss. He missed those goodnight kisses.

He poked her shoulder. "Katie? Katie?" Marta came by and closed the door to just a crack so the couple could have more privacy.

"Katie?" No answer. In his mind, he saw her turn to him like she had so many times before. "Katie? I have a problem and I don't know what to do." He paused. *Can she hear me?*

"I met someone. Don't be mad. She's never going to replace you. But I'm lonely, and there's been no one who could understand me like you did. Then I meet this girl. It was like a God-ordained thing you know? It was weird how we met. And she's a bargirl. You know those places you never liked me going with Tomo?"

He sat down next to her and brushed her hair back. "I tailspinned and I was unfaithful with some of these girls. I'm so sorry. I was so lonely and needed to feel like I mattered to someone. It was wrong. I realize that. I'm so sorry, Katie. I was feeling bad, and I prayed to God to make me stop. Then I ran into her at this bar. Just so you know, no sex. I told her all about you. She says you are still with me. I hope so."

He held her hand. "We get together once a week. I sing karaoke now. Can you imagine? She makes me try new things. I eat Thai food now. I've eaten crickets, and she's got me back in the gym again. She's young. She calls me Papa. I give her money to take care of her mom and sister. I think she has daddy issues. She got me to try fantasy football. I took her to the Paradise Club. Our old table. I hope you're okay with that. I swear I could feel you smiling from above."

He took a deep breath. "Anna is mad at me. I'm not welcome at Anna's. She said I'm being unfaithful to you. I don't know what to do. Should I stop?" It was weird but Glenn thought he heard Katie's voice. *Are you happy?*

He squeezed his eyes shut, then opened. "I am happy, Katie. It's a different happy from us. I wish you'd come back, and we could be happy like that again. She gets me, you know? Like you did . . . like you do."

Confusion and frustration seeped into his mind and heart. His eyes were getting hot, tears blurring his vision. He laid his head on her bosom and sobbed. "Please come back, Katie. Please come back. I need you. I'll stop seeing her, I promise. Just come back." He was rocking back and forth now. She used to hold him and whisper, "shhhh" in his ear. She'd say, "It'll be okay," over and over. Till he was spent.

The whooshing sound of the ventilator sounded like "shhhh." And for a split second, he heard her voice again. *It'll be okay, be happy.*

It was her voice; he could swear it was. It didn't come from her body, but somewhere above or around him. He felt a warmth, and his eyelids grew heavy. They were together again. She was on the bed and he sat by her. She was smiling and laughing about something he'd said.

Marta peeked in. He was asleep, head on his wife's chest. To Marta, it looked like he'd been crying. But there he was with that weird smile. Sweet dreams, she guessed. It was always like this. She brought in a blanket and covered him with it.

96

OASIS

He woke up the next morning, refreshed. In between meetings, he stared at nothing on his computer screen and absent-mindedly signed stacks of approvals already vetted by Debbie and Mike. His only thoughts focused on recollections of the disastrous second date he'd had, or at least the way it ended. Bits of memory flashed back here and there.

He recalled the obscene amount of wine he'd drunk in the last twenty minutes before blacking out. He remembered her trying to stop him, then saying, "Yes, Papa, you can have one more. I take care of you tonight."

He relived falling off the stool at Anna's and remembered two arms swooping in and scooping him up before he buckled to the floor. *She truly is my bodyguard.*

He vaguely recalled stumbling out the door at Anna's and had some memory of her carrying him with one arm and navigating double oak doors to get outside. *Damn, she's strong!*

He retraced his steps in the parking lot. He could still hear the crunch of her heels on asphalt as she trudged step by step with him to her car. He could still feel the kindness in her voice as she told him there was lots of time, take his time, be careful, or something like that. *How did she not sprain her ankle carrying me?*

He tried to coax more from his brain. He saw himself sitting in her car, then falling backward, or did she reach over and lay him down? He heard himself praying to God not to let him puke in her car.

One memory was very clear. As she drove him home he'd asked, "Do you do this for all your customers?" He would always remember the are-you-fucking-kidding-me look she gave him in reply. "Papa, go to sleep."

She really did take good care of me. Wonder why Anna didn't call me a taxi? A lot of girls, not just bargirls, would have called a taxi. This must mean something. Who does this unless there's something there? Not sure what to say. On impulse, he fired off a text.

> I don't have a lot of people in my circle I trust my life with. You're one of them. Thank you for getting me home safe and taking care of me all night. Have a great weekend.

 You are welcome ☺

Across town, she tucked her phone away just as Jae returned to their lunch table.

The mood between her and Jae was lukewarm at best—in truth, it was more like subdued hate. Jae kept telling her all would be good if she only got rid of the old guy. She kept promising it would happen, but they had to do it right because Glenn was such a powerful man. She alluded to the dead Chinatown Merchants executives found in the river. This kept Jae at bay, although each passing day found him getting more and more pissy.

Tuesday nights found him brooding, albeit with his penis inside one of the girls from the Starfall Lounge. In his mind, Jae thought more and more that if Glenn were that strong, he might have to take him out first.

For her part, she was simply stalling. There was one more event in her life she wanted to share with Glenn. Then she could bear not being with him, physically anyway. The heart and soul were different matters.

Meanwhile, Tuesdays continued to be an oasis to her. *I only need two or three more times with him. Just have something to remember. And give him something to remember. One day when he forgive me for leaving him, he have good memories. I will make sure of this.*

————————

She was waiting for him the following Tuesday. Brimming with excitement, she could hardly contain herself. She gave him a big hug as soon as he walked through the door. "I pass, Papa! I pass!"

He'd never felt such a surge of pride before. He lifted her off the ground and twirled her around. "Yes, yes! I knew you could do it! That's my girl!" The barflies were used to this already. Some muttered congratulations. One asked for drinks on the house. Glenn bit and bought everyone a round.

They sat in their booth. "Papa, come to my ceremony next week?"

"When?"

She checked her phone. 11:00 a.m. March 26. It was on a Tuesday morning.

Concerned just for a moment, he said, "Sure."

She saw the look on his face. "Don't worry, Papa, we still have our time that night."

He rustled up a smile. "No. Maybe I should give you a break. You go out with your friends and family." *And your secret boyfriend or whoever else you're always hanging me out to dry for.*

"We see, Papa. I let you know, okay? Tonight, we have pre-celebration?"

They closed down the bar for the first time in two months. No cousin. No dog. No inventory. Lots of kisses. And this time, the after-hours security guard paid no mind to the white Audi sitting alone in the parking lot with its fogged-up windows.

97

CITIZENSHIP

The citizenship ceremony was held at the Federal Building. Some fifty individuals from twenty-one different countries became United States citizens that day. It was a melting pot of cultures, half of which were Filipino and Vietnamese, and surprisingly, one each from Canada, Ireland and Israel. The patriotic citizenship oath administered brought back memories of the one he'd taken before shipping out to boot camp.

Glenn was the only non-Thai who went to see Maya take the oath. No other customers, or "support friends," as she called them. A group of Thai women surrounded her as soon as the ceremony was over, Chloe among them.

Maya caught up with Glenn after the hug-fest with the women. "My sisters from other mothers. Love them. They my family here." She seemed happy, except that it was a Tuesday. "What you wanna do tonight?" she asked him tentatively.

He sucked in his cheeks, rubbing his chin. "I don't know. Why don't you take the night off and celebrate with your friends?"

She paused, searching his face for any hint of trouble, of little boy trouble. "Maybe." She was hesitant. "I call you . . . I text you later?"

He hugged her and turned to leave. *I got no problem letting her party with her friends. I don't want to see all her other customers, and she'll ignore me all night anyway. Might as well not be there.*

Vey from Thai Garden caught up with Glenn. "You coming tonight?"

A bit confused, he answered. "What do you mean?"

It was Vey's turn to look surprised. Pointing back to the group of Thai women, Vey said, "We have party for Maya. Other customers and friends come too."

Glenn shrugged his shoulders. "Up to Maya."

Vey's look of surprise turned to confusion. The gears were turning in her head. She got a look like only a big sister could have when little sister screwed something up again. She smiled. Not a happy smile. It was a please-forgive-her-rudeness-and-stupidity smile. "I email you later." Glenn gave her a thumbs up and left Vey, Maya and the others to their celebration.

––––––––––

Driving back to the office, he reflected on that hug fest. Unknown to Maya and thanks mostly to Mike's research, Glenn knew about all the women—Maya's "sisters." There was the massage palace owner, the Buddhist temple devotee, and of course, Chloe. There was also Bella, who was big at the Buddhist temple and had recently divorced her Army husband. In Glenn's mind, she was right on schedule, divorcing a military man after ten years to claim half his pension.

Glenn knew who had kids, who was divorced, what occupations they had, and who had once been bargirls. One of the "sisters," married to an Air Force officer who was overseas, juggled two boyfriends here in town.

Walking into his office, his mind was still at the Federal Building. *Interesting bunch. Should be a very, very interesting party. Do I seriously want to go? Shit, I don't need to see a parade of her customers lining up to buy her shots and steal kisses. I don't care if she calls them friends or support group or whatever. And dammit, I don't need to run into this boyfriend or whoever she keeps running off early to go see.*

But curiosity gnawed at him. *Who was it? One way to find out.*

Weariness crept in. *Geez,* he yawned, *I'm exhausted. It's been a year working on this, being her cheerleader and coach. Months of quizzing her on Tuesdays and finally, she's a citizen.*

His Google calendar buzzed. He looked down. *Still gotta take care of some business. Burned a lot of daylight picking up her flower bouquet, writing out her card, and waiting for the ceremony to start.*

His calendar showed back-to-back phone conferences the rest of the day and into the evening. *Today's a good day. First chance to counsel Tony since his election. The newest council member. Been a long one, that campaign, complete with recount hearings before the state Supreme Court.*

I'm tired now. Gonna be even more tired later. I really could not care less if she wanted to celebrate with her friends. Pretty much I'm not part of her world there. I'm not part of any world except for 180 minutes every week. I might as well be a holographic image to her.

Several hours later, distracted by his phone meetings, he hadn't noticed it was late afternoon already. Finishing up with the newest council member, he saw two texts that came in one after the other.

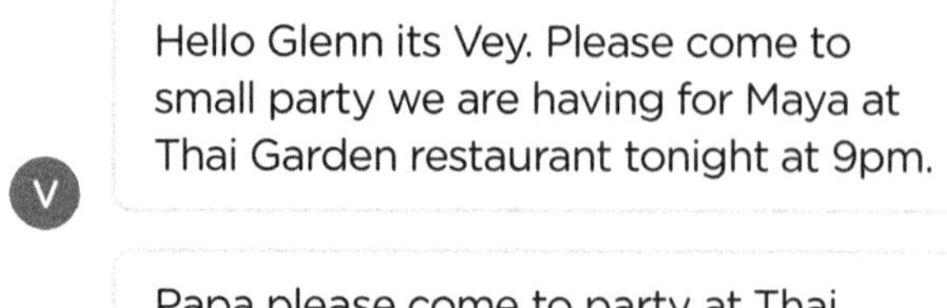

He finished up with the council newbie. "Thanks, Tony. No, that election was all you. Well, maybe the prayer I gave on election night helped!" He stared at the texts. *One after the other? Didn't know Vey had my number. She must have taken it to Maya hard.*

While Maya's other "sisters" didn't know Glenn, Vey considered Glenn her friend and brother. He had helped her out several times at the restaurant. Had Glenn understood Thai, he would have overheard several conversations, always with cover-up smiles, in which Vey told Maya that he was good for her and called Maya an idiot for treating him like shit sometimes.

Glenn checked his Instagram account. Maya posted a pic of the gang at the Mai Tai Bar having a grand time. It was four o'clock. *Is anyone still going to be standing at nine? They look sloshed already.*

He went to the hospital to check on Katie. He entered the room just as his phone died. As always, he charged it in the outlet next to her ventilator. He popped open a Diet Coke and settled down to talk story with her. "Hey Katie, she did it. She's official now. I feel like I did something in her life, you know? More than just being some guy who gives her money and sings songs. Now she can go to beauty school and be on her way to her dreams."

He drained half the can of soda. "Tony wants to start something up with me where we use his position with his law practice and really help people, you know? The reason why we got him in there. Lot of exciting stuff going on. You always liked Tony and the good he can do. Maybe we run him for mayor in eight years."

He brushed back her hair, stroked her cheek with the back of his hand and sighed. "I miss you, Katie. She doesn't understand politics like you do. She doesn't understand me like you do." Again, he felt something stir in him. *It's okay. Be happy.*

Eight o'clock came quickly enough. "Well I gotta go see our girl, Katie. Love you."

He pulled his phone off the wall and started it up. Two texts buzzed up immediately.

One at 7:00 p.m.:

Papa is it ok if I just celebrate with my friends tonight and I'll see you later next week?

The next, one hour later at 8:00 p.m.:

hi Papa I here at the restaurant and it's okay

His phone buzzed right after he opened the texts. She was on the line. *Musta got the read receipts.*

He didn't pick up, still staring at the two texts, irritated. *Crap, she and Vey must have been going back and forth all afternoon about me coming to the party or not. Then she pulls a veto at 7:00, and when I don't answer she panics then says its okay?*

He laughed out loud. *She's the one that plays the no-response mind game. Wonder how she feels now about not getting an answer right away?*

He went back to Katie. Rubbed her shoulder. "Good night, Katie."

On his way out, all kinds of scenarios played out in his mind. He saw a bunch of Maya's friends and family and a group of customers who were familiar with her. He saw her flirting back and forth between customers, other family and friends. *Shit this, I wonder if she's going to be little miss flirt like the night with the construction crew, or even worse, her birthday.*

There were questions too. *Is the mystery boyfriend there now? Is he going to be there when I get there? What is waiting for me at the restaurant?*

His stomach started to knot up. Anna's voice haunted him. *You know, Glenn, you've heard the country song. Love is not a one-way street. It's two ways and certainly not one way from your perspective, and sometimes if you love the girl you gotta bend to her needs even if it rips your heart up. That's love, Glenn*

His phone buzzed again. Another text.

She almost sounds like she's pleading.

ok

I gotta keep it simple. Don't want to say anything wrong. I can tell she's on edge. Probably thinks I flipped out. Well good, she should feel the stress sometimes.

Glenn walked into the restaurant and was greeted by a sea of people. It was a packed house. The restaurant was also playing host to a vacation travel multi-level marketing club.

Tucked away in the corner of the bar area were Maya's sisters he'd seen earlier. There were also two cross-dressers in all their glam glory. They had the attention of one of the bar patrons, who was oblivious to what was waiting for him south of the border.

Glenn surveyed the entire scene. The sisters were drunk, slurring and singing Thai love heartbreak songs. The cross-dressers were more attractive than a lot of bargirls he'd met. *Wow. It's a circus. First time I ever heard karaoke sound like mountain lions fighting. And that guy really should beware of beautiful women with deep voices and Adam's apples.*

He took a deep breath and squared his shoulders. *This oughta be good.*

98

DUPED

Vey came out from around the bar to greet Glenn.

Maya stayed behind the bar. "I'm the bartender tonight!"

He scratched his head. *That's funny. It's her night and Vey is making her work? Makes sense, I guess. Vacation club in full throttle.*

Glenn looked around. *I don't see any of her customers. No police captain. No boyfriend. Like the ceremony earlier. Only her Thai sisters. Am I the only one invited? Maybe phantom boyfriend was here, and she sent him home? No way. Too far-fetched. This is reality, not some romance novel.*

Glenn sat at one end of the bar and expected Maya to come out and greet him, but she stayed behind the bar and pointed to her friend Bella, the Buddhist temple devotee. "Bella will take care of you." *Why so formal? She's treating me like I'm some guy just walked in off the street.*

Glenn turned to Bella. *Oh well, good chance to get know her friends.*

As the night wore on, it became clear to Glenn that Maya was not coming out from behind the bar. She spent a lot of time pouring drinks for all her guests including him but didn't say more than ten words to him all night. When she wasn't pouring drinks or screaming Thai at her friends, she was behind the bar texting on her phone. *Who is she texting?*

Glenn was transfixed on a guy he didn't recognize in the corner, who was also texting all night. *Is that the phantom boyfriend? Are they connecting by text? I heard of boyfriends keeping tabs on their girls by showing up at work and tethering them by text. Is this what's going on? She shoulda let me stay home.*

By 10:00 p.m., the vacation club throng had dwindled to a six-person mini-group. Vey had one waitress working the group and was handling the bar. Vey and Maya were behind the bar chattering in Thai. No fake smiles. Vey was talking rapid fire, pointing at Glenn. Maya wore a frown. Glenn was on guard. *She's being scolded. Vey's making her come to me. This is not going to be good.*

The guy in the corner called out to Vey, gave her a huge hug, and left. False alarm.

Maya came out from around the bar but instead of going to Glenn she went to her sisters and started trading shots with them. Glenn was stuck right in the middle of the vacation club mini-group. After 5 glasses of champagne, 2 shots of scotch, and 5 beers he was feeling no pain and certainly not bored. A buxom young woman leaned into him, her breath heavy with Crown. "You're cute. I got daddy issues, babe. Try me?" It was loud enough for Maya to notice.

Maya's glare could have cut metal. She threw a balled-up napkin at Glenn. "Papa, I love *you!*" The buxom young woman caught the hint. She lightly rubbed his crotch and whispered, "See you, Papa."

Glenn caught Maya's eye. She was smiling in that, fuck-you-you're-mine-and-don't-talk-to-anyone-but-me way. *Seriously? Now you pay attention to me?*

Vey couldn't understand why they were sitting three seats apart. She managed to get microphones to both and clicked on their favorite Elvis selection.

Glenn glanced at the clock while singing: 11:00 p.m. They were singing their song, sitting three seats apart. *Was she waiting for me to come over? Why didn't she come to me? She's not even looking at me! This is the most dry ass rendition of the song we ever sang.*

Her sisters were a drunken mess. Only Bella stayed in control and took charge, getting everybody in their cars with sober drivers and sending everyone home.

The party unraveled quickly, almost if it was a planned finish. Everyone said their goodbyes and left Glenn and Maya alone at the bar, with Vey tending. The vacation group moved to a booth. *Finally, I'll have some time to spend with her. Maybe I'll go home a little earlier, 12:30.* He walked over and sat next to her.

"Hey Maya, I didn't get to tell you congrat—"

Glancing at her phone, she cut him off. "Papa, you have to call Uber now."

"What Uber? Still early."

Her face scrunched. "Papa, you have to go. I have to leave."

"Okay, let me take a piss first." In the men's room, he swayed as he drained his bladder, thinking he wanted another beer, and that the night was a little too early to call it quits. *What the shit? Night's too early. I'm staying. I made a new friend tonight and she's still here.*

He walked up to Maya from behind and tapped her shoulder, bent over and whispered in her ear. "Yeah, I think I'm gonna stay but it's okay, you can go." Something started nagging at his mind. *Does she have someone else to meet elsewhere? Okay, then. Go see him or her or it. We'll sort this shit out later.* "Go, I promise I'll be okay. Just one more beer."

She once told him she wouldn't leave him alone again to get drunk out of control.

Her shoulders slumped and her face frowned in frustration. He expected her to tell him to finish his beer and she'd stay with him, as she'd done so many times before.

But not this time. Her voice rose two octaves. "I have to get up at 5:30. You have to go now. You have to call Uber. Do you want me to take you home?" He thought for a moment and said, "Okay." They'd hardly seen each other that night and he thought he'd at least have a few minutes with her on the drive home.

Bluff called. Her face contorted. She changed her mind. "I think I drank too much tonight. I don't wanna drive in town. Can you call Uber now?!"

He raised his hands, palms out to her, as he backed toward the door. *There's no arguing here. She's about to make a scene. Why the fucking urgency? There's never been in this kind of rush before. Fuck this and fuck her.*

He turned and walked out the door clicking on his Uber app. A driver was three minutes away. She came outside. He walked away into the parking lot. She followed, pleading. "Don't be mad, please don't be mad at me."

He turned to her. Never heard her voice so shrill. He managed only a flat smile. The corners would just not turn up. He mustered the most pleasant voice he could. "I'm not mad."

They sounded like grunts to her. She needed him out. Jae insisted he wasn't going to be held off anymore. He didn't like being at the restaurant earlier and being shooed out, for him, the Tuesday night old guy. He was bringing his boys.

There wasn't much time for more talk as the Uber appeared. He turned to her. "I'm never gonna be part of your world, am I, Maya? Only a fantasy, right? You didn't want me here. You didn't want to be seen with me tonight in front of your sisters. I'm never gonna be more than a good customer, a support friend, am I?" He shouldn't have, but he'd already started. He was lashing out.

She was frustrated. She saw Jae's car behind the Uber. She was trying to keep him from getting killed, or worse yet, killing someone. "Why you say that? You don't know! I invite you party with my family. You see any other customers? Not special enough? You see anybody else other than my sisters?" They stood in silence. The Uber car pulled up. Before he could get in, she took one step forward and kissed him goodnight in the tender way she always did. "Next week we go out?" He didn't answer. He climbed into the car and slammed the door shut. As the Uber reversed, he saw her getting into her car.

Glenn lashed out at no one in particular in the back seat of the Uber. His mind was a mess. *So what she invited me. So what if I was the only customer? It's still my night and I still gave her money. So what she sang our song with me. She wasn't even standing next to me. She was two chairs away all night. So what she kissed me goodnight. Seems like she was doing that as a consolation prize*

Glenn licked his wounds like a wounded animal, like a wolf that stepped into a bear trap. The little boy made a major appearance. The Uber sped across town. *Why couldn't she just leave? Why not let me have one more beer? Vey would've taken care of me.*

Somewhere in the back of his mind he remembered all the times he told her not to worry and he ended up shitfaced, worked, or roofied. *But I'm better than that now. I would have had one more beer and I would have left. Why was it so important that I leave? So she has to meet somebody. Then go. Probably at the bar. I only wanted to have one drink with her. Did she know this was our fifty-second Tuesday? A whole year of Tuesdays.*

The Uber pulled up in front of his condo. Glenn leaned forward. "Driver, can I get you to take me someplace else?"

"Sure, where do you wanna go?"

"Down the street to the other bar."

"You got it." They were there in two minutes. To Glenn's relief he didn't see her car.

"Where next?" the driver asked.

"Home." He had a few beers in the fridge. And then something hit him hard. A thought came to him slowly and then it exploded in his head. He argued with himself. *If somebody was coming to Thai Garden, then why does she leave? I saw her getting in her car. I saw her pulling out of the driveway behind us. And then a sickening thought. No way! Did she double back?*

I'm not gonna be able to sleep tonight unless I know. He laughed to himself. *I'm gonna go there and like anything else with us, find out she's gone. She really did go home.* "Hey, can you take me back to the restaurant?"

"Sure, let me call this in."

They were two blocks away and Glenn got a text from Maya.

He bounced his head off the window. *Idiot me! I just spent another $20 on Uber solely to soothe my stupid neurotic personality.* "Hey man, turn around at the restaurant and take me home."

"Sure thing."

They turned into the restaurant's driveway and that's when Glenn saw the white Audi.

99

BETRAYAL

Glenn threw a hundred onto the front seat. "Wait for me." He walked through the door. He looked left then right.

Off to the left, the mini-group had moved to the bar. Glenn put his index finger to his mouth—the quiet signal—as the regulars saw him enter. One guy nodded, and then they all turned back to each other.

Glenn took two steps forward and turned right. *She's home, my ass!*

They were in the first booth. She was on the inside facing the door. Jae was to her left with his face in her neck. Her eyes were closed. To Glenn, she looked like she was enjoying it. Glenn followed the line of Jae's left arm to the point where it disappeared below the table. It wasn't hard to imagine Jae's hand between her legs.

Remembering their first meeting, he heard her clear as day: *What we have is fantasy, just happy while we together.*

But what he saw looked real, not fantasy. He could see Jae's tongue lapping at her neck like some character in a weird Japanese porn flick.

Jae bit her neck, and she winced. Her eyes opened a bit, enough to see Glenn. Her eyes widened, surprise mixed with panic and remorse. Their eyes met as she sat frozen. Glenn turned away just as she mouthed, Glenn, sorry. He didn't see it.

Jae stirred. She pulled down her top, putting Jae's mouth to her nipple. She needed to distract him. Somehow dry her tears, regain composure, put on a smile and move on. She thought of her family. She thought of Glenn. Two tears dropped, and she sobbed and heaved once. Jae thought she shuddered. "Like it, huh, babe," he muffled, about to look up. She pressed down on his head.

Glenn jumped in the Uber. The last time he caught her with someone was Eddie. She pleaded it was only kissing in the private room. Even so, Chloe said she was drugged on ecstasy, the drug that lowered a woman's inhibition. *I was okay with it. Let it go. Sabai. This time. Different. No drugs. Out in the open. Fuck this shit. No more. I thought we were real. She played me.*

It wasn't a long ride but Rihanna's "Take A Bow" came on as soon as they hit the freeway. *Melodramatic,* he thought, turning to the window, lights flashing by. *What timing, the song about cheaters, pretenders and wannabes.*

It was only 12:30 when the driver dropped him off. *I can't believe I took the day off tomorrow because I thought we were going to close the bar down. For Pete's sake, I coached her through this. This should have been* our *party.*

His throat was dry, tight. *Need another beer, a cold one, and company.*

There was a bar he hadn't been to in over two years. It was a ten-minute walk away. He almost ran.

He walked in, sat at the bar, and off to the side saw the forty-year-old mama-san he'd fucked twice during an afternoon session two years before—the summer of sin, he called it. She had just opened the bar, had no girls working for her and was feeling horny. So that afternoon, she closed the bar, locked the front doors and turned up the AC, and the two had their way with each other for a couple of hours. Then the night shift bartender had arrived, and they'd gone to a back room for another hour.

She was sitting at the bar, surrounded by three gentlemen who had to be at least seventy years old on average. He was hoping she wouldn't recognize him. Holding court with what looked like her stable, awash in their attention, she seemed not to notice him at all, and that put him at ease.

The elderly Korean man working the bar gave him his beer and there wasn't much else to see. *At least I won't get into trouble.* Then a hag of a woman with loose-fitting dentures scooted onto the stool next to him. "Hi, how are you?"

He nodded.

She touched his arm lightly. "Would you like some company?"

He was careful not to make eye contact. "No, thanks." *Certainly not you anyway.* This was one of those places with ultraviolet lighting because it was a strip bar, and he was having a hard time focusing.

It wasn't like Lynh's bar. It was one big room, a bar area, with four booths in the corners of the room turned to the wall to give patrons privacy while negotiating whatever they could with the girls.

While Lynh's bar was known as family-style, this place was known for its full service. Most patrons didn't really care what the women looked like as long as they had mouths and vaginas and didn't cost much. One jukebox played hip-hop stripper music while the sixty-year-old stripper was on stage and '80s and '90s pop playlists the rest of the time. The stripper got paid extra when she incorporated cigarettes and ping pong balls into her act.

The old lady pressed. "What do you want?" *Maybe I only want you to go away. Good grief! Am I so desperate for company that I'm going to end up with this person?*

Then his eyes focused. He saw someone off to the side in a booth in a dark corner of the bar. She followed his gaze, and she asked again. "Anything I can do for you? What do you need, honey?" Glenn pointed to the corner of the bar. "Her."

The hag waved at the corner. A woman so beautiful that he forgot Maya for a split second came forward. Her name was Vivian.

100

ENTER VIVIAN

Exquisite was the word that came to him. He blinked as she approached. *She's Asian, maybe Eurasian. Looks Vietnamese, French stock.* He noticed her skin, like ivory. With her chestnut hair in a ponytail, light makeup and full lips, she sported a very sexy natural look. He was immediately aroused as soon as he focused on her mid-length light blue satin cocktail dress with a slit up the left side.

She took his hand and led him to a booth in the back. She straddled his hips, trapping his hand under her. She was wet with no panties, and he was hard instantly. She lowered the top of her dress and pulled his head to her breasts. Her nipple popped into his mouth. Primal instinct took over—almost.

He wanted it so bad but summoned every ounce of willpower. "Stop. Please stop."

She eyed him curiously. "What, baby? Everything okay? You come already? I clean you up." The accent was Vietnamese, but the English was properly spoken.

Out of breath and panting, his blood was racing. "No. No." *Gotta cool down.* "A few more minutes and I might. Not here for this."

She looked him over, and she could smell nice all over him. *Not the usual,* she thought, *and he's hurting.* She covered herself up. Then put her hand to the side of his face. "What is it baby? Tell me. Let me help you."

He searched her face. She seemed genuinely concerned. He told her the whole story. No sex. Married. Need to be clean. Maya. Fantasy. Reality. Tonight.

She was expensive. He bought five shots at $40 each. She listened for an hour. She held him. She kissed his forehead. It might have been fantasy or an act; he didn't care. She was good at it, showing compassion. *Just need a warm body to hold me,* he justified to himself, *need to hear a kind voice tell me it's gonna be okay.*

But he was guarded. *No mommy here. Not looking for it. Not taking it. But I can feel it.* Oxytocin ran through his brain. *Is this what crack feels like to an addict?*

She caressed the side of his face.

He leaned into her hand. "I'm done with her. Maybe I visit you from now on?"

"You can, honey. Always here." She was a little over forty but looked thirty. Slim. Curvier than Maya and more endowed. "What on your mind, baby?"

"I want to kiss you."

"I don't kiss, baby." Straddling his lap again, she looked down. His longing expression touched her heart. She leaned forward, pinched his lips together and kissed him. "No tongue, okay? I don't know you."

He was a bit amused. *I don't know you either. Smart of her to pinch my lips. Other guys must try to slip her the tongue.* "No tongue, promise."

She kissed him again. *He likes to kiss. Only kiss.* She kissed him off and on all night. Like butterflies flitting in and out.

She rubbed lip gloss on her lips. "You kiss good, baby. You can come anytime."

She leaned back to get a better view of his face. She could tell. His mind was someplace far away. "But you love her? You love her, you should give her another chance. Give her chance. You go see her. You not happy, you can always come here. I make you happy."

It was late, past 2:00 a.m., but she stayed for him. Mama-san came to chase him out, then took a long look at him, smiled and walked away. She chattered something in Vietnamese to Vivian. Vivian glanced back at Glenn wide-eyed. *Two hours with mama?* She smiled at him, felt his hardness under her, and got off. *Too bad. It's been a while.*

She walked him to the door. "Good night, Glenn. I hope I see you again. She reached out with both hands, pulled him close and kissed him. Gently. Softly. No pinching. Her lips were not as soft as Maya's but hungry and searching.

He walked into his apartment at 3:00 a.m. He imagined Maya and the neck biter guy having sex somewhere. *No missed calls. No texts. No voice message. Guess I'm not that important. Give her another chance? Rather give Vivian a chance.*

101

FAMILY > LOVE

Across town at Thai Garden, the midnight casino was winding down, with only the hardcore regulars in attendance. Jae sat at the baccarat table, nursing a winning streak, with Maya standing next to him. She yawned. "Baby, I go now. Work tomorrow."

He looked up with a half-sneer. "Bullshit, babe. You think I'm some fool customer. I know you don't work at the beauty place anymore. Cut the crap and get me another drink."

She glared at him. "Why you so mean to me now?"

He softened. "Sorry, babe. Long day."

"Long day for me too, you know. I get citizenship you don't even come see me."

He turned fully to her. "I did come see you, but they wouldn't let me in after the ceremony started. And I came tonight, and you kicked me out. For what? For him?"

The honeymoon period with Jae had ended over the past month. Most of their quarrels centered on Maya not seeing Glenn anymore. "He's not customer. He's my papa. I don't have other customers anymore. I leave them all for you. Not go bar anymore. Only see papa. Please be okay. He need me."

He took a swing at thin air. "And what, you need him? You have daddy issues. I'm your daddy, bitch. I'm your sugar daddy. What is he? Your sugar granddaddy? Your sugar great-granddaddy?"

Looking down, she fiddled with her keys, thinking of Glenn. *He my little boy too.*

Chloe eavesdropped from the next table and decided she had enough of Jae bullying her sister. She went over behind them and stuck her finger down her throat, puking right in front of Jae and Maya, catching a bit of Jae's shoes.

Jae jumped and banged into the gaming table, scattering cards, chips and dice. "What the fuck? Oh shit!"

Chloe looked up at Maya. "Sister so sick, help me." Maya looked at Jae.

Jae was trying to wipe Chloe's crap off his shoes and didn't even bother to look up. "Go, just go! I'll see you tomorrow."

It was 4:00 a.m. They were down at the beach, sitting on the sand. There was a full moon. The tide was coming in, with waves lapping at the shoreline. It was just them and the bottle of tequila they'd swiped from the restaurant.

Chloe passed the bottle to Maya. "What you going do now?"

Maya took a stiff drink. "Finish tequila. Go home. Go sleep. Not wake up. Hee hee."

Chloe took the bottle back. "Okay, me too."

They sat there for five minutes, not saying a word, the bottle half empty.

Maya reached for the bottle. "Chloe, what do I do?"

Chloe's eyes were glazing. "What you mean what you do? I been telling you what to do for long time already. Stay with Glenn. Eddie was a dick. Luke was a dick. Jae is a dick with a dick. Jacob is a dick with a badge."

Maya shrieked with laughter. "Why you even bringing Jacob up?"

"I dunno. We talking about dicks so he popped into my head."

They laughed some more. Jacob was a police captain and one of Maya's first customers. She'd made the mistake of dating him. Arrogant, persistent, narcissistic. Just like Jae. Maya's weakness, always seeing a man's aggressiveness as his desire for her—validation at its core for her.

Maya buried her head in her hands. "I think I made mistake with Jae. He fuck other girls. Not nice to me anymore. Maybe I'm doing something wrong?"

"No, Maya. He smooth. Smoother than Eddie. Smarter than Luke. Make you think your fault. We know the type. Real pimp mind. Twist your mind. Always make you think your fault."

Maya frowned. *Chloe right. But hard to see when I'm with him.*

Maya didn't want to think about Jae anymore. "How things with Reyn?"

"Okay. He's not a dick. But he know how use his. Five times last weekend!"

They giggled like schoolgirls.

Maya squeezed Chloe's forearm. "I'm happy for you, sis. You happy?"

Chloe gave a slight nod—half yes, half no. "He make me work

restaurant. Quit bar. I don't have to take care of family like you. So no need that much money. He help me with rent. When time right, I go live with him. Restaurant not easy. Not only sit and sing and drink. He teaching me to be like regular woman—not bargirl. Want me out of the business."

Chloe stared into Maya's eyes to make sure Maya understood what she was about to say. "Hard, Maya. Making regular money not easy. Gonna be hard for you too."

Maya frowned again and leaned back. Time for another subject change. "Caleb send me letter. He want me back. He come back soon. I told him we talk when he get back."

Maya sat up. "Chloe, he stationed someplace else soon. If I stay here, I have no place to live. He say if I don't go, then divorce now. No pension, Chloe. Maybe I stay with Caleb little while more. Maybe I go with Caleb."

Chloe grabbed at Maya's arm. "No, Maya. You know about his anger. And you know he had second wife."

Maya hooked Chloe's arm, and laid her head on her sister's shoulder. "No, Chloe. He said I come back and that over."

Chloe's eyes widened. "You mean he still with her? C'mon Maya! You know what going happen. You go back. He have you here. Her over there. All other girls all the time while at sea. You all alone. Not happy. He come home. Get mad. Hit you. By then you fifty years old. No chance at love. You hang from a tree." Maya winced. She thought of Glenn's mom.

Chloe continued. "Jae? Same thing. You know he's a player. My friend from Lucky Seven say he have girlfriend there. Uncle Jimmy told me too. He not serious about you. One year tops. He's done with you."

All emotions drained from Maya's face as she hung her head. "I die alone then. Work hard at bar. Maybe DJ with Vey. Take care family. One day make enough money, pay for house. Go back Thailand."

Chloe lifted Maya's face to hers. "But Maya, you US citizen now. Not your property anymore. How you going work in Thailand?"

Maya squared her jaw. "I find a way."

Chloe shook her head. Maya forgot how hard it was to pay for rent and food. "What about Glenn?"

Maya finished the last of the tequila. "What about Glenn? Chloe, he married. I cannot wait."

Chloe shot back. "You willing to die alone? Why not wait, stay good friends with Glenn?" Checkmate. Chloe had her.

Eyes closed, Maya took a deep breath in and held it, then exhaled very slowly. Chloe nodded slowly, deliberately. She knew. *We about to get to the real reason. The real confession. Why no Glenn.*

Maya reached for Chloe's hand. "I don't want to hurt him anymore. You see how many times I hurt him already? He so patient. I walk away from him at bar, remember the time you brought the customer? Then with the cops? Then with the construction crew? Then I mess with Eddie, then Jae? I get mad, I have Deth come on a Tuesday night."

Chloe squeezed her hand as if to say, I'm here for you.

Maya squeezed back. "I don't trust myself, Chloe. I dunno what wrong with me. Lynh is right. I'm man crazy. Some nights I get bitchy with Glenn cuz got guys nearby. Young, rich looking, fun guys. And I really want to go be with them. But I promise him I stay so I stay, but all irritated and bitchy."

Memories of his patience with her flooded her mind. "He so patient, Chloe. So kind. I can treat him like that, and he still give me money to send back home. But I know him too. I see his face. He hurt. He go home. Post shit about pain on Instagram. Tell me it's about work. But it's what I do to him, Chloe."

She let out a small sob. "I love him, Chloe. I love him like I never love anyone before. There, I said it."

Maya was on a roll. It was confession time. "He's my angel. I thought I was his angel. He so weak in the beginning. Then so strong now. I need him. I wait for Tuesday every week. But I hurt him all the time. I hurt him tonight, Chloe. You saw his face? No? I did. I hurt him. Hurt me so much when I hurt him. I'm done with that, Chloe. He deserve better, much better."

Chloe sat silently. Wishing they took another bottle of something, anything. She searched her sister from another mother. Something tugged at her heart. *They for real. She love the guy. Was going to leave the guy because she love the guy. I must be tired. Sounds like Thai TV drama.*

The sun was peeking over the horizon. Early morning joggers were eyeing these two disheveled—what were they? "Let's go home, Maya." Chloe looked left. Maya was out. *Me too then.* They lay there till a lifeguard woke them up two hours later.

––––––––––––––

Maya climbed into her own comfortable bed. Rusty was waiting. No text from Glenn. *Must be really upset. He always text. Maybe best this way. I should text. See if he's okay. Maybe I text him just to see? Sabai. Let it go for now. See what happen later.* She fell asleep holding Rusty.

She didn't know she was losing Glenn, fast.

102

REBOUND

Four hours after leaving Vivian, Glenn woke with the feeling of her voluptuous lips still on his lips. Instinctively he checked his phone for calls and texts, disappointed to find no text from Maya except the one from last night.

Liar. Telling me she was at home when she was with that guy.

There was no other text from her. *No sorry. No explanation. I guess that's that. Maybe I should text her?* He shook it off.

There were thirty-two texts from various council members and political influencers ahead of the budget hearing scheduled for that morning. Embroiled in city budget battles the whole day, Glenn finally slumped onto the couch in his office a little past 5:00 p.m. There was no text from Maya. *Really? Is that how she wants it?* Another meeting, dinner and a workout later, he was off to see Vivian.

She greeted him with a long hug and a kiss. There was no lip squeezing. "Remember, no tongue. You promised. Come, baby. Talk."

She led him to a booth. "I know you like me. But you on rebound right now, you know? Be careful. Other girls would work you. If you was an asshole, I would work you. But you nice. Can tell. Good looking too. I would date you but you married, you have wife, you have girlfriend, I don't know how many girlfriends."

She took his hand and wrapped his arm around her. "Tonight relax. Let V be your friend, okay? No need money. I buy my own." She leaned backward, nuzzled his neck and kissed him. She had no idea why she felt so close to him. Maybe she knew one too many scuzzbag customers. Maybe this one was real. Maybe for once in this sordid walk of life, she could do something decent. Or maybe she liked his little boy looks.

He liked her next to him. Her curves fit him like a comfort pillow. To her offer of a free night, he said, "Nah, V, business is business. You need to take care of your two little dogs." *Two dogs. More like two kids. Her Instagram account had pics of the kids all over. Divorced six months ago after five years. Guess she had to come back to the bar biz. Shoulda kept her account private, or does she want stalkers like me to find out?* "Take it as a gift, okay?"

She pushed back. "Too much, Glenn." She looked at the money and the way he handed it over. *That other girl . . . no wonder she get spoiled. No wonder she gets jealous.* She put it back in his hand.

He appreciated her gesture.

In return, he cupped her chin and kissed her, a little longer than he should have.

She didn't back off, instead she returned his kiss.

He grew hard as she played with him. He swallowed loudly, looking uncomfortable.

She backed off, created space between them. "Sorry. Don't mind me. I like to play." She smiled.

He burst out laughing. His stress left him like an outgoing tide.

She retook his hand and put it around her, leaning into him. "What's on your mind? Her?"

He kissed her shoulder. "You."

She kissed him. "Never mind me. Glenn, do you love her?" She knew. This is where she said nothing, no matter how long, until he had time to think. She remembered asking her ex the same question before he walked out. She knew men don't take the time to think with the head on their neck, only the head in their pants. She snuggled up to him and waited.

It was a few minutes before she looked up to see his faraway look. "Glenn, do you love her?"

He blinked twice. "I think so. Yes."

She turned and took both his hands in hers and kissed each. "Why? Think Glenn. Important. I'm not going anywhere. Here for you. But you must think. I know you love her. I can make you happy right now, but I cannot make you love me. That comes with time. Time you two had."

He held onto her hands like they were lifelines. "But V, I don't think she loves me. She said this whole thing . . . fantasy."

Vivian reached up, pulled him to her, and kissed him, lightly biting his lower lip. "Not always hundred percent fantasy Glenn. Even this kiss. Always some part of the girl wants it. Some part of her wants you, Glenn. If you love her, then next step go find out how much she wants you."

She chose to let her words sink in and had her own thoughts to consider. *The girl stupid. Just google this guy and you'd find out he was a good man. If she don't want him, I'll take him. If I'm the stand-in for the wife, not a problem either. I make him mine. But useless if he still wants her. I will be friend for now. Just help him decide. She sounds stupid enough to piss him off again, and then he knows how to find me.*

He was staring at his beer. She turned his face to her. "Glenn, why you love her?"

Images flashed in his head. He thought of all the nice things Maya did. *She hand fed me. She cooked for me. She was protective of me. She got me to try new things. She taught me karaoke. She patiently taught me cards. She encouraged my career move. She taught me not to let others' opinions stop me from doing what I thought was right.*

She cleared out her Tuesday nights. She showed up just about every Tuesday—for me. She was there for me, maybe she came late or left early, but she always came. Sick, in a bad mood, mad at me, yawning tired, didn't matter, if she was in town on a Tuesday, she always came. With her, I felt special. I felt loved. I finally knew what it was like to be Billy.

Vivian had her own thoughts. *I dunno if I could sit with someone three-to-four hours at a time. My clients usually done and out in forty-five minutes. In and out, easy money, fast money, name of the game.*

She leaned into him. *Maybe this girl not a spoiled gold digger. I wouldn't do it unless . . . I really liked the guy. More than really like the guy. Almost love . . .*

Vivian listened to him, held his hand, pulled him to her and covered his forehead with butterfly kisses. But mostly she listened with all her attention. She slipped in some advice when she could. "Glenn, go back to her. Give her another chance. Even with all the shit she gives you, you still get something from her that is very valuable. She's like some treasure you been looking for all your life and now you found it. Just because she screwed up again, doesn't mean you run away. You work it out with her. If there is something in your heart left for her, then go to her."

"But V, she was all over that guy."

"No Glenn. Sounds like the guy was all over her, not the other way around. You don't know what was going on. Stand up. Look in some of the other booths. You think these girls in love with these guys?"

He scanned the room and saw familiar scenes—Academy Award

performances all around.

She pulled him back down. "Not nice to stare, Glenn."

She continued. "Sounds like you have mommy issues, Glenn. No worries. Any night she does not make you happy, I will take care of you. You might have to wait a bit if I have a customer, but I'm never more than an hour with anyone. If you leave her, we can take a chance together, if you need. And I'll stop playing with you, okay? So you can honor your wife."

No kiss this time. He leaned over and hugged instead, breathing her in. This gesture—the Vietnamese kiss—touched her. She sounded like a perfect plan B, but that made Glenn feel like he was treating her cheaply. He dug out the two Benjamins she'd rejected earlier. "V, take it. Better than any psychotherapist fees I ever paid." He put it in her hand and wrapped her fingers around it. "Please, V."

Seconds passed. Then she put it in her purse. "Thank you, Glenn." Her sons needed new shoes. This was a godsend.

"I gotta go, V."

"Hope to see you around, Glenn. No need to wait till she makes you unhappy to visit. I'll be here, okay?" She hugged him tightly, kissed him and sent him off. She sat down and said a prayer for him. It'd been a long time since she prayed. *Me the Catholic schoolgirl gone bad. Maybe I'll go back to church. Guy like that, like fresh air in the sewer. I hope that girl knows how lucky she is.*

She frowned. *That girl so stupid to let him go.*

———————

While Glenn was embroiled in city matters earlier that Wednesday, Maya lay in the dark all day, dry heaving, oblivious to anything other than her head feeling like concrete. She managed to crawl over to her phone once to let Vic, her Wednesday regular, know she had food poisoning and was too sick to go to work.

And while Glenn was with Vivian that night, Maya chose physical pain over emotional pain and drained an old bottle of wine till it was empty, and so was she. He hadn't texted her all day. *He out of my life. Maybe I should text him? See if he blocked me? I hope he's okay. He must be hurting. I wish I was there for him. But I'm the one that hurt him. So not good. This is not good. This is never going to be good.*

Her phone fell out of her hand as she passed out. A picture of Glenn and her on their first Paradise Club date stared up at her. A very happy couple.

103

LOVE IS PATIENT

Glenn spent the following day in the weekly Thursday meeting of city executives, council members and the congressional delegation on the city's homeless problem. He continued to spar with Clifford over what was more important to the town—concrete buildings or people. There was bad blood between money-hungry developers backing Clifford for mayor and those supporting the Vice-chair, with whom Glenn was aligned. They glared at each other throughout the meeting.

When his blood wasn't boiling over idiots like Clifford, he thought back to Maya and what Vivian said. *Was Maya acting with that guy? I mean, I didn't really see much. It was more like a snapshot.*

Vivian's words came back to him: "Look in some of the other booths. You think these girls in love with these guys?" *Yeah, but the girls at Vivian's place, they were working. Maya was at the restaurant after her party. But still, a snapshot. I didn't even let her explain. Not that she's trying hard to reach me.*

The meeting on the homeless issues was over—another impasse, which then spilled over into helping the elderly. The only thing Glenn remembered was Clifford saying he worked hard to create his retirement portfolio, and any old person that didn't plan right deserved what they got. *Damn, only one way to help the people that need it the most. I gotta get this guy outta here. Get the Vice-chair in. Admiral said the Group will go all out the next four years to help right this city.*

He went to visit Katie that night. "Hi, sweetheart." He brushed her hair back and settled in, bringing a chair up to her side. He held her hand and talked about his day, including the impasse with Clifford. An hour later, Marta came by. "Glenn, I'm going home early tonight. Do you need anything?"

"No, Marta. Thanks. Hubby should be happy, eh?"

"Hope so. Our anniversary."

"Congratulations, Marta!"

Marta felt uncomfortable. A happy time for her, but her friend sat there with his wife, or what used to be his wife. *There's hope. There's always hope.* She'd seen a lot on this floor. *There's always hope until that's all you have.* "Good night Glenn." She left the door open a crack.

It was a long day for him. "I gotta go, Katie. I love you. I'll always love you. We'll be together again one day. I know it."

On the drive home, thoughts of Maya crept into his head. *Still no text from her. Fuck her then.* Vivian's words made their way into his brain: "Why do you love her? Looks like you found your treasure. If you love her give her another chance. Not all fantasy, Glenn. Some part of it real."

He sat on his sofa in the dark with a full longneck open. He sniffed the bottle, got up, went to the kitchen and poured it down the drain. Sitting back on the sofa, he thought, *I need a clear head.*

He sank to his knees and prayed.

> *Dear God . . . Dear Father, I need You. I need*
> *something. I don't know what to do. I should*
> *walk away right? She's just a bargirl, right? You've*
> *touched me 24/7 all my life. Always giving me favor,*
> *blessings and yeah, so much mercy I don't deserve.*
> *So why do You have her in my life?*

Silence. *Must be a reason. But now she's gone.* Then out of the blue, he heard it.

Go back. Forgive.

He lifted both palms up. "Seriously? I don't mean to test You, Father, but I need some kind of sign. Like, can You tell me what she was doing with the guy? Tell me that's not her guy. She looked happy, you know? I never even got to touch her like that. If they were that intimate, who am I?"

She loves you.

He cocked his head and gave the side-eye upward. "Okay, I'm hearing You, Father, but I can't really hear You. I don't know it's You. I think I want to hear You tell me, 'go back' so I think it's a sure thing. I don't know. Can't You just appear like in the burning bush and talk to me? Like talk so I can hear for real and not some passing-thought small voice in my head?"

He lay his head on the sofa. "Either way, Father, I pray that You bless her. If she's happy with the guy, then great, bless them both greatly, Father. As for me, You know, if You can, bring Katie back to me?"

He looked upward. "If not, then Maya? I just want her to be happy. We can be friends. Something more than fantasy. I'm tired of the fantasy. I want real. Sorry to whine so much, God. I know You got this. And I know sometimes it's about Your plan, and not mine. No matter. You always make it turn out okay for me."

And he heard it, clear as day.

Patience, my son.

A peace came over him. He kissed his ring. "Got You, Abba. Amen. I'll wait on You."

He slept like a baby. Something was about to happen. Something always happened when he felt this way. After all, love conquers all.

While Glenn was spending his Thursday warring at City Hall and later chatting with Katie and God, Maya was having a different kind of day. Twelve hours earlier, her Thursday morning started with Rusty's barking, silenced by the pillow she threw at him. Extremely dehydrated and still dry heaving, she tried to drink water but threw it back up. *Trouble. Alcohol poisoning. Happened before. Need help.* She crawled to her phone. "Chloe. Sister. Help me. In trouble. Yeah, not eat two days. One bottle wine last night. Tequila bottle empty too. Not good."

Maya spent the rest of the day in the ICU. Chloe walked her into the house that evening. Rusty softly nuzzled her hand. "So sorry, boy. Mommy okay now." She poured some food into his dish and checked his water. He didn't leave her side.

Chloe rubbed Maya's shoulders. "Call Glenn, sister. Text him. Be the first this time."

Maya shook her head. "No, Chloe. Over. He didn't text me. I don't text him. I'm out of his life. Better this way."

Chloe wondered why it kept coming to this. She remembered her sister's confession two nights before: "I don't want hurt him anymore. You see how many times I hurt him already? I don't trust myself, Chloe. I love him. I love him like I never love anyone before. But I hurt him all the time. Hurt me so much when I hurt him. I'm done with that Chloe. He deserve better, much better."

It was almost as if Maya was replaying her own words. She fell into Chloe and cried on her shoulders. Chloe held her till the sobs became a soft snoring.

Near midnight Maya woke with a start. Chloe was watching TV. "You okay now, sister?"

"Yeah honey. Maya back now. Sabai. Done. Gone. Next day better."

Chloe handed Maya her phone. "He text you yet?"

Maya looked at her phone. "No. Better this way Chloe. Trust me."

Chloe rubbed her chin. "What if he text you? You block him yet? What you do if he text you tomorrow?"

"No. I should block him. I don't, but. Not know what to do if he texts. Just see what tomorrow bring." Maya scrolled through the rest of her twenty-nine text messages, all from Jae. "Crap, I forgot to tell him I was sick."

Chloe got up to leave. Reyn was texting her as well. "Don't worry, honey. I call Jae for you already. Tell him you have woman problems. Good as new tomorrow."

"Thank you, Sis."

Maya waited at the door till she couldn't see Chloe's car anymore. Then came back into the house.

Rusty bounded into her lap. *What will tomorrow bring? Will it be day after day of wondering where he is? Who he with? What he doing? Is he okay? When I stop thinking of him?*

She rubbed Rusty's belly. *At least I don't hurt him no more. I hope Katie wake up for him. For now focus on family. I take Jae's shit as long as he take care of me. Gotta deal with Caleb too. Take care of family. One day I will be happy. Maybe Jae go back to how he was.*

It was a long day. She fell asleep staring at her phone—the same picture of Glenn and her she had been looking at the night before.

104

ANSWERED PRAYER

Glenn walked into the office Friday morning with a spring in his step that his secretary hadn't seen in a while. She looked up from the briefing folder she was prepping for him. "So what gives you so much energy on a Friday morning, boss?"

"Not what, Deb," he said pointing upward, "but who."

She grinned and was happy for his energy, knowing what a packed calendar he had first thing that morning.

Apart from the regular end-of-week grind, the Vice-chair was getting ready for a weekend of campaigning, and other council members wanted a piece of Glenn that morning before working with their own staffs.

Debbie had her hands full managing the traffic outside his door until the line finally cleared up. Glenn then hunkered down in his office to catch up with reviewing legislation and procurement forms when she popped her head in. "Um, Glenn, sorry to bother you."

"What's up Deb? I thought I said no visitors, nobody. Only the Vice-chair or Tony."

She walked in and closed the door behind her. "I know. I heard you before. But there's someone here to see you, and she doesn't have an appointment. She sounds pretty sure you'll see her. Sounds like an immigrant or something. Seems very desperate to see you. I was about to call security. But maybe you might want to pop your head out just in case? I put her in the first chair outside so you can crack the door and take a peek."

He swiveled toward her. "Thanks, Deb. What's her name?"

"Chloe."

Glenn nearly fell out of his chair. "Umm . . . yeah, tell her to come in. This is family, Deb. Send her in."

Debbie ran out and showed Chloe in. "Do you want coffee or tea?"

Glenn waved at Chloe. "She's talking to you."

Chloe smiled. She shifted in her seat and spoke softly. "Coffee good. How much?"

Glenn smiled. "No, Chloe, on the house."

Debbie glanced at Glenn. *On the house? Family, my foot.* She had a thirty-year-old son in construction that liked to go to certain bars. Professional as always, she gave Chloe the class-A treatment. She went, came back and set the coffee before Chloe. She turned to Glenn with an "anything else?" look.

He saluted. "Thanks, Deb."

As soon as Deb closed the door, he came around the desk and sat next to Chloe. "Everything okay? Is Maya okay?"

Chloe smirked. "Miss her already, huh?"

He pinched his nose bridge. "Chloe, don't tell me to say sorry again. I don't have any reason to say sorry to her. If she had a boyfriend, she should have just said he was coming and I woulda stayed away . . ."

"And what, brudder, sulk? You know she not like you mad or sad."

He leaned back. "What does she care?"

Chloe sipped her coffee then turned back to Glenn. "She care, brudder. That guy nothing to her. Take my word. She just in tough spot."

He bit his nail. "But Chloe, I saw. He had his hand down her crotch. Her head was back, and she looked like she was enjoying it. She don't do that with customers, so must be the boyfriend, right?"

She poked him right in the middle of his forehead. "Why all lawyers so stupid?"

He pushed her finger away. "Wait . . ."

"No, you wait Glenn. You saw his hand under table. Where her hand?"

He thought back. "Under table."

"Yeah, stupid, holding his hand, keeping him away."

He cocked his head—his tell, admitting he was wrong.

She was cross-examining him now. "You saw her head back looking happy?"

"Yeah. Definitely looked happy."

She poked him in the chest this time. "Stupid. You know with all the scumbag try stuff with her, including this asshole? She always think of you to get her through! You so dumb. She was thinking of you. Always think of you when rough times."

"Me? Why me?"

She examined his face for any hint of clarity. "You that stupid, Glenn? You don't know?"

Chloe felt a surge of surprise. *He don't know. He really think this all fantasy.*

"Never mind, Glenn." She decided Maya would have to tell him herself.

Glenn was in Chloe's face. "Don't know what, Chloe?" He thought he might hear what he wanted.

She pushed him back, gently. "Never mind. But you lucky she like you enough to kick you out of restaurant that night."

He did a double take. "What the shit are you talking about? Did I hear you wrong? She kicked me out to be with him. How is that lucky?"

She had the look of an exasperated babysitter. "Brudder, he was there earlier. Before you come. She kick him out before you come, for you."

His face was contorted, confused, near frustration.

She was almost hissing, trying not to yell. "The guy was coming back, brudder. Coming back with his thugs. Coming back to take you out!"

She let that sink in. "Maya know you can handle. She remember time you said you only know how kill to defend. That sound bullshit to me but she not take chances. Didn't want you hurt or get trouble. She care enough to piss you off, Glenn."

He sat in silence, gears clicking. He looked at the Bible on his desk. Suddenly realized his questions from yesterday just got answered.

I don't mean to test You, Father, but I need
some kind of sign. Like can You tell me
what she was doing with the guy? Tell me
that's not her guy. She looked happy, You
know? I never even got to touch her like
that. If they were that intimate, who am I?

He prayed under his breath. "Thank you, God."

Glenn smiled weakly, sheepishly, but with renewed energy. "Where is she today, Chloe?"

"She usually help at Thai Garden lunch crowd."

"Okay. I'll go see her. Then again, maybe. Umm . . . I'll think about it."

She got up to leave. "Good luck, brudder."

He rose from his chair. "Are you going to be there?"

"No, I work at the other restaurant. Day job. No more bar."

"Really? Is that why I don't see you around anymore? I always thought you were in the other room."

It was her turn to be sheepish. "No. Honest American woman now."

"Great, Chloe. Maybe you help your sister, huh?"

She took a step closer and poked his chest. "No brudder, maybe *you* help my sister."

They hugged, and he saw her to the elevator.

Walking back to his office, he said to Debbie. "Cancel my lunch today. In fact, cancel my whole afternoon."

She was already dialing numbers on the phone. "Fine, Glenn. Vice-chair asked for fifteen minutes, though. And Tony wants to see you."

"I'll go see Vice-chair now. Tell Tony tonight, okay? BJs."

"You're gonna get fat, you keep going there."

"We'll see, Debbie."

It was never more than ten minutes with the Vice-chair. Glenn was back in his office, staring out his corner office window. He rubbed his face and took several deep breaths. *What's happening here? Okay. Vivian. I go see Vivian. Find another girl. Another mommy. But she sends me back?*

He picked up his Bible and flipped through it without really looking for anything. *Then God says in his small voice to go back. I ask for a clearer voice. And then he sends Chloe. What did Chloe say? She was doing all that for me? She thinks of me during rough times? And I thought Chloe was about to tell me this was for real, not fantasy.*

He massaged his neck, trying to recall their exact conversation: "You that stupid Glenn? You don't know?"

"Don't know what, Chloe?"

"Never mind, Glenn."

He stretched his arms over his head and cracked his knuckles. *I shoulda pressed her. But here we are. Vivian. God. Chloe.*

Hope gingerly crept back into his soul, followed closely by optimism. *Must be a sign that we were meant to be together. Love does conquer all. I was wrong. We can work this out. Have a happily ever after.*

He plopped onto the sofa rubbing his chin. *I'll text her. If she answers right away, then she likes me. Maybe waiting for me. If no text right away, I'll just drop it. Maybe.*

Time for lunch today?

Ok. Thai Garden at noon?

See you then

He smiled and kissed his phone. *That was quick. Like she was waiting for it. We can work this out. But I need to know who that guy is. I need to hear it from her.*

He imagined getting an answer that left him feeling special, like he was the only one that counted. Hope turned into optimism then shifted to near joy. Love found its way back into his heart again. *They say, anything can happen with God*, he thought.

He forgot. They also say, God's will be done.

105

HURT THE DOG

Maya's morning had started calmly. She slept in, gave Rusty his medicine when she awoke, and then took him for a long walk along the docks where the Navy ships were moored. Caleb would be back soon. In a year, they'd be divorced, and she would settle in with Jae. There was no room for Glenn in the picture.

Rusty yapped playfully, signaling time for his midmorning snack. "Okay, boy, we go home now. You love Mommy, right? At least you love Mommy. Don't ever leave me, boy." He barked twice, then once more for emphasis. Hunger ruled the day, and treats were waiting at home.

Her phone buzzed as she walked into the house. *Must be Jae. I forgot to call him about tonight.* It was Glenn.

Time for lunch today?

Her heart froze. Time stood still. Adrenaline poured through her system and endorphins flooded love into her heart. Tears of joy welled up uncontrollably. Impulsively, she fired back.

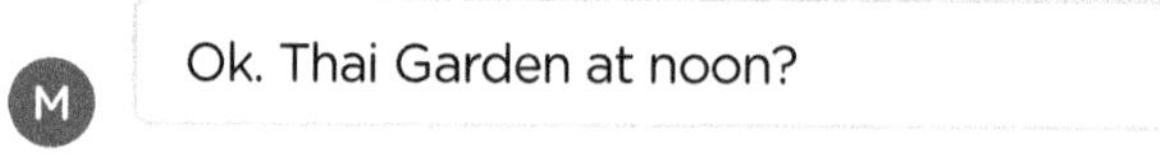

See you then

She answered before she could think. *What will I do? But I'm so happy. I want to see him. He texted me! I feel so special. I don't have to beg. I never have to beg with him. He's a real man.*

Oh, but what do I do?
She threw treats at Rusty for a game of fetch and eat.
I have to let him go. I will hurt him again, and he will come back again, and I will hurt him even more. This has to stop.
I must be the strong one. One last time. For both of us.
She sat on her bed with Rusty. She had had only one other dog in her life, when she was a little girl. She'd called it her little boy. Grandpa warned her that it was not a pet. He said it was still a puppy and would be tender for only a while longer.

Grandpa was old school. No one in the village ate dog anymore except the old people. But then came the tough season when the monsoons killed the rice crop. They were starving and hadn't had meat in three months. Killing the ox needed for heavy farm labor was out of the question.

Her little boy was the only other source of protein for the family. She took the pup to town and let it run off. *Run away, boy, okay?* But the pup had found its way back home in the middle of the night. She knew Grandpa would be up soon and didn't know what to do. Grandpa had said it was time.

She took her little boy to the fields and beat it with a stick till it ran away. She swallowed her sobs and hoped Grandpa would not hear the dog's yelps. It kept coming back, and she kept hitting it with her stick till its back was raw. The dog finally stopped running back to her. It stopped six feet away.

She'd always remember that look. Hurt in any creature is unmistakably found in the eyes. And it was the same, whether man, little boy, or dog. Her heart broke. *At least you have chance out there, little boy.* She threw the stick at it. He snorted, then ran off.

Grandpa beat her senseless that morning. *We should eat you maybe.* Her only thought as she took blow after blow. *My baby still alive.*

She reflected on the lesson she learned then. *Only way to make dog go away is hurt it. Same with men. I love you, Glenn. Don't hate me forever okay?*
She texted Jae.

> **M** Sorry sick last two days. Better now.
> Lunch today?

> **J** That's my girl. Ok

> **M** Thai Garden 11:30?

J: Again? How about Japanese?

M: No baby, please? want aunty's papaya salad today

J: Yah. Cool. See you

106

BLACK FRIDAY

Driving over to the restaurant, Glenn could barely concentrate on traffic. The butterflies in his stomach felt more like bats. He kept wondering and hoping, *Can this work out? Are we for real? So I had to be the first to cave again. So what? Worked out before.*

He pulled up to the restaurant, right next to her white Audi. Three days after having his world crash and his heart crushed, he was back at the crime scene. *Three days. Long enough for Jesus to live again. So can I.*

He paused right outside of the entrance to gather himself. *I owe Chloe. I was overthinking this. Chloe made sense. She never did me wrong. She brought us back together the last time. She's still playing angel sister.*

His thoughts turned to Maya. *I don't expect too much time if she's working. Just want her to know the pipeline's open. Always another Tuesday around the corner. We can make this work. Was Chloe going to tell me it wasn't fantasy? Maybe Maya does have feelings for me? I won't press it today. Only want another Tuesday, then we can see where we go from there.*

Taking a deep breath, he opened the door and heard her laughing. *She's in a good mood. Thank you, God.*

Then the world crashed again. She was sitting on Jae's lap, back facing the entrance, hand feeding Jae garlic shrimp. Jae saw Glenn over her shoulder. "What the fuck is he doing here?"

Jae stood, pushing Maya off to the side.

She stumbled to her feet. "No, wait, Jae, I talk to him." This was not what she wanted. She jumped between them.

She shrieked when Jae took her by the hair and threw her back into the booth.

Glenn's fists clenched. "That's what you like, Maya? Well, have a great life!" It was all Glenn could do to keep it peaceful. *Why say yes to lunch if he was going to be here?*

Glenn glared at Jae, declaring, "You can have her," then stepped back toward the door.

Jae sprang forward, yelling, "Hey, old man, not yet. We're gonna finish this."

Maya tried to stop Jae, who then backhanded her, flying her back into the booth.

Glenn turned fully; fists clenched again. "Leave her alone! You fucking leave her alone!" Glenn took one step forward. He desperately wanted to go to her to make sure she was okay.

Her lips quivered as she rubbed her arms, where she was already bruising. Terrified, she shook her head at Glenn and mouthed *No, Glenn, please go, just go.*

It was showtime. She found her voice and tried her best to sound mad. "Glenn, go. I'll call you later."

Jae's eyes bugged, and his nostrils flared. Through clenched teeth, he screamed, "Bullshit! *This ends now!*"

Jae continued his rant, spurring Glenn to come at him. "You gonna call your high powers on me? Put me in the river? Jus' you and me, old man. Let's go. Winner take all."

Sabai. Sabai. Sabai. Glenn repeated it over and over, hoping some veil of calm would descend.

Fuck Sabai. Glenn planted himself and took his stance. "I don't want trouble. Just let me talk to her one last time and I'm out. Son, you don't want this."

Jae raged on, egging Glenn even more. "Who you calling 'son,' Grandpa! That's what she calls you. Grand. Fucking. *Pa!*"

Maya reached out to Jae and tugged at his sleeve. Jae slapped her hand away. She yelped and cringed back into the booth.

Voice raspy, Glenn nearly growled, like in some Eastwood movie. "Step aside, you piece of silver spoon shit."

Jae whipped out his knife and lunged.

Like he practiced at the dojo, Glenn took one step back and pivoted, letting the knife slice right past where his heart would have been. Glenn caught Jae's wrist with his right hand and levered his left hand on Jae's elbow, then pulled Jae around and slammed the thug's head into the glass door.

It was over. The door cracked into a giant spider-web. Jae was out. Glenn kicked the knife away. Vey ran over and put a closed sign on the door and locked it—no cops today. Aunty and Vey were tending to Jae, trying to stop the blood. Vey chattered to someone in Thai, "Call doctor Yang from down the street!"

Maya's heart was pumping pure adrenaline. She never imagined Glenn this way —the little boy-turned-protector knight. She looked at Jae—the smooth operator-turned-coward and had to bring out a knife. *Grandfather back home would do same as Glenn.*

Glenn looked her way. "You okay?"

She wanted to run to him. "Yes." She said it softly. *His face. Still look hurt.*

He breathed a little harder than usual. "So. Grandpa, huh?"

She shook her head. *He believed the shit?* "No Papa, never. Always my Papa. Not mean old. I told you."

He leaned against the bar. "What's this all about, Maya? I thought *we* were going to have lunch. Talk."

She put on her best poker face. *Must remember. This for him.* "He come, Papa. I couldn't say no."

"Why? Why couldn't you say no? You always cannot say no? Only say 'no' to me?"

She moved to the edge of the booth but stayed seated. *Not true. Say "no" plenty times to others to clear Tuesday nights.* "Papa let's not do this now. Go home. We talk later?" *He not gonna leave. I know him.*

"When, Maya?"

She stood up, hands on hips, eyes narrowed. "Not now, Papa! Okay?"

His adrenaline was still pumping after the fight. He was overthinking again. "What? Pushing me out the door again so you can be with him? Why do you need him? Why not me?"

Her hands were at her side, fists clenched, shaking. "I don't need him, Papa. *And I don't need you!*" *Oh Buddha, please be with him, don't him hurt so much.*

He was unraveling. "Screw you. You need nice guys like me to validate who you are, to prove that you're more than a worthless piece of fuck whore garbage for guys to have masturbation fantasies over. This is nothing but some stupid playacting to you isn't it? Doesn't matter if you hurt people and screw people's lives!"

He was mad.

She wasn't. She hurt for him. She saw it in his eyes. *He acting out. Little boy. He not mean anything. Just saying whatever to hurt me. He not good at this.*

The words were so unnatural for him. She wanted to reach out, to swipe his face and say, it's okay, you don't have to be like this. Then hold him and let him diffuse.

Inside her mind, she was shaking her head. *He cannot take care of me.*

Not my family. He needs take care of his wife. I'm not marriage breaker. Jae not stop fighting either. This going to end bad. I'm man crazy. I'm gonna hurt him over and over. Not want him hurt anymore. He deserve someone better out there. Someone. Not me.

She took a deep breath and let it out. *Now. Be strong.* She remembered her puppy at the edge of the field.

She was on him, shoving him before he could react. "I had enough of you already! You damn right all this playacting! I told you this all fantasy. You like our date? Paradise Club? I go there so many times. You think that impress. I have guys take me Japan and Thailand and Vegas. You take me your old man club? You customer. I'm bargirl. You give me money. You get fantasy. What young girl like me like you for no money? I told you when we started. It business. Only fantasy!"

It was the performance of her life.

He stood there, fists clenched, gritting his teeth, shaking, while teardrops trailed down his cheeks.

What Maya saw melted her heart, but she dug down deep. *Need to keep going. Showtime.* "So I'm whore to you now? What about you, you worthless piece of shit. You a dumb stupid fat little boy that not grow up. You use money to make big shit and make people like you. Fat little ugly boy with money, nothing else. You know it. You nothing. That's why you throw your money around."

She didn't have to say anymore. She needed to hurt him bad, and she succeeded. He grew still, his fists unclenched, and the tears stopped. His face and eyes were something between scowling and glaring, but mostly empty. This dog wasn't coming back. She turned away, crossing her arms, to give the impression that she was done.

Her eyes were closed. Two teardrops streaked down her face. *If I hear him coming, give him finger and run to the bathroom. I'm so sorry, Glenn. I love you always. You safe now, from me.*

He wasn't about to plead anything to the back of her head and walked out the door, numb. The fantasy was over, replaced by a nightmare.

Vey stood behind the bar in shock. She reached for her phone and punched in Chloe's number.

PART FOUR

107

REFLECTION

Driving back from the restaurant, the butterflies that fluttered in his stomach on the way there were long dead, as was hope and love. *This can't be. All the signs were there. What went wrong?*

He walked into the office, looking like he had chains hanging from his neck. Deb thought he had the flu. "Cancel everything, Deb. Reschedule with apologies. Wait. Any fallout?"

Deb looked at his calendar. "It's friendlies. The environmental group at 2:00 p.m. They wanted to update you or Vice-chair on the latest legislation going around. And then the homeless coalition at 4:00 p.m. Just routine drop-ins this afternoon."

He was thankful that Deb made it a practice always to end the week with friendlies. "Have Mike take the 2:00 p.m. and reschedule the 4:00 p.m. With apologies."

She had the phone going. "Oh, and you have your end of week with Mike at 5:00 p.m."

He stopped for a second. "Cancel that too. Tell him to take the night off."

He closed the door, went to his desk, sat in front of his computer and stared at the screensaver for the next three hours.

Father, this can't be. Did I hear You wrong? All the signs were there. You said she loved me. I said I need more. I asked questions. You sent Chloe. I know You sent her because she answered the questions I asked. What happened? Were You lying? Playing a trick? Punishing me? Teaching me? Teaching me what?

Self-pity drowned out any answer from above. Had Glenn's soul quieted enough to discern the voice of truth, he would have heard God explain He wasn't lying and that she did love him—loved him enough to sacrifice the one thing she desired the most, a chance to be with him always.

Glenn's eyes burned hot as he struggled to keep tears from flowing, a battle he lost soon enough.

I thought this was for real. How could she do this? How can a human being be so mean? Tell me come there and he's there? She knew I was walking in at noon. She could have met me at the door. She could have texted me. She could have canceled. She could have at least unstuck herself from him. But no. It was like she scripted it. Like she wanted to hurt me.

He searched his phone for their picture at the Paradise Club to remember how beautiful she was that night. The images of her and Jae together the last three days wiped out all the beauty from any image he had of her. *So that's the real her. That's how she really is. That's how she really feels. Well, take a bow, girl, cuz you really had me thinking we had something.*

It didn't take long to scroll back through a year of Tuesday night memories with her.

The first time they met. The first song. The first dance. The first kiss. Playing cards. Dinners at the bar. Exclusive Tuesdays for him. Crickets. Chicken feet. The night she sent a customer home to be with him. Their champagne date and how they held hands all night. His first birthday— the first time he'd ever had a cake. His second birthday. Her singing to him. Their outside dinner date. Magic at the Paradise Club. Their second Paradise Club date, when she stayed the night to care for him.

He remembered what she'd said at that first Club date: "I told you I will always be here for you. And if I'm not, close your eyes. Find me in your heart. Love conquers all, Glenn, near or far, this life or next, you will always find me in your heart. And I will always find you in mine."

Was it really fantasy? It seemed so real. He closed his eyes and searched his heart. But today's words crushed what good memories he had and snuffed out whatever love was left in his soul for her. Words that would haunt for a long time: "I had enough of you already! You damn right all this playacting. I told you this all fantasy. I told you when we started. It's business. You a dumb stupid fat little boy that never grew up. You are nothing."

He was emotionally done, mentally drained and spiritually dead. He could feel the love drain as he played that scene over again. *Funny*, he thought, *no pain, only emptiness. That's a good sign, I guess.*

On the way home, he bought a bottle of scotch. Falling on the sofa, he brought the bottle to his lips and took three hard swallows. The shock of the day was wearing off, with pain and emptiness spreading like cancer. *Can't breathe right. I feel lost. Lonely.*

The tears came. *Hey God, are you there or what? What's this all mean? Why'd you take me down this path? Love conquers all. Looks like love just got body slammed!*

You said she loves me! She's a bargirl. I don't mean anything to her. I'm an ATM with legs. That's the joke isn't it? What relationship? I'm so special? I don't think so. All that good stuff on Tuesday is just part of the package. True? Untrue? I think true.

The bottle was half drained. He got a familiar feeling. *Here we go again. Isn't this how it all started that summer or even that time we broke up?*

He remembered fucking the crap out of all the girls in all the bars surrounding Lynh's place: Candy, Ivanka, Tricia, Penny, Min, Laney, Cherish, Cherry and a few others whose names he never bothered to get. There were nights when he had two or three at a time. After a month, the endless sex didn't provide the ego boost he craved.

He took another swallow. *Wonder who I visit first?* He shook his head. *This sucks. I'm not even excited. I'm not gonna go to orgy city again.*

Then Vivian popped into his head.

> *Any night she does not make you happy I will take*
> *care of you. You might have to wait a bit if I have*
> *a customer, but I'm never more than an hour with*
> *anyone. If you leave her, we can take a chance*
> *together, if you need.*

He remembered her butterfly kisses, and something stirred between his legs. *I want her. I need her.* The same need he had two summers ago came roaring back. The same need that kept him going to Maya came down on him like Thor's hammer. *I gotta have Vivian.* He was on autopilot now.

108

PASSION CALLS

He half-walked, half-stumbled the ten minutes it took to get to her bar. The elderly Korean bartender who'd first served him met him as he came through the door. It was eight o'clock on a Friday night. The regulars were just coming in. Glenn looked around and squinted in the ultraviolet environment. "Hey boss, Vivian here?"

"Not here."

Misunderstanding what the old man said, Glenn turned to the man and asked, "Where? In the booth already with someone? I can wait. Can you tell her Glenn's here?"

There was a crowd gathering. Age didn't stop the old man from whipping open five beers and three jacks in seconds. "I mean she gone. Not work here no more. Her and mama fight."

Glenn felt a couple of girls standing behind him, ready to pounce. He fought the urge to take them right then and there into the back room. "If you see her, can you tell her I dropped by?"

The old man nodded and watched Glenn wobble out of the bar.

Glenn got out just in time and leaned against the wall outside. The world was spinning. Scotch always had a delayed effect on him. *Now what? No Maya. No Vivian. Lynh's bar? No. Someone new? No.*

The beginnings of a hangover and vertigo took his mind off being lonely. The pain in his head eclipsed what his heart felt. *I need to chill someplace. Don't want to go home.*

He was in and out of three or four bars before he found one where none of the girls recognized him as the Thai girl's high roller. He was about a half-mile from home. He dug out his wallet and slipped a Benjamin in his sock. *Better keep enough money to taxi home.*

The bartender's name was Shawn. Glenn slid two Jacksons his way. "Hey Shawn, not here for any action. Can I just chill here at the bar?"

Shawn slid the money back. "Be a man. If you don't want the girl, tell her 'Go away'."

Glenn knocked back the water Shawn put in front of him. *Novel idea. Shoulda done that two years ago. Oh yeah, that's right, I was too worried about hurt feelings.*

Across the way, he saw an interesting sight. Some guy, clearly out of his element, was nursing a beer, looking very nervous. Two girls had already hit him up, but he shook his head vigorously. The bar wasn't going to make money off him tonight.

Then the mama-san brought over a girl for him, and there were some hushed tones, with the girl nodding no and looking shy and looking to leave. She had a look like let's-not-bother-this-guy. The mama-san leaned over and said a few things to the man, and he nodded yes.

The mama-san said "Thank you" and left the girl, who just sat. The guy eased up after a few minutes and bought her a drink without her asking. *Now, where have I seen that before? Dammit! It's a bar trick. This whole two past years with Maya started with a bar trick!*

A young Korean girl came up behind him wearing only a gold thong bikini. "May I keep you company?" She took his hand and slapped it against her ass.

Glenn was intrigued. *Soft voice. Polite opening. Vulgar pitch. Her ass feels good.* He slowly pulled her closer.

A hand came out of nowhere and pushed the girl away, gently but firmly. Some words were said in a mixture of broken English, Korean and Vietnamese, and the girl left. Glenn turned. It was Vivian.

She examined his face and put her palm to his forehead. "You're burning up. How much did you have?" She turned to the barkeep. "Shawn, can you get him more water?"

Shawn brought the water. She scooted onto the barstool next to him. "Uncle Billy called and said you were looking for me. He said you weren't in the best shape. He should have told you to wait. I would have come and got you."

He looked at her like a lost puppy.

She brushed back his hair. "I got worried, so I came looking for you. I knew you were around somewhere. I put out calls. Shawn called me as soon as you walked in. Said you were about to get pounced on."

"You . . . you looked for me?"

Glenn was touched. *She came looking for me. On a Friday night? So she left all her customers to look for me?*

She dipped a napkin in the water, wrapped it around some ice cubes, and started pressing against his forehead, then his neck. The coolness eased off the vertigo. "What happened Glenn? You and Maya not doing good?"

He shrugged, looking uncomfortable. "Don't really want to talk about it. We're done."

That's all she needed to hear. "Let's go."

"Your bar?"

She took his hand. "No, my place."

109

WEEKEND TO FORGET

Their tongues were locked in a tango as soon as she closed the door behind them. They never made it to her bedroom. The first time was in the hallway, two feet from the door. The second time was in the shower. They finally made it to her bed. He wanted sleep. She grabbed his dick and rubbed the tip softly. "Oh baby, you want me to be your Maya tonight?" That was all he needed.

He woke up the next morning to her sucking his dick. *This girl is crazy!*

The next forty-eight hours was an endless cycle of sex, eat, shower and sleep, with assorted chores in between. She had men's clothes in her closet, and oddly enough, they were a near perfect fit.

"My ex and you about the same size." She stared at his crotch. "In every way." She smiled lasciviously.

Monday morning came. He called in sick. Right after noon, there was a knock at the door. She went to answer. Glenn could hear Mike's voice through the door. *How the hell?*

Glenn opened the door. Mike's voice was a monotone. "Surprise."

"How'd you know I was here?"

Mike rolled his eyes. "Oh, come on. This is me."

Glenn leaned against the door. "So what gives? I called in sick."

Mike rubbed his face. "Don't blame the messenger. Vice-chair called me in. Then the Admiral called me in. Have you checked your phone lately? You have at least four texts and three voicemails from me."

Glenn reached for his phone. It was dead. In all the sexual mayhem, he'd lost sight of the fact that his phone needed daily charging.

Mike crossed his arms. "Vice-chair's waiting. He went by your place. You weren't there. That's when he called me." He then turned to Vivian, who'd managed to cover up with a robe. "My name is Mike. No last name. Just Mike. And you are?"

Glenn cut in. "Never mind." He was dressing and said, "I gotta go."

She took a pen from her purse and wrote her phone number on Glenn's hand. Then took his other hand and shoved it down her panties, where she was wet. She turned his face to her, made eye contact and kissed him hard. "Something to remember me by."

———————

Glenn walked into his office and stopped at the doorway. Two of his guest chairs were occupied. The Vice-chair rarely visited like this. This was the first time for the Admiral, whose baritone voice was unmistakable. "Close the door, Glenn. Come in. It's your office, after all."

Glenn walked to his desk cautiously, guard up. *This is not going to be good. Maybe they're firing me. Off the campaign. Out of the group. How bad can it be? I did call in sick. All the texts and voicemails said was, we needed to talk.* "So, gentlemen, to what do I owe the pleasure and honor of this visit?"

The Admiral started. "I'll be brief. Thank you for coming in. Especially when you are sick." To Glenn, the last statement didn't sound believable. The Admiral continued. "I hope you got the sickness out of your system this weekend. I understand you had quite the treatment regimen."

Glenn fiddled with a pencil on his desk. *He knows. How does he know? A tail? GPS? Doesn't matter. Making me would be duck soup compared to some of the international stuff we've done.* "It depends, Admiral. I hope I don't have a relapse." He tried to smile, to bring some levity into this meeting.

The Admiral leaned forward, elbows on the desk, fingers together. "Son, you better damn well make sure you are cured as of now." He slammed his fist down for emphasis. "The other side made you. One of their peons spotted you with your new friend. They want to make light of your visits to places of ill repute. The Group is clamoring to replace you, both as part of the Group and as campaign manager."

Glenn twirled his pencil between his fingers. "Are you serious? My going to see Maya is an issue?"

The Admiral leaned back. "She has a name. Your weekend tryst has a name?"

Glenn perked up. *He doesn't know about Maya. They're talking about Vivian.* "What do you want me to do?"

The Admiral looked up something on his phone. "We've discredited the peon. Planted drugs in his workplace. And we've floated the story that you were at a bachelor party this weekend, and as boys will be boys, you were embarrassed to be in a place you hadn't been in since your own bachelor party."

The Admiral scrolled to another entry. "Mike is back at her apartment now, explaining the situation and ensuring she does not come around here. By the way, you'll wash off that number on your hand, here, in my presence."

Glenn dug some rubbing alcohol out of his desk and started scrubbing. "Admiral, in my defense . . ."

"You have no defense, Glenn. You got careless. We can't have that during this campaign. Your single days are over. You are still married to Katie. Act like it."

Glenn leaned back. *Dammit. I love the guy, but that's it. Not taking this crap from anyone.*

Glenn caught the Vice-chair's gaze and could feel his longtime friend telepathically telling him, *Don't do anything stupid. Let's talk first.*

Glenn took a deep breath in and exhaled slowly.

The Admiral took this as his cue to leave. "Glenn, before I leave, let me hear you say you understand what I said today, and that you'll get your act together."

"I got you, Admiral. It's done. Out of my system." *Easy to say, I guess, since Maya is already out of my life.*

The Admiral got up and started to the door. The Vice-chair stayed put. The Admiral turned at the doorway. "Glenn, I know it's difficult since Katie had her accident. We can better control the situation once we have our new mayor elected. I know about the other girl too. If you get serious again, and if it makes you happy, we can find ways to make everybody happy. Just work with me, and only after we have a new mayor. Do you hear me?"

Glenn nodded.

The Admiral half-turned to the door. "For now, keep it in your pants. For our sake and this city's sake. Clifford would bury you if he got the goods on you." With that he turned and was gone.

Fifteen seconds later, the Vice-chair plopped onto the sofa, and Glenn joined him. "Pleasure having you down here, Vice-chair."

"Cut the crap, Glenn. You know it's "Jerome" in here. We've done too much."

"Okay, Vice-chair."

"Fuck you and your protocol. And fuck your penis too. You really hate me that bad? You gonna take up with some bargirl and get me raked on the front page?"

"Hey Jerome, it wasn't like that. We're friends, or something like that.

Or we used to be."

Glenn gave his longtime friend the abridged ten-minute version. He ended with the last conversation at Thai Garden and the hope that there was some shot at redemption. "After that, I lost it and went on a binge this weekend. After I lost Katie, I've been a mental basket case."

The Vice-chair sighed. He'd had his own days on the bar circuit. "I'm sorry to hear that, buddy. But maybe it *is* just a fantasy. I mean you only meet in the bar, you buy her drinks, she doesn't give you her real identity, she has social media pages that show a different side to her."

Confused, Glenn's thoughts drifted between Maya and Vivian. *Am I really cut off?* He thought of Vivian comforting him—his arms around her, her arms around him, butterfly kisses, snuggling with her curves. He'd already forgotten that nothing escaped the Admiral.

The Vice-chair snapped his finger. "Come back to Earth, man."

The Vice-chair leaned forward, and Glenn met him halfway. "Man, you know we've been working on this for so long. Can't have anything mess it up. I'm counting on you. Clifford has an army trying to get him elected."

The Vice-chair was almost pleading. "There are only eight months left. I need you to stay on the job. I don't know what kind of shit you're into, but . . ."

"Okay, Jerome. I got you. I got the Admiral. No more." *Not sure how I'm going to do this. I'll find a way. I always find a way. Maybe I just suppress it till after the election.*

After some unrelated shop talk, the Vice-chair headed for another meeting. This left Glenn to send a text to Mike.

> The midlife crisis is over.
> Come back to the office.
> We have an election to win!

110

CAMPAIGN RALLY – INDEPENDENCE DAY

They were twenty-four points behind in the polls. It took all the mental fortitude he had to suppress his feelings so he could concentrate on winning. He killed what emotions he had for Maya, replaying that last day over and over in his mind, letting it burn into his psyche, and letting hate bury love deep into his heart.

By day he had twelve Council staff members at his beck and call. At night, he headed an organization of 3,000 volunteers. He'd done it before, but back then, he had Katie waiting every night to smooth things over. He still visited her every night, telling her all about the day, then falling asleep, head on her bosom.

Over the next three months, he worked savagely on legislation during the day and even more savagely at getting his friend elected at night. Maya rarely crossed his mind.

In ninety days, he won the trust of the key volunteers and supporters.

The populace was warming to the Vice-chair as mayor. Jerome was young, the future was here, and talk among the town's influencers was that the new mayor could do anything with someone like Glenn by his side.

The summer's biggest campaign event was a July Fourth rally with twenty-four thousand supporters at the football stadium. Glenn's job was to introduce the candidate.

As "Don't Stop Believin'" played over the sound system, Glenn ran out on stage with a microphone—arms raised, hands clapping above his head, exhorting the entire stadium to clap along. The lights went dark and right on cue, the crowd hit the flashlights on their phones. Pinpoints of light danced in the dark all over the stadium, turning the evening into a night of shooting stars.

And then he held the microphone out to the masses, and twenty-four thousand voices sang back, exhorting one another to keep believing, never stop believing. The song ended with a thunderous cheer, and the stadium lights came back on. Glenn looked off to the side. For a split second, he remembered that first night he and Maya had together and had one fleeting thought: *I wish she could see me now.*

For a second, the hate was gone, and she was there with him, singing and dancing. Just for a second, and that's all it took for love to come flooding back in, waging war with the hate lodged in his heart. Somewhere in the heavens, an army of angels lay siege to the legion of demons that had held Glenn's heart in their claws for the past three months.

The crowd's roar jerked him out of his trance. He held up both hands and ad-libbed, leaving his speech in his pocket. "Love conquers all," he shouted. "and we're gonna win because we love this city! Everything we do, it's because we love each other, love our city, and love our friends and families! We're gonna make this city the best one ever!"

The crowd erupted, even louder than before. "Don't stop believing!" Glenn called out. "We're just getting started! Three months ago, we were twenty-four points behind in the polls, but we're gaining every day. Today we're only fifteen points behind, and the opposition is scared! They're scared because of you!"

The crowd roared, as people clapped and stamped their feet on the ground. It was thunderous. "And here's the man who will take us there! Give it up, everybody, for our next mayor!"

Then Jerome came running onstage, and they high-fived before Glenn made his exit. Standing off to the side, Glenn was on an adrenaline high. But he had no one to share it with. Images of Maya flashed uncontrollably in his mind. He barely heard Jerome's speech—and didn't have to, since he'd written it.

A couple of hours later, after the crowd had gone home happy, the campaign volunteers were having their own party, blowing off steam and celebrating the night. Jerome joined Glenn in the green room after giving his field ops team a pep talk. Their half-hour, two-man strategy debriefing ended with one final question from the candidate. "Did we really gain nine points on them?"

"Yep. Get some rest, Jerome. Tomorrow's another day."

They said their goodbyes and walked out to their cars together. They could still hear the field ops team behind them whooping it up. The unprecedented event had sent ripples through the populace. This new young guy was taking on the elite, and he was gaining.

Exhausted, Glenn got in his car. *Skipping Katie tonight. Need rest.* But as he turned onto the highway, the adrenaline was still coursing through his body, and Maya made her way back into his soul. Images of her on different nights flashed into his mind. Love and hate commingled with pain and pleasure. On autopilot, he took a detour.

He pulled up in front of Thai Garden, parking ten yards behind the white Audi. *She's in there. I guess with whoever. That guy. I hope she's happy. Text her? Tell her I'm here?*

Then her words came back in a flash.

> *You a dumb stupid fat little boy that never grew*
> *up. You just use your money to make like you*
> *somebody. But that's all you are. Fat little ugly boy*
> *with money, no other worth.*

Three months of suppressed pain bubbled up from his psyche like pre-vomit bile.

His knuckles screamed white as he strangled the steering wheel. His mouth a thin line, he stared straight ahead. Hot tears ran down his face. The white Audi turned to a blur. Love and rejection cross-sectioned into a white-hot burst of pain.

He looked upward and simply uttered, "Why?"

He slapped the dash. "Oh, Father, she's like a sickness. I'm weak. She treats me like this and I'm still here in the parking lot like a lovesick puppy? Help me, Father. I can't do this anymore. And if I can't have her, then what's the sense?"

With that, he broke down. Sobbing, he head-butted the steering wheel so hard the whole car shook.

Then a soft voice, as always.

Love yourself as I love you

He was sure he'd given himself a concussion. His head throbbed, and he felt a lump forming between his eyes. Absorbing what he heard in his head, he thought inwardly. *Love myself . . . as you love me? What does that mean? Isn't it the other way around? Love others as you've loved me?*

The voice again.

> *You cannot truly love if your soul is empty. You cannot*
> *love if you have no love to give. You cannot love if you are*
> *always chasing that same love from others. Love yourself*
> *first. Fill yourself with love. Then let that love spill over to*
> *others. Love will conquer your hurt. Love conquers all.*

Love yourself as I have loved you. Love conquers all.

He strained his inner ear for more, but the voice was gone.

Glenn suddenly felt calm. Like a news highlight, all his accomplishments and values scrolled through his mind giving him, a sense of who he was. The goals of a better city saturated his soul and reignited his life purpose. For the first time in his life, he felt he knew himself and what he was about and felt that was enough.

And for the first time, he saw Maya clearly. A scared little girl in a big person's world, trying her best to make life work. And he loved her for that, and only that. He saw clearly her needs and not his.

A thought inched into his mind as he recalled their last night. He recalled the story of her dog in Thailand—a story she told him blind drunk one night, early in their relationship, sobbing and biting her lip. *Did she really mean to hurt me? Or was she trying to save me?*

He started typing on his phone.

Wondering how you are. No. Erase

How are you? No. Erase.

I'm outside. Can you see me? No. Erase

He put his phone down. *She mighta already blocked me. I can't get over the last things she told me. Maybe she did that so I'd go away? But why? Things were so good.*

He stared at the restaurant door as if his thoughts could go right through it and into her head. *Hey Maya, you woulda been proud of me tonight. I sang. For you. For us. I love you always. Even if you don't.*

He picked up his phone, erased the text, and went home.

Inside, Jae was passed out at the baccarat table. Maya stared at her phone.

Glenn is typing . . .

Glenn is typing . . .

Glenn is typing . . .

She stared intently, squeezing her phone. *Come on, Glenn, say something, press send. Here for you. Waiting.* Then the thread went cold. It was like a dagger through her heart. She ran into the bathroom as the tears started to flow.

111

CAMPAIGN RALLY – LABOR DAY

Two months later, the campaign nailed another milestone at the annual Labor Day picnic, where the big labor unions publicly endorsed Jerome. These were blue-collar folks with families, trying to make a living with barely enough for school supplies. Glenn had broken the news over the past month. The developers got rich on the backs of the local construction trade. The hoteliers made big bucks on the backs of the hotel workers. The rank and file needed a new champion. He gave them his friend, the Vice-chair, the next mayor.

That morning the team learned they were only eight points behind in the polls. There was no need for a blaring introduction. There were no gimmicks this time and no speeches. He instructed his team to have the candidate reach out and touch each person there. As the candidate waded out into the crowd, people gathered around him shouting encouragement. Everyone was still talking about that magical Fourth of July at the stadium, but now they really knew who Jerome was.

Glenn watched from afar, smiling. It was Jerome's moment, not his. The Admiral walked up beside him, quietly and unexpected. "Great job, Glenn."

Glenn hissed, "Whoa!" and jumped to the side, in a ready stance, fists up. "Shit, how did you do that? And how'd you get past my security?" *Must be ninja blood in this guy. Never seen him like this before.*

The Admiral looked like a crusty old guy in a Vietnam vet's hat, dark glasses and a sleeveless camo jacket. *What the hell*, Glenn thought, *is that a Navy Seals tattoo?*

The Admiral spoke calmly. "There's a lot you don't know about me. And your security? That's my security, remember? Can't take a chance with the power brokers pissed at you now. They're not worried about Jerome. They know you're the mastermind. Your 'love conquers all' campaign is starting to resonate nationally, Glenn. The whole country's watching what's going on here. Keep it up!"

Glenn left Jerome in Mike's capable hands and walked the Admiral to his waiting car. "Just a few more months, Glenn. You given any thought to what you want to do in the new admin?"

"Little soon, isn't it, Admiral? Don't want to jinx this thing."

"You need to think about it, Glenn. You want to go back to your young friend, that's fine. We can keep you in the shadows. But now you're almost as popular as Jerome. People are already talking about you for mayor next time around and Jerome as governor. Something great for this whole state."

Glenn was silent. *Mayor? Governor? I'd trade it all for one more Tuesday with her. One more real Tuesday.* "I'll sleep on it, but I'm one hundred percent for Jerome right now. But I promise I'll think about it, Admiral. Whatever's best for the people, right?"

The Admiral sized him up. Saw it in Glenn's eyes. *We can always find another mayor. Having him in the shadows is just as well.* "We'll talk again, Glenn. Eight points behind. Get to it, boy!"

Glenn found his own car, climbed in and gunned the engine. He hadn't been to Thai Garden since after the stadium event. On impulse he drove over and pulled into the lot. It was after nine, but the white Audi wasn't there. *Maybe too early? Or maybe she doesn't work here anymore?*

The hurt from the last time had faded. All he could remember were the good feelings. *Where are you?* For the first time in a long time, he cracked open his Instagram account. Her account was gone. *Where is she? Changed her account again. Text her? No. I won't be able to take it if she doesn't reply or worse yet, goes off on me. Maybe she even blocked me. Can't risk a tailspin. Too close to the win.*

He sat back, his eye on the bench outside the restaurant. *We sat there. We kissed there. That night I first came to see her here. Chloe set it up. After that shit storm with those Chinese pricks. I let her beat me that night. I let her cry on me that night. We stayed up all night. It was a Thai fest. We walked out arm in arm and kissed in her car as the sun came up. You telling me that was fantasy? I don't care what you told me, Maya. I'll always love you. Maybe. One day. After all, love conquers all.*

He went home, passing the 7-Eleven. He smiled as he drove by.

112

CAMPAIGN STRATEGY

A month later, he walked into the campaign's weekly Saturday morning strategy session. It was all hands on deck, with just five weeks remaining before the election. Glenn and his fifteen team leaders oversaw various aspects of the campaign, squished into a small conference room one of the non-profits let them use.

Nicknamed the war room, the place had maps all over the walls, with demographic notes on multicolored Post-its and colored pins marking strategic sign-waving points. Coffee cups and pastries littered the big table. Starbucks. Seattle's Best. Dunkin. Krispy Kreme. Costco. All accounted for. The fruit plate was untouched.

He walked in and headed for his usual place at the head of the table, with Jerome off to one side. Here, Glenn was the boss. "Settle down, folks. We got a lot to talk about."

Mike ran in. "Make it short. Christine Mendoza from KCBD wants to talk to you."

"Why me? You're the press guy. Why not the candidate? I'm a waste of time."

Mike grinned. "No you're not. You're the news item. Wife in a coma. Best friend's campaign manager. Actually, I thought I was your best friend."

Glenn turned back to his agenda. "I'm busy."

"Boss, you gotta do this. She's the most popular reporter in town. If she loves you, she loves Jerome, and then all the news stories she does are about *us*."

Jerome was listening in. "Glenn, don't get all sanctimonious now. If she wants to talk to you, talk to her. If I'm elected, you're gonna be the deputy mayor. Get used to it. Talking to the press will be your job too. Just do it. Whatever helps the people, remember?"

Glenn shot Jerome a fuck-you look.

Jerome signaled likewise. "You know I'm right."

Glenn turned to Mike. "Okay. I'll do it. Ten minutes. Wait. Tell her to come in here."

Mike's eyes widened. "What? This is the war room. She'll see our strategy."

Glenn slapped his back. "Just do it," he said, and Mike hurried back out the door.

Glenn turned to the team. "Okay, folks. Lots to do. First thing I want to report: Polling says we're in a dead heat. Even." The meeting erupted in whooping. Then Christine Mendoza walked in, trailed by her cameraman, and the room quickly went silent. "What the fuck?" someone blurted.

Jerome leaned over. "I hope you know what you're doing."

Glenn stood up and waved. "Good morning, Christine!"

She nodded back. An investigative reporter in her prime, Christine Mendoza had been a thorn in local government's side for at least ten years. As a cub reporter, she'd made her mark by ferreting out housing department officials who'd embezzled federal funds—and stashed them in their personal accounts right under the then-mayor's nose. Now she struck fear in anyone who had anything to hide. Civil servants made up the bulk of her confidential informants.

Glenn cleared his throat. "Thank you for coming, Christine. I'll be with you in a sec. I think I speak for our next mayor when I say the next administration will be working *with* the media, and not at odds with them. That's something that will bring this city back to where it can be, where it *should* be. If we had anything to hide, it would be a different story. But we have nothing to hide here. The transparency of our administration for the next eight years, God willing, starts now."

He made a sweeping gesture around the room. "You're in our war room. Your camera guy can record all the crucial information that our opponent needs to win. But we're trusting you with it. A sign of good faith. This is what the press will be seeing going forward."

Christine turned to the cameraman, who nodded and shut off his gear, then set it down on the floor.

Glenn continued. "Okay, folks. Let's not gawk. Christine is a guest. But as I was saying, we're in a dead heat. Our message is, one city, one government, for all people. Everybody deserves love. And that's what we're going to do. We're going to take care of the people that need it. The more they need it, the more we give."

Glenn pointed upward. "And we give for the honor of giving." Not everybody in the room agreed with Glenn's religious views, but they understood him and where his heart was, and that was enough for them.

Christine Mendoza had only one thought. *Wow.*

The meeting broke down into smaller groups. Mike took Jerome aside to brief him on the day's events, and Glenn walked over to Christine with his hand extended.

She shook it enthusiastically. "That was quite a performance."

Glenn's face resembled a puzzled emoji. "That was an everyday thing. Short and to the point. Like my wife described me."

She laughed. *This guy has a sense of humor too.* "Is there a quiet place we can go?"

"Not here."

"You don't have an office?"

Glenn looked around. "No, everything's open space here. You go to war; you sleep, eat and work with the troops. Let's step outside."

She liked this guy. *Something genuine. Really cares about people.*

The camera guy was setting up. Glenn started off. "So why me? How can I help you today?"

She had seen enough. In truth, she'd used the interview as a pretense to investigate closed-door campaign tactics. She'd already been turned away by the other side. She had anticipated the same treatment today and had planned to use footage of closed doors to crucify back-room campaign officials in general.

She signaled to Camera Guy. "Actually, all we'd like is some b-roll of you talking about the campaign and its main themes."

Glenn's features relaxed, and he rubbed his face. "Okay, great. Want me to start, or you want to prompt?"

"Why don't I prompt?" She asked what the campaign was about, and he was on a roll.

"This campaign is about making people happy again—the homeless, the elderly, the unemployed all deserve a happy life. But let's not forget the rank and file that make up the backbone of our workforce—the folks who work with their hands to make all of our lives better, and who work toward the day that their children will have better lives too."

Christine had been raised by a single dad who worked three jobs to give her the best life possible. He was a construction worker by day and a hotel laundry worker by night, and on weekends he hired out as a handyman. As Glenn spoke, she decided to do what she could to give Team Jerome a fair shot.

Glenn walked Christine and her camera man out to their van. As they pulled away, he offered one parting shot. "Give a shout anytime you need.

If you can't find me, well, you already know Mike has a way of getting me."

She gave a quick salute from the car. "Thanks, Glenn. Good luck!"

That night in bed, Glenn was exhausted. *One more month to election night. I wonder if Maya's going to be there?* He drifted off. He was with her again. Their first date . . .

> *Maya? Yes, Glenn? If I win. I mean, if we win.*
> *Yes, Glenn? You will win, Glenn. Okay. If we win,*
> *will you come see me at the election night party?*
> *Yes, Glenn, I will. And if I lose? You will not lose,*
> *Glenn. But if you do, you come see me and we'll get*
> *stinking drunk. My treat. Okay. My treat first round*
> *anyway, then you pay rest. She laughed and he*
> *joined in. Glenn? Yes, Maya? You will win. I know.*
> *You will win.*

He woke the next morning with the biggest smile he'd had in a while. *The dream was so real. It was as if we were just together. Will she come? Maybe we'll lose and I'll go to the bar. Oh Maya, I miss you. Where are you? What have you been doing?*

It had been seven months since they'd parted ways.

113

REWIND BACK

Seven months earlier . . .

You a dumb stupid fat little boy that never grew up!

That's what she'd said. Maya leaned against the restroom sink at Thai Garden, watching her tears trickle down the drain, along with everything she and Glenn had had over the past two years.

Hunching forward, her shoulders shook and her heart ached as Glenn's pained visage appeared to glare at her from the mirror.

Oh, Glenn, I love you so much. I'm sorry I hurt you. You safe from me now. You will be happier without me. I love you always, Papa.

Outside, Vey was on the phone, spitting out the details to Chloe: Maya come, Jae come, Glenn come, Jae and Glenn fight, Jae go down, Glenn say shit, Maya say shit, Glenn leave, Maya cry.

Chloe tried all afternoon to reach Maya.

Maya finally answered that night. "Hello, sis."

"What you do, girl," Chloe scolded.

"I release him, Chloe. He can be happy now." *Why she not on my side? She should know. I told her already. She not remember? At the beach?*

> *I don't want hurt him anymore. You see how*
> *many times I hurt him already? He so patient. I*
> *walk away from him at bar, remember the time*
> *you brought the customer? Then with the cops?*
> *Then with the construction crew? Then I mess*
> *with Eddie, then Jae? I get mad, I have Deth come*
> *on a Tuesday night. I don't trust myself, Chloe. I*
> *dunno what wrong with me. Lynh is right. I'm man*
> *crazy. I love him, Chloe. I love him like I never love*
> *anyone before. But I hurt him all the time. I hurt*

*him tonight, Chloe. You saw his face? No? I did. I
hurt him. Hurt me so much when I hurt him. I'm
done with that, Chloe. He deserve better, much
better.*

Chloe stared at her phone, disbelief marbling her face. *After all I did?
How many breakups I fix? This time I went to his office. Everybody hot shit,
they all stare at me but I don't care. I still see him and explain for you. How
you kick him out because Jae was coming with his gang. How you don't like
what Jae do to you. How you think of him.*

Chloe took a breath in, cricked her neck, and breathed out. "Sister,
what the fuck! What you . . ."

"Chloe, I don't want to talk no more. Jae and I talk after. I told Jae no
worries. I'm his now. No more bar. Jae say other girls are other girls. I'm the
wife. He take care me, family. We have kids."

Maya took a quick breath in. "I'm not second wife. I'm first wife. Okay
with me. Uncle Jimmy find day job for me. His assistant. He say daytime
husband and wife together not good, too much fight. Need to be apart so
happy when go home."

Chloe fell back on her sofa. "What you do for Uncle Jimmy?"

"Day job, Chloe. Like you." Maya couldn't see Chloe rolling her eyes.

"You really gonna be happy with that jerk?"

"What else I got, Chloe? Glenn wrong. He say I can be whatever I
want. I'm just bargirl. No school. What I got? Nice purses. Jewelry. Rusty
my main treasure. I must take care of him too. Doctor say diabetes worse.
Medicine cost more money." Rusty shifted in her lap, and she scratched
him behind an ear. *Mommy take care of you, boy. Don't leave mommy, okay?*

Chloe bit her lip, rubbing her temples. *She think about this at all? I
thought the other night just the Cuervo talking.* "What about Caleb?"

"He and I ten year next year. The deal was we divorce after. Then Jae
and I will marry." Maya hugged Rusty tight. *Sorry, boy, we be okay without
Daddy. I promise.*

Chloe kicked the coffee table lightly. "But sis, Caleb say he want you
back?"

Maya rubbed her neck. "I only say we talk. I let him know. I will be
his wife till divorce. Marry is marry. I told Jae too. He have to wait. He say
'okay.'" *This best, Chloe. Don't leave me. Be my support, sis. Please.*

Chloe's face turned a shade of red. "He say 'okay' cuz he fuck around
other girls!"

Maya closed her eyes and took a deep breath. Sabai. Sabai. "That's okay, Chloe. One year. He still single. I don't fight. I'm not single either. I will take care Caleb. Get divorce. Then Jae. Till then, Jae can do whatever. We just good friends till then. Uncle Jimmy bless us long time ago he said."

Maya knew she didn't sound convincing. She barely convinced herself. "He can be nice, Chloe. Vegas, he good man. Only thing, Glenn around make him mad. Me at bar make him mad. How Reyn was with you. Right? Now no Glenn, no bar. He better now. I know for sure."

She was lying to Chloe. Worse, she was lying to herself. "Caleb back soon. I will go back to him. Work for Uncle Jimmy. Friends with Jae. Wife to Caleb. Next year divorce. Marry Jae. Family okay. Happy ever after?"

Chloe's shoulders slumped. "Yeah, except for you." *Stupid. So stupid. So fucking stupid.*

Maya's eyes reddened by the second. She cleared her throat. "Don't worry, Chloe. Caleb think I still work bar. I will spend nights with Jae, then go home to Caleb. Jae have boys night out Friday and Saturday. I will go out with you sisters or spend time with Caleb and Rusty. Still have wife duty to Caleb."

Chloe looked at her watch. Almost time to meet Reyn. "You get money for family, Maya?"

"I don't worry, Chloe. Jae give me money, thousand dollars every Saturday for gamble at Thai Garden. I tell him I lose all money. But I win and send home. Soon have money to buy house. Uncle Jimmy's job let me take care Rusty and whatever else I need."

Maya heard Chloe sigh and continued. "I will go beauty school soon. GI bill. I get stipend too. Jae say he take me world cruise when we marry. Chloe, I have to go. Uncle Jimmy waiting."

Chloe kissed the phone for luck. "Okay. Call me later sis." *I'm done. Let karma decide from now. I will be there for her no matter.*

Uncle Jimmy was not waiting. If only Chloe could see. Tears were streaming down Maya's face. On her Mac laptop, every picture she had of Glenn was open. She hugged her pillow tight and sobbed.

114

BAD SUMMER

Caleb returned from deployment two weeks after Glenn's fight with Jae at Thai Garden.

Rusty was happy Daddy was home. Caleb and Maya went back to the five-star revolving restaurant they'd enjoyed the night before his deployment. He took her hand in his. "So, what do you think? Songkhram in a month. Go back and visit Mom?"

He still called Maya's mother Mom. Maya had already told her family what she planned to do, where all the money had been coming from, and why she was doing this. "Caleb, let's stick to original deal. I'm your wife till ten years and you make rank, and then we separate. Okay?"

He flipped her hand off his. "You found someone? The old guy?"

She took a sip of her wine. "No, Caleb. You and I both young. Can start over. I know you have second wife. No need for two wives. Just have one. Take care her."

His eyebrows raised in surprise. *She knew?* "What about you?"

She smoothed her napkin on her lap. "I will be okay. You were—are—good husband. Thank you. I not forget. Always appreciate. You bring me to America. Land of opportunity. I'm okay if I work hard. I work bar little while more then quit. Vey want me be DJ with her. With GI Bill I go beauty school and have my own clients. One wedding, makeup hair and DJ make two thousand dollars."

He didn't like it. He wanted her. But if not, his second wife already told him she wasn't staying with him if half the pension went to Maya. *If she's leaving me, this is bullshit, she's not getting the pension. My boys that watched the house said some guy stayed over. I just need proof.* He never gave a thought to his own infidelity.

He narcissistically switched to charm mode. "Yup. Okay. Back to the upstairs downstairs?"

She nodded. "Yes, Caleb."

He smiled, something that looked more like a sneer. "It was a good run wasn't it?" At least there was some hope. "Same deal once a month?" He was leering now.

Her eyes downcast, hands in her lap. She took a deep breath and looked up, staring into his soul. "Yes, Caleb. I'm still your wife. I will do my duty."

He raised an eyebrow. *She looks unhappy. Fuck her. I don't care. Pussy is pussy, and she's still hot.*

Three months after Caleb's return, Maya came home on a clear June night after being with Jae to find boxes stacked up on the sidewalk. Rusty was tethered to the boxes, barking. Looking up the walkway, she could see the house was dark, though she thought she saw the blinds move in her bedroom window.

Caleb was staring through the blinds. It was his bedroom now. The teenaged cashier from the base exchange was on her knees, servicing his every whim. He knew how to twist their young, needy minds. It was easy with their military fathers overseas. Treat them right and they'd live to make you happy.

He was enjoying his wife's anguish. Maya tried the door. He'd changed the locks. She knocked loudly. His car was in the driveway. She called him, but he'd blocked her. She walked back and forth between the stacks of boxes and the house. A couple of MPs rolled up. "Everything okay, ma'am?"

"Yes, okay, officer." She smiled. The base cops moved on. They were friends of his, on call to drag her off base if necessary.

She was labeled—fraud, sham, whore. Someone in his posse, expert with social media, had found a photo. The Facebook page belonged to some guy named Jae. Her face was cropped out, but her body was turned just enough to see the phoenix wings tattooed on her back and the mole on her shoulder.

Facial recognition software was amazing. Most people did searches on faces. This social media guy did it on the mole on her shoulder and the tattoo on her back. Apart from the usual Facebook pages they knew of, Jae's was the only unknown that popped. They analyzed the picture. Couldn't see the face, but it was definitely Maya wrapped around the guy in some swanky hotel room.

Jae had taken the picture that last night on their trip. She'd protested, and he'd pretended to delete the picture from his phone. Later, he posted it to a trophy website—post after post of girls bedded by him and his frat brothers over the years. To be nice, he cropped her face out before posting.

That was the picture she found in an envelope Caleb had taped to one of the boxes. A note read:

> *Dear soon to be ex-wife,*
>> *See the picture. We're through. See the divorce papers. It's an official summons by a Navy judge advocate for divorce based on infidelity. You can appeal. Get your own lawyer. For now, no house, no medical, no GI Bill so no beauty school, no stipend, and no pension.*
>> *You shoulda kept your pants on. I remember calling you that night and you told me you were alone in your room, and that you were up there with Chloe. That blanket wrapped around you and the guy is the same blanket in your Instagram photo of only yourself. Big bullshit.*
>> *You can have Rusty. He costs too much. Enclosed is $100 for you to find a place for the night.*
>>> *Sincerely,*
>>> *Your soon to be ex-husband*

Her friend Bella had divorced her Army husband after ten years. Bella would later tell her she had no case. Maya's pension was gone.

She called Jae, who got upset and told her to take a taxi to his place. He was an angry drunk, especially after losing money, and most especially after having to send his girlfriend home without blowing his seed for the night. Rusty came running in and knocked over a vase. Rusty yelped, then growled after Jae kicked him.

She got between them. "No, don't!"

He kicked her too, then threw Rusty in the hall closet and slammed the door.

Then he was on her. "Give me some, girl! You owe me this." Like so many times before, she could hear her mother. *Just close eyes. Go happy place.* She closed her eyes. She remembered the night she first met Glenn.

She could feel Jae ready to come, but he wasn't pulling out. She thrashed about trying to get out from under him. "Nooooo . . . We not supposed to till marry!"

There was no pulling out. He buried it deep and came in her like he was branding her. Caleb always used a condom, so she didn't use pills. Jae pulled out halfway, then pumped a half dozen times for good measure. It was too much, and she passed out. He sneered and went upstairs. In the morning, she woke to Rusty barking from inside the hall closet, a pool of dried semen between her legs. Jae was gone.

That was her first night living with Jae, and the following days and nights weren't much better.

When she refused him one night over the Labor Day weekend, he beat her. She threw a punch that glanced off his arm without any harm. "Why you do this? I'm your wife. Respect?"

He slapped her against the wall. "Bullshit, bitch! You're not my wife, and you're not going to be my wife. You're a skank bargirl. What makes you think you're going to be the wife of an international CEO?"

He was tired of her being there every night. He wanted to fuck his girls in his bed, in his house, with his sheets, and not have to go home after being in their tiny studios or in the back room of some bar. He wanted them two or three at a time, with cocaine, and then wanted to just roll over to sleep while they found their own way home.

In another life, he and Caleb could have been best friends. And he was tired of that damn dog too.

She pleaded. "Calm down, baby. I'm sorry. I'm ready. Let's do it."

He spit at her. "Get out. Get out now!"

"Wha. . . what?"

"I. . . said . . . get . . . *out!*" He cracked his fist into her ribs. She doubled over, and he kicked her in her head.

It was midnight. Her head was ringing. She called Chloe as he stood over her. Her broken ribs made her yelp each time she sobbed. She looked up at him like a beaten dog. "I come for my stuff tomorrow."

"Fine. It'll be outside."

Inside of five months, she'd been kicked to the curb twice. This time there was no optical shop to take her in. Only Chloe.

115

BARGIRL AGAIN

Chloe had moved in with Reyn a few months before. Maya slept on their couch for the rest of September until she healed. In hushed tones, Reyn told Chloe that Maya had to leave; his son was asking too many questions. In truth, Reyn did construction work for Uncle Jimmy and Jae, and they had given him an ultimatum.

Maya went back to working at a bar in a seedier part of town. Lynh wouldn't take her back. None of the other mainstream bars would take her. She was stained, with a reputation for being a marriage wrecker. Eddie's wife made good on her threats to talk shit among the mama-sans. Maya was also tagged with a scarlet letter—married to a service member and cheating on him with customers.

Jae also put out word that any bar that took her would lose out. He didn't care about the seedier places. And she was barred from the one avenue she was counting on to get back home: Thai Garden, still running Uncle Jimmy's gambling operations, also closed its doors to her. It felt just like the time the restaurant in Wyoming had kicked her to the curb, warning her not to come back for fear of what Caleb would do.

She shared a crowded apartment with three women in their fifties who still worked as bargirls. They'd been too proud to put out in their younger days but were now giving hand jobs for fifty bucks, blow jobs for a hundred, and spreading their legs for two hundred. Sex for pay was physically faster and emotionally easier than interacting with the cheaper customers, spending an hour begging for two or three shots amounting to maybe $20-$30 take-home.

These repulsive customers reminded her of Gollum, that ugly creature in the hobbit movies. These monsters came in with no intention of buying shots for the girls. They brought their own beer and saved what cash they had for their weekly sex-with-a-live-person sessions. They laughed with each other afterward, making it all about male conquest. Part of the package was having the girls fawn over them. It was demeaning at best, and the women all self-medicated with alcohol or drugs.

Maya still had her looks, so she got away with giving hand jobs for a hundred dollars a crack, in addition to shots here and there. It paid the bills. She convinced herself that hand jobs were a form of massage and the guy coming was his own thing. Lying to herself again.

But it got around that she needed money. One night she had to give a blow job just to make rent. Spitting out pubic hair was disgusting, but at least the guy wore a condom. She knew some paid extra for the natural feel. The other women told her that one day she'd need to provide more services. Fucking for money was inevitable if you stayed in the trade too long.

Maya was at an all-time low. Once a roommate offered a hit of something that would make her "feel good, forget." She wanted to escape so badly but said no. She went back to her room and felt her baby bump, a present from Jae. *No. I'm having this one. His name is Glenn. He will grow up fine. He will go to school, play sports, do well in studies, and go to college. He will work at a bank and go to law school. Become something, someone. Someone like . . .*

It always ended there.

116

ELECTION NIGHT

The seedy bar was dead. No customers. Maya and two other hostesses sat at one end of the bar in a queue, each waiting their turn with the next guy through the door. The late news came on the flatscreen, and she heard a familiar voice that made her heart jump. She smiled instinctively. A warmth rushed through her soul.

> *Someone once told me not to let what others think*
> *stop you from doing what's right or what makes you*
> *happy. This campaign was right. This campaign is*
> *about making people happy again—the homeless,*
> *the elderly, the unemployed, all deserve a happy*
> *life. But let's not forget the rank and file who make*
> *up the backbone of our workforce. Those that work*
> *with their hands to make the lives of others better.*
> *We all deserve a better life as well as the promise*
> *that their children will have better lives too.*

"I'm Christine Mendoza, reporting for KCBD News. You've been listening to Glenn Forrester, the campaign manager for this victorious campaign, stirring up the crowd, and he joins us now for a few words. Mr. Forrester, the mayor-elect just gave a rousing acceptance speech and named you deputy mayor if you'll accept. Will you?"

Maya called to the barback to turn up the volume. There was Glenn on TV being interviewed! What a difference eight months makes. Two hundred forty days since she had last seen him at the restaurant. From time to time, she'd gotten wind of what he was doing. She saw him on the news. Her cop friends told her about this guy working behind the scenes at City Hall. Big changes were around the corner, and even people who hated politicians were feeling right about their beloved city once again. Corruption was a bad word again.

Glenn's face glowed, sweating just a little. "Hey, Christine. Just call me Glenn. First, all glory to God. It's His plan. Second, it's Jerome's . . . I mean, the mayor-elect's night. With all due respect, we'll create a search committee and give the city the best person for the job."

The reporter looked into the camera and turned back to him. "That's exactly what he said you'd say. But he also said that as mayor, it's his right to pick his deputy."

Glenn scratched the back of his head, "He's right Christine, the city charter does say that, and it's not even subject to Council confirmation. But hey, tonight's not the night to pick anyone else. It's about having picked the right person for the biggest job. Tomorrow we'll start with the rest, beginning with a new deputy mayor."

Maya put her hand to her mouth. *He did it! He going to be somebody now. Fix things like he always wanted.*

Her heart swelled with pride. Tears welled up. *I'm so proud of you, Glenn. I wonder about you. Sometimes I see you on TV. You look so tired. Sometimes you look scared. Sometimes you look mad. I wish I was there for you. Tonight you happy—tired but happy. I'm happy for you. How I wish I could see you. I saw you text in July. But you don't send anything. Who support you now? Who your Tuesday nights?*

Maya thought Glenn looked like he wanted to run away. She couldn't help her grin. *Still little boy.*

The reporter held Glenn by the arm. "Do you think you can do the job?"

"I think I might make the short list, but we'll leave it to an independent search committee. That's the first step, forming the committee."

The reporter held fast onto his arm. "Thank you, Glenn. Any other comments?"

"Christine, someone once told me, don't let what anyone thinks stop you from doing what's right or what makes you happy. This campaign was right."

She signaled her cameraman for a close-up. "And who told you that?"

He paused and looked into the camera. "An angel from heaven, Christine, an angel from heaven."

The reporter let him go, and with a wave, he was gone.

Sitting at the bar, Maya couldn't help smiling. Her soul was soaring. It felt like he was talking to her. Angel from heaven—that's what she told him Maya meant.

She thought of that first night and how shy he'd been, and the night she coaxed him to sing and what she told him: "Do what you like, what make you happy, don't care what other people think."

Whenever he brought problems to the bar, she would tell him, "You can do it. Do what make you happy. No matter what others think."

She left the bar soon after the news ended. There were no customers, at least not any she wanted to touch. Not tonight anyway. Back home, she remembered their first big date.

He told her back then about the exciting things happening at City Hall and how the campaign was shaping up. Going to war always excited him, the adrenaline was infectious, and she was equally excited for him.

Maya? Yes, Glenn? If I win. I mean, if we win.
Yes, Glenn? You will win, Glenn. Okay. If we win,
will you come see me at the election night party?
Yes, Glenn, I will. And if I lose? You will not lose,
Glenn. But if you do, you come see me and we'll get
stinking drunk. My treat. Okay. My treat first round
anyway, then you pay rest. She laughed and he
joined in. Glenn? Yes, Maya? You will win. I know.
You will win.

She wanted to smile, but sadness eclipsed her joy for him. Her lips a tight line, she struggled to smile. *Sorry I'm not there Glenn. I break promise again. Better I'm not there.*

She wondered if he even remembered the promise to be there for him. Then she cried into her pillow. Rusty curled up with her. He was moving slowly lately. She knew he needed to see the vet. She thought they would as soon as she saved up the money. It was a cash-upfront situation now. She looked in her bag. If she didn't eat tomorrow, she would have just enough.

There was a knock on the door. "You have call." The four women shared a landline. Personal phones were luxuries for low-in-demand whores.

Chloe gushed. "You see?"

"Yes, Chloe. So proud of him."

Chloe dabbed her eyes with tissue. "He was talking about you, Maya. I was there that night you told him that. He still thinking of you. Call him, Maya!"

Maya's mouth was a thin line. "No. I hurt him too much last time. I don't hurt him again. And now he important. Best not to have bargirl in his life. Happy to know him one time. So proud. He will do well. He will help everyone. Best this way."

Chloe ran her fingers through her hair, wanting to tear it out strand by strand. *She love him that much. The one person that can help her, and she not call him. She love him that much.*

117

HOLLOW VICTORY

After his interview with Christine Mendoza, Glenn walked back to the victory bash in progress and grabbed a cold one from a cooler brimming with beer.

Standing at the edge of the party, he watched over Jerome, who stood across the room surrounded by well wishers—captains of industry, major donors, lobbyists and assorted others who made hobnobbing with people in power their business. The political games had already begun.

There were mini-celebrations clustered around the room, as a band blasted Journey and other '80s and '90s cover songs. Glenn kept an eye on two young campaign staffers celebrating their first election victory, dancing and singing "Don't Stop Believin'" at the top of their lungs.

They looked like a guaranteed hookup. Glenn made a note to himself to have Mike keep an eye on them. Looking around the room, Glenn erased the first mental note and made a follow-up note to let what happens happen. The atmosphere was getting raucous, and there was about to be more than one hookup.

He crushed his beer can and pulled two more from the cooler. Still on the outskirts, he reflected on the last eight months. The campaign had gone from twenty-four points behind to winning by a full five points. A near thirty-point swing in eight months that some called a miracle.

The day after the fight at Thai Garden, he dove into the campaign and never looked back. Over the last few months, it was always her voice that kept him going. He heard her in his head every day—*You can do it! No matter what other people think, do what you think right.*

It was almost as if they were still together. But that last day. It still hurt, though he had since come to terms with God over that. He wished it never happened, but one hope drove him throughout the campaign. Her promise during their first date at the Paradise Club. *Where is she? She promised she'd be here.*

Yes, he was going to be the deputy mayor. So much good was about to happen. But as the night wore on, a fog of loneliness slowly crept over his heart. He had completed his mission. What he suppressed at the Admiral's order was slowly making its way to the surface. Not even the raucous election night celebration could stem the impending gloom for him. The iceberg was straight ahead. He just didn't know it.

Why am I not ecstatic? It feels so blah. I don't even want to be here. Maybe I'll try Thai Garden again tonight? Maybe the bar? I'm done with the campaign. The group can't be mad if I go see her.

He opened his third beer. *She promised. The address for this party was all over social media and the news. She promised. She broke another promise. I guess it was fantasy. For her anyway. For me, those three hours a week were the only reality I knew. Everything else was as if I was in an alternate universe.*

He crushed his third can. *I wish you were here, Maya. The family wants to let Katie go. I think I'm ready now. It's time for her too. I asked Mom to wait till after the election. If there was a goodbye involved, I wanted to do it with all my heart.*

I wish you could be with me, Maya. I need you.

118

SAY GOODBYE

Glenn spent the following week wrapping up the campaign, organizing transition meetings, setting up the deputy mayor's office, and continuing to spearhead needed legislation against a lame-duck executive branch.

On Friday afternoon, he got a call from Katie's mother. It had been more than three years since the tragedy. The family had been considering whether it was time for her to go home to God.

"Hi, Mom."

After small talk and congratulations on the election and new job, Katie's mother got serious, as only a parent could. "We need to talk, Glenn. The election is over. We're ready to let go. Are you?"

Now that Maya was gone, Katie was all he had. But he was ready to let go. He'd learned who he was from Maya. Love conquers all. While no longer with him, he could love Katie from near or far, whether she was there with him or just in his heart. "Yes, Mom, I'm ready to let go. Shall we let God decide? Take her off the machine and see?"

It broke Mom's heart, too. She had never told him, but she loved Glenn like he was her own. She knew his problems but never wanted to interfere. Never wanted to take the place of what he must have held in his heart for his own mother.

———

It took a week to get the family together on this. They met in Katie's room on a Sunday afternoon. He wanted her involved somehow. It was sunny outside with blue skies and some puffy white clouds. The smell of brownies and coffee filled the room, a present from Katie's mother. The sound of the ventilator and the buzz of the life support monitor had been part of the audioscape for years.

The voices were serious and weary at the same time. Her father was reluctant. Some family members, more spiritual than others, said it was a killing. They backed off when Glenn told them they could pay the hospital bills. Her parents had thought about mortgaging their house to keep Katie comfortable. Glenn knew Katie wouldn't have wanted this—the equity in the house she grew up in was her parents' retirement package. He'd leave it to God to decide. Legally, the decision was his.

He wished he could ask Katie what to do. For a split second, he thought he heard her. *Why are you so worried? Just do it. Everything will be okay.* It sounded like what Maya would say, but it was Katie's voice. And it came from above.

Mom spoke up. "Glenn, what do you want?"

He hung tight to his Bible. *What would Katie have wanted? She was practical. She loved God. If there was no chance, she'd want to return to her heavenly Father so she could watch over us all from a cloud somewhere. Mostly she'd want to stop being a burden to everyone.*

Somewhere in his deep subconscious, he also knew she'd want him to have a life again.

The sun was shining outside. He stared out at the blue sky and took a deep breath. "I'd like to hear the doctor tell me again there is no chance. Then I'd want a second opinion."

Dr. Heller had been the lead on the case since the night they brought her into the emergency room. He stood up so all could hear. "We never say 'no chance,' Glenn. But the chances of recovery are less than one percent. Do you understand that?"

Next to Dr. Heller stood another physician who had been introduced as Dr. Sarcovich, brought in that morning for a second opinion consult. "I'm afraid my colleague is correct, Mr. Forrester. Every diagnostic we've run shows no brain activity, and her systems are shutting down."

Glenn had read a few stories online of life returning after the ventilator was taken off and thought maybe that's what was needed. He took another deep breath. "Okay, let's do it and give it up to God, with everyone present. Let's make it a party—a welcome home party, either to the Father or to us."

Deep in his heart, he was hoping for a miracle. That the machine would be turned off and she'd breathe on her own, then wake from a deep sleep. *Hope is all I got. She'll wake up and we'll spend hours catching up and making plans.*

They gathered again on the following Monday. Everyone who could be present was there. Her mom and dad, and his brother-in-law. Some cousins. Brad, his best man and training partner. It had taken this to bring the two friends back together after their fallout at the dojo. There were others. Doctors. Nurses, including Marta. Even a nurse tech who'd retired had come back to say a final goodbye.

Glenn continued to cling to hope. *Father, I really need a miracle. I can say, Your will be done till I'm blue in the face, but I really, really want her to breathe on her own, then wake up, stretch out her arms, and give me a hug.* The mere thought warmed him.

Dr. Heller explained the procedure. The doctors had consulted with one another. In hushed tones, they predicted there would be no chance she'd breathe on her own once the machine was off. It would be a matter of minutes. Glenn was by her side. The family laid hands on her and prayed. Mom had one hand on Katie and the other on Glenn. Brad stood beside his best friend. It was the wedding all over again.

Glenn prayed. *What if? What did the Book say, if three or more are gathered in His name?*

They all prayed and asked for God's will. It was time.

Glenn climbed into bed with her and lay beside her while the nurses gently did what they had to. He whispered in her ear. "It's okay. Over soon. I love you."

The procedure to stop ventilation was peaceful. No trauma. No suffering. The whooshing sound ceased. Her breathing was shallow with small sips of air. He could tell. It would stop at any moment. For the first time, the soft sound of the bedside radio was noticeable: Ed Sheeran's "You Look Perfect Tonight." They'd danced to this at the Paradise Club one night while celebrating a double-digit wedding anniversary. They called it their new wedding song—a song about two kids falling in love and finding each other perfect even with huge obstacles in front of them.

All the tubes had been removed. Glenn sat up and cradled her, or tried to. He pulled her close. It was easy to pull her onto his lap.

Mom saw what was happening and helped position Katie's arms and hands, so it looked like he was cradling her, rocking her to and fro, with her arms around his neck, head on his shoulder. Someone turned the radio up.

He barely heard the words. He was cheek to cheek, whispering in her ears. "I wish I had more time with you. I really wanted to grow old with you. We were supposed to die together, remember? Like that movie. Don't go. Please don't go. But if you have to, wait for me up there. I'll be there sooner than you know."

He rocked her. He nuzzled her neck. He held her head to his shoulder and felt her nuzzling him. The tears were flowing freely now, and he remembered the first time they met . . .

It was the first day of business school, and they were standing outside of the classroom, waiting for the previous class to clear out.

She remarked how scared she was. He said, don't worry, and told her she looked smart. She had smiled at the compliment. Later she'd say he looked mean. They ran into each other at the vending machine afterward. They learned they both had the next class together too, after a three-hour break.

The three hours went by fast. They talked as if they'd been friends for life. It was so easy, he thought later. Why couldn't the girls he dated be this easy to get along with? They talked about anything. Mostly about recent loves gone bust and never wanting relationships again. There was a lot of laughter, but neither could ever remember what it was about. They'd had thirty years of laughter since.

By the next class, they were study buddies promising each other they'd work together, and also serve as a buffer against any new relationships until graduation. That didn't last long. Their first kiss happened after she helped him put up his student council campaign posters all over campus.

So many memories. After their first two weeks of dating, he landed a coveted on-campus job as a software programmer. Katie said she'd meet him for lunch the next day to celebrate, but Glenn was so engrossed in the new job that when he checked his watch, he was horrified to see it was well past 2:00. There were no cell phones then, so he ran all the way to the library. Of course she'd already gone home, he figured, but he had to check.

Rounding a corner, out of breath, he stopped short. There she sat, holding the lunch she'd made for him. His soda sat in a pool of condensation, the ice long melted. She looked up slowly, her eyes puffy, and cried out. She'd kept waiting when most would have left and never come back. Standing next to her, he held her head and stroked her hair, whispering, "I'm so sorry."

It was the first of many such apologies, big and small, as Glenn worked his way up the corporate ladder. Yet she always waited patiently— and forgave. Eventually, she learned to carry a paperback to fill such moments, and more recently a smartphone loaded with games and puzzles. And always she greeted him with a smile and hug.

But that day, he took the sack lunch from her—a lunch that was cold where it was supposed to be warm and vice-versa—and ate every bit of the warm, soggy tuna sandwiches and the cold and rubbery French fries. He even finished off the watered-down Diet Coke.

It was difficult to eat with a lump in his throat and his foot in his mouth. But he looked back on that lunch as the most love-filled, delicious meal he'd ever eaten. How she looked that day, sitting on the bench waiting for him, haunted him and mesmerized him for the rest of the time they were together, even now. That's when he made up his mind he would spend the rest of his life with her. This woman, he realized, would never leave the way Mommy had.

He flashed forward to the night they celebrated their first-date anniversary, dancing in the darkness of the computer lab to a Carpenters song playing on a beat-up radio. So poor, they shared a Burger King Whopper and a single Diet Coke.

He flashed forward again to their graduation together—she'd slowed her studies and he'd taken summer courses to make that happen. He held her hand during the ceremonies. They were the first in both their families to graduate from college, such a proud moment for both clans. As they sat there in their graduation gowns, the only thing on his mind was how happy he felt being next to her.

Years of joy followed. Every Christmas, right at midnight, they danced in the dark to the same Carpenters song. They had no kids, so they spoiled each other. Christmas. Valentine's Day. Easter. Fourth of July picnics. Her birthday. Their anniversary. His birthday. Annual trips to Vegas. Now all of these memories flashed by. Sights, sounds, smells, feelings, all came rushing back.

In recent years they'd had more time to spend together at the Paradise Club—working out for him and the pool for her. They showed up five nights a week—they were known as Uncle and Aunty to the younger members and Mr. and Mrs. Fitness to all others. One night, a party upstairs was playing a favorite song, and they danced cheek to cheek, in workout garb, next to the pool.

Later in the evenings they were usually poolside under the stars, enjoying the club's free munchies and, of course, the Diet Cokes. It was their thing, going over their Facebook pages together, being the first to like and heart the other's posts, sometimes with a sassy comment.

And then with a shudder, a last gasp and a long exhale, she was gone. Her breathing stopped. Outside the nurses saw on the monitor that her system had shut down. Flat line. They had muted the alarm. He held on to her tightly as the song ended. *You look perfect,* he thought, *yes you do,* as he bent over and kissed her still warm lips.

He lay her down gently. Grabbing her hand, he wiped his face with her palm. It looked like she was wiping his tears. He'd shown her this years before; how his mother used to comfort him. She did it over and over through the years, just when he needed that little extra to get through life's stresses. She did it tears or no tears because it was the one reassuring touch that would calm him. Today there were tears. Hot, salty tears that did not stop. Again and again, she wiped them away for him.

His eyes finally went dry. He bent over and kissed her again. And then he crumbled. With one heavy sob, he buried his head in her bosom and cried. He clutched at her shoulders and stroked her hair. They could hear him say, don't go, don't go, wake up, wake up. Anguish filled the room. All the suffering gasps and heaving sobs of a little boy who'd lost someone very dear.

The nurses couldn't bear it and left the room. Marta broke down crying, as did some of the family. Brad stood by Glenn, his own tears flowing, hand on his friend's shoulder, ready to hold him up if his legs went weak. Mike stayed by the door, always on the watch over his boss and friend. Anna arrived and flanked Glenn opposite Brad. Mom alone from the family stayed. She hugged Glenn from behind and cried her own tears. For her, for him, for both of them.

He realized too late that he wasn't ready to let go.

119

INTO THE VORTEX

Glenn spent the next four hours in the hospital chapel with Katie, sitting with her mom, receiving visitors. News traveled fast, and among his friends, Jerome was one of the first in line, followed by Debbie. Jerome ordered Glenn to take a week off and charged both Mike and Debbie to make sure Glenn followed through.

Meanwhile, Brad took on the mantle of family caretaker once again. At Glenn's wishes, private burial services were scheduled for the following Sunday. Anna made arrangements for the after-burial wake at the Paradise Club. After that, Brad, Anna and Mike all remained by Glenn's side.

Sometime after the last of the visitors had come and gone, Mom reached for Glenn's hand, lacing her fingers in his. "It's time to go, Glenn." Glenn sat numb, his breathing steady. Anna took his other hand, their last harsh words forgotten. Together, Mom and Anna gently coaxed Glenn to stand and say his final goodbyes.

At her bedside he gently kissed her lifeless lips. *This isn't goodbye, Katie. I'll think of you every day. You'll always be a part of me.* He smiled at that. *You woulda loved to hear me sing "Tattoo."*

He turned, and the room began to spin. Anguish filled his heart, ripped apart by death's hard finality. His knees buckled. Brad and Mike were right there to catch him.

Back in Glenn's apartment, Brad, Mike and Anna stayed late. "Guys, I'm okay," Glenn lied, putting up the brave front. "Really, I'm okay. It was time. Need to get some sleep now."

The three looked at each other, not buying it. Brad went to the fridge and came back with four beers. A toast to Katie, and then four empty bottles chunked down on the coffee table.

Brad turned to Glenn. "I'll stay the night, buddy."

"No, Brad. It's cool. Really, all. I'm good. Today was closure time. No more binges."

It was a suicide watch. The three had discussed it after what had happened earlier. Not easily apparent, but something had snapped today. Glenn didn't look normal. Anna saw it in her bar customers all the time. "What was the word?" Brad had asked. Mike said it. "Unhinged."

Glenn leaned back on the sofa and was soon snoring.

Mike rubbed his chin and turned to Brad. "Did you . . ."

"Yep," Brad said, holding up a small bottle of tranquilizers. "He'll get a good rest tonight."

Anna found a blanket and placed it gently over Glenn. Turning to Brad, she said, "See you in the morning? Six o'clock?"

They'd agreed beforehand. Brad would stay the night. Anna would take over after that. Mike would come after work to take the next night shift, if needed.

Glenn spent the next two days gathering Katie's personal items with her mother. By Wednesday evening, Brad, Mike and Anna agreed the babysitting was no longer needed and left him alone. All three had fallen behind in their own work lives.

That night, Glenn found himself alone for the first time since he'd said goodbye to Katie. He sat in silence on the couch, staring at their wedding portrait, placed lovingly on the coffee table. He decided that was where the picture should be, in a place of honor. Next to the picture was her college graduation picture, to remember her in their early years.

He spoke as if she were there. "I miss you so much. I always thought you'd be back here one day. We'd watch our favorite shows and play footsies. We'd go to the Club at night to work out, and sometimes have dinner and visit Anna." He sighed, hands trembling, lips quivering. "We were supposed to grow old together."

He hugged a sofa pillow hard, crying into it, mouth open with no sound, every fiber of his soul in anguish at the tortured ripping apart of his heart.

He wiped away his tears. Like so many times before when he longed for Katie, his thoughts turned to Maya for comfort. Only this time, there was no Tuesday to look forward to.

Just the thought of Maya gave him comfort. *Maybe,* he thought, *I can just reach out. It's okay if there's no response. Just letting her know I'm thinking of her is enough.*

Deep in his subconscious, he craved a connection, any connection, with the one person on earth that could replace the yearning for Katie.

He punched up his Instagram account for the first time in months. *She's gone! Her Instagram is gone! Is she blocking me?*

He dialed her phone. "The number you have dialed has been disconnected or is no longer in service."

He shook his head. *She changed her number?*

She was gone. Glenn didn't know: Hard times for her meant no phone, no computer, no social media.

He needed to see her. It was overwhelming. *So this is what it feels like to fall off the wagon,* he thought. A freefall, tailspin, downward spiral. He grabbed his keys.

First stop, the bar. "Hey Tia, Maya here?"

He hadn't heard Tia's coo in ages. "Not here, love." *Something wrong here,* she thought. "Glenn why don't you stay? Catch up?" He was gone without even a goodbye.

He walked into Thai Garden. It was empty. Vey looked up, but he was gone by then. He went to every hostess bar, even the seedier ones. *Maybe she doesn't work anymore?*

Had he looked in the private room of one of the seediest bars, he would have found her—providing a hand job for a hundred and fifty bucks. Looking in the private rooms or private booths never even occurred to him. In his mind, she wasn't like that.

He was lost. The last thing he remembered was sitting at Kimmie's bar, asking for the bottle of Hennessey and tossing his credit card to Kimmie. Mount Vesuvius was about to blow.

The next thing he felt was a cold shower, with Brad standing over him—two days later.

120

MAYA FOUND

Friday morning, Mike sat in his cubicle, staring at his phone. He'd sent two texts to Glenn the day before and another one that morning. No reply. An investigator's sixth sense gnawed at him. He called Brad.

"Hey, have you heard from him by any chance?"

"No, I texted yesterday about the burial, but nothing."

"You think . . . ?"

"Shit . . ."

They both thought back to their suicide watch earlier that week.

Mike and Brad broke into Glenn's condo and found a real mess. He was unrecognizable, almost like a tormented animal, and he smelled like one too. They discovered his diaries, with almost every entry for the past two years focused on Maya.

> *. . . met someone reminds me of Katie*
> *. . . makes me feel like I can do anything*
> *. . . soothes my soul*
> *. . . makes me laugh*
> *. . . gives my life purpose again*
> *. . . miss her*
> *. . . love her*

Entry after entry said the same thing in different ways. She was important. She gave him life. She sustained him. What she meant to Glenn beyond the bar now became reality for Brad and Mike. While Brad tended to Glenn, Mike went to look for Maya.

———

The next day, thanks to his sources, Mike found her. The bar was an awful place—dank and dimly lit like an abandoned photo darkroom. The stench rising from the carpet was tequila mixed with tobacco smoke, masked only by the odor of Febreze. Even for a Saturday night, business was abysmal. As he walked in, he saw a rat scurry up the wall into the ceiling. He took it all in. *Charming,* he thought, *just charming.*

He slid into the booth where Maya was with a customer without a thought about interrupting the scumbag's fantasy night. *She needs to know,* he thought. *Glenn needs her.* The customer told Mike to fuck off and like an enraged grizzly bear, Mike stood back up to all of his six-foot five-inch height and his 420 pounds. "Come again?"

Maya whispered to her customer, "I'll be with you in ten minutes, honey," and sent the guy scurrying. It turned out to be more like thirty minutes, but the guy was not about to piss Mike off.

Mike smiled, or tried. "How you doing, Maya? Remember me?" *She looks like shit. Like the whores in* Les Miserable *but with even more makeup.* He breathed through his mouth. The stench was getting to him. *Man, she doesn't smell good. And this place—it ought to be torched.*

She brushed her hair back, hiding her hickey-covered neck with a scarf as best she could. One of her false eyelashes hung limp, giving her once beautiful eyes a kind of Picasso effect. "I'm okay. Long time no see, Mike. How you? How Glenn?"

"We're good, Maya. You heard about the election?"

"Congratulations. Saw on TV. Happy for Glenn."

Mike nodded. "You know about Katie?"

She sat up. "No. She woke up?" She felt hope—the first time in months, she felt any kind of hope.

Mike shook his head. "They took her off the machine last week. She went home to God."

She cocked her head. "She die?"

"Yes, Maya. She died."

Her spirits plummeted. She clutched at her heart. *Oh my boy, my little boy.* She teared. She was no good at holding back the tears anymore. "Is he okay?"

"No, Maya. The graveside services are tomorrow. He didn't want a funeral. Just skip right to the burial. He held it together through the campaign, but this past week . . ." Mike didn't know how to describe what he and Brad had found.

She clutched at his forearm. "What, Mike?"

He covered her hand with his. "No one could find him. We think he'd been on a rampage. He never answered the door. His apartment looks like a crack house. Brad and I broke down the door. Found him in bed. Empty bottles and vomit everywhere. He had pictures of Katie all over." He let it sink in. Wanted the next part to be clear. "Maya, his PC was on. He had pictures of you open, too."

She blinked twice. "He going to be okay?"

A server walked by. Mike ordered a beer and a lucky shot for her. She bowed her head in appreciation. "Heads up, Maya. This is me. Anyway, Brad's cleaning him up. We didn't know how much you meant to him. He kept a diary. He wrote down every good thing that happened between you two. We were wrong about you. We thought you were a gold digger. We didn't know he forced his money on you, to help your folks. He wrote about how he had to force you to take money."

She nodded. He continued. "He wrote about how you made him feel. We both knew about his mommy issues. He fought it all his life. Only you filled the gap Katie left behind. If we'd only known."

They clinked bottle to shot glass—the word "cheers" just didn't suit this place. "Don't feel bad, Mike. I pushed him away, you know."

"We know. He wrote about that too. He said everywhere he went, some song reminded him of you. Everywhere he went, every woman he saw looked like you. He really loved you. And he believed still that his love would win out one day. He wrote over and over that love conquers all. He ever mention that to you?"

She motioned him to stop. Putting her hand to her chest, she inhaled—a labored breath. Then a couple more long breaths, in and out. It had been awhile. She remembered all those times they'd talked about love. The connection between two souls. Neither distance nor time would keep love apart. "We talk all the time about that."

He took a swallow of his beer. "Yeah, he really loved you. But he wrote that you didn't. It was a fantasy. Was it? I talked to Anna. She said she met you. She swears you two had something, but you told her it was money only." He caught her eye and held it. He wanted to see her eyes when he asked the next question. "Maya, was it really money only?"

She fiddled with her shot glass. He signaled for another, and this time she asked the server in her broken Vietnamese for a real drink with alcohol. It would come out of her cut. *Never mind,* she thought, *need something strong for this talk.* She knocked it back as soon as the server brought it. Mike waited patiently. "Maya, was it money or was there love?"

She slid the shot glass to the edge of the table. "No, Mike. Not money only." She explained her family situation. She explained what being married meant to her and what Glenn's marriage to Katie meant to her. And finally, she described her issue, her fear of hurting Glenn. She broke down in tears as she explained all the times she hurt Glenn. "Got it, Mike? I'm man crazy. I will hurt him. I hurt him so much. His face. Too hard to take when I hurt him."

Mike pulled out Glenn's diary. "Yeah, Maya. He understood you're man crazy. Someone named Tia and some crazy guy he knows explained it to him. He might have hurt, but he never blamed you. Look here."

He showed her a page where Glenn had said she was worth it. "And Maya, when was the last time you hurt him? If you go by his diary, it was a while ago—something about a construction crew?"

She nodded. The night someone kept pouring her fully alcoholic Crown shots and not the watered-down version. "He almost leave me that night."

He opened another page. "That's right, but he wrote that something happened. You came back to him?"

She nodded. "I turn around. I see his face. My hunger gone. I almost run back to him."

Mike pointed at the bottom of the page. "Says here you left those guys in the middle of a song and came back and finished the song with him. And something happened after the bar closed? He doesn't say much, but he says it was hard to believe it was all fantasy after that night."

She smiled. Recalled how they kissed like high school kids in the parking lot till the security guard chased them away. "He say all that?"

"Yes, Maya. Did you do any man crazy stuff after that? I didn't find anything else after that entry."

She thought about it. "No." It hadn't dawned on her till then. *Maybe problem can fix. Maybe can manage.* She shook her head. *Not sure. But only one way I don't hurt him.*

He called for another beer. "So you overcame." He smiled. "So, love does conquer after all."

She changed the subject. "Why you here?"

It was his turn to pause. On his third beer, he took a long swallow. "This town's in trouble. We got a good mayor, and we need a good deputy mayor. But the deputy mayor right now is a basket case. If it takes asking you to be in his life to straighten it out again, then that's that. A message, straight from the Admiral."

"Who is Admiral?"

He leaned his massive frame back. "Glenn ever mention his night job?"

She nodded.

"The Admiral is Glenn's night job boss."

She nodded again. Hope crept into her heart, then scurried back out.

He fiddled with the bottle label. "Glenn always hoped that Katie would be back. At least he had a warm body to go visit every night. Now he's only got a patch of grass and a headstone. He needs an anchor."

She dabbed her eyes. She thought back to the night at his house and all those pictures of the happily married couple. "Mike, I'm not able to replace Katie. Not even close."

Mike shrugged. "Not asking you to replace her. Just be you. We saw it. Two years ago. Basket case. He meets you. He rebounds. Like a warrior out of *The Lord of the Rings*."

Her eyes, her tone, were part hope and part skepticism. "What you want?"

"We don't know. Open your mind?"

She looked around at the dump she was in. "I dunno." *Maybe this ticket out. Maybe karma finally help.* His face the last time they were together haunted her. Maybe it was that or because she did not eat for two days, but she was thinking she could not do it. She spoke softly. "No, Mike. I don't want to hurt him again."

Mike's massive shoulders slumped. *Maybe I just kidnap her? Who would know?* "Okay, Maya. We will honor you. But did you love him?"

She looked across the table at him and held his gaze. "Yes, Mike. I loved him. I still do."

He sat back. *And there you have it. I guess I will carry her out of here.*

She felt her baby bump suddenly kick. It was the first time. *A sign?* She looked up. "Mike, take me burial? Maybe I think better after? Want see him, but don't want him see me. Can?"

He lifted his giant hand for a high five. She smiled for the first time since election night. They had spent two hours together. The scumbag customer was long gone.

121

UNDER A SYCAMORE TREE

Katie was laid to rest late on a blue-sky Sunday afternoon with only family and close friends in attendance. Her final resting place was next to a running stream partially shaded by a sycamore tree. On a nearby hill overlooking the burial service, Mike stood dwarfing Maya with the sun behind them.

Maya could see Glenn bent over the casket, hands outspread. Even from this distance, she could hear him crying over the sound of the wind and the rustle of trees. An elderly lady held him from behind. Another man stood at his side, hand on his shoulder. They let him cry till he was ready. Maya sank to her knees and cried too.

She looked on, absorbing his pain and feeling his agony throughout her entire being. Every instinct screamed at her to run down to him. She wanted to yell, *I'm coming baby*, like the night she ran back to him at the bar.

As a pastor read from the Bible over the casket, Maya offered her prayers to Buddha and out of respect intoned, "Dear Glenn's God, please watch over him and give him happiness again."

Maya waited with Mike till only the mortuary workers remained. *He hurt with me around*, she thought, *but he hurt more without me. My little boy. Oh Glenn, I wanted so much to run down there to you. Hold you. Make everything all right. Wipe your face. Tell you all okay.*

She brushed her hair back. *Maybe love conquer all. Conquer my man crazy. I'm not Katie. Only me. I can love him, take care him.*

She recalled her own words to him on their big date:

I told you I will always be here for you.
And if I'm not, close your eyes. Find me in
your heart. Love conquers all, Glenn, near
or far, this life or next, you will always find

> *me in your heart. And I will always find*
> *you in mine.*

She only now remembered her promise and turned to the big man next to her. "Mike, what you want me to do? I do what you want me to do."

He stroked his chin. *There is a God. This is coming together.* "Wait for me to get back to you, Maya. Here's some money. For whatever you need." The Admiral had personally okayed the expense.

She pushed the money back. "I don't want it, Mike. I have pride. Can you take me home?"

Mike could see what Glenn saw in her. Katie would have reacted the same way.

122

REBOOT

Maya was on the phone as soon as she returned to her drab apartment. Rusty was more alive than usual. It had been a long time since Mommy smelled like happiness.

Chloe was setting dinner for Reyn and his son when her speed dial went off. She mouthed "Maya" to Reyn. He mouthed, "It's dinnertime." Pointing to his watch, he mouthed "after." She answered, anyway. "Maya, cannot talk now . . ."

Maya cut her off. "I'm going back to Glenn."

Chloe collapsed onto the kitchen floor. Reyn and his son ran over.

Chloe looked up at Reyn. "She going back to Glenn."

He helped her up. "Go! Take it in the bedroom."

Chloe scampered off, phone at her ear. "Hello, Hello? Tell me. What going on?"

Maya relayed everything that had happened the last few days. Mike's visit. Her confession of love. The burial. Mike asking her to go back to Glenn. "What do I do, Chloe?"

"Are you dumb? Go to him! He not have wife. You don't have husband. His friends like you. What more you need?"

"But I might hurt him again, Chloe."

Chloe threw her phone at her pillow, then picked up again. "What? Same old story, sis. The guy said, you fix already. You fix when you run back to him. That time with the construction guys."

"Maybe Chloe. Maybe lucky that night."

Chloe whacked her head with her phone and winced. "Not lucky, Maya. You say all the time. Love conquer all. He say all the time. Love conquer all. Then give love a chance here. His diary tell the real story. He truly love you. Let him decide whether he hurt or not."

Silence on the other end. "Maya, why you call me? How you feeling?

Right now, what you feeling?"

More silence. "Maya!"

Tears fell on Maya's pillow. Rusty licked what tears were on her face. "Happy, Chloe. I feel happy. I want to go to him. I want to make him happy. I know I can make him happy."

Teeth flashing, Chloe's face burst into a smile. "That what you call me to say? So why you ask me what to do? You know what you want. Go to him! Now your baby have father. Then you make more baby. Aunty Chloe babysit. Maybe your baby have cousin soon."

"Chloe! You and Reyn . . ."

"I'm not saying. This not about me, Maya. We talking about you. Go. Karma say you suffer enough already. Time to be happy. True? Not true?"

"True." For the first time in a very long time, Maya cried tears of happiness. Rusty felt it. He bounded around the room barking and jumped onto the bed and into her lap. Still sniffling, Maya said, "Chloe, you help. You there for me?"

Chloe rolled her eyes. "Gee shit, sis. You have to ask? He brudder to me too, you know." *I not telling her I see him for her—twice. This gotta work. Oh, Buddha, give Maya her man. Oh, Jesus, if Buddha cannot, can you help here? You Glenn's God, right?*

"Maya, what now?"

Maya sniffled. "I dunno. Mike, the big guy, say wait for him to call. Oh Chloe, so much hopes and dreams. I help him fix city. I make food for him every night. I take food his office. I make sure he rest . . ."

"Ayyyy—and you give him good sex! Heehee!"

Maya burst out laughing. Rusty barked along. She wished Chloe were there with her. "Shut up, Chloe. I do this right. Not till marry. Everything else okay, but no sex."

Chloe was wide-eyed. "You shitting me?"

"No. His God and Bible important to him. Say no sex before marry. I honor his God."

Chloe shook her head, still smiling wide. "Okay, sis."

"And I make sure he not forget Katie. I don't replace her. I make sure we take care of Katie's mother too."

Chloe was staring at a calendar. "And when wedding?"

Maya's eyes twinkled, first time in months. "Soon, I hope! I'm horny for him so much!!"

They were laughing like old times. Like two teenagers in high school.

Maya's voice calmed. "Chloe, I need to go now. Reyn waiting, huh?"

"Don't worry, Reyn. But I promise Riley ice cream today."

She wiped the last of her tears. "Ohhh. You sound like mommy."

"I have two kids, both easy to spoil."

Again, more laughter. After hanging up, Maya opened her arms to Rusty. "Here, boy. You about to have a papa again!" He sprang into her arms with more energy than she'd seen in a while.

Karma finally on my side. We will be happy. Live long life. He need to get used to crickets and papaya salad. I can eat hamburger and hot dogs.

She rubbed her baby bump. *And our son will grow up like his new father.*

We take it slow. Meet again. Whatever his Admiral wants, I do. I will come for you, Glenn. Don't worry. I'm here for you.

Her mama-san from the dingy bar was calling—time for work. She ignored the phone. No work tonight. She fell asleep with Rusty at her side, a faint smile on her face. Barely audible, she was singing "Don't Stop Believin'" in her dreams.

123

HOMESTRETCH

After the burial, the four friends retreated to Anna's bar for a wake she was hosting for Paradise Club members. While Glenn was busy with his guests, Brad and Anna huddled with Mike at the corner table, where Anna did her nightly paperwork. Mike took up half the table as he leaned over. "I found her! Admiral's orders. Get the guy on his feet any way we could."

Anna signaled to her barback for three beers, drafts, in mugs. "Where'd you find her? How? What's she doing now? Who's she with? What's the plan?"

The barback set three mugs in the middle of the table and a bowl of peanuts. Mike shoved a handful of nuts in his mouth and washed it down with half a mug. Anna and Brad waited patiently. Anna spoke up. "Take your time, Mike. Want a steak dinner too?"

Mike finished his beer. "So, Anna, you read the journals Brad and me found? True love, right?"

Anna signaled for another round. "From his side, yes. From hers? I couldn't figure it out. I told you I thought I saw a real connection, but, in the end, she told me she was in it for the money. Pretty convincing she was." Anna thought for a moment. "But the way she carried him out that night. So caring. And now we know from his diary that she took care of him all night."

Brad prodded Mike. "So give us the where-what-how details."

Mike took a sip from his second beer. "She works at this seedy dive across town. The place looks like a fire trap and smells like the sewer backed up in there. The asshole she was with last has influence in the bar community and put out the word to keep her from working anywhere better."

Mike swallowed at the thought of how she'd looked when he found her. "Get this: She's treated like a whore among whores. Stained. The story is she's a marriage wrecker who cheated on her serviceman husband. The top-tier bars all turned their backs on her, and the restaurant where she worked did the same. So that left only the worst places, and she was giving hand jobs and blow jobs to make ends meet. She don't look that good either. And . . . she's pregnant. "

Anna brought her hand to her mouth. Brad shifted. "His?"

"No, not Glenn's. From what I understand that influencer prick forced himself on her without protection. Then a few months later, he kicked her out. Not only that, her Navy husband summarily divorced her on infidelity charges. She came home one night, and all her things were on the street. That influencer prick took a sex pic of them in Vegas and posted it on his brag site; and the Navy guy found it."

Anna was wringing her bar towel. "The poor thing. How the hell could she end up like that?"

"The prick played her. Promised her a good life if she got out of the bars and if she dumped Glenn. So she did, then she lost all her good clients, along with Glenn. What she tells me is she loved Glenn but didn't want our boy to be unfaithful to Katie, so she made up some story about them being all fake to piss him off enough so he'd leave."

Brad jumped in. "Yeah, did you read that part of his diary talking about how painful that was? But he softened the last few months. His gut hunch was that it was real and he wanted to try again and let love take its course."

Mike nodded. "There's something else. He didn't mention it much in the diaries, but she calls it her sickness. She said that she's man crazy and that she hurt him several times when she blew him off to be with other men."

Brad finished his first beer. "I remember that in the journal. He also said she was done with that, though, or that's what he believed."

Mike leaned back. "I remembered that too. So I asked her if she thinks it's still a problem—I told her the diary talks about some night at the bar with a construction crew. She left him to party with these guys that night, but then she came back to him. She thought about it, and I think it was a revelation for her to think she might have licked the problem. That helped turn the corner."

Anna absorbed it all. *The poor girl. I should have known it was real. Stupid Lynh planting seeds in my mind.* "So Mike, did you ask her up front how she feels?"

"Yeah, I asked her point-blank: Does she love him?"

In unison, Brad and Anna nearly shouted, "So, what'd she say?"

Mike held up his hands. "She said, 'Yes.' She loves him. All her heart and all kinds of other teary, gooey stuff."

All three sat back and let the moment sink in. Anna broke the suspense. "What about the Navy husband? Did she really cheat on him?"

Brad held up his hand. "I got this one. The guy is a prick. A woman in every port. And several on base. My sources tell me he beat her several years ago, but she agreed to stay so he could make rank. If she stayed with him for ten years, she got half his pension. They agreed to this. As the ten years got closer, I guess he got cold feet and looked for any evidence against her. He kicked her out one night with no warning. A real dick."

Anna shook her head. "I hope these assholes get what they deserve."

Brad cracked his knuckles. "The Navy husband—I took care of that already. He'll be losing rank next month for fucking around with the base commander's seventeen-year-old niece."

Mike cracked his own knuckles in reply. "And the prick and his high-roller uncle who's been running their company are about to be raided by the IRS, courtesy of the Admiral."

Anna feigned awe at these two alpha males and all their knuckle cracking. *Men!* she thought. *Still, I'm glad karma is dishing out punishment to those assholes.* "So have you told Glenn what she said? About loving him?"

Mike was playing tabletop soccer with a peanut. "No, not yet. I thought maybe tonight. To cheer him up."

Anna flicked the peanut Mike was playing with off the table. "No, don't. Glenn should hear it from her."

Brad was next. "I agree. Mike, does Glenn even know you found her?"

Mike finished his beer. "No to that too. I didn't want him running off to that part of town. He is the deputy mayor, you know."

Anna recalled Mike's description of how disheveled Maya looked. "I'd love to get a chance to clean her up too. Mike, you should get her out of that hellhole. She can stay at my place for a while."

"Yeah, I can do that. Admiral also okayed some spending money for her. Never took him for a softie."

Brad finished his beer. "Don't let the Admiral catch you saying that."

Glenn walked by. "You guys want to get out of here? How's BJ's in thirty? Might not be a good idea to leave me alone in a place with booze. I just need to chill, and I haven't really thanked you for taking care of me this past week. How about it?" He counted all the empty mugs. "Or maybe you've had enough already."

Mike shot back. "You kidding? Two of Anna's cheapskate-sized mugs barely tickle my piss tank." Anna lobbed her wipe rag at Mike.

Glenn slipped out at ten o'clock with Brad and Mike in tow. Anna was running a little behind them.

It was the usual crowd at BJ's. Directly across from City Hall, it was considered the neutral zone—a mix of locals, military, elected officials from both parties, and a significant number of staffers from the executive and legislative branches.

The place was brightly lit, with one bank of TVs tuned to a boxing match and another bank showing baseball, basketball and some off-season football. The Monday midnight crowd was still going strong, awash in whiskey, beer and all manner of bar food. Country music alternated with hard rock. The waitresses wore short shorts and showed ample cleavage, and friendly was the mantra. The air smelled sweet, like the piped-in air at a Vegas casino.

The four of them hoisted mugs of beer. A bottle of Hennessey and shot glasses made up the table centerpiece. Glenn took the lead. "Here's to new beginnings," he toasted, in a nod to the election results.

Mike raised an eyebrow at Anna and Brad. *Here's to double meanings.* They were thinking about Glenn and Maya.

Glenn punched the big grizzly in the arm. "Where were you today?"

Mike feigned shame. "Sorry, boss. Admiral asked me to do something."

"Since when does he call you direct? You're my crew."

Mike shifted in his chair. "He knew you were busy today. Didn't want to bother you."

Glenn persisted. "What was it about?" *What could possibly be so important that the Admiral would call Mike, on this day of all days?*

Anna tried to help. "Do we have to get into your spy business tonight? It's been a long day. I was working at a bar. Now I'm trying to relax at a bar . . ."

Glenn held his hand up. "No biggie, Anna. Sorry, Mike. Just—you know. It's Katie, and you're family. You coulda said something."

Brad pushed some tater tots over to Glenn. Anything to divert.

Glenn ignored them, so Mike reached. Glenn pulled the plate out of Mike's reach. "Well?" *What's his problem? So evasive. What is going on?*

Mike jerked his eyes between Brad and Anna for help. "It's the Admiral, Glenn. He needed something."

Glenn drained his beer and brought his mug down hard. "Don't look at them. What was it?" *Something wrong here.* "Big guy, tell me . . ."

"Geez, Glenn let it go. Someone had to babysit Maya."

Glenn's mouth dropped. There was stunned silence around the table. Glenn couldn't believe he'd heard her name. The other two couldn't believe the big bear had spit it out so easily.

Mike crammed a handful of tots in his mouth. Then finished his beer.

Glenn pushed Mike's beer to the side, out of his reach. "Come again?" Mike kept quiet.

Glenn tapped the table with his index finger. Three times in rapid succession. Tap-tap-tap. "Mike?"

It was the longest exhale of Mike's life. "Okay. But I was just following orders."

Brad tried to buy time. "Maybe this isn't the best time. We're all tired . . ."

"Then go home, Brad." Glenn wanted to hear this.

Mike continued. "After we found you. While Brad was cleaning you up." Glenn winced. Looked over to Brad as if to say, thank you, bro, and sorry I just snapped at you.

Mike's shoulders heaved as he breathed. "I called the Admiral and gave him a situation status report. He said to go find Maya and try to bring her back. Something about how you'd done everything he asked you to."

Glenn recalled the meeting when he discovered the Admiral knew about Maya:

> *Glenn, I know it's difficult since Katie had her*
> *accident. I know about the other one too. If you get*
> *serious again, and if it makes you happy, we can*
> *find ways to make everybody happy. Just work with*
> *me, and only after we have a new mayor. Do you*
> *hear me? For now keep it in your pants. For our*
> *sake and this city's sake.*

Mike turned to Glenn, explaining in rapid fire. "So I found her. Talked to her. She wanted to be at the burial. But she didn't want to distract you. So I stayed with her in the background. At the top of the hill." He was pleading. "Bro, I was there. It was Katie. I wouldn't miss it."

There was only silence afterwards. Anna and Brad exchanged glances. Mike's eyes were moist. Glenn got up and reached out to Mike. It was a sincere brotherly hug.

Glenn reached for the Hennessey. Poured four shots. He took his in hand. The others did the same. He lifted his glass. "To the Admiral!"

He set the glass down and leaned back. *Maya? She was there?* So many questions. They ripped through his brain in seconds.

Four tables away, a military type sat nursing a beer. An odd sight with a Georgia Bulldogs cap and aviator shades, apparently taking in the boxing match. His back was turned to Glenn's group, but Caleb Finnegan could still see their reflection in the mirror behind the bar. In front of him was a summons from the Navy Judge Advocate General's office—a court martial summons for conduct unbecoming a military member. The end of a career.

124

CONSEQUENCES

After the four of them toasted the Admiral, Glenn leaned back in his chair. Fifty-two Tuesdays scrolled through his head. The joys. The pains. The breakups. The makeups. Holding hands under the table. Kissing outside in the parking lot. Champagne dates. His birthdays. Nights at the Paradise Club. And the night she stayed all night to care for him. Tuesday after Tuesday. Their Tuesdays.

He remembered a conversation he'd had with the Admiral:

You want to go back to your friend, that's fine.
But now you're almost as popular as him. People
already talking about you as mayor in eight years . . .

He brushed his hair back. *Me? Mayor? I'd trade it all for one more Tuesday with her. One more real Tuesday.*

Anna reached out and squeezed Glenn's hand. He squeezed back and let go to fold his hands together, and bowed his head. *Father, if I could have one more Tuesday with her. I know it's fantasy. But one more time. One more good Tuesday. To carry me for the rest of my life. One more time, to last a lifetime. Your will be done.*

He looked up. His friends were looking on, concerned.

He smiled at Mike. "So? How is she? She still with that guy? How's things with her cousin, the Facebook husband?"

Then his brow furrowed. "So why did the Admiral do this?"

Mike nearly coughed up his peanuts. "Boss, are you kidding? We read the diaries. The Admiral didn't have to. He already knew. This girl is good for you. You got problems. We all got problems. She's your fix. She's no Katie. But better than anything else out there. And this city needs you to be at the top of your game."

Glenn shook his head. "Seems weird to me. But I'll take it. So, Maya?"

Mike repeated his last two days activities for the second time in a night. He stopped short of revealing Maya's true feelings for Glenn. "She's not what you remember."

Glenn rubbed his eyes, then his face, then raked his hair. "So what then? Where is she? Can I call her?" His head clicked with calculations. *What time is it? Is she working? Is there time?*

"She got no phone, boss, at least not a cell phone."

Glenn half grinned. "That's why no social media!" *So she wasn't blocking me.*

Discomfort etched across Mike's face again. "Yeah, boss."

Glenn drummed the table with his fingers. "So no more guys in her life? She say anything about me?"

Anna kicked Mike under the table. Her way of saying watch it, let her tell him.

Mike kept mum.

Glenn took it the wrong way. "I don't care. It's okay. She's moved on." He looked up. *Father, just one more time?*

Anna gave Mike the stink eye, then turned to Glenn. "Glenn, don't say that. You do care."

Glenn pounded the table. "So what should I do, Anna? Life is short. For three hours of every Tuesday I was happy—mostly anyway."

He glanced around the table. "In her I found my mother, approval, affection, my self-worth and everything in between. Whatever hole Katie left behind, Maya filled it. Maybe not perfectly, but I could live with it."

His throat dry, he opted for a glass of water. "But it wasn't real, and if she wants no part of me and there's no chance for a future . . ." His voice trailed off, remembering her words again:

> *I had enough of you already.*
> *You damn right all this playacting.*
> *I told you this all fantasy.*

Anna gritted her teeth, fighting the urge to tell him. "I dunno, Glenn. Why not go see her? She cared enough to come to the burial. Just see her. Once. And see where that goes."

Glenn thought Anna was channeling Chloe. He recalled Chloe saying the same thing over and over after every bump in the road:

Before you do something stupid, stop. Just sit here.
No need talk. But before leave, agree to try next
Tuesday again."

Glenn took a shot of the Hennessey. Its warmth consumed him. He started to remember the good feelings. *Three hours a week. If I can be happy just for that short time, I'll deal with the rest of the week. Was it a lie? She said it was. Was she telling the truth? Did she even know herself? I'll never know. And now I don't want to burst that bubble. Maybe I'd rather live the lie happy, then seek the truth unhappy.*

He turned to Anna. He remembered their last conversation about Maya:

Don't bother bringing this girl back here again. And
if you keep seeing her, don't bother coming back
here period. And when she takes you for all you
got—your money, Katie's money, your house, your
dignity, shit, your wedding ring too . . . don't bother
crying to me!

"Anna, weren't you the one who said she was a gold digger? You sounded pretty sure last time. What changed?"

It was Anna's turn to squirm, and Mike relished kicking her under the table. Turnabout was fair play. "Honey, I'm not saying to go propose to her. I'm saying go see her. Get her out of your system. Or maybe she's changed. Assess the situation, then see your path forward. She came to the burial. Maybe I was wrong?"

It was Brad's turn. "Brother, maybe you should just think about it the next couple of days. It's been a long day. You just laid your wife to rest. Then you find out all this about your . . . your love . . . on the same day. Lots for your system to process. Just let it ride. Talk to God. Talk to Katie. She's up there now."

Inside his head, Brad was thinking they could use the time to prep Maya. He knew Glenn would give Maya a chance, and it would be the best day of Glenn's life. But for now, Glenn looked to Brad like he needed rest.

Anna jumped in. "Sounds like a plan." She wanted Maya to herself, partly to apologize for the role she'd played, and to make it right for both of them.

Glenn played with his shot glass. *Another one? Nah. Done. Need to think. Yeah, a couple days to think. Maybe pray. Tired. Drunk. She came to the burial. She must care. Somewhere in there, she must still care. Why would she come to the burial? Why not just tell Mike to fuck off? Maybe she needs money? Wants to use me again. But she turned down Mike's money. I gotta hear it from her.*

He turned to his friend. "Mike, the Admiral sent you to bring her back to me. Did you succeed?"

Mike moved his leg out of Anna's striking distance. "Boss, that's for you to deal with. I think what I did was lay the foundation for you two to talk. She didn't say anything about seeing you, but she didn't tell me to piss off either, you know. The decision is yours man."

"Do you think if I asked, she'd see me?"

Mike scratched his neck. "One way to find out. man." *Geez*, Mike thought, *this is like going to the prom.*

Glenn's eyelids were getting heavy. Out of the blue, he heard one of the servers say, "Don't worry, honey, just do what makes you happy!" She was talking to another bar patron about what, Glenn didn't know. He saw them high-fiving like he and Maya used to. And maybe it was imagination, but he heard a voice—Katie's voice—saying, *"Go!"*

He turned the shot glass upside down. *I'll think about it. Give it a shot. Go see her. Maybe we start as friends again.* "Hey Mike, give it a couple of days, then can you set something up? And while we're at it, set up something, so my trust covers her and the kid. It'll give me a cover to go talk to her. I'll give her the paperwork. *If* we move forward, then great. If not, something to remember me by."

Mike raised an eyebrow. "You sure about that, Boss? I don't think she'll take it."

"That's her choice. Just make it happen, okay?"

Glenn leaned back. Peace eluded him, but hope was making its way back into his heart. Faith was sure to follow. Love conquers all. *One day in the future?*

Glenn didn't know the future was nearer than he thought.

———————

None of them saw it coming. The guy in the Georgia Bulldogs cap strode quickly to the table. He extended his hand toward Glenn, cocking the gun as he came. Glenn saw the gun barrel first. Jungle training instincts kicked in as he pushed away. Dropping backward, he felt the bullet graze his chin. Meanwhile, Brad covered Anna and Mike threw himself at Georgia Bulldog, knocking the gun out of his hand. It was over in seconds with a sickening, cracking sound, as Mike broke the guy's back over the bar.

Two off-duty cops rushed over. Recognizing the new deputy mayor, they saluted and said they'd take it from there. Glenn returned the salute as only former military would. "Fellas, can you take my statement tomorrow? Got something to do."

Mike turned to him. "Not staying?"

Glenn gathered up his wallet and keys. "No. That was a sign. Life is short. Tell me where she is, Mike. I have to see her now. I coulda been killed. I'm not waiting another minute to tell her how I feel."

Brad jumped in. "Tomorrow, Glenn. That's adrenaline talking. You should rest."

"Rest? No, brother. Rest when we die, remember?"

Mike laid a hand on Glenn's shoulder. "Yeah, boss, you should rest up. Plus, we can't have the deputy mayor showing up at that dive. She might not even be there. And worse, man, what if you catch her doing something you don't like and go nuts again?"

Glenn picked Mike's hand off him. "Dammit, Mike, tell me what bar and where her apartment is. So I'm the deputy mayor? Then I'm ordering you."

"Suit yourself." Mike blurted out the name of the bar, and Glenn winced. He'd heard about the place. It wasn't a bar—it was a brothel that served liquor, and a drug haven to boot. He'd heard enough. He wanted her out of there, now.

"I'm going. You guys can come too if you want. If you think I'm gonna go nuts."

He got up and left, with Brad and Mike close behind. Anna alone stayed back to give her statement to the cops.

He wanted to go to her. *Hey, take a ten-minute break. Send the guy home. Like you did once. Let's meet tomorrow. Let's meet the next day. After all, it'll be Tuesday. Just one more time. See where it goes.*

He'd had a few beers and shots, but so what? It was only ten minutes away. He turned onto the main drag. Two intersections away, the light turned yellow. He gunned it. A biker came out of nowhere. He swerved. Didn't see the truck coming.

They heard the crash clear back at BJ's.

125

FINALLY, TOGETHER

The surgical team worked on Glenn through the night and into the morning. The doctors moved him from the recovery room a day later, a Tuesday.

Mike went to get Maya that evening, and when she walked into the room, she gave a quick gasp. Glenn lay sleeping, unrecognizable, tubes everywhere, face swollen, head bandaged with a neck collar, an oxygen mask covered swollen lips and a broken nose. An IV morphine drip kept time. An electronic monitor flashed and buzzed with each heartbeat. The oxygen machine hissed.

Mike walked over and gently nudged Glenn. Opening his eyes, Glenn turned his head from Mike to Maya, and smiled, or what looked like a smile. Maya tried hard to smile back as she walked to his side. "You look bust up," she said in her sweet accent that he hadn't heard in ages. It looked like tears in Glenn's eyes, but she couldn't tell. He mouthed, "You look worse."

This time she smiled without effort. Mike pulled up a chair for her. She sat and took Glenn's hand instinctively.

Glenn mouthed, "I'm so sorry for the way it ended."

Maya squeezed his hand and said, "Stop, you had me at 'Huh'."

It was their inside joke. Glenn shook a bit. Maya could tell he was laughing. To Mike, it looked like a coughing fit.

His voice a raspy whisper, Glenn said through his mask, "No, really, let me say what I have to say." Glenn seemed to have renewed strength as he took in Maya's face. She looked worried, sad, and happy at the same time. Glenn thought, *Was this for real? Or was it another lie?*

Slowly he continued, more audible as his voice returned. He took off his mask. "I don't care what was real and what wasn't. Those Tuesdays were the best nights of my life. I felt alive. I felt understood. I felt loved."

He closed his eyes. He took a deep breath. It wasn't enough. He tried to put his mask back on but couldn't quite do it. Maya reached over and helped. He opened his eyes. "Can we do it again? Can we do Tuesdays again? I miss you so much."

She brushed back his hair. "How about every night for you, Glenn?"

He said it slowly. "What?"

Maya glanced at Mike then back. "You mean Mike not tell you?"

"Tell me what?"

She pursed her lips. "How I feel about . . . you?" Glenn stared blankly. She thought he looked confused. She couldn't tell. She understood though, that Mike hadn't told him. *Not yet,* she thought, *change subject.*

Maya wasn't sure what to say. Was Glenn going to even remember this? "Sure, we can do Tuesday," she said softly. "We can do this again. Just get better. Same time, same place. Maybe in the cafeteria downstairs?" She wanted to give him hope. For now, it looked like he needed rest. The color was draining from his face, and it was a struggle for him just to stay awake.

Glenn tried to keep his vision from blurring. He wanted to look at her as long as he could. *Stupid morphine,* he thought.

Mike stepped in. "Hey boss, maybe you should rest." Glenn cocked his head toward Mike ever so slightly, and even in Glenn's present condition, Mike knew what that meant. "So okay, have it your way. I'll go check in with the nurses outside."

Maya tried to coax Glenn to sleep. "You really need to rest. I will come back tomorrow. We do it again when you better."

Glenn wasn't sure if she'd be back. "No, now. Like we used to. Be my girl, just for now. Pretend we're going places together. Your village in Thailand. Pretend for me how you're going to help me in the city, and that you'll be my bodyguard. Don't forget, you were going to adopt a son for us. I'm still godfather, right?"

She nodded, rubbing her baby bump, not sure if he could see.

He squeezed her hand. "Make sure he goes to Harvard, finance and Law. Well, Yale Law is okay too."

She squeezed back. "Okay, Glenn, when time come, we take him there together okay?"

He smiled. *She's all in with playing the fantasy.* "I'm so sorry I called it playacting. I don't care if it is. Can we do it again? Right here?"

Maya stared at the place where his brown eyes should have been. Still holding his hand, she leaned over and kissed his forehead. "Sure, what do you want to talk about?"

For the next ten minutes, they talked about everything they'd ever discussed. Her dog, her mom, her sister, the house in Thailand, his campaign, his work, beauty school, her beauty business.

He sighed. "I know you can do it. You're gonna do great things. You're gonna be more than a beauty consultant. You're gonna save the world, I know." He erupted in a coughing fit; the excitement overwhelmed him.

Glenn was tired, but he wanted this night to go on forever. It was a familiar feeling.

"Maya?"

"Yes?"

He opened his eyes to make sure she was there and not a dream. "Can you sing for me?"

She looked around the room. "Here, in the hospital?"

He managed to nod. "Yeah, just close the door."

She kissed the back of his hand. "What do you want to hear?"

She could tell. He was weak. All his strength went into staying awake and holding her hand. "Sing anything."

Maya cleared her throat and sang Britney Spears' "Everytime." Then she sang their song—Elvis's "Can't Help Falling in Love."

Her voice trailed off as she realized Glenn was asleep. She moved a bit, and he squeezed her hand.

"Glenn, you need to sleep."

"No, rest when we die, remember?"

The emotion was too great for her, but she suppressed it like she had so many times before.

He repeated himself. "I love our playacting Maya. You make me so happy. I'll take whatever I can get." *But I need to know. I need to hear. Was it real? Was it fantasy?* He held her hand, thinking it was time to ask, to finish what he'd set out to do the night of the accident. "Maya, was it really all fantasy? Is this real? Where are we? Are we real?"

She was choking back sobs. Tears dripped onto his arm. She held tightly to his hand with both of hers. It was time. "Yes, Glenn. We are real. This is real. Not fantasy. Always was real. Always love you all my heart."

She could feel him squeeze her hand tighter, trace of a smile on his face. His heart was full. Never happier. His mind was racing. *She loves me. Always has. All those good times. Kisses. Real. Genuine. Authentic.*

Time rewound two years. Every doubt vanished. Every hope confirmed. He'd never felt more love in all his life.

Then time flashed forward. In his mind, he saw himself helping her through beauty school and pictured her doing makeup and hair for weddings and proms, and he saw the family they were going to be. *She's gonna be great. I'll go to New York with her. J.Lo, here we come. Our kids will only know love in our house.*

She sat watching over him as he slipped in and out of consciousness. He was murmuring happily like a child dreaming of toys and candy. Her heart beat fast. She could sense his happiness, the same feeling on the best of their nights. She had so much more to say.

She held tight to his hand "We will be happy now. I cannot replace Katie, but I will try. I will take care of you, Glenn. I will be by your side always. I will not leave you. I will be your angel. Here for you. You will get better. We will see the places we always talked about. Do the things we wanted to do. I will help you save the world. Just get better."

It was so natural to say these things. "Glenn, I love you so much. Get better. Rest. I will be back tomorrow."

He looked her way. "I love you, Maya." She blushed, glowing warm. Somewhere in his mind, Glenn was in a happy place. Back with Maya again, sipping drinks, laughing and looking through the karaoke books. She brushed his hair back. He closed his eyes.

Suddenly his breathing stopped. "Glenn!" She squeezed his hand. "Oh my God! Papa!" She called for Mike, who looked in then ran for help. It was a long few seconds, and Glenn finally opened his eyes and looked at her, then breathed his last. Her beautiful face was the last thing he saw. His hand went limp in hers. The bedside monitor flatlined.

Nurses and doctors clamored into the room, moving her aside. His hand slipped from hers.

Oblivious to the commotion, she blew a kiss. *You can rest now, Glenn. Be happy with Katie.* A tear rolled down her cheek. Then another. Then another.

It was their fifty-third Tuesday together.

126

COMMENCEMENT

Twenty years later.

Cambridge, Massachusetts was in full bloom. Cool breezes blew through the trees under bright blue skies, in the time between the cool of spring and the heat of summer. Harvard University's 390th commencement was nearly underway.

Mother and son were getting ready—a private moment in their hotel room just blocks from campus.

The young man sat facing his mother, her purse on her lap. "Do you think he would have been proud, Mama?"

She took his hand in hers. "I know he would have been. I know he is. A degree in finance from Harvard. That was his dream you know."

He nodded. "I know, Mama, you've told me many times. Do you think he'd be upset that I'm going to Yale Law?"

She shook her head slowly. "No. He always said Harvard or Yale—it didn't matter. What mattered was what you did with the degree."

He looked into her eyes. "I wish I'd known him."

She brushed his hair back. "You do. Just look in the mirror, into your own heart. He is there. You act so much like him. Always wanting the world to be a better place. Never backing down from anything. And you're still shy about singing, just like he was."

Like a little boy, he puffed his chest. "Not shy when you help me, Mama."

She smiled. "Just like him."

He'd heard the story so many times. The shy politico who'd come into Mama's working place one night and learned to sing karaoke, but only after a young, uneducated bargirl stuck a microphone in his face.

She sighed and reminisced. "He was always so nice to me. He was nice to everybody. Like family. He bought clothes for Tia's kids. He bought ice cream for Mei's kids. The bar, the girls, were like family to him. Never admitted it, but when the crime boss threatened the bar and us girls, he ended all of them. Your Uncle Mike told me later: He was almost cut off from the most powerful political insider group in the state because he broke the rules. He did it for me . . . for the girls at the bar. And he never said a word."

She held back tears. "Always kind to me. Patient with me. I was so young. Still a wild child, they called me. Clubbing, drinking, dancing, wild nights were my thing. And yet, once a week, a quiet night with him. Sometimes it was easy, comfortable, fun even. Sometimes, my demons took over, I saw other men . . . I wanted . . . needed to be with them. I had issues. It was hard . . . for me, for him too . . . it was hard."

He scooted off his chair and sat at her feet as he'd done as a child.

She smiled down at him. "Through it all, he was kind, patient . . . a gentle soul. He never gave up on me, even when I mistreated him. Every time I did something stupid, he forgave me. I ran after other men, and he just waited patiently for me. Till I came to my senses."

She brushed her son's hair back. "A mama-san I worked for called him a stupid, cowardly dog for waiting so patiently. But she was wrong. It took a real man to love so unconditionally. I didn't understand till I read his diary and saw how close he was to his God. His God, now my God and my Lord Jesus. Each time I did something stupid, his God would say, forgive, love, be patient, His grace is sufficient and always, love conquers all.

"I understand now. He tried to explain back then, but I wouldn't have it. Too many people told me I'd have to give up my family beliefs and culture. I should have listened when he said the Buddhist path and devotion to Christ could co-exist."

Her son nodded. He'd gone to temple with his aunties but always kept God and Jesus in his heart.

She looked out the window. "And he kept believing in me. He kept saying I could do great things. I could be more than a bargirl. More than a beauty consultant. Once we connected, he sent me encouragement every Saturday. He said he'd spend the morning thinking of me and praying for me, then send me something. I almost lost them all, those texts, so I took my favorites and made a book, an old-fashioned paper one that I could carry around."

She reached into her bag and handed him a booklet with worn pages lovingly caressed over the years, and finally laminated to preserve the tears and kisses left on each page. She traced her fingers over his words, reliving how she felt when she'd first read these texts.

Keep striving. You are a beautiful person inside and out. You will make the world a more beautiful place.

Stay positive. You are a good person. Doesn't matter what others think. What matters is what you think.

Keep caring. You are a kind daughter and sister. Trust and believe in yourself and life will take care of the rest.

Keep going forward. Follow your heart. Believe in your dreams. Believe in yourself. The universe believes in you. I believe in you. Those that love you believe in you.

Never back down. Do what you need to do. Take care of what you need to take care of. Stay strong and positive, and everything will be okay.

Keep moving. I believe in you and all that you can do. The present and future is yours. Make it happen. The universe has your back. I got your back.

Be passionate. Whatever is happening, believe . . . keep reaching . . . you can do it . . . and I'm with you all the way. Always praying God's best for you.

Keep believing. Enjoy life. It's up to you to make it a good one.

Be happy. Don't stop believing . . . ever. Life believes in you if you believe in yourself. Love life and it will love you back.

Keep dreaming. I'm so proud of you. I would give you the world, but you already own it.

Live crazy, love hard, laugh lots. You're awesome.

Be blessed. Wishing you happiness wherever you go. God bless you always.

She took the booklet back from him and thumbed through its worn pages. "When we were apart that last time, when I was getting kicked around, living like a whore, I would read his texts over and over. They were my treasure . . . knowing that in my life someone cared for me. Those words kept me alive then and have kept me going for twenty years now." *Has it been that long? Seems like just yesterday we were singing, "Don't Stop Believin'."*

She caressed each page. "He said I'd make it someday. He kept saying, don't stop believing. I didn't believe in me, but I believed in him, and so I kept going. I believed in the fact that he believed in me. Do I make sense?"

He nodded vigorously. "Yes, Mama."

She reached down and wiped his face, the way he liked. "I know you know all this, and it must be hard to have your old mama keep telling you these stories over and over."

He took her hand. Kissed her palm. "No, Mama. I love these stories. It's like he's right here with us."

She took a quick deep breath. "Well, here's something I never told you. After the funeral, your Uncle Mike told Katie's mother about me."

"You mean Papa's first wife?"

"Yes. He told the mother how important I was to Glenn after Katie was bedridden. He showed her the part of the diary that said I was the only one who could fill the void left by her. I couldn't imagine such a thing. It's one of the reasons I ran away from him."

She stared at a picture she kept in a locket. "The mother came to me at the funeral. I was sitting slumped over in the back. She saw the hurt in my eyes, in my face. I felt defeated—like my world had ended. She hugged me, a good long time, rubbing my back, saying, thank you, and saying, it's going to be okay. If that was all I got, then it would have lasted a lifetime."

She was tearing up again. He handed her a tissue. "But then she took my hand and brought me up to the front row. They brought another chair and put it next to the empty one reserved for Katie. They let me sit there. With the family. With the others who really loved him. I cried. I was sad. I was heartbroken. But I also felt Katie's spirit. He once told me that he felt she blessed us from heaven. I was happy then and at the funeral, a part of me was happy again. He was with her again. How could I not be happy for him?"

She dabbed her eyes and beamed at her son. "At the funeral, so many people said nice things about him. They shook my hand, and the mother introduced me as his special friend. Many important people, but what got to me were all the old and poor and even homeless people who came to see him one last time. He had been their beacon of hope. Word got out. One by one they filed past his casket—their champion."

She looked out the window, remembering a far-off time. "I decided then—dedicate myself to helping others who needed a champion. The city would take care of these people, but your father and I had always talked about helping the girls that ended up in the business with no other future. I would give them one."

She sighed, almost sobbed, lost in the past. Her son had seen this many times. "He was so kind, so gentle like . . . a little boy. I got to see that side of him. I loved him dearly for it."

He paused before asking. "Mama, do you regret not having more time with Papa?"

She looked wistful, reaching out to caress her son's cheek. "No regrets. Only thankfulness. How can I regret? In those few minutes we experienced more love than some do in years of marriage."

She put her hand on her heart. "After the funeral, it was so hard. I came home to an empty house. He left a hole in my heart. All alone. All I had was memories, the songs we sang, the stories we shared. Such wonderful memories. I prayed and went to sleep, dreaming that I was with him again. And in my dream, I was able to hold him, to tell him from my heart, he was all I was thinking of."

She blinked back tears. "I've dreamed of him and loved him deeply for twenty years. And I don't know how to explain it, but I've also felt his love for me and you. He was right, you know. Love does conquer all, across distances and even time."

Her son nodded. He'd felt it too all these years. She took her son's hands in hers. "I didn't know it at the time, but the day of the accident, he had your Uncle Mike arrange for his trust to be left to us—left his whole estate to us. He'd found out about you and was so worried about you, your future."

She choked up. "He didn't even know how I felt about him. He didn't care. He just loved me, unconditionally, like Jesus." She started to sob and drew a letter from her bag that was worn and torn from reading and rereading.

The young man had read the letter many times. It was a message that brought them all together as one.

> *Love is forever. Those that we love are ours forever, if not in this life, then in the next. And while separated by here and there, we are still connected by the memories and feelings we have in our hearts.*
>
> *Some part of your loved ones will still be with you. You will find them in your heart. You will feel their spirit and sense their presence, like the warmth from a fire. You will hear their voice (or bark), faintly but clearly. You will feel their touch (or nuzzle), softly, like the wind. In time, you will remember fondly the good times, the tears will stop, and you will smile. And you will know that you will be together again.*

*If our loved ones means that much to us, we
have a duty to find a way to continue living, and to
honor and cherish all the memories made and love
shared. You must remember this, to keep living, for
Rusty, for your mom, for whomever you shared life
here with. They would want you to.*

The son reached out and hugged his mother. *Let her cry*, he thought.
She whispered, "He had so much love for others, for me, for you."
"I know, Mama. I know. We make sure Papa's love continues, right?"
More composed now, she wiped away her tears and inhaled-exhaled.
"Yes, my little boy." She ruffled his hair. "And I'm so glad you're not afraid
of the microphone. We can't have our commencement speaker be shy, can
we?"
"I'll do my best, Mama."

127

LOVE CONQUERS ALL

At the commencement ceremony in Harvard Yard, the young man sat with the others on stage, waiting his turn to speak. Gazing over the audience, he wondered how his father would have felt. Of course, he knew this man hadn't been his biological father. But he'd taken his name and, through his mother's stories, his father's love for the world—a love he'd felt all his life.

He'd heard the story of how Papa, as he had come to know him, made sure that he and his mother were cared for, and how he'd left his estate to them with the stipulation that she attend beauty school and graduate. This financial support had allowed his mother to go to school full time, without working, and to pay for their living expenses and child care until she could establish herself.

He read the other letters Papa had shared with his mother and the notes she'd taken about what it took to make it in politics. And he'd first learned about God from his father's diary, reading about patience, forgiveness, kindness, helping others less fortunate, making the world a better place, and God's abundant grace. He'd read these over and over growing up, forming character traits and values that exceeded anything that any random DNA strains could provide.

He took a deep breath as he was introduced as Harvard's 390th commencement speaker and strode to the podium. In the front row he saw his mother, who mouthed, you can do it, and he smiled back.

"Dean Rykroft, distinguished faculty, honored guests, fellow graduates, friends and family, and especially—my mother.

"I stand before you today, proud of this institution and this country, and all the lives that have been bettered by both. I am especially proud because making my life better was what my father was all about. He died before I was born. I did not know him, nor were we connected by blood.

But we were bound by the love he had for my mother, the love she had for him, and the love she gave me from both of them.

"My mother came to this country as a visitor from the third world. She met a man she helped back on his feet, and in doing so, she found herself, her dignity, and her passion to help her family back home—as well as to help others find beauty within themselves.

"Papa didn't know until his last day on Earth that my mother loved him, but he always knew that he loved her. And this was enough. He was patient, forgiving and kind, and he knew in his heart that love would conquer all. And so it did. For a brief time, they shared a love that only God could bring about.

"My Uncle Mike told me that all Papa ever wanted was to be special to my mother. And he was, and is, even today. I hope he can hear me when I look up and say, 'Papa, you're special to me too, and you always will be.'"

The young man choked up. It was so quiet and still. Then a gentle voice arose from the front row. "My son, you can do it. Finish, please." At that, the crowd erupted in applause—for the strong woman who had helped her son get here today.

He smiled. Cleared his throat.

"I believe some of you already know about my mama. She was a bargirl when she met Papa, but she worked her way through beauty school when I was still a baby and then opened her own shop. Over the years, she adopted many young immigrant girls whose only option was the sex trade, and gave them what they needed to work in her business or go on to school. She opened beauty salons up and down the coast to help in this effort, then opened more overseas, in Thailand, Laos and Cambodia. In time, she became CEO of an international school of beauty with more than 340 franchises and schools in five countries, including twenty in the United States.

"Papa always said she was good with people—about identifying their driving motivation—and that she could either use that skill as a bargirl, or take a step up and save the world. She chose to save the world, one person at a time.

"Every young woman deserves the chance for the kind of love that Papa had for my mother. And that's why I'm especially proud to announce that today, my family's Papa Foundation has received final clearance to partner with the World Health Organization—toward the goal of ending dependence on the sex industry in the third world."

Now the applause was clamorous, and the young man paused, staring off into the distance as if seeing someone from afar.

"And it all started because Papa's love helped Mama find the courage to endure any obstacle with hope and grace, without condition, without reservations. To inspire her to do better. To assure her there was always one person who believed in her wholeheartedly.

In the end, what I've learned most from my father is that love conquers all. We may be separated by distance or time, but if that love is ingrained in our hearts, it will conquer any obstacles we face. And if that love is ingrained in the hearts of the people we touch, they in turn will overcome their own challenges."

Overwhelmed with emotion, he paused, staring down at his handwritten speech on the podium. There was more, but now he put aside his notes. Trembling, he lifted a clenched fist to his mouth and bit a knuckle to fight back the tears.

He breathed in and composed himself. Standing straight, he looked out over the audience, and spoke again, this time without notes.

"I think you would have liked my father, and he would have liked you. He would have told you that in life, it's okay to be angry and frustrated, as long as we can also be patient and forgiving. He would have said the world is filled with evil—all the more reason to show kindness to those who need it most. Most of all, he would have told you to *love*. Love yourself and love others. And let that love conquer all and burn brightly forever, to help guide others to happiness.

"Thank you for letting me share this love with you today. Good luck, my fellow graduates. I love you, Mama. I love you, Papa."

In the wild applause that followed, Maya was on her feet along with everyone else in Harvard Yard. The young man felt his own hot tears welling up in his eyes, and he bit his lip, trying to be brave. He knew that Glenn was smiling from above. Then he closed his eyes and let the tears fall.

A gentle afternoon breeze caressed his cheeks, like a hand wiping away his tears.

> *Love conquers all, near or far. In this life or the next, you will always find me in your heart. And I will always find you in mine.*

ABOUT THE AUTHOR

650

G. K. Nakata has written all his life—mostly legal briefs and financial analyses. He delved into fiction after stumbling into a Honolulu, Hawai'i hostess bar and, he says, "the adventures just started rolling off my pen." A cabinet member in a previous city administration, Nakata has been involved in more than twenty political campaigns at both the city and state levels. How did a veteran of the political wars end up writing a love story? "I walked into the bar one day, made a few friends, drank a few beers, sang some songs, and watched everyday people having everyday interactions— then asked, what if?"